Ladies' Night
&
Save the Date

ALSO BY MARY KAY ANDREWS

Sunset Beach

The High Tide Club

The Beach House Cookbook

The Weekenders

Beach Town

Christmas Bliss

Spring Fever

Summer Rental

The Fixer Upper

Deep Dish

Savannah Breeze

Blue Christmas

Hissy Fit

Little Bitty Lies

Savannah Blues

Ladies' Night & Save the Date

Mary Kay Andrews

St. Martin's Griffin New York

These are works of fiction. All of the characters, organizations, and events portrayed in these novels are either products of the author's imagination or are used fictitiously.

www.stmartins.com

The Library of Congress Cataloging-in-Publication Data
is available upon request.

ISBN 978-1-250-26001-7 (trade paperback)

Our books may be purchased in bulk for promotional, educational, or business use. Please contact your local bookseller or the Macmillan Corporate and Premium Sales Department at 1-800-221-7945, extension 5442, or by email at MacmillanSpecialMarkets@macmillan.com.

First Edition: June 2019

10 9 8 7 6 5 4 3 2 1

Ladies' Night

In memory of my brother, John Joseph Hogan,

who left this world too soon.

Miss you, Johnny.

1

If Grace Stanton had known the world as she knew it was going to end that uneventful evening in May, she might have been better prepared. She certainly would have packed more underwear and a decent bra, not to mention moisturizer and her iPhone charger.

But as far as Grace knew, she was just doing her job, writing and photographing Gracenotes, a blog designed to make her own lifestyle look so glamorous, enticing, and delicious it made perfectly normal women (and gay men) want to rip up the script for their own lives and rebuild one exactly like hers.

She peered through the lens finder of her Nikon D7000 and frowned, but only for a moment, because, as Ben had told her countless times, a frown was forever. She made a conscious effort to smooth the burgeoning wrinkles in her forehead, then concentrated anew on her composition.

She'd polished the old pine table to a dull sheen, and the available light streaming in from the dining room window glinted off the worn boards. With her right hand, she made a minute adjustment to one of the two deliberately mismatched white ironstone platters she'd placed on a rumpled—but not wrinkled—antique French grain-sack table runner. She replaced the oversized sterling forks, tines pointed down, at the edge of the platters. Should she add knives? Maybe spoons? She thought not. Spare. The look she was going for was spare.

Edit, edit, edit, she thought, nodding almost imperceptibly. Less was more. Or that's what Ben always claimed.

Now. About that centerpiece. She'd cut three small palmetto fronds from the newly landscaped driveway . . . No, she corrected herself. The builder's Web site referred to it as a motor court. The palmettos were giving her fits. She'd arranged them in a mottled, barnacle-crusted pale aqua bottle she'd plucked from a pile of random junk at the flea market the weekend before. They should have looked great. But no. They were too stiff. Too awkward. Too vertical.

Grace replaced the palmettos with a cardboard carton of lush red heirloom tomatoes. Hmm. The vibrant color was a good contrast against the nubby linen of the runner, and she loved the lumpy forms and brilliant green and yellow stripes on some of the irregularly shaped fruits. Maybe, if she placed the container on its side, with the tomatoes spilling out? Yes. Much better.

She grabbed a knife from the sideboard and sawed one of the tomatoes in half, squeezing it slightly, until seeds and juices dribbled out onto the tabletop.

Perfect. She inhaled and clicked the trigger on her motor-driven shutter. Click. Click. Click. She adjusted the focus so the pale gel-covered seeds were in the foreground. Now, she zoomed out, leaving the tomatoes as red blurs, so that the old ironstone platters were in focus, their age-crazed crackles and brown spots coming into sharp relief.

"Very pretty," a voice breathed in her ear.

Grace jumped.

Ben rested a hand lightly on her shoulder and studied the vignette.

"Is that for tomorrow's 'Friday Favorites' post?" he asked.

"Mm-hmm," Grace said. "I tried the palmetto fronds and, before that, a basket of seashells, and then some green mangoes, but I think the tomatoes work best, don't you?"

He shrugged. "I guess."

"What?" Grace studied his face, as always, craving his approval. "The tomatoes don't work for you?"

"They're nice. In an artsy-fartsy kind of way," he said.

She pushed a strand of light brown hair off her forehead and took a step back from the table. She'd spent an hour putting the table together, and she'd been fairly pleased with the effect she'd achieved. But Ben didn't like it.

"Too country-cutesy?" she asked, glancing at her husband. Ben's trained eyes missed nothing. He'd been in the ad business forever, and no detail was too small or too insignificant. It was why they made such a great team.

"It's your blog," he reminded her. "And your name is on it. I don't want business stuff to impinge on your editorial freedom. But . . ."

"But what? Come on. I'm a big girl. I can take it."

"The Aviento folks sent us a big crateful of pieces of their new fall line," Ben said, hesitating. "Treasures of Tuscany, the new pattern is called. It's for the giveaway you're doing on Monday. I was thinking maybe you could put the tomatoes in one of those bowls they sent."

Grace wrinkled her nose. "That is seriously the ugliest pottery I have ever seen, and it looks about as Italian as a can of Chef Boyardee."

"You don't have to set the whole table with it. Just maybe put some of the tomatoes in one of the bowls. They *are* spending a lot of money advertising with us now, and it would be good if they could see their product . . . you know."

"Stinkin' up my 'Friday Favorites' tablescapes," Grace said, finishing the sentence for him. "Did you promise them I would use it editorially? Tell me the truth, Ben."

"No!" he said sharply. "I would never try to influence you that way. But would it hurt to maybe try a couple shots with one of the bowls. Or a plate?"

"I'll try it out. But if it looks as crappy as I think it will, I'm not going to run it. Right? I mean, you promised when we monetized the blog, we wouldn't be whoring me out by using the advertisers' product in a way that would compromise my aesthetic."

"It's your call," Ben said, picking up one of the tomatoes and examining it. "These are weird looking. What kind are they?"

"Don't know," Grace said, gently taking the tomato from him and replacing it on the table. "J'Aimee picked them up at the farmer's market."

"Kid's got a good eye," Ben said. He glanced back at the table. "How long before you're done here?"

"Maybe an hour? I guess I'll try some shots with the Aviento stuff. Then I need to edit, and I've still got to actually write the piece." She glanced down at her watch. "Good Lord! It's after six. I've been piddling around with this tabletop for hours now. Why didn't you say something?"

"Didn't want to interrupt the genius while she was at work," he said. "But since you brought it up, is there any actual food to go on these pretty plates?"

"Nada," she said apologetically. "I'm sorry. I completely lost track of the time. Look, I'll just take a couple more shots with the Tuscan Turds, then I'll run down to Publix and pick up some sushi. Or maybe a nice piece of fish to grill. I can have supper on the table by seven. Right?"

"Finish your shots," Ben said easily. "J'Aimee can pick up supper."

"No, I'll go. I've had J'Aimee out running errands all afternoon."

Ben dropped a kiss on her forehead. "That's what assistants are for, Grace."

"But I hate to bother her," she protested. "She just went back over to the apartment an hour ago."

Grace gestured in the general direction of the garage, which was at the back of the "motor court." J'Aimee, her twenty-six-year-old assistant, had been living in the apartment above the garage since she was hired three months earlier. Her battered white Honda Accord was parked in the third bay, beside Ben's black Audi convertible.

Their builder had referred to the apartment as a mother-in-law suite, or even a nanny suite. But Grace's mom lived only a few miles away on Cortez and she wouldn't have moved to this "faux chateau," as she called it, at gunpoint. Ben's mother lived quite happily down in Coconut Grove. And since the fertility specialist still couldn't figure out just exactly why Grace couldn't get pregnant, the apartment, for now, was the perfect place to stash an assistant.

"Finish your shoot," Ben said, settling the matter. "I'll walk over there and roust J'Aimee. In fact, I'll ride to Publix with her."

"Thanks," Grace said, going back to her camera. "You're the best."

Ben gave her a gentle pat on the butt. "That's my girl," he said.

Grace went into the kitchen and found the heavy wooden crate with the Aviento shipping label sitting on the polished black granite countertop, pausing, as she always did, to flick a crumb into the sink. She hated the black granite. Even the tiniest fleck of sea salt showed up on it, and she seemed to go through a gallon of Windex every week, keeping it shiny.

But Ben and the builder had ganged up on her to agree to use it, after the granite company offered the countertops at cost in exchange for a small ad on Gracenotes.

She was soon immersed again in her work, barely registering the familiar roar of Ben's car as it backed out of the garage. Grace looked up in time to see that he'd put the Audi's top down. He did a neat three-point turn and gave her a carefree wave before he sped down the driveway, his forearm casually thrown across the back of the passenger seat, and J'Aimee's long red hair flowing gracefully in the wind.

Ben reminded her of Cary Grant in *To Catch a Thief*, a golden boy, elegant, aloof, mysterious, maybe even a little dangerous? She reflected briefly on how unfair life really was. At forty-four, Ben was six years older, but you'd never know it from looking at him. He never gained weight and never seemed to age. He kept his tennis tan year-round. His gloriously glossy dark brown hair still didn't show a speck of gray, and the faint crow's-feet around his eyes lent him the look of wisdom, not imminent geezerdom.

Grace, on the other hand, was beginning to spend what she thought of as an alarming amount of time on maintenance. At five-four, even five extra pounds seemed to go right to her butt or her belly, and she'd begun coloring her sandy-brown hair two years earlier, at the suggestion of Ruthanne, her hairdresser. Her face was heart-shaped, and only thirty minutes in the Florida sun left her round cheeks beet-colored, giving her even more of the look of a little Dutch girl when Ruthanne got carried away with the blond highlights. Ben insisted she was still as pretty as the day they'd met six years earlier, but they both knew that with Grace's blogging career about to take off, she would have to be that much more vigilant about her appearance.

Blogging? A career?

If anybody had told her two years ago that she'd make a living out of journaling her quest for a more beautiful life, she would have laughed in their face. And if anybody told her that she would become enough of a success that Ben would quit his career to run hers? Well, she would have politely written that person off as a nutcase.

But it was all true. She and Ben were on the very verge of the big time. This house, a 6,500-square-foot Spanish colonial located in a gated golf-course community had been one of the subdivision's model homes, and the builder, whose wife was an avid Gracenotes reader, had given them an incredible deal on it in exchange for a banner ad across the top of the blog. Most of the expensive upgrades on the property—the landscaping, the pool and spa, their amazing master bath—had also been trade-offs for advertising.

She'd always loved writing, and had tinkered with photography for years, but once the blog took off, it had somehow caught the eye of magazine editors and television producers. In addition to having their own house featured in half a dozen magazines, writing, photography, and decorating assignments had begun coming her way. She'd become a contributing regional editor for *Country Living* and *Bay Life* magazines, and next month, they were going to start working with a production company out of California to shoot a pilot television show of Gracenotes for HGTV.

All because of her silly little blog.

She couldn't say why she awoke so suddenly. Normally, Grace fell asleep the moment her head hit the pillow, and she slept so soundly Ben often reminded her of the time she'd slept through Hurricane Elise, not even stirring when the wind tore the roof totally off the screened porch of their old house in a slightly run-down Bradenton neighborhood.

That night was no exception. She'd retreated to her office after dinner, writing and rewriting her Gracenotes post and fussing over the photographs before, finally, shortly before eleven, pushing the SEND button and crawling into bed beside her already-slumbering husband.

For whatever reason, she sat straight up in bed now. It was after 1:00 A.M. Her heart was racing, and her mouth was dry. A bad dream? She couldn't say. She glanced over at Ben's side of the bed. Empty.

She rubbed her eyes. Ben was probably downstairs, in the media room, watching a tournament on Golf TV, or maybe he was in the kitchen, looking for a late-night snack. Grace yawned and padded downstairs, already planning her own snack.

But the downstairs was dark, the media room deserted. She went out to the kitchen. No sign of him there, either. The kitchen was as spotless as she'd left it three hours earlier, after finishing up the last of the dinner dishes and packing up the faux-Tuscan pottery. Not even a cup or a spoon in the sink.

Grace frowned, and this time she didn't bother to worry about wrinkles. She checked the downstairs powder room, but the door was open and there was no sign of her husband. She ran back upstairs and peeked inside the two guest suites, but they were empty and undisturbed. She walked slowly back to the bedroom, thinking to call Ben's cell phone. But when she saw his cell phone on his dresser, along with his billfold, she relaxed a little. And then she noticed the keys to the Audi were missing, and her heart seemed to miss a beat. She went to the window and peered out, but saw nothing. There was only a quarter moon that night, but it was obscured by a heavy bank of clouds. The backyard was wreathed in darkness. She couldn't even see the garage.

"It's nothing," she told herself, surprised to realize that she was talking out loud. She shrugged out of her nightgown, pulling on a pair of shorts and a T-shirt, slipping her feet into a pair of rubber flip-flops. "He's fine. Maybe he's out by the pool, sneaking a midnight cigar."

The sandals slapped noisily on the marble stairs, the sound echoing in the high-ceilinged stairway. She ditched them by the back door, carefully switching off the burglar alarm before stepping out onto the back patio. She paused, put her hand to her chest, and could have sworn it was about to jump out of her body.

"Ben?" She kept her voice low. It was pitch black, except for the pale turquoise surface of the pool and the eerie green uplights on the date-palm clusters at the back of the garden. Cicadas thrummed, and in the far distance, she heard a truck rumbling down the street. She crept forward, her hands extended, edging past the pair of chaise lounges perched at the edge of the patio, feeling the rough-textured coral rock beneath her feet.

Gradually, her eyes adjusted to the dark. There was no glowing cigar tip anywhere on the patio or the garden. She glanced toward the garage. No lights were on in J'Aimee's upstairs apartment, and the garage doors were closed. Was Ben's car there?

For a moment, a train of scenarios unspooled through her imagination. Ben, passed out, or even dead, at the wheel of his car, an unknown assailant lurking nearby. Should she retreat to the house, find some kind of weapon, even call the police?

"Don't be an idiot," she murmured to herself. "You're a big girl. Just go look in the garage. You live in a gated community, for God's sake. The only crime here is dogs pooping on the grass."

She tiptoed toward the garage, skirting the electronically controlled metal doors, heading toward the side door, trying to remember whether or not it would be unlocked.

Luckily, it was. The knob turned easily in her hand, and she stepped inside the darkened space, her hand groping the wall for the light switch.

And then she heard . . . heavy breathing. She froze. A man's voice. The words were unintelligible, but the voice was Ben's. Her hand scrabbled the wall for the switch. She found it, and the garage was flooded with light.

A woman squealed.

Grace blinked in the bright lights. She saw Ben, sitting in the driver's seat of the Audi. He was bare-chested, his right hand shielding his eyes from the light. His hair was mussed, and his cheeks were flushed bright red.

"Grace?" He looked wild-eyed.

And that's when she realized he wasn't alone in the car. Her first instinct was to turn and run away, but she was drawn, like a bug to a lightbulb, to the side of that gleaming black sports car. The top was retracted. She looked down and saw that distinctive mane of flame-red hair.

J'Aimee, her loyal, invaluable assistant, was cowering, naked, making a valiant effort to disappear into the floorboards of the car.

"What the hell?" Grace screeched as she yanked open the passenger-side door.

"I'm sorry, Grace, I'm so sorry," J'Aimee blurted, her eyes the size of saucers.

J'Aimee's clothes were scattered on the floor of the garage, and, come to think of it, that was Ben's shirt—his expensive, pale-blue, custom-tailored, monogrammed, Egyptian cotton shirt that Grace had given him as a birthday gift—that was flung over the Audi's windshield.

With the passenger-side door open, Grace saw, at a glance, that her husband was nearly naked, too—if you counted having your jeans puddled down around your ankles as naked.

For a moment, Grace wondered if this was some bad dream she was having. Hadn't she just been asleep a moment earlier? This couldn't be happening. Not Ben. Ben loved her. He would never cheat. She shook her head violently, closed her eyes, and reopened them.

But this was no nightmare. And there was no mistaking what she'd just interrupted. Suddenly, she felt a surge of boiling hot rage.

"Bitch!" Grace cried. She clamped a hand around J'Aimee's upper arm and yanked her out of the car in one fluid, frenzied motion.

"Ow," J'Aimee whimpered.

Grace flung her against the side of the car.

"Stop it," J'Aimee cried. Her face was pale, with every freckle standing out in contrast to the milky whiteness of her skin. For some reason, Grace, in an insane corner of her mind, noted with satisfaction that J'Aimee's breasts were oddly pendulous for such a young woman. Also? Not a real redhead.

"You stop it!" Grace said, drawing back her hand.

"Jesus!" J'Aimee screamed. She raised her arms to cover her face, and for a moment Grace faltered. She had never hit anybody in her life. She dropped her hand and glared at the girl.

"Now, Grace," Ben started. He was wriggling around in his seat, trying in vain to surreptitiously pull up his pants. "Don't get the wrong idea. Don't . . ."

"Shut up, just shut up!" Grace shouted, her eyes blazing. For a moment, she forgot about J'Aimee. She flew around to his side of the car, but before she could get there, Ben had managed to slide out from under the steering wheel, zipping up his pants as he stood.

"How could you?" she cried, raining ineffective punches around his head and shoulders. She was aware that her high-pitched shrieks sounded like the howls of a lunatic, but she was helpless to stop herself. "You? And J'Aimee? My assistant? You were screwing her? Under my own roof?"

He easily caught her fists and held them tight in his own. "No!" Ben lied. "It's not what you think. Look, if you would just calm down, let's talk about this. Okay? I know this looks bad, but there's a logical explanation."

"Like what? The two of you snuck out here to the garage while I was asleep and you decided to have a business meeting in your car? A clothing-optional meeting? And suddenly, J'Aimee decided to give you mouth-to-penis resuscitation? Is that the logical explanation for this?"

"Calm down," Ben repeated. "You're getting yourself all worked up . . ."

Grace saw a flash of movement out of the corner of her eye and looked over just in time to see J'Aimee scoop up her clothing and make a run for it.

"Oh, no," Grace said. "You're not getting away from this." J'Aimee darted out the door, and Grace went right after her.

"Stay away from me," J'Aimee cried, running in the direction of the house. "I'll call the police if you come near me . . . It's aggravated assault."

"You don't know the meaning of aggravated," Grace shouted. She flinched when her bare feet hit the lawn, damp from the automatic sprinklers, but ran after J'Aimee, who was surprisingly slow for a young woman unencumbered by clothing. She picked up her speed until she was only a few yards behind her former assistant. She reached out to try to snatch a handful of J'Aimee's hair, but her prey danced out of reach.

"Don't you touch me," J'Aimee cried, backing away. "I mean it."

But Grace was quicker than even she expected. She managed to grab J'Aimee's arm, and the girl screamed like a stuck pig.

Lights snapped on at the house next door. A dog began barking from the back of the property.

"Get away," the young woman screeched, dropping her clothing onto the grass and windmilling her arms in Grace's general vicinity. "Get away."

Now they heard the low hum and metallic clang of the garage door opening. Grace glanced over her shoulder to see Ben come sprinting out of the garage. "Are you insane?" he called. "For God's sake, Grace, let her go."

In her fury, Grace turned toward her husband, and in that moment J'Aimee slipped out of her grasp. While Grace watched, speechless, J'Aimee scampered, naked, around the patio. A moment later, she'd disappeared behind the thick hedge of hibiscus that separated the Stantons' property from their nearest neighbor.

"Go ahead and run, bitch!" Grace screamed. "You're fired. You hear me? Your ass is fired!"

Ben was walking slowly across the grass, his hands raised in a cautious peace gesture. "Okay, Grace," he said, making low, soothing sounds at the back of his throat, the kind you'd make to coax a cat out of a treetop. "Oh-kay, I know. You're upset. I get that. Can we take this inside now? You're making a spectacle of yourself. Let's take it inside, all right? I'll make us some coffee and we can sort this out . . ."

"We are *not* going inside," Grace snapped. "Coffee? Are you kidding me? You think a dose of Starbucks Extra Bold is going to fix this? We are going to stay right here. Do you hear me?"

"The whole neighborhood can hear you. Could you lower your voice, please? Just dial it down a little?"

"I will not!" His calmness made her even crazier than she already felt. Grace megaphoned her hands. "Hey, people. Neighbors—wake up! This is Grace Stanton. I just caught my husband, Ben Stanton, screwing my assistant!"

"Stop it," Ben hissed. "I was *not* screwing her."

"Correction," Grace hollered, lifting her voice to the sky. "She was blowing him. My mistake, neighbors."

"You're insane," he snapped. "I'm not staying around listening to this." He turned and stomped off toward the house. "We'll talk when you've calmed down."

"One question, Ben," Grace called, running after him. She grabbed him by the shoulder to stop his progress. "You owe me that."

"What?" He spun around, rigid with anger. She noticed three small love bites on his collarbone. Hickies? Her forty-four-year-old husband had hickies? A wave of nausea swelled up from her belly. She swallowed hard.

"How long? How long have you been fucking her?"

"I'm not . . ." He shrugged. "Come inside. All right?"

"How long?" Grace felt hot tears springing to her eyes. "Tell me, damn it. This wasn't the first time, was it? So tell me the truth. How long?"

"No matter what I say, you won't believe me," Ben said quietly.

"Tell me the truth and I'll believe you," Grace said.

"No," he said softly. "Not the first time. But we can fix this, Grace."

"Fix it?" Grace exploded with pure, white-hot rage.

"Fix it," she said, lifting her voice to the heavens. "He's been screwing her for a while now, and he thinks we can fix it."

"That's it," Ben said. "I won't stand here and let you humiliate me like this."

"Don't you dare walk away from me," Grace called.

"I'm gone," Ben said. True to his word, he stalked away toward the house.

She raced to the back door, to discover that he'd locked her out.

"Let me in, damn it," she screamed, pounding on the kitchen door.

Nothing. She kicked the door. Still nothing.

She looked around for something, anything, to break the glass in the door. Just then she spied the heap of clothing J'Aimee had discarded in her hasty escape.

Grace scooped up the clothes and returned to the back patio. She craned her neck in the direction of the hibiscus hedge, hoping she might spot J'Aimee's bony white ass back there, hiding in the foliage or, better yet, being gnawed on by the neighbor's dog, a vicious-tempered chow mix named Peaches. But nothing moved in the shrubbery.

She had an idea. She stepped onto the patio and found the light switch for the outdoor kitchen, with its granite counters and six-burner gas-fired barbecue.

Earlier in May, her Gracenotes blog had dealt with barbecues.

Mr. Grace and I are fortunate to live in Florida, where grilling season never ends. But just because we're dining outdoors doesn't mean I serve burnt hot dogs on spindly white paper plates. I love to spread a white matelassé bedspread diagonally across our glass-topped patio table and anchor it with a pair of heavy black wrought-iron candelabras, or, if it's a windy day, I'll place votive candles in old Mason jars anchored with a layer of bleached-out seashells. Especially for casual occasions like this, you do not have to have a set of matched plastic dishes. I'll let you in on a secret: I hate matchy-matchy! Instead, I have an assortment of mismatched Fiestaware plates picked up at junk shops and yard sales over the years, in bold shades of turquoise, green, pink, yellow, and orange. Paired with silverware with ivory-colored Bakelite handles, and oversized plain white flour-sack dish towels bought cheap from Ikea, and a bouquet of brilliant zinnias cut from the garden, they telegraph the message to guests: the fun is about to begin!

Speaking of fun, Grace chortled as she tossed J'Aimee's clothes—a T-shirt, pair of shorts, bra, and pink thong panties—onto the counter and then reached into the stainless steel bar fridge and found herself a perfectly chilled bottle of Corona. She didn't really like beer all that much, and there were no lime slices handy, but she'd just have to make do. She uncapped the bottle and took a long, deep swig, and then another. She pushed the IGNITE button on the front burner and the blue flame came on with a satisfying whoosh.

The beer wasn't bad at all. She took another sip and tossed the panties onto the burner. The tiny scrap of synthetic silk went up in flames and was gone in a second or two, which was a disappointment. The shorts made a nicer display, and she watched the blaze for two or three minutes, reluctantly adding the T-shirt and then, after another five minutes, the bra. The bra, which had heavy padding, smoldered for several minutes, sending up a stinky black fog of smoke.

She looked around for something else to add to the fire, and remembered Ben's shirt, still draped over the windshield of his Audi.

Ben loved expensive things. But Grace, raised above her parent's working-class bar in the nearby fishing hamlet of Cortez, could never quite get comfortable with the luxury goods that her husband had grown up with as the pampered only son of a Miami bank executive. The day she'd bought the shirt at Neiman-Marcus, for $350, she'd walked away from it twice, finally forcing herself to pull the trigger and buy the damned thing.

Grace stood in the open doorway of the garage, scowling at the Audi. If the shirt was Ben's favorite, the Audi, a 2013 Spyder R8 convertible, was beyond his favorite. It was his obsession. He'd bought the Audi without consulting Grace, right after they signed the pilot deal with HGTV. Ben wouldn't disclose what he'd paid for the car, saying only that he'd "worked a deal" on it, but when she checked the prices online, she'd discovered that the thing retailed for $175,000! She'd somehow managed to swallow her resentment over not being included in the decision to buy the new car, telling herself that if Ben, who handled all the family finances, thought they could afford the car, then she shouldn't worry.

She walked around to the driver's side, snatching the shirt off the windshield. Looking down, she noticed the keys were still in the ignition.

The next thing she knew, she was using the shirt to wipe down the bucket seat's leather upholstery—just in case. She slid beneath the wheel and turned the key in the ignition, smiling as the powerful engine roared to life.

Ben didn't exactly prohibit her from driving the Audi, but he didn't encourage it either, telling her it was "a lot of car" for a woman and pointing out that her experience driving a stick shift was limited, although she'd learned to drive on her father's beat-up manual-transmission Chevy pickup.

Maybe, Grace thought, she'd just take the Audi for a spin around the neighborhood. Wouldn't that just fire Ben's rockets? She hoped he was watching from one of the upstairs windows. He'd have a stroke when he saw her behind the wheel. She eased the car into reverse, carefully backing it out of the garage.

Maneuvering an expert three-point turn, she was about to head down the driveway when the kitchen door flew open.

"Grace!" Ben yelled. "What do you think you're doing?"

"Going for a drive," she said cheerfully, raising the Corona in a jaunty salute.

"The hell you are," he barked, walking toward her. "You've been drinking and you're in no shape to be driving. Get out of my car."

"Your car?" she raised an eyebrow.

"You know what I mean," he said. "You've had your fun. This is taking things too far."

Too far? Grace revved the Audi's engine and slammed the car in first, screeching past Ben, who was a shouting, raving blur. Now she was at the edge of the patio, knocking over chaise lounges and the wrought-iron table with its jaunty green umbrella. The limpid turquoise surface of the pool was straight ahead. She closed her eyes, held her nose, and stomped the accelerator. The shock of the water was a final reminder. This was no nightmare. She was awake.

2

Grace had grown up living above a marina, but she was only an okay swimmer. Still, she could dog-paddle and manage a serviceable backstroke when the occasion demanded. The shock of the cold water disoriented her momentarily, but seconds later she managed to kick herself free of the Audi and power up to the surface, blinking and gasping for air.

As soon as she surfaced, the enormity of what she'd just done came crashing down. She pushed her hair from her eyes and saw Ben, standing at the side of the pool, staring down at her, wild-eyed and more agitated than she'd ever seen him. "Jesus, Grace!" he shouted. "My car! What have you done to my car?"

He wasn't alone. A uniformed police officer stood at his side, training a large flashlight over the pool. Grace wished she could dive back down to the bottom, maybe hide in the Audi's trunk. Just until things got a little less crazy.

"Ma'am?" The cop was young, with close-shorn hair and a look of concern that was noticeably absent from her husband's face. "Are you all right?"

Grace coughed and brushed a strand of hair from her face, dog-paddling to stay afloat. "I'm all right," she said cautiously, flexing her toes and examining her hands just to make sure. Not a scratch, she thought, which pleased her. After all, she was homicidal, not suicidal.

"You're not all right," Ben snapped. "You're fuckin' nuts."

"Ma'am, could you come out of the water now?" the cop asked.

Grace looked around the backyard. "Where's the slut?" she called.

The cop looked confused. "Who?"

"J'Aimee. The slut. I'm not coming out if she's still here."

"Who's Jamie?"

Grace jutted her chin in Ben's direction. "Ask him." Her legs were getting a little weary from all the dog-paddling, so she floated onto her back and stared up at the sky. It was a gorgeous evening. The clouds had cleared, and the stars sprinkled in the deep blue heavens looked so close she felt she might just reach out and pluck one. It was too bad she couldn't just float here for a long time, enjoying this view.

"Sir?" she heard the cop say.

"It's not Jamie, it's J'Aimee," Ben said. "And she's our assistant. The woman my wife assaulted earlier this evening. Grace chased her off. I don't know where she's gone."

"Our assistant?" Grace said. "I thought she was my assistant. Of course, that was before I found her assisting you earlier this evening." She turned to face the cop. "I caught them, doing it, right there in the garage. In the front seat of the Audi. So you see why I want to make sure she's gone, can't you?"

The cop was blushing now, which made him look even younger. He coughed and crossed his arms and looked over at Ben. "Is that correct?"

"No, it's not correct," Ben said. "My wife thinks she saw something she didn't, and now she's blown everything completely out of proportion."

"Blown!" Grace called, her legs pumping underwater, her voice abnormally gleeful. "You got that right, buddy. Only I wasn't the one doing the blowing, was I?"

"You're disgusting," Ben said. He turned to the cop. "She's been drinking, obviously."

The cop gave Grace a stern look. "Ma'am, have you been drinking?"

"I had half a beer," Grace said. "You want me to take a Breathalyzer? Want to draw some blood?" She held her arm above water, as though he might tap a vein right there and then.

While he was considering that, the radio clipped to his shoulder began to crackle. He turned his back to her, spoke into it briefly and then turned around again.

"I think you need to come out of that pool now," he told Grace. He turned to

Ben. "You told the dispatcher you were afraid she might get hurt. Or hurt somebody else. Are you still concerned about that?"

Ben shrugged. "I suppose not."

"What about you?" the cop asked Grace. "Did your husband strike you, or threaten to harm you in any way?"

"Not really," Grace admitted.

"What about this J'Aimee person? Do I need to get a statement from her?"

Grace swam to the shallow end of the pool and pulled herself up on the coral rock patio. The May night was warm, but she shivered as the water streamed off her body.

Ben's voice was low. "That won't be necessary."

"I want to get a statement from her," Grace called, standing up. She pointed toward the hibiscus hedge. "She went that-a-way."

Her teeth were chattering and she hugged her arms around her torso. "Excuse me," she told the cop. "I'm just going to get a towel to dry off."

Grace found a thick yellow and green striped beach towel in the cabinet at the edge of the patio and wrapped it around herself. She took another towel and wound it around her head, turban-style. Suddenly, her legs felt weak. She sat, abruptly, on the edge of the only chaise lounge she hadn't mowed down on her way to the pool.

The young police officer looked down at her with an expression of unspeakable pity. "Are you sure you're all right? You didn't hit your head or anything?"

"My head is fine," Grace said, tears springing to her eyes. She couldn't say the same of her heart. Her chest felt like it might explode.

"What happens now?" Ben said, his voice gruff. He was standing ten yards away, keeping his distance so her craziness didn't rub off.

"Unless one of you wants to file a complaint, nothing happens," the cop said. "I'd suggest you take your wife inside and get her some dry clothes."

"She can get her own clothes," Ben said.

"Also, considering the, um, circumstances, I think it would be best if you did not both spend the rest of the night here," the cop went on. He looked over at Ben. "Maybe you could call a friend? Or get a motel room?"

"I'm not going anywhere!" Ben said, outraged. "This is my home." He looked over at Grace. "Besides, I can't exactly leave, since my car is currently resting on the bottom of the pool."

"Don't worry, I'm going," Grace said, struggling to her feet. She glanced in the direction of the house. She could see the lights she'd left on in their bedroom, and the kitchen light, too. The house looked enormous, like something she'd seen in a magazine layout. Or a real estate ad. It didn't look real to her. Not like a home. Nothing like a home.

The cop looked from Ben to Grace. His radio crackled again. "Are we done here?"

"We're done," Grace said wearily.

Ben stomped off in the direction of the house. A moment later, he switched off the exterior lights, throwing the yard into sudden darkness. The cop gave a nervous cough, but he didn't leave. He switched on his flashlight, but held it down at his side.

"Um," he said, and she could see that he was blushing again.

"I swear, I'm not going to do anything violent," Grace said. "I'd just like to tell you that, for whatever it's worth, I'm really a very normal, peace-loving person. I've never, ever done anything like this before."

She peered at his face, to see if he believed her.

"Look," he said hesitantly. "I didn't want to say this in front of your husband. But I'm a big fan of your blog."

"You read Gracenotes?" Grace wasn't sure if she should be embarrassed or flattered. "Really?"

"Oh yeah. I even subscribe. My girlfriend and I just moved in together, and we're fixing up our place, and we both really enjoy Gracenotes. Next weekend, we're even going to paint our bathroom ceiling the same color you painted your powder room."

"Waterfall? That is so sweet!"

"Well, we're going to cut the strength fifty percent, like you suggested in your blog," he said. "But Amy, that's my girlfriend, she's already painted the walls Cloud Cover. How do you think that will look?"

"It'll be great," Grace assured him. "That's one of my favorite whites. And Benjamin Moore is an excellent paint. I use it all the time."

Am I really discussing paint colors with a cop? Within an hour of my life imploding?

"Great," the cop said. He reached into his pocket and brought out a business card. "Hey, uh, I'm sorry about tonight. Don't quote me, but I kinda don't blame you for what you did with his car. I mean, what kind of douche bag does something like that?"

"The kind I'm married to, apparently," Grace told him. She took the card, and he held up his flashlight so she could read it. "Officer Strivecky."

"Pete," he said. "My cell phone number is on there, if you need me again tonight. I'm on shift until seven, okay?"

"Okay," she said, touched by his kindness. "Thanks for not arresting me."

"You've got a place to go?" he asked. "It's really not a good idea for you to stay here."

"Don't worry," she said, feeling a shiver run down her spine. "I'm just going to throw some things in a bag, and then I'm gone. My mom lives over on Cortez. I'll head over to her place. You couldn't pay me to spend another night here, now that I know what's been going on right under my own nose."

"I could hang around," Pete Strivecky said, gesturing in the direction of the house. "Make sure he doesn't try anything tricky."

"He won't," Grace said. "He's a douche bag, like you said, but he's not a dangerous douche bag."

He turned to go.

"Officer Strivecky? Pete?"

"Yeah?" he said, pausing at the edge of the pool, glancing down at the submerged Audi.

"Do you mind if I ask how old you are? You look too young to be a police officer."

He laughed. "I get that all the time. It's the red hair and freckles. I'm twenty-six. Been on the force for three years now."

"Twenty-six," Grace said wistfully. "So young . . ." She nodded her head in the direction of the house. "Seems like a long, long time ago."

"Yes ma'am," he said.

She had an idea. "Hey. Send me a photo of your bathroom after you're done, will you? For the blog? I'd love to see how it turns out."

"I'll do that," he said. "And you take care."

An open bottle of Chivas Regal stood on the kitchen counter. She could hear the sound of the television coming from the media room. The door was firmly closed, but he'd turned up the volume on the surround sound, and she recognized Bruce Willis's voice. He was watching one of the *Die Hard* movies again.

For Ben, watching the bad guys blow up buildings and try to shoot down airliners just never got old.

She ran up the back staircase to their bedroom. On her side of the his-and-hers bathroom suite, she peeled out of her sopping wet shorts and T-shirt, stopping only to drape them neatly over the towel bar beside her Jacuzzi. She grabbed a cosmetic bag from a drawer in her dressing table and swept in some random toiletries: her shampoo and conditioner, deodorant, and her vitamins. Her hand hovered over the Clomid pill bottle. She'd been scheduled to start her second round of the fertility drug at the start of her next period, in two weeks.

It had taken Grace two years to talk Ben into seeing a fertility specialist. An only child herself, she'd always wanted children. Ben claimed to want them, too, although he didn't see why they couldn't just "wait and see" if she'd get pregnant what he called "the natural way." Finally, two months ago, he'd relented. "Now or never," was the way Ben looked at it.

"Never," Grace said now, tossing the pills into the trash. She wondered if he'd already started sleeping with J'Aimee when she'd begun taking the Clomid. But she couldn't think about that right now. What was done was done. And she—and Ben—were done.

Standing in her walk-in closet, she dressed quickly in a pair of white jeans and a favorite navy-blue knit top. She slid her feet into a pair of Jack Rogers sandals. Opening a suitcase on the top of the island that housed her folded clothes, she dumped a handful of random things: panties and bras, some shorts and tops, and a pair of jeans. She threw her running shoes and socks on top of the clothes, then zipped the suitcase.

Grace stepped into the bedroom and looked around. One last time, she told herself. At the silver framed photos of her and Ben in happier times, at the paintings she'd collected and hung on the walls, at the gorgeous custom-made linen drapes. It was the nicest room she'd ever owned, and she was getting ready to walk right out of it.

She found her purse on the tufted velvet bench at the foot of the bed and slipped the strap over her shoulder. Picking her suitcase up, she made her way back down the stairs. She stopped in her office, shoving her laptop computer and a handful of file folders into an oversized tote bag. She dumped her camera bag on top, hefted the tote onto her other shoulder, and made her way awkwardly to the kitchen door.

The Chivas bottle was gone from the kitchen counter and the door to the media room was still closed. From within, Bruce Willis was kicking ass and taking names.

Grace paused by the door. She raised her hand to knock, but changed her mind. She went out the kitchen door, walked to the garage, and got into her own car, a four-year-old Subaru. "Now or never," she whispered aloud.

3

Grace was idly switching channels on the big wall-mounted television at the Sandbox, her mother's bar on Cortez, a spot only seven miles, but light years, away from Grace's house on Sand Dollar Lane.

"Leave it on channel four," Rochelle said. "Please."

Grace gave her a look. "You know I always watch the morning news on four," Rochelle said. "I hate that weather guy's hair on channel eight."

Grace gave a martyred sigh and did as she was told, turning back to her mother's favorite channel, just in time to see a reporter standing in front of her very own front yard.

"Holy crap," Rochelle whispered. "Is this what I think it is?"

"Good morning," said the reporter, a black woman who'd been a local television mainstay for as long as Grace could remember. Camryn Nobles. Grace stared at the television. How the hell had Camryn Nobles gotten past security?

"I'm at the exclusive gated community of Gulf Vista on Siesta Key, where police were summoned this morning to what they termed an escalating case of domestic disturbance. But what makes this story newsworthy, in fact, fascinating, is that the principals involved in the incident are a nationally known domestic goddess—and her husband—or is it safe to say, soon to be ex-husband?"

The camera panned to show a pale-pink stucco two-story Spanish colonial revival mansion with red tile roof sprawling across a swath of emerald green lawn dotted with colorful beds of tropical flowers and half a dozen black-and-white Sarasota County sheriff's deputy cars, as well as a fire truck, an emergency rescue ambulance, and a large black tow truck. A traffic helicopter from the Tampa CBS affiliate droned overhead.

"You're a media event," Rochelle said, and Grace shot her another look.

"If this palatial house and grounds look familiar to many of you," Camryn Nobles said, her voice lowering to a confidential tone, "it's because this is the home of lifestyle blogger Grace Stanton, who writes the wildly popular Gracenotes blog. The house has been featured in numerous national publications, and Ms. Stanton has been a frequent guest on network shows like *Oprah, Ellen,* and, yes, even the *Today* show, and of course our own *Suncoast Morning!* where she's been practically a fixture over the past two years, as a lifestyle expert."

Now Camryn was talking again, strolling around to the side of the house, down a long coral-rock driveway toward the rear of the Stanton mansion.

"Grace Stanton is a successful interior designer and a hometown girl who grew up in modest circumstances in nearby Cortez," Camryn said. "After moving to South Florida and marrying, she had a thriving design practice before moving back here to the Suncoast in 2009. Husband Ben, forty-four, was an advertising executive who gave up his career two years ago in order to devote all his energies to maximizing his wife's burgeoning lifestyle business. Grace and Ben Stanton are fixtures on the local social scene; in fact, they hosted a charity party for the local children's shelter right here in this lovely poolside setting back in October. But authorities say this bucolic scene turned ugly sometime after midnight. Here's the tape police have released, of the panicky 911 phone call they received at one fifteen A.M. from Ben Stanton. And we want to apologize to our viewers, in advance, for the somewhat graphic language in this tape."

"Yeah, I'm gonna need some assistance here. My, uh, my wife, she's out of control."

The female 911 operator sounded bored. "*Sir, are you in physical danger?"*

"What? I don't know. She went crazy on me. I've never seen her like this. Look, I think you better get an officer over here before she does hurt somebody."

Shrieks were clearly audible in the background. And then came Ben Stanton's muffled voice.

"Grace, what are you doing? This isn't funny. Are you crazy? What the... Get the hell away from there!"

In the background came the sound of a car door slamming, then a high-powered motor revving, tires squealing across pavement. And then, a loud splash.

"Christ! Grace, what the hell have you done? Jesus H!..."

"Sir? Do you have a life-threatening situation there?"

Stanton's voice, when he came back on the line, was grim. *"If she hasn't already drowned, I'll kill the bitch myself."*

"Turn it off, please," Grace said, turning her back to the television.

Rochelle dialed down the volume, but she kept watching.

Camryn was back on camera, walking toward a patio area lined with a lush hedge of sea grapes. Graceful coconut palms and hibiscus shrubs were scattered about the patio, which included a fully outfitted kitchen and thatch-roofed tiki bar.

The reporter gestured in the direction of a two-story, three-bay garage. "The police won't say what sparked the altercation between Grace and Ben Stanton last night, but I spoke off camera to a neighbor who claims to have overheard what she termed 'a spirited exchange' between the married couple last night. That neighbor says the source of the problem was Mrs. Stanton's stunning twenty-six-year-old female assistant, who has been living in a garage apartment on this property for some months now. The neighbor also says that in the early morning hours before dawn today, that assistant, whose name we aren't divulging, fled in terror through that hedge," Camryn pointed to the sea grapes, "wrapped only in a beach towel."

"Neither of the Stantons were available for comment at airtime," Camryn went on, still walking toward the patio, "But despite the lack of witness statements, or cooperation from the parties involved, there are some simply inescapable conclusions we can draw about what went down here last night."

The camera pulled back to show a three-car garage, with all three parking bays empty, and then panned over toward the swimming pool, a shimmering free-form turquoise oasis set on a patio of more coral rock. The shallow end of the pool had coral rock steps that descended into a separate, enclosed whirlpool spa. And the deep end?

Camryn Nobles stood at the edge of the pool and looked down, the camera following her gaze. A lime-green canvas beach umbrella floated tranquilly on the surface of the water, as did four chartreuse vinyl lounge cushions. Totally submerged and barely visible beneath the water was an ominous-looking oblong black form.

"And that," Camryn said, her voice somber, "appears to be Ben Stanton's 2013 Audi Spyder convertible, which retails for approximately 175,000 dollars."

Rochelle Davenport pointed the remote control and finally, mercifully, clicked it off.

"You really drove a car worth 175,000 dollars into the pool?" Rochelle asked her daughter.

Grace shrugged. "I doubt he paid that much for it. Knowing Ben, he worked some kind of advertising trade-off with the dealer."

"This is just so unlike you," Rochelle said. "I mean, I don't blame you for what you did, but it's just so not you."

"Temporary insanity," Grace said. "That's the only explanation I can think of."

"You could have drowned," Rochelle said. "Did you think of that? You'd have left me a childless widow."

"And then Ben could have collected on that two-million-dollar life insurance policy we bought last year," Grace muttered. "I gotta change that."

"It was a dumb thing to do," Rochelle insisted. "Seriously."

"I couldn't have drowned. The top was still down," Grace said, suddenly returning to her normal, logical self. "I guess it got kind of hot in that garage, while she was . . ."

"Giving him a blow job?" Rochelle said helpfully.

"Yeah. In the front seat of the Audi."

"I also can't believe Ben just let you drive it into the pool," Rochelle said. "How exactly did that happen?"

"I can't discuss that right now," Grace said, staring moodily into her iced tea glass. "It makes my head hurt."

Rochelle reached behind the bar for the industrial-sized bottle of ibuprofen she kept there, shook two into her hand, and handed them to her daughter.

"Thanks," Grace said, swallowing the pills. "Have you got any food around here? I've always heard that heartbreak kills your appetite, but I haven't eaten in twelve hours, and, I swear, I could gnaw my arm off right now."

Rochelle pushed one of the plastic laminated menus across the bar.

Grace looked down at the Sandbox menu, which, as far as she knew, hadn't changed in at least fifteen years. "Buffalo wings. Stuffed potato skins. Stuffed potato skins with Buffalo-wing sauce. Onion rings. Fried oysters. Fried shrimp." She looked up at her mother. "Seriously? How are you still alive, eating this stuff all this time?"

"I don't eat this crap," Rochelle said, nonplussed. "You kidding me? I'd be big as a damned house."

She allowed herself a satisfying glance in the mirror over the back bar. At fifty-nine, Rochelle was proud of her still-trim figure. She took good care of herself, slathered herself with sunscreen before taking her two-mile walk along Bradenton Beach every morning, colored her hair a soft brown at home, and allowed herself a single glass of heart-healthy red wine or the occasional beer most evenings. She'd quit her pack-a-day smoking when Grace was still a baby, and her doctor said she had the bone density of an eighteen-year-old.

"I microwave myself a nice Lean Cuisine for dinner, usually. And for breakfast, I juice."

"You juice? As a verb?"

"Don't get snotty with me," Rochelle said. She nodded at the oversized Oster blender on the back bar. "Felipe, this real nice Mexican guy, comes in here with his soccer team on Sundays, his mom runs a produce stand at the Red Barn, and he brings me all kinds of fresh produce. Spinach, kale, chayote, strawberries, pineapples, mangoes. Herbs, too. I like mint and ginger. I put it in with everything."

"That doesn't sound too bad, actually," Grace admitted. "You got anything like that you could fix up for me? Not kale," she said, wrinkling her nose. "But any of that other stuff?"

"Sorry," Rochelle said. "I used up the last of the fresh stuff this morning. I could maybe make you a sandwich. Would a BLT offend your delicate sensibilities?"

"That'd be great," Grace said, resting her cheek against the bar and folding her arms over her head. Her shoulders heaved, and she let out a muffled sob. It was the first time Rochelle had seen her cry since she was a teenager, and it wrenched her heart just as it had back then.

Rochelle hesitated, but then reached over and smoothed her daughter's mussed hair. "Don't worry, sweetie. We'll fix this. We'll figure it out."

Grace raised her head and looked at Rochelle, tears streaming down her cheeks. "Fix it? That's exactly what Ben said, 'we can fix this.' And then he admitted it wasn't the first time. How do we figure this out, Mom? I loved him. I thought he loved me. But it was all a lie. Everything was a lie. What do I do now?"

Rochelle handed her a paper towel. "Blow your nose. Dry your tears. Eat something. And then we'll call your Uncle Dennis and take the bastard to the cleaners."

"Uncle Dennis is a real estate lawyer," Grace said, sniffling. "He doesn't do divorces."

"No, but he's been divorced twice himself, so he'll know who we should call, and who we should avoid."

Grace took a gulp of tea. "I'm not even sure I want a divorce."

"You're kidding," Rochelle said. "You caught Ben having sex in your garage with your assistant, who he's surely been screwing at your house all these months, and you're not sure it's over?"

"I don't know," Grace wailed. "This is not the way I thought my life would go. I don't understand any of this. I thought I would have a forever marriage, like yours and Daddy's."

Rochelle considered this, started to say something, then changed her mind. Now was not the time.

"Have you talked to Ben since last night?"

"No."

"Any plans to talk to him?"

Grace shrugged. "I've got to go over there and pick up some more clothes pretty soon. And I'll have to figure out what to do about the blog, and the HGTV pilot and all the rest of it."

Rochelle busied herself putting together her daughter's sandwich. She popped two slices of bread into the toaster, slapped some bacon on the griddle, and picked up a fat red Ruskin tomato from a bowl on the back bar. She had the knife poised to slice it when Grace spoke up.

"Could you peel that, please?"

Her mother shot her a look of annoyance. "I fixed you a million BLTs in your childhood, and now, suddenly, you have to have your tomatoes peeled? La-de-damn-da."

Grace stood up and came around the bar. "Never mind. I'll make it myself if it's that big a deal."

"It's not a big deal. I just don't get why it's necessary. The peel has the most vitamins."

"That's not true," Grace said flatly, taking the knife from her mother and proceeding to pare the skin from the tomato.

Rochelle stood back with her hands on her hips. "Who says it's not true? It's absolutely true."

"According to who?"

"I forget," Rochelle said stubbornly. "Maybe I heard it on one of those cooking shows."

Grace shook her head and reached into the refrigerator for a head of lettuce. She peeled a leaf from the head and gave a martyred sigh.

"What now? You don't like my lettuce?"

"I'm just not crazy about iceberg," Grace said. "Romaine is so much tastier. And prettier, not to mention better for you, since we're talking about vitamins."

"I like iceberg," Rochelle said, her tone frosty. "It's what I've always bought. It was always good enough for you up until now."

Grace fixed her with a look. "Are we going to get into this again? I'm sorry, Mom, if I like nice things. Sorry if it somehow offends you that I outgrew my childhood taste for Kraft macaroni and cheese and frozen Tater Tots and casseroles made with cream of mushroom soup and canned onions rings. And Asti Spumante." She shuddered involuntarily at this last listing.

"That chicken casserole used to be your favorite," Rochelle said. "You insisted I make it for your birthday dinner every year."

"I was a kid," Grace said. "I grew up and my tastes changed. Refined, if you will."

Rochelle rolled her eyes and built the sandwich. She placed it on a plate, deftly cut it in half on the diagonal, and handed it to Grace.

"Thanks," Grace said. She took the sandwich and moved back to her barstool, chewing slowly.

Rochelle wiped the bread crumbs from the cutting board. "This split-up could get pretty messy, pretty fast, you know. Ben is involved in every aspect of your business. You can walk away from him, but can you walk away from everything you've built up in the business? Not to mention the house?"

Grace shrugged to indicate she had no answers, and kept chewing.

"Counseling?" Rochelle offered. Grace shook her head violently and took another bite of her sandwich, and then a sip of her iced tea.

"All right," her mother said, glancing meaningfully at the neon Budweiser sign that hung over the mirrored bar back. "It's after eleven now. My lunch trade is gonna start trickling in here pretty soon."

"I can take a hint," Grace said, finishing off the last of her sandwich. She pushed the empty plate aside and stood. "I'm gonna go upstairs to my old room and try to get some work done. I'm doing a giveaway of this hideous Tuscan pottery on Monday, and I've got to write that blog post and figure out what I'm writing about tomorrow."

She picked up her laptop case. "You've got Wi-Fi, right?"

Rochelle wrinkled her brow. "I guess. They hooked up some kind of Internet doohickey when I changed cable providers back in the spring."

"Password?"

"Who knows?"

"Never mind, I'll figure it out myself," Grace said. She headed for the stairway that led to the family's upstairs living area, and then stopped and poked her head around the doorway. "If Ben calls here looking for me, you haven't seen me and don't know where I am."

"Gotcha," Rochelle said. "I hope he does call. I'll give the son of a bitch an earful."

"Thanks," Grace said, offering a wan smile. "It's good to know you've got my back."

"I do," Rochelle assured her. "I'm your wingman, right?"

Grace pushed the bedroom door open with her hip. She'd decorated the room herself, at the age of fourteen, and not one single thing had changed in all these years.

She'd been in her Laura Ashley phase then. She'd longed for the pink and white striped wallpaper she'd seen in a *House Beautiful* layout, but with no money to spend, she'd laboriously taped and painted pink stripes over the cheap knotty pine-paneled walls that her mother had previously slathered with white paint. Grace found a crappy $9.99 faux-mahogany four-poster bed at the Salvation Army and painted it white, then stenciled a sappy design of green vines, pink daisies, and blue ribbons across the headboard.

Grace kicked at the worn and stained beige wall-to-wall carpet on the floor. She'd begged and pleaded with her father to let her rip up that carpet—the same stuff that covered every surface in their apartment, but Butch had been adamant. "Do you know how much money I spent on this stuff?"

She settled onto the faded pink chintz bedspread and opened her laptop, clicking onto the logo for Gracenotes. She reread the post she'd written the previous evening, which seemed like something from a previous life. There were already forty-seven comments posted. Had any of her readers seen the news about the flamboyant scene at her house? She decided against reading the comments. Maybe later.

Instead, she concentrated on writing Monday's post, going ahead with the topic she'd already settled on a week ago: how and where to find great deals on discounted designer home fabrics. Soon she was typing away, copying and pasting images of favorite fabrics and room settings, copying Web site links, losing herself in the process of creation.

When she looked up from her work, she realized that two hours had passed. Her cell phone, lying on the nightstand, had not rung, and no beeps had signaled an incoming text message. She'd halfway expected Ben to call, either downcast and contrite, or furious and full of threats. The silence seemed ominous. No matter. She glared at the phone, daring it to ring. She would not call him. Not ever. Let the swine call and beg her to come crawling back.

Grace went back to her work. She checked for typos, misspellings, links that didn't work, pictures that were improperly sized. Finally satisfied with her work, she pulled up the Gracenotes blog page, and clicked on the sign-in and password buttons.

A red highlighted italicized sentence flashed on the screen.

Invalid password. Try again?

She frowned and winced as she retyped the password. *GracenBen4ever.*

Invalid password. Check for misspellings?

Not possible. She typed the word again, with the same results.

Reset password?

She checked her e-mail, waiting for the message to alert her that her new password had been sent. But when she opened the e-mail, she stared down at the message in disbelief.

New password may not be reset. Invalid user name. Please contact technical support if you believe this message has been sent in error.

She fumed and dialed the number provided, waiting on hold for ten minutes. Finally, a young man who identified himself as Hans came on the line.

"Hello," she said briskly. "My name is Grace Stanton, and I write a blog called Gracenotes. I've just spent half an hour trying to get access to my dashboard so I can write a new post, but I keep getting error messages, and, finally, I got a message telling me that I can't set a new password, because I have an invalid user name. But it's not invalid. I've been writing this blog for three years under the same name. So I can't understand what is happening."

"Let me just check that," Hans said. She could hear his fingertips flying over a keyboard. "Just a moment," he said, putting her on hold.

A moment later he was back on the line. "Mrs. Stanton?"

"Ms. Stanton," Grace said pointedly.

"Right. Um. The thing is, you don't have access to the blog dashboard."

"I know that," she said sharply. "That's why I'm calling you. Because I need access. It's my blog."

"Wellll," he said. "From what I can tell, the domain owner has changed the user sign-on and password. That would explain why you're locked out."

"That can't be," Grace said, feeling her face get hot. "I'm the domain owner. The blog is Gracenotes. I'm Grace Stanton."

There was a long meaningful silence on the other end of the line. "Actually," Hans said, "according to our records, the domain owner is Ben Stanton. And apparently, he's changed the access."

"He can't do that," Grace cried. "Change it back. It's my blog. I started it, I write it, I own it. And I want you to change it so I can have access to my own blog."

"I'm sorry, Ms. Stanton, but I don't have the authority to do that," Hans said. "Now, is there anything else I can help you with?"

Downstairs, in the bar, Rochelle was pouring a longneck Sweetwater Pale when she heard an unearthly shriek coming from the direction of upstairs.

Frank, a mailman who'd just come off his shift, gave her a questioning look.

"My daughter," Rochelle said apologetically. "She's having some marital issues."

4

Three days had passed since Grace had walked out of the house on Sand Dollar Lane.

They were three of the longest, most miserable days of her life. During the days, she tried to help out around the Sandbox, working behind the bar, waiting tables, even doing a brief stint as a short-order cook, until her mother unceremoniously fired her from that job after she caught Grace substituting ground turkey for ground chuck in the bar's signature Sandbox burger.

"I know you mean well," Rochelle said, ordering her out of the kitchen. "But my customers don't care about saturated fats or sodium or antioxidants. They just want a big, greasy, salty burger on a puffy, white, highly processed white bun. With maybe a slab of gooey yellow cheese on top. And they definitely don't want a side order of smug advice about healthy dining."

Evenings, Grace locked herself up in her bedroom, spending hours writing blog entries she couldn't even post. When she finished writing and editing, she slipped out to the second-story deck overlooking the Cortez marina. Growing up, she'd hated that marina. She hated the stink of the diesel fuel burned by the boats and the shrill cries of seagulls wheeling overhead as the shrimpers and commercial fishermen returned to the docks with their catch. She'd hated the greasy water lapping against the seawall, and the constant ebb and flow of fishermen and regulars who regarded the Sandbox as their home away from home.

Most of all, Grace hated the fact of where she lived. In high school, the guys she dated thought it was awesome that she lived right on the water, and above a bar! But she didn't want to live on a marina. She wanted a regular suburban house, with a grassy green lawn, and although she loved her parents, she longed for a father who worked in an office and wore a necktie, with a mother who stayed home and played bridge and got her hair done every Thursday.

The only ties Butch Davenport owned were bolo ties, which he wore with his ever-present violently colored Hawaiian shirts. As for Rochelle, who cut her own hair, Grace was fairly sure she didn't even know how to play bridge, although she was a demon at pinochle.

For some reason, the sights and sounds of the marina, and the bay that flowed beneath the weathered gray boards of the docks, were now oddly comforting. When sleep wouldn't come, and it rarely did, she crept out to the deck, in her nightgown, and sat for hours, her knees tucked to her chest, staring off at the sparkling black water and the shadowy hulks of the fishing vessels tied up at the dock.

That first morning Grace had moved home, Rochelle found her like that when she arose at seven to make coffee.

Her mother sank into the chair next to her, wordlessly handing her a steaming mug. Grace nodded her thanks and sipped.

"Gonna be another hot day," Rochelle said finally, looking at the pink-tinged sky.

"Hotter than the hinges of hell," Grace agreed, repeating one of Butch's favorite sayings.

"You sleep any?" Rochelle asked.

"A little," Grace lied.

"I've got some Ambien, if you want," her mother offered.

Grace stared at her, shocked. The only drugs she'd ever known her mother to take were baby aspirin.

"Don't look at me like that," Rochelle said. "The doctor gave 'em to me, after your daddy died. I only took the one. Slept for fourteen hours straight, and when I finally did wake up, I'd eaten most of a pecan pie somebody brought to the house after the funeral. I looked it up on the computer. It's a real thing. Sleep eating, they call it. Hell's bells, I eat enough when I'm awake. I don't need a pill that makes you eat a whole pie without even remembering it."

Grace was forced to smile.

"You hear anything from the asshole?" Rochelle asked.

"Not a word," Grace said.

"Are you okay for money?" Rochelle asked.

"For now," Grace lied.

Rochelle knew it for the lie it was, but didn't call her daughter out on it. Instead, she sighed and gave Grace a sideways glance. "I think you better give your Uncle Dennis a call."

When she couldn't access her blog, Grace reluctantly called Ben, leaving a voice mail when he didn't pick up. Three days later, Ben still wasn't returning Grace's phone calls. But he'd been a busy little worker bee during that time. He'd changed the PINs for their joint checking and savings accounts, and although she'd gone to the bank in person, twice, and argued with the branch manager, she still couldn't make them understand that her estranged husband was freezing her out of her own hard-earned money. He'd canceled her AmEx and Visa cards. And when she'd gone to her gym to try to work out some of her frustrations in a Zumba class, she'd been greeted with the unwelcome news that her membership had been terminated, since the gym was no longer able to debit her checking account for her fees.

"Call Dickie Murphree," her Uncle Dennis said, when she finally got him on the phone. "I finally got smart and hired him the second time around. He's the best divorce lawyer in town. Didn't the two of you go to high school together?"

"Dickie! Of course," Grace said, her black mood lifting, just a little. "That's a great idea. Dickie took me on my first real car date. I haven't seen him in a couple years."

"Give him my best when you call," Dennis said. "And tell him I hope I never have to see him again. No offense."

She called the law offices of Murphree-Baggett-Hopkins twice a day, for two days in a row, each time asking the receptionist to please have Dickie call her about an urgent matter.

"He's in court," the receptionist told her. "I know, but I'm an old friend," she said, giving the woman her maiden name. Might as well start getting used to it again, she thought glumly.

Things really were getting pretty dire.

As much as she dreaded another confrontation, she had to talk to Ben. Aside from business matters that had to be settled, she needed more clothes, her treasured interior design books and magazine files, and the macro lens for her camera. Also panties.

Finally, she decided on an ambush. Grace dressed carefully for the outing, as carefully as she could considering the fact that her hastily packed suitcase contained three faded T-shirts, two pairs of yoga pants, her jogging shorts, and a pair of skinny white jeans that she hadn't actually been able to fit into in two years.

Now though, the jeans zipped with ease. Heartache, she thought ruefully, was the ultimate diet aid.

She tried calling Ben one more time, and when her message went directly to voice mail, she resolutely got behind the wheel of the Subaru and drove the ten miles to Siesta Key, her stomach roiling so badly that once, a mile from the house, she had to pull off onto the side of the road to barf on a white oleander bush.

On the way over, Grace rehearsed her lines.

"Hello, Ben. I know you've been avoiding me, and you're probably still furious about me driving the Audi into the pool, but hey! I'm still furious about finding you and J'Aimee doing the nasty in the front seat, so why don't we just call it a tie and figure out a way to get through all this with some courtesy and civility?"

She thought that was an excellent opener. And she would follow it up by letting him know that he would absolutely HAVE to unfreeze the bank accounts and credit cards and restore her access to the blog.

"It's my business, Ben. It's called Gracenotes, for God's sake. Your preventing me from participating in it is foolish and shortsighted."

That would get him. Ben was *all* about business. Since he dealt with all the blog's advertisers, he would certainly want to keep them happy to keep the ad dollars flowing. Right? Surely he would be reasonable, now that he'd had some time to think things over rationally. Right?

Up ahead, Grace spotted the thick emerald green embankment that meant she was approaching Gulf Vista, their subdivision. A stately row of royal palms, underplanted with thick beds of asparagus ferns, lined both sides of the road, and a classic arched white stucco bridge crossed over a canal. A hundred yards ahead, she spotted the security gate and felt a sharp, unexpected wave of panic so strong that she had to clutch the steering wheel to keep from turning around and fleeing in the opposite direction.

Stop this! She told herself sternly. This is a business transaction. No need for emotion. Be strong.

She pulled the car alongside the electronic card reader and swiped her plastic key card through it, waiting patiently for the heavy iron gates to slide open.

Nothing. The gate didn't move. She wiped the card on the leg of her jeans, a trick she'd used many times when the finicky card reader refused to open sesame.

Grace tried three more times with the same results. Despite the fact that she had the Subaru's air-conditioner thermostat on the subarctic setting, she could already feel sweat beading up on her forehead. Her mouth was dry, but her hands as they gripped the key card were clammy.

The driver of the black Lexus behind her car tapped his horn impatiently, but Grace had no place to go. The gate wouldn't open, and there were two more cars behind the Lexus.

The driver tapped his horn again. Finally, near tears, Grace rolled the window down and leaned out to address the situation. "I'm sorry," she called, waving her key card. "It's not working. Can you back up so that I can back up?"

The driver, an older man with silver hair, gestured impatiently. Finally, all three cars backed up so that Grace could get out of the line. She parked her car on the shoulder of the road and went to the guard shack, whose dark tinted windows obscured those inside. She felt limp and defeated, and she hadn't even gotten to the house yet, a destination she was already dreading.

She tapped on the guard-shack window, and finally a uniformed security guard, a middle-aged guy with a graying military crew cut, opened the door. She was grateful for the cold blast of air-conditioning. The guard stepped outside and Grace recognized him at once.

"Oh, hi, Sheldon," she said, favoring him with a smile. "I'm so glad you're on duty." She held up her key card. "I'm Grace Stanton. My key card won't work. Can you fix it for me?"

He frowned slightly, taking the card, turning it over and over to examine it closer. "Looks okay."

"I know, but it won't work," Grace said.

"Hang on a minute," Sheldon said. He stepped back into the guard booth and closed the door. A mosquito buzzed around her face, and she swatted it away. The sun beat down on her head, and she was sure she was about to melt.

The door opened, but only an inch or two. The security guard's friendly smile had vanished. Now he glowered at her. "Sorry. I can't help you."

"What?" Grace said, startled. "Why not?"

"I can't discuss it," Sheldon said, and he started to close the door again, but before he could, Grace grabbed the doorknob.

"Wait a minute," she said, feeling her face growing redder by the moment. "What's going on here? Why won't you fix my key card?"

He glanced around, to make sure he couldn't be overheard. As if!

"I can't help you because your card has been deactivated."

"That's ridiculous!" Grace said. "Is this because of . . . my marital situation? Did my husband call up here and tell you people to keep me out? He has no right! I live here. At 27 Sand Dollar Lane."

"I don't make the rules, ma'am," Sheldon said. "All's I know is, according to the computer, you are no longer listed as a resident of Gulf Vista."

"He can't do that," Grace said, her teeth gritted. "Please! Look, I don't want to make a scene . . ."

"Then don't," Sheldon said. He held up a walkie-talkie. "My supervisor told me to tell you that if you have a problem with the card situation, you should contact an attorney. Until we have some kind of a legal document stating otherwise, I can't let you in." He reached around and gently removed Grace's hand from the doorknob. "Sorry."

Grace heard a light beep of a car horn. A white Lincoln rolled up beside her and the passenger-side window slid down. Anita McKenna, an older woman she knew slightly from the country club, gave her a friendly smile. "Hi! It's Grace, right? Are you having car problems? Anything I can do to help?"

"Anita! Hello," Grace said eagerly, stepping closer to the car. "Actually, I am having a little issue . . ."

There was a tap on her shoulder. She turned to find Sheldon standing directly beside her. "Mrs. Stanton? My supervisor thinks it would be a good idea if you would just move along now." He held up his walkie-talkie again.

Grace felt her spine stiffen. "I was just . . ."

Anita McKenna looked from Sheldon to Grace. "Oh," she said. "My goodness. I didn't realize." The window slid up again, and the Lincoln breezed through the gate.

She called Dickie Murphree's office twice more on her way to back to Cortez. Finally, his receptionist allowed her to leave a voice mail message.

"Dickie," she said, fighting back tears. "It's Grace Davenport. I've been calling and calling. I really need to talk to you. I've left Ben. Maybe you saw it on the news? Now he's frozen our bank accounts, cut off my credit cards—he's even fixed it so I can't get back to our house to pick up my clothes and things. Please, Dickie. Please call me."

Grace was pulling into the crushed-shell parking lot at the Sandbox when her cell phone rang. She saw that the caller was Murphree-Baggett-Hopkins.

"Hello?"

"Hiya, Gracie," Dickie said. "I just got your message. Sorry it took me so long to call you back. I'm in trial this week, and the damned judge just now cut us loose for a lunch break. How's your Uncle Dennis?"

"He's fine," Grace said. "He sends his best. Look, Dickie, if you listened to my message, you know I'm in big trouble. When can I come see you? To talk about my situation?"

"Wellllll," Dickie drawled. "I'm not sure that's a good idea."

"Why not?" Grace asked, stunned. "Uncle Dennis said you're the best divorce lawyer in town."

"Hell of a guy, your uncle," Dickie said, chuckling. "He sure gets himself in some damned interesting jams, doesn't he?"

"Why isn't it a good idea for me to come see you?"

"Awwww, Grace," Dickie drawled. "You know I think the world of you, don't you? We had some good times, way back there in high school, didn't we? You broke my heart when you threw me over for that basketball player, sophomore year. What was that guy's name? He went on to play college ball at FSU, didn't he? It was years before I got over you."

"That's sweet, Dickie," she said impatiently. "His name was Calvin Becker. Could we discuss current affairs? Like my divorce?"

"The thing is, we can't talk, Grace," Dickie said. "It ain't even really proper for me to be talking to you right now, but I figured I owe you an explanation."

"What are you explaining?" Grace asked.

"That I can't represent you. Because I already agreed to represent Ben."

Grace put the phone down in her lap. She closed her eyes and rested her head against the steering wheel, utterly defeated.

"Grace?" Dickie's voice rose faintly from the phone. "Grace? Are you there?"

She pushed the disconnect button.

5

I take it things didn't go well with the asshole," Rochelle said, pouring her a large glass of iced tea and pushing it across the bar. "Drink that. It's sweetened. You're losing weight so fast it's starting to scare me."

Grace took a sip of the tea and sucked on an ice cube. "I never got to see Ben. I couldn't get through the security gate. He had my key card deactivated."

"Bastard," Rochelle said, pouring her own glass of iced tea. The lunch-time rush hour was over, and only two people remained at opposite ends of the bar, one watching the Rays game on the TV, the other staring intently down at his smartphone.

"Did your uncle's lawyer ever call you back?" Rochelle asked.

Grace stirred her tea with a straw. "Dickie Murphree. Yeah, he called. But I can't hire him."

"Why not? Just because you dated years ago?"

"I can't hire him because Ben beat me to it," Grace said, lifting her eyes to meet her mother's. "Yeah. Ben has already hired the best divorce lawyer in town. Face it, Mom. I'm screwed."

"No, you're not," Rochelle said. "The Yellow Pages are full of divorce lawyers. You can't swing a dead cat in this town without hitting a lawyer. We just need to find you the right one." She drummed her fingers on the bar's scarred wooden surface. A minute later, she disappeared into the kitchen.

When she reemerged, she handed her daughter a well-worn business card.

"Mitzi Stillwell, Attorney at Law?" Grace asked, lifting one eyebrow. "Who's she?"

"A lawyer I know," Rochelle said. "Give her a call."

Mitzi Stillwell didn't waste much time with niceties. She'd been practicing domestic law for a dozen years, and she generally believed her clients needed the truth more than they needed coddling.

She listened for fifteen minutes while Grace recounted her tale of what she now thought of as the meltdown, nodding and occasionally jotting some words onto a legal yellow pad.

"So," Grace said, when she'd finished. "What do you think? Can you help me?"

Mitzi tapped the pen against the legal pad. "You walked away from your own home—even though your husband was the one screwing around on you?"

"Yes," Grace said.

Mitzi cocked her head and a strand of gray-flecked dark hair fell across one eye. She was in her early fifties now, but when her hair started graying twenty years earlier, she'd chosen not to color it—just to give herself the look of an older, more experienced jurist. At home, she favored bright colors and clothes designed to show off the figure she worked hard at maintaining, but in the courtroom, Mitzi mostly chose expensively tailored business suits in neutral colors, with just enough feminine detailing to remind her clients—and prospective jurors—that she was a woman in charge.

"You know, Grace, it's supposed to work the other way around. You're supposed to kick his butt out of the house."

"Sorry," Grace said. "I'm new at all this. It never occurred to me to ask him to leave. Anyway, after I sank his car, I'd pretty much made the statement I needed to."

Mitzi laughed. "I've handled hundreds of divorces over the years, but you're my first client to drown a car." She half stood and bowed in Grace's direction. "Awesome. Although probably not prudent."

She sat down again and looked at her notes. "How are you for money?"

"I'm broke," Grace admitted. "Ben froze our bank accounts. He canceled my credit cards. I had to borrow money from my mom to buy gas to drive over here today."

The lawyer nodded. “Nothing unusual about that. We'll have to try to get the court to order your husband to come to a temporary financial agreement between the two of you.”

Mitzi doodled something on her legal pad, then considered whether or not to share some unhappy news with her client. She hesitated to pile more bad news on Grace Stanton, whose life had taken an ugly turn for the worse ever since she'd drowned her husband's sports car two weeks earlier.

Grace caught the meaning of her lawyer's pitying glance.

“What?” Grace said, tucking a lock of hair behind one ear. “You're giving me that look.”

“What look?” Mitzi asked.

“It's the look doctors give their patients before they tell them they've got an incurable disease. The look my college professor gave me right before he announced I'd pulled a D in statistics. The look that Ben gave me right before he admitted that night with J'Aimee wasn't the first. Come on, Mitzi. Spit it out.”

Mitzi sighed. “Your divorce case has been assigned a judge, and we've got a date for an initial hearing.”

“But that's good news, right? The faster we get things settled, the faster I can get my life back on track.”

“It would be good news,” Mitzi agreed. “Except that you drew Stackpole.”

“Who's he? One of Ben's old drinking buddies?”

“If only,” Mitzi said. “If we could prove he had some kind of association with your ex, that would be grounds for recusal, which would be great. But I doubt Ben and Cedric Stackpole have ever met.”

“Then, why is he bad news?”

“Because,” Mitzi said, “Cedric N. Stackpole Jr. is unofficial head of the He-Man Woman Hater Club.”

“Why?”

“Nobody knows. Stackpole just hates women in general and women plaintiffs specifically.”

“But, he's a judge. I mean, judges are impartial, right?”

“Supposed to be,” Mitzi said. “Only Stackpole never got that memo. He's a notorious misogynist. I've been lucky. I've only had one other divorce in front of him in the past.”

“How did that go?”

Mitzi's eyes strayed to the row of framed diplomas on the wall opposite her desk. "Hmm? Don't ask. My client got shafted. Her husband abandoned her and her two small children, left them basically penniless while he lived it up, funneling their marital assets into a dummy corporation. We had clear proof that he'd hidden assets, but Stackpole refused to hear a word of it. But because she finally had to go out and get a job to support herself and the children and eventually hooked up with a decent guy and allowed him to move in with her and the kids before the divorce was final, Stackpole decided she was an unfit mother. Gave the ex custody of the kids, forced her to move out of the house and sell it and split the proceeds with the ex, who was already a millionaire several times over."

Mitzi shook her head at the memory. "The ex didn't even want the kids. He just didn't want to pay her child support. It was brutal."

"How can a judge get away with that kind of thing?" Grace asked, horrified. "Can't you report him or something?"

"That's not how it works, unfortunately," Mitzi said. "We're just going to have to hope for the best. We'll lay out the facts; Gracenotes is your business, carries your name, and is written and photographed solely by you. By locking you out of your own Web site, Ben has essentially hijacked your name, which is trademarked, right?"

Grace shook her head. "I was *going* to trademark it, but I just never got around to it. I guess I assumed Ben would take care of that."

"Unfortunate," Mitzi said. She scribbled a note to herself. "All right, the good news is, at least we know what we're dealing with."

"If that's the good news, I don't want to hear the bad stuff," Grace said. She gathered her papers and went home to figure out her next move.

6

They'd gotten there early. The courtroom was half-full, and another hearing was still under way. Mitzi Stillwell led her up the right-side aisle and gestured at a vacant seat toward the front third of the room.

Grace studied the judge, who sat erect in his high-backed chair, listening intently. He looked to be in his late forties, with receding strawberry-blond hair combed straight back from a high forehead, steel-rimmed glasses, and a long, narrow, unsmiling face. "Is that our judge?"

"That's Stackpole, in the flesh," Mitzi said.

"I thought he'd be older," Grace said.

"He was two years behind me in law school at UF," Mitzi said. "And he was a pain in the ass, even then. But a politically connected pain. He was appointed to the bench at forty."

A uniformed bailiff, a young black woman with startling platinum marcelled hair who was standing at the side door to the courtroom, caught Mitzi's eye and gave her a very slight shake of the head.

"We gotta keep quiet," Mitzi murmured. "Or he'll have that bailiff toss us out."

A lawyer standing at the table on the left front side of the room stood and spoke into a microphone. "Judge, we'd like the court to view this video my client shot of her husband, while he was terrorizing my client." Grace couldn't see the lawyer's face, just the back of his balding head, and his neat, dark suit.

An older woman sitting at the opposite table stood. "Your honor, we have not seen that video, so we're going to oppose that being introduced into evidence."

The judge gave her a mirthless smile. "We'll all see it together right now, shall we, Ms. Entwhistle?"

"My client was deliberately goaded into an altercation by Mrs. Keeler's boyfriend. For months now, she and Luke Grigsby have repeatedly violated the terms of their custody agreement by either delivering Bo hours late, or not at all, at times when my client was scheduled to have Bo."

"Well, Ms. Entwhistle, I don't see where you've notified the court about that," Stackpole said evenly.

"No sir," Ms. Entwhistle said. "My client was trying to keep things amicable and civil, for the sake of the child. On the day that video was shot, Bo was to have been dropped off at his father's house before lunch. Mrs. Keeler was aware that Bo had a T-ball game at four that afternoon. My client even sent her a text message reminding her of that fact. But she was a no-show. She never notified my client of Bo's whereabouts, instead dropping him off at the park half an hour after the start of the game, and without his team uniform or his glove. The child was distraught, in fact, in tears, because he thought he'd let his team down."

The opposing lawyer stood up. "Judge, if you watch our video, you'll see that if there were indeed any tears, which my client states there weren't, it was probably only because Bo was afraid that Wyatt Keeler, who also happens to be his coach, and who obviously has a volatile temper, might be angry at *him*."

The man who'd been sitting at the table beside the female lawyer shot to his feet. He was coatless, but dressed in a pale yellow long-sleeved dress shirt and a blue necktie. He looked to be in his late thirties or early forties. His clean-shaven head was deeply tanned and gleamed in the glow of the courtroom lights. "That's not true," Wyatt Keeler called out, his voice cracking with emotion. "My son has never been afraid of me. He was crying because it was a big game, and Callie and Luke couldn't be bothered to get him there in time to play."

"That's enough, Mr. Keeler," the judge snapped. "Anything else, and I'll have the bailiff remove you from this courtroom." He closed his eyes for a moment and pinched the bridge of his nose. "All right," he said, gesturing to the same bailiff who'd already shushed Grace and Mitzi. "We're about to be running late. I want to see this video right now."

A moment later, a projection screen had been set up at the front of the room and the overhead lights dimmed. The video, grainy and depicting jerky movements, obviously shot from a cell phone.

As Grace and the other observers in the court watched, they saw Wyatt Keeler, dressed in a bright turquoise T-shirt with MARASOTA MAULERS in script lettering across the front, come storming toward the camera, his eyes narrowed, jaw set angrily, fists clenched.

"Hey, man," he called. "I'm not done with you."

Now the camera showed a second man, with dark, slicked-back hair, wearing khaki slacks and a red polo shirt, walking hurriedly toward the camera. He wore dark sunglasses. *"Make sure you get all this, Callie,"* he called, glancing over his shoulder. An unseen female voice said. *"I got it."*

Now Wyatt Keeler charged toward the other man, grabbing him from behind by the shoulders and spinning him around. It looked like he was saying something, but their voices were muffled.

The woman's voice rang out. *"Get your hands off him, Wyatt."*

Sunglasses man easily shook himself free of Wyatt Keeler's grasp and went jogging away with Wyatt Keeler following at a steady clip.

"Back away, Wyatt," the woman's voice called. *"If you put your hands on Luke one more time, I am calling the cops. I mean it, too."*

Wyatt Keeler looked right at the camera, stricken. His pace slowed and his facial expression softened, slightly. The camera moved back a little, now showing a gleaming white Trans-Am in the foreground.

"Don't do this, Callie," Keeler pleaded. *"Bo needs me. You can't just take him away like this. I won't let you. This is his home."*

"Not anymore it ain't," Luke Grigsby taunted. He was almost at the driver's side of the Trans-Am. *"You call living in a double-wide trailer a home? The kid doesn't even have his own room. He's coming with us to Birmingham, and there's nothing you can do to stop us."*

"Fuck you, Luke," Wyatt Keeler's voice rang out crystal clear. He was advancing again, his face menacing.

"Get in the car, Callie," Luke said loudly. *"Come on, before this maniac hurts somebody."*

Luke opened the driver-side door and started to slide onto the seat. The camera was moving now, so the footage was even jerkier and out of focus. Even with that, Grace watched, appalled. Grigsby's head popped up above the car door. *"See you later, alligator,"* he said, smirking, just before he closed the door.

Wyatt Keeler lunged toward the car. *"The hell you say,"* he bellowed, smashing his fist into the rolled-up car window.

"Stop it, Wyatt," the woman yelled. Her shrill scream pierced the cool courthouse air. The video stopped abruptly, and a moment later, the lights in the courtroom were turned on again.

Grace stared, wide-eyed with horror at the now-white screen.

"Ms. Entwhistle?" Judge Stackpole's face was deadpan. "I can see why you didn't want the court to view that video." He turned toward Wyatt Keeler. "You, sir, are lucky that gentleman did not file assault charges against you. Frankly, what I've just seen here turns my stomach."

Wyatt Keeler bowed his head and buried his face in his hands.

His wife's lawyer saw an opening and dove right in. "Judge, as you can see, Wyatt Keeler is not a fit father or role model for a young child. We'd ask the court to grant my client's application to go ahead with her planned move to Alabama with her fiancé, Mr. Grigsby, and of course, we want to have the previously agreed-to custody settlement amended to reflect that. Mrs. Keeler would be willing to allow Bo to visit his father for monthly supervised weekend visits, and she'd also be open to discussions about alternating holidays and, possibly, summer visits of up to a week. Again, to be supervised by a neutral party."

Wyatt Keeler raised his head. "One weekend a month? This is my son we're talking about."

"Quiet, Mr. Keeler!" Stackpole boomed.

Betsy Entwhistle stood and placed a warning hand on her client's shoulder. "I apologize for my client's outburst. He won't do it again. And I'll add that he is not proud of his behavior that day. But judge, that video was choreographed and shot by Mrs. Keeler and Mr. Grigsby. It's just as important to note what you don't see as what you do. For instance, that video doesn't show Mr. Grigsby deliberately baiting my client . . ."

"I saw all I needed to see," Stackpole interrupted, waving his hand dismissively. "Mr. Keeler?"

Betsy Entwhistle gave a brief nod and her client stood.

Stackpole's eyes drilled into the hapless Wyatt Keeler. "Regardless of what that video did or did not show, I find the actions shown there to be alarming, bordering on criminal." He looked over at the opposing lawyer. "When do Mrs. Keeler and Mr. Grigsby intend to relocate to Birmingham?"

After a brief whispered conference, the other lawyer cleared his throat. "Early August, Judge. Although Mr. Grigsby will move there immediately, Mrs. Keeler needs time to settle things here. But we'd ask that your custody order become effective immediately."

Stackpole thought it over. "I don't see any need for a rush. I'm going to take this under advisement. I have some thoughts, and I'll issue a ruling, probably by the end of business today." He glared at Wyatt Keeler. "And you, sir, are to stay away from Mr. Grigsby. If this court hears of even a hint of any more aggression from you, I'll issue a temporary restraining order. Is that understood?"

"Understood," Betsy Entwhistle said.

"Understood," her client echoed.

Stackpole flicked his eyes over at Callie Keeler, who was dressed in a demure pale-blue, long-sleeved dress. "Mrs. Keeler, if there are any more incidents, you're free to take that back up with the court again."

"Oh, I will Judge," Callie said, her high-pitched voice sounding defiant. "You better believe I will."

Stackpole jerked his head at the bailiff. "Ten-minute recess. Then I'll hear my next case."

Mitzi touched Grace's arm. "Let's make a bathroom run before they call us." Grace followed her lawyer out of the courtroom and down a long, narrow hallway.

As they walked, Grace spotted Wyatt Keeler. He was sitting on a wooden bench, focused on conversation with his lawyer. He was deeply tanned, and from here Grace could see that his dress shirt was ill-fitting, the collar too big, the sleeves too long. The shirt had obviously just come from a package, as the factory fold marks were still visible.

The other lawyer looked up just as they were passing. "Hey, Betsy," Mitzi murmured, nodding. "Looks like Stackpole is in rare form today."

Betsy Entwhistle rolled her eyes. Her client turned, noticing the two women who'd been in the courtroom earlier, and blushed, then looked down at his hands. For the first time, Grace noticed that his right hand was heavily bandaged.

"He's a peach, isn't he?" Betsy said. "I saw you sitting in the courtroom. Are you on his docket today?"

"Unfortunately," Mitzi said. She gestured toward Grace. "This is my client, Grace Stanton."

"And this is my nephew, Wyatt Keeler," Betsy said.

Wyatt Keeler offered them a solemn smile, revealing choirboy dimples. His eyes were a deep chocolate brown, framed with stubby dark lashes. He was seated, but he had the lean, lanky look of somebody who spent a lot of time outdoors. "I hope you fare better with that guy than I did," he said quietly.

Up close, Grace thought, he didn't look quite as much like the deranged goon he seemed in the video shot by his wife. Up close, he looked sad. Defeated.

"I was just telling Wyatt he's lucky Stackpole didn't order him to be castrated," Betsy said.

"He did seem pretty worked up today," Mitzi agreed. "I was kind of surprised, since it's usually the wives he's antagonistic towards."

"That damned video didn't help us any," Betsy said bluntly.

Mitzi glanced down at her watch. "Whoops. Sorry, but we've got to make a pit stop before Stackpole readjourns."

"Good luck in there," Wyatt said.

They slid into their seats at the front of the courtroom just as the bailiff at the rear of the room was closing the doors.

Mitzi Stillwell shot Grace a sideways glance. "You okay?"

Grace nodded. "As good as I'm gonna get." She turned halfway in her chair and looked around the courtroom. There was no sign yet of Ben and his lawyer. She didn't know whether to be glad or mad.

"What happens now?" she asked, turning back to her attorney.

"It should be pretty cut-and-dried," Mitzi said. "We've asked the judge to order Ben to mediation for a financial settlement, since he's so far resisted all our efforts in that direction. We've produced plenty of documentation that the business is yours and that he's put you in an untenable situation. Even Stackpole should agree that you are arguably the rainmaker for Gracenotes."

"And then?"

"Then we figure out a way to divide up the marital assets, seek a final decree for you, and Stackpole pronounces you unmarried."

"You make it sound easy," Grace said.

Mitzi shrugged. "Not easy. The statutes don't want to make it too easy to get a divorce. But if Stackpole makes Ben play by the rules and divvy up the goods, this shouldn't be too terribly complicated from hereon out."

Grace heard footsteps coming up the center aisle of the courtroom and turned slightly before swiveling violently back toward Mitzi. "He's here," she whispered. "Oh, God. I don't think I can breathe."

She still hadn't laid eyes on Ben since the night she'd driven his Audi into the pool on Sand Dollar Lane. He strode past her, eyes front, and sat at a table directly to the right of the one where she sat. He was dressed in a conservative charcoal suit, sharply pressed white dress shirt, and a purple silk tie. His glossy hair looked freshly cut, his black Gucci loafers were polished to perfection. He was carrying a briefcase Grace hadn't seen in years, and he busied himself now, snapping it open and sorting through file folders.

Grace felt something tighten in her chest. "Breathe," Mitzi instructed quietly. "In. Out. You can do this, Grace. Don't let the bastard get you rattled."

"I *am* rattled," Grace said, feeling her face flush. She felt a hand clasp her shoulder and looked up.

Dickie Murphree smiled down at her. "Gracie," he said, his hand lingering on her shoulder. "It's great to see you."

Dickie looked much as he had the last time she'd seen him, at an expensive restaurant on St. Armand's Circle, not long after she and Ben had moved back to town. Had it been three years ago? His thinning brown hair was a little too long in the back and he had a rakish mustache and that same impish smile he'd used so effectively to get his way all through high school.

"No hard feelings, right, Grace? This is just one of these things. You'll get past this, and you'll be fine. Right?"

No hard feelings? Grace felt her jaw drop. With Dickie's help, Ben had effectively impoverished her. Right this very minute, she was wearing the dressiest clothing she possessed, a pair of her mother's cast-off sandals, and an ill-fitting rayon knit dress she'd picked up for $3.60 at a thrift shop near the hospital. No hard feelings? Not long ago, Grace wouldn't have used this dress as a dishrag. Dickie didn't wait for her reply. He nodded now at Mitzi, flashing his easy smile. "Hey there, Ms. Stillwell."

"Dickie." Mitzi gave him a curt, dismissive nod.

He finally removed his grasp of her shoulder and slid onto the chair next to Ben's.

Ben was still busily sorting file folders, avoiding meeting her eyes.

"Exhale," Mitzi said quietly. "Think about a happy place. Picture yourself there."

"I don't have a happy place anymore," Grace whispered. "Ben got custody of it."

"Then try this. Picture your ex with his dick caught in a rattrap."

Implausibly, Grace began to smile. As the image formed in her mind, she began to giggle. Horrified, she clamped her hands over her mouth, but not before the giggle became a guffaw. Ben's head turned sharply. His eyes narrowed and he looked, briefly, disgusted. He glanced at the back of the courtroom and gave an almost imperceptible shrug before returning to his paper shuffling.

"Feel better?" Mitzi asked, a smile playing at the edge of her lips.

"Much," Grace said. Her eyes followed Ben's gaze toward the back of the room. Sitting in the last row, wearing a form-fitting chartreuse dress and dark sunglasses, a raven-haired woman was staring down at her cell phone, her fingertips racing over the keyboard. Probably sexting Ben, Grace thought.

"I don't believe it," Grace said, her mirth short-lived. "She's here. Right in this courtroom. She's wearing sunglasses, and I think she's dyed her hair, but that's definitely J'Aimee. I can't believe he had the nerve to bring her here."

Mitzi turned all the way around in her chair to have a look, not bothering to hide what she was doing. "Oh. The green dress, right? What is she, about thirteen? Did he have to sign her out of homeroom?"

Just then, the blond-haired bailiff strode past them to the front of the room. "All rise for the Honorable Cedric N. Stackpole," she intoned.

7

Mitzi laid out the case neatly before the judge, letting him know that Ben had locked Grace out of their home, canceled her credit cards, and denied her access to their joint checking and savings accounts.

"Your Honor," Mitzi said, gesturing toward Grace, who was sitting straight in her chair, eyes forward, like an obedient schoolgirl on her first day of class, "Mr. Stanton has effectively impoverished my client. She has no funds, no home, and no way to make a living, thanks to him."

"No way to work?" Stackpole looked startled. "Now how is that possible? Didn't you tell me Ms. Stanton was some kind of professional writer?"

"Yes sir," Mitzi said. "Ms. Stanton is—or she was before all this happened—one of the most successful lifestyle bloggers in the country."

"A blogger?" Stackpole's high forehead wrinkled and his lips thinned in distaste. He waved his hands in the direction of the neat printouts Grace had made of six months' worth of Gracenotes. "Do you mean to tell me Ms. Stanton here makes a living writing this material?" He picked up one of the sheets and skimmed its contents.

"Recipes? Pictures of sofas? Directions for painting an old table? This looks like some kind of hobby to me, Ms. Stillwell."

Grace's heart sank. Mitzi had warned her that Stackpole might not take her work seriously.

"No sir," Mitzi said sharply. "Not a hobby in any way. Ms. Stanton's blog has 450,000 followers. That's just people who have subscribed to her RSS feed. Her blog receives 1.3 million unique visits each month. Since Gracenotes was monetized, which means Ms. Stanton started accepting paid advertisers, the site has consistently generated twenty thousand dollars a month in revenues."

"Impressive," the judge admitted.

Mitzi beamed. "We think so. Judge, Gracenotes is named for Grace Stanton. It was conceived by her and it is written and photographed solely by her. There are no other outside contributors. In other words, this blog is intellectual property, and, as such, it belongs to her. But Ms. Stanton's estranged husband, Ben Stanton, is deliberately blocking her from access to her blog."

"I see," Stackpole said. He swung his head to the left, smiling at Dickie Murphree.

"What do you say to that, Mr. Murphree?"

Dickie thrust his hands in his pockets and gave an exaggerated shrug. "Obviously, Judge, we'd refute just about everything Ms. Stillwell has just said. Grace Stanton is free to write whatever she wants, whenever she wants, and, as far as I know, there's nobody stopping her from doing that. The Internet is a big ol' marketplace, and there's plenty of room in it for everybody, last I heard."

"Mm-hmm," Stackpole said. "And what do you have to say about the dire financial situation of your client's estranged wife? Ms. Stillwell makes a convincing case that your client has effectively cut off her access to all the couple's marital assets."

Dickie's face registered what passed for genuine shock. Grace wondered if Dickie had ever done anything in his life that was genuine.

"Judge, I would just point out to you that Ms. Stanton is the one who initiated all the turmoil in this marriage. It was she who abandoned my client, moving out of their home, of her own accord, after a violent outburst. And, I would add, she did so in a manner that was calculated to humiliate and embarrass my client—not just in front of this couple's immediate neighbors, but in front of everybody in this community, and across the country, for that matter. If her business has been damaged, that is Ms. Stanton's own doing."

"He went there," Mitzi muttered under his breath. "I should have known."

"I'm afraid I don't understand," Stackpole said.

The lawyer clapped a reassuring hand on Ben's shoulder. "Your Honor, I deeply regret having to trot this out again. My client certainly didn't want me to drag all this out in the open again, but sometimes, sir, you have to get these things out in the open."

"What things?" Stackpole asked, leaning back in his chair.

Dickie let out a long, anguished sigh. "Well, ahhh, it's a long story, Judge."

Mitzi stood up. "Your Honor? If Mr. Murphree is referring to the matter I think he is, that matter has no direct bearing on the issue of my client's right to her share of this couple's marital assets. And I strongly object to his trying to introduce it here today."

"What matter?" Stackpole asked, looking peevish.

Dickie shrugged. "The matter of Ms. Stanton intentionally driving my client's 175,000 dollar Audi convertible into the swimming pool of their home on Sand Dollar Lane, thus destroying it. The matter of her assaulting and slandering my client's employee."

"What?" Stackpole's eyebrows shot up. "When was this?"

"The night of May eighth," Dickie said. "Ms. Stanton misunderstood some communication between my client and his employee and flew into a rage. My client eventually began to fear for his life and locked himself into his home and called the police, who, unfortunately, arrived on the scene after Ms. Stanton destroyed the Audi."

Stackpole gave Grace a stern look. "Is this true?"

Grace's voice came out in a squeak. "It's true that I drove the car into the pool, yes sir. But it's not true that I assaulted J'Aimee. I would have, but I couldn't catch her. And anyway, she was my assistant, not Ben's. And it's a joke to think that Ben would be afraid of me. But Your Honor, you haven't heard the whole story."

"That's right, Judge," Dickie said quickly. "You haven't heard how Ms. Stanton raised such a ruckus that their entire neighborhood could listen in on this private marital spat. And I'm assuming you didn't see the network news footage of the aftermath—including footage showing Mr. Stanton's personal vehicle sitting at the bottom of his pool?"

Stackpole's eyebrows shot up. "It was on the news?"

"I had nothing to do with that," Grace offered.

"Enough!" Stackpole glared over the top of his glasses at her.

Dickie held up a small plastic rectangle. "I have the news footage right here on a flash drive, if Your Honor would like to see it."

"I don't intend to do any such thing," Stackpole said. "Let's get back to the matter of finances. Mr. Murphree, I want your client to come to some kind of equitable agreement with Ms. Stanton." He flipped through the files before him.

"Ms. Stanton? Your attorney has asked for what seems like an exorbitant amount of money to pay your monthly expenses. I find it hard to believe a resourceful woman like yourself can't live on $2,000 a month. My own wife manages quite nicely on that amount."

"But Judge," Mitzi sputtered. "Ms. Stanton is entitled to much more than that. She has business expenses involved in writing and producing her blog. And she'll need to find a place to live. She can't continue to live in her mother's very small quarters. And furnishings . . . Besides, it's really immaterial how much allowance you give your wife. Ms. Stanton was the primary breadwinner in this marriage . . ."

Dickie shot to his feet. "That's not true! Mr. Stanton incorporated Gracenotes. He managed the business, sold advertising, dealt with every aspect of the business, and built it up from a small-potatoes hobby to the entity it is today. He, in fact, is the CEO of Gracenotes, Inc., and the owner of the domain name, among other things. It was Ms. Stanton's choice to be paid a weekly salary on a work-for-hire agreement, because she did not want to be troubled with the business of running a business."

"What?" Grace shrieked, then quickly covered her mouth with her hands. She tugged urgently on Mitzi's hand. "I never agreed to any kind of a weekly salary," she whispered. "Ben just drew money out of the corporate account and put it in our personal checking account. I left all of that up to him and the accountant."

"Judge," Mitzi began, but Stackpole wasn't listening.

"Two thousand a month," he said firmly. "It was apparently Ms. Stanton's decision to leave this marriage, so I'm afraid she'll have to deal with the repercussions of that."

"Thank you, Judge," Dickie said quickly.

"That's not all," Stackpole said. He took his glasses off and rubbed the bridge of his nose. "Ms. Stanton, I find myself at a loss for words as far as your behavior in this matter goes. This is the second instance today of parties to a divorce acting in dangerous, violent, even criminal behavior. I'm troubled by that. Deeply troubled."

"Judge, if you'd just listen to what provoked my client," Mitzi began, but Stackpole held up a hand to stop her.

"There can be no justification for the wanton destruction of property or for harassment or assault on a third party. This is just the kind of thing that escalates, until we have domestic violence, armed stand-offs, and God knows what."

"It won't happen again," Grace said in her meekest voice.

"It certainly won't," Stackpole agreed. "We'll see how you do with this new financial settlement, while the two of you work out the other details of your divorce settlement. But in the meantime, Ms. Stanton, I want you to begin seeing a therapist who is an expert in divorce, uh, counseling. Immediately. Dr. Talbott-Sinclair does excellent work, as you'll see." He glanced down at his calendar. "I believe she has a group meeting on Wednesday. If she can fit you into her group meeting tomorrow night, that will give you six weeks.

Mitzi stared at the judge. "Your Honor, are you also ordering *Mr.* Stanton to attend these group sessions?"

"No," he snapped. "Mr. Stanton seems to have his anger issues under control. Now, Ms. Stanton, if Dr. Talbott-Sinclair signs off on your rehabilitation, then I'll take that into consideration when I see you later this summer. Understood?"

Grace could do nothing but nod. Inside was another story. Inside she was screaming.

But Mitzi wasn't done. "Judge, we still need you to rule on the matter of ownership of Ms. Stanton's business. As it stands right now, Ms. Stanton has been deprived of access to her blog, which in effect deprives her of making a living."

"Why can't she just start another blog?" Stackpole asked, gathering up his papers and shutting the file in front of him. "Nobody's keeping her from writing, are they?"

"Mr. Stanton is keeping her from writing," Mitzi said, sounding weary and out of patience. "He is in effect hijacking her intellectual property."

"Talk to me in six weeks after your counseling," Stackpole said. He jerked his head in the bailiff's direction. "I can feel my blood sugar getting low. Let's break for lunch."

Mitzi was stuffing papers into her briefcase. Ben stood and began to stride past, but Grace reached out and grabbed his sleeve.

Ben looked down at her with a blank expression. "Don't do this," he said, his voice chilly.

She jumped up. "Do what? Ask you to answer my lawyer's phone calls? Ask you to treat me with some kind of fairness, some kind of decency, even if our marriage is over? Why are you doing this? If I can't write my blog, neither of us makes any money. You realize that, right?"

Dickie was at Ben's side now. "Now, Gracie. This is very inappropriate. You heard what Judge Stackpole just told you. You need to get your issues under control. If you have something to say to Ben, you need to have your lawyer bring it up with me."

Ben looked her in the eye. "That means no more phone calls. No more showing up at the gates at Gulf Vista, embarrassing the security guards. You wanted it over, Grace, so that's what you've got. It's over. You get on with your life, and I'll get on with mine."

He carefully pried her fingers from the fine fabric of his suit coat, then picked up his briefcase and strolled toward the door, where J'Aimee was already standing, waiting for him. She grasped his arm and, just before walking out, turned and shot Grace a triumphant smile.

8

It was four o'clock on a steamy Tuesday afternoon and Jungle Jerry's Olde Florida Family Fun Park was nearly deserted. There were no families present, and not much fun in evidence.

A quartet of blue-haired tourists from Michigan were taking advantage of the "buy one, get one" coupon they'd found in that day's newspaper. They were having a nice enough time, wandering the crushed-shell footpaths, admiring the unusual flora and fauna, especially the wading pool full of preening pink flamingos.

If they noticed that the temperatures were in the high nineties, and the humidity at 2,000 percent, they didn't remark upon it. Instead, they fanned themselves with the yellowing cardboard Jungle Jerry's Fan Club fans they'd bought for $1.99 in the gift shop and inhaled the heady fragrance of frangipani and ginger lily.

The four paused in their leisurely tour to stare up at the gnarled crimson boughs of a particularly eye-catching tree. "What the heck is this?" asked the only man in the group, a spry seventy-six-year-old who was actually the youngster of the crowd.

Wyatt Keeler happened to be nearby, trimming dead branches from an oleander bush that seemed particularly stressed by the summer's dry spell.

He was dressed as he always was at the park, in a khaki shirt bristling with epaulets and with flap pockets and embroidered Jungle Jerry patches, matching khaki cargo shorts, lace-up work boots, and, of course, his ever-present safari hat.

Wyatt walked up to the group and gave them a welcoming smile, flashing his dimples. Old ladies were crazy for the dimples. He gave the tree trunk a loving pat, as though it were a beloved family pet, which, to Wyatt, it essentially was.

"This is a gumbo-limbo tree," he volunteered. "It's one of the more unusual species we have in the park. It's Latin name is *Bursera simaruba*, and it's a native of tropical regions like Florida, of course, as well as Mexico, the Caribbean, Brazil, and Venezuela. Some people call it the 'tourist tree,' because the bark is red and peeling—like a lot of tourists we see down here in the wintertime."

The Michiganders laughed at this and themselves by association.

"Interesting," murmured one of the women, a sturdily built eighty-five-year-old widow in a pink sun visor.

Wyatt felt himself suddenly cheered by his own speech, and by the interested comments from these tourists.

The very oldest member of the group, a spindly legged ninety-year-old in a thin cotton housedress, stepped closer and peered at Wyatt's Jungle Jerry's name patch, which had faded into obscurity from years of laundering.

"You're not Jungle Jerry," she said sharply. "You'd be too young."

"No ma'am. I'm Wyatt Keeler," he offered her his hand. "Jungle Jerry was my grandfather. He bought this place in 1961, when it was still a commercial orange grove."

One of the women did a little full-circle turn. "You don't see a lot of orange trees here now."

"That's right," Wyatt said. "My grandfather, Jerry Brennan, bought six hundred acres here on County Line Road, back in the day when this was considered way out in the boonies, and he thought he'd become the orange king of Manatee County. And he might have done it, too, except that this area experienced a record-breaking frost in 1963. Temperatures dipped into the low teens and stayed there for three days. My granddad didn't know enough about citrus growing back then to know that he needed to fire up the smudge pots. He lost most of his orange trees in that freeze, and most of the family money, too."

"Too bad," the man muttered.

"Fortunately," Wyatt went on, "he met my grandmother, Winnie, not long after that. And *her* family still had some money. Granddad's family had once owned a little amusement park back home in Tulsa, and, since tourism was going great guns in Florida then, he decided maybe he could take the old orange grove and convert it into what he called a kiddie park."

Wyatt gestured to a rusty jungle gym partially obscured by a hedge of orange-flowering shrubs. "He put in all kinds of rides and playground equipment, and because my grandmother Winnie loved flowers, the two of them also started planting new trees and shrubs as they took out the dead orange trees."

"It's lovely now," the ninety-year-old said. "We used to bring our grandchildren here when we all came down every spring. Whatever happened to all your wild animals? I was just telling my friends, there used to be lions and a tiger, and do I remember a zebra?"

"Yes ma'am," Wyatt said with a laugh. "We had all that and more. My granddad watched a lot of those old Tarzan movies in his younger days. He bought the animals from a traveling circus that had gone bust. A lot of circus outfits used to winter down in this area, you know. He'd always loved animals anyway. So he named himself Jungle Jerry, and he got a retired lion tamer to teach him a few tricks of the trade."

"I thought I remembered a lion show," the woman crowed. "So that was the real Jungle Jerry?"

"The one and only," Wyatt said. "We had the big cats, plus Zoey, that was the zebra, and an elephant, and even a Florida black bear, right up until the late seventies. After my granddad retired, my dad took over, and he phased out most of the large animals."

The woman in the sun visor glared at Wyatt. "They didn't . . . kill them. Tell me they didn't."

"Not at all," Wyatt assured her. "Those animals were like my grandfather's own kids. Boo-Boo, he was the bear, he died of natural causes the same year granddad retired. Monty, the lion, and Tonga, that was the tiger, they retired to an exotic animal shelter in Ocala. Daphne, our elephant, was donated to the Lowry Park Zoo over in Tampa."

The four tourists all seemed relieved. "I love all the tropical birds you have around here," said the woman in the baggy shorts.

Wyatt put his fingers to his lips and gave a long, shrill whistle. They heard a flapping, and suddenly a huge gray parrot flew down from the top of a nearby poinciana tree and perched on Wyatt's shoulder.

"Oh!" one of the women said, clapping her hands in glee.

The bird nuzzled Wyatt's ear, then dipped its neck and poked her head into the right breast pocket for a treat.

"This is Cookie," Wyatt said. "She's an African gray, a total diva, and the star of the parrot show. I can't take any credit for her, though. The birds were my mom's idea."

"Weren't there monkeys, too?" the ninety-year-old inquired.

"You've got a good memory," Wyatt said. "The monkeys were here when I was a little kid. But when this neighborhood started going residential, with all the subdivisions closing in, we were getting a lot of complaints, especially since the little boogers were too clever and kept getting out of their pens and frightening the neighbors. Eventually, all of them were adopted out."

Cookie found a parrot pellet in Wyatt's pocket and began chewing contentedly.

"That was certainly interesting," the old man said, pumping Wyatt's hand again. "This is a grand place you've got here. We're a little surprised to have it all to ourselves today."

Wyatt was not surprised. But he made a valiant effort to keep up a good front.

"You just happened to catch us on our slow day," he lied. "But you come back later in the week, and the crowds will be here, I guarantee."

That was a lie, too. They hadn't had what you could call a real "crowd" at Jungle Jerry's in months and years. Okay, decades, if you wanted to be brutally honest. In this post-Disney era, families got their kicks in air-conditioned comfort, with audio-animatronics and movie-quality special effects. Animal rights advocates didn't approve of exotic birds performing quaint tricks like riding a tiny bicycle on a high wire, and kids were bored silly just looking at a bunch of plants and trees.

Jungle Jerry's had shrunken significantly over the years. Right now, they were at around a hundred acres, since Jungle Jerry's son-in-law, Wyatt's father, Nelson, had been forced to sell off a chunk of land to pay inheritance taxes after Jerry's death.

Wyatt had never intended to work in the family business. He'd been a horticulture major in college and had gone to graduate school at Clemson for a degree in landscape architecture, which was where he'd met Callie Parker, a twenty-two-year-old graphic arts major from Orangeburg, South Carolina. He and Callie had been in a fever to get married, such a fever that he'd canned the idea of getting his master's and dropped out of grad school to get a job working for a mail-order nursery in Greenville.

He'd worked there for four years when his mother called to beg him to come home to run Jungle Jerry's. Nelson had suffered his first heart attack, and Peggy, his mother, had just been diagnosed with breast cancer, although she didn't tell him that until after he and Callie moved back to Bradenton.

Peggy lived just long enough to hold Bo, christened Nelson William Keeler II, before succumbing to the cancer.

The first few years at the park, Wyatt had worked furiously to try to turn the tide at Jungle Jerry's. He'd advertised, joined civic associations, networked like crazy. He'd phased out the old kiddie rides, which were rusting safety hazards anyway, and had begun emphasizing ecology and the botanical aspect of the park. And at first, things seemed to be working. Attendance crept up. Callie came to work at the park, designing posters and ads. Bo took his first steps chasing after Beezus, a gold-capped conure. They weren't getting rich, but they were young and happy. And dumb, Wyatt reflected now. At least, he was.

They'd bought their first house in one of the newer subdivisions nearby and enrolled Bo in the neighborhood school, one of the best in the school district. Wyatt was working crazy long hours at Jungle Jerry's, and Callie was doing some sporadic freelance work. Most of the other families on their block were like them, young marrieds with one or two kids. They cooked out together, took the kids en masse to Holmes Beach—all the things you did when you were young with not much money.

The one bachelor on the block, Luke Grigsby, was a salesman with a chemical company. Luke was the neighborhood fun guy. He wore cool clothes and drove a sharp white Trans-Am. His home was the biggest, newest house on the block, and since he had a pool, he entertained frequently.

Every year Luke threw a big, crazy Halloween party. Everybody competed to come up with the most outrageous costume. Wyatt wasn't a big one for parties, but Callie loved dressing up. That year, she decided they should go as Aladdin and Jasmine, the characters from the Disney movie.

Wyatt reluctantly allowed himself to be talked into wearing a turban, idiotic-looking billowy pants, and, worst of all, a short embroidered vest over his bare chest. For her own costume, Callie outdid herself. She took one of her old bikinis and covered the top and bottoms with hot-glued gold sequins, then attached some kind of filmy fabric to the bottoms to make harem pants. She bought a felt fez, cut a hole in the top, and pulled her blond ponytail through, then made herself a veil with more of the filmy fabric.

Callie refused to let Wyatt see her in her costume until the night of the party. When she stepped out of the bedroom, he couldn't believe this was his wife.

She'd swept glittering blue eye shadow on her eyelids and outlined them in black liner. Her breasts jutted out of the skimpy sequined bikini top, and her harem pants skimmed right above her pubic bone. She wore half a dozen jangly gold bracelets on each arm, huge earrings, and little gold sandals. As a final touch, she'd somehow attached a huge plastic rhinestone in her belly button.

Callie's eyes danced from above the veil obscuring the lower half of her face. She did a little pirouette followed by a suggestive hip grind that sent her bracelets jingling.

"What do you think?"

"Where's the rest of it?" Wyatt asked.

She pouted. "What's that supposed to mean? You don't like it?"

He looked over his shoulder, toward the kitchen, where the teenage babysitter was trying to con Bo into eating his dinner. "I like it just fine if we're staying home tonight—just the two of us," he said in a low voice, running a finger down her bare arm. "But don't you think it's a little, uh, I don't know, risqué for a neighborhood party?"

"No, I do not," Callie snapped. "I've been working on this costume for weeks. Yours, too. And that's all you can say? I look risqué?"

He shrugged. "You asked."

"Well I don't care what you think. I think I look hot. And cute." She grabbed a gold beaded clutch purse and opened the front door. "Are you coming?"

He went to the party, had a couple beers, talked football with a couple of the guys, and watched glumly from across the room while his wife knocked back half a dozen wine coolers and then proceeded to strut and shimmy and flirt with every guy in the room.

Callie was doing a tipsy but highly suggestive belly dance with Luke out on the patio when Wyatt tapped her on the shoulder. She whirled around, then frowned when she saw it was her husband. "What?"

"It's eleven thirty," he said pointedly. "We promised we'd get Melanie home by midnight."

"It's Friday night. There's no school tomorrow! Just call her and tell her we're going to stay later," Callie said. "It's no big deal."

"It actually is a big deal," Wyatt replied. "She's got to get up early because she's taking the SATs tomorrow."

"Oh, for God's sake," Callie said. "Just when the party is starting to crank up." She looked over at Luke and gestured at Wyatt. "Meet Aladdin—he traded his magic carpet for a wet blanket."

"You don't have to leave," Wyatt said stiffly. "I'll go, since she drove herself over to the house."

"You mean it?" Callie's face lit up, her pout forgotten. "I won't stay that much longer. I just want to hang around long enough to see who wins the costume contest."

Luke laughed and wrapped an arm around Callie's shoulder. "You already know who won—lady." He gave Wyatt a wink. "Don't worry about her. I'll walk her home myself. Okay?"

What could Wyatt say? Callie planted a perfunctory kiss on his forehead. He walked the two blocks home, paid the babysitter, and walked her out to her car. He looked in on Bo, who was fast asleep, then went to bed. Alone. He woke up at 3:30 A.M., glanced at the clock, and then back at Callie's side of the bed. She wasn't there.

He couldn't sleep. Finally, Wyatt got up. He peered out the front window, just in time to see Luke and Callie stroll slowly up the sidewalk. The window was open, and the curtains billowed in a faint breeze. Callie's giggle floated on the night air, and Luke said something in a low voice. She leaned heavily on the arm Luke had around her waist. As Wyatt watched, they stopped just short of the driveway. Luke pulled her from the sidewalk into the shadow of their neighbor's Florida holly tree. Wyatt's heart stopped. His hand clutched the curtain fabric as he watched his wife wrap her arms around Luke's neck, press herself up against his chest, and pull the neighborhood fun guy into a long, deep kiss.

As he walked back to their bedroom, Wyatt checked the dial on the clock radio on his side of their bed. He made a note of the time. 3:47 A.M. It was the moment time stopped in what he thought had been a perfectly happy marriage.

9

Callie never did come to bed that night. She was asleep on the living room sofa in the morning. Her fez was on the floor, her hair mussed and spilling over the sofa cushion. The blue eye shadow and black liner were smeared into raccoon circles under her eyes. One breast peeked all the way out of the bikini top.

"What happened to Mommy?" He hadn't heard their barefoot son pad into the room. Bo stood looking down in horror at Callie.

Wyatt pulled an afghan over Callie's shoulders and scooped Bo up into his arms. "She didn't feel so good last night when she came home from the party, so she slept out here. Come on, sport, let's get you some breakfast."

Months later, after the trial separation, after the tears and accusations and denials, Wyatt knew, in retrospect, he should have said something the night of the Halloween party. Maybe if he'd let Callie know what he'd seen, told her he loved her and didn't want to lose her, maybe things would have turned out differently. Or maybe he might have admitted he didn't love her enough. Not enough to fight Luke for her.

But things didn't turn out that way. Eventually, Callie admitted that she and Luke were in love. Eventually, she told him the marriage had been in trouble for a long time. And so Wyatt did the decent thing. They agreed it was important for Bo's life to retain some degree of normalcy. Callie would keep the house so that Bo could stay in his school. Wyatt was thirty-eight years old, with a failed marriage and an ailing business.

Wyatt moved out of their little house and into a battered double-wide trailer at Jungle Jerry's that had once been the living quarters for a security guard—from back in the day when they actually had the funds and the need for a security guard.

When it came time to start divorce proceedings, his Aunt Betsy offered to handle his side, pro bono. They somehow worked out a time-sharing agreement, with Bo splitting his time between the two of them. Wyatt's dad, Nelson, moved into the second bedroom of the double-wide to help out with child care for Bo on the weekends and after school on the days Bo stayed with Wyatt.

Wyatt was shocked at how fast his marriage unraveled and dumbfounded at the changes in Callie once she and Luke moved in together.

Or had she been somebody else all along? Wyatt would never be sure.

Their temporary custody-sharing arrangement got off to a rocky start. On the first weekend Bo was to spend with Wyatt, he got a tearful call from his son on Friday night, hours after Callie was to have dropped him off at Jungle Jerry's.

"Daddy?"

"Hey, Bo," Wyatt said, relieved to hear his son's voice. "Grandpa and I are waiting on you. We're having your favorite, mac 'n' cheese."

Bo sniffed, and then, in a thin, wobbly voice, "Mom says if you want me, you gotta come pick me up."

Wyatt frowned. That had not been the agreement.

"Sure thing," he said. "I'll be right over."

Now Bo was crying. "But, I'm not at Mom's house. I'm at Luke's friend's house, and it's way far away."

He heard Callie's voice in the background. "Just tell him you'll see him in the morning. Your dad will understand."

"But I wanna see Daddy," he heard Bo wailing, and his heart sank.

"Oh, for Pete's sake," he heard Callie say.

And then she was on the phone, her voice crisp and unapologetic.

"Look, Wy, we've had a little change of plans. We went over to St. Pete Beach with Luke for a work thing, and with Friday traffic and everything, we're just not gonna make it back in time tonight. You understand, right? I'll drop him off first thing in the morning."

"This is crap, Callie," Wyatt protested. "You were supposed to bring Bo here as soon as school was out, four hours ago. Now you call me and tell me you took him all the way to St. Pete? And I'm supposed to be okay with that?"

"You're supposed to be okay with doing what's good for your son," Callie snapped. "Luke's friends live right on the beach here, and they have a pool, and Bo was having a blast until he all of a sudden decided he needed to talk to you. The next thing I know, he's blubbering and saying he wants to leave. And if we leave now, with traffic and everything, he'll be asleep by the time we get him there anyway. So what's the difference if you get him tonight or tomorrow morning?"

"The difference is, I haven't seen him in three days," Wyatt said, feeling his chest tighten with anger. "I made plans for tonight, with Dad and Bo."

"Whoop-dee-shit," she said. "Fine. Whatever. I'll pack his ass up now, and we'll get in the car and drive him all the way back over there so you can see him. Asleep."

Wyatt took a deep breath. "I wish you wouldn't cuss in front of him. But all right, he can stay. As long as you have him here first thing in the morning. And since you've got him tonight, I want him to spend Sunday night with me."

"Great." She hung up without another word.

10

Gracenotes

Despite what you might think, I am definitely not a neat freak. My desk is frequently a disaster area, and dust bunnies are not an endangered species at my house. But truthfully, I get deep personal satisfaction out of making my surroundings beautiful—and comfortable.

I've learned a few tricks that make housekeeping less drudgery and more delight. For one thing, I try and tidy up every night before bedtime. Dishes always get put in the dishwasher—is there anything more depressing in the morning than a sinkful of greasy crockery? I spritz the sink and kitchen counters with my favorite all-purpose organic cleanser, watered-down white vinegar.

In the morning, after I've showered, I use more of my diluted vinegar-water spray to freshen up the tub and shower surfaces, and I keep a special "squeegee" under my bathroom sink to allow me to wipe down the glass shower door before it gets any annoying water spots or streaks.

On the Wednesday after her court appearance, Grace flipped the last of the heavy wooden chairs onto the tabletop. She dipped the mop in the bucketful of scalding soapy water, then, with rubber gloved hands, wrung out the excess soap. She swished the mop back and forth across the Sandbox's gritty linoleum floor, halfheartedly listening to the morning news roundup of traffic accidents, taxpayer revolts, and local political skullduggery.

The smell of coffee somehow managed to waft through the biting aroma of Pine-Sol. Her mother was standing at the bar, holding out a freshly brewed pot.

"Come on, hon," Rochelle urged. "It's early. You can stop for one cup. That floor ain't going nowhere."

It was barely eight o'clock. Grace had been up since six, taking a run along the quiet predawn streets of Cortez while it was still relatively cool, then starting in on her new ritual of swabbing down the restaurant, from floor to ceiling.

Out of boredom and desperation, in the weeks since she'd moved in, Grace had been waging a one-woman war on the Sandbox's decades-old accumulation of grease, grime, and clutter.

She'd started in the storeroom, clearing out an entire Dumpster's worth of antiquated equipment, a deep fryer her father had always meant to fix, an ice machine that had stopped working ten years earlier, boxes and crates of old business records, food service catalogs, and broken chairs and tables.

From there she'd moved on to the kitchen, ruthlessly tossing anything and everything that wasn't essential to their food-service operation. She'd inspected every glass, dish, and piece of cutlery, consigning anything chipped, bent, or discolored to a crate she'd allocated for the local homeless shelter's soup kitchen.

Along the way, she'd had to abandon all her old, genteel ideas about housecleaning. Diluted vinegar and baking soda were useless in her dust-busting efforts here. Now, her weapons of choice included every industrial-strength, commercial-grade cleaner she could find at the local janitorial supply house.

Grace set her mop aside, peeled off the rubber gloves, and sipped her coffee. She gestured around the room. "I feel like I'm finally making some headway, don't you?"

Her mother shrugged. "Place doesn't even smell like a bar anymore. You've scrubbed away every last trace of the Sandbox ambiance."

"Mom, that wasn't ambiance, it was crud. Years' and years' worth of baked-on, smoked-in, ground-down crud. This place was gross. Can't you just admit you like it better clean?"

Rochelle rested a hand on the old mahogany bar. "I liked it the way it was," she said pointedly. "We were shabby before shabby got cool. Now it's like a hospital operating room, for God's sake. Who wants to grab a beer and a burger in a hospital?"

"There's a difference between shabby gentility and run-down and decrepit, and it's really not so fine a line," Grace said. "Our regulars may grouse at first, but you wait, they're gonna appreciate pouring beer from a pitcher without a busted spout or eating with a fork without bent tines."

"*My* regulars don't know what a fork tine is," Rochelle said.

Maybe, Grace wanted to tell her, if we clean this place up, change the menu, and raise our standards a little, maybe we'll attract a clientele that actually will pay $15 for a decent dinner entrée.

But before she could lob another useless argument into Rochelle's court, she happened to glance up at the television and stopped, midsentence.

Rochelle followed her gaze. "Aw shit. Here we go again."

The morning news hour had segued into *Sunrise Sarasota,* one of those chatty, morning-magazine-format shows. The cohosts, an unbearably perky husband-and-wife team named Charley and Joe, were doing an "In the Kitchen" segment that had the wife, Charley, attempting to crack a Florida lobster shell while the husband, Joe, was being tutored in the finer points of crafting a table setting.

When Grace heard an all-too-familiar voice, a high-pitched nasal twang, she turned around to stare at the wall-mounted television above the bar.

The guest coaching Charley and Joe through their cooking segment was none other than J'Aimee. Her J'Aimee, or rather, Ben's J'Aimee.

Rochelle grabbed for the remote to change the channel, but Grace was faster, snatching it up from beneath her mother's fingers, then staring, dumbfounded, at the television.

"Don't go away!" Charley was saying. "We'll be right back with Gracenotes-style blogger J'Aimee.

"What?" Grace shrieked. "Gracenotes-style blogger? Seriously?"

"Just turn it off," Rochelle said soothingly. "Tune it out. This means nothing. You're just going to get yourself all worked up for nothing."

"It's not for nothing," Grace said, still staring up at the television. "This is all Ben's doing." She scrabbled around on the bar, looking for her phone.

"I'm calling my lawyer," Grace said, scrolling through the numbers on her contact list. "He can't do this. He can't promote her as a Gracenotes blogger. He can't turn her into me!"

"Looks like he already did," Rochelle said, under her breath.

Grace got Mitzi Stillwell's voice mail. "Mitzi! This is Grace. Turn on *Sunrise Sarasota* right now! Ben has J'Aimee on there, promoting herself as the Gracenotes-style blogger. You've got to do something, Mitzi. Call the judge, get an injunction or something. Call me back, okay?"

The commercial break was over, and Charley and Joe were back with their guest.

"Look at that whore!" Grace ranted. "See how good she looks? I swear, Ben's gotten her a makeover. She looks almost classy."

J'Aimee was wearing a sleeveless hot-pink dress, her newly dyed dark locks worn in a simple upsweep.

"They must have put some kind of concealer on that barbed-wire tattoo she has on her right bicep," Grace muttered. "And I think maybe she got Botox on her lips. You see how full they are now?"

Rochelle shrugged. "I never paid that much attention to the girl, to tell you the truth."

J'Aimee was now openly flirting with Joe, batting her artificial lashes at him, giggling and playfully flicking a dinner napkin at him . . .

"Hey! That's my damned napkin." Grace scrambled up on one of the barstools to get a closer look at the television. She pointed at the screen. "Those are my hand-blown Mexican wineglasses." She felt tears welling up in her eyes. "I carried those all the way back from Puerto Vallarta on my lap.

"And look. She's using that fugly damned pottery from my Gracenotes sponsor. That's strictly a Ben move."

She sank back down on the barstool, unable to take her eyes off the television. Now J'Aimee was placing a centerpiece in the middle of the table. It was a large, shallow glass bowl, heaped with shiny green Haas avocados.

"I always like to use fresh local fruits and vegetables in my table settings," she told Charley, adjusting one of the avocados. "It gives a party a sense of authenticity, don't you think?"

"Authenticity?" Grace howled. "She didn't know an avocado from an orange before I hired her."

Rochelle quietly removed the remote control from Grace's clutch. She aimed it at the television and clicked.

"You're getting yourself all worked up for nothing," she said. "So what if she's on television? So what if Ben has her writing a blog with your name on it?

She's not you. She's just a cheap little floozie. You are the real thing. You're butter and she's . . . she's not even Parkay. Ben will figure that out soon enough. Your readers will figure it out. Everything will work itself out."

"No, it won't," Grace said tearfully. "She's stolen everything from me. My house, my husband, my napkins. That was my wedding silver she was setting the table with. My Repoussé silver, Mom."

Rochelle sighed and folded her weeping daughter into her arms. "It'll be okay, Grace. Really it will. I know it hurts right now, but you'll get through this. You will. I'll help you."

Grace looked up at her. Tears streamed down her face. Her eyes were red-rimmed and her nose was snotty. She sniffed loudly. "How, Mom?"

"I just will," Rochelle vowed. She grabbed the bottle of spray cleaner Grace had left behind the bar. "Look. I'll let you clean the office next, okay? You can throw out whatever you want, and I won't say a word."

After the judge refused to give her back her blog, Grace promised herself she would *not* look at Gracenotes. But that afternoon, once she'd filled the Sandbox's Dumpster with dusty files and years' and years' worth of old *Sports Illustrated* and *Florida Sportsman* magazines, Grace opened her laptop and clicked on the icon for her blog.

"Oh no she didn't," she murmured, looking at the home page. Everything had changed. Including the name. It was now Gracenotes for Living, with J'Aimee! The new banner was in a nearly unreadable font, in a garish orange and teal color combination. The rails on both sides of the page were filled with tiny, one-inch squares advertising everything from *New Unbelievable Anti-Aging Serum!* to bank credit cards to cruise ship vacations to *Pet Meds by Mail!*

"Horrible," Grace said, shaking her head. "Heinous." She counted three dozen ads on the home page. Ben must have been having a field day, she decided, maximizing and monetizing to his greedy heart's content.

She read the previous day's post. It was titled "How to Buy Furniture."

"Hmm. Scintillating," Grace said. As she read, she felt sick. The entire blog was really a thinly veiled advertorial for Room in a Box, a wholesale furniture company with franchise operations all over central Florida. The same furniture company whose banner ad now took up the entire top of the home page.

Room in a Box's marketing people had been pestering Grace for more than a year to write about their furniture. They'd even had the nerve to ship a faux-leather recliner chair to the house—as an inducement/bribery for Grace to write testimonials about their product line.

"No way," Grace had said, as Ben cut the cardboard crate away from the chair—which actually came with a remote control allowing it to recline, vibrate, and even play music. "Pack that thing up and tell UPS to come back and get it. I don't even want it to stay here overnight."

Ben knew it was useless to argue with her. Obviously he'd waited until he no longer had to argue with her. Grace was gone, and with her had gone any hint of editorial standards.

She couldn't read any more of this drivel. She closed out the blog, opened a file, and began to type, her fingers flying over the keyboard.

By four that afternoon, she'd registered a new domain name for herself, TrueGrace. Maybe not the most original name, she admitted, but it would serve its purpose, hopefully letting her readers know this blog was the real thing.

This time around, she promised herself, the blog would be all hers. And for her first post, she decided to go public with what had happened in her life and to her old world.

No more prettying things up, Grace decided. She was still writing, deleting, revising, when she looked down at her watch and realized it was nearly 7:00 P.M. She hit the SAVE button, closed her laptop, and reluctantly went downstairs.

Rochelle was behind the bar, pouring a beer for an older woman Grace didn't recognize. She looked up in time to see Grace heading for the Sandbox's front door.

"Where are you headed?" Rochelle called.

Grace grimaced. "To my so-called therapy group."

"Looking like that?"

Grace looked down at herself. She was wearing a faded lime-green Sandbox T-shirt, white shorts, and flip-flops, the same outfit she'd changed into after her morning run. Her hair was knotted in a limp ponytail and she wore no makeup.

"The judge said I had to go," she said, her chin jutting out defiantly. "He didn't say I had to dress to impress."

Rochelle handed the beer to her customer and hurried around the bar to her daughter's side. "Honey, you don't want to go in there with an attitude," she said, her voice low. "Maybe these sessions will actually be helpful. Maybe you should keep an open mind. Or at least do something about your hair."

Grace sighed. She reached into the glass display case where they kept the Sandbox-branded merchandise, the koozies, tees, bumper stickers, and key chains. She grabbed a baseball cap with the Sandbox logo embroidered on the bill, jammed it on her head, and looped her ponytail through the opening in the back of the hatband.

"Better?" She didn't wait to hear Rochelle's answer.

11

Grace had to check the street address on the therapist's door to make sure she'd arrived at the right place. This was a shrink's office? It was a drab one-story stucco storefront occupying the end slot in a strip shopping center that also boasted a Vietnamese nail salon, a hearing aid salesroom, a business called the Diaper Depot, and a tattoo parlor. The dusty plate glass window was boldly lettered in gilt-edged black letters; PAULA TALBOTT-SINCLAIR, L.S.W. FAMILY AND MARITAL COACHING, DIVORCE DIVERSION, EMOTIONAL HEALING.

"Emotional healing," she muttered to herself, taking a last sip of lukewarm coffee before getting out of her car. "Right. Like that's going to happen." There were four other cars in the otherwise empty parking lot. One of them, a shiny black VW bug, boasted a yellow smiley-face bumper sticker with the motto "Change Happens." Had to be the therapist's car, she decided, hating her on the spot.

Paula Talbott-Sinclair's reception area wasn't much more impressive than her storefront. Worn and faded brown indoor-outdoor carpet, a low-slung olive-green pleather sofa, and a couple of armless chairs. There was a receptionist's desk, with a computer terminal and telephone, but no sign of a receptionist. Only a clipboard with a hand-lettered sign on the desktop: DIVORCE RECOVERY GROUP MEMBERS, PLEASE SIGN IN HERE. There were three other names on the sign-in sheet, all women, Grace noted.

The door on the wall opposite the front door was slightly ajar, and Grace heard the low hum of voices. She wrote her name on the sign-in sheet, hesitating a moment, before jotting down Grace Davenport.

"Hello?" she said softly, approaching the door. A woman popped her head out. Grace guessed she must be in her midforties. Her heart-shaped face was framed with a cascade of sandy-blond curls, and she had startlingly blue eyes behind wire-rimmed glasses. She was dressed in a figure-hugging sleeveless black tank top and tight black yoga pants, with a gauzy black shawl draped around her bony shoulders. And she was barefoot.

"Oh hi," she said brightly, looking Grace up and down. She grasped both of Grace's hands in hers and squeezed. "I'm Dr. Talbott-Sinclair, although in group, we all just use first names. So I'm Paula. And you must be Grace Stanton?"

"Actually, it's Davenport," Grace said. "If you don't mind."

"I see," Paula said, pursing her lips. "Well, that's something we're going to want to talk about, isn't it?"

"Taking back my maiden name?" Grace asked. "Does the judge have a problem with that?"

Paula cocked her head and blinked. "The question is, Grace, do you have a problem with it? Is this something you're doing out of anger? Because we can't have a healing when our hearts and minds are full of bitterness. You'll come to see that, I think, eventually, in group."

"It's *my* name," Grace said, feeling unusually obstinate. "I was a Davenport for way longer than I was in Stanton.

"All right," Paula said, pushing the door open. "Let's hold that thought. For now, come on in and meet the other members of group."

The inner office consisted of a large glass-topped desk and a swivel chair, in the corner of the room. It had the same brown carpet as the outer office and a pair of smallish windows that were covered with a set of shiny bronze drapes in a cheesy sheer fabric. Five folding chairs were arranged in a semicircle around a high-backed brown leather chair. A row of framed diplomas was stretched across the wall above the desk, and three women, all of them looking ill at ease, were clustered around a small wooden table that held a coffeepot and a stack of Styrofoam cups, talking in subdued voices.

"Ladies," Paula said, her voice rising to let them know she had an important announcement. "Ladies!"

The women turned their attention to the newcomer. If Grace had any expectations about what her divorce recovery group would look like, this wasn't it.

"Don't I know you?" A tall, elegantly dressed black woman approached Grace, hands on her hips, studying the newcomer intently. She wore her hair in a sleek bobbed cut, and the first thing Grace noticed about her were her almond-shaped eyes and her luxuriously thick fringe of eyelashes. Fakes?

"I, I'm not sure," Grace said, stuttering a little. Wasn't group therapy supposed to be anonymous? Wasn't Paula Talbott-Sinclair supposed to protect her identity?

"Wait, I've got it," the woman snapped her fingers. "Gracenotes! Am I right? You're the lifestyle blogger who drowned her husband's 175,000-dollar ride. Damn! I covered that story, and it got picked up by all the networks." She patted Grace's shoulder. "Nice goin', girlfriend."

Grace felt her face flame with embarrassment. So much for anonymity.

"You! You're that reporter! Camryn. Camryn . . . something. You snuck into our subdivision, trespassed, talked to all my neighbors." She lowered her voice. "Did you follow me here today? Don't you people have any sense of decency?" She looked around for the therapist, ready to chew her out.

"Relax," Camryn said, chuckling. "Me, follow you here? Don't flatter yourself. I'm here for the same reason you are."

Grace narrowed her eyes. "You drove your husband's car into a pool?"

"Not quite," Camryn said. "Let's just say what I did do didn't set well with some parties."

Another woman walked up to join them. She was younger than Camryn Nobles but older than Grace, petite and slender, with sun-streaked shoulder-length blond hair pushed back from her forehead by a pair of designer sunglasses. Her skin was flawless, and she was dressed casually, in white capris and a flowery pink and orange tunic top and gold sandals. She wore a fine gold chain around her neck, and dangling from it was a whopper of a diamond, three carats, at least, Grace estimated.

"Hey, y'all," she said, in a honey-dipped drawl. She glanced over her shoulder at Paula Talbott-Sinclair, who had seated herself in the swivel chair and was looking expectantly at the door. "Are you thinkin' what I'm thinkin'?"

"What's that?" Camryn said.

"Well, I'm just wondering what kind of dog-and-pony show we've lucked into here. I mean, did you get a look at this shopping center? I've been living in Sarasota all my life, and I have never, and I mean ever, stepped foot in a place like this. What kind of a therapist has her offices between a tattoo artist and a diaper store?"

"The kind who charges three hundred dollars a session," Camryn said. "Obviously she's not spending what she makes on overhead."

"For real," the blonde said. "And the thing is, my lawyer says I probably can't make my ex pay for these sessions. Even though I'm not the one who was fuckin' around on the side. I'll tell you, that damned Stackpole has my lawyer runnin' scared."

"Stackpole!" Camryn said with a snort. "He's the judge hearing your divorce?"

"That's the one," the blonde said. "You too?"

"Unfortunately," Camryn said. She looked at Grace. "How about you?"

"Afraid so," Grace said. "My lawyer says he hates women. Especially women lawyers."

"My lawyer's a man, and I still got the shaft," Camryn pointed out.

"Me too," the blonde said. "Well, I guess we're in this together, huh? By the way, I'm Ashleigh. Hartounian."

"I don't think we're supposed to tell our last names," Grace said.

"Why not?" Camryn shot. "I got nuthin' to hide. Anyway, y'all both know my name, so why shouldn't I know yours?"

Grace sighed. "Whatever. I'm Grace Davenport."

"I thought your name was Stanton," Camryn said.

"It was. I'm taking back my maiden name."

Camryn rolled her eyes. "I'll bet the judge is gonna love that." She turned toward Ashleigh. "So, is your ex Boyce Hartounian? The plastic surgeon?"

"You know him?"

"Only his reputation," Camryn said. "He did an eye lift for one of my girlfriends at the station. I swear, she looks ten years younger."

"Boyce is good, all right," Ashleigh admitted.

Camryn took a step closer and examined the younger woman's face. "How 'bout you? Did he do some work on you?"

"Some," Ashleigh admitted. She lifted her shoulders. "He gave me these boobs, not long after we started dating. And for our first anniversary, he gave me Reese Witherspoon's nose."

"Damn," Camryn said. "Those boobs are fine."

The fourth woman in the room wandered up, looking distinctly uneasy. She was older than all of them, in her early fifties. Her dark brown hair was streaked with gray, and a thin network of crow's-feet radiated out from her eyes. She was neatly dressed in a pale gray linen blouse and gray slacks.

"Hello," she said quietly. "I guess I should introduce myself? I'm Suzanne."

"Ashleigh."

"Grace."

"I'm Camryn. Look here, is the judge hearing your divorce named Stackpole?"

Suzanne looked startled. "As a matter of fact, yes."

"Uh-huh," Camryn said, nudging Grace. "And did you do something ugly to your ex? Maybe act out a little bit, something like that?"

Suzanne's face paled. "I can't . . . I don't . . . I won't . . ."

"Never mind," Grace said. "Whatever you did, I'm sure your husband deserved it."

Suzanne bit her lip. "I still can't believe I went through with it. And I can't believe I'm here, tonight. It all seems so surreal."

"What's surreal is the fact that this group is all women," Camryn said. "This isn't group therapy. It's ladies' night."

"A really, really, expensive ladies night," Grace put in.

"Ladies . . ." Paula called from her seat at the front of the room. "Let's get started, shall we? I'm expecting one more member to join us, but I think we'll go ahead and get started. So take a seat, if you will."

Grace sat down on one of the folding chairs and crossed her legs. The other three women did the same.

"Well," Paula said, giving them a bright smile. "I take it you've all introduced yourselves to each other. Ashleigh, Grace, Camryn, and Suzanne. Tonight is an important night for all of you. Right? It's the night you all start the healing. And the forgiving."

"No way," Camryn muttered under her breath.

"Excuse me?" Paula said sharply.

"I said, no way," Camryn said defiantly. "That judge can order me to come to these bullshit counseling sessions. And he can order me to pay through the nose for the privilege of coming here. But he cannot make me forgive what Dexter Nobles did to me."

She crossed her arms over her chest. "And neither can you."

"I see," Paula said. She nodded at Ashleigh. "What about you, Ashleigh? Did you come here with an open mind tonight?"

"I came with an open checkbook," Ashleigh said. "That's the best I can do right now."

Camryn guffawed and Grace managed to stifle her own laugh.

"Grace?" Paula's look was expectant.

"My husband has locked me out of my own home," Grace said, feeling her throat constrict. "He's frozen my bank accounts. Canceled my credit cards. I have no way to support myself. I'm living with my mother, tending bar to pay for gas money. He's living in a two-million-dollar home, shacking up with my twenty-six-year-old former assistant. So no, right now, I'm really not ready for what you call a healing."

Paula frowned. "All this negativity. I find it very sad. Very disappointing."

Too damn bad, Grace thought. She glanced over at Camryn Nobles, and then at Ashleigh Hartounian. Their faces were impassive. Suzanne's face was scrunched in concentration.

"We've got a lot of work ahead of us," Paula said after a moment. She went over to her desk, picked up a stack of old-fashioned black-and-white-spattered composition books, and handed one to each of the women.

"This," she said. "Is your divorce journal. I want all of you to get in the habit of writing in it, at least once a day, although several times a day would be most helpful."

"Write what?" Ashleigh demanded.

"Everything. Anything. We're going to be doing some visualization exercises that I think will be helpful. And I'd like you to search, really search your souls, for the truthful answers to some questions I'm going to pose to all of you. Because, in here, honesty is everything."

Paula waved toward the windows. "Out there, with your family and friends, you can hide your pain. You can cover it up, sanitize it, deny it. But in here—with group—I expect nothing less than absolute honesty."

She opened the bottom drawer of her desk and brought out a boxy Polaroid camera. She walked briskly to the semicircle of chairs and snapped a photo of Grace, before Grace had time to object. When the photo ejected from the camera, the therapist handed it to Grace and moved on, pictures of Camryn and Suzanne, then Ashleigh, handing each woman her photo.

Grace stared down at the Polaroid, watching as the pale gray of the film disappeared and a grainy image of herself came into focus. She was shocked at what she saw. Her formerly full, round face looked gaunt. Her hair hung limply from a center part that emphasized her dark roots. She hadn't bothered with makeup that day, hadn't actually bothered with it at all since the day she'd been turned away from the security gate at Gulf Vista. There were dark circles under her eyes and deeply etched grooves at the corners of her mouth. It struck Grace that she couldn't remember smiling, not in days. She looked sad. Sad and old, and defeated.

She glanced at the other women. Camryn and Ashleigh didn't look any more pleased with their photos. In fact, Ashleigh had pulled a compact from her Louis Vuitton satchel and was busily applying more lipstick. Suzanne stared at her photograph as though she'd never seen a picture of herself before.

Now Paula handed Grace a stapler. "I want you to staple the Polaroid to page one of your divorce journal. This is your before picture. Now, turn the page and describe what you see in yourself in this photo. Tell me where you are, today. What you're feeling about the place you're in, right now, emotionally. If you like, you can write about this experience you're having, your first night in group. Be honest. I know you all resent me, resent being here. I expect that." She looked down at her watch. "I'm going to give you fifteen minutes to write. And when I come back, I want you all to be ready to share what you wrote with the rest of the group."

"What if I don't feel like sharing?" Ashleigh asked, tossing her hair behind her shoulder. "What if I don't feel like writing anything?"

Paula's smile was tight. "Oh, Ashleigh. You know Judge Stackpole made your attendance at group mandatory as a condition for granting your divorce, right?"

"How could I forget?" Ashleigh asked.

"It's not as simple as just showing up," Paula said. "Judge Stackpole knows some people will just go through the motions, simply so they can get that divorce decree. Despite what you all think, I must tell you, Cedric Stackpole is really a very wise man. So he's asked me to be very clear about his expectations for all of you." She smiled.

"Each week, I'll be reporting in to Judge Stackpole about your progress in group. And if I feel that you're only coasting, just giving group therapy lip service, I won't be able to sign off on your attendance report."

"Attendance report?" Ashleigh asked. "Like in kindergarten? Are you serious?"

"Very serious," Paula said. "You have fifteen minutes to write. Starting now." She walked out into the reception area, closing the door firmly behind.

Grace began scribbling on the second page of the journal.

I can't believe I have been "sentenced" to group therapy. I have nothing in common with these other women. I don't see how hearing their pathetic stories is going to help me get over what was done to me. I don't need therapy. I need a divorce. I was betrayed by my lying, cheating, dirtbag husband. You want to know how I feel? I feel different ways, different days. Most nights, I can't sleep. I don't know what's happening with my life. How will I make a living for myself? Where will I live? I can't keep living with my mother, but right now I don't have a choice. I have no choices at all. That's what I think I resent the most about all this. The feeling of powerlessness, of being helpless. It's so damned unfair. And I'm supposed to get over all of this? I'm supposed to reach a point where I don't feel this rage, bubbling up inside me, threatening to boil over at any moment? Most of the time, I am CONSUMED with anger. And when I'm not, I'm just sad. So damned sad. And lonely. Everything I had is gone. I'm thirty-eight. And alone.

"This is bullshit," Camryn Nobles was saying, as she made bold, looping lines of script on the open page of her journal. "My lawyer didn't tell me anything about having to write in a journal, or having to report to therapy, like a high school kid to study hall. I'm calling him tonight, just as soon as I get out of here. That bullshit judge can't make us do this shit."

"Shh," Ashleigh whispered, jerking her head in the direction of the door. "She'll hear you and tell the judge what you called him."

"I don't care what she tells that damned judge," Camryn said fiercely. "I'm not in his courtroom now. This is America. Not some damned banana republic, where he gets to lay down the law and make us salute every time he farts."

Grace laughed despite herself. "Maybe you could do an exposé of the judge for your television station."

"Maybe I will," Camryn shot back. "Just as soon as I get my divorce from Dexter Nobles, I might just do that."

The room was quiet then, with only the scratching sounds of their pens as they scrawled their thoughts across the cheap notebooks.

After she'd filled two pages of her journal, Grace looked at her watch. "It's been thirty minutes. Where do you think Paula went?"

"Who cares?" Camryn said. "This whole thing is a charade."

"I'm gonna go check on her," Grace said. "I've had a long day. I just want to get out of here."

She walked across the room, opened the door, and peeked out into the reception area. Paula Talbott-Sinclair was slumped down in the chair behind the reception desk, her chin resting on her chest. She was snoring softly.

Grace stood there for a moment, uncertain what her next move should be. Then she heard the front door behind her open.

A man stepped inside the reception area, looking uncertainly around the room.

He was tall and lanky, and sunburned. He was about Grace's age, she guessed, and at first she thought he was completely bald, until a closer look revealed a fine dark stubble of hair covering his scalp. He was dressed like a workman, in baggy khaki cargo shorts, a grimy-looking faded khaki safari hat, and high-topped lace-up work boots. His eyes were dark, nearly black, with an astonishing fringe of thick, luxuriant lashes. And dimples. It was the dimples that reminded Grace that she'd seen this guy before, and recently.

"Hey," Wyatt Keller said, scowling at her. "I'm looking for Dr. Talbott-Sinclair?"

Grace nodded in the direction of the slumbering therapist. "You just found her."

12

Is this a joke?" Wyatt asked, narrowing his eyes. He pulled a slip of paper from his pocket and reread the card the judge had forced him to take. Then he took a closer look at Grace.

"Didn't we meet . . ." he hesitated. "In court?"

"That's right," Grace said.

"I'm supposed to be here for the, uh, divorce recovery group," he said.

"Well, you're late," Grace snapped. "It started thirty minutes ago. Not that you missed much."

"Damn," Wyatt said. "The bridge was up. I've got a sick bird, and I had to run her to the vet's office, and the asshole vet tech wouldn't wait for me to get there, and the office was closed by the time I got there, and I had to stop at a drugstore and buy some meds . . ."

"Really?" Grace sniffed. "That's the best you can do? The dog ate your homework?"

Wyatt bridled. "It's true. Anyway, what do you care?"

Grace shrugged. "I don't. I just care about getting out of here. Right now. I've had enough 'sharing.' "

Wyatt nodded in the direction of Paula, who hadn't stirred despite their odd conversation.

"What's wrong with her?"

"Don't know, don't care," Grace said. "It's eight o'clock. My time's up."

She marched over to the desk and shook the therapist's shoulder. "Paula," she said loudly. "Hey, Paula. Wake up."

Nothing.

"Is she sick or something?" Wyatt asked, taking a step closer. He reached out and touched the side of her neck, looking for a pulse.

"Who's that?" Paula's eyes flew open and she swatted his hand away. She looked wildly around the room. "What's happening?"

"You told us to write for fifteen minutes, but it's now been more than thirty minutes," Grace said. "I came out here to check on you, and found you dead asleep. Or passed out."

"Ridiculous!" Paula said. She stood, fluffed her hair, and straightened her clothing, looking like Stevie Nicks after an epic bender. "I was meditating, waiting on the group to complete their visualization exercise."

"Who are you?" she asked, looking Wyatt up and down.

"I'm Wyatt," he said. "Judge Stackpole said I had to come see you. For divorce recovery group."

He said the words with such distaste, that Grace almost laughed out loud.

"Didn't the judge tell you our sessions start promptly at seven?"

"He told me," Wyatt said. "But I had a family emergency. And the bridge was up. But I'm here. I've been here for . . ." he looked down at his watch, and then at Grace, his dark eyes pleading.

"Twenty minutes," Grace volunteered. "We weren't sure whether or not to wake you."

Paula studied Grace's face carefully. "Really?"

"It's true," Grace said, with a shrug. "You can ask the others. We were all waiting for you to come back and take a look at our journals, to see if we did what you asked."

Paula waved her hand distractedly. "Never mind that. It's late. I'll read them next week."

"So . . . we can go now?" Grace asked. "All of us?"

"Didn't I just say that?" Paula asked.

She went into the inner office and clapped her hands for attention. "All right. That's the session for tonight. I'll see everybody next Wednesday, at seven o'clock. Remember to bring your journals."

She turned and handed Wyatt a notebook. "And next week, please be on time."

Camryn and Ashleigh stood quickly and headed for the door, while Suzanne was still jotting in her notebook. "Ladies," Paula said, gesturing toward the newcomer. "Before you go? This is Wyatt. He'll be a part of group for the next few weeks. I'd like you to welcome him to our little circle of healing. Wyatt, this is Ashleigh, Camryn, and Suzanne. And you already met Grace."

Suzanne looked distressed. "Uh, Paula, no offense to him, but I thought this was just a women's group? Nobody said anything about men being part of it."

"We welcome anybody with an open, willing heart to group, Suzanne," Paula said.

"Hey," Wyatt mumbled, blushing slightly as the women carefully looked him over.

"Hmm," Ashleigh purred.

"What's your story?" Camryn wanted to know. "Did Stackpole sentence you, too? I thought he only hated women."

"Never mind that," Paula said. She grabbed her camera and snapped a picture of the startled Wyatt. When the photo had developed, she handed it to him.

"What's this?" he asked, gazing down at the picture. It was not what you'd call a flattering image. The harsh overhead lights cast his face in deep shadows. He needed a shave, he noted, and there was a distinct sweat ring around the collar of his shirt. Also? There was a tell-tale white dribble on the shoulder of the shirt. Parrot poop, from Cookie, who'd insisted on riding on his shoulder the whole way to the vet's office.

"That's your before picture," Paula told him. "Staple it in the book. And the journal is your homework assignment. I want you to write in it at least once a day, every day, more often if you can. Tonight's assignment is to write about how you feel about where you are in your emotional journey."

"Ohh-kay," Wyatt said slowly.

"And Wyatt? As the ladies can tell you, the one thing I insist upon in group, besides punctuality, is absolute honesty. No whitewashing. No lies. Understand?"

Camryn snorted. "He's a man. They're genetically programmed to lie."

"Telling a man not to lie is like asking him to pee sitting down," Ashleigh agreed.

"Ladies?" Paula said wearily.

Wyatt had had more than enough. He could feel the hostility radiating out of every woman in this room. Man-hating ball busters, every one of them.

"Also?" Paula held out her hand. "Your counseling fees must be paid in full, in advance of each session. Did your attorney explain my fee structure? You understand I don't accept personal checks? Credit cards, although no American Express, or a cashier's check."

"She told me," Wyatt said. He reached into the pocket of his shorts and pulled out a tightly rolled bundle of money. The bills were faded and creased, and as he counted off each of the six fifty-dollar bills he thought of what that money should be going to. Groceries. New tennis shoes for Bo, and, now, payment on his ever-growing vet bill.

He pressed the money into Paula's hand.

"Cash?" She looked down at the bills as though he'd just handed her one of Cookie's bird turds.

"Yeah," he said. "Can I get a receipt for that? My lawyer told me to make sure and get one. To prove to the judge that I was here."

When he finally got outside the therapist's office, he took a deep breath of the hot, humid night air. May, and it was already sweltering. Well, that was Florida. Anyway, it felt good to be outside. It had been freezing in that damned office. And all those women, staring at him, like he was some kind of spawn of Satan.

Just because he was a man. Betsy had warned him it would probably be like this. "It's a divorce recovery group, honey," she'd said. "A bunch of sad, mad, depressed, repressed women. All of 'em blaming all their problems on some man who done them wrong. Just sit there and take it, and with any luck, six weeks from now, Judge Stackpole will sign off on your divorce and you and Bo can get back to living your lives."

He'd parked at the far end of the parking lot, mostly because he didn't want anybody riding by to know he was going to see a shrink. As he approached the truck now, he saw a woman standing beside it, bending down, looking in the open window.

It was that woman from group. What was her name? Grace, yeah. Grace.

He quickened his step until he was right beside her.

"Is there a problem?" he asked gruffly.

She looked up, puzzled. She had nice eyes, Wyatt thought, when she wasn't pissed off.

"You really do have a bird in your truck," she said, wonderingly.

"That's what I tried to tell you," Wyatt said. "What? You think every man is a liar?"

She ignored that, concentrating on Cookie, who was roosting on the steering wheel, her head tucked under her wing, eyes closed.

"It's a parrot, right? What kind?"

"African gray."

"Aren't you afraid he'll fly away, leaving the window open like that?"

Wyatt laughed. "Cookie? Nah."

"You said he's sick? What's wrong with him?"

"She. Same old thing," Wyatt said. "Cookie will eat any damned thing she can get her beak around. One of the kids at the park fed her something today. A gummy worm, probably. It, uh, didn't agree with her digestive system."

Grace looked closer at the slumbering bird. "Looks like she pooped all over your steering wheel."

"Yeah," Wyatt said with a sigh. "She's bad to do that."

She turned and pointed at his right shoulder. "I think she got your shirt, too."

"I would make a joke about getting shit on by everybody, but I wouldn't want you to think I'm bitter," Wyatt said.

Grace straightened. "Are you?"

"Oh yeah," he said easily. "Isn't everybody bitter about something?"

She thought about it. "I'd hate to think so, but yeah, it seems that way to me these days. Although maybe my mom isn't. God knows why, but I really think she doesn't have a bitter bone in her body."

"I've got enough bitter for both of us," Wyatt said.

Grace was looking at Cookie again. "You said something about a park. Do you work for the city or the county?"

"Hell, no," he said emphatically. "I work for myself. At Jungle Jerry's."

Her face lit up. "Jungle Jerry's," she said delightedly. "I remember that place! We used to go there every year on field trips for school. I used to love the parrots and the little Key deer. They were so adorable. Do you still have the parrot show? Where they ride the little toy bike on the high wire?"

"Yeah," Wyatt said, feeling himself thaw a little. "Cookie here is the star of the show. When she isn't eating Popsicle sticks and Happy Meal toys."

"Jungle Jerry's," Grace said wistfully. "I haven't been there in years and years. In fact, I didn't even know it was still there."

"You and everybody else in Florida," Wyatt said. "But we are definitely still there, right where we've always been.

He hesitated, then reached in the pocket of his shorts and pulled out a bright orange card. "That's a free pass. If you're not doing anything some day, you get in free with that. Bring your kids, if you want. It's good for the whole family."

"No kids," Grace said lightly. "Just me."

"Guess that's just as well," Wyatt said. "Since you're getting a divorce, right?"

"Yeah," Grace said. "Just as well. Since he turned out to be a scumbag."

Her mouth hardened and her eyes narrowed, and she looked like she had earlier in the evening, when he'd first walked into the therapist's office. Wyatt found himself missing her smile already, and wishing he could do something to bring it back.

"Guess I'd better go," he said, unlocking the truck.

"Me too," Grace said. "Gotta go home and write in my divorce journal."

"Yeah." Wyatt opened the driver's door and slid onto the seat. "Hey, uh, thanks," he said.

"For what?"

"Covering for me with the therapist," Wyatt said. "I can't afford to get crossways with her, or that damned judge."

"It's okay," Grace said. "Sounds like we're all in the same boat. Divorce-wise," she added.

"Yeah, divorce-wise."

She gestured at Cookie, who was awake now, and hopping up and down on the steering wheel.

"Will your parrot be okay?"

"She'll be fine," Wyatt said. "I'm gonna pick up some Pepto-Bismol at the Seven-Eleven, and see if that settles her down any."

"Hey. Does she talk?"

He laughed. "When she wants. If she likes you."

Grace leaned into the car, and Wyatt caught the scent of her, faintly soft and sweet, like the flowers in the park after a spring rain. She held her hand out, and Cookie happily stepped onto her outstretched index finger.

"Ohhh," Grace breathed. "Is this okay? She won't bite, will she?"

"Not usually," he said.

"Hi, Cookie," she said.

The bird cocked her head and blinked. "Wassup?"

Grace giggled just like one of the kids at Jungle Jerry's. "Cookie want a cookie?" She looked over at Wyatt. "Dumb, right?"

The parrot inched her way up Grace's forearm, until she was perched on the crook of her elbow.

Now Grace was getting nervous. "She won't try to fly away, will she?"

"No such luck," Wyatt said. "She knows where her bread is buttered. Literally."

"Gimme a beer," Cookie demanded. "Gimme a shot of whiskey. Gimme some peanuts."

"You don't really give her beer and whiskey, do you?"

"Nah," Wyatt said. "She just says that for the shock value. But she really does love peanuts."

Grace smiled again, and Wyatt found himself smiling back. "I better get going. It's trivia night."

"You play trivia?"

"Not really. I'm terrible at it. Actually, it's trivia night at the bar where I work, and it gets pretty busy about this time."

"You work at a bar?"

She bristled. "Anything wrong with that?"

"No," he said hastily. "Not at all. Which bar?"

"It's just a hole in the wall. Over in Cortez. You never heard of it."

"Try me."

"The Sandbox."

He grinned. "I know that place. My whole softball team used to go there after games. So it's still there? I heard the owner died a while back. What was his name? Butch?"

"Butch Davenport," Grace said. "Yeah, he's been gone a couple years now."

"You knew him?"

"He was my dad," Grace said. "My mom runs the place now. I moved in with her, after the split with my ex." She held her arm out straight and laughed as the bird waddled down her forearm and back into the truck.

"Good night, Cookie." She looked in at the bird's owner and was surprised to see him smiling at her, flashing those choirboy dimples.

"Good night, Wyatt."

"See you next week," he said.

13

Wyatt found his father asleep in the battered leather recliner in the tiny living room, the remote control still clutched in his hand, the television turned to the Cooking Channel.

"Pop." He shook the older man gently. "Hey, Pop. C'mon. Why don't you go on to bed now?"

Nelson yawned and stretched. "I'm waitin' for Rachel Ray to come on. I like those quickie recipes of hers."

"You like that cute ass of hers," Wyatt retorted. "Anyway, her show just went off. Go on to bed, okay?"

Nelson pulled himself out of the chair with effort. He was only seventy-four, but a lifetime of physical labor around the park had left him feeling every ache and pain this time of night. "I gotta make Bo's lunch and put a load of clothes in the dryer."

"I'll do it," Wyatt said, giving his father a gentle push in the direction of his room. "Everything go okay around here tonight?"

"Sure thing," Nelson said. "Bo and me, we had some hot dogs and coleslaw for dinner. He ate up every scrap I fed him. That kid's got a hollow leg for sure."

"Don't I know it," Wyatt said ruefully. "He's already outgrown the pants I bought him at Easter. And his toes are coming out of the top of his sneakers."

"How's Cookie?" Nelson asked. "The vet fix her up?"

"The damned vet tech closed up before I got there," Wyatt said. "Anyway, I think she'll be all right. I just put her up for the night. Anything else going on in the park?"

"Slow," Nelson said. "Like all week. No sense in staying open when there's nobody around. I locked up the gates around seven thirty." He brightened. "We got that Brownie troop coming tomorrow. Fourteen little girls, and the troop leaders and some mamas. I put some sodas in the snack-bar fridge, and I thought I'd go pick up some candy to sell in the morning."

"Skip the candy," Wyatt advised. "Just get some fruit—maybe some grapes and apples and stuff. These scout leaders don't let the kids eat the kind of junk we used to eat."

"It never killed you," Nelson pointed out. He started toward his room, then turned around.

"Callie called."

Wyatt sighed. "What now?"

"I don't know," Nelson admitted. "She wouldn't talk to me. Just ordered me to put Bo on the phone. I did, and when he hung up the phone from talking to her, he burst out crying. I should've told her he was outside playing and couldn't come to the phone. That's what I get for being honest. And stupid."

"Did he say why he was so upset?" Wyatt asked, his heart sinking. Callie knew damned well he'd be out of the house tonight, at his so-called divorce recovery group. She'd been sitting right there in the courtroom when the judge ordered him to attend.

"Oh yeah," Nelson said. "Callie told Bo she and the asshole are picking him up right after school on Friday, because they're going to Birmingham this weekend, to look for a new place to live."

"Dammit," Wyatt said. "I told her it's Scout's birthday party Friday. Anna's taking all the kids to that new water park, and then they're going out for pizza afterwards. Bo's been talking about it for two weeks now, ever since he got the invitation in the mail."

"Remind me who Scout is?"

"She's Bo's best friend, and she's our shortstop on the T-ball team. Anna is her mom."

"That's right," Nelson said. "Bo's had his bathing suit laid out on his dresser since Saturday. Poor kid. Now he'll have to miss it. All because Callie can't stand to see him have a good time unless it's something she engineered. Isn't there anything you can do?"

"I doubt it," Wyatt said, his jaw tensing. "It's her weekend. Technically, it starts as soon as he gets out of school on Friday. Never mind that most Fridays she calls me at the last minute and has me pick him up because 'something's come up'—like she wants to get her nails done, or she and the asshole are slugging down margaritas at The Salty Dog."

"Damned shame," Nelson muttered.

"And I can't call her anyway," Wyatt said. "Since she got the judge to forbid me to contact her, unless it's in writing."

"I know she's a woman, but she oughtta be horsewhipped," Nelson said angrily. "And that's my opinion on the subject."

Wyatt opened the bedroom door and undressed in the dark. He heard the soft rustle of sheets.

"Dad?"

He went over to the narrow twin bed and sat on the edge. He ruffled his son's light brown hair. "Hey, buddy," he said. "What are you doing awake?"

"I tried to wait up for you, but I fell asleep," Bo said.

"You're supposed to be asleep," Wyatt chided. "You're a little kid. You need a lot of sleep so's you can grow another six inches before tomorrow morning."

"I'm really mad at Mom," Bo said. "She says we have to go to dumb old Birmingham this weekend, and I have to miss Scout's birthday party."

"I know," Wyatt said. "Granddad told me, and I'm so sorry. I know how much you wanted to go to that water park."

The little boy sniffed. "Cory went there for his cousin's birthday. He says they have a killer wave machine that'll make you pee your pants just looking at it. And water cannons. They have water cannons so strong you could knock a kid down with 'em. I told Mom I didn't want to go to Birmingham. I told her I don't want to move there, and I don't want to live with you know who."

"Oh, Bo-Bo," Wyatt said. He rubbed his son's back, feeling the warmth of his skin through the thin fabric of his Lightning McQueen pajama top.

"Dad?"

"What, buddy?"

"I got so mad at Mom, I called her a bad name. Did Granddad tell you that?"

Wyatt had to stifle a laugh. "He didn't mention it. What kind of bad name did you call your mom?"

The child hesitated. "Granddad told me if I said it again, he might have to wash my mouth out with soap like he did when you were a kid."

Now Wyatt did laugh. "I'll tell you a secret on your granddad, Bo. He's all hat and no cattle."

"Huh?"

"That means he just talks a good game. He never washed my mouth out with soap. Not ever. Now, what kind of name did you call your mom? Just between us guys?"

Bo dropped his voice to a whisper. "I called her a shit."

Wyatt was glad for the cover of darkness, because his grin split his face in two. Then he forced himself to sound stern.

"Well, son, that's not a very nice thing to call your own mother."

"I was very, very, very mad at her."

"I know you were. But you can't go around calling people a shit, just because they made you mad."

"She called me a shit first," Bo said.

"When was this?" Wyatt asked, surprised.

"Right after I told her I wanted to stay with you this weekend and go to Scout's birthday party. She said, 'listen, you little shit. I am picking you up Friday right after school and that's final.' "

Wyatt tried to choose his words carefully. Betsy had warned him that he was on thin ice with Callie, now more than ever.

"I don't think your mom should have called you that, Bo," he said finally. "But that doesn't make it right for you to use bad words. Right now, your mom is really mad at me, too, because I don't want her to take you so far away from me. So, she might say some stuff to you that she doesn't really mean, because she's actually just mad at me. But, Bo, even if she says mean things sometimes, your mom really loves you. We both do. Right?"

"I guess so. But I still don't want to go to stinkin' Birmingham."

Wyatt leaned over and kissed his son's cheek. "Sleep now."

He climbed into the matching twin bed and pulled the worn sheet over his chest. The old walls in the mobile home were paper-thin, and he could hear his father snoring in the room right next door. A moment later, he heard the soft in and out of his son's drowsy breathing. For once, he was glad of the cramped quarters in their makeshift house. He reached out his hand and let it rest lightly on Bo's wrist. For tonight, anyway, Callie could not pull them apart.

14

On only their second night of what she'd begun to think of as divorce camp, their counselor, Paula Talbott-Sinclair, looked, Grace decided, a hot mess. Her eyes were red-rimmed, her thick black mascara smeared. She seemed not to notice that her haphazard topknot of blond curls was coming undone or that a fine sprinkling of crumbs adorned one strap of her turquoise tank top.

She'd lit a stick of incense, and the pungent white smoke drifting through the room made Grace's eyes water and her nose itch.

"Everybody here?" Paula asked, looking around the room. She gave Wyatt Keeler a droopy-eyed wink. "Wyatt, I see you made it on time this week. That's good. Verrrry good."

She was slurring her words, Grace thought. Was she drunk, stoned? She looked around the therapist's office. Nobody else seemed to notice Paula's condition. Maybe it was just her imagination.

"Now," Paula said, giving her hands a clap that sent her half dozen bracelets a-jingle. "Who wants to read from their recovery journal?"

Silence.

"Nobody?" Paula frowned. "Friends, we have to share here. It's part of our healing process. So who will break the ice? Am I going to have to call on somebody, or will you volunteer?"

"I'll go," Camryn said. She was dressed in gym clothes tonight, a snug-fitting fuschia Nike shirt, black bike shorts, hot pink running shoes. She'd wrapped a hot-pink scarf around her hair and had ditched the false eyelashes.

Camryn opened her black-and-white notebook and cleared her throat. "Okay," she said hesitantly. "Here goes."

She traced a line of writing with her fingertip, took a deep breath, and began reading.

"I feel like a victim. It's my job as a journalist to interview people, to tell their stories, convey their experiences. So here is my experience, and I am going to tell you exactly how it happened and how it makes me feel, and the hell with anybody who wants me to say I am sorry, because I am not sorry.

"My husband, Dexter Nobles, is scum. He lied to me, he lied to our daughter, he lied to all our friends. Bad enough he cheated on me, but no, he had to do it with our daughter's best friend. A twenty-year-old! So how do you think that makes me feel when I look in the mirror? When I look at this picture of myself, I'm reminded of the victims I interview at a crime scene. Like the old lady who gets pistol-whipped by a thug on a street corner, or the guy whose car is jacked at a gas station. I used to wonder, what was that old lady doing out that time of night? Or why did that guy drive through that part of town in a new Mercedes? Were they that clueless? But now I know, a victim isn't asking to be jacked or pistol-whipped, or cheated on by somebody they used to love. I know it because I'm a victim. I'm somehow less than I used to be. And I don't like it worth a damn."

Camryn paused and looked up at the others, and then at Dr. Paula Talbott-Sinclair. "There's a lot more, but you get the idea."

Paula's eyelids drooped, then fluttered. "Very . . . revealing." She was quiet for a moment, her blond topknot resting against the leather armchair's headrest, her eyes closed.

"Are we supposed to talk about what Camryn wrote?" This from Ashleigh, who was leaning forward, her hands clamped on her knees.

Paula's eyes remained closed. She waved her hand. "Go ahead."

"Your ex actually did that? Screwed your daughter's best friend? Like, even in your house?"

"Repeatedly," Camryn said. "In my house, my bed, my living room. In motels, and in the apartment she shared with my daughter. Did I mention this girl is our daughter's roommate?"

"Ooh," Ashleigh said, wide-eyed. "That is cold."

"Stone cold," Camryn agreed, her smile evil. "But I dealt with the bitch."

"What? More talk of revenge?" Paula's eyes flew open and she seemed to rally for a moment. "None of that," she warned. "No revenge talk. That's regressive behavior."

Ashleigh rolled her eyes.

"Whoosh next?" Paula asked, blinking rapidly. "Audrey?"

"It's Ashleigh. And yes, I can share."

Paula tilted her swivel chair backward, then around, so that her back was facing the group.

What the hell? Grace looked wordlessly at Camryn, then at Wyatt, who shrugged.

Ashleigh opened her notebook with a flourish and began reading, her voice breathy, dramatic.

"I look good. I mean, why should I let the fact that Boyce mistakenly believes he is in love with somebody else give me an excuse to let myself go? Working for a plastic surgeon, I see all kinds of women. I see middle-aged women who are trying too hard, desperately trying to stay young, and I see young girls who think a smaller nose or higher cheekbones or a tighter ass will change their lives, make them something they're not. But I'm not like that. Boyce fell in love with me—the real me. I am the same person he fell in love with, just a few years older. That whore he's with now? I know where she lives. I watch her come home—sometimes he's with her. I want to call her up, laugh in her face, tell her, 'just you wait. You think he's in love? Think he'll stay with you? Hah! What you don't know is this: you're just like a carton of yogurt at Publix. You've got an expiration date, only you can't see it, cuz it's stamped on your ass. You won't even know it, until one morning Boyce Hartounian locks you out of your condo and stops payment on your new Benz.'"

Ashleigh closed her notebook, looking expectantly at the others. "Well?"

Suzanne Beamon cleared her throat, and all heads turned to stare at her. She'd barely said a word since the group started, hadn't even looked any of them in the eye yet.

"That's an interesting metaphor for marriage, the thing about the expiration date," Suzanne said. "I'm an English teacher," she added apologetically.

"You're really watching your husband's new girlfriend?" Grace asked Ashleigh. "Isn't that a little creepy?"

"Isn't it actually stalking?" Camryn put in. "The judge finds out about that, he's not gonna like it."

"He won't find out," Ashleigh said. "What goes on in group, stays in group, right, Paula? Everything we say here is confidential, that's what you told us."

No answer.

Camryn got up and gently swiveled the therapist's chair around so that it was now facing the group. Paula's head rested at an awkward angle on her shoulder, her mouth was slack-jawed with a tiny thread of spittle trailing down her chin, but her eyes were closed.

"Passed out cold again!" Camryn stepped back so the others could see for themselves.

Suzanne knelt on the floor beside Paula Talbott-Sinclair and pressed two fingers lightly to the pulse point on her throat, relieved to find an even, steady beat. Her dark brown eyes were intent behind the tortoiseshell frames of her glasses.

"She's not dead, thank heavens. So, what do we do now?" she asked, looking to the others for guidance. "Should we call somebody, make sure she gets home okay?"

"Who would we call?" Grace asked, looking around the office. "We don't even know if she's married. Or where she lives or anything else."

Camryn walked to the desk in the corner, sat down, and boldly began searching through the desk drawers, a journalist to the last.

"Here's her purse," she said, drawing a small multicolored crocheted handbag from the bottom desk drawer.

Suzanne frowned. "Is that really necessary? It's such an invasion of privacy." She shuddered. "I'd hate for a bunch of strangers to go pawing through my purse."

"We're not strangers. We're her 'friends,'" Camryn said, making air quote marks. She unknotted the drawstring closure and pulled out a small leather billfold. She flipped it open to the driver's license.

"According to this, she lives over on Anna Maria Island," Camryn said, lifting one eyebrow. "Obviously, she spends her money on a mortgage, not on the rent on this dump." She dumped the rest of the pocketbook's contents on the desktop, taking inventory as she examined each object.

"Lipstick, just some cheap drugstore crap. Hand sanitizer. Car keys." Camryn held up the key. "Big surprise, granola girl drives that VW Bug out front." She put the key back in the bag. "Cell phone."

She tapped the phone's screen, looking, in vain, for a call history. "Cheap-ass phone, too," she complained.

"Hello!" she said brightly, holding up a small brown plastic pill bottle. "Here's something interesting."

She squinted down at the tiny print on the bottle's label. "Why do they make the writing so small? Melasophenol?"

Ashleigh snatched the bottle away. "Here, let me. I was married to a doctor."

Camryn calmly reclaimed the pill bottle. "And I was married to a lawyer, but that doesn't make me Perry Mason." She opened the bottle and spilled two different colored capsules into the palm of her hand. "These are all that's left. Sleeping pills, I bet."

Ashleigh picked up one of the capsules. "Believe me, honey, they haven't made a sleeping pill I haven't sampled. Well, the label says melasophenol, which is a fairly mild tranquilizer, but this blue one here"—she held it up—"isn't melassophenol, which is actually a pale yellow tablet." She held up the other pill, which was pale yellow. "She's mixing tranqs with something else. Which might be the reason she's so out of it."

She leaned over and lightly ran a finger down the sleeping therapist's cheek. "Paula? Yoo-hoo. Anybody home?"

The woman didn't stir, didn't flinch.

"Clinically speaking, I'd say she's out for the night," Ashleigh concluded. "I say we blow this place. It's so depressing, I'm tempted to borrow one of these babies. And I would, but I've got plenty better stuff at home."

Grace wanted to leave as badly as anybody else. But. "You really think we should just leave her like this? I mean, what if she has like, respiratory failure or something? Or chokes on her vomit or something? You read about that with celebrities."

"You want to take her home with you, be my guest," Ashleigh said, heading for the door. "But I bet she won't be happy when she wakes up and figures out you people went through her purse and dragged her out of her office, unconscious."

Camryn hurriedly stuffed the pill bottle and the billfold back in the pocketbook. "She's got a point, you guys," she said. "Right now, I do not need to piss

Paula off and get the judge pissed off at me." She placed the purse back in the desk drawer and quietly closed it.

"I say we leave her like she is and just go. And I don't know about you guys, but I could definitely use a drink. Who's in?"

"A drink sounds fabulous," Ashleigh said, nodding vigorously. "Grace? Wyatt?" At the last minute, she included the quietest member of the group. "Suzanne?"

"I wouldn't mind a drink," Grace admitted. "But let's at least put her on the sofa in the reception area, make her comfortable. If she stays like this much longer, she's going to have a hell of a headache when she finally wakes up."

Without saying a word, Wyatt leaned down, scooped Paula into his arms, and carried her to the outer office. He set her carefully down on the sofa cushions, placing a pillow beneath her head. She snored loudly.

Ashleigh followed him out to the reception area, watching Wyatt with an appreciative eye. "Good work," she purred. She sat down on the edge of the sofa and unceremoniously lifted one of Paula's eyelids. The therapist did not stir.

"Out like a trout," Ashleigh proclaimed. "Wyatt? What about that drink?"

"I don't know," he said uneasily. "My day starts pretty early. And I've got my son tonight."

"It's just barely eight," Camryn said, coming up behind him. She turned to Grace. "What about you?"

Grace did not intend to spend any more time with these people than necessary. Still, a long night stretched before her. And she was getting sick of her own company.

"Tell you what," she said, wondering if she'd lost her mind. "We can go to my mom's bar. The Sandbox? Do you know it? Over in Cortez?"

"Cortez?" Ashleigh wrinkled her pretty little nose. "Isn't that kind of a dive bar?"

"Exactly," Grace said.

"Perfect," Camryn said. "I love a dive bar. Let's roll." She turned to Suzanne. "Are you coming?"

"Well . . ." she said, her brow furrowed. "I told my daughter, Darby, I wouldn't be late."

"You won't be," Camryn said. "One drink. Think of it as group therapy."

"I guess one wouldn't hurt," Suzanne said finally. "I don't think I've ever been to Cortez. Is it very far?"

"Ten minutes," Camryn said. "I did a story over there a couple months ago. You can follow me. I'm in the white BMW sedan."

"What do we do about locking up?" Grace asked, glancing around the room.

"Nothing," Ashleigh declared. "What self-respecting thief would want any of this crap? Look, Paula will probably wake up in a couple hours and either sleep it off here or take herself on home. Either way, it's her problem, not ours."

15

It was a slow night at the Sandbox. Rochelle was seated on her stool behind the bar, halfheartedly watching *Dancing with the Stars*, when Grace walked in, followed by three women she'd never seen before.

Grace gestured toward a table in a darkened corner of the bar, and they all slid into the booth and gave her their drink orders.

"Margarita for me," Ashleigh said. "On the rocks. No salt."

"Vodka tonic, double lime," Camryn said. "I don't suppose you have Grey Goose?"

"Nope," Grace said calmly.

"Stoli?"

"Nope. We've got any kind of vodka you want, as long as you want Smirnoff." It was one of Butch's favorite lame jokes, and Grace was surprised to hear herself using it.

"Suzanne?" Grace was also surprised that Suzanne Beamon had actually come along. She was seated at the far edge of the booth, anxiously checking out her surroundings, as though she'd never been in a bar before.

"Oh. Uh, just club soda, if you don't mind."

"Club soda?" Ashleigh gave Suzanne a playful tap on the shoulder. "Come on, Suzanne, chill out a little."

Suzanne's nose turned pink. "I have to drive home tonight, and I live over in

Bradenton. I don't dare risk giving my ex any more ammunition with which to torture me."

"Good point," Grace agreed. "Be right back."

Rochelle raised an eyebrow as Grace approached where she was seated.

"My divorce recovery group. Paula passed out again, halfway through the session, so we decided to come over here for a drink."

"Interesting," Rochelle said, looking over her daughter's head at the group arrayed around the table. "Didn't you tell me there's a guy in your group? Where's he?"

"At home with his little boy," Grace said. "Just us girls tonight."

The drinks came. Ashleigh took a long sip of her margarita. "So . . . who's going to go first?"

"First with what?" Grace asked.

"You know. The dish. What really happened with all of y'all's marriages. How everybody ended up in 'divorce recovery' with all of us outlaws."

"It's not that interesting," Suzanne said, her voice low. "We were betrayed. End of story."

"Oh, I disagree," Camryn said quickly. "Grace, for example, has a fascinating story."

"You should know," Grace put in. "Anyway, everybody already knows what I did and how I ended up as one of Paula's people. Everybody in Florida knows, thanks to you, 'girlfriend.' "

"Not me," Suzanne said. When the others voiced their disbelief, she added. "I don't watch much television. Anyway . . . I guess I've been caught up in my own drama."

"Come on, tell it," Ashleigh urged Grace. "We want to hear your side of the story."

Grace gave a condensed version of the swimming pool story. "Afterwards, when I was driving over here, thinking about it, I couldn't believe that was me. Grace Stanton? Well, Davenport, now. I didn't plan to do it. I'm not a person who acts out like that. But I guess you never know what you're capable of until you're put in a situation like that."

Camryn snorted. "It was just a car. And you know he had insurance on the damned thing. As for planning something? Oh, hell yeah, I'm big on planning. Especially when it comes to that kind of thing. You know that quote, 'revenge is a dish best served cold'? I am all about that."

Suzanne leaned across the table. The small candle lit her face, giving it a greenish glow. "Did you catch your husband and that girl?"

Camryn's expression changed, hardened. "No. And that's what makes this whole thing so nasty. Our daughter, Jana, caught her daddy, in bed, with her best friend and roommate."

"Oh no." Suzanne looked sickened.

The other women at the table were silent.

"Awful," Suzanne mumbled.

Grace blotted the tabletop with a paper napkin. "Did you confront him?"

"Oh yes."

"Did he admit it?"

Camryn shrugged. "What was he gonna do, call his baby girl a liar? And then I found that little DVD of his."

She turned to Grace, rattling the ice cubes in her now-drained glass. "You think I could get another one of these?"

Grace turned toward the bar, caught her mother's eye and held up Camryn's glass. Rochelle nodded and a moment later arrived at the table. She didn't seem in a hurry to leave, either. So Grace introduced her to the other women, Rochelle went to refill everybody's glass, and before Grace knew it, Rochelle had pulled a chair up to the edge of the booth.

"You mentioned a DVD?" Ashleigh asked, after the introductions had been completed.

"Uh-huh. The fool hid it inside the family Bible. I guess he thought Jesus loves a liar and was counting on forgiveness. But not from me." Camryn shook her head. "Not after what I saw."

"Porn?" Suzanne's nose wrinkled in distaste.

"You could say that," Camryn said. "Dexter had been a busy little boy, filming his very own self. Getting ready for his 'dates.' And yeah, he lied about that, too, Treena wasn't his only 'Forever Your Girl.' Uh-huh, yes. That was the theme song for his date nights. Paula Abdul's 'Forever Your Girl' was his turn-on tune. But what really turned him on was the sight of himself in the mirror, prancing around in his red satin thong."

"Eeewww," Grace said. She shuddered. "Just . . . eewwww."

"I used to really like that song," Ashleigh said sadly.

"You'll have a whole new appreciation for it if you see that video," Camryn said tartly. "You got a smartphone?" She held out her hand. "Give it here and I'll show you how to find it on YouTube."

"No thanks."

"So . . ." Rochelle interrupted. "How did the video get on YouTube?"

"I put it there," Camryn said. "Oh, yes I did. Dexter Nobles, in the flesh—a whole lotta flesh! Getting dressed in his lil panties, getting ready for business meetings, lunches. County Commission meetings. Oh, he loved the feel of that satin under his suit when he was doing county business."

"You really did that?" Ashleigh asked, glancing down at her phone.

"Sure did. And it's gotten over twelve thousand hits," Camryn said.

"And that's what got Judge Stackpole on your case," Grace said. "Right?"

"His lawyer got the video taken down, but as soon as he did, other people put it right back up there. It's gone viral."

"Does your daughter know you put it on YouTube?" Suzanne asked.

Camryn sighed. "I didn't tell her. But she found out. She's furious. Not speaking to me." She looked around the group. "Does that seem fair to you? Dexter's the one who cheated, the dirty pervert. But she's mad at *me*—for outing him."

"Kids don't want to know bad stuff about their parents," Rochelle said.

"Dexter and I? We'd been living separate lives for a long time now," Camryn admitted. "I guess we stayed together for Jana. I don't miss his sorry ass. Not a bit. But I miss my little girl."

"She'll just have to get over herself," Ashleigh said. "Like you said, he's the pervert. The cheater. I bet she'll come around."

Camryn managed a wry smile. "Hope so. Now what about you, Miss Ashleigh? What did you do to earn yourself a spot in divorce recovery?"

"It's really not that big a deal," Ashleigh protested. "Nothing like what you guys did. I mean, it's a paint job, okay? The whole thing got blown way out of proportion."

"Why don't you just go ahead and tell us everything that happened?" Grace asked. "After all, you heard what happened with us."

Ashleigh pulled her compact from her satchel, checked her makeup, fixed her lipstick, and flipped her hair behind her shoulders.

"So . . . you already know who my husband is. Boyce Hartounian. We met when I was working as an insurance billing clerk in his office." She looked over at Rochelle. "Boyce is one of the top plastic surgeons in Florida. He is *the* man for boobs, in case you're ever interested. And, of course, he was married at the time, but honestly, Beverly, that *cow,* was totally a joke. So that happened."

"Wait," Grace interrupted. "What happened? Did we miss something?"

"They split up," Ashleigh said. "She hired this weasel of an investigator, and there were some unfortunate photographs, and what with that, well, Beverly did very, very well for herself in the settlement."

Suzanne interrupted. "I'm sorry, but I'm going to have to go." She opened her pocketbook and placed a five-dollar bill on the table. "Will this be enough?"

"More than enough," Grace assured her. "Are you sure you can't stay?"

"I really can't," Suzanne said, looking flustered. "My daughter, Darby, still isn't used to the idea of her father being gone. She gets anxious if she's alone at night."

"How old is she?" Camryn asked.

"She'll be eighteen in October," Suzanne said. "A senior this fall. This split-up has been very hard on her."

She looked around the table. "Good night, everybody. Thanks for including me."

Camryn watched Suzanne leave the bar. She turned to Grace. "There's something very odd about that woman. Afraid to leave an eighteen-year-old at home alone? And she still hasn't told us a thing about herself."

"I think she's probably just very shy," Grace said. "An introvert."

"I don't know about you guys, but I am *dying* to know what she did to her ex," Ashleigh said. "It's those quiet ones who always surprise you with something outrageous."

"Speaking of outrageous," Camryn said pointedly.

"Okay, sooooo. Boyce and I have been married, what, four years now? And it was amazing."

"And then?" Grace asked.

"My biggest mistake was quitting my job. Boyce told me he didn't want me working so hard." She shook her head ruefully. "I never even saw it coming."

"Hello?" A man's voice bellowed. "Rochelle? Where the hell are you?"

Their heads swiveled. A grizzled, shirtless old man wearing baggy shorts that hung below his kneecaps stood at the bar, banging the wooden surface with his glass.

"Pipe down, Milo," Rochelle hollered back. She stood. "Hang on. I want to hear this. I'll be right back."

Rochelle scurried behind the bar, scolding her regular as she drew him a beer.

"Your mom seems nice," Ashleigh told Grace. "Did you say you're living together? Where?"

Grace pointed her index finger upward.

"Here? You live above a bar?"

"I grew up here," Grace told her. "There's an apartment upstairs, two bedrooms, living room, dining room, kitchen. It's not fancy, but I guess you get used to it. At least it's close to the beach."

"I'm back," Rochelle slid back onto her chair. "You were saying?"

"Long story short, Boyce wanted me out of the office because he was having a fling with this slutty little drug rep named Suchita." Ashleigh laughed bitterly. "He even took her to the same suite at the Ritz where he used to take me, back when he was married to Beverly."

"That's just plain tacky," Rochelle said. "But how'd you find out?"

Ashleigh flipped her hair over her shoulder. "One of the girls in the office spilled the beans that he was getting friendly with the Juvenesse rep. I knew it was this Suchita chick right away. I parked across the street from his office and followed them to the Ritz."

Tears welled up in her eyes. "That was *our* place! Afterwards, I followed her back to her house, and when I saw the neighborhood she was living in, I knew it was true. No drug rep can afford to live in Newtown. So I decided to fix her little red wagon. Teach her a lesson."

"There was a Home Depot a couple miles away," Ashleigh continued. "I went home and changed into my guerrilla warfare outfit: black T-shirt, black Theory slacks, black Tory Burch flats. Then I went back after midnight. I painted HE'S MARRIED in these big, scary red letters all across the front of her house. Oh yeah, and on the front of her Beemer."

"You wore Tory Burch on a covert mission?" Camryn looked offended.

"They were last season, and I'd worn them to death," Ashleigh said. "So that's it. See?" She glanced around the table. "The whole thing just got blown way out of proportion."

"I'll bet," Rochelle said, helping herself to a sip of Grace's pinot.

"I know, right?' She turned to Grace. "Apparently in this state it's considered some kind of capital offense or something if you paint all over your husband's mistress's house. And then there was some crap about defacing private property . . . I let my lawyer deal with all that. I paid some fine. But then!" She paused for effect. "Stackpole found out. And he literally blew his stack!"

"And that's how you ended up at Ladies' Night," Rochelle said. She picked up Ashleigh's empty glass. "Anybody ready for another?"

Camryn frowned. "Better not. The station put me on 'probation' after they found out about the YouTube video. My lawyer says the only reason they didn't fire me is because I'm a community institution. I'm not but forty-two. And they act like I'm friggin' Betty White or something. Plus, I have 26,345 Facebook fans."

"You're only forty-two?" Ashleigh leaned way across the table to study Camryn's face. "Have you ever thought of Botox?" She traced a finger over Camryn's forehead, and down to her upper lip. "Because I could totally hook you up. Boyce showed me how to inject myself. It's really easy-peasy."

Camryn drew back. "Uh, thanks just the same. I don't think I'm up for any DIY Botox sessions at this time."

Ashleigh sighed and looked at her watch. "Guess I'd better get on home, too." She fumbled around in her billfold, finally finding a twenty-dollar bill, which she laid on the tabletop. "Thanks, ladies. It's been fun."

Grace hung around downstairs, long enough to help count out the cash register, wash the last of the dirty glasses and dishes, and turn off the neon WE'RE OPEN sign on the front door.

"That's a fascinating group of women you've got going there," Rochelle said, as she trudged up the stairs to the apartment.

"I don't know that I'd call them fascinating," Grace said, three steps ahead. "Bat-shit crazy is more the word that comes to my mind. I was a little worried about Ashleigh. She was slamming those margaritas pretty seriously."

"No worries," Rochelle said. "They were actually fakearitas. I just barely passed the tequila bottle over 'em."

"Good thinking," Grace said. "And I will admit it's just a little bit comforting to put things in perspective and find out there are people who've done worse things than me."

"Yeah . . ." Rochelle agreed. "I might need you to show me how to look at that

YouTube video that Camryn was talking about. You know," she added hastily, "just to help you put things in perspective."

"I keep thinking about Paula, the therapist," Grace said, when they got up to the living room. "She was really zonked. I don't feel so good about leaving her all alone like that."

"What else could you do?"

"I could have made sure she got home okay," Grace said finally. She turned around and headed for the door.

"You're going back to check on her?" Rochelle asked.

"Yup."

16

The strip shopping center looked even gloomier after midnight. Empty beer bottles and discarded fast-food wrappers littered the asphalt pavement. Blue lights flickered from behind the tattoo parlor storefront, and she could see a burly, bare-chested man inside, reading something on a computer screen. There were only three vehicles left in the parking lot, and neither of them was the shiny yellow VW. But one was a pickup truck.

Grace pulled along beside it and rolled her window down. "I thought you had to get home to your little boy."

"I did," Wyatt said. "He's asleep. My dad's there, so it's cool."

"You came back to check on her too, right?"

Wyatt Keeler got out of the truck and walked over. "Paula's gone," he said sheepishly. "I looked in the windows of the office, and I could see the sofa, so she's definitely not there. I checked around back, too, just to make sure her car wasn't there."

Grace let out a long breath. "That's a relief."

"Yeah," Wyatt said. He thumped the roof of her car. "Guess I'll head back home. See ya."

Grace didn't start her car just then. "You're not such a bad guy after all, are you?"

He raised an eyebrow. "Who said I was?"

"I was in the courtroom the day your ex's lawyer showed that video, remember? You put a fist through that guy's car window. It looked pretty scary from where I was sitting."

He sighed. "If I had it to do over again, I'd have turned around and walked away. Next time I will. What if I told you my side of the story?"

"What? Here?" Grace looked at the clock on her dashboard and considered. "Can we go someplace else? This place gives me the creeps. Gus's is just down the road."

She followed him in her own car to a brightly lit doughnut shop a few miles away. Seated at the counter, just a few stools away from a couple of goth-looking teenagers, Wyatt ordered coffee and two apple crullers while Grace ordered an iced tea—and a chocolate-iced cake doughnut.

He looked surprised.

"I usually don't eat a lot of sweets, she explained. "But I've been losing weight, since, you know, and anyway, their chocolate doughnuts are the best. Ever."

"You know this place?" He looked around. The dull green linoleum floor tiles were chipped and cracked, the red leather booths were held together with duct tape, and the white tiled walls were lined with yellowing framed newspaper clippings and faded family photos.

"Yeah, we used to come to Gus's all the time when I was a kid," Grace said. "It was a big treat."

"So, you really grew up here? Living above the Sandbox?"

She nodded. "How about you?"

"Sarasota. Kinda like you. We didn't exactly live above the company store, but we did have a house right around the corner from Jungle Jerry's."

"Right," Grace said. "I almost forgot."

The waitress brought their food, and Wyatt took a huge bite of his cruller. "Sorry," he said, in between chews. "I missed dinner tonight. I'm starved."

He washed down the first doughnut with coffee. "You've lived here, always? Never moved away?"

"I went to college at Florida State, which is where I got my interior design degree, and after college, I moved down to Miami. We moved back here a few years ago."

"Miami. Is that where you met your husband?"

"Afraid so. What about you? Where did you meet . . . what's her name?"

"Callie. We met while I was in grad school at Clemson. But for some reason, I thought it was more important to get married than finish my master's. I was working for a seed company in South Carolina, and Callie was pregnant with Bo. Jungle Jerry's was in rough shape, and my dad really wanted to retire, and my mom was begging me to come back down here to run it. She'd been diagnosed with cancer then, but she didn't want that to influence my decision. Anyway, we came back, Bo was born, and my mom died just a few months later."

"I'm sorry," Grace said.

"She got to hold him right after he was born, babysit him a few times, before she got really sick," Wyatt said. "And we named him after her father, which really tickled her."

"How old is Bo?"

"Six," Wyatt said. "Just finished first grade." He reached for his cell phone, scrolled through his photos, and held it out for her to see.

A sturdy freckle-faced boy with soft brown bangs and his father's dimples grinned into the camera, showing off two missing front teeth. He wore a baseball cap set back on his head and had an aluminum bat resting on his right shoulder.

Wyatt touched the screen with his fingertip. "Kid lives and breathes baseball. He's as crazy about it as I was at that age."

"Very cute," Grace said, taking the phone to study the little boy better. "What position does he play?"

"He's a catcher. Like I was. I tried to get him to play shortstop, told him he didn't want to be crawling in the dirt like I did the whole time I played ball, but he was determined to catch. He's not bad, either, even if I am his dad. And his coach."

She handed his phone back.

"So. I know you said you don't have kids. Ever want them?"

Her face colored, and he instantly knew he'd made a misstep.

"Sorry," he said. "That's a pretty personal question. Forget I asked."

Grace picked at the chocolate frosting with her fingernail. "That's okay," she said finally. "I do want kids. Well, I did. I'd started seeing a fertility specialist . . ." She blushed again. "I guess it's a good thing it never got that far." She gave him a sideways glance. "I don't know that I'm cut out to be a single parent."

"Sometimes, you don't have a choice," Wyatt said grimly. "I never thought I'd be a single dad, that's for sure. But I'm not sorry we had Bo. He's the best thing that's ever happened to me."

She broke off a piece of the doughnut and chewed. "You asked me if I wanted to hear your side of the story. About why you busted out that car window. I would like to hear it, if it's not too painful."

Wyatt held up his hand. The bruises were still a vivid greenish-black. "Pain? Me? Nah."

"Callie and Luke were gaming me, for months. That day at the ball park was the last straw. I coach Bo's T-ball team. Callie had the game schedule. I gave it to her myself. But all spring, she'd drop him off late for the games half the time, without his glove or his shoes, or even his uniform shirt. It got so I bought extras of everything and kept 'em with me. But I'd sent him home with the spares the week before. That day? They didn't bring him until the second inning—and again, with no equipment. Poor Bo was so upset, he was in tears. Luke acted like it was nothing, just blew me off. Told me if I didn't like it, too damn bad."

Wyatt flexed his right hand and winced. "You saw how I reacted. Not my finest moment."

He'd finished his doughnuts and his coffee. Grace broke off half her doughnut and placed it on his empty plate.

"Really?"

"Yeah, I think I just wanted a taste. To remind me of old times here. You know how that is?"

He gobbled the doughnut. "I'll tell you a secret. I feel the same way about Krystal's sliders."

"Ick," Grace said. "Not the same thing at all."

"Krystal was where my granddad would take me on Saturdays, for lunch, when I was a kid," Wyatt said. "Just the two of us. He'd order me two sliders, and he'd eat four. Right out of the paper sack, in the front seat of his old tan Buick Regal. Every once in a while, not that often, but sometimes, if I have Bo on a Saturday, we ride through the Krystal, get ourselves a bag of sliders, take 'em out to Holmes Beach, sit on the sand, and scarf 'em down."

"Sweet sentiment, but still, ick," Grace said. "Does your ex know you do that?"

"If she did, she'd probably sic the Department of Child Welfare on me."

"Not to mention Judge Stackpole," she added.

"You saw how he treated me," Wyatt said, leaning back on his stool, "How did you do?"

"Let's put it this way," Grace said. "Not great. Mitzi—she's my lawyer—is trying her best, but we still can't get his lawyer to respond to us, and I'm still essentially locked out of my business. He's supposed to be 'giving' me two thousand dollars a month, but I haven't seen a dime yet. And, oh yes, that money he's 'giving' me? It's mine anyway. All this while he transforms his new girlfriend into Grace 2.0." She fluttered her eyelashes. "Does that make me sound bitter?"

"Kind of," Wyatt said. "But then, I'm on a first-name basis with bitter these days. Right now, it looks like Bo's going to be moving to Birmingham by the end of summer, and so far, there's not a damned thing I can do about it. Yeah, technically I can see him weekends, but how do I pull that off when he's living nine hours away? I can't afford to buy a plane ticket every weekend, and anyway I've got a business to run. Or what's left of a business."

"That's really rotten," Grace said. "I can't believe any mother would deliberately deny a child the chance to see his father. It's just cruel."

"Callie's into cruel these days," Wyatt said. "She'll do anything she can to punish me. And the weird thing is, I can't figure out what I did to make her hate me like this. She wanted out of the marriage, I let her out. She wanted the house, I gave it to her." He shook his head and yawned.

"Yeah," Grace said, standing up and stretching. "It's pretty late for me, too."

"Thanks for listening to me vent," Wyatt said. He hesitated. "I got the feeling, back there at Paula's office, all of y'all were ready to tar and feather me. Just for being a guy."

Grace shrugged. "Everybody in that room is there because a man dumped on her."

"Hey, a guy dumped on me, too," Wyatt said. "Remember?"

"Right."

They paid at the cash register and walked out to their cars. Wyatt looked back at the old-timey neon GUS'S DONUTS sign. "I gotta remember this place. Bo would love it."

"If you feed that child Krystal sliders and Gus's for the same meal, I'll report you to Stackpole myself," Grace threatened.

"Hey," Wyatt said. "Thanks for listening to me tonight."

"You're welcome," Grace said, meaning it. "See you next week."

"If Paula's conscious. Do you think she's really on drugs?"

"She's definitely on something," Grace said. "My mom would say she's one ant short of a picnic."

Wyatt laughed. "One brick shy of a load. I can't believe I have to come up with three hundred dollars a session for this crap, on top of all the child support I'm paying Callie."

"Do you think it would do any good to report her?" Grace asked, fumbling for her car keys.

"Report to who?" Wyatt asked. "Stackpole? I'll mention what's going on to Betsy, but I already know what she'll say. 'Shut up and turn up.'"

17

Grace sat cross-legged on her bed, her laptop balanced on her lap, tapping away at the keyboard.

Lately, I've gotten interested in the farm-to-table movement. Here on Florida's Gulf Coast, where I live, there's the tendency to think farms are all in the Midwest, or up north. But that's not true. We have amazing small farms all around us. Citrus growers, of course, and small avocado groves, but once I started looking around, I was surprised to find honey producers, organic chicken and egg farmers, and even small family "row-crop" farms producing gorgeous lettuces, tomatoes, peppers, cucumbers, corn, and, of course, strawberries. In addition, we're lucky here to have local seafood brought to port by fishermen who keep us supplied with fish, crabs, and shrimp caught right in the gulf and bay, and beef from the cattle farms that have been in the interior parts of this area since I was a little girl.

My mother's generous friend Felipe brought us a bushel of white corn on Sunday. Picked that morning, it had the sweetest taste you can imagine. We feasted on it for dinner, but then I started thinking of new ways to combine it with other locally produced goodness, and I came up with this corn-crab chowder recipe. It utilizes the corn, plus sweet blue crabs, which are being harvested here right now, not to mention red bell peppers and jalapeño peppers, readily available anywhere. I hope you'll try this at home, and let me know what you think.

She glanced over at the notes she'd scrawled in the kitchen earlier in the day. The corn-crab chowder really had been a triumph. She'd diced sweet yellow onions, jalapeños and red peppers, and some garlic, then sautéed them in bacon drippings in the cast-iron Dutch oven. Rochelle had grumbled about what a pain in the ass it was to cut all the corn off the cobs, but once she'd dumped them in the bacon drippings, along with diced tiny new potatoes and added chicken broth, the aroma wafting through the Sandbox kitchen had been irresistible. After the corn had simmered for twenty minutes or so, Grace had dumped in the crab. It was just back-fin crab, because Rochelle insisted you really didn't need lump claw meat for a soup, and, although crab was in season, her supplier still charged her $6.99 a pound.

Half-and-half was carefully added to the corn and crab mixture, along with a generous sprinkling of Old Bay seasoning—at Rochelle's insistence. As that simmered another five minutes, Grace diced up the crisp bacon she'd set aside from the pan drippings.

She'd gone outside to snip chives from the pots of herbs she'd started growing by the Sandbox front entrance, and when she reentered the kitchen, she caught her mother, standing over the stove, the Old Bay tin poised over the pot of chowder.

"Hey!" Grace protested, snatching the can from Rochelle's hand.

"I was just adjusting the seasoning." Rochelle dropped a wooden spoon into the big stainless steel sink.

"It doesn't *need* any more adjustment," Grace said, through gritted teeth. "Do you know how much salt is in that stuff? Not to mention the sodium in the bacon?"

"I don't need to know. I just know you can't make soup—especially soup with corn and crab, without a good douse of Old Bay," Rochelle retorted. "I've been making soup for way longer than you've been alive, young lady, so don't go lecturing me on salt. Or on cooking."

Grace bit her lip. She wanted to remind her mother that she was already on medication for high blood pressure and that her doctor had been urging her to cut back on sodium. Instead, she began snipping the chives into a milk-glass custard cup. "If you want more Old Bay in your soup, you can keep the shaker by your bowl. But please don't add it to the pot. Please?"

"Hmmph." Rochelle began tossing dirty dishes into the sink, a sure sign that she was miffed.

Ignoring her mother's tantrum, Grace found two old ice cream sundae glasses and placed each on a white plate. She started for the bar, to grab the sherry bottle, then, quietly, picked up the Old Bay can and took it with her. Just in case.

She turned the burner down to low and added a splash of sherry to the soup. Tasted, then added another splash.

A few minutes later, she made diagonal slices in the loaf of Cuban bread that had been delivered to the restaurant that morning, dribbled olive oil over the slices, and ran them under the broiler just long enough to toast them a light brown.

She placed a slice of bread on each plate, then dipped a ladle into the Dutch oven, carefully spooning the chowder into each sundae glass. A sprinkling of chives and diced bacon topped each glass.

Grace grabbed her camera and began snapping photos.

"Who serves crab chowder in a sundae glass?" Rochelle asked.

"I just like the way it looks," Grace said, snapping away. "Eccentric."

"Weird," Rochelle muttered, watching from the sink. "Are we eating or shooting?"

"Eating," Grace said, setting the camera down. "But if the finished product tastes as good as it looks, I think this will make a terrific blog post."

She grabbed two blue and white striped dish towels from the stack on the stainless steel prep counter and draped them over her arm before picking up the soup dishes and pushing her way through the swinging door into the bar.

Grace unfolded the dish towels and spread them out as a placemat on the bar. She grabbed a couple of wineglasses, poured in some white wine, and stood back to look. Finally, she added a paper-thin slice of lemon to the side of each plate for a shot of color. Pleased with the effect, she went back for her camera and took a couple more exposures. "Let's eat," she called, over her shoulder.

Rochelle eyed the place settings at the bar. "Pretty fancy, just for Saturday lunch for the two of us."

"You eat with your eyes, as well as your tastebuds, you know," Grace said, refusing to let her mother bait her.

"Hmmph," Rochelle said. But she dipped her spoon into the soup, tasted, and closed her eyes.

"Well?"

Rochelle took another bite of the soup. "Not bad. Not bad at all." With a fingertip, she fished a small limp green fragment from her soup and held it up for Grace to see.

"What's this?"

"Sorry," Grace said. "It's just a sprig of tarragon. I was supposed to remove it before I served the soup, but I got distracted. So . . . you really like it?"

"I do," Rochelle said. She dipped a piece of toasted bread into the soup and chewed.

Grace ate slowly, pausing to make notes on her ever-present yellow legal pad. Next time, she thought, she might do cheese toasts to go along with the soup, maybe adding slivers of goat cheese to the bread before broiling. She pondered the soup's consistency, finally deciding she'd need to add an immersion mixer to the kitchen equipment at the Sandbox, so that in the future she could puree part of the soup. Her own immersion mixer was back in the kitchen at the house on Sand Dollar Lane. Ben's house.

When Rochelle finished her soup, she got up from her seat, found a piece of chalk, and began writing on the blackboard on the wall by the cash register.

Today's SPECIAL—CORN CRAB CHOWDER à la GRACE. $10.

"You really think the customers will like it?" Grace asked, secretly pleased. She'd been living with Rochelle for nearly two months, and it seemed like the first time she'd done something in the kitchen or the bar that Rochelle approved of. "And more importantly, that they'll pay ten dollars for a bowl of soup?"

"They'll lap it up," Rochelle predicted. "We just won't tell 'em how healthy it is. And if anybody gripes about the price, I'll show 'em my bill from the seafood wholesale house."

They'd had a busy evening. One of the local softball leagues was having a tournament, and word had apparently gone out that the Sandbox was the place to meet after the games.

The first batch of soup was gone by 7:00 P.M., and Grace made another gallon, using up all the crab in the big walk-in cooler. At 9:30, she had to tell Rochelle to "eighty-six" that night's special.

A loud groan rose up in the bar as Rochelle crossed the special off on the blackboard.

They were both exhausted by the time Rochelle's late-night shift, consisting of Almina, a young Latin woman, and her husband, Carlos, showed up to take over at 10:00.

While Rochelle showered in the apartment's only bathroom, Grace settled down to write her blog post, referring to her notes and editing and refining the photos she'd shot earlier before uploading to her blog, accompanied by a list of local farms, complete with their links.

It was after midnight when she tapped the PUBLISH button. She viewed the blog in its final form and smiled. "Take that J'Aimee," she muttered, right before padding off to take her own shower.

Sunday morning, Grace was still sleeping when she heard the cell phone on her nightstand ding softly, signaling an incoming message.

She sat up and yawned, looking out the window. It was barely daylight. But the message on her phone woke her in a hurry.

HAVE U SEEN YR OLD BLOG TODAY?

The text message on her phone was from ShadeeLadee, one of her earliest Gracenotes followers and another lifestyle blogger based in Miami. Over the years they'd met at various blogger meet-ups and gotten friendly, and, although ShadeeLadee had a real name, which was Claire King, Grace always just called her Shadee.

Grace clicked over to what she thought of as Faux Gracenotes, and swore. Loudly.

The photo was the exact one Grace had posted on her own blog, but with the headline Grab Some Crab.

Beneath it was Grace's corn-crab chowder, which J'Aimee (or more likely Ben, Grace decided) had rechristened Crab-Corn Bisque. She'd cleverly changed the recipe in the slightest ways, calling for a sprig of rosemary instead of tarragon and decreasing the amount of half-and-half. But otherwise, it was Grace's recipe. And it was definitely Grace's photo.

"Oh, hell no!" Grace exclaimed. She scrolled down to see the number of comments J'Aimee's post had garnered. There were seventy-six, and it was barely 7:30 A.M. on a Sunday, usually her slowest day for blog traffic.

She quickly typed in a comment of her own. "THIS RECIPE AND PHOTO WERE HIJACKED FROM TrueGrace.com. To see the original, much better, recipe, click over to here." And she added a link to her own blog.

Most likely, Ben, whom she assumed was the blog's administrator, would delete Grace's comment and block her from trying to comment again, but Grace didn't care.

She opened her own blog. Nothing. Her new banner was there, but the only thing beneath it was a vaguely worded link. She instinctively clicked on it, and immediately regretted it. The link took her to the vilest, most sickening display of pornography she could have imagined.

Grace stared at the screen in stunned silence. How? She didn't have to ask who had done this, who'd not just erased her blog post, but sabotaged her entire blog. It was Ben, that she knew. She just didn't know how.

How could he have infiltrated her blog? She had a new protected password; he couldn't have accessed it, or could he?

Fuming, she left the blog and went to check her e-mail. Her in-box showed she had eighty-eight new messages.

She read the first one, from another lifestyle blogger, Shana, of Design or Die, and cringed.

Grace, what's going on with you? Your blog has been hacked, and it's not only got a porn link, it's infecting anybody who opens it with a virus. Love ya, girl, but for the sake of my readers, I'm removing you from my blogroll until you get your act together.

The next e-mail was from Nathan Woods, an influential interior design blogger with nearly half a million followers. Grace had been on cloud nine the day Nate had e-mailed to tell her how much he loved her post "Window Treatments That Ought to be Outlawed," which he'd privately called "Swags for Hags." He'd done two cross-promotions with Grace that had gained her a slew of new followers, and had even given her invaluable business advice about which advertisers to avoid on her own blog.

Nathan's e-mail was terse and to the point.

What the fuck is this??? It was followed by a link, which took her to an infamous online forum called SnarkSauce, where contributers posted venomous items about Internet celebrities.

I HATE NATE was the post's headline.

Closet queen Nathan Woods's tenuous hold on the title of "Biggest Boozer" has never been challenged, but recently the Manhattan-based designer and blogger was knocked down a rung when textile giant F. Shumacher & Company ended their five-year contract with Woods, whose lame-ass line of botanical-based fabrics never quite lived up to its early promise. Apparently the only person in the tightly knit New York design community who was surprised by the move was Woods himself. Insiders tell me Woods is also about to be asked to leave his post as contributing editor at Architectural Digest. Also? We hear Woods's love interest, boy-about-town Marc Klein has moved out of Nate's East Village love nest. Stay tuned y'all!

Although the posts on SnarkSauce were usually anonymous, the Nate item was signed. *Grace from Gracenotes.*

Her fingers flew over the keypad. "I never wrote any such thing. This is all Ben, my soon-to-be ex. You have to believe me, Nathan, I would never, ever write anything like this. Ben has hijacked my blog, and he's sabotaging me every way he can. I don't know why he's decided to do this, but I'm going to get this post taken down, and make SnarkSauce print a retraction. I swear."

A moment later, she saw that Nathan had replied. His message was succinct. "You are dead to me."

Grace was devastated. She closed the laptop and put it on the floor, like a diseased thing, best avoided.

18

Grace stormed downstairs to find Rochelle sipping coffee at the bar. "I'm going to kill Ben, so help me. Right after I tear that little bitch J'Aimee limb from limb."

"What've they done now?"

She poured a mug of coffee for herself and plopped onto the barstool next to her mother's. "I spent hours yesterday making that crab soup, photographing it, editing, then writing and posting my blog. Hours!"

"So? If you're still fishing for compliments, I'll say it again. The soup was damned good."

"The soup was amazing," Grace cried. "And the photos were amazing. So amazing that Ben lifted the recipe, nearly word for word, and the photos, my photos, and put them on J'Aimee's blog. And, somehow, he managed to erase my blog post. In its place, he put a link to the foulest, most degrading porn site on the planet. A site that, if you were to click the link, would give your computer a virus."

"You're sure it was Ben?" Rochelle asked.

"Who else? It had to be him. I can't figure out how it's possible, how he could figure out the password to the new blog, but somehow he did."

Rochelle rolled her eyes. "What a slimy bastard. It's a damned shame Ben wasn't locked in the trunk of that car when you drove it into the pool."

"And that's not all he did," Grace said. "When he was done hijacking my blog post, he hopped all around the Internet, poisoning people against me. He left nasty comments on my friends' blogs signed with my name, and he wrote this incredibly bitchy piece on SnarkSauce about Nathan Woods and signed my name to that, too."

"Who's Nathan Woods? And what's SnarkSauce?" Rochelle asked. She could never keep all this Internet stuff straight.

"Oh, Mom, you've seen his show on Saturday mornings. He's probably the best-known interior design blogger in the country. His blog has like, I don't know, probably seven hundred thousand followers. He did a cross-promotion with me back in February, and my analytics took a crazy jump, just because of my exposure on his blog."

"You still haven't explained SnarkSauce," Rochelle reminded her daughter.

"I don't know if anybody can explain SnarkSauce. I guess you'd say it's hater central for lifestyle bloggers. People post these vicious remarks about well-known bloggers. I never read it, but Ben always did. He thought it was hilarious. That's how I know it must have been Ben that wrote that crap. Now Nathan is furious with me. He says I'm dead to him. And all my other blog buddies hate me, too, all because of Ben."

Grace banged her head on the bar top. "Why me? Why?"

"Did you let these people know it wasn't you that wrote the stuff? That it was Ben, trying to get even with you?"

"Of course! But I don't think anybody believes me. People are dropping me from their blog rolls and defriending me on Facebook. At this rate, I won't have a single friend in the business." Grace jumped up and paced back and forth in front of the bar, close to tears.

"Grace?" Rochelle's voice was stern. "Sit down and listen to me." She caught her daughter by the elbow. "Sit."

"What?" Grace knew she sounded like a spoiled brat, but she couldn't help herself.

"Anybody who thinks that you would be capable of doing something like that doesn't really know you. And if you tell them you didn't do this stuff, and they still don't believe you, well, screw 'em. They were never your real friends at all."

"But they were," Grace insisted. "You don't know what the blog world is like. We read each other's blogs and comment and cross-post and guest blog. And we see each other at meet-ups, once or twice a year. I care about these people, and they care about me."

Rochelle shook her head. "No, they don't. Did any of these so-called friends call you after your big breakup with Ben was all over the news? Did any of them drive over here, take you out to lunch, or just give you a shoulder to cry on when you needed it most?"

"That's not how it works in my world," Grace said stubbornly.

"Then your world is seriously screwed up. You've gone through a lot in the past two months, but as far as I can tell, not a single friend has stepped up. And not just these so-called blogger buddies of yours. Where are your old girlfriends? The couples who used to come to all those dinner parties you used to throw all the time?"

Grace clutched her coffee mug so tightly she thought it might crush. "I don't know," she whispered. "A couple left me messages on my phone. But I was just too embarrassed to call them back. After a while . . ."

"They quit calling," Rochelle finished her sentence. "Fair-weather friends, every last one of 'em."

"I guess Ben got custody of all our old friends." Grace blinked back tears, and wondered if her tear ducts would ever dry up. "And that hurts, too. I try to keep busy, to keep from dwelling on everything, but everyday, it's like something else happens, another slap in the face. My blog? I know it seems silly to you, but, Mom, this is my work. If I don't have a marriage, and I don't have any friends, and then, somehow, I can't even make a living, what the hell else do I have? What kind of life is this?"

Rochelle handed her a paper towel. "Dry your eyes, honey. This is the life you've got, so put on your big-girl panties and make it what you want it to be. All your old friends are gone? Find some new ones. Ben's attacking you. Counterattack. Stay on the offensive. The best way to do that, from where I'm sitting, is to figure out a way to do what only you can do, and then get on with it. Everything else will take care of itself."

"How?" Grace's voice quivered with emotion.

Rochelle threw up her hands in surrender. "I don't know, Grace. I'm not Dr. Phil. But you can't just give up and sit around and whine. That's not how we raised you."

She leaned closer to Grace, rested her forehead against her daughter's. "Figure out what you want. And then go get it."

. . .

She hadn't had all that much contact with the Gracenotes advertisers. That had been Ben's department. But she'd had some correspondence with the bigger, most important ones: Home Depot, Levolor, Benjamin Moore, Viking, a big carpet manufacturer, and DeWalt, a power tool manufacturer.

Now Grace scrolled through the contacts on her laptop, searching them out, mentally composing the message she'd send.

Dear Sir: Just wanted to take the time to thank you for your past support of Gracenotes. Unfortunately, a situation has arisen that I wanted to make you aware of. I am currently in the middle of an unpleasant split from my husband, Ben. The result is that although Gracenotes.com is still online, I am no longer authoring or associated with those posts. I've started a new blog, TrueGrace.com, and I hope you'll take a look at it. In the meantime, you should know that Ben is actually lifting my intellectual property—my writing, my recipes, and my photographs—and publishing them on Gracenotes, representing them as original. I also believe he's actually engaging in sabotaging my career as a blogger, by posting potentially libelous, scurrilous, negative comments and material on other lifestyle blogs and signing my name to them. I know your company values your brand and identity too much to underwrite these kinds of activities, and I hope you will take the appropriate steps to ensure that your company is not associated with individuals who rely on devious, underhanded, negative activities. All best, Grace Davenport (formerly Stanton), the True Grace.

She pushed the SEND button and, for the first time in weeks, felt like herself. The real Grace.

19

Grace had never been what you would call athletic. She'd been a book nerd as a kid, always happier inside with a book than outside with a racket or a club or playing a sport that made her sweaty.

It was only after her sophomore year of college, when she'd gained not just the freshman fifteen but a whole twenty pounds, that she'd reluctantly taken up running. She'd kept it up, off and on, since then. Running to keep her weight down or the stress of daily life at bay.

Lately, she'd started running for sanity. Since the split with Ben and moving into the apartment above the Sandbox, she'd taken to waking before dawn. Sometimes she read; sometimes she worked on her blog; sometimes she laced up her running shoes and hit the road.

Reading again through all the e-mails in her in-box left her feeling infuriated and helpless, even a day later. Ben—or somebody—had done a thorough job of poisoning her Internet presence. Using her name, he'd posted inflammatory blog comments on every single blog from her old blog roll. She knew this because nearly all of the bloggers had e-mailed to tell her that she was dead to them, too.

She had to get away. It was still dark when she slipped down the stairs and let herself out the Sandbox's side door.

Grace wasn't fast, and her running form left much to be desired. She popped her earbuds in, pressed the PLAY button on her iPod, and loped down the street. The route she'd developed took her along the winding roads that paralleled the Gulf of Mexico. If she looked to her left, she could see blue skies, sometimes catch patches of blue-green surf through the tree line of shaggy Australian pines and palm trees.

After crossing the bridge from Cortez, she ran through Bradenton Beach, on to Holmes, and Anna Maria. After an hour, her nylon tank top was drenched with sweat, her gym shorts plastered to her butt. Even her ponytail dripped sweat onto her shoulders.

The last mile of her run was actually more of a cool-down walk. She did a run-walk on the beach for a half mile or so, keeping her eyes on the surf line, scanning for any shells, watching the seagulls and sandpipers. At one point, she stopped and stared at a huge gray heron, poised, motionless at water's edge. The bird never flinched as Grace approached and stood, marveling at its elegant blue-gray plumage. Eventually, she moved on, but the heron did not.

It was early Monday morning, so the streets of Anna Maria were quiet. She loped up one sandy, narrow street after another, walking, fuming. Every once in a while, she felt a faint breeze coming through the tree line. The houses on these streets were cottages, many of them bearing real estate signs indicating they were vacation rentals.

This was a new neighborhood to Grace. She slowed to a stroll, appreciating the modest concrete block or frame structures, so unlike the rambling, overblown megamansions on Gulf Vista. She wished she had her camera to capture the early morning sun, the tropical gardens of palms, bromeliads, crotons, bougainvillea, and hibiscus.

Grass was sparse here. Instead, the small yards seemed to consist of dense plantings of vines and ferns and flowers. Lizards darted across the narrow sand-strewn road, and she saw hummingbirds hovering over the thick hedges of ixora with their star-shaped coral blossoms.

It seemed the whole world was still slumbering, until she came across a house that stood out like a sore thumb on this block of neatly maintained homes. The curb was heaped high with trash, the yard weedy and strewn with dead palm fronds and fallen limbs. Barely visible, behind an overgrown hedge of ficus, she could see a glimpse of faded white siding.

Also blocking her view was the mountain of refuse. Two big city-issued receptacles were spilling over with plastic bags of garbage. Alongside these were sodden cardboard boxes overflowing with old clothes and shoes and more. A stained king-sized mattress leaned against the receptacles and was propped up by two cheap fiberboard nightstands.

Grace heard a screen door slam, and, as she watched, an old man muscled a long rattan couch through the doorway and into the yard. He cursed softly as he pushed and shoved the sofa to the curb.

"Hey," he said, barely noticing Grace. He dumped the sofa, wheeled, and went back into the house.

Something about that sofa caught her eye. She glanced at the house, to see if the man was watching, but he'd disappeared.

The rest of the discards at the curb were junk, cheap, soiled, ruined junk. But this sofa . . . Grace squatted to get a better look.

The rattan arms formed huge pretzel-like shapes. It was a three-seater, and it looked, she thought, like it could be by Paul McCobb. The rattan wrappings were in surprisingly good shape, and all the seat supports looked intact.

A moment later, the screen door slammed and the man reappeared, this time with a wheelbarrow heaped with thick cushions covered in a hideous orange and rust synthetic plaid fabric. He dumped the cushions without comment and wheeled back inside.

Grace was intrigued. She walked across the street, down the block, and then doubled back again. It was like a floor show whose second act she couldn't bring herself to miss.

By now, an armchair had joined its matching sofa. And the man with the wheelbarrow was back, this time bringing a low-slung, boomerang-shaped rattan coffee table with a yellow pine top, which he unceremoniously dumped on end. The table's top, Grace saw, was marred with cigarette burns and water rings, but the legs and the rattan wrappings were in fairly decent condition.

The man looked annoyed at having a spectator. He was tall and thin, with a high forehead and thinning gray hair and a lit cigarette dangling from one corner of his mouth. He wore a pair of loose-fitting khaki slacks and a shapeless gray T-shirt.

"Can I help you?" he asked.

Grace blushed. "Did somebody die?" she blurted out.

"I wish," he said. His voice was gravelly. He set the wheelbarrow down, took a wrinkled handkerchief from his back pocket, and mopped his face.

"My damned tenants moved out and left me with this mess," he said, removing his eyeglasses and wiping them down.

"That's awful," Grace sympathized.

"You don't even know," he agreed. "Three months back rent owing, not to mention they trashed the house so bad, I don't know how long it'll take me to get it into shape to rent again."

He was gazing at her, taking in her sweaty, disheveled appearance. "Don't I know you?" He gestured at her ball cap, with the Sandbox logo. "Maybe from the bar?"

Now that he mentioned it, she did think he looked familiar. "Maybe. I'm Grace Davenport. Rochelle's daughter."

"Riiight," he said, wiping his hands on his pants and shaking her hand. "And I'm Arthur Cater. I knew your daddy. Took him fishing a couple times. Butch was a great guy. How's your mama gettin' along?"

"She's good," Grace said. "We miss him, but if you know Rochelle, you know she's a tough old bird."

"She is that," he said with a laugh.

Now he gestured toward the mountain of trash. "Should have trusted my gut instinct. But they were a young couple, and my wife felt sorry for 'em. Famous last words."

Grace gestured toward the mound of trash. "You're throwing all of this out? Not even calling Goodwill to come pick it up?"

He snorted. "Goodwill wouldn't take this mess. Would you? Mildewed, pee-stained. They had dogs, even though the lease specifically forbids pets, and they swore they didn't have any. So everything is crawling with fleas."

Grace shuddered and took a tiny step backward.

He flicked his handkerchief at the rattan sofa. "This was my grandmother's. She left me the house, and this was always in it, as long as I could remember. We've been renting this house, furnished, with no problems for fifteen years, and then these bums move in, and now it's not fit for the dump."

He was mopping his neck. "You see anything here you want, be my guest."

"The rattan furniture is actually very pretty," Grace ventured. "Probably from the forties. You're sure you don't want to keep it? Maybe have the cushions redone?"

"Nah," he said dismissively. "We got a house full of furniture. And my wife doesn't like this old grandma stuff." He studied her. "There's an end table and another armchair inside, that goes with this set, if you think you might want it. Course, you'd have to haul it off yourself."

"I just might want it," Grace said, surprising herself. And then she had an idea.

"Would it be all right if I came inside, took a look at the furniture?"

"You got a clothespin for your nose? And if you get bit up by fleas, don't blame me."

The walkway to the front door was brick, but it was barely visible beneath the tendrils of vines and weeds that grew up in the sandy yard. The house was raised up from ground level on concrete block piers. It had a steep gabled roof with slatted wooden air vents near the V-shaped peak and a half-shed tin-roofed porch with large wooden brackets supporting the overhanging porch eaves. The siding was aluminum, and it was pulling away from the house in several spots.

Arthur Cater yanked open the screened door, and she followed him inside.

It took a moment for her eyes to adjust to the dim light. She was on a screened porch, or what was left of it. Most of the rusty screens were torn, and in some cases, they were missing entirely. Two cheap plastic armchairs were overturned, and the painted wooden floor was littered by overflowing trash bags.

Her new friend pushed open the front door. "After you," he said with a flourish. She was greeted with a pungent smell—a mixture of urine, mildew, and stale cigarette smoke.

"Oh my," she gasped, forcing herself to breathe through her mouth.

"Now you see what I'm dealing with," he said.

The front of the cottage was basically one room. They were standing in the living room. Its windows were cloudy and smeared with dirt. Venetian blinds hung crazily from one hook on a long window that looked out on the porch. The rattan armchair was pushed up against the wall, heaped with an old sleeping bag and pillow, and a matching end table rested, upside down, atop it.

"That's it, right there," the man said. "And I warn you, it's heavier than it looks."

Grace upended the table, setting it on the filthy avocado-green shag carpeting. Its top had more water rings and cigarette burns, but she loved its rounded-off triangular shape. She gingerly removed the bedding from the armchair and concluded that it, too, was in sound shape, although the cushion was ruined.

"You really don't want these?" she asked Arthur, who'd walked to the other end of the room. Which was a dining room, from the looks of it. The only furniture here was a flimsy card table and a pair of old-timey folding aluminum beach chairs with rotting plastic webbing. A cheap brass chandelier dangled over the table, but only one of its candle arms was lit.

"What?" He turned around. "Nah. But I would have liked the dining room furniture that used to be here."

Grace went over to join him. "They stole your furniture?"

"Yup," he said. "Mahogany table and chairs, and a buffet kind of thing. Those were my mama's. I thought about taking 'em out of here, but we didn't have room at the house, and I thought they'd get ruined if I left them in the garage." He shrugged. "I'd love to know how they got that heavy stuff out of here. They didn't have but one car, and that was a crappy little Kia."

"Mm-hmm." Grace wasn't really listening. She was taking a good look at the house itself now.

It was a typical Florida cracker house, she thought. These walls were board and batten, probably old pine under the multiple layers of paint and dirt. The ceilings were quite tall, also board and batten, although they'd never been painted. Through a tall doorway, she could see into the tiny galley kitchen.

"Okay if I look around, Arthur?" she asked.

"Just watch your step," he advised, heading back toward the porch with another load of trash.

A single grungy window over the kitchen sink let in feeble light. Grace found a light switch, and as the ceiling fixture flickered on, half a dozen cockroaches skittered for the shadows. She shuddered, but was not surprised. Roaches were as much a part of living in Florida as palm trees and sunshine. Her least favorite part.

The kitchen was something of a time warp. The countertops were speckled gray formica. The cabinets were wooden, with gummy-looking chipped white enamel paint. There were two wooden upper cabinets, one on either side of the sink, and two lower ones, each topped by a drawer. The cabinet doors were all ajar, and she could see a sad assortment of mismatched pots and pans, some cloudy glasses, chipped plates. An old avocado-green stove sat at the far end of the counter, its surface spattered with grease and food particles. A small saucepan with an unspeakable layer of burnt . . . something . . . sat on the front burner. The oven door was open, and when Grace closed it she saw another scattering of roaches.

Turning around, she saw the refrigerator. It was a somewhat newer model than the stove, but its white surface was freckled with rust. To the left of the fridge was another counter, with a pair of wall-mounted upper cabinets. Beneath the counter there was nothing but an open space, where an evil-smelling plastic trash can was tipped on its side.

Through a second doorway was a short hall. An open door showed the bathroom. The black-and-white penny-tile floor was now a grimy gray. The sink, commode, and bathtub were pale pink, which meant, Grace knew, that they probably dated from the early fifties.

There were two more doors, both closed. Grace was about to open one when she heard a faint scratching sound coming from inside the room.

She took a step back. Rats? She took another step back.

Arthur poked his head inside the hall. "I wouldn't open that door unless you wanna get attacked," he warned.

Grace decided she'd seen enough of the house.

"Bad enough those lowlifes trashed the house like this," he said. "They went off and left their damned dog behind. I ask you, who moves out and leaves a dog behind?"

"No," Grace said, appalled. "There's a dog in that bedroom? Can I see it?"

"Look all you want," Arthur said. "I penned her up in there because with me coming and going outside, I was afraid she'd run out and get hit by a car. I'm no dog lover, but even I couldn't stand that."

20

As she and Arthur talked, the scratching grew more intense, and now it was accompanied by a series of high-pitched yips.

She put her hand on the doorknob. "Don't say I didn't warn you," Arthur said.

Grace pushed the door open and stepped inside the bedroom, where a small brown bundle of fur began leaping at her knees in a frenzy of barking and yipping.

"Heyyyy," Grace said softly, bending down to get a closer look. The dog leapt into her arms and began lavishing her chin with a soft pink tongue.

"Oh my God," Grace said, holding the reeking animal at arm's length. "You poor thing."

Her best guess was that she was some kind of poodle mix. But it was hard to tell because the dog's fur was filthy and matted. Its liquid brown eyes were cloudy and tinged with some milky substance, and there were speckles of dried blood on its muzzle.

She set the dog down gingerly and wiped her hands on the seat of her shorts. The dog sat back on its haunches and looked at her expectantly.

"Pathetic, ain't it?" Arthur asked, standing behind her in the hallway. "She'd been locked up in this room, I don't know how long, when I got over here this morning." He jerked his head in the direction of the bedroom. "You can see the mess she's made. Not that you could blame her."

The room was, as Arthur said, a disaster. Even mouth-breathing could not contain the stench.

Grace picked the dog up again and stepped into the hallway, closing the door to the horrors within.

"What will you do with her?" Grace asked, still holding her at arm's length.

Arthur reached into the bathroom and found a threadbare bath towel. "Here. Wrap her in this. She's got fleas pretty bad."

As Grace wrapped the towel around the dog, she felt it shivering violently.

"I think she's sick, too," she said, looking up at Arthur.

"Gotta be," he agreed. "I give her a bowl of water when I found her this morning, and what was left of the sausage biscuit I had out in my truck, but there's no telling how long it had been since she'd been fed."

"Those people should be tracked down and put in jail for something like this," Grace said fiercely. She swallowed hard, feeling nauseous.

"I've filed a report with the sheriff's department, but there's no telling how long they've been gone. I know the wife, well, I guess she was his wife, I don't really know, but she did mention at one point that they had family in Alabama."

He looked down at the shivering bundle of fur in Grace's arms. "I was gonna take her to the animal shelter. Later on. But if you'd take her, that'd be a whole lot better." He reached out and scratched under the dog's chin, and she wriggled in delight. "She's kinda cute, in a homely sort of way."

Grace looked down at the dog and sighed. "She seems like a sweetheart. But I'm living with my mom, above the bar. And if you know Rochelle, you know she doesn't believe in having inside pets."

"And my wife has got three big ol' tomcats, and they don't like dogs any more than I do," Arthur said. He took the dog from Grace's arms, opened the bedroom door, and set her back inside before firmly closing the door.

The dog's plaintive whines tore at Grace's heart.

Arthur knew how to deal with such a thing. He stalked out to the living room and began loading his wheelbarrow with more trash.

Grace wanted not to hear the dog's cries. "How long do you think it'll take to get this place cleaned up?" she asked.

"Who knows? However much time it takes, it's more than I can spare,"

Arthur said. "We usually spend the summer up in North Carolina. Fixing to leave next week, until this happened."

"I have an idea," Grace said slowly. "It's kind of crazy."

"Crazier than me letting these folks do me out of three months' back rent?" Arthur asked.

She took a deep breath. "What would you think of letting me fix the place up for you?"

"Why would you want to do something like that?" Arthur asked, his eyes narrow with suspicion.

"I'm an interior designer, and I write a blog about home design and home improvement," Grace said. She gestured at the dank room they were standing in. "This little house actually has good bones. It's small, but it could be terrific. I could make it terrific. And I could photograph it and write about the process. If you'd let me."

She was already writing the blog posts in her mind, picturing the rooms, stripped of their filth, the cottage returned to its old Florida vernacular architecture. Let J'Aimee try to copy that!

Arthur shook another cigarette out of the pack in his breast pocket. "I don't know . . ."

"Okay," Grace said easily. "As I said, it was just an idea."

He lit the cigarette and inhaled. The smoke smell was actually an improvement. "What would you charge for something like that?"

"Uh, nothing," Grace said. And then she hurriedly backed up. "That is, you'd need to pay for the materials." She did a 360-degree turn around the room. "Paint, new light fixtures."

"Carpet, for sure," he added.

Grace stubbed her toe into the shag carpet. "What's under here, do you know?"

"Wood floors, best I remember," he said. "God knows what kinda shape they're in. We've had carpet down, ever since I can remember."

"Best-case scenario, rip up this carpet and refinish the wood floors," Grace said. "It's way cheaper than buying new carpet, and if you put down a good finish, your next tenants shouldn't be able to ruin it."

She walked out to the kitchen. "I'm thinking you'll need new appliances in here." She knelt down and peeled at an edge of the vinyl-roll flooring. "This stuff would have to come up, too. So either refinish if there's wood or put down new vinyl."

He nodded. "I was gonna have the stove and fridge hauled off, probably tomorrow."

"How much were *you* thinking it would cost to get it ready to rent again?" Grace asked.

Arthur pursed his lips and flicked his cigarette ash onto the carpet. "With appliances—there's a washer and dryer on the back porch, and they're ruined, too, I'm thinking a couple thousand."

"With appliances? I'm thinking at least five thousand," Grace shot back. She'd walked out to the porch and was staring out at the overgrown yard. "The screens out here are all shot and you've got rotten framing, too."

She turned around. "How about the air-conditioning? Does it work?"

"Window units," he said, pointing to a rusting brown hulk that stuck out of the front living room window. "Couple smaller ones in the bedrooms. They do the job. Or they did, up until now."

Grace put her hands on her hips. "What do you charge for rent? If you don't mind my asking?"

"Four-fifty a month," he said. "And we pay utilities."

"Oh, Arthur," she said with a knowing smile. "This house has such potential. And you're only, what? A block from the bay? If we fixed this place up—I mean, really fixed it up, cleaned up the yard, got it landscaped, maybe put in a little central air unit . . ."

"No central air," he growled. "Think I'm made of money?"

"It couldn't cost that much," Grace said. "How many square feet here?"

"A little under a thousand," he said.

"If you're paying for the electric, you're spending way more money now with three old window units," Grace said. "I bet if you put in a new efficient central unit, you'd save enough to pay for it after just a couple years. Plus, once I've got it fixed up and looking great, you're gonna get more rent anyway, and definitely attract a better-quality tenant."

"You make it sound so easy," Arthur said. "You have any experience fixing up houses? Or handling investment properties, for that matter?"

"I've fixed up three old houses," Grace said. "And my ex-husband and I had a little two-bedroom, two-bath in Bradenton that I did this very same thing with. That one, I gutted to the studs. By the time we sold it, a year ago, we were getting $1,200 a month. Unfurnished."

"Ex-husband?"

"About to be," Grace said casually. "We split a couple months ago. That's why I'm living with my mom right now."

"Sorry to hear it," Arthur said.

"I'm not," Grace said, lifting her chin. "So? What do you think?"

"Have to run it by my wife," he said. "Five thousand. You're talking about a lot of money."

She decided to push her luck. "Five thousand, more or less. I haven't even seen those bedrooms. And we don't know what shape the floors are in."

He chewed on that for a minute or two. "All right. Assuming my wife doesn't hate the idea, you've got a deal."

"Great!" Grace beamed. "What about the rattan furniture? It's really good stuff, Arthur. I love it, but I don't actually have a place I can use it right now. Once I get this house cleaned up, it'll be perfect in the living room. Is there a place we can store it until then?"

He yanked his head in the direction of the back of the house. "There's a garage out back. Guess I could lock it up out there for now."

She couldn't believe what she'd just done. Gone out for a run, found a set of cool old furniture, and ended up with a new decorating gig and several months' worth of potentially fabulous, totally original blog posts. This was a nonpaying gig, sure, but she couldn't wait to dig in, turning this toxic-waste dump into a treasure.

"When can I get started?" she asked, trying not to sound too anxious.

"As soon as you like," Arthur said. "I'll get the worst of this crap hauled off tomorrow. Meet me over here then, and I'll give you a key."

"How will we work out paying for the materials?" Grace asked. "I'm, uh, kind of tight on funds while I wait for my divorce to play out."

"I'll set up a draw for you at the hardware store," Arthur said. "Just keep the receipts. Oh, and there's just one more thing. Part of the deal, you might say."

"Yesss?" Grace felt her throat tighten. She knew it was too good to be true.

He walked toward the hallway. A moment later, he thrust the stinking, shivering bundle of fur into her arms. "You keep the dog."

21

She didn't dare tell her mother what she was up to. It was nearly 9:00 A.M. by the time she'd walked home with her bundle tucked under her arm. She thanked every holy force she could think of that it was Monday, and Rochelle had gone out do the week's grocery shopping.

Grace dragged a washtub from the carport and filled it with water from the garden hose.

"It's okay, sweetie," she cooed, keeping one hand on the dog's back for reassurance. "We're gonna get you cleaned up a little. This won't hurt, and you'll feel a lot better afterward." She squeezed a little of her own shampoo into her hand and gently rubbed it into the dog's fur.

The animal whimpered a little, but Grace rubbed and cooed and breathed through her mouth as a vile stream of brown water surged off the quivering animal.

When finally the water had turned clear, and she could see no more crust in the dog's fur, Grace wrapped her in a beach towel. Upstairs in her bedroom, she set the beach towel on her bed and turned her blow-dryer to cool, running it back and forth over the little dog's damp fur.

Even though she was now semiclean, the poor little thing still looked so pitiful, Grace could have wept.

"Okay, sweetie," she said, ruffling the dog's ears. "There's a vet over on

Anna Maria. I think we'll just run over there to see if they'll take a look at you."

It was Grace's first time in a vet's office. The receptionist looked up at her with a blank expression.

"So . . . you don't know anything about this dog?"

"No. Basically, she'd been abandoned, in a house. Locked in a bedroom, and I don't know for how long. When I got her, she was kind of bloody. I think she'd tried to scratch her way out. I gave her a bath, but I think there's probably something else wrong with her. Because she keeps shivering."

Grace looked down at the little brown dog, huddled under the swaddling of beach towel. "But you're a good girl, aren't you, sweetie?"

The girl had been typing on the computer. She looked up. "That's her name, Sweetie?"

"Uh, sure," Grace agreed. It was as good a name as any.

"It's slow right now," the girl said, clicking over to another page of her computer. "I think Dr. Katz can see her pretty soon. Can you wait?"

"The vet's name is Dr. Katz?" Grace suppressed a giggle. "Really?"

The girl rolled her eyes. She'd heard it all before. "Really. How did you want to pay today?"

Grace hesitated. "Cash, I guess."

"You can sit over there," the receptionist said, pointing to a chair. She held out her arms and Grace handed the dog over, towel and all. "It's okay now, Sweetie," the girl said softly. She reached into a glass jar on the counter and gave the dog a biscuit, which she eagerly snapped up. Then she disappeared behind a swinging door.

Grace sat in a hard vinyl chair and read a magazine about schnauzers. She hadn't realized there was so much to say about schnauzers, but apparently there was. On the opposite side of the waiting room, an elderly lady cradled a pet carrier in her lap. A huge tabby cat nearly filled the thing, its tail sticking out through the wire-mesh door.

Thirty minutes later, the receptionist was back at the desk. "Sweetie Davenport?" she called.

Grace suppressed a giggle. It was as though she'd acquired a new baby sister. "Yes?" she said, standing.

"Dr. Katz is back with Sweetie, in examining room one," she said. "You can go back and talk to her."

The veterinarian was a compact blond woman, in her late forties. She wore a short white lab coat that had silk-screened cartoon images of dogs and cats on it.

Sweetie was lying on a stainless steel examining table, and the vet held one hand on her back, slowly stroking her fur. When the dog spotted Grace, her stubby brown tail beat a tattoo on the table.

"Hi there," the vet said, nodding at Grace. "You've got a very good little girl here. She let me examine her, and she didn't make as much as a squeak."

"Is she okay?" Grace asked.

"A little deyhydrated," Dr. Katz said. "And she's got an intestinal parasite, and some wounds on her paws, which are infected."

Grace felt her throat tighten with anger. "The people who owned her, they just left her, locked in a bedroom of the house they'd been renting, and took off. She'd apparently been trying to dig her way out. We don't know how long she'd been there when the landlord found her today."

"It happens," Dr. Katz said, ruffling Sweetie's fur. "I'm sorry to tell you we see all kinds of cruelty to animals. It's upsetting, but not unusual."

"What can you do for her?"

"I'd like to keep her overnight. Put her on some IV fluids and get her started on antibiotics," the vet said. "We don't have any idea of her medical history, but given the fact that she was abandoned in this condition, I think we should assume she's never had any shots. We'll give her parvo and rabies shots, and start her on worm meds. And," she added, "give her a good flea dip."

"Right," Grace said. She hesitated. "Look," she said, her cheeks flaming with shame. "I'm in the middle of a divorce, and right now I just don't have a lot of money. I'm living with my mother, and getting a dog was the last thing I'd planned. How much will all this cost?"

Dr. Katz put a hand on her sleeve. "Don't worry too much about that. Let us work on Sweetie a couple days. We'll call you Wednesday and let you know what time you can pick her up. We do have a special rate for people rescuing strays, and we can always work out a payment plan, if need be. Does that sound all right?"

"Yes," Grace said. "Thank you! I'll be honest with you. I've never owned a dog, and wasn't looking for one. But I couldn't just leave her there and let her be dropped off at the dog pound."

"Good for you," Dr. Katz said.

"Can you tell me anything about her?" Grace asked. "Like what breed she is, or how old?"

Dr. Katz continued to stroke Sweetie's head. "She's no puppy. Judging by her teeth, I'd say she's probably at least four years old. It's hard to tell without doing DNA testing, but I feel confident that she's got a good bit of toy poodle in her, maybe some cocker spaniel, too. Considering what she's been through, she's surprisingly calm and docile. Once we get her feeling better, she'll make you a loyal, adoring little buddy."

Grace's eyes rested on Sweetie's big brown ones. She could have sworn the dog was grinning at her.

"And Grace?"

"Yes?"

"I think she's housebroken! I was examining her, and she started to whimper, so we took her out to the dog run, and she did her business right away."

Now Grace returned Sweetie's smile. "Thanks, Dr. Katz. That's the first good news I've heard today."

22

She spent Tuesday working in the bar and fuming over Ben's sabotage of her blog. But early Wednesday morning, Grace bounded down the stairs to the bar, her camera bag in hand.

Rochelle had the blender going, whipping up an evil-looking green concoction. She shut it off, poured the sludge in a glass, and sipped, all the while taking in Grace's work ensemble, which consisted of a pair of thrift-store jeans, oversized T-shirt, and cheap tennis shoes. "No run this morning?"

"Nope," Grace said, unable to suppress a grin. "I've got an actual job." She poured herself a mug of coffee and snagged a banana from the fruit bowl on the bar back.

"Is that so?"

"Yup."

"How'd you get this job? Where is it? What's it pay?"

Grace couldn't remember when she'd been this excited at the prospect of working for free.

"You won't believe it, Mom," she said. "When I was out for my run Monday I passed this really rundown house over on Anna Maria. There was a huge pile of junk at the curb. Obviously, somebody was doing a clean out. I stopped to look, because this guy had just dumped a great old midcentury rattan sofa. And then he added more pieces, and I kind of struck up a conversation with him. The house had been a rental, but the tenants trashed the place and skipped out on the rent, and the guy I met was the landlord. The rattan was really good stuff. Very collectible, so I asked him if I could have it, although God knows where I'd put it. He invited me inside the house—which was a disaster area, but it could be really wonderful."

"Slow down," Rochelle ordered. "You went into a house with a strange man? Are you nuts? What if he'd been some kind of deviate or something?"

"He wasn't a deviate; he actually knew Dad," Grace said. "So he was complaining about how long it was going to take him to get the place fixed up to rent again, and I asked him if he'd let me do it. You know, as a before-and-after story for the blog. And he said yes!" Grace was practically jumping up and down.

"How much?" Rochelle asked.

"I finally got him to agree to a minimum budget of five thousand dollars, although I think it'll probably run more than that," she said.

"He's paying you five thousand? Honey, that's great," Rochelle said. "I'm so proud of you."

Grace shook her head. "No. He's not paying me anything. The budget to fix up the house is five thousand. Or more. I'm doing the work for free. So I can do a before-and-after series for my blog. Wait 'til you see this place, Mom. It's over on Mandevilla, on Anna Maria, about a block from the bay. It's a real old-timey Florida cracker house, with the pitched roof and the screened porch. All the inside walls are the original pine. Right now, there's some skanky carpet on the floors, but I'm sure there's hardwood under there. It's got a tiny little galley kitchen, again with the original cabinets. I'm thinking I'll take the doors off the upper cabinets . . ."

"Wait," Rochelle said. "You're going to do all this work? Without getting paid? How is this a good thing?"

"Because it's design work," Grace said. "I'll be rehabbing a historic old cottage. It's what I love to do! And I can photograph it from every stage and blog about it. And that is something that not even Ben and J'Aimee can rip off."

She dug into her camera bag and brought out some Benjamin Moore paint chips, rifling through the colored cards until she found the one she wanted. "Here. Dove White. I'm thinking of using it for all the interior walls. The house is kind of dark inside, because of the porch overhang, so I want to brighten it up, make it look crisp and clean. Have you ever seen a prettier white?"

"You know all white paint looks the same to me," Rochelle said. "But if you say it's the best white ever, I believe it."

"I might do the kitchen another color, maybe a soft aqua, something like that," Grace mused. "But I want to get it all defunked, have a clean slate, before I make too many design decisions."

"What's the owner going to say about all those design decisions? And who is it? You said it's somebody who knew Butch?"

"He doesn't care what I do, as long as I get it presentable and ready to rent again," Grace said. "He'll be the perfect client—especially since he's leaving soon to spend the summer in North Carolina. I won't have him breathing down my neck, second-guessing everything I do. Oh yeah. His name is Arthur Cater. He said he used to take Dad fishing on his boat."

"Arthur Cater? He's your client?" Rochelle rolled her eyes.

"What's that supposed to mean? No, never mind. I don't want to hear it. I am not going to let you rain on my parade. Whatever you know about him, keep it to yourself."

"I wasn't gonna rain on your parade," Rochelle said. "Arthur's an okay guy. He used to come in here a lot, when they lived on the island, back before he got fancy and moved over to Longboat Key. There's just one thing I want you to know about him."

"Whatever," Grace said, packing up her paint chips impatient to get started on her new project. "Can I have the key to the shed? Thank God I didn't get around to cleaning out Dad's tools. All my stuff is still back at Sand Dollar Lane. I don't even have a hammer or a pair of pliers to my own name now. And I want to get that nasty carpet pulled up this morning. First thing."

Rochelle went into the kitchen and came back with a key ring, which she handed to her daughter. "Just know this about Arthur. He is the world's biggest cheapskate. He's got tons of money, but he didn't get that way throwing it around. He will nickel and dime you to death. Your dad used to say Arthur was so tight he squeaked when he walked."

"I don't care," Grace said, cramming her sweat-stained Sandbox ball cap on her head. "I've dealt with cheap and I've dealt with difficult. I'm just happy to have a job again."

Arthur Cater was standing in the driveway of the house on Mandevilla, directing two Hispanic day laborers as they loaded the avocado-green stove into the back of an ancient rust bucket of a pickup truck.

"Hey, Arthur," Grace greeted him.

"So you didn't have a change of heart, huh?" He took in her work clothes and toolbox.

"No way," Grace said. "Did your wife give us the thumbs-up?"

Arthur mopped his face with his handkerchief. "She says you're a big-deal interior designer. She's all excited now. Says she reads your blog and she can't believe I could trick you into working for nothin'."

Grace laughed. "She doesn't know I'm the one who tricked you, does she?"

He gestured toward the house. "I got over here right at sunup this morning and set off a couple of flea bombs in there. I just opened up all the windows, so you should be all right to go in now." He reached in the pocket of his own faded blue jeans. "Here's the keys. Front and back doors, and the garage." He nodded at his workers, who were bringing the washing machine out on a furniture dolly. "I had the fellas put all that furniture in the garage, and put a tarp over it. There's some other odds and ends out there you can maybe use."

"All right," Grace said. She took her camera from around her neck and stepped into the street, clicking off a few frames.

"Stand right there by the mailbox, will you Arthur," she called. "I like to document everything, right from the beginning."

Arthur stood awkwardly by the curb, his hands thrust in his pockets. "You don't want pictures of this ugly old mug," he growled. "It'll break your camera."

"Let me be the judge of that," Grace said, stepping backward to shoot. "Arthur, do you have any idea when this house was built?"

"Let me see. Well, I'm seventy-three, and we've got old family pictures of my grandma, standing out front of this house with me in her arms. I know my grandpa bought the house, probably sometime in the thirties. It looked a lot different back then. There was no front porch, no real trees, just some scrub palmettos and sand, and where the kitchen is now, was a porch they used to cook on. There was an old wood cookstove out there. My grandpa used to fry mullet on it Friday nights. Hard to believe they raised seven kids in this little bitty place, isn't it?"

It was just a little after nine, but the sun was already high in the sky, the summer heat relentless. Grace walked all the way around the house, photographing it from every conceivable angle, swatting at mosquitoes and stopping to pick off the sandspurs clinging to her ankles. She prayed no snakes were lurking in the thick underbrush. Despite that, the more she saw of the house, the more she liked. Virtually nothing had been done to change the house in the years since the porch had been added. In a way, she decided, it was a very good thing that Arthur Cater was a cheapskate.

When she got back to the front of the house, Arthur was standing by the truck, waiting on her. He handed her a slip of paper. "Here's my phone number. You call me if there's a problem, hear? I set up a draw for you at the hardware store. And my wife said I should tell you she'd like it if you'd e-mail us some pictures as you go. She's all jazzed up about this project of yours. Good thing we're leaving town, or she'd be over here all the time, sidewalk superintending."

Grace stood on her tiptoes and planted a kiss on Arthur's grizzled cheek. He looked surprised, but not displeased. "All right then, get to work," he ordered. He drove off with the two laborers in the back of the truck, wedged in among the rusted appliances. A moment later, he was backing down the street toward where she stood at the curb.

He hung his head out the open window. "Meant to ask you about that little dog," he said, failing miserably at pretending he didn't care. "How's she doing? Did you find somebody to take her in?"

"Sweetie is going to be just fine," Grace said. "They kept her overnight at the vet's office, giving her some IV fluids and some antibiotics. I'm going to pick her up this afternoon. And I'm going to keep her myself, until I figure out something else."

"Sweetie, huh? Dumb name for a dog."

Grace paced every inch of the cottage interior, snapping photos and making notes. She found an old broom in a tiny utility closet off the kitchen and swept up an entire village of dead insects. Then she cranked up the music she'd downloaded onto her iPod, adjusted the tiny little speakers, pulled on her work gloves, and got down to business.

A veteran of the remodeling wars, Grace donned a paper face mask before tackling the carpet. It was a hot, filthy job. The carpet was so old and brittle, hunks of it tore apart in her hands as she pried it from the nail strips along the baseboards. But when she pulled up the thin foam padding and got the first glimpse of the intact oak floors, she got a new burst of energy. By noon, when she took her lunch break with a sandwich and a bottle of water she'd brought from home, she'd pulled up all the carpet in the bedrooms, rolled it up, and dragged it out to the curb.

She was buzzed with adrenaline, dancing around the smaller of the two bedrooms doing a creditable accompaniment to Adele's "Rolling in the Deep," using the broom as a makeshift microphone. The music echoed in the high-ceilinged empty rooms, and she whipped her sweat-dampened hair from side to side as she cataloged the all-too-familiar misery of a lover done wrong.

Grace didn't hear the front door open. Didn't hear anything except the music, until she happened to turn around and see Ben, standing in the doorway, arms folded over his chest, watching her performance with no trace of amusement.

Her face flamed. She grabbed for the iPod and shut it off.

For a moment, she couldn't think of anything to say. Her throat went dry, and all she could think of was how idiotic she must have looked to him, dancing around a filthy house, in her filthy clothes, playing air guitar with a broom.

Then she got mad and found her voice again. "What are you doing here?" she asked, clutching the broom, because she needed to clutch something. It was the first time she'd seen him since their day in court.

He was dressed for golf, in a spotless white polo shirt, crisp black shorts, golf shoes, his aviator sunglasses pushed back off his forehead.

"I came to see the floor show," Ben said. "Good thing it's free."

"How'd you know where to find me?" Was he following her?

"Your mother told me you were working at a house over on Mandevilla. You're not that hard to find. She really, really doesn't like me, you know."

"That makes two of us," Grace snapped. "I'm surprised she actually spoke to you at all. But then, probably you lied to her. Lying seems to be your good thing."

He smiled. His orthodontics were a thing of beauty. "I told Rochelle I had something to give you. I guess she assumed it was money."

"But it's not."

"No," Ben said. And his smile dissolved, like Alice in Wonderland's Cheshire cat. "No money. Just some advice."

He took a step into the room. "I got a call this morning, from Anna Stribling, at Home Depot. It seems she had some 'concerns,' as she called them, about the originality of our material on Gracenotes."

"Oh?" Grace wondered if he could see her hands shaking as she clutched the broom.

"Yes. She was specifically wondering if J'Aimee's corn-crab chowder recipe was original. Because, she said, she'd had a disturbing e-mail from you, accusing us of stealing your material."

"Which you did. A blatant rip-off," Grace said. "My photos, my recipe, my everything. And that's what I told her."

"But you don't have any proof of that, do you?" Ben raised one eyebrow, amused.

"Because you hacked into my Web site and erased it. And put that filthy porn link on there," Grace fairly spat the words at him.

"And you don't have any proof of that, either."

Ben took a step closer. She could smell his elegant cologne. The Clive Christian 1872 that sold for $310 a bottle at Saks. Everything about Ben was elegant. "What I told Anna during our chat today is this. I told her that you're delusional. That you're bitter and jealous and emotionally fragile. I mentioned that you're in court-ordered counseling. I think she felt a lot better after our conversation. In fact, I know she felt better, because Home Depot just agreed to take a bigger Gracenotes banner ad starting next month."

Grace clamped her lips together to keep her jaw from dropping. She hoped Ben wasn't close enough to detect the sense of defeat that swept over her, threatened to knock her off her feet and destroy her hard-won equilibrium.

Ben towered over her—intimidation through proximity was his motto. "Don't fuck with me, Grace," he said, his voice light and even. "You'll get mowed down every time. Know this. If you send out any more of those incendiary e-mails, I'll haul your ass back to court in a New York second. And that judge will be only too happy to shut you down for good."

She took two steps backward, nearly tripping over the damned broom. "Get out," she said, recovering quickly. She poked the broom at his spotless two-toned golf shoes. "OUT!"

He stood his ground. She jabbed at his ankles. "I said out!" He chuckled, shook his head, and strolled for the door, with Grace right on his heels. He'd left the door open, and now she saw an unfamiliar car in the driveway, a gleaming ebony Porsche Pantera.

"Nice car," she spat.

He gave her a mock bow. "Glad you like it, since I have you to thank for it.

And you know? I actually like this one much better. It handles so much smoother."

She finished ripping out the rest of the carpet, without the music, now that Ben had managed to poison that source of joy. Slowly, she swept the living room and dining room floors, taking grim satisfaction from the cockroach body count.

Grace retrieved her cleaning supplies—bucket, mop, sponge, and spray cleaners—from her car and attacked the filthy windows, using an entire roll of paper towels on the front room. Logistically, it made no sense to spend so much time cleaning a house that still had so far to go in the rehab process, but she did it anyway, inhaling the scent of the strong pine cleaner as she filled her bucket with hot water.

When she found herself humming as she mopped, she got her iPod and turned it on again. The music filled her head and helped erase, temporarily, the image of Ben, smug, self-important, all-powerful Ben. "Gonna wash that man right out of my hair," she muttered, dumping the gray mop water down the toilet and flushing it with a flourish.

Finally, satisfied that the surface layers of crud had been eradicated, along with Ben's overpowering cologne, she set down her mop and picked up her camera again.

She photographed the front rooms, pleased with the way the afternoon sunlight slanted in, leaving atmospheric shadows on the old oak floors. She was so absorbed in her work she was startled at the sudden rattle of rain on the tin roof of the porch.

Time to go, she thought. She had to pick up Sweetie at the vet's office, get cleaned up before her Wednesday-night "therapy" session, and, in the meantime, figure out how to hide a dog from her mother.

23

Wyatt Keeler stood in front of the tiny closet he shared with Bo, barefoot and dressed only in his cotton boxers, and felt gloom. He walked over to the closet, opened the door, and his mood did not improve. He hadn't thought about clothes in months, not since the breakup with Callie. Okay, maybe even before that. His style guidelines in adulthood had gotten simple; he liked clean, and he liked cool. As in temperature, not trendiness.

At one time, he'd prided himself on being a sharp dresser. Just the right label jeans, good-quality classic shirts, ties and jackets. Nothing too flashy or outrageous. He'd learned a lot from his fraternity brothers in college. He'd been, like the ZZ Top song, a sharp-dressed man.

No more. Now, he idly plucked at the meager assortment of shirts and pants hanging limply on the wire hangers. "Dude," he muttered under his breath, "you are really, really lame." Finally, he found a pair of presentable navy blue Dockers and a short-sleeved plaid dress shirt that had been a Father's Day gift from Callie. The J.C. Penney price tag still hung from the sleeve.

The pants fit reasonably well, but they were wrinkled. He put on the shirt, then padded out to the living area, where Nelson was eating a chicken potpie at the dinette and reading the sports section. "Dad, do we own an iron?"

"Dunno," Nelson mumbled, his fingers poised over the box scores. "Your mother always handled that." He glanced up, looked surprised. "Since when do you iron?"

"Since now," Wyatt said. He checked under the kitchen sink, then on the top shelf of the hall closet, to no avail. "Screw it," he said, tossing the pants into the dryer.

While he was waiting for his pants, Wyatt went back to the bathroom. Feeling foolish, but somehow lighthearted, he brushed his teeth, again, and flossed. Back in the bedroom, with the door closed, he checked himself out in the cloudy mirror on the back of the closet door.

He wasn't a bad-looking guy. His teeth were straight, he was clean-shaven. After that crack Callie had made about his baldness he'd thought about letting his hair grow out again, just to prove he had plenty, but later he'd changed his mind. Screw Callie. He worked outside in the blazing Florida sun all day, and it was just much cooler without hair. Obviously, she liked a guy with hair. Luke wore his hair deliberately shaggy, like a surfer dude, although the guy had clearly never been anywhere near a surfboard. And Wyatt had always secretly suspected Luke of being a bottle blond.

Luke, Wyatt thought, had a body like the Pillsbury Doughboy. Big, pillowy hips, blobby butt. He was a desk jockey and looked it. But a successful desk jockey.

Now Wyatt turned and surveyed his own body, sucking in his gut—okay, just a little. He had wide shoulders, and all those years of hard labor at the park left him with the pects and abs to prove it. He was just a shade over six feet tall.

Callie'd always claimed his eyes were what made her start flirting with him at that bar back in Clemson, all those years ago. That and the dimples. His eyes were a mud color, he'd always thought, but he had his mother's eyelashes, thick, black, Bambi lashes, as she called them.

A lot of good they'd done him lately.

What the hell. He fetched the pants, got dressed, put on his grandfather's gold watch. For maybe the millionth time, he looked at the plain gold wedding band on the ring finger of his left hand. He'd taken it off dozens of times, put it back on again the same number of times. He couldn't say why. Callie had replaced her wedding rings with the flashy diamond "engagement" ring Luke had bought her. Was it technically possible to be engaged while you were still married? Maybe he'd remove his own ring once the divorce was final. He only knew it wasn't time. Yet. Probably this made him a double loser. He took a deep breath and picked up the truck keys from the dresser.

"You goin' to church?" Nelson asked. He'd moved to the recliner in front of the television and found the Braves game. He was dressed in an old T-shirt and a pair of faded pajama bottoms. *Geezus H.*, Wyatt thought. *Save me from ever wearing pajama bottoms.*

"Church? No. Remember, Dad? I told you. I've got to go to that divorce therapy session."

"Oh, right," Nelson said vaguely. "And Bo's at his mom's?"

"Yes," Wyatt said patiently. "Bo is with Callie tonight. "I'll pick him up Thursday. Remember?"

Every night he replayed this same scene. Nelson would ask where Bo was, and Wyatt would tell him. Most of the time, his father seemed perfectly with it, lucid, same old Nelson. But in the evenings, he got . . . vague. Wyatt told himself his father was fine. He was still physically fit, strong as an ox. He ran the concession stand in the park, took tickets, helped out with the never-ending landscaping and maintenance. But in the past year, Nelson had begun a slow, almost indefinable slide. Sometimes, he needed help with the bank deposits. He got aggravated if there was even the slightest deviation in his carefully mapped daily routine.

Wyatt worried. But hell, he worried about everything. Like now. He doubled back to the bedroom, hung up the dress pants and the plaid shirt. He rolled up the sleeves of the white dress shirt he'd worn to court and put on his nicest pair of shorts. And what he thought of as his dress shoes, a pair of leather flip-flops. At least he felt like some version of himself.

Paula Talbott-Sinclair greeted them all in the reception area. Her usually flyaway hair had been tamed and twisted into a sleek, artful chignon. She wore a long wispy yellow and green flowered dress with bell sleeves that made her look like a butterfly, bright coral lipstick, and her usual dozen or so bracelets. She wore gold gladiator-style sandals, and tonight she seemed lucid and bright-eyed. She was, Grace thought, a woman transformed. Which made Grace immediately suspicious.

"Hello, friends," she said, grasping the hand of each group member as they arrived at the office. She made a show of having them all sign in, inviting them to have coffee, asking them how their week had gone.

Grace was surprised when the first person she saw was Wyatt. He'd obviously taken pains with his appearance tonight. "Hey," she said, sidling over to him at the coffee machine. "You look nice tonight."

"No parrot poop, right?" He looked embarrassed. "You look nice, too. But unlike me, you always look good."

"You wouldn't say that if you'd seen me a couple hours ago," Grace assured him. But she was glad he'd noticed. On her last thrifting excursion, she'd found a pair of nearly new black DKNY capris at the Junior League for three dollars and a simple acid-green polished cotton wrap blouse, which set her back ninety-nine cents at the hospice shop. The blouse was sleeveless, and she thought it was flattering to the new tan she'd acquired from all that running. With the black ballet flats from Target and a wide gold bangle bracelet she'd borrowed from Rochelle, this was the nicest outfit she owned, and she'd spent less buying it than she had a tube of lipstick in her old life.

Wyatt nodded his head in Paula's direction. "Obviously, she found her way home last week."

"Look. She's even wearing shoes. Maybe she's got a hot date afterward," Grace murmured.

At the stroke of 7:00 P.M., Paula began herding them to their seats. "Please be seated," she said, clapping her hands. Paula looked around the room, taking a silent body count. Grace prayed she would overlook the oversized totebag she'd stowed under her folding chair.

"So," Paula began, her voice in a slightly higher-than-normal pitch. "We've completed two weeks of recovery therapy. At this stage of your process, I hope you're beginning to feel a little more comfortable in your own skin. We've talked a little bit about how you see yourselves, following the breakup of your marriage. And I'd like to continue that discussion this week, with having you share from your journals."

Paula's cell phone was in her lap, and while she spoke, her eyes continually watched it.

She gazed around the room. "Who haven't we heard from?"

Wyatt and Suzanne slumped down in their chairs, ducked their heads, hoping they wouldn't be noticed. It was painfully clear the therapist had no memory of what had transpired in their previous session.

"I don't think Suzanne has shared with us yet," Ashleigh volunteered.

"I'll just bet you were that kid in elementary school who always reminded the teacher she hadn't assigned homework, just before the bell rang," Camyrn said, giving Ashleigh the evil eye.

Suzanne's olive skin flushed.

"That's right," Paula said. "Thank you, Ashleigh. Suzanne?"

Grace felt a sharp pang of sympathy for Suzanne, hunched down in her chair, eyes glued to her journal. Her face was pale, with two bright spots of pink on her cheeks, but her face was beaded with a fine sheen of perspiration.

Suzanne was dressed in a dull, unflattering beige dress and scuffed brown leather sandals. It was as if she was wearing her own brand of camouflage, to blend into the surroundings.

"Uh, well," Suzanne stuttered and blinked rapidly. Grace noticed that the damp palms of her hands had begun to make the ink on Suzanne's journal run.

Suzanne's voice was low.

"Once, I was a wife," she began, reading in a stilted monotone.

"I was a lover, a mother, a teacher, a mentor. I had value, to others as well as myself. And then I discovered my husband's treachery. He was cheating on me, with one of my coworkers. I didn't confront him. I kept telling myself it might not be true. I became obsessed with checking on him, on her, confirming my worst suspicions. I figured out where they were having their trysts. I followed him. I checked into the same cheap motel room after they'd left, and I told myself I would take some pills and kill myself, in that same bed, and it would be the perfect, poetic justice. Just another Shakespearean tragedy. But I couldn't even do that. Even after I knew, I did nothing. I was paralyzed. He loved someone else. She was younger, prettier, cleverer, sexier. How could I compete with her? I was a failure, at everything, especially marriage. If I couldn't keep Eric, how could I be a success at my job? How could I be a good mother to my daughter Darby? So I have stopped trying, because if I don't try, I can't fail. Every day I shrink a little more. Soon I'll be invisible. Will anybody notice? Will Eric?"

Suzanne closed her notebook, but didn't look up.

"Oh, wow," Ashleigh breathed, breaking the silence. "You actually slept in the same motel room they'd just screwed in? That is all kinds of crazy."

"Ashleigh!" Camryn's eyes blazed. "Will you please shut the *fuck* up?"

Paula didn't appear to have heard Ashleigh's comment. She was staring down at her cell phone, reading something on the screen.

Now, she looked up, realized the group was expecting some comment from their therapist.

"That was very powerful, Suzanne," she said, beaming, and then looking around at the others. "Any comments? Thoughts?"

Wyatt twisted his wedding band. "I've been there," he said, finally. "I couldn't put it in words like you just did, Suzanne. But yeah, every day, when I think about it, letting some other guy just take my wife, just stepping aside and letting her leave? What a loser I am. So who could blame her for leaving me for him?"

"You're not a loser," Grace said fiercely. "None of us are losers. Just because my husband didn't value me—all the things I am? That doesn't change who I am. But it changes who he is. Somebody who lies. Somebody who cheats." She sat up. "My ex came to see me today. And I finally saw him for what he is."

"Oooh, girl," Camryn said. "Was he begging you to take him back?"

"No." Grace thought about it for a moment. "He just wanted to grind his heel in my face. Punish me some more, make me feel like crap. Let me know he'll always have power over me."

Suddenly, Paula stood up. "Very nice, Wyatt and Grace. Excellent work, sharing with our friends. Let's take a little ten-minute break, and then we'll come back and, um, I have a surprise for all of you. Also? Who haven't we heard from yet?"

"Me," Wyatt said reluctantly.

The others shot out of the room like first graders at recess. All except Suzanne, who sat demurely in her chair, ankles crossed, hands in her lap.

Grace slid into the chair beside hers. "Suzanne? That was really wonderful, what you wrote. I think all of us saw something of ourselves in what you've gone through."

Suzanne brightened, just a little. "So, you don't think I'm the queen of crazypants?"

"You? Nah. That title belongs to Ashleigh," Grace said. Out of the corner of her eye, she saw a small pink nose pop out of the top of her tote bag. "Oh, Lord," she breathed. "I've gotta go outside for a minute. So—will you come to the Sandbox tonight, after? Just for a little while? At least so we can discuss what's up with Paula?"

Suzanne brightened. "So, it's not just me? There is definitely something weird about her. Weirder than usual tonight, because she's actually acting normal!

About the Sandbox, I'd come, but it's just such a long way there and then home again."

"If you like, you can leave your car here and ride over there with me," Grace offered. "I'm sure one of the others will give you a ride back afterward."

"Maybe," Suzanne said. "Let me think about it, okay?"

"Friends," Paula began, once their break was over, her face flushed with excitement. "I didn't want to announce this earlier, because, well, I wasn't sure it was going to happen. But I got a message just before our break, and it appears that we are going to have a guest joining us tonight. I, for one, am incredibly honored that he's taking time out from his very busy life to be with us." She glanced down at her watch and, then again, at her cell phone.

She took a deep breath. "I'm sure he'll be along shortly. In the meantime, I'd like us to think about options." She looked around the room. "From what you've told me, all of you feel you've been badly hurt by your spouses. Of course, since we don't have your partners here with us, I only have your version of events that led to your breakups."

Camryn snorted. "We're the ones got ordered to be here, Paula. If you want Dexter Nobles's version of what happened, feel free to drag his ass in here."

"Camryn?" Paula frowned at her. "Sharing time is over. Now. All of you have spoken of your feelings of powerlessness and inferiority. Now, I'd like you to explore what options you have, going forward with your lives."

A man cleared his throat. All heads swung in the direction of the reception-room door. "Er, hello?"

Paula jumped up from her chair and clapped her hands in glee. "Judge Stackpole! Your Honor, we're so glad you could be here!"

24

Judge Cedric N. Stackpole Jr. was dressed in his version of business casual and Grace's idea of what not to wear to divorce therapy. A black short-sleeved knit shirt with the top button fastened—although Grace saw the glimmer of a thick gold chain resting amidst a tuft of chest hair sticking out over the top button. Very shiny, very faux-distressed, very obviously brand-new jeans, belted and worn navel-high. Highly polished black slip-ons, no socks.

His thinning reddish hair was slicked back with some type of hair product that he'd obviously bought in bulk in the eighties.

He nodded curtly at the group, and cracked something similar to a smile at Paula.

"Hello, hello," he said briskly, his hands thrust awkwardly in his jeans pockets. "Uh, Dr. Talbott-Sinclair invited me to drop in tonight, just to see how everybody is doing. Er, uh, I hope you are all listening closely to her message. Because, uh, if more people like you all came to sessions with therapists like Dr. Talbott-Sinclair, there'd be lots less work for judges like me." He seemed to think this was a hysterically funny line. "Right?" he asked. "Judges might not have jobs. Right?"

Paula's laughter trilled up and down the musical scales. "That's right!" she said, clasping her hands. "Very intuitive, Your Honor."

Grace didn't dare cut her eyes sideways to the left to see Camryn's reaction to this. Instead, she pretended to study the journal on her lap. Through lowered eyelashes, she could see Wyatt, on her right, his arms folded across his chest, glaring directly at the judge, barely disguised hostility emanating from every pore.

"Well," Stackpole said, "please don't let me interrupt. I'll just sit here in the back of the room, and you all go on as though I weren't here."

Like that's gonna happen, Grace thought. She glanced nervously down at her tote bag, but for now it was very still.

Paula stood and faced the group. Her hair was neatly combed, and Grace noticed she'd reapplied her lipstick and powdered her nose during the break. And was the neckline of her dress tugged just a little lower? Showing just a hint of cleavage that hadn't been visible before?

"Most of you are here because in the heat of the moment or, perhaps, after some very deliberate but ill-thought-out reasoning, you decided to strike out—violently, publicly, even *criminally,* against your spouse. Probably, you reasoned, 'this person has hurt me, and my only option is to strike back.'" She nodded at Grace.

"Isn't that right, Grace?"

"No," Grace heard herself say. "That isn't what happened at all."

Paula gave her a patronizing smile. "We'll come back to that."

"What I'm trying to say," Paula went on, "is that whether you know it or not, you had options at the time you acted out, and you have options now. Do you stay, or do you leave? Forgive? Forget? Neither?"

"Huh." Wyatt shook his head. "That ship has sailed, Paula."

"Yeah," Camryn put in. "I already left, or rather, I kicked his butt out the door. You want me to forget? How do I erase the image of him in bed with my twenty-two-year-old daughter's best friend? I wish I could forget it," she said, throwing up her hands in surrender. "What's that drug they used to give women during childbirth? Scopolamine, yeah, the twilight drug. You feel the labor pains, but after, you have no memory of the pain. You tell me how to find the equivalent of Scopolamine for what he did to me and my family."

Grace's mind flashed again to the scene of Ben and J'Aimee in the darkened garage. She closed her eyes and willed the scene to disappear, the same way she had nearly every night since it had occurred.

"That's right," Suzanne murmured, pressing her fingertips to her forehead.

"I don't have any drugs to give you," Paula said, her face flushing. She was looking past Camryn and the others, directly at the back of the room, where Stackpole sat.

Grace heard a little gasp at this, but then, at almost the same time, she felt the tote bag at her feet move. She dropped her journal to the floor as a cover, reached in, and scratched the warm furry head there, felt a tiny pink tongue rasp against the palm of her hand. She stole a backward glance at the judge, who was staring down at his watch, pointedly tapping the crystal. She sat back up again.

"I can tell you, though," Paula said, her voice rising, "that until you spend time figuring out what went wrong with your marriage, until you stop blaming yourself, your partner, the other lover, you will never move past those scenes like the one Camryn describes. Even if your marriage is irretrievably, undeniably finished now, there was a time when you had hope. You had love. Whatever your version of love is. Next session, I want you to try really hard to get past your bitterness and write down one quality, perhaps one anecdote, that might explain what drew you to your partner. What about that person made you happy?"

"That's easy. It was the big ol' honkin' ring he gave me," Ashleigh whispered, with a giggle, fingering the bauble she wore around her neck.

Paula hadn't heard, as usual. "I'll see you all next week."

Grace looked at her watch. It was barely 7:30 P.M. Why was Paula suddenly in such a hurry to end the session? When she looked up again, she saw Stackpole speeding toward the door with the look of a man with a mission.

25

Sandbox?" Camryn murmured, as the group drifted out to the parking lot.

"I'm in," Ashleigh nodded vigorously. She turned to Suzanne. "You coming?"

"Well, I guess I could. I did tell my daughter I might be a little late," Suzanne said.

Grace looked at Wyatt. "How about you?"

He hesitated. Camryn tugged at his arm. "Oh, come on. You can't hold out forever."

"I thought this was a girls-only thing," he said. "No boys in the tree fort?"

Ashleigh gave him a wink. "For you, we'll lower the rope ladder. Right, ladies?"

A hastily scribbled RESERVED sign was taped to the booth in the corner. Rochelle hurried over to the table when Grace pushed through the front door. "They're coming tonight, right?"

"Yeesss," Grace found herself slightly annoyed at her mother's eagerness, but she couldn't say why. While Rochelle returned to her post behind the bar, she slipped outside with the tote bag, and when she returned five minutes later, the rest of the group were arranged around the table, each with a drink in front of them. She slid into the booth beside Wyatt, who was sipping a beer.

"What was going on with Paula tonight?" Ashleigh asked.

"Here you go," Rochelle said, as she placed a glass of white wine in front of Grace and a big basket of freshly made popcorn in the center of the table. She plunked herself down beside Camryn at the opposite end of the booth.

"Why?" Rochelle wanted to know. "What was Paula doing?"

"She was, like, sober," Ashleigh said. "All dressed up. With shoes and everything. She actually kind of looked like what I pictured a professional therapist would look like. It was kind of crazy."

"Mm-hmm. Mama was definitely on some new meds tonight," Camryn agreed. "There were a couple times tonight she managed to almost sound coherent. Not that I agree with any of that forgiveness crap she was selling," she added hastily.

"I couldn't get over how changed she was. And when Judge Stackpole came in, I was really struck by the transformation," Suzanne said. "It was like she was hoping for his approval. Dying for it."

"The judge showed up?" Rochelle asked, her eyes widening.

"Asshole," Wyatt muttered, staring down at his beer.

All the women turned to look at him at once. "Can't help it," he said defensively. "He's gonna ruin my son's life, letting Callie drag him off to Birmingham. How often will I be able to get to Birmingham to see him? Every other month? Probably not even that. Even if I could forgive her, I'll never forgive him, if I lose my kid."

Ashleigh waved the straw from her half-empty margarita glass in the air. "I think Paula's got a big ol' school-girl crush on Stackhole."

"Stackhole, that's good!" Rochelle said. "What do you think, Grace?"

Grace had been surreptitiously slipping a handful of popcorn in the direction of the tote bag, which was between her feet. She was distracted by the soft snuffing sounds and hoped the din of the bar would drown them out.

"Well . . . I agree, Paula was definitely on her best behavior tonight. And I did wonder about Stackpole's appearance. Why was he there? Paula told us she reports to him on our progress. Doesn't he have anything better to do than sit in on our sad little sessions?" She turned to Suzanne. "Do you think maybe there's something going on between them?"

"Maybe," Suzanne said, her voice tentative.

"Eeew," Ashleigh said, wrinkling her nose. "Paula and that . . . old man? And isn't he married or something?"

"He's not all that old. My lawyer, Mitzi, was in law school with him. When he was appointed to the bench, he was the youngest judge in Florida. But, yes, he's definitely married," Grace said. "During our hearing he made a point of telling my lawyer that his own wife has no problems running his household with two thousand dollars a month."

"Which pays for what?" Rochelle asked. "I'll bet he doesn't expect her to pay a mortgage or utilities or insurance for that."

While they batted ideas around, Camryn was busily typing away on her iPhone. "I've got the Florida judiciary Web site here," she announced, thumbing down the page. "Gimme a minute. Okay, here it is. Cedric Norris Stackpole, age fifty-one. B.A., University of Florida, 1980. J.D., University of Florida, 1983. Appointed to the bar, 2000." She looked up. "Wow, a judge at forty. That's impressive, even if he isn't." She scrolled a little more. "Married, 1999, to the former Eileen Bolther of Kissimmee."

"Bolther? Why is that name familiar?" Suzanne asked.

"If she's a Bolther and she's from Kissimmee, she must be related to Sawyer Bolther. As in Bolther Groves and Bolther Beef. Two of the biggest cattle and citrus growers in Florida. Not to mention Bolther Bank and Trust," Camryn said.

"How do you know all this stuff?" Ashleigh asked.

"I'm a reporter. I don't know it off the top of my head, but I get paid to know how to find it out," Camryn said. "I covered the last three governor's races, and, as I recall, Sawyer Bolther was one of the biggest campaign contributors to that last joker we elected. So that gives you an idea how ol' Cedric got named a judge at the ripe old age of forty. His wife's family is politically connected."

"What about Paula?" Suzanne asked. "I'm a little curious about her, I have to admit. She's such an enigma. After those first two sessions, I'd written her off as a total fraud, or at least a deeply troubled person with some kind of substance-abuse issues. But tonight?" She looked around the table for consensus. "She actually said a couple things that I thought made sense."

"Like what?" Wyatt asked. "I mean, I'm not disagreeing."

"I can't quote her directly," Suzanne said, flustered. "It was something about taking the time to figure out what went wrong with our marriages, putting blame aside, and just, you know, taking a look at what the problems really were."

"Wasn't the fact that everybody's husband or wife cheated on them the big, overriding problem?" Rochelle asked.

"A problem? Or maybe a symptom?"

All heads turned toward Grace. She shrugged. "I don't know anything. I probably know the least about marriage of anybody here. I thought my marriage was just peachy, until it all went up in flames. I'm not saying I want Ben back. If I ever did before, the things he's done since I left have opened my eyes to the kind of person he is. I keep wondering how I didn't see the real him."

"Sometimes, maybe we do see the real person, but we convince ourselves that we can live with him, or somehow change him, just by loving him enough," Rochelle said.

Grace stared. Where had this come from? And why did Rochelle keep hanging around?

"Dexter changed, once he had a taste of success, once he got into politics," Camryn said. "In college, when he was at Morehouse, and I was at Spelman, he wrote poetry! Yes, he did. He was this shy, skinny, geeky mama's boy. Not anybody I ever would have taken a second look at. But one of my sorority sisters was dating his roommate, and she begged me to go out with him, as a favor so the two of them could get some privacy on a Friday night. I asked him to a mixer, and it turned out the guy could dance. I mean, dance! Later on, he admitted he'd been watching Michael Jackson videos for years, learning his moves. I thought that was so sweet. You know? That's the Dexter I fell in love with. He had ideals. He wanted to change the world."

Camryn sipped her drink. "I don't know him now. Obviously."

"Would any of you take your husbands—or wives—back, if they wanted to come back?" Ashleigh asked.

The table got very quiet. "I'd take Boyce back," Ashleigh volunteered. "But, I mean, there'd have to be some changes. For one thing, I'd go back to managing his practice. Some men you just have to keep on a short leash. I know he doesn't love that tramp he's seeing. She's not even his type! I've learned my lesson, I'll tell you that." She grinned mischeviously and leaned forward. "I'll tell you something else, too. When he comes back—I'll be a lot more adventurous. In the bedroom, you know? Keep him guessing."

Grace felt herself blushing. She'd just met these people. There was no way she'd ever talk about her and Ben's love life—especially with her mother sitting right there!

Ashleigh pointed at Camryn. "How about you? If Dexter wanted you back—would you do it?"

"Oh, hell to the no," Camryn said. "How could I respect myself if I took him back? I know what a sleaze he is. Jana's sad about us breaking up, but I want her to know, as a black woman, she needs to have some standards. I don't want her settling for second-rate, or thinking it's okay for some brother to cheat on her and degrade her. Besides? He's been dipping his pen in a lot of ink. And I know Dexter. I know he wasn't wearing a condom for any of those close encounters. Who knows what kind of diseases he might be carrying around?" She shuddered. "We hadn't been sleeping together for months anyway, but just to be sure I got myself tested as soon as I saw that little DVD of his. Somehow, I got lucky. Everything tested negative."

"How about you, Wyatt?" Camryn asked pointedly. "You've been pretty quiet all these sessions."

"Yeah," Ashleigh agreed. "I'd just l*ooove* to know how it feels when the shoe is on the other foot."

Wyatt's face colored. "You don't think women cheat on their husbands? Look, it's different with me."

"Because you've got a penis? And choices?" Camryn asked.

"Because I've got a six-year-old son to raise," Wyatt half stood, obviously roused. "I've got to put my kid first, and myself second."

"What if you didn't have a kid? Or what if she broke up with the other guy?" Ashleigh persisted.

Wyatt glared at her. "Can we just drop it?"

"No, we can't," Camryn snapped. "Can you quit being macho man long enough to answer an honest question?"

He eased back into his chair, some of the fight gone out of him. With his thumb, he twisted his wedding band around and around. "You read all these statistics about the children of divorce. They don't do as well in school, have emotional problems. I don't want that for Bo."

"Listen, Wyatt," Rochelle said, reaching down the length of the table and grabbing his hand. "Shrinks can come up with all kinds of statistics to make people feel guilty. What kind of home will you be raising Bo in if he knows you and Callie hate each other? Kids aren't dumb. They can sense things. And what happens if you take her back and she decides to go off with some other guy?"

Wyatt's face contorted and Grace wished she could kick her mother under the table. Instead, she spirited some more popcorn into her tote bag.

"Suzanne?" Now Rochelle was concentrating on the least forthcoming member of the group.

"What about you? Would you take your husband back?"

Suzanne seemed to shrink into her chair. "Our situation . . . is unique," Suzanne said. "I'm sorry. You've all been so open and honest. I feel like a voyeur, sitting here, contributing nothing. I'm still . . . still trying to sort out my feelings." She took a deep breath and started again.

"Let me try to explain. I come from a very religious Catholic family. My father dragged us to Mass every Sunday. My mother was very pious. From the outside, we looked like the ideal family. Inside?" She shrugged. "He cheated on her. Always. Made her life miserable. She'd never worked outside the home, what was she going to do? Leave him? Besides, we Catholics don't divorce, right? So she stayed, a martyr to the end. Why did she put up with his crap? My two sisters and I swore a pact that we would never, ever fall into the same trap she did.

"Damned if we didn't. Tricia's husband is a closet drinker. Eileen? We think he abuses her, but we don't have any proof, and even if we did, she has kidney disease, and she needs his medical benefits. And me? Eric and I lived together off and on for eight years. When I was thirty, and still working on my Ph.D., I got pregnant with Darby." Suzanne's small, sad face suddenly lit up. "It was a huge surprise. I'd had ovarian cysts in my twenties, and my doctor told me I probably wouldn't have children."

Suzanne took several deep breaths, sucking in more oxygen to fuel her narrative. The others waited, willing her to continue. "Even then, I waited until Darby was two, just to be absolutely sure, before I agreed to marry Eric. I thought we had something good, you know? Not perfect, but a much better marriage than my parents'."

"You poor thing," Rochelle said. She stood quickly. "Don't say another word, okay? I need to see if everything's all right in the kitchen. Can I get anything for anybody?"

Ashleigh raised her nearly empty margarita glass. "I could use a freshie."

Grace could feel her jaw tightening. Did she dare suggest that Rochelle stick to bartending instead of marriage counseling? Probably not.

"Listen, Suzanne," Grace said gently, "don't feel like you have to talk, if you don't feel like it. We all understand."

"No!" Suzanne said, taking a gulp of her tea. "I think this is probably good for me. I've never discussed my family's . . . marriage issues, to anybody. Ever. Not even with my best friend. Not even with my sisters. So thanks, for listening. And not judging."

"Oh, you are just so welcome," Ashleigh said, looking around the table for consensus. "Isn't this awesome? I mean, I feel soooo much better, hearing what you guys have been through. If I didn't hate the whole idea of paying three hundred dollars an hour to Paula, I would think just being with you all was totally worth it."

Camryn had her chin propped on her hands. "Yeah. I can't believe Stackpole is making us pay Paula that much money for the privilege of watching her fall asleep and drool on herself once a week." She grimaced. "Speaking of sleep, I've got to be at the studio at six, to tape an interview with some exercise diva, and if I don't want to have king-sized bags under my eyes, I better get out of here right now." She stood, pulled money from her billfold, and placed it on the tabletop.

"Grace, tell Rochelle I said 'bye. See y'all next week!"

Ashleigh yawned widely. "I can't believe it's not even ten o'clock and I'm this sleepy. Guess I need to take off, too." She stood up and slapped her backside. "My new trainer is making me do this really intensive booty camp, starting tomorrow." She added some bills to the pile on the table. "I'll just run by and tell Rochelle never mind on the drink," she added. "I probably don't need the calories anyway."

"I hate to ask," Suzanne said, turning to Grace. "But is it too much trouble for somebody to give me a ride back to Paula's office?"

"I'd be happy to take you, but the front seat of the pickup is loaded with sacks of bird feed and crap for the park," Wyatt said apologetically. "Didn't want the chance of it getting rained on."

"I can take you," Grace said. She was painfully aware that that the tote bag at her feet was starting to wriggle, and every once in a while a small brown muzzle would pop out. "Be back in a minute."

By the time she got back to the table, Suzanne and Rochelle were deep in conversation. Wyatt was standing, looking around, unsure of his next move.

"If you're going to take Suzanne back to Paula's office, why don't you let me ride with you?" He was trying to sound casual, cool even. "It's not that great a neighborhood."

26

There were now a dozen cars in the shopping center parking lot. The lights were on in the tattoo parlor, heavy metal music blaring from within, and a trio of imposing black Harleys were parked on the sidewalk in front of it. Suzanne leaned over the front seat console. "Here's my car." She pointed to a silver Prius. "Thanks again, Grace. Wyatt. See you next week."

Grace pulled alongside Suzanne's car and waited until she'd started the car and eased out of her parking spot.

"Hey, look." Wyatt pointed at the very end of the parking, where a black Lexus had just pulled into the space nearest the end. As they watched, Paula emerged from the passenger's side of the sedan. She slammed the car door, and then, while they watched, she kicked the tires. Next, she ran around to the driver's side. She was screaming something, slapping at the car windows, pounding, but the driver never cut the engine, instead throwing the car into reverse. Its tires screeched and skidded as the driver slammed it into drive and sped out of the parking lot, turning left onto Manatee Avenue.

Paula stood, hands on hips, watching it go. Then, she walked back, unlocked her office door, and disappeared.

"Oh my God," Grace said. "Do you think that's Stackpole in the black car? Looks like they were having a knock-down, drag-out fight, huh?"

"Only one way to find out," Wyatt said, leaning forward to keep his eyes on the car.

"I'm on it," Grace said, pulling out of the shopping center. Traffic was light that time of night, and she could see the Lexus's red taillights only half a block ahead of them.

"Good of him to be such a safe driver," Grace said.

"If it's Stackpole, the last thing he wants is to get pulled over by a cop," Wyatt pointed out.

Grace followed the Lexus west on Manatee, for five blocks. It stopped at the light at West 75th and put on its blinker to turn left. Grace pulled behind the Lexus and did the same. "You think this is really a good idea? Following Stackpole—or whoever is in that car?"

"We're just two people out for a drive. No big deal. You're not speeding and you didn't even drink all your wine, right?"

"That's right."

"And I had a beer, over the course of two hours," he said. He glanced toward the backseat. "How's the dog?"

She grinned sheepishly. "How'd you know?"

Instead of answering, he reached around and pulled the wriggling dog out of the bag, setting her carefully on his lap.

"She popped her head out of there a couple times, back at group," Wyatt said. "It was all I could do to keep a straight face. Every time she heard your voice, the whole bag would move—she was wagging her tail so hard." The dog stretched its neck and rewarded Wyatt by licking his chin.

He held it at arm's length, checking its undercarriage. "Hello, little girl," Wyatt said, rubbing the top of the dog's head, then scratching its belly. "What's your name?"

"Meet Sweetie," Grace said. "The new kid on the block."

Sweetie put her front paws on the passenger window, straining to see out the window.

"Where'd you get her?" Wyatt asked.

"Sweetie has kind of a sad story." While she recounted the tale of the dog's rescue, her adoptee climbed over the console, wriggling its way under Grace's arms. "But she's feeling better now. The vet fixed her up, gave her some IV meds, kept her overnight."

"And you got yourself a dog," Wyatt said. "What's Rochelle think about that?"

"She doesn't know," Grace admitted. "My mom is not really what you'd call a pet person. You can't really blame her, I mean, we live above a bar. So I'm guessing I'll try to keep her a secret, until I figure something out."

"Do you think you'll be getting your own place pretty soon?"

"I hope so," she said fervently. "I'm too old to be moving back in with the folks. You've seen what Rochelle's like. I love her, but she's . . . got an opinion about everything. If my asshole husband will start making the payments the judge has ordered him to make, and if I can get my blog up and generating income, I hope I can move out, sooner rather than later."

"What are you going to do with Sweetie until then?" Wyatt asked. "You can't keep hiding her in a purse."

"I know. She does seem pretty laid back. She's house-trained, so that's a big plus. The vet said she was amazingly calm while they treated her, and she's been so good all night tonight, not making a peep, just sleeping in my tote bag."

Grace scratched the dog's ears affectionately. "She's really a very chill little girl. My plan is to keep her in my room with me at night and sneak her down the back steps first thing in the morning, for a potty break."

"What about during the days?"

"That house where I found Sweetie? It's on Anna Maria. I was out for a run and spotted this cool old rattan sofa in a pile of junk on the curb. I struck up a conversation with the landlord, this old guy named Arthur, who, it turns out, used to be kind of fishing buddies with my dad. He invited me in to see the house. It's a wreck right now, but it's got wonderful potential, and it's in a great location—a block from the bay. I'm going to be working on it, fixing it up, redecorating it for Arthur, getting it ready to rent again. I'll be photographing and writing about it for my blog. Sweetie can stay there with me during the day while I work on it. In fact, I'm thinking I'll write her into the story, too. It was her house, after all."

"Look, he's turning up ahead," Wyatt said, pointing at the Lexus. "He's headed back out to the beach. I bet he lives out there."

"Not at Cortez, for sure," Grace said. "We're not fancy enough. I bet he lives at Longboat Key."

"You're probably right." Wyatt said.

Grace stayed back a few car lengths but made the same turn. She kept on Cortez Drive, passing the turnoff for the Sandbox in the fishing village, crossing the bridge over the Intracoastal Waterway and into Bradenton Beach. At the light at Gulf Drive, the Lexus signaled to make a left turn.

"Well, he's definitely not going to Anna Maria," she said, following as the black car turned south.

The moon was nearly full, and as they followed the road paralleling the ocean, they could catch occasional glimpses of silvery water through the thick fringe of Australian pines and sea grapes lining the road in the intermittent patches of undeveloped land.

Grace smiled, as she always did when passing the sign for Coquina Beach. "That was our beach, growing up," she said. "How about you, which beach did your family go to?"

"Holmes Beach, mostly," Wyatt said. "Once I could drive, though, I was too cool for school. A bunch of us used to hang out at Siesta Key, where the rich girls were—or so we thought."

As they drove, the landscape changed from sparsely developed to the manicured civility of Longboat Key. High-rise condo complexes hugged the shores of the gulf on the right and the bay on the left, and imposing stucco homes painted in sherbet hues were set back behind hedges and gates. Grace slowed when she saw the Lexus's brake lights and then turn signal.

She waited until it made the left turn into a sprawling development called Lido Bay. "Should I keep following him, you think?" She glanced over at Wyatt. "If it's Stackpole, I really don't want him to notice us."

"Up to you," Wyatt said. "I don't want to get us in trouble either, but I'd like to know if it really is Stackpole."

He looked out the window at the homes lining the neatly landscaped street. All the homes were done in a similar hybrid Tuscan/Spanish-mission style, with stucco walls painted in pinks, peach, apricot, and buff, with red barrel-tile roofs. "Nice real estate," Wyatt said. "Wonder what these homes sell for?"

"Hmm, four or five years ago they were probably selling for seven hundred to eight hundred thousand dollars," Grace said. "The ones on canals or directly on the bay used to go for over a million. Now? You could probably move in here to a perfectly lovely home for under three hundred thousand."

"If I had three hundred thousand, I wouldn't want to live here," Wyatt said. "Too cookie cutter for my taste. Huge houses all jammed in here together on these little-bitty lots. Anyway, that's never gonna happen."

The Lexus made a wide left turn, and, as Grace started to follow, its brake lights went on. "Better slow down," Wyatt said. "Maybe turn off your lights. We don't want him to see us."

Grace pulled to the curb four houses down from the driveway where the Lexus turned in and, as suggested, cut her headlights.

"Come on, Cedric," Wyatt quietly urged. "Get out of the car and let us see your pretty face."

"Damn!"

As they watched, the garage door slowly, soundlessly rolled up, and the Lexus pulled in, with the garage door rolling down right behind it.

Grace burst out laughing, and after a moment Wyatt laughed, too. "Well, that was certainly anticlimatic," she said, turning around and driving out of the subdivision.

He was still sizing up the real estate. "Even with the real estate market in the toilet, that subdivision was pretty high cotton," he mused. "Wonder what kind of money a judge makes in Florida?"

"Don't know," Grace said. "But remember, Camryn said his wife's family is loaded. So maybe it's her money. Or maybe he does well in the stock market. Or he's cornered the market for black-market Oxycodone."

He gave her a startled look.

"Just kidding," she said. "Remember, we don't even know if that really was Stackpole. It could be anybody. It could even be Paula's husband, if she has one."

"Don't think so," Wyatt said. "Remember, we checked her driver's license. Paula lives on Anna Maria. Not Longboat."

"I'd love to know what that fight was about," Grace said, after a moment. "Paula seemed so different tonight, and then, wham, something really upset her apple cart."

She reached down and scratched Sweetie's silky brown ears. The dog hopped across the console to Wyatt's lap and scratched at his door, whining.

"Uh-oh," Grace said. "I think somebody needs a pit stop."

"Why don't you pull over up here at Coquina Beach," he suggested. "It's a nice night, and I haven't been to the beach since all this crap started with Callie. We can take her for a walk, if you want."

She raised an eyebrow. "You know dogs aren't allowed on the beach, right?"

"I won't tell if you won't," he said. "Besides, Sweetie's been such a good girl, she deserves a little treat, right Sweetie?"

The dog's tail beat a tattoo on the window.

"I swear she knows her name already," Grace said.

She parked the car beneath one of the towering Australian pines and clipped a leash to Sweetie's new pink collar, extracting a plastic bag from her tote bag.

Grace slipped off her shoes and Wyatt did the same with his flip-flops, and they left them, side by side, in the soft white sand at the parking-lot edge. After Sweetie had taken care of business and Grace had disposed of the plastic bag, they took the boardwalk over the dunes, past gently waving fronds of sea oats.

The tide was out, and the moon bathed the beach with a silvered pearlescent sheen. The ocean surface was as calm as a puddle after a summer storm, lapping gently at the edge of the shore. Only the faint breeze rippled the water.

Sweetie paused and looked startled when her feet first touched the damp sand, then sat on her rump and gave Grace a quizzical look.

"Come on, girl," Grace said, tugging gently at the leash. "Let's walk."

"I'll bet she's never been to the beach before," Wyatt said.

Grace tugged again, and finally the little dog stood and began trotting toward the water. She got all the way to the surf line, stopped, and looked back at her mistress.

"It's okay," Grace coaxed. "You can get your feet wet. Give it a try."

To demonstrate, Grace waded in, letting the warm ocean water lap against her ankles. "It's like bathwater," she told Wyatt, who followed her in.

The dog edged in and immediately scampered back onto the dryer sand, barking as the wavelets edged toward her.

"Okay," Grace agreed. "You walk on the sand; we'll walk in the water."

"Can I take her?" Wyatt asked. Grace handed over the leash.

"Come on Sweetie," Wyatt called, veering onto the beach. "Let's run!"

He broke into a trot, and the dog obediently followed behind. After less than a hundred yards, though, Sweetie ran toward the shell line, where mounds of crushed seashells and seaweed marked the high-tide line.

Sweetie sat, barked, and began nosing in the shells, digging frantically and occasionally stopping to give an excited yip.

"What's she doing?" Grace asked, when she caught up to the pair.

"She smells something" Wyatt said. "I think she must have some terrier in her, the way she's going after it."

Suddenly, the little dog yelped. She backed away slightly and gave a menancing growl, barked again, crouched, and growled again.

"It's a ghost crab," Grace laughed, as the pale creature scuttled away. She bent down and picked up the dog. "Stay away from crabs, Sweetie. Crabs are not your friend!"

They walked down the beach in companionable silence, with Sweetie meandering along, sniffing the air and occasionally stopping to growl at imagined threats to her security. After half a mile or so, by unspoken agreement, they turned and walked back toward where the car was parked.

A concrete picnic bench was perched under the shadows of one of the big old pines. "Let's sit for a little bit," Grace suggested. She sat on the tabletop and placed Sweetie in her lap. Wyatt sat beside her.

"We used to come out here and go 'parking' in high school," she said, with a sigh. "Seems like a long time ago."

"When I was in high school, we liked someplace a little more secluded," Wyatt said. "There was this dead-end street over on Holmes Beach. You could pull your car way up under the trees, and it was on a little bit of a rise, with a perfect view of the water. Although"—he laughed ruefully—"I don't remember being that interested in actually looking at the water back then. I was a horny little bastard, back in the day."

"And now?" Grace turned to look at him, her gray eyes teasing.

He hesitated, but stood abruptly, brushing sand from the seat of his pants. "I don't remember."

She felt her face aflame with embarrassment, jumping to her feet and startling the dog, who yipped her reaction. "We should probably go."

"Look. I'm not divorced yet. You're not divorced yet. I'm pretty sure this is against every divorce-recovery-group rule Paula ever thought of."

"This?"

He sighed. "You know. Us getting together. Gotta be against the rules."

Something inside her rebelled. Against rules, and best intentions and common sense. That mischevious smile of hers was back. "I won't tell if you won't." She tilted her face up, waiting to be kissed.

And then . . . he coughed politely. She opened her eyes and saw that he was putting on his shoes.

. . .

Ever since they'd pulled over to the Coquina Beach parking area, Grace had been anticipating this moment. Wondering what she would do if Wyatt tried to kiss her. Or even touch her.

Okay, maybe she'd been wondering all of the above since the minute he'd walked into Paula's office earlier in the evening. Not that he hadn't been kinda hot the other times, unshowered, dressed in his Jungle Jerry's safari work clothes. She didn't usually go for all that down-and-dirty muscley, manly type, but somehow, on Wyatt, it worked. Then, tonight, he'd obviously made an effort to look good. Was it for her? And had he noticed that she'd dressed up tonight, too? She hadn't anticipated how crazy all of this was making her feel.

It had never occurred to her that they would come this close—and he would so totally and completely shut her down. Dammit, she was no good at flirting after all this time.

But maybe Wyatt didn't know that.

Grace cursed all that stinking moonlight. She gathered her keys, her shoes, and her dog and stomped off toward the car.

"Jesus!" Wyatt's voice was hoarse. He grabbed her arm as she was unlocking the car. "Don't think I don't want this, Grace. I do. More than I can tell you, I want it. But where do we go from here? It makes no sense."

She spun around to face him. "I don't care. I don't want to make sense. I just want to be held, and be kissed." She raised her eyes. "By you. Does that make me a criminal? Or some kind of a slut?"

"No! Of course not. Don't call yourself that."

She felt her jaw clench. "That's how you're making me feel."

She placed Sweetie on the backseat, brushed the sand from her feet, and sat in the driver's seat, with the engine running. A moment later, he got into the car.

"Grace?"

She didn't answer, just pulled the car out of the lot and onto the beach road, keeping her eyes straight ahead. Sensing the tension in the air, Sweetie whined from the backseat, but Grace kept her back stiff.

"Look," he said, running his hand over his gleaming head. "I'm playing way out of my league here. You know?"

"No, I don't know."

He closed his hand over her shoulder, but she wrenched it away. He tried again. "You are incredibly beautiful, smart, and sane, and nice."

"Sane?" She raised one eyebrow. "Nice? What kind of left-handed compliment is that?"

"I don't know!" he shouted. "I don't know anything. I haven't been with another woman in eight years. Okay? I have no idea what I am saying or doing tonight. My instincts say go for it, but I'm afraid, all right? What happens if you and I . . . start something? Where does it go?" You say you'd never take your husband back, but maybe you'll change your mind. How do I know?"

"How do I know you won't take Callie back?" she retorted. "Right now? I just don't care. I really don't. I'm tired of worrying about what might happen. I've got no control over anything: your marriage, what's left of my marriage, that asshole judge, my career. From now on, I'm going to do just what everybody else in this world does. I'm going to do what feels good. And the *hell* with the what-ifs."

"I don't have that luxury," he said quietly.

27

It was the most erotic sensation she could ever remember having. She was having smoking-hot, crazy sex—under a Hawaiian waterfall of all places. Or she guessed it was a Hawaiian waterfall, from the profusion of flowering orchids and waving palms surrounding them. She couldn't see her lover's face, but my God, his body was sleek and hard and muscled and tan all over, and he had magic hands that did the most amazing things, and it seemed to go on forever and ever, until he had her body humming like a concert violin. And then, just as she was about to climax, a gigantic parrot swooped in and landed on his shoulder. "Gimme shots, gimme beer," the parrot called. Her lover turned his head. It was the honorable Cedric N. Stackpole Jr.

The horror made Grace sit straight up in bed so abruptly that Sweetie, who'd been nuzzled on the pillow next to hers, yelped.

"Shhh!" Grace bundled the dog into her arms and hugged her close. "It was just a dream, Sweetie. No, not a dream, a terrible, terrible nightmare." She shuddered at the memory of it. Looked over at the nightstand to realize it was five in the morning. "Stupid men," she said, pounding the bed with her fist. "Stupid, stupid men!"

Sweetie hopped off the bed and made a beeline for the bedroom door. "Okay," Grace said wearily. "Let me put some shoes on."

. . .

The only good thing about waking up early from a nightmare was getting to work early, Grace decided. It was still dark outside when she unlocked the door of the house on Mandevilla and switched on the lights.

Dark outside, but sweltering inside. She set Sweetie down on the floor, then ran from room to room opening all the windows she'd closed the previous day. She sniffed the air. The house reeked of Pine-Sol, in a good way, but there were still strong undernotes of mildew and pet smells, not to mention more dead bugs.

It took two more trips to retrieve the rest of the day's supplies, which included a pair of old box fans she'd found in the shed back at the bar. She set one fan in the window of the living room and another in the back bedroom where Sweetie had been imprisoned and switched them both to the HIGH setting.

The little dog apparently hadn't been totally traumatized by her time living in the house. She trotted from room to room, her nails clicking on the wooden floors, and had a high old time in the kitchen, barking and growling at a cockroach in the death throes.

Her plan for the day had been to carefully assess the house and work out a list of priorities and a timetable. But her mood, following the previous evening's disastrous encounter with Wyatt, and the revolting sex dream that had followed, left her in no mood for assessments.

"Right," she said briskly. She wheeled in the huge plastic trash can she'd borrowed from the shed, lined it with a black contractor's bag, snapped on her rubber gloves, and began emptying the kitchen cabinets of their contents.

She'd considered trying to salvage the pots and pans and dishes left behind, but one glance at their cracked and battered status convinced her to discard them, too. When the house was done, she'd bully Arthur into letting her buy new cookware.

With the cabinets empty, Grace took another look. In a perfect world, she'd rip out all the upper and lower cupboards and fit the kitchen with inexpensive Ikea cabinets, ones with Shaker-style door panels, with matching drawers. She'd outfitted their little rental house in Bradenton with the exact same ones, spending less than seven thousand dollars for everything, including hardware and countertops. She didn't have that kind of budget here.

Instead, she got out her cordless electric screwdriver and removed all the upper-cabinet doors, setting them aside, just in case she found another use for them down the line. The kitchen immediately looked better.

The gray aluminum-edged Formica countertops were funky but age-appropriate for the house, and the deep porcelain-over-cast-iron sink was filthy, but she knew a good cleaning with Bar Keepers Friend would make it shine again.

Grace gazed out the kitchen window and saw the first orange streaks of daylight at the edge of the overgrown yard.

On an impulse, she clipped a leash to Sweetie's collar and walked out the kitchen door, drawn to the glorious glow. They walked the block to a sandy lot that overlooked the bay, and the two of them stood there, basking in a Technicolor Florida sunrise. Whoever ended up renting the little house on Mandevilla would have the privilege of watching that same sunrise whenever they liked. Maybe she would have to make it a habit to get over here every morning in time to do the same thing. It wasn't a bad way to start the day.

She turned to go back to the house, resolving to start ripping up that revolting vinyl kitchen floor. It would feel good to jab something inanimate with a knife, a pry-bar, a chisel, or anything sharp she could put her hands on.

For months now, Wyatt had been meaning to take down the sprawling thirty-foot-tall Brazilian pepper tree that had taken over the area near his grandmother's old orchid slat-house. As he set out on his golf cart with his weapons of battle—chain saw, ax, and ladder—he grimly decided that today, Wednesday, was as good a day as any.

The Florida Department of Agriculture had placed the Brazilian pepper, a nonnative invasive "shrub," on its hit list of noxious plants. It was definitely a pushy interloper—with its massive crown of branches, it shaded out anything else in its path, and it grew so rapidly he hadn't noticed it had sprung up and taken over the old orchid-house area.

Though it was a typical summer day, with temperatures promising to rise to the nineties, he knew enough about the Brazilian pepper's near-poisonous sap to take precautions, outfitting himself in long pants, a long-sleeved shirt, work gloves, and blue bandanna on his head. He set up the ladder next to the trunk, fastened a rope to the chain-saw handle, and began climbing into the canopy. When he'd gone as high as he could, he steadied himself against the main trunk, hauled the chain saw up from below, and fired it up.

The roar and the whine of the saw as it chewed its way through the brittle wood made a huge din, and the gas fumes filled his nostrils.

For two hours, Wyatt hacked away at the tree, dropping the limbs to the ground, steadily moving downward as he decimated the upper canopy.

Twenty feet aboveground, with a buzzing chain saw in hand, he was focused only on the tree, the chain saw, and avoiding falling out of the tree.

By noon, his clothes were sweat-soaked, his face was itchy from the pepper-tree fumes, and the tree itself was looking like a grotesque, defoliated skeleton. He considered going back to the house to shower, change clothes, and grab lunch but went back to work instead. The pepper tree, like Callie and Luke and their lawyer and Judge Stackpole, was his nemesis. And this one he intended to cut right down to the ground.

"Jesus, son!" Nelson recoiled at the sight of Wyatt when he came tramping into the house. "What the hell did you do to yourself?"

"To me? Nothing. It took me all day, but I cut down the pepper tree, sprayed the stump with the legal equivalent of napalm, then raked up every limb, leaf, and seedpod I could find and hauled it all off to the dump."

Wyatt collapsed onto one of the wooden kitchen chairs. "I'm whipped. What's for dinner?"

"Beanie-weenies, Tater Tots, cornbread, coleslaw. Doesn't your face hurt?"

Wyatt stripped off his gloves and put a finger to his cheek, which, come to think of it, did feel kind of hot and swollen to the touch. The backs of his hands were covered in a nasty red rash, too.

"Guess I better hit the shower," he said. "I might be having a slight reaction to the pepper-tree sap."

"If that's slight, I don't want to know severe," Nelson said.

The face of a monster stared back at Wyatt in the bathroom mirror. His entire face was mottled red and swollen, his nose a puffy red blob, his eyes rimmed in pink. Dime-sized welts ran down his neck and to the V of where his shirt collar had been open.

When he took off his shirt he saw that his chest was also streaked with angry crimson slashes. He unzipped his pants and stepped out of them, as well as his boxers, and looked down.

Holy shit! His crotch was covered in blisters. *Everything* was red and inflamed—and not in a good way. He turned on the shower full force and jumped in, letting the cool water sluice over his head and chest. He grabbed a bar of soap, lathered up, but the first touch of the soap to his chest felt like a splash of acid.

Wyatt dropped the soap and looked down again. Not good. How the hell had this happened? He'd been so careful, with the long pants and shirt, high socks, work boots, gloves. And then he remembered and would have smacked himself in the face if that face hadn't felt like an open wound just then.

He'd had to pee. And who could unzip and do all the rest wearing work gloves? He must have gotten some of the sap on his hands, and then, well, his boys. Which were now itching like a son of a bitch.

He tried to think back to a college class he'd taken on noxious plants. They'd studied poison ivy, oak, sumac, and a few others, and, of course, over the years, working in landscaping and now running Jungle Jerry's, he'd run into all of the above. But he couldn't remember anything about the hazards of Brazilian pepper.

After gingerly toweling off the inflamed skin, he found a bottle of Calamine lotion in the medicine cabinet and slathered it all over himself. Within a few seconds, the thick pink goo had dried and started to cake and crack. And he itched, God how he itched.

Wrapped in nothing more than a towel, he carefully stepped over the clothes he'd just discarded. In his bedroom he donned the loosest pair of cotton shorts he could find and an old, threadbare cotton T-shirt.

Wyatt sat down at the kitchen table as his father was taking a pan of cornbread from the oven. "Does it feel as bad as it looks?" Nelson inquired, after he'd served his son a plate heaped high with food.

"Worse," Wyatt said, pointing toward his crotch. "It's . . . everywhere."

"Ow," Nelson grimaced and poured him a glass of iced tea. "I think we've got some Benadryl around here somewhere. That might help some."

"Maybe after dinner," Wyatt said. "I'll fall asleep with my head in the plate if I take it now, and I've got some stuff I need to do tonight."

They cleaned up the kitchen, and Nelson retired to his recliner to watch his nightly roundup; *Wheel of Fortune, Jeopardy,* and the Rays game.

Wyatt sank onto the old sofa and tried not to think of his inflamed privates while he leafed through the paper, but he was so acutely uncomfortable he gave in shortly after eight and went looking for the bottle of Benadryl.

"Okay, Dad," he said, poking his head out from the hallway. "I'm turning in."

"Hmm?"

"I'm going to bed," Wyatt repeated.

"Did you ever talk to your Aunt Betsy?" Nelson asked, his eyes glued to the television.

"No. Why would I?"

"She called here looking for you. Guess you must have had your phone turned off."

Wyatt came around and stood directly in front of the television, the only way he knew to get his father's attention this time of night. "Dad? What did Betsy say?"

"Hey! Come on now, it's the bottom of the inning, two outs, and we've got the bases loaded."

"What did Betsy say? Did she have news? Come on, Dad, this could be important."

Nelson waved his hand in irritation. "How'm I supposed to know what she wanted? She just said to call her. Not tonight, she had something goin' on. Now, can I watch my game?"

Wyatt called her anyway and left a message on his aunt's phone. The itching was driving him nuts, but he resisted taking the Benadryl. At 9:30 he called and left another message for her, and at ten, in desperation, he texted. *WHAT'S UP? DAD SAID YOU CALLED.*

Thirty minutes later, his phone dinged and he lunged for it. Betsy's message was clear as mud. *CAN'T TALK, CALL U IN A.M.*

Finally, sometime after ten, he popped some Benadryl and fell into an uneasy sleep, imagining all the bad news his attorney might be saving up for the next morning.

28

Betsy Entwhistle was sitting at a table near the window of Eat Here, her favorite breakfast spot in Holmes Beach, when she spotted her nephew making his way through the parking lot, a baseball cap pulled down low over his face, sunglasses covering his eyes.

She sighed. She hated the bruising Callie was giving Wyatt. He'd been a good husband and a loving father, and the little idiot thought she could do better with that punk Luke? She'd known Callie was trouble from the start, and she'd told her sister, Wyatt's mom, that, in confidence. In confidence, Peggy had agreed wholeheartedly. But Wyatt was in love, and they both hoped things would work out.

"Hey," Wyatt was almost out of breath. He dropped into the chair opposite hers. "What's going on? What couldn't you tell me last night?"

"Good Lord, what have you done to your face?" Betsy reached over and tipped back the bill of his cap, removed the sunglasses. Wyatt's handsome face was a crimson, contorted mess. His eyes were nearly swollen shut, his nose and cheeks covered with red blisters that crawled down his neck to his chest. His hands were covered with a similar eruption.

"I took down a tree at the park yesterday, and I've had some kind of reaction to the sap," Wyatt said. "Just tell me what's going on, would you? Have you heard from the judge?"

"Honey, that's not just a reaction," Betsy said. "Your eyes are nearly swollen shut. Have you seen a doctor?"

"I don't need a doctor," he insisted. "It's like poison ivy. I put some Calamine on it and it's some better."

She pressed her lips in disapproval. "I'll tell you what's going on, but then I'm taking you to see my dermatologist. Wyatt, that stuff is in your eyes. What if you lose your eyesight?"

"Okay, whatever," he said. "Would you please talk to me now?"

Betsy took a sip of her coffee. "Don't you want some breakfast? I ordered you some pancakes and bacon."

"Betsy!"

"Okay. Here it is. I got a call from Stackpole's clerk yesterday. It seems Callie is claiming you've been interfering with her time with Bo. He wants to see you in his office this afternoon."

"Me?" Wyatt was incredulous. "I haven't done a damned thing. I don't even call Bo anymore when he's with her. Whatever she's telling the judge, it's total bullshit, Betsy."

"I know it is, but Stackpole doesn't," Betsy said.

"Did the clerk give you any details about this so-called interference?"

"Something about a birthday party Bo was supposed to go to this past weekend?"

"Yeah? What about it? Callie deliberately planned a trip to Birmingham with Fatso, supposedly to look at houses. She knew last weekend was his best friend Scout's birthday party at that new water park, but she planned the trip anyway and insisted Bo had to go. Bo was furious with her." He laughed. "He confessed to me that he called her a shit."

"It's not funny, Wyatt," Betsy said.

Wyatt slapped his hat on the table in disgust. "I didn't tell him to call her that. In fact, I told him it wasn't nice to call his mother names, although, privately, I can think of lots worse names to call her. And incidentally, he says Callie called him a shit first, and I happen to believe him. So that's what this is about? Some name-calling? Seriously?"

"It's worse than that," Betsy said. "When Callie went to pick him up at school on Friday, Bo wasn't there. She claims she called you, but you never answered her phone call."

"Wait? Are you telling me Bo went missing? And this is the first I'm hearing of it?"

"Calm down," Betsy said. "I did some checking. Apparently, Bo never had any intention of going on that trip to Birmingham. He told Scout's mom, Anna, his mom wanted him to spend the night with her and go to the party, and Anna, not knowing any better, took him home from school with her, and on to the party."

"That little con artist," Wyatt said. "I don't know whether I want to pat him on the back or whack him on his butt. But I still don't see how Callie can say any of this is my fault. It was her weekend to have Bo. I didn't call him, didn't pick him up, didn't hide him from his mom."

Betsy shrugged. "Don't kill the messenger, okay? Callie's made a serious charge, and Stackpole, in his totally random way, seems to find her story believable. So we're going to see the judge this afternoon." She looked over his shoulder and saw the waiter approaching with a tray of food. "Right after we get you your pancakes. And see my dermatologist."

"Sir, remove those sunglasses and that hat," the Honorable Cedric N. Stackpole said, as soon as Wyatt and Betsy were seated in his office.

Wyatt shrugged, took off the glasses and the baseball hat. Stackpole cringed. "Are you having some medical issues?" he asked brusquely.

"An allergic reaction to some underbrush he was clearing," Betsy said. "He's gotten a cortisone shot and he has some steroid cream. He'll be fine."

Callie was sitting in a chair on the judge's left side. She was dressed in a short pink skirt and a tight-fitting black tank top that displayed yet another tattoo, and glimpses of her abdomen whenever she moved. She leaned forward and grimaced. "You look like something out of a horror movie." She glanced over at her lawyer. "I don't want my son to see him like that. It's upsetting."

"I'm fine," Wyatt said, clenching and unclenching his fists. "The swelling has already started to go down. It's not contagious. Bo has seen me with poison ivy before."

"Let's stick to the subject at hand, shall we?" Stackpole said. He looked down at a file on his desk. "Mrs. Keeler, you're alleging that Mr. Keeler is interfering with your son's visits with you? Something about a birthday party?"

"Bo knew we'd been planning this trip to Birmingham, to look at houses,"

Callie said. "Wyatt knew it, too. We'd been planning the trip for weeks, and then suddenly, Bo was having a fit over going, because of some little party a friend was having. When I went to pick him up from school on Friday, he wasn't there!"

She leaned across her lawyer and glared at Wyatt. "You put him up to this. And I know it."

"Put him up to what?" Wyatt demanded. Betsy gave her client a small headshake, warning him not to be baited.

"Bo deliberately lied to his friend's mother, told her I wanted him to spend the night with them that night, so he could go to the party! He even packed a bathing suit and pajamas and hid them in his school backpack," Callie said. "He never would have done that on his own, not without his father giving him the idea."

The judge eased back in his leather desk chair. "Mr. Keeler, did you suggest to your son that he disobey and lie to his mother?"

"Absolutely not," Wyatt said. "This is the first I'm hearing about any of this. Bo did tell me his mother had scheduled a trip out of town, and he was upset over having to miss his friend's party that he'd been looking forward to for weeks. He even admitted he called his mother a bad name. But when I told him that wasn't acceptable behavior, he told me his mother called him that name first."

Stackpole raised an eyebrow. "What kind of bad name?"

"Bo told me his mother called him a little shit," Wyatt said calmly.

"Ridiculous," Callie snapped.

Stackpole's head swung in her direction. "Do you deny calling your son that name?"

Her face reddened. "Bo's been hostile to me for the last few months. He acts out, talks back. Whenever he comes back from a visit with his father, he's belligerent and defiant. And he's openly disrespectful to my fiancé."

"Mrs. Keeler, did you call your six-year-old a 'little shit'? Yes or no?"

Callie burst into tears. "He's my little boy! How would you like it if your son told you he hated you? How would you like it if you went to pick up your son and he refused to get in the car? I may have called him that, in the heat of the moment, but I never meant it."

Wyatt folded his arms across his chest and looked away. Callie loved to turn on the waterworks whenever she was backed into a corner. It was her go-to tactic. He wondered if Stackpole would fall for it. Betsy claimed the judge hated women, but Callie seemed to be the exception to that rule.

Betsy saw an opening and went for it. "Judge, Mr. Keeler is also concerned about his son's behavior. If Bo is unhappy after returning from a visit with my client, it's because he is uncomfortable seeing his mother living with a man other than his father. Bo is upset over the breakup of his parents' marriage, which is totally understandable, and I want to address that in a minute. But in the meantime, Mr. Keeler would like to know more about this past weekend. If Bo wasn't at school when Callie went to pick him up, why didn't she notify my client?"

"I left him a voice mail!" Callie said. "He never returns my calls. I basically assumed Wyatt had Bo."

"But she didn't know that," Betsy said calmly. "Did she do anything else to check up on her son's whereabouts? Question the teachers at the school? Go over to my client's home to see if Bo was there? Did she call his friend's homes to see if he'd gone home with one of them?"

"I just told you, I figured Bo was with Wyatt." Callie glared at Betsy.

Stackpole frowned. "Mrs. Keeler, did you leave town for the weekend without knowing your son's exact location?"

"We had to get on the road," Callie said, her voice shriller by the minute. "We had dinner reservations. It's a long drive to Birmingham, and I was positive Bo was with his father. I never would have left Bo home alone. And it turned out fine! He was with Anna."

Betsy went in for the kill. "He could have been abducted, Judge. My client relied on Mrs. Keeler's representation that his son was in her custody for the weekend. He had no knowledge that Bo wasn't where he should have been. And we find that very disturbing."

"As do I," Stackpole agreed. He looked Wyatt up and down. "Mr. Keeler, Dr. Talbott-Sinclair tells me you've been attending her divorce-recovery sessions, and I, ah, noted your presence there this week when I stopped by. She seems pleased with your progress."

He swung around in his chair and considered Callie, who was dabbing at her crocodile tears with a Kleenex in a valiant effort to look brave and vulnerable.

"Mrs. Keeler?"

"Yes?" she whispered, her lower lip trembling.

"If you and your son are having relationship issues, perhaps you'd better spend more time working on your relationship with him, and less on your fiancé."

Stackpole said the word "fiancé" as though it were some revolting sexual practice. Wyatt felt his spirits start to brighten.

"A young, impressionable boy needs a father in his life. Mr. Keeler had that regrettable episode at the baseball park, but he seems to be making some progress handling his anger and hostility. I'm starting to rethink the wisdom of allowing you to move your son so far away from his father."

Yes! Wyatt wanted to jump up, fist-bump Betsy, maybe even hug Stackpole. Nah, not that. But still.

"Now, Judge," began Callie's lawyer, who'd been noticeably silent until now. "Mrs. Keeler's fiancé has already accepted a job in Birmingham and put his home on the market. It's going to work a real hardship on them if you prevent them from moving . . ."

"I'm not preventing anybody from doing anything, yet," Stackpole interrupted. "I'm just saying I'm rethinking. I still want to wait a few more weeks to make sure that Mr. Keeler completes his therapy, and I want to hear reassurances from Dr. Talbott-Sinclair that there won't be any more episodes of violence before I rule on this custody issue."

"Thank you," Wyatt said fervently. "Thanks very much, Judge."

Stackpole was staring at Callie, eyes narrowed.

"And Mrs. Keeler?"

Callie blew her nose on the tissue. "Yes, Your Honor?"

"The next time you are in my presence, I do not want to be assaulted with the vision of your body piercings. Is that clear?"

Callie looked down and yanked her top over the diamond-studded navel ring winking from her abdomen.

Wyatt waited until they were in the elevator to gather his aunt into a bear hug. "You did it!" he exclaimed. "Finally, a win for our side."

"Not a win, necessarily, but at least a point for our team," Betsy conceded. "I can't believe that little . . ."

"Shit?" Wyatt grinned.

"Shit works, although I *was* going to call her an ignorant slut," Betsy said, returning her nephew's smile. "No offense."

"None taken," Wyatt said. "You were awesome in there, the way you kept on about how Callie just left town, not knowing where Bo was."

"I wasn't just grandstanding. It really is appalling that she was so focused on her little trip she didn't even care enough to make sure Bo was somewhere safe. In the past, I just thought Callie was a selfish, stupid, self-involved little twit. But now I'm starting to wonder how fit a mother she is."

Sobered, Wyatt nodded in agreement. "I keep telling myself she really does love Bo, but since she hooked up with Fatso, Callie's changed. It's like she's turned into this eighteen-year-old party animal overnight. She wasn't always like this. She was a good mom. She wouldn't even let Bo sleep in his nursery until he was, like, eighteen months old, because she'd read all this crap about Sudden Infant Death Syndrome. He slept in a bassinette in our bedroom or in bed with us, until I finally convinced her he'd be okay in his own room. Maybe we got married too young. Maybe she's just immature. Maybe this, the tattoos, the piercings, the clothes, maybe it's all just a phase."

"I hope you're not making excuses for her," Betsy said. "She's thirty-six. It's a little late for her to be in a 'phase.'"

"Hell no, I'm not making excuses for her." Wyatt pulled his baseball cap on again. "Maybe I'm making excuses for me, for letting her go without putting up a fight."

"Don't beat yourself up," Betsy said. "Callie and her lawyer are doing enough of that. You're a good guy. Remember that, okay? And don't go getting soft on me." She made a fist and thrust it into his face. "And if you start thinking about taking her back, I'll punch out *your* car window."

"No worries there," Wyatt said.

"Listen," Betsy said suddenly. "Did I understand Stackpole right? Did he actually sit in on your therapy session the other night?"

"Yep," Wyatt said.

"So weird. What was he doing there?"

"Paula said she invited him," Wyatt said. "But there's something definitely . . . kinky going on between the two of them."

"Kinky and Stackpole are not two words you necessarily think of together," Betsy said. "Kinky how?"

"There's a vibe between them. And everybody in the group noticed it. Paula was positively giddy that he showed up. In fact, she was stone-cold sober, which is a major change."

"Your therapist? You mean she's not usually sober? Wyatt, what's going on with this group?"

The elevator dinged, and the doors opened. They emerged into the courthouse lobby. Betsy pulled Wyatt by the arm, gesturing for him to sit on a bench.

"Talk," she ordered.

"Paula's stoned out of her gourd during most of our sessions," Wyatt said. "The first one, I got there a little late, and she was passed out cold. I had to wake her up to make sure she realized I was there. On a good night, she's just vague and glassy-eyed. During our second session, the light was getting dimmer, if you know what I mean, and then after we got back from break, she zoned out again. We actually left her on the sofa in the reception area. But before we left, just to make sure she hadn't overdosed or something, we checked her purse and figured out she's mixing tranquilizers and sleeping pills."

"Don't you think that's something you might have mentioned to your lawyer?" Betsy scolded.

"Wouldn't do any good," he said. "Like I was telling you, Stackpole showed up at our last session. Paula was on her best behavior, all dressed up and proper and professional. She actually ran the session."

"She doesn't usually?"

"Not really," Wyatt said. "But this week was different. She had her act together, and was so excited about him being there, it was kind of pathetic. He made a stupid little speech, about what a good thing it was we were all doing, blah, blah, blah. And it was going good, and all of a sudden Paula just ended the session. We're supposed to be there an hour, and it wasn't even thirty minutes."

Betsy was shaking her head. "How on earth did he find this woman? And if she's obviously on drugs, like you say, why would he refer people to her?"

Wyatt glanced around the lobby and lowered his voice. "I'll tell you why, but you're not gonna believe it. Because he's in her pants."

"Shhh!" Betsy yanked him up by the arm and hustled him out of the courthouse.

"Oww," Wyatt winced and she loosened her clutch.

"In my car," she said, making a beeline for the parking lot.

. . .

When they were in Betsy's car, with the air conditioner blowing at full blast, he gave her the whole story. Or as much of it as his pride would allow.

"Wednesday night, after Paula let us leave early, we all went over to the Sandbox, like we always do."

She gave him a fishy look. "Tell me that's not a strip joint."

"All those women? You know I'm the only guy, right? The Sandbox is a bar. In Cortez."

"That dumpy little fishing village?"

"It's not all that dumpy," Wyatt said. "Anyway, the Sandbox is a classic dive bar. It's even got an original Ms. Pac-Man. One of the women in the group, Grace, her mother owns it, which is why we go there."

"Who's we?"

"Everybody in the group. Me, Grace, Camryn, Ashleigh, and Suzanne. Like I said, I'm the only guy. At first I thought they were gonna scratch my eyes out, because they've all been shafted by their husbands, and they all hate men, but we're cool now."

"You were telling me about Stackpole being, as you indelicately put it, in your therapist's pants? What makes you think that?"

"For one thing, you had to see them in the same room together. Paula was all giggly and flirty. And then, well, there was this other thing."

"Tell me." Betsy dug in her pocketbook, pulled out a stick of gum, offered it to her nephew, then took one for herself.

"Okay, but you're not gonna like it," he warned.

When he'd finished recounting his story, Betsy sighed. "You're right. I reallllly don't like what you guys did."

"Do you happen to know where Stackpole lives?" Wyatt asked eagerly.

"I have no idea. But I would imagine he probably lives somewhere over on Longboat."

"How about his car? Do you know what kind of car he drives? Like I said, this was a Lexus."

"Stackpole is as conservative as it comes, so whatever he drives, I'd be willing to bet it's a big American-made land yacht."

"Hey!" A light came into Wyatt's eyes. "Do judges have assigned parking spaces? Here at the courthouse?"

"Probably," Betsy said. "God forbid a judge might have to drive around and hunt for a parking spot like the average Joe."

She sighed. "I suppose you want me to swing through the county parking deck to check this out?"

Wyatt leaned over and pecked her on the cheek. "Did I ever mention that you're my favorite aunt?"

"I'm your only aunt," Betsy said. But she started the car and went on the prowl.

29

Transformations and Dirty Laundry

Dear Readers: If you've managed to follow me over here to my new blog, TrueGrace, from my former blog, you know that my personal life has been dealt some, uh, "challenges" lately. My marriage came off the rails in a fairly spectacular way, I've left my husband and lost my home, and now my former blog has been co-opted by my estranged husband and my former assistant. It sounds like it should be a funny story, but unfortunately there's no punch line.

Somebody—and I have a good guess who that is—has been sabotaging me professionally, wiping out my blog posts, leaving nasty comments falsely attributed to me on other blogs, and just generally smearing my good name in the blogosphere. I won't make any accusations, but I would like to assure all my readers, and other bloggers, that I have never and would never engage in such scurrilous behavior.

On a positive note, my life these days is a clean slate. And I have an exciting new project to share with you! Over these next few weeks and months I hope you'll follow along as I rehab, restore, and redecorate a wonderful original 1920s cottage.

Mandevilla Manor, as I call it, is a classic example of a vernacular

Florida cracker cottage. Built of heart pine on a raised cinderblock foundation, it has the original pine board and batten walls, oak floors, and an airy screened porch.

I discovered this diamond in the rough when I was out for a morning run recently. I noticed a huge pile of trash sitting on a curb, which meant a house was being cleaned out. As I watched, a gentleman dragged a fabulous 1940s rattan sofa to the curb. When I struck up a conversation with Arthur, who turned out to be the landlord, I learned that his deadbeat tenants had vacated the house after thoroughly trashing it.

The house has been in Arthur's family for three generations, and he was disheartened by all the work it would take to make it habitable again.

At Arthur's invitation, I toured the house, and, although it was filthy and in terrible disrepair, I could easily see all the charm just waiting to be rediscovered. So Arthur and I worked out a deal. He has provided a tiny budget, and I will provide the vision—and the sweat—to bring Mandevilla Manor back to life.

This will be a true shoestring operation. I'll be shopping at discount centers, thrift stores, and yard sales, and, yes, I'll probably be doing some Dumpster diving and curb cruising. Since my budget is so small, I'll be providing most of the girl power myself. As you can see from this first batch of before and "in process" photos, I've already torn down all the yellowing venetian blinds and ripped up all the nasty old carpet. The kitchen cabinet doors have been removed, and that ugly vinyl flooring is currently under attack. Watch this space for frequent updates!

One other thing. Meet my new BFF, Sweetie. She is an adorable poodle mix who was cruelly locked in a bedroom at the cottage and abandoned by her former owners. Can you believe she is the first dog I have ever owned? Sweetie is an expert at watch-dogging and cockroach wrangling, and she works cheap—just a little kibble and a lot of love. Life is full of twists and turns, dead ends and detours, isn't it? Lose a husband, gain a dog, take a run, find a house to transform.

I can't wait to see what the next chapter of my life will bring.

Grace uploaded all the before photos she'd taken of the little cottage, resizing and writing captions as she went. The last photo she posted was her favorite,

Sweetie, posing on the front steps of the cottage, ears pricked up, tongue lolling, as though to say, "Hey, check me out!"

She held her breath and clicked the PUBLISH toggle on her new blog's dashboard.

"Just try and hack me now, Ben," she muttered to herself. She'd knocked off work on the cottage at noon, just so she could come home and re-create her blog. One more time. She'd chosen a new, easier platform, WordPress, and gone through every security move she could think of to foil any other attack on her blog, including running a malware program that would pinpoint and hopefully eliminate whatever method Ben had used to sabotage TrueGrace.com.

"Everything new" was her motto this time around. She didn't have the graphics knowledge Ben had, and she sure didn't have any of her former advertisers. But her new platform was clean and simple. The writing was brutally honest, and from the heart. The photos of Mandevilla Manor were clear, and Grace felt certain this project would resonate with all the homeowners, thrifters, and DIY-ers in the world, in a way her old blog never had. How many people, after all, could relate to a three-hundred-dollar Belgian linen tablecloth like the one that had adorned the dining room table at Sand Dollar Lane? Were there really all that many hostesses who wanted recipes calling for black truffle oil and imported pink sea salt?

After she published the blog post, she copied the URL and e-mailed it to every lifestyle blogger she'd ever read, explaining to them that Gracenotes had been taken over by Ben and apologizing, again, for any spurious negative comments they might have seen floating around on the Internet.

I've reinvented myself, and my blog. I'm TrueGrace now, and I would love it if you'd drop by and check out my new project. And since I'm starting from scratch, I'd be humbled if you saw fit to add me to your blog roll.

Grace lolled back on her bed pillows and closed her eyes. It was nearly six. She'd been hunched over her laptop for hours. She was tired and sore from being down on her hands and knees hacking away at the kitchen floor. She told herself she was in no mood for divorce-recovery group. And she really dreaded seeing Wyatt Keeler again after her clumsy and humiliating encounter with him after their last session.

She was surprised to find that she was looking forward to seeing the others. Camryn's wisecracks and brutal honesty never failed to entertain her. Suzanne, quiet, vulnerable Suzanne, seemed close to revealing whatever secrets were tormenting her, and even that gold-plated gold digger Ashleigh was at least good for comic relief.

And yes, she was definitely curious about Paula after witnessing her encounter with the mystery Lexus driver. She got dressed and slipped Sweetie into her now-familiar tote bag, giving her a doggie treat to chew on and keep quiet.

A hastily scrawled note on the back of an envelope was taped to Dr. Paula Talbott-Sinclair's office door.

DUE TO FAMILY EMERGENCY NO GROUP SESSION TONIGHT—PTS

"What's going on?" Ashleigh Hartounian stuck her head out the window of her red BMW and called to Camryn Nobles, who was standing in front of the office door, fuming.

"No session tonight," Camryn said.

"Whaaat?" Ashleigh scrambled out of her car and joined Camryn on the sidewalk in front of the office. She peered into the office window, but there was nothing to see.

"What are we looking at?" Grace asked, as she walked up to the two women.

"See for yourself." Camryn gestured toward the note taped to the door.

"Huhh," Grace said, frowning. "And there's no sign of life inside the office?"

"None that we could see," Ashleigh said. "So what do we do now?"

"We don't spend three hundred dollars on Paula's bullshit, at least tonight," Camryn said.

"Oooh, that's exactly how much the pair of shoes I've been stalking at Saks are," Ashleigh said, rubbing her hands together in glee. She bowed in the direction of the door. "Thanks, Paula."

Camryn adjusted the strap of her pocketbook on her shoulder. "Since I had to clear my calendar anyway, should we go somewhere and grab dinner?"

"Absolutely! I know this adorable new bistro at Saint Armand's Key," Ashleigh said. "If we hurry, we can still get in on happy hour martinis."

Grace glanced at her watch. "What about Suzanne? Shouldn't we wait for her? I'd feel bad if she came all the way over here just to turn around and go home again. She's always so quiet, but I get the feeling we're the only ones she can really talk to."

"Although she hasn't really told us anything at all," Ashleigh pointed out. "I'm thinking whatever she did to get Stackpole to order her to therapy must have been really, really radical. And scary."

"Scarier than writing on her husband's mistress's house and car with blood?" Camryn asked.

"I told you, it wasn't blood. It was only red paint," Ashleigh said. "Although now I kind of wish it had been blood, which would wash off, because I was in such a hurry when I did it, I grabbed oil-based paint. And since my lawyer is making me pay to have the bitch's house and car repainted, it's costing me a fortune."

As they talked, a Prius rolled up to the office.

"Oh good, here's Suzanne now," Grace said. "Looks like the gang's all here."

"What about Wyatt?" Ashleigh asked. "We can't leave him behind."

"It's five after," Grace said. "Maybe he's ditching us tonight."

"Who's ditching us?" Suzanne asked as she joined the group. "And why are we all standing out here on the sidewalk?"

"Paula's got some kind of family emergency," Grace said, pointing at the note on the door.

"Allegedly," Camryn added. "We're just talking about going out to dinner, since we're all here anyway. Care to join us?"

Suzanne hesitated. "Well, since I'm here anyway . . . but what about Wyatt?"

Grace made a show of checking her watch again. "He's probably not even coming tonight. Look, we better get going if we're going to Saint Armand's. You know how crowded it gets there."

"Saint Armand's?" Suzanne's face fell. "I, well, never mind. You all go on without me. I'll get something to eat on the way home."

"No, Suzanne," Grace protested. "We don't have to go to Saint Armand's, if you have a problem with that. We could go anywhere."

"What's your problem with Saint Armand's?" Ashleigh asked. She was promptly given a not-so-subtle elbow in the ribs from Camryn.

"Why don't we just go over to the Sandbox, like we usually do?" Camryn said. "I'm not really in the mood for a twelve-dollar martini tonight anyway. Your mom serves food, right, Grace?"

"Sure, anything you want, as long as it's fried."

"Then it's settled," Camryn said. "Suzanne, do you need a ride? I can drop you back here afterward."

As they headed for their cars, Grace took a quick look around, mentally crossing her fingers and hoping Wyatt would not drive up as they were leaving.

When she got home, she bounded up the outside stairs at the Sandbox, unlocked her bedroom door, and opened the top of the tote bag. Sweetie climbed out, yawned widely, then hopped onto the bed.

"Good girl," Grace laughed. "I'll be back in a couple hours or so, and we'll take a quick walk before bedtime." She scratched the dog's ears and earned a generous tail wag for her efforts.

"You're early," Rochelle said when Grace strolled into the bar. "But I already reserved your table. Where are the rest?"

"They'll be along," Grace said, moving toward the table. "Could you bring some menus when they get here? We're going to have dinner."

A few minutes later, Rochelle appeared with menus, a glass of wine for Grace, and a basket of popcorn for the middle of the table. "Did your therapist pass out on you again?"

"She wasn't there," Grace said, helping herself to a handful of popcorn. "There was a note on the door saying she'd had some kind of family emergency. Very cryptic. Very mysterious."

"Does anybody really believe Paula had an emergency tonight?" Ashleigh speared a french fry with the tip of her fork and chewed slowly. "I mean, I find it hard to believe Paula even has a family. She's just so . . . spacey. I mean, can you imagine having her for a mom? Or a wife?"

"It might not be something with a child or a husband," Suzanne said timidly. "Maybe she has elderly parents. A friend I teach with has to use up every day of her sick leave and vacation time caring for her mother and her aunt, who both have dementia."

Grace tore off a piece of her patty melt and chewed slowly. "I was thinking it could have something to do with Paula's behavior last Wednesday night. She was definitely on edge."

"Family emergency, my ass," Camryn said. She squirted ketchup on her burger. "I knew all along there was something odd about that woman . . ." She broke off her sentence.

"Oh, my precious baby Jesus! Will you look at that boy's poor face?"

They all turned to see what she was talking about. And that's when they spotted a familiar-looking figure, threading his way through the maze of tables and chairs in their direction.

He was still dressed in the neatly pressed navy slacks and dress shirt he'd worn to court earlier in the day, and the bill of the baseball cap was still tilted low over his eyes, but he'd removed the sunglasses.

"How'd he find us?" Grace muttered, but as he got closer to the table and she saw his face, she gasped aloud.

"Hey, ladies," Wyatt said. He pulled a chair from a nearby table and sat down. He nodded curtly at Grace. Before he could say anything else, Rochelle arrived with a pitcher of beer and two glasses. She poured one and handed it to him, then sat down and poured a glass for herself. Rochelle reached out and gently touched Wyatt's cheek. "Your face! Did you fall into a fire-ant hill?"

"Not exactly. I did something even stupider. I purposely cut down a Brazilian pepper tree."

"That's bad?" Camryn asked.

"It is if you're allergic to the sap, which I apparently am," Wyatt said. He tried to smile, but his stiff, swollen lips were nearly immobile. "I know it looks pretty gnarly, but this is actually an improvement. My aunt dragged me to a doctor, and he gave me a cortisone shot and some steroid cream, so I'm starting to feel semihuman again, even if my face does look like a piece of raw meat."

Ashleigh leaned her body across Suzanne's to get a closer examination, and to give her pseudo-professional opinion. "Hmm. It looks like the eruptions haven't scabbed over. That's a good thing. I'd hate for you to have scars all over that pretty face of yours."

Wyatt ducked his head, obviously embarrassed by all the attention.

"What can I get you to eat?" Rochelle asked. "Hamburger? Wings? Loaded potato skins?"

"Nothing, thanks," he said. "I had a late lunch after my date with Stackpole."

"Stackpole?" Grace stared, wondering what he'd been up to, halfway dreading the answer.

"Yeahhh," he said slowly. "It's kind of a long story." And then his face cracked painfully, but he smiled anyway.

"Well, since Paula called off our session, we've got all night," Camryn said. "So don't keep us in suspense."

He filled them in on Callie's efforts to get him into hot water with the judge, and how his lawyer had instead managed to turn the tables on her.

"Wyatt, that's huge!" Suzanne said, beaming. "I'm so happy for you." She looked at the other faces around the table. "We're all happy for you."

Grace saw Wyatt watching for her reaction. "It's great, really," she said. "For once, the good guy comes out ahead with that clown Stackpole."

"Thanks, Grace," he said. "Maybe he'll change his mind about you and Ben, too."

"I wouldn't count on that," Grace said. "I'm a woman, remember? I'm the gender he loves to hate."

"Did you, uh, tell everybody about last week?"

Grace blushed at the memory.

"What?" Ashleigh demanded. "Did something happen after we left here?"

"You might say that," Wyatt said. Had Grace imagined it, or had he actually winked at her? She'd hoped to avoid any mention of their late-night chase the previous week.

"We don't actually know for sure that the car was Stackpole's," she put in, when he was done.

"Although . . ." Wyatt was trying his best not to look smug, but it was a hard-fought battle. "Today, while I was at the courthouse, my aunt and I took a drive through the county parking deck. Did you guys know judges get assigned parking spaces?"

"They probably don't even have to pay for 'em, either," Camryn said. And then she perked up. "Stackpole drives a Lexus?"

"A black one," Wyatt said, "with a little Florida gator decal in the lower left corner of his rear window."

Grace grinned despite herself. "So, it was Stackpole!"

"Maybe," Camryn cautioned. "Half the judges in this state probably have a UF Gator sticker on their car. And of those, there's probably a whole bunch of them who drive a black Lexus."

"But there's only one judge in Manatee County who drives a black Lexus with a UF sticker *and* who resides at 4462 Alcazar Trace, Longboat Key. And that is the Honorable Judge Cedric N. Stackpole Jr." Wyatt said.

"You're sure?" Grace asked.

"Yup. Betsy did an online search. It's him."

"Well, I'll be damned," Rochelle said. "What do you think that means?"

"I knew it!" Ashleigh said. "You can always tell with those straitlaced types. They're the biggest horn-dogs on the block. And, of course, they're *always* married."

"It might not mean anything," Grace cautioned, although she hoped against hope it did. "Maybe they were just having a professional meeting, and he told her he didn't like the way she was conducting our group session."

Camryn was drumming her long acrylic fingertips on the tabletop. "Okay, y'all, I'll tell you what I think it means. I think it means a hard-nosed piece of investigative journalism will unveil a web of intrigue and paybacks between a respected local circuit court judge and a disgraced therapist. And I think, maybe, just maybe, it might mean a daytime Emmy for a certain hard-hitting member of the News Four You I-Team."

She held up her iPhone. "I've been doing a little dirt digging on my own."

30

Paula Talbott-Sinclair," Camryn said, pausing for dramatic effect, "used to live in Oregon. But three years ago, the state revoked her professional license. She moved to Florida sometime after that and set up an office here, but she's not licensed by the state of Florida to be a clinical therapist. So how does she get away with charging three hundred dollars an hour for a group session? And more importantly, when the phone book is full of marriage counselors, why does Stackpole insist people like us attend counseling sessions with her?"

"Do we know why they revoked her license in Oregon?" Suzanne asked. "And does the state of Florida require her to be licensed in order to be a therapist here?"

"This is Florida, honey," Camryn told her. "Just like we attract every kind of poisonous reptile, bug, or plant, every whacked-out criminal, huckster, or con artist, we also get every loony-toon variety of self-appointed therapist on the planet. Even though Florida seems to have pretty strict licensing requirements for therapists, there's always a loophole. So you could still call yourself something else, hell, you could call yourself a divorce whisperer, and as long as you have a business license from the county, you're good to go. Paula does have that. I checked. As for why Oregon took away her professional accreditation, I'm working on it, but it's slowgoing. All these state licensing boards have layers and layers of confidentiality rules. I've got an intern at the station working on trying to dig up the particulars, but so far we're getting sandbagged."

"I wonder if her losing her license had anything to do with drugs?" The others at the table turned to look at Grace.

"She's obviously impaired, at least some of the time. And we did find those sleeping pills and tranquilizers in her purse," Grace reasoned. "Camryn, can your intern check to see if she's had any drug arrests, or something like that?"

"I can ask," Camryn said. "But this kid's no rocket scientist."

"I don't care what she's done or how she lost her license," Suzanne spoke up. "Paula is obviously troubled, but I honestly believe she cares about us. I don't know about you guys, but she's helped me. A lot. I feel sorry for her. Can't we help her, instead of making her part of an exposé?"

Ashleigh laughed. "You think she's helped you? I mean, no offense, Suzanne, but you've never said one thing in group about what happened in your marriage. All we know is that your husband's name is Eric and he cheated on you with another teacher at your school."

"Ashleigh!" Grace chided.

"I don't care," Ashleigh tossed her honey-colored tresses. "We've all opened up our innermost secrets, and she just sits there, every week, with her lips zipped."

"Something you might try once in a while," Camryn said.

"No, Ashleigh's right," Suzanne said. "I haven't been open. And that's not fair to you or me. That's one reason I was so disappointed our session with Paula was canceled tonight. That question she asked us Wednesday night—the one about a moment with our spouse when we were happy?" She gave a sheepish smile and pulled her journal out of her pocketbook. "I wrote ten pages! Which is hard for me to believe right now, but I did."

"Well? Are you gonna read it?" Ashleigh asked, daring the others to shut her up.

Suzanne glanced at the table directly behind them, where two grizzled fishermen sporting three-day beards and sweat-stained T-shirts lolled backward in their chairs, obviously interested in their conversations. "It's sort of private," she whispered.

"Let me handle this," Rochelle said. She stood, hands on hips and faced the table. "Miller, Bud, you guys need to pay up and move on." She jerked her head in the direction of the door. The men scowled but pulled some rumpled bills from their pockets, threw them on the table, and ambled toward the bar.

"Nuh-uh," Rochelle called, following in their wake. "You two are done for the night. Unless you plan to actually buy a drink or some food."

"Oh no, Grace, make her stop," Suzanne blurted. "I don't want your mom to chase off paying customers for me, especially your regulars."

Grace rolled her eyes. "They're her regular deadbeats. That's not even their real names. She just calls them that because that's what they order. A Bud and a Miller. But only one. They eat a boatload of popcorn and generally annoy all our paying customers. Plus, they stink to high heavens. And they're crappy tippers. Believe me, they'll be back tomorrow. They're shameless barflies."

Rochelle shooed the men out the front door, then returned to the table. "What were you saying, Suzanne?"

Suzanne took another deep breath. "If you guys really want to hear it, I think I'm ready. Don't worry," she added hastily. "I won't read all ten pages. I'll give you the abridged version."

She took a gulp of wine and laughed nervously. "Liquid courage, right?"

"It was a Saturday night, and our daughter Darby was playing in an out-of-town soccer tournament. I guess I am the ultimate soccer mom. Usually Darby and I share a room during the tournaments, because Eric rarely goes, and I love giggling and gossiping with her. We are so much closer than most moms and daughters. But this time, Darby specifically asked me not to go because she wanted to room with her two best friends, so I stayed home.

"At first, Eric and I didn't know what to do with ourselves on a Saturday night alone! We talked about going out to a nice restaurant, but it was raining out, so instead we stayed home. Eric did something he hadn't done since the years when we first moved in together. He fixed me my favorite dish and cleaned up the kitchen, too. After dinner, we opened a good bottle of wine, and we sat on the sofa together and dialed up a movie on Netflix, a silly little chick flick. But it made us laugh, and parts of it were so romantic. I was stretched out on one end of the sofa, with my shoes off, and Eric was giving me a foot massage. And it was just... so sweet, and tender. I just, I don't know, got really turned on."

Suzanne stopped reading. "I can't... I can't believe I am reading this out loud. My heart is pounding so hard right now, it feels like it might jump out of my chest."

"You're doing great," Rochelle said, patting Suzanne's hand.

"Thanks," Suzanne said, her voice sounding wobbly. "I think I'll be okay if I just don't look at your faces while I read. Dumb, huh?"

She stared down at the notebook. "Uh, I'm going to skip over this part." She blushed furiously, flipping the notebook pages. "And this. Nobody wants to hear this."

Ashleigh's hand shot up. "I do."

"Damn, Suzanne," Camryn drawled. "Ashleigh's right for once. Don't be such a scaredy-cat. You had relations with your husband? Why is that such a big deal? We're all grown folk here. You said you were going to read, so read already and quit making us beg for the good stuff."

"Sorry, sorry, sorry," Suzanne said, fanning her face with her hands. She turned back to her starting point and began to read again.

"Eric couldn't believe I was actually initiating sex with him. And I couldn't either. But I did. I undressed him, right there on the sofa, and he undressed me, and we . . ."

She bit her lip.

"We did it! We had sex in the family room, on the same sofa where Darby does her homework every night. Eric made me leave the lights on and everything. I don't know what came over me that night, but it was all different. I did all the things he's been begging me to do for years. Tried different positions. I talked dirty to him. He loved it."

Suzanne whispered, without looking up at the others. "I loved it."

"We were different people that night. We were who we used to be, before life reshaped us. Mutated us. I can't remember ever achieving that sense of intimacy before, even when we were dating. I thought maybe that night would change our marriage. I thought the next morning, I would get up and make us a late breakfast in bed, and we would make love again and everything would be different. But it wasn't. Still, that was the happiest I've ever been with Eric. It made me remember how we used to be."

Suzanne closed the notebook and folded her hands on the cover.

"Wow," Grace breathed. "Just, wow. The next morning, after your night of grand passion. What happened?"

"Nothing. I woke up, and Eric had gone for his ten-mile run," Suzanne said, her shoulders slumped. "When he got back, he disappeared into his office for the rest of the afternoon. Then, Darby got home from the tournament, and, well, things went right back to the way they'd been."

"Did you ever talk about that night?" Wyatt asked. "Did you tell Eric how much you enjoyed it? Or try doing the same thing again?"

"No," Suzanne said, her voice small. "The time just never seemed right. And not long afterward, I . . . discovered he was cheating on me. So there wasn't any point to any of this, was there?"

"You had fabulous sex! There's always a point to that," Ashleigh said.

After the laughter died down, Grace brought up something that had been on her mind since the first night she'd met Suzanne.

"Suzanne, you say you and Darby are really, really close. And it sounds like you're pretty wrapped up in her life and her soccer and everything. I'm wondering if maybe you're too involved."

"Yeah, maybe you're one of those helicopter parents I hear about," Ashleigh said. "Why do they always call them that, I wonder?"

"Because those are the parents who're always hovering right over their kids' shoulders, doing their work for them, or interfering with teachers or coaches, or whatever," Camryn said. "I did a story about it. It's a real problem."

"Helicopter parents? That's ridiculous," Rochelle scoffed. "You've never had kids, Grace or Ashleigh, so you don't understand. Suzanne is a great mom. Darby's a senior this year, right, Suzanne? So this is will be her last year at home before going off to college. It's totally understandable that you want to be part of her life. When Grace was in school, I never missed a class play or one of her tennis matches."

"Maybe," Wyatt said, carefully choosing his words, "you got so wrapped up in your daughter's life, you forgot to pay enough attention to your husband. Maybe Eric felt, I don't know, neglected?"

"Spoken just like a man!" Rochelle snapped. "Honest to Pete, I am so tired of hearing men make excuses for their own bad behavior. If her husband was feeling neglected, maybe he should have gone to those soccer tournaments with them, instead of sleeping with any woman who caught his eye. Right, Suzanne?"

"Maybe," Suzanne said quietly. "Maybe if Eric was feeling abandoned, he could have told me that. Or maybe I should have made more of a point of including him. I just don't know anything."

"You knew enough to kick his cheating butt to the curb," Rochelle said. She glanced over her shoulder and saw a tall black man with a gleaming bald head standing pointedly in front of the cash register at the bar. She jumped up. "Oh, Lord. There's Garland, from the health department. Hold that thought," she told Suzanne. "I'll be right back."

Five minutes later, Rochelle returned to the table, grim-faced, with Sweetie clutched firmly under her arm.

She glared at Grace. "Of all the dumb luck. Garland drops in for a beer, and this little mutt comes scampering down the back staircase and into the kitchen." She thrust the dog at Grace. "You know anything about this?"

Grace sighed and held the wriggling dog against her chest. "This is Sweetie. She was left behind at Mandevilla Manor. I know you don't like dogs, but . . ."

"But you decided you'd bring her here to the Sandbox. Are you crazy? We can't have a dog in a restaurant. You want the health department on my ass? I could lose my license, if Garland decided to report this."

Grace glanced over her shoulder. Garland gave her a stern look and waggled a finger at her. "I'm really sorry. I thought I'd closed my door tight. I don't know how she got out. I'll take her back upstairs."

"And then find her a new home, tomorrow," Rochelle said firmly.

Grace carried Sweetie to her bedroom and examined the door where the dog had scratched and clawed to escape.

She carried Sweetie into the bathroom and set her down on the floor. Sweetie gave her a quizzical look. Grace sat on the edge of the bathtub, to lecture the dog at eye level.

"I know you don't like being penned up, but you just can't go downstairs, or you'll get me kicked out of my mom's house. And then we'll both be homeless." She pulled a treat from her pocket and tossed it to Sweetie, who caught it and retreated beneath the pedestal sink to savor it.

"Stay here for now, and we'll figure something out tomorrow," she promised, giving her a final, reassuring head scratch.

. . .

When Grace got back to the bar, the group was still having a spirited discussion and Rochelle was back behind the bar. She set a fresh basket of popcorn on the table and tried to avoid her mother's disapproving stare from across the room.

"What did I miss?" she asked.

"Just a lot more man bashing," Wyatt said, helping himself to a handful of popcorn. "The usual."

Camryn rolled her eyes. "It seems like Suzanne's husband was jealous of all the time she spent with their daughter, so that's his excuse for having an affair?"

"Affairs. Plural," Suzanne said quietly. "But I wouldn't really characterize them as affairs. More like one-night stands, from what I could find out."

"Oh, no." Grace blurted. "That's so awful."

"Like my asshole husband," Camryn said disgustedly. "Men really are such shits."

"Thanks," Wyatt said. He stood up and pulled some money from his pockets. "On that note, I think I'll just take my sorry, shitty man self on home and let you girls continue the vagina monologues." He did a little half bow. "Ladies?"

Camryn reached out and caught him by the elbow as he started to walk out. "Don't be such a wuss, Wyatt. You know I wasn't talking about you."

"Don't go!" Ashleigh pleaded. "We really don't hate all men. Well, I don't. I don't know about the others." She turned to Suzanne. "You tell him."

"Please stay," Suzanne echoed. "We want to hear a man's point of view. Right, Grace?"

She could feel Wyatt watching her, one eyebrow cocked expectantly.

"Right," she said finally, looking anywhere but directly at him.

Camryn tugged impatiently at his arm. "Come on, dude. Sit back down. Don't make us beg."

"It's getting late," Wyatt said, his resolve ebbing a little.

"It's not even nine o'clock yet," Ashleigh pointed out. "And didn't you tell us your little boy stays with your wife on weeknights?"

"We alternate days. I pick him up after school tomorrow," Wyatt admitted.

Camryn was steering him back toward the table. "What about you?" she asked, after he'd sat down again. "You've got a kid. Did you ever resent your wife spending more time with your son than with you?"

Wyatt took a sip of his beer. "Maybe when Bo was just a baby, yeah, I probably felt a little left out, especially when Callie was nursing him. Things got better after the pediatrician convinced her she could pump breast milk and let me take the early-morning feedings so she could get some sleep."

"You did that?" Grace turned to him in surprise.

"Sure," Wyatt said, shrugging. "It was kind of cool. I'd take Bo out to the living room, give him his bottle, and we'd watch cartoons until we both fell back asleep. I swear, he loved *Phineas and Ferb* when he was only six weeks old. He'd laugh his little ass off."

Camryn shook her head. "Dexter Nobles used to sleep right through those midnight feedings. And I don't remember him changing all that many diapers either."

"Eric changed a lot of diapers, and sometimes he'd sit up and read aloud to me while I nursed Darby," Suzanne said wistfully. "I kind of miss those days."

"He read to you? That's so sweet," Ashleigh said. "What did he read?"

"*Harry Potter,* actually," Suzanne said. "A college classmate who was living in the U.K. sent us the first book as a baby gift for Darby. Another nice memory I'd completely forgotten about."

"How about you all? Suzanne asked, polling the others. "Did anybody else come up with any deeply repressed happy moments?"

Ashleigh wrinkled her nose. "I didn't really get that question when Paula asked it. See, I was happy right up until Boyce started up with that Suchita chick."

"Any one, particular memory?" Suzanne queried.

"Oh yeah," Ashleigh said, dreamy-eyed. "One of the drug companies had a 'seminar' for plastic surgeons in the Napa Valley back in the fall. They put us up in this fabulous old inn in the wine country. Boyce and I drove over to Calistoga and did a couples-only mud bath and massage . . ." She giggled. "We got pretty naughty. I ended up with mud in the most *interesting* places . . ."

"Spare us any more smutty details," Camryn said drily. "We get the picture."

"Your turn," Ashleigh said, pointing right back at her. "And don't try telling us you were never happy. You were married longer than any of us, right? There must be some reason you stayed with your husband all those years."

Camryn sighed. "The last really happy time? I'd have to say it was that first

Christmas Jana was old enough to understand about Santa Claus. Dexter bought her this ridiculously expensive Victorian dollhouse with about a million itty-bitty pieces to it. That night, after we put her to bed, we put on my Johnny Mathis CD, and he popped a bottle of champagne he'd been saving for a special occasion. We stayed up drinking and laughing and dancing to Johnny Mathis. "I Saw Mommy Kissing Santa Claus" came on, and the next thing you know, we'd forgotten all about that dollhouse . . ." She blushed. "I sound like Ashleigh now, spilling about our sex life. Of course, that was fifteen years ago."

"You've really been that unhappy all this time?" Grace asked.

Camryn rested her elbows on the table and propped her chin on her hands while she thought about it.

"I guess I was going with the flow. At one point, when Jana was about eight, I realized things weren't great. But then Dexter made partner at his law firm, and I finally got hired on at News Four. We bought the new house with the pool and we put Jana in private school at Saint Stephen's, which was not cheap. And I thought, why rock the boat? Things will get better. But they never did. I should've ended it a long time ago. Before things turned ugly like this."

"Graaaaccce?" Ashleigh tilted her nearly empty glass. "Is your mom coming back? 'Cause I could use another of her 'ritas."

"I'll get it," Grace stood.

"And then it's your turn to share," Camryn said, making quote marks with the fingertips of both hands. "So don't think we're going to forget."

Rochelle deliberately turned her back to Grace when she walked behind the bar. "I'm fixing Ashleigh another fake margarita," she told her mother. "Could you add it to our tab?"

"Is the dog locked up?" she asked pointedly.

"She's in the bathroom, taking a nap," Grace assured her. "It won't happen again."

"We're waiting," Wyatt said pointedly, when Grace returned to the table with Ashleigh's drink.

She stuck her tongue out at him. "I notice you haven't read from your journal tonight."

"But I shared. And it was honest and it was meaningful," he taunted. "Right, ladies?"

"Come on, Grace. Your turn." Ashleigh noisily sipped her fakearita.

"Okay, okay," Grace grumbled. She pulled her notebook from her bag and skimmed what she'd written.

"I'd never lived in a real house, until Ben and I bought our first little place in Bradenton. It was the worst house on the street. Concrete-block and less than a thousand square feet. Two tiny bedrooms, one miserable bath that didn't even have a shower, a galley kitchen so narrow that when you opened the oven door it almost touched the cabinet on the opposite wall. The countertops were plywood covered with plastic tile."

"Sounds dreamy," Camryn said.

"I knew we could make it dreamy. But we had zero money to work with."

Ashleigh waved her hand in the air. "Excuse me, Grace, but when does the happy-memory part come in? Because, so far, this is all sounding pretty grim to me."

"That was just the setup. The prologue," Grace said. She flipped through the pages of her notebook and began reading.

"I was working for a big developer in Sarasota, designing their model-home interiors. This was before the economy tanked, when condos were selling as fast as they could put them up. Ben was an account executive with an advertising and marketing company. We'd work all day, then go straight to the house, change clothes, and work 'til one or two in the morning, go back to the condo we were renting, fall into bed, then get up and do the same thing the next day. For six months, we worked every weekend. Some nights we were too tired to even drive home, so we'd just crash on a mattress on the living room floor. Neither Ben nor I had any real do-it-yourself skills. So we taught ourselves. It was all a huge adventure, and we were in it together. We just figured if we messed up, we'd rip it out and start over. We were absolutely fearless. One night, I wanted to put up this ten-inch cove-ceiling molding in the living room. We had exactly enough to do that one room, and I knew it would be fabulous. Ben bet me I couldn't do it. And of course, I totally messed it up and ended up in tears. He took pity on me, took over, and somehow made it work. But it took hours. It was close to midnight by the time we ate our dinner of Chinese takeout and cheap jug wine, sitting on overturned plastic joint-compound buckets. We got silly drunk and ended up naked, hosing each other off in the backyard. And Ben won the bet, so you can probably figure out what happened next. I can't remember a happier time in our life together."

Grace closed the notebook. She heard a soft exhalation of breath from somewhere behind and turned just in time to see Rochelle, scurrying back toward the kitchen.

"Good night," Grace said, walking out into the Sandbox parking lot with the others. They'd discussed what to do about Paula but hadn't come to any kind of consensus. "Let's see what happens next Wednesday," Suzanne had suggested, and short of any other brilliant ideas, they'd agreed to do just that.

She'd turned to go back inside. "Hey, Grace?" She turned and saw Wyatt, standing in the shadow of a clump of palm trees.

"Hi," she said.

"Can I talk to you?"

"Okay." She leaned up against the bumper of his truck and squinted to see his face in the flickering green and red light cast by the bar's neon sign.

"Wow. That rash or whatever it is on your face really looks painful," she said.

"The stuff on my face isn't the worst of it," Wyatt said, grimacing and jerking his chin downward, toward his belt line.

"Oh." She caught his meaning and grimaced, too. "Sorry."

"I'll be okay. As soon as I get home, I'll, uh, apply the cortisone cream. And take some Benadryl and drift off to la-la land."

"I hope you feel better," she said, sounding cold and insincere, even to herself.

"I hope you mean that," Wyatt said. "I know I screwed up at Coquina Beach."

Grace stepped sideways in order to escape the flash of the neon, to hide her confusion and embarrassment.

Wyatt cleared his throat. "Look. I'm not good at this crap. I wasn't good at it when I was a teenager, and I sure as hell haven't gained any momentum with age. I just wanted to tell you . . . don't write me off. Okay? I really, really like you. The other night? That was great. Really, really great. I wanted to kick myself in the ass afterward."

Grace just looked at him.

"Is any of this making any sense to you?"

"Not really."

He sighed. "Instead of divorce recovery, they should have dating-reentry therapy. For dweebs like me who never figured this stuff out."

She had to laugh then. "Dating reentry. Not a bad idea. Maybe you should suggest that to Paula. If we ever see her again."

"The point is, I think maybe I had a breakthrough when I was at Stackpole's office with Callie today."

"Oh?"

"She hates me. My wife, soon to be ex, hates me. I don't exactly know why, but she does. And to tell you the truth, I'm not so crazy about her, either. Maybe your mom is right. Maybe Bo is better off if we just split up and get on with our lives."

"And if Callie gets her way and moves to Birmingham and takes Bo with her?"

"Right now, Stackpole seems like he's switched sides. But whatever he decides to do, I'm gonna fight that as hard as I can, to keep them from taking him away," he said, his jaw tightening. "Not just because I'd miss my son, but because I know those two aren't fit to raise him. He's an afterthought to them. A bargaining chip."

Grace did what she'd been wanting to do all evening. She reached out and brushed his face with the palm of her hand. He caught her hand in his and kissed the back of it.

"For a guy, you're not so bad," she said.

He pulled her closer, wrapping his arms around her waist. "And for a man-hating ball buster, you're not so bad yourself."

She leaned in and closed her eyes.

The screened door from the kitchen flew open, and Rochelle stuck her head out. Her voice echoed in the still evening air. "Grace? Your goddamn dog was upstairs whining to get out."

Sweetie scampered out into the crushed-shell lot, looked up at Grace and Wyatt for only a moment, then discreetly trotted around the palm tree to complete her toilette in private.

31

Grace scooped the little brown dog up into her arms. Sweetie squirmed in ecstasy, covering her chin and neck with kibble-flavored kisses. "Poor little girl," Grace said. She looked at Wyatt over the dog's ears. "Sweetie hates being locked up. I think she has the doggie version of post-traumatic stress disorder. So that's that. I've got to figure out something else."

"She really won't let you keep a dog? Not even after you explain the circumstances?"

"She's not a dog person. And anyway, it's against all kinds of health codes," Grace said. "Guess I'd better start looking for an apartment."

"Can you afford that?"

"Not really."

He hesitated. "Look, I was going to suggest this anyway. Why don't you let me keep Sweetie at my place?"

"Oh no," Grace interrupted. "I found her and adopted her. She's my responsibility."

"Just hear me out. You could keep Sweetie with you during the day while you're working at the house on Mandevilla, and she could stay with me over at Jungle Jerry's, nights, and any other time you need her to. She'd love it there. The whole place is fenced in, so there's no way she could run off and get hurt. She can sleep in the house with us at night. I'll fix her a bed right beside Bo's.

He'll be crazy for her. He's been bugging me to get him a dog, and I was going to, but then Callie started busting my chops about that, claiming I'd just be doing it to get back at her."

"I don't understand how your having a dog affects her," Grace said.

"Luke's allergic. Or so he claims. Funny, though. He has this huge Siamese cat, and that doesn't seem to bother his allergies. The cat hates Bo, scratches him every time it gets a chance."

"I don't know . . ." Grace hugged Sweetie to her chest. "It's crazy, but I'm already so attached to her. She sleeps on the pillow next to me. And she's such good company."

"It'd just be 'til you get your own place," Wyatt promised. "Think of it as temporary joint custody. But I swear, I won't pull any of Callie's custody crap."

Grace scratched Sweetie's chin. "No alienation of affection? No bribing her with special dog treats?"

He held up his hand in the Boy Scout pledge. "I'll never drop her off late for visitation or forget to bring her leash."

"Well . . ." Grace sighed. "I guess that will work. If you're really sure she won't be an imposition."

"She won't be. I can take her home right now, if you want."

"I'll just run upstairs and get her stuff," Grace said. Wyatt held out his arms, and she reluctantly handed Sweetie over.

Five minutes later she was back, having hauled an overflowing black trash bag down the outside stairway from her room.

"All of that? You haven't even had her a week and she already has more stuff than I do." Wyatt took the bag and set it on the front seat of the truck.

Grace edged around him and began showing him Sweetie's belongings. "Her bed is in the bottom here. But, like I said, she likes to sleep with me."

"Who wouldn't?"

She frowned. "Is that a line? Somehow it doesn't sound right, coming from you."

"I got lines," Wyatt said. "I've got moves, too. I'm a little rusty from lack of practice, that's all."

She lifted two stainless steel bowls from the bag and set them on the seat. "Here's her water bowl, and here's her food bowl. I put the dog food in here, too. I give her a cup in the morning and a cup in late afternoon."

"Got it."

Grace handed him a pink leopard-print leash with lime-green banding. "Here's her leash. I let her out first thing in the morning. But she won't go right away. You have to walk her around a little bit, let her sniff things out before she picks her spot."

He handed the leash right back to Grace. "You keep this one. I'll get her one that's a little less, uh, girly."

"Nothing too butch," she warned him. "And no camo. Sweetie has standards." She went on unloading the bag.

"Here's her Greenies. I give her one last thing at night."

He wrinkled his nose. "Greenies?"

"They're supposed to promote healthy teeth and gums. And help with the whole doggie-breath thing."

"You're kidding."

She raised one eyebrow, which shut him up, then continued with her inventory. "Brush."

"Brush," he repeated.

"Pillowcase."

He held up the pink and white striped case with a questioning look.

"It's the one I usually sleep on," Grace admitted. "I read that dogs can get separation anxiety. This one smells like me. So she won't feel like she's in a strange place. Just put it in her bed, okay?"

"Okay."

She went back to unloading the bag. "Flea and tick medicine. She gets it once a month."

"Once a month."

"Heartworm meds. Again, once a month. I put it in the middle of a little peanut butter sandwich, so she won't figure out it's good for her."

"Peanut butter," he repeated dutifully, putting the meds back into the trash bag. "Is that it?"

"One last thing," she promised. "Chew toy." She reached in the bag and pulled out a nude Ken doll.

Wyatt held the doll up to the light and examined the teeth marks ringing Ken's overly tanned buttocks.

"Is this supposed to be symbolic?"

"Not at all," Grace said. "The first night I brought her home, Sweetie was rooting around in the closet in my bedroom and she found it in a box of my old toys and dolls. She loves Ken. It's the cutest thing, the way she carries him around in her mouth."

"You couldn't let her chew up a Barbie doll?" He handed the doll back to her.

"She likes Ken," Grace said, with a shrug.

He handed the doll back to her. "If it's just the same to you, I'll get her a ball or a squeaky cat or something else to chew on while she's at my place."

Grace looked down at the Ken doll. "I'll take this over to Mandevilla and keep it there for her."

"Good." Wyatt propped the little dog on his forearm. "Say good night, Sweetie."

Grace caressed the dog's ears and gave her one more head scratch, then looked up at Wyatt.

"Call me if you need me. Really. Like, if she won't sleep or she starts that scratching-at-the-door-and-whining thing, I could come over and calm her down."

Wyatt cupped Grace's chin in his hand. "She'll be fine. Stop worrying. I'll bring her over to you at Mandevilla first thing in the morning." He set the dog down gently on the passenger seat and closed the door.

"I'm there by eight," Grace said, following him around to the driver's side. "You won't forget to give her the pillowcase, right?"

He got into the truck and leaned out the open window. "Stop being such a helicopter parent."

She opened her mouth to protest, but she didn't have a chance, because suddenly he was kissing her. Both his hands were tangled in her hair, and he pulled her right up against the door and teased her lips open with his tongue. The kiss lasted another minute or so, and left Grace breathless and dazed. And hot. When a car pulled alongside the truck, she reluctantly pulled away.

"See?" Wyatt said, grinning as he put the truck into reverse. "Moves."

32

The little cottage—okay, he could call it a cottage, but it was really a glorified double-wide—was ablaze with lights when he pulled the truck under the carport. Wyatt tucked Sweetie under one arm and carried her and her luggage inside.

"Home sweet trailer," he said, setting her down on the vinyl floor. She took a few tentative steps and sniffed one of Bo's discarded flip-flops before picking it up in her mouth and turning to him, as if asking permission.

"Knock yourself out," Wyatt said generously. "It's way better than a Ken doll, right?"

He could hear the television in the back room. "Dad? He called loudly. All his conversations with Nelson had to be at top volume these days. He walked toward the tiny den and poked his head around the doorway. The recliner was facing the television, but there was no tell-tale tuft of white hair poking above the headrest. "Dad?"

The chair was empty, the television turned to a *Law and Order* rerun. A plate with the remains of a chicken potpie sat on the folding TV tray beside the recliner. Wyatt felt his pulse blip. He passed the open bathroom door, knocked softly on Nelson's closed bedroom door. "Hey old man," he called. "You sleeping?" When there was no answer, he opened the door to find the room empty and the bed still made, the worn quilt folded neatly at its foot. The room smelled like his father, like Old Spice and Bengay. But where the hell had the old man gotten to?

He opened the back door and peered out into the darkness. "Dad?" Nothing. He gave a soft whistle and Sweetie dropped her flip-flop and trotted over, her nails clicking on the harvest-gold vinyl flooring. "Come on girl, let's take a walk and find Granddad." Now he wished he'd taken that ridiculous pink leash.

"Stay here," he told the dog. He went out to the carport and rummaged around until he found a length of clothesline. Back in the house, he found a flashlight and fashioned a makeshift leash from the rope.

His heart was pounding as he stepped out of the cottage. It was nearly ten. His father was usually fast asleep by now, either in his recliner or his room. Nelson's car, a gas-guzzling Olds, was parked in the carport, its hood covered in a fine haze of cobwebs and pine needles. He seldom drove it anymore, claiming his night vision was fading, but Wyatt suspected his father probably realized his driving days were mostly over. Now he noticed that the golf cart was missing. He cursed softly.

Sweetie sat on her haunches and looked up at him expectantly. What was it Timmy used to tell Lassie in those old Nick at Night reruns? "What's that girl? Granddad fell down the old well?" Only Sweetie was definitely not a collie, and as far as he knew, there were no abandoned wells at Jungle Jerry's Olde Florida Family Fun Park.

"Let's take a walk," he said in a surprisingly calm voice. Sweetie inched forward, testing the air with her nose, and then set off at a trot. For lack of a better idea, Wyatt let her take the lead, playing the flashlight over the curtains of green. It was a typical summer night in Florida, the air nearly dripping with humidity. Clouds of mosquitoes swarmed his already-inflamed face, and the smell of night-blooming jasmine blanketed the thick spongy air. Sweetie trotted on, heading past the huge old banyan tree with its sinister-looking tracery of roots draping from the elephant-gray lower limbs, and around the reflecting pool with its island rookery for herons and egrets nesting in the moss-draped cypress trees. The moon was nearly full and its reflection was a butter-yellow orb in the black water of the pool. Every hundred yards or so, the little brown dog stopped, sniffed, and then readjusted her course.

Sweetie, Wyatt thought, had a lot more hunting dog in her gene pool than he would have guessed.

They were just rounding the Nursery Rhyme Garden, with its two-story concrete Mother Hubbard shoe when a pair of sharp cracks pierced the still night air. Wyatt knew that sound. It was Nelson's double-gauge shotgun.

Sweetie pricked up her ears and took off at a surprisingly fast full run, with Wyatt following close behind, the flashlight's beam bouncing off the landscape. She was barking now, excited and on full alert. She made a sharp right turn at the stand of crimson-flowering royal poinciana trees, and Wyatt realized she was headed for the area they'd always called Birdland, because it was where all the tropical bird cages and the parrot-show amphitheater were located.

The little dog barked as she ran, and Wyatt's mind conjured up every conceivable tragedy as he sprinted through the thick tropical foliage. Maybe his father had gotten confused and wandered off into the darkness, on the golf cart, armed with his favorite old shotgun. Maybe he'd imagined an intruder and gone to investigate. None of the story lines flashing through his imagination had a happy ending.

Finally, Sweetie skidded to a stop. She sat on her haunches, her ears folded back, a deep, guttural growl rising in her throat, aimed at some unseen enemy lurking in the darkness.

Silvery moonlight revealed Nelson Keeler, sitting on one of the splintery green-painted benches ringing the amphitheater, his shotgun resting across his pajama-clad knees. In the round, chicken-wire-ringed aviary nearby, Cookie, the African gray parrot, hopped agitatedly from foot to foot. "Shots and beer, shots and beer," the bird muttered.

"Hey, son!" Nelson exclaimed, spying him. Sweetie stayed where she was, on full alert, growling menacingly.

"Dad?" Wyatt sank down onto the bench beside his father. "What's going on?" He was out of breath, bewildered. "What are you doing out here?"

Nelson pointed into a clump of ferns and bromeliads ringing the aviaries. "I got the sumbitch. One clean shot. The second for insurance."

Wyatt's heart sank. For months now, the park had been the target of petty criminals. Twice, they'd managed to break into the gift shop, stealing less than fifty dollars' worth of cash, some cases of coke, and some stale candy bars. Another time, they'd gone farther into the park and attempted to cut through the wire to steal the parrots, apparently thwarted by the hue and cry raised by Cookie and the others. Although Wyatt viewed the crimes as a nuisance, Nelson had been enraged at the idea of anybody breaching the admittedly lapse security at Jungle Jerry's.

A dozen years earlier, they'd had the park wired for an alarm system and installed motion-detector cameras. Now, though, the technology was outdated and the cameras were inoperable. And they didn't have the money to install a new security system.

For a week or so, after the last break-in, Nelson had taken to patrolling the grounds on the golf cart Wyatt used for landscaping, finally growing bored after encountering nothing more than a few errant fruit rats on his nocturnal rounds.

Had his father shot and killed some young punk? Wyatt took a deep breath. "Who'd you get, Dad? Where is he?"

"Over there," Nelson gestured. "He slunk off into the ferns. See the blood? He's dead, though. I guarantee you. I nailed the sumbitch."

Wyatt's stomach turned as he observed the fine spatter of bloodstains on the crushed-shell walkway. He stood, and Sweetie took that as a signal to advance. She crept forward, her round belly scraping the sand, her nose sweeping back and forth. Five yards from the clump of ferns, she sat straight up on her haunches and growled again.

He held his breath as he played his flashlight over the greenery. Sweetie stayed close to his side on high alert. Finally, he saw where the trail of crimson ended. At first he thought it was a clump of Spanish moss. But as he grew closer, he spied a muzzle in a ghostly shade of gray, and then what looked like the emaciated body of a dog. He turned and glanced back at his father, who'd risen on shaking legs to follow them to the spot.

"What the hell is that?" Even as he said it, he realized what the form was.

"Coyote," Nelson said grimly. He turned and pointed to an aviary at the edge of the amphitheater. The wire door was ajar and the tree-limb perch was vacant. Brilliant red and yellow scarlet macaw feathers littered the cage floor. "Sumbitch got Heckel and Jekyll. I'm sorry, son."

The two macaws were the park's most senior residents, having been bought by Wyatt's grandfather in the late sixties. At one time they'd been a featured attraction in the parrot show, but now the colorful birds were officially retired from active duty. Wyatt patted his father's shoulder. "Not your fault, Dad. I'd heard about coyote sightings in and around town, but for some reason it never occurred to me they might turn up here."

"The hell it wasn't my fault," Nelson said gruffly. "I'm the one who fed all the birds today. I guess I must have left the macaws' cage unlatched. They were so old and lazy, it probably never occurred to them to try to fly away. The damned coyote had already finished 'em both off by the time I heard Cookie screaming and got over here on the cart."

Wyatt went to Cookie's cage, unlocked it, and reached in. He extended his hand and the bird gingerly walked up his arm to his shoulder. "Hey, Cookie," he said. "You're one hell of an alarm system." The gray parrot cocked its head and seemed to wink at him. "Gimme a beer," she said. He fished in his pocket and brought out a bird treat instead. "Performance bonus," Wyatt said. When the parrot finished chewing, Wyatt placed her back in the aviary and locked and double-checked it. Then, he walked around and checked the other cages. Marilyn and Lana, the cockatoos, were huddled together in the far corner of their cage, and Elvis, the huge blue and gold macaw, improbably, seemed to be sleeping.

"Okay, everybody's safe and accounted for," he said finally. "C'mon, Dad, it's late. Let's go home. I'll come back in the morning and bury the coyote." Wyatt took the shotgun from his father and placed it in the cargo hold of the cart, then climbed behind the wheel. Sweetie hopped up onto the bench seat beside him.

Nelson lowered himself into the cart, looking down at the dog in surprise. "Who's this?"

"This is Sweetie," Wyatt said, backing the cart up and heading down the path toward the house. "She's gonna be staying with us for a while." He reached over and ruffled the dogs' ears. "I think she'll fit in nicely around here, don't you?"

The old man regarded the dog with a practiced eye. "Got a lot of poodle in her. Maybe some schnauzer or cocker spaniel. Poodles used to be great hunting dogs, before they started being bred as silly show dogs. Did you know that?"

"I didn't," Wyatt said.

"Where'd you say you got her?"

"A woman in my divorce-recovery group found her in an abandoned house. She's living with her mom right now, over in Cortez, but the health regs don't allow a dog to live in a bar, so I said Sweetie could stay with us until Grace moves into her own place."

"Cortez?"

"Yeah. Her parents own the Sandbox. You remember that place?"

"Sure. Used to take you there when you were a little kid, after we'd been over at Holmes Beach. You used to love their cheeseburgers. This Grace, is she Butch Davenport's daughter?"

"Yeah. Did you know him?"

"Everybody in Manatee County knew Butch Davenport. He was quite a character. Is he still around?"

"No, he passed away a few years ago. Rochelle, Grace's mom, runs the Sandbox now."

"And what's your connection to this Grace person?" Nelson frowned. "You going out with her? Hanging out in dive bars like the Sandbox with her? Before your divorce is final? You better hope Callie and her lawyer don't get wind of that."

"Callie is living with her boyfriend, and has been for months now, so I don't think she has anything to say about my personal life. Anyway, like I just told you, Grace is in my divorce-recovery group. The whole group goes to the Sandbox after our meetings, just to sort of unwind. I have a beer or two and come home. End of story."

"But you like this girl."

"I do," Wyatt nodded. "She's a nice person. You'd like her, too."

"You sleeping with her?"

Wyatt felt his face burn. "Jesus, Dad! No. Where'd you get an idea like that?"

Nelson shrugged but said nothing else.

Wyatt pulled the golf cart under the carport and switched it off. Nelson unfolded himself from the seat, grunting with the effort, clutching the side of the cart for balance, swaying a little as he stood, trying to catch his breath.

And it struck Wyatt again: his father was aging before his eyes. The vagueness, forgetfulness, especially in the evenings, these had crept up and even accelerated since Wyatt had moved in with him. Nelson had always been strong—even into his sixties; he was fit and used to hard physical labor. Now, though, his gait had slowed and his energy level was diminished. It was all he could do to putter around the gift shop or the office a few hours in the morning before he returned to the cottage for a nap and endless hours of television.

He followed Nelson into the cottage, making sure the old man got safely into his bed before walking around the cramped cottage, switching off the lights and the television. The thin walls seemed to close in on him, choking him with claustrophobia. Sweetie followed close on his heels, seemingly sensing Wyatt's restlessness.

He held the back door open. "Come on then, let's go for a midnight ride."

. . .

As the cart jolted along the shell pathway, the headlight picked out the shaggy, overgrown landscape. Just like his father, Jungle Jerry's was aging, and not gracefully. Even the moonlight did not become it.

In his mind, Wyatt ticked off the unending items of maintenance that needed tending to. The gift shop's roof was leaking badly. He'd patched it so many times himself that the patches outnumbered the original asphalt roofing. The crushed-shell parking lot was pocked with potholes and washouts, and half the neon in the Jungle Jerry's sign had burned out.

In the park itself, dead or half-dead trees stood, waiting to be trimmed or cut down. The flower beds were choked with weeds and vines, and the abundant rain-forest plants swallowed whole sections of the pathways. His earlier visit to the amphitheater reminded him that half the benches there were rotted or splintered and all of them needed painting or replacing. The aviaries his grandfather had built decades ago for the tropical birds were rusting and were too small by current-day standards.

And that was just the physical plant, Wyatt mused. With only three employees—him; Joyce, his bookkeeper, ticket taker, and gift-shop manager; and Eduardo, who helped out with maintenance and landscaping—there were never enough bodies or hours or funds to get everything done.

Probably, Wyatt thought, he should have been smarter about all this. Six years earlier, not long before Bo's birth, a developer had offered to buy the park from the family for what seemed like a stunning amount of money—three million. His parents had considered taking the money and making the deal, but Wyatt, young and stupid and full of plans and dreams for the family business he intended to nurture for his unborn son—had urged them not to sell. How could they let a shopping center and yet another condo complex erupt on this gorgeous garden his grandparents had worked so hard to create?

Even then, Jungle Jerry's was struggling. They weren't losing money, but they weren't making much money either. Wyatt was certain he could turn things around. He'd taken marketing classes in college, had all kinds of ideas to drag the park into the twenty-first century. Callie had been furious with him. How could he be so stupid? All that money would have set them up for life! She'd raged at him for weeks after his parents turned down all that delicious money.

And then, before he could even get a Web site designed for the park, the economy tanked. Their attendance figures plummeted, and developers quit calling. Every month, the aging park went deeper into debt.

Wyatt steered the golf cart through the empty parking lot, hanging onto Sweetie's collar to keep her from flying off as the cart jounced through the potholes.

He fought the urge to surrender to the melancholy mood of the evening. Not everything in his life was crap. Earlier in the day he'd won one tiny battle against Callie. Starting tomorrow, he would have Bo for the weekend. He glanced over at Sweetie, sitting erect on the golf cart beside him. And maybe, just maybe, he would find a way to convince the dog's real owner that he wasn't such a total jerk after all.

33

She'd set her alarm for 6:00 A.M. Her to-do list for Mandevilla was long and getting longer, and she was eager to get to work. Grace opened her laptop and clicked on the comments section of TrueGrace.

This was her favorite part of blogging. Styling, photographing, writing, editing, and coming up with new ideas fed her creative soul, but hearing from readers was what kept her motivated. When she'd first started writing Gracenotes, she would stay up for hours after publishing a post, clicking and refreshing, anxious and nervous to see if anybody out there in the darkness was reading her work.

Now, she gasped. More than three dozen readers had left remarks about her last post. She clicked over to her dashboard and saw that over two hundred readers were now subscribing to the blog feed, meaning they would be automatically notified whenever Grace posted a new article.

A typical post on Gracenotes, where she had 239,000 subscribers, would have generated a couple hundred comments. But she was starting over now, from scratch, and each and every one of these readers and commenters were like gold for TrueGrace.

"Yay," she said, in a small voice. Then, louder. "Oh hell yeah, yay!"

Scanning the comments, her smile grew wider. "Go, Grace," said Justamom32.

"Love your new blog. So much more approachable and attainable," commented Wild4Style.

Of course the naysayers showed up for the party, too. "I liked your old blog better." Or, "Why don't you take some photography classes and get yourself a decent camera?" And, "Not much new or original here. All your ideas are tired and clichéd." All of the negative comments, not to her surprise, were anonymous. Her finger hovered over the delete button for a moment, but then she read a note left by Rinquedink. "Hey, Grace, don't let those bitches get you down. Haters gonna hate, taters gonna tate."

Ben had always monitored the comments on Gracenotes, deleting anything that even smacked of criticism. No, Grace decided, she would only delete comments that were obscene, libelous, or obvious spam. She'd let her readers make up their minds themselves on what was spurious.

The final comment made her laugh out loud. "I've deleted that fraud, faux Gracenotes, from my feed. You really are the one, true Grace. Wishing blessings for you and the ex-husband genital herpes." It was signed CindyLouWhoo.

When she got out of the shower, Grace checked her e-mail and saw that she had responses from six of the bloggers she'd contacted to request a place on their blog roll. The first message she clicked on was from a lifestyle blogger who called herself Eleganza.

Eleganza's real name, as everybody in the blogosphere knew, was Kennedy Moore. She'd been a contributing editor at several of Grace's favorite, now-defunct shelter magazines, including *House and Garden* and *Southern Accents.*

Grace knew Kennedy's backstory by heart. She'd been an interior designer, like Grace, and then, in the late eighties, after her children were off to college, had gone to work in the magazine world. Along the way, she'd weathered a divorce, remarried, and, within the past five years, lost her adored second husband and then her job at *Southern Accents.*

Kennedy had reinvented herself as one of the first professional lifestyle bloggers, writing witty, original posts; posing question-and-answer sessions with big-name designers; and sharing photos of the transformation of Hedgehog Cottage, her own small farmhouse in rural Connecticut. Eleganza, which featured her very personal take on interior design, cooking, entertaining, and affordable luxury, was hugely influential in Grace's world.

Grace held her breath as she clicked on the e-mail.

Congratulations, Grace, for landing on your feet again. The little house on Mandevilla is a gem, and I can't wait to see what clever tricks you'll come up with to make it shine. I was sorry to hear of the end of your marriage, but as I know all too well from past experience, endings are really all about beginnings. I'll be happy to add you to my blog roll. As soon as you get one of your rooms furnished, please send me pics and we'll discuss you doing a guest post for Eleganza. All best, K.

If the room had been larger Grace would have turned a backflip. A guest post on Eleganza was at the top of her blogger bucket list. Kennedy Moore's blog was the biggest-drawing lifestyle blog in existence, with more than three million subscribers. Her advertisers ranged from Home Depot to Tiffany to Coke. And now, TrueGrace would be on the very short, very select Eleganza blog roll. She flopped back on her bed, kicking her legs in celebration.

Quickly, she read the other responses. All but one were warm welcomes from bloggers who'd formerly included Gracenotes on their blog rolls.

The sixth e-mail contained a sobering message.

Dear Grace. I'd be only too happy to add TrueGrace to my blog roll, but I just can't. I think you should know that certain people are out there making veiled threats to anybody who gives you a hand. Since my husband was laid off his job last year, my little blog and the money it generates is our family's sole income. Unfortunately, I can't afford to make any enemies right now. Wishing you all the best, PeanutButter&Jedi.

Grace blinked. Was Ben actually contacting other bloggers and threatening anybody who helped her? Obviously, the others who'd agreed to add her name to their rolls either hadn't been contacted by him or just didn't feel threatened.

PeanutButter&Jedi was an emerging mommy blogger from Denver whose blog had been one of the first Grace added after establishing Gracenotes. Susan, its author, was the mother of four young boys, including a set of triplets, and Grace loved reading her wry accounts of decorating their home on a budget, thrifting, and her inventive recipes.

She felt a tiny stab of fear. What, exactly, was Ben threatening? His contacts with their advertisers were extensive. Maybe he'd casually dropped a hint to those same advertisers that anybody associated with Grace was poison? Whatever he'd done, it was enough to scare off Susan at PeanutButter&Jedi. And how many others?

It didn't matter, she decided. Ben would do whatever he could do. J'Aimee could preen and poach off her blog, but she would never be anything more than a poser.

Suddenly, Grace's path seemed very clear. She thought back to that first house she and Ben had restored together. They'd had nothing but sweat and perseverance. It was a cliché, but they'd made lemons out of lemonade back then. She would do it again, she vowed. Without Ben, without his connections, without money. And without fear.

34

Grace stood in the paint aisle at the hardware store on Friday morning, staring at the huge display and its thousands of one-inch color chips. What she wouldn't do for her trusted paint fan-decks, with all the notes she'd scrawled on the backs of the cards and the yellow Post-it notes reminding her what paint strength and finish she favored for all her favorites. But the fan-deck, along with all her old files and design library, in fact, all her old life, were back at Sand Dollar Lane.

She knew she wanted the equivalent of either Farrow & Ball's White Tie or Pointing, two very specific whites for the walls at Mandevilla. Farrow & Ball itself was out of the question. Imported from England, it was just too expensive. She liked Benjamin Moore, too, which was what she'd used at Sand Dollar Lane, mostly because the Benjamin Moore paint store in Sarasota was one of her blog sponsors. She had shelves and shelves of BM paint at her old house. Now, however, neither paint would work for her tiny budget on Mandevilla. She sighed. Cheap paint always just looked shoddy to her eye, and using it would require at least three coats, which would take up too much of her precious time.

She walked around to the clearance endcap and scanned the assorted cans of "oops" paint cramming the shelves.

There was a logical reason these cans were marked down; they were mistints, custom colors that had been rejected by the original customer. Most of the gallon cans were in shades she deemed either truly heinous—a neon bubble-gum pink, a muddy-looking taupe, a sickly green that reminded her of gangrene—or they were just unsuitable for a simple vernacular cottage like Mandevilla.

She did, however, find six gallons of an innocuous white in Benjamin Moore's low-VOC paint, marked down to ten dollars a can. That she could afford. Grace pulled a can from the shelf and studied the dab of paint on the tin lid. This paint had been custom-tinted, so it didn't have a color name or a formula. The shade was what she'd always thought of as a "dead white." But maybe if she had it tinted?

The clerk at the paint counter was a middle-aged man in a red apron. Grace set the oops can on the counter. "Help you?" he asked.

She gave him her sweetest smile. "Hi there. I'm wondering if you can add a little something to this paint to brighten it up a bit?"

He looked puzzled. "Like what?"

"Well, I was thinking you could add a little black to tint it, to see if I like it better."

The clerk took a closer look at the paint can. "Sorry. This is an oops paint. See, the sign says all paint is "as-is." That means we don't remix or add tint."

Grace sighed dramatically. "Look, it just needs the teeniest amount of black paint. I'm trying to match it to Farrow and Ball's Pointing shade. It wouldn't take very much time, and I would be soooo grateful?"

This approach had always worked for her in the past—at furniture showrooms, fabric houses, plumbing-fixture showrooms. A sweet smile and a plea for mercy, especially with men, had always been a winning formula in the past.

The hardware store clerk, though, seemed immune to her charms. "Sorry. Store policy. Can't help you." He went back to working on a display of weed killer.

And Grace went back to the clearance counter, where she loaded up all six gallons of the dead white, along with a pint of black latex paint. She would just have to experiment with mixing her own paint. She added in two gallons of white latex enamel for the trim, a paint tray, a five-gallon plastic bucket, canvas drop cloth, and rollers and brushes, sighing, again, at the thought of her workshop back at Sand Dollar, where all of her painting equipment and tools were lined up neatly, ready for her next project. At the last minute she plucked six Benjamin Moore paint cards from the display, to give herself an idea of the shades she was trying to achieve.

When the cashier added up all her purchases and applied them to the account Arthur Cater had set up for her, she was shocked that she'd already managed to make a four-hundred-dollar dent in her five-thousand-dollar budget.

It was nearly nine by the time she pulled up to the new cottage. Wyatt's pickup was parked out front, but he and Sweetie were walking around the yard, inspecting the property.

Grace's heart skipped a little beat. She told herself it was because she was happy to see her dog. But maybe Wyatt Keeler had a little to do with it, too.

He was dressed in his khaki Jungle Jerry's safari shirt, cargo shorts, and work boots, and he was bare-headed, stooped over, examining some kind of weedy shrub near the right edge of the porch. He had, Grace reflected, a fine-looking butt, tanned, muscular calves and thighs, and an admirable set of shoulders across a nice, broad chest.

"Sweetie!" Grace called. The dog turned and looked at her and, after a moment, came bounding over. She gave an excited little yip and jumped up into Grace's outstretched arms.

Wyatt followed in her wake, but he did not jump into her arms. "I was just checking out the yard. Hope you don't mind."

"It's a disaster," Grace said, "like the inside of the house. If you've got any landscaping advice, I'd love to hear it. How'd Sweetie do last night? I hope she wasn't too much trouble."

"No trouble at all. I would have been here sooner this morning, but I had to bury a coyote."

She raised an eyebrow. "A coyote? Around here?"

"In the park. My dad heard the parrots raising a ruckus last night. Turned out to be a coyote. By the time he got to the old amphitheater, where we have the aviaries, the damned thing had already finished off two of our parrots."

"Oh no! Not Cookie. Please tell me the coyote didn't get Cookie," Grace said.

"Fortunately, no. Cookie's cage was locked up tight. But our macaws, Heckel and Jekyll, weren't so lucky," Wyatt said, his expression grim. "Dad shot the varmint before he could do any more damage."

"That's awful," Grace said, feeling a chill go down her spine. She hugged Sweetie closer and shivered, despite the ninety-degree heat. "Could a coyote attack a dog?"

"Maybe," Wyatt said. "But after what happened with the macaws, I won't let her roam around off a leash at night. She doesn't seem inclined to go very far from me anyway, which is probably a good thing."

"You're not kidding." Grace breathed. She set Sweetie down carefully in the yard. "So. What do you think of my little project?"

"Great house," Wyatt said. "I love these old Florida cracker places. Not too many of them left around here."

"I know," Grace said, warming to her subject. "Do you want to see the inside?"

He glanced at his watch. "Can I have a rain check? Dad's a little worn out from his big adventure last night. I need to stick pretty close to the park today."

"Sure," Grace said, feeling a little let down.

"This yard could be really pretty with some work," Wyatt said, gesturing at the shrub he'd just been examining. "You've got some nice specimen palms in the front here, and that hedge of gardenias by the porch is in pretty good shape. Might want to spray it for aphids and trim it a little."

"What about this pathetic yard?" Grace asked, stubbing the toe of her sneaker into what was left of the crabgrass- and sandspur-infested patch of sand. "What could I do with it that won't eat up my fix-up money?"

Instead of answering, Wyatt walked away, pacing it off. He bent down, kicked at something in a patch of crabgrass, stood, and grinned. "You've got an old sprinkler system here, did you know that?"

"No!" Grace said, bending down to look. "You think it works?"

"I'd have to take a closer look," Wyatt said. "But if the lines are intact and the system is in place, that's half the battle. You can replace the old sprinkler heads and even buy new timers if necessary, but with those in place, you'd be able to replace the lawn with something hardier and keep it watered until it's established."

"A new lawn would do wonders for the curb appeal," Grace said. "But that'd cost thousands and thousands. And I don't even have hundreds and hundreds. Maybe that's something Arthur would be interested in doing down the line."

"Arthur?"

"Arthur Cater. He's the owner. He's kind of a tightwad, but my big hope is that once he sees what I've done here, he'll loosen up give me a little more money to work with."

"This yard isn't that big," Wyatt said. "I was walking around before you got here, just kind of brainstorming. You've got a lot of planting beds and borders that are all overgrown with weeds right now, but if you weeded and mulched them and put an edging around them, you're left with just a nice little swath of green up front here and one in the back. The sides of the house are mostly shaded by those oaks, and they're underplanted with some beat-up old hostas and leather-leaf ferns and begonias, but again, get that cleaned out, separate the hostas and give them some breathing room, and it'll be fine."

"What about the backyard?" Grace asked. "Pretty disgusting, huh?"

"It needs work, yeah. But it's not impossible. I'd get rid of that old tin storage shed first thing. It's falling apart and you don't need it anyway with that big garage. You've got the start of a nice fruit grove back there."

"Really? I just thought they were a bunch of old half-dead bushes. They're all overgrown with moss and half the branches look dead."

"They need some help, for sure," Wyatt said. "But you've got a couple of tangerine trees, a ponderosa lemon, a lime, a grapefruit, and a kumquat." He laughed. "You could set up your own fruit stand."

"I might if it were my house," Grace said. "But it's Arthur's. And it's a rental house."

"Have you thought about asking him if he'd rent to you?" Wyatt asked.

"Only since the first minute I saw it," Grace said wistfully. "I could do so much with this place, if it were mine . . ."

"But?" He crossed his arms over his chest.

"I told him when I've finished with it, it should rent for at least $1,500 a month, this close to the beach and being on Anna Maria. That's more than I could afford."

"But you're doing all this work, essentially for free, right?"

"So that I can photograph and write about it for TrueGrace," she said. "It's that kind of trade-off. Essentially to get material for my new blog."

"Maybe you could work out some kind of arrangement with the guy," Wyatt said. "You don't know until you ask."

"Maybe . . ." Grace said hesitantly.

He glanced at his watch again. "Okay, gotta go. What time should I pick her up this afternoon?"

"Her?" Grace was lost in thought.

"Sweetie. Remember?"

"Oh, right." She laughed. "Just come whenever it's convenient. I'm gonna try to finish ripping up the kitchen floor today, and then I hope to get started painting. It'll be a late night. So come whenever you like. I'll be here."

35

The music boomed through the empty rooms of the old house, echoing off the wooden floors and high ceilings. Grace poured a gallon of white paint into the five-gallon bucket. Yup, too dead white. She pried the lid from the can of black paint and dipped in a plastic measuring spoon. A quarter of a teaspoon to start. It wasn't scientific, but it was the best she could do. She took the wooden paint paddle and started to swirl the black into the white. Hmm. Not bad.

She dipped her index finger into the paint and smeared a bit of it on her Benjamin Moore paint chip. Not quite enough oomph, for lack of a better word, but not a bad start either. She added another eighth of a teaspoon and repeated her test.

Better. Grace slipped one of her father's old T-shirts over the tank top she'd worn to the hardware store. Its hem touched the top of her thighs and nearly reached the ragged hem of the faded blue cutoffs she'd picked up at the animal-rescue thrift shop in Bradenton. She hesitated for a moment, then stripped off her bra. It was kinky, she knew, but for some reason, she'd never been able to paint in a bra. She knotted her hair in a ponytail and tied a bandanna over the finished coiffure. She was good to go.

She'd already taped off one wall of the living room and spread out her canvas drop cloth. Now, she dipped a trim brush in the bucket and brushed it onto the wall in a two-foot-wide square. She stood back and checked the effect. It did not suck. She moved her equipment to the long wall opposite the front door and painted a swatch there. Maybe?

She fired up the box fan she'd placed in one of the dining room windows and pried open all the rest of the windows that hadn't been painted shut. It was still hot in the house, but she was pleasantly surprised when the cross-ventilation at least kept the warm air moving. Grace still wasn't convinced that the ancient window-air-conditioning units actually worked, and, anyway, the house still needed airing out.

While her test paint swatches dried, Grace went back into the kitchen. She'd managed to pry up most of the harvest-gold vinyl flooring, but what she'd found underneath was a nasty surprise. Plywood sheeting. No heart pine, like the rest of the floors, just plywood. And it was speckled with bits of mastic that had been used to glue down the vinyl. Whatever she did with these floors, she'd have to get rid of all those gobs of goo. It made her back ache just thinking of it.

The first day she'd set up her laptop in the house, she'd been thrilled to discover she could piggyback off a neighbor's wireless Internet. Now she clicked over to her blog again and read another handful of comments, all positive, except for one from someone calling herself Freebird.

Wow, what happened to that showplace mansion you used to live in? Oh that's right, your hubsand kicked you out for a real woman. This place is a pigsty and a waist of time. Save the paint and buy a box of matches and a can of gas instead.

She was positive Freebird was really J'Aimee, who couldn't spell to save her life.

Leaving TrueGrace, she clicked over to Craigslist. She'd done some preliminary shopping and discovered that even the cheapest stoves and refrigerators at the big-box chain stores would put a worrisome dent in her budget. Maybe, she thought, she could find a bargain on Craigslist. Stainless steel would be nice, but she'd be happy with nearly-new good quality white appliances if the price was right.

She typed stoves into the search bar and came up with a list of nearly two hundred possibilities, ranging from the ridiculous—"Free stove, only one burner works, door has to be duct-taped. Must pick up today." To the sublime: "Viking 48-inch stainless steel pro series dual fuel, six burners, 12-inch steel griddle, simmer plate, convection/gas oven, electric broiler, Like new, $6,000."

"This is more like it," she muttered, reading a listing for a, "Like-new GE Profile refrigerator, and electric range, removed from model home, still in warranty, $200 must pick up." She e-mailed the owner, asking about availability, and then logged off.

Grace walked back and forth between the paint swatches, debating whether or not the white would work. Was it too cold? Too gray? She held the Benjamin Moore paint chips up against the walls for comparison. It wasn't Farrow & Ball, that was for sure. She would never be able to duplicate the depth of color or matte finish of the English paint, but this color? Yeah. She nodded. It was a happy, clean white, and a huge improvement over the current dirty taupey-pink walls.

She finished taping off all the trim, cranked up the tunes on her iPod, and went to work. Grace had always secretly enjoyed painting and had done a lot of it in her early days as a single career girl and then in the first few houses she and Ben rehabbed.

But at Sand Dollar Lane, she'd happily relinquished the job to the contractor. All those soaring cathedral ceilings and huge window walls and stairwells, not to mention the miles and miles of moldings and the window frames themselves, were too intimidating. Besides, Ben insisted it was time to have everything in the new house "first-class."

"You're going to be photographing the house all the time, and we're gonna shoot videos here, so how will it look to your readers and followers if they see streaky or chipped paint?" he'd said.

Now, she worked quickly, rolling the paint to the beat of the music. Unlike most people, she loved the smell of wet paint, especially mixed with the leftover fumes from all the Pine-Sol she'd used to get rid of the funky white-trash odors the house had absorbed.

She didn't stop for lunch until after she'd finished the living room and the dining room. Then, she took her sandwich, a bottle of water, and a ripe peach out to the front porch, where she sat in an old aluminum-and-plastic-webbed lawn chair she'd found in the toolshed. Sweetie sat at her feet while she ate, gobbling up whatever crumbs Grace tossed her, then curling up in a sunny spot near the screened door for a nap.

Grace stood up and stretched. She'd considered starting on the paint in the kitchen, but since she still didn't have a solution for the kitchen floors—and because she dreaded the thought of painting the old cabinet boxes and drawers, she decided to move on to the bedrooms.

It was no good trying not to play the "if I lived here game." She'd been trying to repress the urge since day one. So while she rolled faux Farrow & Ball on the larger of the two bedrooms, she allowed herself to daydream.

The room had two decent-sized windows that looked out to that big, deep backyard.

If I lived here, I'd replace those windows with a pair of French doors and build a big, wide stoop that ended in a little patio made of old mellow bricks. Maybe I'd have some kind of trellis partially enclosing it for privacy. I'd plant a pink climbing rose on the trellis, and I'd have a pair of lounge chairs out here. Or maybe I'd even have a fabulous outdoor shower, with one of those giant rain-shower heads.

The closet in the bedroom was nowhere near big enough to be a real master-bedroom-sized closet. The closet in the house on Sand Dollar Lane was bigger than this bedroom.

But if I lived here, I wouldn't need a huge closet. I don't need a lot of clothes anymore, so that's a blessing in disguise. Maybe I'd look for a big old armoire or a chifforobe, or even one of those oversized entertainment cupboards that are a dime a dozen now that everybody has a flat-screen. I'd paint it a dusty, weathered gray-blue, and I could look for old leather suitcases at estate sales and thrift shops, and I could store my extra clothes there and stack them on top of the armoire. And I'd find a great bed, maybe use a pair of twin headboards, something rattan or tropical? This house seems to scream for that Old Florida/British Colonial look.

Grace dragged the drop cloth over to a new section of wall. She didn't really know why she even bothered using one. The wood floors were already spattered with old paint and pockmarked with nail and tack holes from the wall-to-wall carpet she'd ripped up. She'd meant to check on the price of renting a floor sander at the hardware store, but she'd been distracted by figuring out the paint situation.

If I lived here, I'd stain the floors two shades darker, and I'd use a matte-finish poly. With the soft white walls and the sunlight coming in through the French doors, they'd have a deep, natural glow. No carpets underfoot, just maybe a striped cotton runner, or possibly a worn old Oriental in pale, faded greens, blues, and browns.

Planning it all out in her head, listening to the music, Grace found her painting groove again. She was dripping with sweat and spattered head to toe with paint, but it didn't matter. She was doing just what she wanted to do, how she wanted to do it, with no interference from anyone. It was a very good day.

She was just starting to move into the second bedroom when she heard the screened door open. "Hellllooo?" A male voice echoed.

"Wyatt?" She stripped the bandanna off her head and ducked into the bathroom to survey her appearance. Disastrous. Epic, Titanic-level disastrous. Her face was flecked with white paint, her arms and legs were flecked with white paint, and she had a giant smear of dirt on her right boob.

"Grace?" His footsteps echoed in the living room. "Are you in here?"

"Be right out," she called, pulling the bathroom door shut. She found an old washcloth in the linen closet, ran the water in the bathroom sink until all traces of rust were gone, and scrubbed her face and arms with it. She sighed. It was the best she could do. Anyway, who was she trying to impress?

When she got out to the living room, Wyatt was walking around, checking her handiwork. And there was a little freckle-faced boy rolling around on the floor with Sweetie, who was engaged in a spirited tug-of-war over what looked like a rag of some sort. Until she got a closer look, and realized they were actually using her discarded bra.

"Sweetie," Grace called, her face in flames. The dog looked up, with a bra strap clenched between her teeth. Grace scooped her up, disengaged the bra, and stuffed it into the back pocket of her cutoffs.

She cut her eyes over to Wyatt, whose chest was heaving with barely suppressed laughter. He was studiously avoiding meeting her eyes.

"Well, hello," Grace said, sitting down on the floor next to the child. Sweetie jumped out of her arms and began sniffing the little boy's shoes. "I bet you're Bo."

The child ducked his head. "Yes ma'am." Sweetie put her front paws on the child's chest and sniffed his neck, wedging her head under his hand until he was forced to scratch the dog's head.

"My name's Grace," she said, extending her hand. "I hear you're going to be helping take care of Sweetie."

"Yes, ma'am," the boy said. "Does she do any tricks?"

"I don't know, Bo. I've only had her a few days. But I think she's a pretty smart little thing. Maybe you could teach her some tricks?"

Bo flopped onto his back and Sweetie dutifully stepped onto his chest and began licking his neck and face, which prompted a huge fit of giggles from the child.

Finally, he sat back up and cradled the dog in his arms. "My dad taught Cookie to ride a bike and talk. Maybe we could teach Sweetie to do that."

Wyatt laughed. "Thanks for that vote of confidence, son, but even though Sweetie is really, really smart and cool, I think bike riding and talking is probably not in her future. How about if we just work on teaching her how to fetch a stick and sit up and bark on command?"

"Cool," Bo said, tickling Sweetie's belly. "Can we start tonight?"

"In the morning, maybe," Wyatt said. He touched a fingertip to one of the newly painted walls. "Man, you work fast. I can't believe you got this whole place painted in one day."

"Not all of it," Grace said. "I was just starting on the second bedroom when you guys showed up. I've still got the bathroom and the kitchen to do, not to mention the screened porch. Those are the rooms that are going to take the most work."

"Still," Wyatt said, walking into the abbreviated hall and then into the bedroom. "When you said this morning that the place was a mess, I was picturing something much, much worse."

"You should have seen it the first day I got here," Grace said, wrinkling her nose. "If my camera had smell-a-vision, I could have totally grossed out everybody on the Internet. It was so, so, nasty. Rotting wall-to-wall carpet, skanky old appliances. Everything was filthy. And that bedroom, where they'd locked Sweetie . . ." She shuddered.

"Are you ready to knock off for the day?" Wyatt asked.

"I don't even know how late it is. I kind of lost track of time."

"It's nearly six," Wyatt said. "Bo and I are going for pizza. We were wondering if you'd like to join us?"

"Pizza?"

"There's a place just over on Holmes Beach," he said. "Arturo's. Nothing fancy, but it's good and it's cheap, and if we get there reasonably early, we can get a table on the beach and watch the sunset."

Grace glanced at Sweetie. "What about her?"

"It's pet-friendly," Wyatt promised. "As long as we get a table outside."

She glanced down at her paint-spattered, braless self. "I can't go like this."

"Sure you can," Wyatt said. "Bo and I don't care. And neither does Sweetie."

"But I do," she said gently. "Certain standards must be maintained. I'll tell you what. Why don't you guys go ahead to Arturo's. I'll get cleaned up and meet you over there in thirty minutes."

"Thirty minutes?" he scoffed. "I've never known a woman yet who could shower and change and show up someplace in that little time."

"Thirty minutes," Grace swore. "If I'm one minute late, the pizza's on me."

At precisely 6:30, Grace hurried through the door at Arturo's. She was dressed in a pair of white capris, a black tank top, and a pair of gold metallic sandals from Pay-Less. Her hair was still wet from the shower and the only makeup she wore was a bit of coral lipstick. A pair of simple gold-hoop earrings sparkled at her ears, and around her neck she wore a necklace made from a tiny nautilus shell she'd found on the beach, hanging from a long thin gold chain. She walked through the main dining room and through a set of doors onto an expansive veranda, where she spied Wyatt and Bo sitting at a table close to the beach.

Wyatt's eyes swept over her appreciatively. He scrambled to his feet and gently pulled his son to a standing position, too.

"You clean up pretty good," he told her, pulling out a chair for her.

"And fast," she reminded him. "Thirty minutes. That might be a new land record for me."

"I guess that means dinner's on me," he said.

They ordered the Arturo's special, which meant a huge pie with everything, including pepperoni, Italian sausage, onions, peppers, olives, and anchovies; a glass of milk for Bo; and a pitcher of beer for the adults.

"Anchovies?" Grace asked, glancing over at Bo, who'd devoured two slices of pizza in the time it took Grace to work her way through one. "Your kid likes anchovies?"

The boy looked up, his face smeared with enough tomato sauce to fashion another whole pie. "I love anchovies!" he exclaimed, his broad smile revealing two missing front teeth.

"I haven't found anything he doesn't love," Wyatt said ruefully. "He's eating me out of house and home. I swear, every week he's grown another two inches."

"I'm the third tallest boy in first grade," Bo reported. "Cory Benton was the second tallest, but he's not going to our school next year, so I'll be the second tallest. Unless I grow some more, and then I'd be the first tallest." He took a gulp of milk and stood up, whispering in his father's ear.

Wyatt nodded. "It's inside, near the bar. Don't forget to wash your hands, and come right back here, okay?"

When he was gone, Grace took a sip of beer. "What a nice boy. I love that he's figured out he's the third tallest."

"He's fascinated with numbers and statistics," Wyatt said, shaking his head. "I do not know where he gets it. There are no bean counters in my family, and certainly none in his mother's. I haven't had the heart to point out to him that if Callie gets her way, he won't get to be the second tallest boy in the second grade at his school, because he'll be going to a new school. In Birmingham."

"Maybe it won't come to that," Grace said.

36

Bo came bounding back to the table. "Guess what, Dad? Scout's here! She and Coach Anna and her dad are eating dinner. Can I go sit with them for a while?"

Wyatt half stood, craned his neck, and spotted Anna and her family in the dining room. Anna nodded and pointed to an empty chair at the table and Wyatt gave her the thumbs-up sign. "Okay, but are you all done with your pizza?"

He eyed the last remaining piece on the tray. His father scooped it up into a napkin and handed it to him, and Bo ran off to join his friend.

"Anna's assistant coach on Bo's T-ball team," Wyatt said casually. "Scout's our pitcher, and Bo's best friend—on days he doesn't think girls are icky."

"What about Bo's father? Does he still think girls are icky?" Grace kept her tone playful.

"No, I'm a reformed girl hater." He reached across the table and tucked a strand of her damp hair behind her ear. "Especially where present company is concerned."

"Good to know," Grace said. "I've been meaning to ask you, how's your dad doing? You said he was pretty worn out today?"

"He's okay," Wyatt said. "I'm just going to have to get used to the idea that he's not getting any younger. All my life, he was this rugged, can-do guy. He literally did everything and anything at Jungle Jerry's: he built buildings, including the gift shop; paved the parking lot; dug the reflecting pond for the bird rookery. It was nothing for him to work a twelve- or fourteen-hour day, come home and play ball with me, and then get up and do it all over again the next day. I think my mom's death kind of took the wind out of his sails. He's only seventy-four, but some days, you'd think he was twenty years older."

"Your dad's seventy-four? Wow. Rochelle is only fifty-eight. How old are you?"

"I'm thirty-eight," Wyatt said. "You wanna see my ID?"

"I trust you," Grace said.

"Dad was thirty-two when they had me, same age I was when we had Bo. Dad went in the navy when he was just eighteen and got out in the late sixties. He and my mom met at an Allman Brothers concert in St. Pete, at the old National Guard Armory there. Crazy, huh? To think about your parents grooving to the Allman Brothers back in the day? My mom was six years younger than him, so she wasn't that old when she had me."

"Rochelle always says she was just a baby when she had her baby. She was only twenty when she got pregnant with me. Of course, my dad was a good bit older, too. He was already thirty, and he'd just bought the Sandbox when she came to work as a waitress. Dad claimed he threatened to fire her if she didn't marry him."

Wyatt thought for a moment. "It still bugs me, you know? That my parents had this long, happy marriage, and I had a happy childhood, and, with all that, I'm still ending up divorced. And you're in the same boat, right?"

"I guess." Grace took a sip of her beer. "I mean, I always assumed they were happy. Lately, I'm not so sure. Little things Rochelle's says. Maybe she wasn't as happy as I always thought. Certainly, I didn't have what you'd call the average childhood, growing up in a bar, but I don't think there was any lasting psychological damage."

"You grew up in a bar; I grew up in a tourist trap, playing with monkeys and parrots. And I always thought that was totally normal. I thought all kids had to shovel zebra poop when they got home from school every day," Wyatt said. His voice turned wistful. "I always just assumed Bo would have that life, too. He really loves hanging out at the park."

Grace's eyes widened. "You mean he won't, because Callie's taking him to Birmingham?"

"Not just that," Wyatt said. "I'm really not sure how much longer we'll be able to hang on at Jungle Jerry's. People don't want to spend a half a day wandering around a park where the big attraction is a bird riding a bike. Nobody cares about a tree that's two hundred years old or an orchid that doesn't grow anywhere else in the world. We're an anachronism. And we're bleeding money."

"It's that bad?" Grace asked.

He shrugged. "This is too depressing. Let's discuss something else. Like your new project."

"It's not depressing," Grace insisted. "It's just reality. Isn't there anything you can do to turn things around?"

"I've tried everything I can think of. Billboards, social media, Groupon offers, coupons in the mail. It helps a little, just never enough. Did you know that up until nineteen seventy, there were at least a dozen roadside tourist attractions, right here in this area?" He ticked them off on his fingers, "Sunken Gardens, Sarasota Jungle Gardens, Weeki Wachee, Silver Springs, Rainbow Springs, the Aquatarium, Tiki Gardens, Six Gun Territory, and that's just the ones I can think of off the top of my head. Lots of them are long gone, but others are still limping along, like Cypress Gardens. The last I heard, most of it had been turned into Legoland."

"I remember some of those places from when I was a little girl," Grace smiled at the memory. "I guess Disney coming to Florida in the seventies probably was the kiss of death."

"That and the interstates bypassing them," Wyatt said. "And people's tastes change. So, Jungle Jerry's is a dinosaur. A really expensive, dying dinosaur."

"What'll happen to it?" Grace asked.

"I'm not sure. We had a hot offer from a developer, right before Bo was born. They wanted to build one of those new urban centers, shopping and office and multifamily housing. My mom was sick; she had cancer—although we didn't know then that it was terminal—and she wanted us to keep the place running. Her father started it. He was the original Jungle Jerry. And like the fool I was, I thought maybe I could make it work." He shook his head. "Callie never let me hear the end of it afterwards. 'We could have been rich. You should have sold out.'"

"And then the economy tanked," Grace said. "How well, I know. Since nobody could sell a new house or condo, they sure didn't need a decorator to design a fabulous model home. And developers and builders probably couldn't afford to break ground on yet another new project with all that unsold inventory sitting around."

"Six months after we turned down the deal, we heard the developer defaulted on all his bank loans," Wyatt said. "So probably, even if we had made the deal, we never would have gotten paid."

"I know housing starts are starting to inch up again. Do you think it's possible that another developer would be interested?" she asked.

"Right now, there's only one interested buyer," Wyatt said, lowering his voice, as the waitress came by their table to ask if they wanted another pitcher of beer.

"Who?"

"The state of Florida," Wyatt said.

"Really? But that's good news, right? What would they do with the park? Keep it?"

"I don't know," he said, sounding irritated. "Dealing with bureaucrats is a major pain. They say they'd turn it into a state park. They say if the state legislature approves their next budget, the money's there, if Manatee County can kick in some money, too. There's a lot of 'ifs' flying around."

"What does your dad think?"

"He says he's okay with the idea," Wyatt said. "But I'm not sure he really understands all it involves. He just knows I'm worried all the time, and that worries him."

"Hey Dad!" Bo ran toward their table with a little girl with blond braids close on his heels. "Anna says we can have ice cream for dessert if you say it's okay."

"Hi Scout," Wyatt said, reaching out and tugging one of the girl's pigtails. "How was your pizza?"

"She *hates* pizza," Bo announced. "She had 'pasketti. And I had some, too."

From the looks of it, Grace thought, Both Bo and Scout had applied as much spaghetti sauce to their faces as they had to their bellies.

"It was dee-lish!" Scout announced. She was kneeling on the patio, and Sweetie was jumping up to lick her face.

"This is Sweetie," Bo told his friend. "We get to keep her at our house at night."

"Cool!" Scout said. "Does she go to your mom's house, too?"

Bo's shoulders sagged. "No. You know who is allergic. But I get to keep her at Dad's, and he's going to teach her how to fetch and stuff."

Wyatt took a napkin and wiped the outer layer of sauce from Bo's face. "Tell Scout's mom I said it was okay for you to have ice cream." He reached in his pocket and took out two dollar bills and handed it to the little boy. "That's to pay for your dessert. Don't spend it all in one place. Right?"

"Okeydoke." The two ran back inside.

"He's the real reason I hesitate to pursue this thing with the state," Wyatt said, nodding in his son's direction. "Dad and I will be okay. Theoretically, we'd come out of the deal with a little money. Enough to pay our bills and keep a roof over our heads. But Jungle Jerry's is Bo's legacy. He's grown up with the park. He thinks Cookie is his little sister. How can I sell that out from under my son?"

Grace met his eyes. "You're asking me?"

He clasped his hand over hers. "I'm asking you."

"It seems to me that Bo's legacy is you. And his grandfather. Times change. You know that as well as I do. I think we have to be flexible to survive. Look at me. When my work as an interior designer dried up—I mean, in this economy how many people need a twelve-thousand-dollar hand-knotted silk rug or eighteen thousand dollars' worth of window treatments? I had to reinvent myself. I had to go back to my roots, making do with what I had, doing most of it myself, with a lot of creativity and not much money. You do what you have to do, right?"

"Yeah." Wyatt sighed. "I just keep thinking, if I could hold on a little longer . . ."

He laughed. "Like I did with my marriage. And you see how well that turned out."

"It was different for me," Grace admitted. "These months, since I walked out on Ben, I've been blaming him for everything. And he's responsible for a lot of it, truly. But I think in the last few years I changed. My belief system and my values changed. It became more about status, having the best, the most expensive everything. Even though I started out writing DIY on Gracenotes, that changed, too. We monetized, got advertisers, and I needed to make them happy in order to survive. Or so I thought."

She took a sip of her beer. "I guess I sold out. And it wasn't entirely Ben's fault. I liked all that free stuff, giving big parties, living in the big house in the gated subdivision. And I loved having what seemed like unlimited resources available for any project I dreamed up. Ultimately, along the way, that's when our marriage started to go south." She gave a wry smile. "Rochelle would tell you I got too big for my britches."

Wyatt scooted his chair over toward her and leaned down to give her an unconvincing leer. "Your britches look just fine to me."

"Wyatt?"

He turned around to see Anna Burdette standing there, with Scout and Bo holding on to her hands. Anna gave Grace a friendly, if curious smile. "Hi there."

Wyatt stood. "Anna Burdette, this is my friend Grace . . ."

"Davenport," Grace finished for him, not wanting to be introduced by her married name. She shook Anna's hand. "I hear Scout's the Babe Ruth of T-ball."

Anna's nose crinkled as she laughed. "To hear Wyatt tell it, you might think so." She was studying Grace's face. "I don't mean to keep staring at you, but I keep thinking I know you from someplace."

"She's a famous blogger," Wyatt said.

Anna snapped her fingers. "Gracenotes, right? Your blog is my guilty pleasure. I read it in the middle of the night when I can't get to sleep."

"Thanks," Grace said. "Actually, I've changed the name. My old blog got, er, co-opted by my soon-to-be ex. Check out TrueGrace, if you will."

"I definitely will," Anna said. "In the meantime, the kids have been telling me about this spectacular little dog named Sweetie. I hear she's going to learn all kinds of tricks over there at Jungle Jerry's."

"She's actually Grace's dog, but she can't keep her where she's living right now, so we're sort of sharing custody. Bo has big plans for her," Wyatt said.

"Anyway," Anna said, "the reason I came by . . . Jack had to go on to work, but I told the kids I'd take them to play putt-putt for an hour or so, if that works for you. I can drop him off back at your place around eight."

"Please, Dad, please, please, please?" Bo was hopping up and down.

"I guess that would be okay," Wyatt said. "But not too much later, right, buddy? We've got a big game tomorrow, and your granddad is making you pancakes in the morning."

"Don't worry, the assistant coach is not gonna risk letting her star catcher suffer from sleep deprivation," Anna said.

"Let me give you some money to pay for Bo's golf," Wyatt said, half standing to get to his wallet.

"Not necessary. I've got buy-one, get-one coupons," Anna said. "Grace, it was nice to meet you."

"My pleasure," Grace said.

Anna leaned over and put her head next to Wyatt's. "She's cute, dude," she said in a stage whisper. "Classy, too. Don't screw this up, 'kay?"

37

Sorry about that," Wyatt said, when they were alone again. "Anna's worried about my love life. She keeps trying to get me 'back in the game,' as she calls it. But she's about as subtle as a slap in the face."

"You haven't dated at all since your split?" Grace asked.

"Me? The only other woman in my life besides Anna right now is Joyce Barrett."

"Who's she?"

"Our eighty-year-old bookkeeper slash office manager. I love Miss Joyce to pieces, but I seriously doubt she's interested in starting a new relationship."

As the waitress passed by, he gestured to her to bring the check. "It's still another hour 'til sunset, and Bo won't be back from putt-putt 'til after eight. Would you like to go someplace else for a drink? Or just take a walk on the beach?"

"Sweetie would probably love a stroll on the beach. And so would I," she said.

Grace stepped out of her sandals and stuck them in the back pocket of her pants, and after a moment of hesitation, Wyatt tied the laces of his Top-Siders together and slung them over his shoulder. They walked through the powdery white sand to the shoreline, and Grace stood and let the mild breeze blow through her hair. They walked for a while, close, but not touching.

The bright blue sky gradually darkened to deeper layers of dark blue, violet, silver, and then ochre and pink. The wind began to whip whitecaps on the incoming waves. Families lingered on beach blankets with coolers of drinks, radios playing softly. Closer to the dunes, at every pathway from the road, knots of people stood beneath the clumps of Australian pines, sea oats, and beach myrtle, waiting for the sundown ritual to begin.

The county had an ordinance against dogs on the beach, but Sweetie stayed close to Grace's side, and, as if by tacit agreement, other law-breaking dog walkers passed by and nodded in a conspiracy of silence.

The sun dipped lower, glowing gold, and when they came to a dune walkover with an empty bench, they sat down to watch the show. Sweetie hopped up onto Grace's lap, and Wyatt stretched his arm across the back of the bench; when his hand brushed the bare skin of her shoulder, she smiled to herself.

She leaned back, resting her head against his arm, and the warmth of his skin on hers felt familiar and exciting at the same time.

"Look," Wyatt said, pointing with his free arm. Out in the waves, the graceful gray backs of a pod of dolphins curved through the water. There were four or five larger ones and three or four smaller ones. "Some moms and some calves," he said.

"I've been watching dolphins in the gulf and the bay my whole life," Grace said. "But it never gets old. I used to love it when we'd go out on my dad's boat and they'd follow us, waiting for us to throw in some bait or a too-small fish."

"Yeah," Wyatt said with a sigh. "Kind of reminds you why you live here, doesn't it?"

"Mm-hmm."

The sun was sinking lower and the clouds above growing purple and midnight blue. "You ever see the green flash?" he asked, his hand grazing her shoulder.

"You mean the thing that happens the moment the sun slips below the horizon? Yes. We used to make a big ceremony out of it when I was growing up. My dad had a cowbell he'd ring at that exact moment."

But there was no green flash tonight, just another bright yellow glow, and then striations of deepening colors.

"This is nice," Grace said, snuggling back against his arm as the air grew cooler. She leaned against his chest, inhaling his clean, woodsy scent, feeling his warmth seep into her bare shoulders.

"You cold?" He wrapped both arms around her. "We could go back to the car."

Grace shook her head. She wondered if he would ever get up the nerve to kiss her again. Or if she would have to be the one to initiate things. In the meantime, she closed her eyes and told herself to enjoy the moment.

At some point, she must have enjoyed the moment so long that she dozed off. When her eyes fluttered open, it was dark.

She sat up with a start.

"What?" Wyatt asked. "You finished your nap?"

She yawned and laughed. "I'm sorry. I've been working so hard every night, I fall asleep as soon as the sun goes down. She glanced at her watch and jumped to her feet, grabbing Wyatt's hand and pulling him up, too. "Come on, Cinderfella. I regret to remind you that at eight o'clock, you turn into a dad again."

He groaned. "I'll text Anna, tell her to play another round of putt-putt. On me. That'll give us another hour, at least."

"No way. She'll think I'm seducing you."

"Anna's a hopeless romantic. She'd probably offer to get us a room."

Grace sighed. "Bo's expecting you to be home when Anna drops him off. I don't want to be the one who causes you to break promises to your son."

"I hate it when you talk sense," Wyatt grumbled.

They walked hand in hand back down the beach, with Sweetie staying close at their heels. Wyatt stood awkwardly beside her car as she unlocked the door. She sensed his nervousness, and found it touching.

She leaned over and kissed him lightly on the cheek. "About that dating-reentry counseling you mentioned—maybe we could take a class together."

38

At exactly 8:15 A.M. Wyatt hopped out of his truck and dashed into the house on Mandevilla. He found Grace sitting on the floor in the back bedroom, taping off baseboards.

"Gotta run," he said, setting Sweetie down beside her. "I promised Bo I'd throw him some extra batting practice before the game."

"Okay," she said. "How about if I just drop Sweetie off to you at the park later? Say six?"

He was halfway out the door, but he turned around, came back, and pulled to her feet. "I thought about what you said last night. Just before you left. You're killing me. You know that, right?"

She smiled. "In a good way, right?"

"Absolutely. See you at six." And then he was off again. A minute later, she ran out to the porch, hollered at him as he was getting into the truck. "I'll bring dinner. What do you like?"

"If you bring it, I'll like it." He threw the truck into reverse and headed down the road.

She was still on the floor, barefoot, dressed in her messy, paint-spattered T-shirt and cutoffs, a bandanna tied over her hair, scooching along on her butt, painting the baseboards, when she heard footsteps in the living room. Maybe Bo's T-ball game was over early? She turned expectantly.

J'Aimee stood in the doorway, looking down at her, eyes blazing with hostility.

Grace scrambled to her feet, dusting off her butt with both hands. "What do you want?" she asked, her voice cool.

J'Aimee was dressed in all black, a sheer, sleeveless black chiffon midriff-baring top worn over a black bra, black skinny jeans, and high-heeled silver-studded black sandals with gladiator-wrapped ankles. With her jet-black dyed hair she looked like a refugee from a bondage flick.

Although J'Aimee was actually about Grace's height, today, in the heels, she glared menacingly down at Grace.

"You think you're pretty damn smart, don't you," J'Aimee said, poking Grace in the chest with her forefinger. "With those bullshit e-mails you sent my advertisers. Me, steal your content? Who the fuck do you think you are?"

J'Aimee's breath was hot on her face. Grace was tempted to take a step backward, but instead stood her ground.

"Me? I'm the person who started Gracenotes. I'm the actual Grace. I'm the person who developed, cooked, photographed, and wrote that corn-crab chowder recipe you so blatantly lifted off my blog to pass off as your own work."

"There are a million recipes for that soup floating around on the Internet," J'Aimee said with a shrug.

"Ben managed to wipe out that post on my page, so I can't prove it, of course," Grace said calmly. "But I've got a new blogging platform for TrueGrace and a new protected password, and I've installed malware now, so tell him not to bother to try to mess with it. Also? I've started watermarking my photos with my TrueGrace logo, so you won't be able to poach my photos anymore either."

"Me? Poach your shit?" J'Aimee's throaty laughter was harsh. "Who are you kidding?"

She took a step backward, her eyes sweeping disdainfully over the room. "So this is your exciting new project? This *shack*?" Abruptly, she turned and walked out of the room, her high heels clacking sharply on the wood floors.

J'Aimee walked into the kitchen, took in the beat-up, doorless cupboards; the gaping spaces where appliances should have stood; the bare, glue-spattered plywood floors. She sniffed and wrinkled her nose in disgust. Just as quickly, she walked into the hallway, peered into the bedroom and then the single bathroom with its outdated tile and filthy tub and toilet.

"You're pathetic, Grace," J'Aimee said, her eyes glittering with malice. "You are desperate and pathetic, like this house. You put yourself out there to all the world on the Internet as this all-knowing authority. Miss Know-It-All: the perfect designer, entertainer, gourmet cook . . ."

J'Aimee admired her own reflection in the bathroom mirror and then stomped out of the bathroom and into the living room. "But you're not even woman enough to keep your husband interested in you. You want to know how long it took Ben to jump my bones after you hired me? A week."

She laughed at the look of shock on Grace's face. "And don't be telling yourself that I'm the little tramp that went after him. He came on to me. Uh-huh. That's right. The first time? Oh, that was while you were out giving a speech to some fancy society women's fund-raising luncheon. I even remember the title of your talk, because I had to type it and print it out for you. 'A House Is Not a Home.' And while you were giving your lame talk, I was back at your house, fucking your husband's brains out." She paused and laughed again. "In your bed."

Grace wanted to knock J'Aimee down, shove a fist in her throat, anything to shut up the torrent of bile spewing from her mouth. But she was paralyzed, speechless.

J'Aimee's smile was mirthless. "TrueGrace? That's what you're calling yourself now? Who are you kidding? Ben was the brains behind Gracenotes. He and I did all the scut work, making it look pretty and effortless, while you took all the credit."

She took another step closer to Grace again, until she was directly in her face. "Look at you now, Grace *Davenport*. Living with Mommy above a shitty bar, hiring yourself out as nothing more than a glorified housepainter." She whipped a cell phone out of the pocket of her form-fitting jeans, and before Grace could stop her, she'd snapped a picture of Grace, standing there, covered in paint, her mouth gaping. "This'll give Ben a good laugh."

The click of the camera lens suddenly snapped Grace back to consciousness.

"Just what is it you want here, J'aimee? You want more material to leave some more snarky, barely literate comments on TrueGrace? Don't bother to deny it either. I know you're Freebird. Since you're living in Ben's pants these days, you might want to get him to explain ISP numbers to you."

Now it was Grace's turn to fight. She put her paint-spattered hand squarely in the middle of J'Aimee's chest, leaving a perfect white handprint on the black chiffon.

"Hey," J'Aimee cried angrily, swatting Grace's hand away.

"You're a fraud, *J'Aimee*," Grace said, rolling the name out with the exaggerated French pronunciation. "Oh. Wait. Even your name's a fake, *Jamie*. You've never had an original idea in your life. You're the kind of bottom-feeding parasite who has to be content with whatever crap sinks to the bottom of the cesspool. But hey, you want my old blog, take it! My house and that bed you seem to love? Help yourself. It means nothing to me now. Oh, and how about my husband?"

"He's mine now," J'Aimee purred.

"And you're welcome to him," Grace said. Suddenly, she remembered something Ashleigh Hartounian had said during their first session of divorce-recovery group, something about her husband's new mistress.

"You are more than welcome to Ben Stanton, that lying, cheating piece of garbage. But here's something you need to know, J'Aimee. You are just like a cup of Publix yogurt."

"Huh? You're crazy."

"Nope," Grace said, starting to enjoy herself. "You, J'Aimee, are just like any other garden-variety skank. You've got an expiration date stamped on your bony little ass. But you won't even know when it's past—until Ben throws you out for something sweeter and newer."

Clearly, J'Aimee had no clever response. "Screw you," she said, her teeth clenched. "Leave my advertisers alone. Quit making trouble for Ben and me, or you will live to regret it." She turned to stalk away.

"No, screw you," Grace said. "Now get out of my house." On an impulse, she managed to land a kick, leaving a perfect impression of her bare foot in faux Farrow & Ball white on J'Aimee's black-clad butt.

For the rest of the morning, Grace fumed. What, she wondered, had prompted J'Aimee to seek her out here? She was obviously worried about her advertisers. Had one of the companies she'd e-mailed dropped their support for Gracenotes? Wouldn't that be poetic justice! When she finished with all the trim in the bedroom she struggled to her feet and went to check the time.

It was nearly twelve thirty. There was a peanut butter and jelly sandwich out in the kitchen, calling her name. But as she was about to put her phone down, the screen lit up with an incoming text from a number she didn't recognize, with a Bradenton prefix.

Got some news about Paula. Meet me for lunch at Rod & Reel Pier, 1 pm?

Who is this? Grace texted.

Camryn. R we good?

She looked down at her messy clothes. She'd have time to wash her hands and face, but not much more time than that. Fortunately, the Rod and Reel was an open-air restaurant at the end of the fishing pier on Anna Maria. She could go dressed as she was.

OK!

She almost didn't recognize the woman sitting at one of the tables by the window. Most of the tables were full of families, tourists, and anglers who'd spent the morning trying their luck fishing for trout or redfish on the pier. Finally, a lone woman in a floppy straw hat and sunglasses waved her down.

"Camryn? Is that you?"

"You see any other black women loitering around here?" Camryn snapped. She fanned herself with her hands. "Lord, Jesus, I'd forgotten how hot it is out on this pier."

Grace shrugged and sat down. "You picked this place, so don't blame me."

"I'm just sayin'," Camryn said. "I come here once a year for the fried grouper sandwich. Best thing I ever put in my mouth, but I try not to eat fried food, so I generally stay away."

"Why the disguise?" Grace asked.

"I'm what they call a minor celebrity in this town," Camryn said. "When I first got in the business, I got a big kick out of having people come up to me at Dillard's or a restaurant. 'Ooh, you're the lady on TV.' Uh-huh. Then I gotta have my picture taken with 'em, maybe autograph something. And I swear, every time I step foot out of my house without makeup or my hair all looking nappy, that's when somebody spots me. You think I don't see them snapping pictures of me with their cell phones, telling their friends at work, 'I saw that Camryn Nobles on channel four at the gym, and girl! Without her TV makeup, she is looking old in the face.' "

"So on Saturdays, you leave off the makeup and wear a hat and sunglasses. Makes sense."

Camryn studied her. "If I went somewhere in this town, looking like you look right now, people would be tweeting and Facebooking my picture all over the Internet."

"I was painting a house when I got your text," Grace said, deciding not to be insulted. "There wasn't time to go home and change. So what did you find out about Paula?"

"Let's order first," Camryn said. The waitress took their orders: fried grouper sandwich for Camryn, mahimahi for Grace, unsweetened iced teas for both.

When their drinks came, Camryn sucked down half her tea. "First off, don't you think it's funny that a supposed marriage counselor is divorced?"

"Maybe not," Grace said. "After all, she's not counseling us on how to hang on to our marriages. She's helping us deal with breakups. So I guess it's not all that surprising that she's in the same boat. How'd you find out she was divorced?"

"I got tired of waiting for our silly little intern to do her job, so I made some phone calls myself. Did some googling, a little investigative journalism. To tell you the truth, I'd forgotten how much fun it is to dig up good dirt. Anyway, yeah. Dr. Paula Talbott-Sinclair has only been divorced a couple years. We already knew she'd been in practice in Oregon—Portland. I called one of the assistant producers at our network affiliate out there, and she knew all about our Paula."

Their food arrived, and Camryn picked up her sandwich, nibbled, and sighed happily. "I'll have to do an extra hour on the elliptical to pay for this, but it's worth every calorie."

Grace was surprised by how hungry she was, so they ate in silence for a while. Finally, Camryn finished her sandwich. She picked up the paper plate with the remaining curly fries and dumped them in a nearby trash bin. "I don't need the temptation," she explained.

"You said that producer knew something about Paula?" Grace prompted.

"Mm-hmm. Paula and her husband, Thorsen Sinclair, were in practice together. He was a psychiatrist; she was a therapist. Connie, the woman I talked to at KTXX, says they were pretty prominent, gave workshops all over the Pacific Northwest on 'mindful marriage,' whatever that is. They self-published a book with the same title. And everything was golden with the Sinclairs. Until he fell in love with one of their patients."

"Oh, wow." Grace breathed.

"Uh-huh. Both couples split up, and it made a nice little scandal, because the husband called the state board and filed a formal complaint against Thorsen and then leaked it to the media out there. Connie sent me a link to the story in the Portland paper. 'Mindful Marriage Melt-Down.' Long and short? Thorsen dumped Paula. After their divorce was final, he married the other woman. And Paula, apparently, fell to pieces. She 'borrowed' one of her ex's prescription pads and wrote herself a bunch of scrips for tranquilizers. But she got caught."

"Did she go to jail?" Grace asked, wide-eyed.

"It was a first offense, so the judge agreed to drop the criminal charges and allowed her to check herself into a rehab program for impaired healthcare givers," Camryn said. "She must have completed it to the court's satisfaction out there, because Connie couldn't find any record of the arrest."

"Poor Paula," Grace said. "I guess she's been through the wringer, just like all of us. But how did she end up all the way out here?"

"Probably got sick of the rain. You ever been to Portland?"

"No."

"I don't actually know what brought her to Florida," Camryn admitted. "What I do know is, she only set up this divorce and life coaching business six months ago. And it seems like it's just barely legal—as long as she doesn't call herself a therapist or a marriage counselor. Which she doesn't."

"I see," Grace said, toying with a piece of lettuce that had slid off her mahi-mahi. "So—is Paula actually qualified to do what she's doing? I mean, I thought she was a quack that first week, but honestly, I think she really is trying to help us. And she has some real insights into what goes wrong with marriages."

"When she's sober or not having a 'family emergency,'" Camryn said, still clearly not convinced. "Her credentials are for real. I checked. Her undergrad degree is from the University of Washington, and she got a master's in clinical social work from Portland State. She belonged to a bunch of professional organizations in Portland and was even on the board of a center for battered women, until her life went to shit."

Grace drummed her fingernails on the tabletop. "Obviously, she's back on the pills, self-medicating. It's such a shame."

"She's a grown-up," Camryn pointed out. "Nobody's making her take those pills. What I want to know is, how did she and Stackpole get hooked up?"

"Good question." Grace considered the woman sitting opposite her at the table. "Camryn?"

"Hmm?"

"Why are you telling me all this?"

"You're a member of the group. It affects you as much as it does me."

"There are three other people in our group. You don't even like me."

"Did I ever say I don't like you?"

"Well, it's not like we're buddy-buddy. You've never called me and asked me to go to lunch or anything."

"I don't *do* lunch, Grace. You want to know about the glamorous life of a morning anchor in a third-tier market? I get up at five in the morning, get on the elliptical, haul my ass to the station. I'm in makeup at six, on air at seven. After I get off the air, I've got meetings, I read the wires, the online editions of *The New York Times, Wall Street Journal, Washington Post, Miami Herald.* Since I still do my own enterprise stories, I've got phone calls to make and interviews to set up, and lots of times I go out on remotes with a camera crew. I eat a take-out salad at my desk, go to some more meetings, make some more phone calls. Oh yeah, and I talk to my lawyer about this freakin' divorce and brood about being single again at my age. And that's my day."

Grace still wasn't convinced. "Why me?"

Camryn considered her over the top of her sunglasses. "Because other than me, you're the only normal person in this group."

Grace started to protest.

"Stop!" Camryn took off the sunglasses. "Wyatt doesn't count. He's a guy. A white guy, and I know it's a new century and we finally have a black man in the White House. And I should be better than this, but I still consider him the man. Ashleigh? Pffft. I won't even go there. You and I? Yeah, we did some stuff to our men, but they had it coming. Ashleigh is just all kinds of flaky. I wouldn't trust her any farther than I could throw her."

"What about Suzanne? She's shy, sure, but she's also smart and compassionate, and she seems to understand people."

Camryn shook her head. "No. I can't put my finger on it, but there is something definitely off about that woman."

"She's an introvert," Grace protested.

"It's more than that," Camryn said. Suzanne is damaged goods. Like it or not, Grace, it's you and me."

"You and me—doing what?" Grace said impatiently. "We don't definitely know that Paula and Stackpole are involved. She's not breaking the law billing herself as a divorce coach. I don't see us blowing the whistle on her because she's got a problem with pills. If anything, I think we should try to get her help."

"Help her?" Camryn looked disgusted. "Who's helping us? Who's helping us pay three hundred dollars a session for a 'divorce coach' who can't keep her eyes open for an hour at a time? Who's helping all those other poor women Stackpole sends to Paula for help? You ever consider that? I have. I hung around outside her office yesterday. Yeah. I saw what looked like three different 'divorce recovery' groups filing in there. Total of fifteen people. All women. I did the math. That's 4,500 dollars. In one day. Do you make that kind of money in one day? I sure as hell don't."

It didn't take long for that to sink in. "What do you want from me?" Grace asked.

"You said your lawyer went to law school with Stackpole? You trust her?"

"Yessss?" Grace said reluctantly.

"Talk to her. Ask her to sniff around. I'd ask my lawyer, but he's a man. And he's from Miami, went to law school down there. Balls of brass, great for negotiating your next contract at the station, but he's definitely not in the local courthouse pipeline."

Grace hesitated. "I'll ask Mitzi what she can find out, but in the meantime I've got an idea of what we can do to help Paula. But I'll need your help. The others, too."

"You bleeding-heart liberals," Camryn said. "What have you got in mind?"

"I'll e-mail everybody else in the group, let them know the plan. Wednesday night, assuming Paula shows up, we ambush her. Do an old-school Betty Ford intervention."

Camryn nodded thoughtfully. Put on her sunglasses, picked up the check. "I like it." She pulled her straw hat down so that it put her face in deepest shade. "Don't tell anybody else, but I like you, too, Grace Stanton."

"Davenport," Grace corrected. "It's Davenport now."

Grace watched while Camryn sped purposefully down the pier toward the parking lot. Had Camryn Nobles actually just befriended her? Were they in cahoots? Conspiring against Stackpole? Her life had just taken another unexpected turn. For the better, she hoped.

39

Grace took the outside stairs to the apartment two at a time. She let herself into her bedroom and set Sweetie on her bed. She knelt beside the bed and whispered into the dog's silky ear. "I've got to take a shower and get ready for tonight. But you have to be really, really quiet, or the bad lady downstairs will kick us both out of here."

Sweetie blinked, gave Grace's nose a lick, then settled herself on one of Grace's pillows, with her head on her paws. By the time Grace emerged from the shower, the dog was asleep. She dressed quietly, in a pair of blue and white seersucker shorts and a scoop-necked white T-shirt that she'd found for a total of five dollars at the Junior League thrift shop.

She found Rochelle downstairs, behind the bar, refereeing a hot argument about politics between two of her regulars.

"You look nice," Rochelle said, raising an eyebrow. "Going somewhere?"

"I promised Wyatt I'd take dinner when I drop Sweetie off for the night," Grace said.

Rochelle frowned. "Is that dog . . ."

"Sleeping in my room. Don't get your panties in a wad. It's just until I round up some food to take over there. He's got Bo tonight. What do little boys like to eat?"

"I never had a little boy, so I wouldn't know. But I can tell you what the big ones like. Meat. Fried things. Cheesey things. Anything with ketchup or barbecue sauce. Or jalapeños."

"Well, it's after five now, and I promised to have dinner there at six," Grace said. "So I don't have time to fix anything healthy from scratch. What are our specials tonight?"

"Wings. Crab burgers. Fried fish bites. Taco casserole."

"God help me, but the taco casserole hits on all the major male food groups," Grace said.

She went through the swinging doors into the kitchen and found the taco casserole on the steam table. Grace scooped up enough of the casserole to fit into a foil nine-by-twelve to-go tray and fitted it with a cardboard top. She was filling another foil tray with salad when Rochelle joined her.

"What about dessert?"

"Maybe just some fruit?"

Rochelle snorted. "If you're ever gonna land another man you've got to get over this healthy fetish of yours." She turned to one of the big walk-in coolers and lifted out a plastic-covered dish. "Never met a man or a kid yet who didn't love my brownie pie," she said, slicing off a huge slab and placing it in a large Styrofoam clamshell. Then she reached back into the cooler and handed her daughter a white can. "Whipped cream. You know what to do with this. Don't you?"

"Get your mind out of the gutter," Grace said primly. She sorted everything into a large brown paper sack. "Thanks, Mom. This will be great."

Rochelle raised one eyebrow. "Don't forget the damned dog."

Wyatt Keeler emerged from the shower to find the other male inhabitants of his home immersed in the Rays game. Nelson was stationed in his recliner command center, and Bo was sprawled on his belly on the floor, his face inches from the television. The room was a disaster. A mound of clean, unfolded laundry took up most of the sofa. Bo's mud-grimed T-ball uniform, underpants, socks, cleats, and sweat-soaked cap were tossed on the floor. The wood laminate coffee table was littered with three days' worth of newspapers; dirty dishes, including a half-eaten potpie; empty Coke cans; and the remains of their fast-food lunch.

"Hey, you guys," Wyatt started, but then he felt his bare foot impaled with a piece of sharp plastic. He stooped over and held up a yellow Lego. "Ow!"

"Dad!" Bo protested. "You messed up my Mega-Bot." He started to scoop up the scattered red, yellow, green, and blue blocks. "I've been working on this all day. Now I gotta start all over."

"Now you gotta clean up this mess," Wyatt told him. Nelson looked up from his chair.

"Both of you," Wyatt said firmly. "We've got company coming in fifteen minutes, so I need all hands on deck here. Bo, pick up all your Legos and stash them in their basket, where they belong. Get your uniform and put it in the laundry room, then clean up all this trash on the coffee table. Dad? Didn't you say you'd fold the laundry and put it away?"

"*You* said I'd fold the laundry," Nelson muttered, bracing his hands on the recliner's arms as he struggled to stand. "And what are you going to be doing while me and Bo slave away in here?"

"I'm going to clean up the kitchen, sweep the floor, and take out a week's worth of garbage. I already cleaned and disinfected the bathroom, so don't either of you dare go in there."

"What if I gotta pee?" Bo asked.

"Take it outside," his father said.

"Who's coming over, the queen of England?" Nelson griped. He was folding T-shirts and shorts and underpants, matching socks.

"It's Grace, Dad's new girlfriend," Bo told his grandfather.

"Who told you Grace was my girlfriend?" Wyatt said. "I never said that."

"Well, she is, isn't she?" Nelson asked.

"Anna said it's okay for Dad to have a girlfriend, since Mom already has you know who," Bo commented.

"Remind me to have a discussion with Anna about minding her own business," Wyatt said. "In the meantime, just get busy, you two. She'll be here in, like, ten minutes. And she's bringing dinner, so be nice. And whatever she brings, pretend like you like it."

"What if she brings fried liver?" Bo asked. "Or lima beans?"

"Or tofu?" Nelson said darkly. "I'm warning you right now. I don't do tofu."

"If she tries to make me eat liver and lima beans, I'll blow chow," Bo said.

"She's not bringing liver or tofu," Wyatt said. "Just remember what I told you. Nice."

"I'm always nice," Nelson said under his breath. He looked over at Bo, who was busily wadding up the newspapers and paper bags and stuffing them under the sofa. "Aren't I always nice?"

Bo gave it some thought. "Mostly. Except when my mom calls."

Wyatt sprayed the chipped Formica countertops with Windex and surveyed the kitchen. He had no idea what Grace's reaction would be to his place. He knew she'd lived in some mansion, because he'd surreptitiously looked at pictures of the place on her old blog. It was huge, with something like five bedrooms and four bathrooms, a screening room, home gym, swimming pool, pool house. Hell, from the looks of it, her pool house was bigger than his crappy little double-wide.

Still, she seemed happy enough, working over at the house on Mandevilla, even admitting she'd fantasized about living there. Maybe she wouldn't turn around and run screaming into the night after she got a look at this dump.

At least it was a fairly tidy dump now. He'd picked some zinnias from the flower bed by the back door and stuck them in an empty jelly jar. The table looked okay, set with his mother's good dishes, the ones with little sprigs of blue cornflowers and gold edges. The silverware all matched, and there were paper napkins at every place, which was a huge step up from the usual roll of paper towels he kept on the table.

But there were only three chairs. How had he missed that? At one time, the dinette set had four chairs, but just a few months ago Bo had been leaning back in his chair when one of the back legs buckled and cracked. He'd meant to try to fix that. But it was too late now. He hurried through the house, looking for an extra chair. Nothing. In desperation, he went out to the carport, found an old plastic beach chair, and dragged it inside. He frowned. It was too short. He went out to the living room, where Nelson and Bo were again wrapped up in the baseball game. He snatched a throw pillow from the sofa and tossed it onto the seat of the chair, just as he heard a knock at the door.

Wyatt wiped his sweaty palms on the seat of his shorts and went to answer the door.

As Rochelle'd predicted, the taco casserole was a hit with the Keeler men.

"Pretty good," Nelson said, scraping a last bit of hamburger, tomato sauce, and cheese from his plate. He pointed at the nearly empty Pyrex dish Grace had used to warm up the casserole. "Is that a Frito?"

"Afraid so," Grace said. "Not very healthy, I know, but . . ."

Before she could apologize further, Nelson reached across the table and scooped up the last remaining spoonful.

"Dad loves Fritos," Wyatt said. "Almost as much as chicken potpie."

"Just the Marie Callender's ones," Nelson said. "Not Swanson. The Marie Callender's are more expensive, but I can usually find a coupon in the Sunday paper."

"Dad does most of the grocery shopping," Wyatt said. "He's a fiend for those coupons. Knows where all the best deals are."

Nelson beamed at the compliment. "Do you like baked beans? Because I've got an extra BOGO for Bush's baked beans at Winn-Dixie this week."

"What's a BOGO?" Wyatt asked.

"Buy one, get-one," Grace said. "And yes, I'd love a coupon, if you've got an extra."

Dinner, she thought, had been a breeze. It was so cute, the way Wyatt had obviously gone to such pains to make a good impression. She looked down at her plate. "I know this china pattern. It's Bachelor's Button, right?"

"Uh, maybe," Wyatt said.

"That's right," Nelson volunteered. "It was our wedding china. Peggy picked it out. Blue flowers were always her favorite."

"Mine too," Grace confided. "Bachelor's buttons, or cornflowers, any shade of hydrangea, iris, those deep-blue pansies with the little clown faces . . ."

"Plumbago?" Wyatt said. "You like plumbago?"

"I love it, especially the ferny leaves," Grace said.

"I grow it in our nursery here," Wyatt said. "We could dig up some clumps and plant it at Mandevilla if you want, maybe a swath of it in front of the gardenias by the porch. The lighter green foliage would be a good contrast against the dark-green gardenia leaves."

"Great idea," Grace said. She looked around the table, beaming at the sight of all the empty plates. "I brought dessert, if anyone's interested."

"I'm interested," Bo said.

"You're interested in any kind of food," Nelson observed.

"Except liver and lima beans," the child said. "Gross."

Grace laughed. "I have to agree with you there. Totally, gag-me-with-a-spoon gross."

She'd sliced the brownie pie into generous squares and arranged them on one of the chipped white plates she'd found in the cupboard. Now, she set it in the center of the table. "My mom's brownie pie. It's her secret recipe, so I don't know what's in it, but we always sell out at the Sandbox."

Each of the males at the table immediately reached for a square. They were all munching happily.

"Bo, I meant to ask, how did your big T-ball game go today?" Grace asked.

"We lost," Bo said, spraying crumbs of chocolate over his plate.

"Not with your mouth full," Wyatt warned.

Bo chewed for a moment, then, his eyes on his father, carefully wiped his mouth with his napkin. "We lost to the stinkin' Pythons. Our archenemy."

"I'm sorry," Grace said.

"But we played great," Wyatt said. "Bo hit a triple and a double. And he hit a smokin' line drive that probably would have homered, except their third baseman, who I totally think is on growth hormones, because the kid is six and he's like six feet tall, made a diving catch."

"But then I struck out. Twice," Bo said sadly.

"Boy, you're batting four hundred," Nelson reminded him. "That ain't too shabby."

Bo eyed the last slice of pie on the plate, his hand hovering just above it, until his father nodded approval.

"Granddad, I'm four hundred for the week, three-fifty for the season. This kid on the Wolverines, he's batting six hundred. Scout's striking out, like, two kids an inning."

"Wow," Grace said admiringly. "You really do know your statistics. Your dad told me you're quite a math wizard."

"He's a freak," Wyatt said, gazing fondly at his son. "But he's our freak."

Bo looked longingly toward the other room. "The game's still on, Dad. Can I be excused?"

"After you two clear the dishes. And thank Grace for the dinner she cooked."

"Don't thank me," Grace admitted. "My mom fixed everything. I just carried it over here."

"Dinner was awesome," Bo said, gathering the dishes.

Nelson stood slowly. “Anytime you want to bring over some more of that taco casserole, please feel free.”

Wyatt looked at Grace, who was starting to gather up the silverware. “That’s Dad’s job,” he said. “It’s not too hot right now. I thought maybe I’d take you on a tour of the park. If you’re interested.”

“I was hoping you’d ask,” Grace said.

40

The golf cart bumped noiselessly along the crushed-shell pathways, an occasional limb or branch slapping harmlessly at Grace's arm. The air was thick with humidity and the scent of damp earth and tropical flowers. It was twilight, and birds and squirrels twittered from the thick tree canopy. And from somewhere off in the park came an unearthly shriek that made Grace startle, so much that she nearly fell off the cart. "What was that?" she asked, clutching Wyatt's arm for balance.

"Peacocks," Wyatt said. "The bane of my existence. If only that damned coyote had jumped a peacock . . ."

"But they're so beautiful," Grace said. "So elegant."

"So noisy and cranky and a major pain in my ass," Wyatt said firmly. "People in the neighborhood around here are always calling the cops to complain that we're torturing animals over here. We can't make 'em understand that it's just normal peacock behavior."

"Why do you have them if you don't like them?"

"Jungle Jerry's has always had peacocks," Wyatt said. "The first pair, Ike and Mamie, were my grandmother's pets. After they died, we thought we were through with peacocks, but no, somebody was always 'gifting' us with new peacocks. People get them because they think they're such a classy addition to a garden or an estate. Then they hear that ungodly banshee screeching and they can't get rid of them fast enough. They don't even ask us. They just drop the damned things off in the parking lot in the middle of the night, like stray kittens."

He pointed to a huge banyan tree a few hundred yards ahead. "They like to roost there." The path wound around the tree and a clearing came into sight. It was ringed with flowering bushes, and a tall rose-covered arch was centered in a swath of grass.

"That's the butterfly garden," Wyatt said, pointing. "And the wedding chapel, in the middle there."

"How pretty," Grace said. "Do you get many weddings here?"

"Not so many lately," Wyatt said. "Couples seem to want to get married at the beach. Anyway, we don't have the kind of upscale facilities a lot of brides want. The only bathrooms are back at the gift shop, and they're not too glamorous. And let's face it, Jungle Jerry's ain't exactly a classy destination."

"That's a shame," Grace said. "It really is a lovely setting, with all the trees and flowers around, and that sort of meadow in the middle. You could bring in a tent and those fancy port-a-potties that are on trailers, with running water and everything. A good wedding planner could pull off an amazing event here."

"Know any?" Wyatt said gloomily. "Me neither."

The path made a sharp left and suddenly they were surrounded on both sides by a dense wall of bamboo. A light rain had begun falling, so she moved away from the open sides of the cart. Grace caught a glimpse of some kind of structure through the curtain of green.

"What's that back there?"

"That's what's left of Jungle Jerry's big-cat house," Wyatt said. He explained about his grandfather's short-lived career as a lion tamer, and how all the big cats had long ago left the premises.

"From what I've heard, they used to really pack 'em in for the shows," Wyatt said. "At one time we had a 'Safari Train' that ferried people from the parking lot back in here. It was really nothing more than a glorified tractor with a bunch of open cars tacked on the back. Dad sold the train for scrap after we farmed out all the animals more than twenty years ago. But the cages and the remains of the grandstand are still back there. Mostly rust and dust. He planted bamboo to try to provide a natural barrier, but he didn't really understand back then how invasive the stuff is. It's a constant, losing battle, trying to keep it from totally taking over every inch of the park."

"I had no idea what all was involved in running a place like this," Grace said, studying Wyatt's strong, stubborn profile. "I'm amazed you've been able to keep it running after all these years."

He turned and flashed her a rueful grin. "No more amazed than me. But it's not like I really had a choice."

Her hand crept across the bench seat and gave his forearm a squeeze. They rode along for several more minutes with nothing louder than the sound of the rain lightly falling and a breeze ruffling the bamboo until the path took a sharp left.

The bamboo hedge ended abruptly in a large field. Rows of flowers and young trees were laid out in straight lines. A tin-roofed shed was off to one side, under the shade of a large tree.

"This is my favorite place in the park," Wyatt said. "My nursery."

He pulled the golf cart up to the shed and jumped out. "We can hang out here 'til the rain stops." A moment later he was back with a pair of rubber boots. "It's pretty muddy," he warned, handing them to her. "You might want to wear these."

Grace slipped out of her sandals and plunged her feet into the boots, which were four sizes too big and reached nearly to her knees. She giggled as she climbed clumsily out of the cart, lumbering forward in the oversized boots.

Wyatt offered her his arm to steady her. There was a picnic bench under the tin-roofed shed, and now he turned, reached under the seat of the cart, and produced a paper bag, which he handed to her.

Grace looked inside and found a bottle of wine and two plastic cups. "It's screw-top," he said apologetically. "But the guy at the liquor store swears it's good screw-top. You like red?"

"Sure," Grace said.

"One other thing." He picked up a can of insect repellent and sprayed his own neck, arms, and legs, and did the same for her.

Grace sat down on one side of the bench, and after a moment Wyatt sat beside her. He opened the bottle and poured a bit into the cup, handing it to her to sample.

"The guy at the liquor store was right. This is yummy." She held out her cup and he filled it, then filled his own. They sat with their backs to the table, looking out over the fields, slowly sipping the ruby-colored wine.

"What all do you grow here?" Grace asked.

"Annuals for the flower beds out front and throughout the park, some perennials and shrubs. I've got some saplings going that I started from seeds or grafts from our existing trees," Wyatt said. He nodded toward a row of palm trees at the far edge of the field. "I've had pretty good luck with the palm trees. Those are four years old."

"Isn't it a lot of trouble to grow all your own plants?" Grace asked. "Especially with everything else you have to do around the park?"

"It's way cheaper than buying from wholesale nurseries, and anyway, I get a kick out of growing our own stock. It scratches my horticulture itch."

"Very impressive," Grace said, tapping her cup against his.

He fumbled in his pocket for a moment, then brought out a carefully folded sheet of paper. "I, uh, well, when I was thinking about you last night, after I got back home and couldn't sleep, I, uh, drew something for you."

She took the paper and unfolded it. "A landscape plan?" It was an elaborate pencil drawing of a garden, with hand-lettered botanical names. Looking closer, she saw "Mandevilla Manor" in neat block letters in the lower right corner of the paper.

"Some nights my mind won't shut up," he said apologetically. "I have to get up and draw. This isn't anything fancy. Just some ideas."

"I get like that, too," Grace admitted. "I'll wake up in the middle of the night with an idea for a recipe I'd like to develop or some crazy scheme for a house. Since I've been working over at Mandevilla, some nights I only sleep a few hours, I'm so stoked. I think that's how creative people operate."

"Callie always said it was how crazy people operate," Wyatt said.

Grace was examining the sketch. "So . . . no more lawn?" She pointed to the tightly packed rows of shrubs he'd sketched for the front yard.

"Very little grass," Wyatt said. "You could change that, if you wanted, but in Florida it takes so much in the way of water and chemicals to keep large chunks of grass healthy. I think it would look better to do these planting beds with native ornamentals, and maybe some seasonal annuals for color. Here," he jabbed a finger, "I'd do a crushed-shell parking pad, and then extend it to a path that winds through the flowers right up to your front door.

"I didn't have time to label everything, but since I know now that you like blue flowers, I'd give you lots of blues and purples, with whites and green and silver," he said.

"If it were my house, it would be perfect," Grace said, leaning over and giving him a peck on the cheek. "I'll keep it. Maybe eventually I'll have a house again, where I could plant something like this. Well, exactly like this."

"Why couldn't you just do it at Mandevilla Manor?" Wyatt asked.

"Arthur would never go for it," Grace said. "I'm still trying to talk him into springing for central air so I can get rid of those hideous rusting window units."

"It wouldn't be all that expensive to install this plan," Wyatt said. "Most of the plants I've drawn I grow right here in my nursery. The big cost would be in the gravel for the parking pad, the pavers, and the walkway. I get that all at wholesale cost."

"And what about the installation?"

Wyatt grinned. "I know a guy. He works cheap. Or in your case, free." He put his arm around her shoulders and drew Grace closer.

She returned her attention to the plan. "Whoa!" She placed her finger on an irregular shape on the plan. "Is this a pool? In the backyard? Are you kidding?"

"It's just a little dip pool," he said. "Nothing like you had at your last address. Nothing big enough to drown a convertible," he added impishly.

Grace gave him the side eye, and then giggled despite herself. She took another sip of wine.

"The backyard is so big at Mandevilla, it would be a shame not to take advantage of it, eventually," he said. "Everything on here could be done in phases. So, phase one is the front yard and trimming and defining the shrubbery on the sides of the house. Phase two would be getting the citrus grove in the backyard looking good. Paint that barn-slash-garage thing, plant some vines to grow on a trellis to try to minimize the scale of it. Phase three would be the dip pool. And the garage-barn is so big, you could section off part of it for a guest house. The side that faces the proposed dip pool, you'd put in French doors or maybe a cool, industrial-looking roll-up bay door to a space that becomes your pool house. At the same time, you'd probably want to put a pair of French doors in that bedroom that becomes the master, so you have access to your little private patio out to the pool courtyard."

"You are really, really good at this," Grace marveled, looking from the plan to him. "Everything you've drawn here, it just perfectly fits the scale and sensibility of that little Florida cottage. Nothing too grandiose, just right, so appropriate. I can actually picture all of it."

Wyatt's face shone with pleasure. "It's cool, you know? Creating something out of nothing? I miss the design aspect of landscaping. The rest of the park"—he gestured around—"it's pretty much a done deal. All I can do is try to keep the wheels on the bus."

Grace leaned her head back against Wyatt's arm and stared up at the deepening night sky. The rain drummed softly on the tin roof. "What if money were no object? What would you do here then?"

"If wishes were horses?" He snorted derisively. She nudged him with her elbow.

"Okay, well, I'd do more to emphasize the specimen plants my grandparents brought here from all over the world. I'd eventually phase out the bird show, but not Cookie, of course. She's part of the family. I'd maybe have a big demonstration garden, showing all the fruits and vegetables that we grow well in this climate. I'd love to work with local chefs, have an outdoor kitchen here and do cooking demonstrations using locally harvested produce and seafood and meat. I'd make the park less about tourism and more of a community resource. And, maybe, I'd even enlarge the nursery, make some of the plants we've grown here available to the public."

Grace sat up. "Those are wonderful ideas! Truly."

Wyatt shrugged. "It'll never happen. Not in my lifetime. But yeah, I've got my plans."

She gave him a level look. "Do I fit into any of those plans? Or am I just another complication?"

"You? You're not a complication. You're . . . ah, hell, Grace."

He turned and gathered her into his arms and kissed her softly.

"Mmm," she said after a while. "I do like your plans." Wyatt's arms tightened around her. His tongue tickled hers, and she wrapped her arms around his neck and flattened herself to his chest. A moment later, his warm hands slipped under her T-shirt, and then under the white camisole she wore instead of a bra. He grazed her nipples with his thumbs and she inhaled sharply and twined her hands through his hair.

"Is this okay?" he whispered in her ear. "Should I stop?"

"Never," she breathed.

His kisses grew more urgent as he pushed the fabric of her T-shirt upward. Grace let her hands slide slowly down his chest, to his waist; then, working them under his polo shirt, she flattened her palms on his bare chest, feeling the warmth, sliding her hands upward, brushing her fingertips across his nipples.

A moment later, by mutual, silent agreement, they were both shirtless. Wyatt pulled her onto his lap, kissing the nape of her neck, the hollow of her throat, cupping her breasts with both hands, teasing his tongue across her tightened nipples while she kneaded his shoulders, raking her nails across his bare back. Her breathing grew ragged as he kissed and caressed and, slowly, pushed her backward onto the picnic bench.

"Mmm," she protested, between kisses. "This isn't going to work, this bench is too skinny. We'll both end up in the mud."

He stopped what he was doing, then pulled her to her feet and, without warning, picked her up and plunked her atop the picnic table. She laughed but scooted back on her behind, and soon he was right there beside her, stretched out on top of the picnic table. He worked one thigh between hers, fumbling for the zipper of her shorts. She found his zipper easily, slid it down, and traced his erection with her thumb, while she pushed his shorts down. He was still groping with the button on the waistband of her shorts when she heard a soft buzzing and then a ringtone that sounded like "Take Me Out to the Ball Game" coming from the pocket of his shorts.

"Dammit!" he muttered.

She laughed. "Can't it wait?"

He sat up abruptly, pulling at his shorts. "That's Bo's ringtone," he said, grabbing the phone. "I gotta answer."

41

Hey, buddy, what's up?" Wyatt said softly, turning so that his back was to Grace. She rested her head on his bare shoulder.

The child whispered something incoherent.

"What's that? I can't hear you, Bo."

"I said, Mom called and she sounded really mad," Bo said, his whisper hoarse.

"Why are you whispering?" Wyatt asked.

"I don't want Granddad to hear," Bo said. "He told me not to call you, but I can tell he's all upset."

Wyatt held the phone away from his face and swore softly.

"What did your mom want?"

"She was yelling at me because she said you didn't tell her we had a big game today and she missed it."

Wyatt rolled his eyes. "We gave your mom a schedule of all the games at the beginning of the season, son. I'm sorry she yelled at you, but I'll call her later and we'll get it straightened out."

"Dad, Mom made me put Granddad on the phone when she got done talking to me. And he got super, super angry. He was yelling and saying bad words. Some of it didn't even make any sense. Now he's breathing kind of funny. Dad, can you come back? I'm kind of scared."

"I'll be right there," Wyatt said firmly. "Don't be scared. You did just the right thing to call me. We're just over at the plant nursery. We'll be back at the house in five minutes."

Wyatt stood and pulled his shirt over his head. Grace dressed hurriedly, straightening her hair, and packed the wine bottle and glasses in the brown paper sack.

"Do you want me to stay on the phone with you while we ride back?" Wyatt asked. Grace climbed onto the seat of the golf cart, and a moment later they were rocketing down the path.

"No, that's okay," Bo said.

"Where is Granddad right now?" Wyatt asked. "Is he awake? What's he doing?"

"He's just staring at the television, talking to himself," Bo said. "It's okay now. He's not dead or nothing."

Wyatt laughed, despite himself. "That's good news. I'm on the way."

"Bye."

Grace gripped Wyatt's arm. "I heard part of that. What's the problem? Is your father okay?"

"To quote my son, 'he's not dead or nothin,'" Wyatt said, his facial features taught. "Callie called to ream Bo out because she missed his game today. Then, after she'd finished making him feel like crap, she got on the phone and picked a fight with Dad. She knows just how to push his buttons. Apparently, he was yelling and ranting and raving at her, and of course Bo overheard all of it, and, naturally, it got him pretty worried. He says Dad is breathing funny, just staring at the television, talking to himself. Bo's a smart kid. I think he senses that Dad is starting to slip a little, and he's protective of his grandfather."

"Thank God for that," Grace said. "And thank God we weren't far away."

"I'll just pack up my stuff and get out of your way," Grace said, as the cart approached the double-wide.

"No! This is not how I wanted the evening to end," Wyatt said. "It's probably nothing. I'll get Dad calmed down and pack Bo off to bed. It'll be fine."

"You need to spend time with them, not worry about me," Grace said. "We can have other nights."

"Really? When? We both work all the time, and the rest of the time, my life is like this," he said, pulling the cart beneath the carport. "Just stay a few minutes, please? Just 'til I get these guys sorted out."

"I don't want to be in the way," Grace protested.

"You're not in the way. I promise," he said, squeezing her hand. "Your being there will probably make Bo feel a little better. He likes you."

"He just likes my dog," Grace said, laughing.

"Whatever works."

Bo met them at the door. He was dressed in his pajamas, and his freckled face looked worried. "Don't tell Granddad I called, okay?"

Wyatt leaned down and hugged his son. "It's a deal."

He walked into the living room, where Nelson sat rigidly in his recliner, muttering incoherently. His face was pale except for two scarlet patches on his cheeks. The television volume was turned all the way up.

Wyatt touched his father's shoulder. He found the remote control and turned the television down. "Dad? What's going on?"

Nelson didn't look up. "That woman got no right to talk to me like that. No respect. No morals. I told her that, too. Told her it looks bad for her son, her living in sin with that man. Did I cuss her out? Hell yeah, I cussed her out. Do it again, too, next time."

Wyatt sat on the sofa. "I'm sorry Callie got you so upset. I'll talk to her about that. But maybe it would be better if you just didn't speak to her at all."

"She called me!" Nelson shouted. "Didn't even know she was the one on the phone until Bo said his mom wanted to talk to me. I told Bo to tell her I was asleep, but she could hear me, and she insisted Bo give the phone to me."

"What did she want?" Wyatt asked.

"What she always wants. She wanted to raise hell with me. Wanted to know where you really were. If you were out with your new girlfriend. She claimed you didn't tell her about Bo's game because you wanted your girlfriend to go to the game instead of her. I told her if you did have a girlfriend it was none of her goddamn business. Then she wanted to know why Bo wasn't in bed, since it was after nine, which is his bedtime at her house. I told her it was Saturday night and there's no school tomorrow and I didn't give a tinker's damn what time he went to bed at her house."

Nelson's voice was rising, his breathing getting shallow. He waved his arms as he shouted, and from the corner of his eye, Wyatt saw Bo, standing, wide-eyed in the doorway. A moment later, Grace was behind him, gently shepherding him into the kitchen.

He leaned forward and grasped his father's arms, forcing the old man to look at him. "Okay, Dad, calm down. I am going to have a discussion with Callie and her lawyer, and tell them that she is not to talk to you anymore. All right? This isn't your fault. But you need to settle down. Did you take your blood pressure meds this morning?"

"What? Hell, who remembers that long ago?" Nelson grabbed for the remote control, but Wyatt held it out of his reach.

Bo sat at the kitchen table, clutching Sweetie in his arms. Huge tears welled in his dark eyes, and he was rhythmically kicking the chrome table leg.

Grace found the foil-wrapped remains of the brownie pie. She cut a generous slice and put it on a plate and poured a glass of milk, which she set in front of the little boy.

Without a word, Bo picked up a fork and took a bite. He gulped his milk and wiped his mouth with the back of his hand. Sweetie wriggled in his lap and licked his neck. Bo giggled.

"She just wants some of your pie, but we can't give her any, because chocolate isn't good for dogs," Grace warned.

She gave Sweetie a mock-stern look. "What? Sorry, little girl. There are no leftovers when you feed three hungry single men." She looked around the room until she found the jar of dog treats she'd given Wyatt. She handed one to Bo, who offered it to Sweetie, who snapped it up without hesitation.

Bo ate a few more bites of the pie. He had a milk mustache and his ears were bright pink as he looked at Grace with open curiosity. "I think my mom is mad because I told her Dad took you out to ride around on the golf cart."

Grace nodded. "She's probably mad at me, not you. But that's understandable."

"She thinks you're Dad's new girlfriend."

"I wonder how she got that idea?" Grace said. "Your mom doesn't even know me."

Bo hung his head.

She laughed, leaned over, and ruffled his close-cut hair. "It's okay with me, but I don't know how your dad will feel about hearing that I'm his girlfriend."

"You're my new girlfriend?" Wyatt walked into the kitchen and swiped the last bite of pie from his son's plate.

"That's what Bo's mom apparently thinks," Grace said. She bustled around the kitchen, packing up the empty food containers.

"Hmm," Wyatt said, looking from Bo to Grace. He nodded at Bo. "Wonder where she got that idea?"

Bo's voice was very small. "I told her. She made me very, very mad when she yelled at me about the game. So I told her you have a new girlfriend who is really nice, and whose name is Grace, and who brought us taco casserole and chocolate pie. I told her I get to take care of her dog. And then I told her I do not want to move to stinking Birmingham."

"Okay," Wyatt said. He looked at the clock on the oven. "It's past your bedtime. How about you tell Grace good night and then go brush your teeth and hit the hay?"

Bo looked like he might put up a fight, but then thought better of it. "Is Granddad okay?"

"He's kind of tired right now, so he just went to bed," Wyatt said. "I think maybe he forgot to take his medicine this morning. Guess we'll have to do a better job of reminding him, won't we?"

"Yes, sir," Bo said. He set the dog down on the floor and stood. "Good night, Grace. Thank you for dinner." He thought for a minute, then added, "And for letting Sweetie stay here."

"I'd better get going, too," Grace said, watching the dog follow Bo down the hallway.

"I could make some coffee," Wyatt offered. "Don't run off just yet."

He poured them each a mug of coffee and sat opposite her at the kitchen table. "Sorry about all the drama," he said, taking a sip. His face hardened. "It's like Callie enjoys stirring up trouble. She hasn't been to a single one of Bo's Saturday games this season. She's always too busy with Luke. Now, suddenly, it's my fault she didn't know about today?"

"It does sound like she's deliberately trying to provoke you, and Nelson," Grace observed. "The question is, Why? What does she get out of it?"

"I'm sure she's got an ulterior motive," Wyatt agreed. "But I have no idea what it could be. And I don't feel like investing a lot of energy trying to predict what her next move will be."

"Maybe just be careful with what information Bo gives her," Grace said. She felt her face warm. "So . . . it's official? I'm your new girlfriend?"

"I hope so," Wyatt told her. "Is that weird?"

"Not weird," she decided. "Different. New. I haven't been anybody's girlfriend in a really long time."

"It's new to me, too," he admitted. "Not at all what I expected when Stackpole ordered me to attend divorce camp."

"Speaking of," Grace said. "I had lunch with Camryn Nobles today."

"Camryn? Why? I didn't know you two were buddy-buddy."

"Neither did I. She's been doing some investigating. She found out Paula lost her therapist accreditation out in Oregon, after she got caught forging her ex-husband's name on some prescriptions for tranquilizers."

"No shit?"

"It's kind of a sad story." Grace filled him in on everything Camryn had confided in her at the Rod and Reel pier and about Paula's new career as a divorce coach.

"We know she's taking pills again," Wyatt said. "I wonder if they have something to do with her family emergency the other night?"

"I'm thinking the same thing," Grace agreed. "Camryn wants to report her to the authorities here. But what good does that do? I think we have to help her."

"And how do we do that?"

"I think we, that is, the group, have to confront her," Grace said. "Tell her we know she's self-medicating and that we know she was in rehab for the same thing. Maybe she'll open up and talk to us."

"Or . . . maybe she'll tell us all to fuck off and then rat us out to Stackpole for spying on her," Wyatt said. "And then we're all really, really screwed with the judge who has life-or-death jurisdiction over our divorces. Have you considered that possibility?"

Grace sighed. "Stackpole's the bad guy in all of this. I really think Paula is like us, another one of his victims."

"But we can't prove they're involved or that Stackpole is doing anything illegal, right?" Wyatt asked. "And in the meantime, it's hard for me to feel sorry for a phony therapist who's ripping us off."

"I disagree," Grace said lightly. "I just don't believe Paula is the one getting as rich as Camryn believes she must be. I'm going to call Mitzi tomorrow, just to let her know what we've found out about Paula. And I think we ought to at least let Ashleigh and Suzanne know what Camryn discovered."

She took her coffee mug and set it in the sink. "But now, I think I'd better head home. Thanks for a lovely evening, Wyatt."

He walked her outside to her car, his arm slung casually over her shoulder. "I just wish things had gone differently tonight. I wish . . ."

She turned and wrapped her arms around his neck. "I wish it, too. It was nice while it lasted, though."

He kissed her. "Nelson wanted me to apologize for him. For ruining our 'date,' as he called it. He keeps asking me if we've slept together!"

"Oh my God," Grace said with a giggle. "I should not be telling you this, but Rochelle keeps asking me the same thing."

"So why haven't we?"

Grace arched an eyebrow in response.

"I'm a slow starter," Wyatt admitted. "But once I build up steam . . . I won't lie. I've been trying to figure out how we can be alone since last week."

"We can't be together at the Sandbox, that's for sure," Grace said.

"Ditto for here," Wyatt said, resting his hands lightly on her waist. "Bo and I share a room, and even on nights he's with Callie, Dad's room is right next door, and the walls in this trailer are like toilet paper."

"Poor us," Grace said mockingly.

"I'll think of something," Wyatt said. He lifted her chin and kissed her hungrily. "Soon. Very soon."

42

The coffee shop was only two blocks from the Manatee County Courthouse in downtown Bradenton. The lunch-hour rush was over, and Grace and Mitzi Stillwell were alone at a booth near the front window, sipping watered-down iced teas while the hostess counted down the money in her cash register.

"I've got a little good news for you," Mitzi said. "After much arm twisting and hand wringing, I heard from Ben's lawyer today. You'll have your first check tomorrow."

"It's about damn time," Grace said. "How'd you manage it?"

"A combination of threats, nonstop phone calls and e-mails, and borderline harassment," Mitzi said. "It's not nearly enough, but it's a start."

"I cannot wait to buy myself a decent pair of shoes. And some new underwear," Grace added.

Mitzi gave Grace a critical glance. "You're looking good, Grace. I think the single life must suit you."

"Thanks. I'm busy, working on a house, and that makes me happy. As for single life? Things are getting, um, interesting."

"Hmm. Interesting as in good?"

"Very good," Grace assured her.

"And how's Rochelle? Do you think she'll ever get back in the game?"

"Mom?" Grace looked puzzled. "Date? We've never discussed it. To tell you the truth, the idea of her going out never entered my mind. Why do you ask?"

"No reason," Mitzi said quickly. "She's not that old, not even sixty, right? My mom married her second husband at seventy, and when he dropped dead five years later, she picked right back up again. She's always got a guy in the wings. Rochelle's a very attractive lady, very young-thinking. I just think it would be a shame if she turned into one of those dried-up mean widow women you always see in every retirement community in Florida."

"Mom. Dating?" Grace couldn't quite seem to put the words together, in her mouth or in her mind.

"Never mind," Mitzi said. "Tell me how it's going in divorce-recovery group. Does your therapist seem to have recovered from her episode?"

"That's why I called you," Grace said eagerly. "Camryn—she's that reporter from channel four. Stackpole sentenced her to group after she put a video of her husband parading around in a pair of red satin women's thong panties up on YouTube . . ."

Mitzi coughed violently, and dabbed at her face with a paper napkin. "Oh my God! That's her husband? Camryn Nobles, News Four You? What's that song he's dancing to in the video? Have you seen it? It's hysterical!"

"No, I haven't seen it. Stackpole made her take it down," Grace said. "But listen to what Camryn found out about Paula."

"Really? I'm impressed. Camryn Nobles figured this out? I always thought she was just a pretty face. Who knew she could actually do real journalism?"

"Paula's not even a licensed therapist in this state. She gets around that by calling herself a divorce coach. Mitzi, she doesn't even have a Web site. So how did she get that successful that fast?"

"Her book?"

"It's only available as an e-book, and *Mindful Marriage*'s Amazon ranking is 367,459," Grace said.

Mitzi chewed on some ice. "Those people in the other divorce-therapy sessions, were they all women?"

"Yes."

"Well . . . if we knew that all of them were referred to Paula by Stackpole, that might be a very useful piece of information," Mitzi allowed.

"How could we find that out?"

"I guess you could ask them," Mitzi said.

"I think our group should have an intervention with Paula," Grace said. "We could confront her about the pills and her odd behavior. But Wyatt thinks if it goes wrong, it could make things even worse for all of us. With Stackpole."

"Wyatt?" Mitzi pursed her lips. "He's the guy we saw in court that day? The one who put his fist through his wife's car window? Are you two seeing each other?"

Grace blushed.

"Is it serious?"

"I hope so," Grace said quietly. "He's a good person, Mitzi. He doesn't deserve the crap his wife is handing him."

"I remember the wife from court. She was a terror."

"You don't know the half of it," Grace told her. "Wyatt is sick with worry that Stackpole will allow Callie to move to Birmingham with his son, Bo."

"About Stackpole," Mitzi said. "I've been asking around, very quietly. He and his wife used to be quite the social butterflies around town. She chaired the big Heart Fund ball last year, and they're members at the Longboat Key Club, where he plays a lot of tennis, but nobody's seen them out and about together much these past few months."

"Maybe the wife found out about Paula."

"Could be," Mitzi allowed. "Or maybe it's just that it's July. The Stackpoles have a house in the mountains in North Carolina. One of those woodsy, social places like Highlands or Flat Rock. I think she spends most of the summer up there."

"And while the cat's away, the rat will play," Grace said. "Mitzi, I just know Stackpole and Paula are having an affair. I can't prove it, but if you'd seen them that night when he showed up at group, it was just so obvious."

Mitzi stirred the dregs of her ice with her straw. "So what? You've only got two more weeks of divorce camp left, and then Stackpole will sign off on your divorce."

"I know," Grace said resignedly.

"Isn't that what we want? You—divorced? Free to get on with your life? Free to have a relationship with Wyatt or anybody else of your choosing?"

"The whole thing with Stackpole and Paula—it's wrong, Mitzi! And there's nothing I can do about it."

"You *are* doing something, Grace. You're building a new life for yourself. The financial aspect aside—I still haven't given up on that—I still think we can argue that you're entitled to your equity in the house since so much of the labor and materials were given to you as compensation for exposure on your blog . . . All that aside, you are doing what I preach to all my women clients. You are not letting this divorce define you. You're not letting bitterness defeat you. Grace, you're a rock star!"

Grace snorted. "I don't even have a place to shack up with the new man in my life! So what kind of rock star does that make me?"

Mitzi's eyes lit up. "Ohhhh. So it really is getting serious with Wyatt. Why didn't you say something earlier?" She dug a key ring from her purse and extracted a key, which she pressed into Grace's hand.

"Here. This is to my condo at Anna Maria. My long-term tenant just moved out, and I'm converting it to a vacation rental. I've bought some furniture and had it painted and recarpeted, but that's as far as I've gotten with the place. Decorating is just not my thing. I've been planning on hiring a decorator to finish it, but maybe that's something you could do?"

Grace flushed and tried to return the key. "Oh, Mitzi, no. I couldn't. I really wasn't asking for your charity. I just needed to vent for a minute."

"I'm not trying to give you charity," Mitzi exclaimed. "I'll pay you, for God's sake! You'd be doing me a huge favor. The management company that's going to handle the rentals has been after me to get the place ready to be photographed for their Web site, but I hate shopping, and I suck at decorating. You'd be doing me a huge favor if you'd agree to fluff the place. Please?" She grinned. "It's not fancy, but there's a sofa and a bed and sheets and towels and a flat-screen television. What more do you need for a romantic evening? Say you'll take the job, and I'll stock the fridge with champagne and chocolate."

"I don't know," Grace demurred, but Mitzi grabbed her hand and closed her palm over the key. "You've got a credit card again, right?"

"Yes, with a five-thousand-dollar limit," Grace said.

"Great. So that'll be your budget for the condo. Five thousand will be enough to get some curtains and some rugs and doodads, won't it?"

"Sure, as long as I don't have to buy the big-ticket items like mattresses or sofas or furniture, I should be able to fluff it for that much. When do you need it ready?"

"Like, yesterday, according to the property-management people. They wanted it done before Memorial Day, but that ship has sailed."

Grace gave it some thought. "Give me two weeks. Is that okay?"

"Works for me," Mitzi said. She reached into her purse and pulled out her checkbook. "Designers work on retainer, right? So, how much?"

"No retainer," Grace said firmly.

Mitzi's eyes narrowed. "Then give me back my key. Because I won't let you work for me for free. Listen to me, Grace. I have to remind my women clients about this all the time. Just because your spouse didn't recognize your worth doesn't mean you have no value. You're a professional interior designer, not some little dabbler who does this as a hobby. Don't devalue yourself by refusing to be fairly compensated. Now. What do you bill out at?"

Grace opened her mouth to argue, then closed it. Finally, she said, "Going rate here is about 125 dollars an hour, but since I won't actually be doing any sketches, and since it'll mostly be a matter of shopping and installing, I charge a hundred dollars an hour."

"Fine." Mitzi wrote the check and handed it to her client. "That's fifteen hundred. If you think it's going to take you more time than that after looking at the place, let me know."

Grace took the check and looked at it. It was written to Grace Davenport, her first paycheck under her born-again maiden name.

"Thanks," she said, her eyes shining with barely suppressed tears. And then she remembered the reason she'd asked for this meeting with her lawyer.

"Okay. What about Stackpole?"

"Oh, all right," Mitzi grumbled. "I'll take a look at his recent dockets to see what other attorneys I know have had cases before him. I'll ask around, to see if any of their clients have been sentenced to divorce camp with Paula Talbott-Sinclair. Satisfied?"

"Yes," Grace said. "Totally satisfied."

"In the meantime," Mitzi wagged a finger at Grace, "stay away from Wyatt Keeler's wife. That woman is trouble."

Grace shuddered. "Don't worry. I have no plans to get anywhere near Callie Keeler."

Wyatt Keeler spent the morning in his tiny office at Jungle Jerry's, staring at a mounting pile of bills. When his cell phone rang and he saw who was calling, he snatched it from his desktop.

"Betsy? Hey! How are you?"

"I'm fine. How's the rash?"

"Mostly gone, thanks to you. Guess I should listen to my elders more often."

"I'll have to remind you of that in the future," Betsy said drily. "Look, I won't beat around the bush. I just got a call from Callie's lawyer. They're asking Stackpole for an emergency hearing."

Wyatt's throat went dry. "What's the emergency?"

"Oh, Christ," Betsy said. "Promise me you will not go crazy when you hear."

"I won't go crazy," Wyatt said automatically. "Now tell me what's going on. Please."

He heard the sound of pages being turned. "Callie is now claiming that Nelson is suffering from acute dementia. Her filing says that when he is not confused and nonresponsive, he is verbally abusive and threatening, and he uses profane language in front of Bo, and he's capable of violence. In short, she's saying that as long as Nelson is living with you, your home is an unfit atmosphere for a child."

"What!" Wyatt put the phone down on the desk. He stood back and kicked his old army-surplus battleship-gray desk so viciously his work boot left a hollow impression in the bottom file drawer.

He sat back down and took several deep breaths.

"Wyatt?"

"I'm here," he said quietly.

"Do you have any idea what prompted this piece of garbage?"

"I do," he said grimly. He quickly recounted Saturday evening's events for his aunt.

"Well." Betsy sighed. "You and I know Callie deliberately provoked Nelson into a tirade. Is any of what she's claiming true? Is your Dad suffering from dementia?"

"No. Betsy, you know what Dad's like. He's slowing down, no question about it. Sometimes, usually in the evenings, he gets a little . . . foggy. And sometimes, again, usually when he's overtired, he can get a little verbally combative. But most days, he's still sharp as a tack. And he's a sweetheart, you know that. He adores Bo. Being around Bo, helping take care of him, it's given him a real sense of purpose. Of responsibility. And it's good for Bo, too. There is no way Dad is capable of violence. Ever! He might rant and rave at Callie, because as far as he's concerned, she abandoned us. But he would never act on his threats."

"That's what I think, too," Betsy said. "But this latest ploy has me worried. Stackpole really chewed her out last time around. I'm thinking she wouldn't risk annoying him again unless she thinks she really has something that will stick."

Wyatt buried his head in his hands. "Oh my God," he said softly. "This is like a nightmare that never ends. She really will stop at nothing."

"I know," Betsy agreed. "Stackpole wants to see us at eleven A.M. tomorrow. In the meantime, I went ahead and made an appointment with Margaret-Ellen Shank. She's a really well-respected geriatrician on staff at Sarasota Memorial. Fortunately for us, she had a really messy divorce a couple years ago, and I was able to help her out. Can you have your dad over there by four this afternoon? She's agreed to juggle her schedule to see him."

"I'll have him there," Wyatt said wearily. "But what do I tell him? He's gotta see a doctor to prove he's not senile so I don't lose custody of my son?"

"Tell him the truth," Betsy said. "I'll see you there."

43

Arthur Cater stood on the porch staring into the doorway at the little cottage on Mandevilla. He wore an ancient T-shirt with chopped-off sleeves; shapeless, colorless green pants; and a dubious expression. He poked his nose inside the living room. He sniffed. His craggy face scrunched into some indefinable expression that threatened to give Grace an anxiety attack.

"What?" she asked. "What's wrong?" She'd spent all day Sunday using a rented floor sander to take the dirty, scuffed finish off the oak floors. She'd worked all night, mopping every last particle of sawdust before staining the floors a rich, dark walnut color. Her arms and lower back were still throbbing from her efforts.

When Arthur Cater called to casually announce his intention to drop by and check on her progress, Grace had only managed to stall him until after her meeting with Mitzi. Her stomach had been in knots all morning, wondering what Arthur's reaction would be to her progress.

Now she had it, and judging by the look on his face, the news was not good.

Suddenly, she got angry. And defensive.

"Arthur," she exclaimed, "it's just paint. If you hate it, I can repaint. But I wanted a higher contrast between the floors and the walls, which is why I chose the dark stain for the floors."

"Hush!" Arthur turned on his heel and walked rapidly out to the porch and into the yard.

Grace stared, speechless. Was he leaving?

No. A moment later he was back, carrying a bulky leather-covered camera. It was an old 35-millimeter.

He stood in the doorway and clicked the shutter. He walked into the dining room and snapped another picture. When he got to the kitchen, he stopped in his tracks.

"Well, I'll be damned." When he turned to Grace, his face was actually wreathed in smiles.

"You did all this?"

"I did," Grace assured him.

"By yourself?"

"With a little help."

He gestured at the secondhand Craigslist range, fridge, and dishwasher. "How the hell did you get those in there?"

"Some guys I used to work with back in my model-home days. Jimmy and Eduardo. I hired them to pick up the appliances in their truck and to install them. I don't do wiring, Arthur."

He gestured at the floor, with its gleaming red-checkerboard pattern. "What's that made out of?"

She gulped. "It's marine-grade plywood. The old linoleum tiles just were not coming up. So I nailed the plywood down, primed it, then taped off the squares and painted it with deck paint. Do you hate it?" She prayed he didn't. Her knees still had bruises from all the hours she'd spent taping and painting.

"It's good," Arthur said, nodding and flashing that rare-as-diamonds smile again. "Better than good. It's great. This floor—it looks just like the tiles my grandmother used to have in here. I'd forgotten that until just this minute."

"How about the open shelves?" Grace asked, still anxious for his approval. "The old cabinet doors were warped and gummy with all those old layers of paint, and the only way to clean them up would have been to strip them all down to the bare wood, and I just didn't have the time or the patience for that."

"Hush," Arthur commanded. He snapped two more pictures of the kitchen in rapid succession. "Wait until my wife sees this." He chortled. "She's said all along that we should just get rid of the darned cupboard doors. She even showed me a picture in one of her magazines, but I told her she was crazy. Just shows you how much I know."

He walked back through the abbreviated hallway and poked his head into both bedrooms, nodding and snapping more exposures.

"I can't believe it," he said, shaking his head. He looked over at Grace, still dressed in a simple cotton sundress for her coffee date with her lawyer.

"A little bitty gal like you got all this done, just like that," he said, snapping his fingers.

If only he knew, Grace mused, the untold hours she'd spent working on the house, for which she'd never be compensated—not in money, anyway.

"So, do you like it?" she asked.

"I do," he said, patting her shoulder awkwardly.

"There's still so much more to accomplish," she cautioned. "The bathroom vanity—I know I told you all the fixtures were okay, but the sink has a leak, and that vanity is all rotted out underneath. I'd like to replace it with a pedestal sink with more of a period look. And the tub—I've scrubbed it and scrubbed it, but it's pitted and chipped, and it's going to look even nastier once I get the bathroom painted. I'd love to have it reglazed."

"Do it," Arthur said expansively. He was in a rare mood, Grace thought. Maybe now was the time to spring the rest of her wish list on him.

She followed him onto the front porch, where he gazed out at the yard. "What the hell have you done out here?" he asked wonderingly.

Grace blushed. "I have a friend, he's a landscape architect, and he gave me some suggestions about cutting things back, reshaping the beds. There's a lot more I'd like to do in the yard, eventually. This house has such incredible curb appeal now, but it could be even better."

"It looks grand," Arthur said, and he was actually beaming. "It looks better than it has in twenty years. Not just the yard, everything."

"I'm so glad you like it," Grace told him. "Once I get some poly on those floors, they'll really look sharp. And then I was thinking, I could probably start furnishing it in the next week or so."

"Fine," Arthur said. "That sounds fine."

"About the air-conditioning, Arthur," Grace began.

He scowled.

Grace picked up a wooden paint-stir stick from her stack of supplies in the corner of the front porch. She poked the outside of the air-conditioning unit protruding from the living room window. A flurry of rust chips fell to the porch floor.

"The salt air has completely rusted this unit out," Grace said. "It's on its last legs. And the other units aren't much better."

"No ma'am," he said firmly. "Why, those units aren't that old. I put them in here myself."

"In 1982. I found the owner's manual in the hall linen closet. Arthur, these units are almost as old as me. They've outlived their useful life."

"Then I'll buy some new ones," he said, his face set in a mulish expression.

"You'll need five window units, at the very least," Grace said, consulting the notes she'd scribbled on her last shopping trip. "I checked at Sears and Home Depot, for the BTUs we need in the main rooms, meaning, the living room, dining room, kitchen, and both bedrooms, that's a little over two thousand dollars."

"Nonsense," Arthur said. "I can buy those units for under a hundred bucks apiece."

She handed him the most recent sales flyer she'd picked up at Sears. "Maybe thirty years ago you could buy them for that, but not these days."

He scowled down at the flyer. "I suppose you're going to keep after me about putting in central air-conditioning?"

"Yes, I am," Grace said emphatically. She handed him another brochure. "That's an estimate I had worked up by a very reliable HVAC guy who my mom uses at the Sandbox. It'll cost less than five thousand dollars! You'll get an up-to-the-minute energy-efficient unit, and there may be tax breaks involved as well. And, since you pay the utilities, there will be a substantial savings on your electric bills."

He ran a bony finger down the printed estimate, frowning. "I never figured to put all this much money in this little house." He looked up at her. "There's hardly any sense fixing it up this grand, just so the next bunch of tenants can come in here and ruin all our hard work."

Now, Grace told herself. Ask him now.

"About the next tenants," she said, fixing him with her most winning smile. "What would you say to renting this place to me?"

"Ah-hah!" he cried. "At last the other shoe drops. I should have known you had an ulterior motive for wanting me to spend all this money."

"I want you to spend what is really a very reasonable amount of money to maintain and improve this lovely property," Grace said, willing herself to keep calm and use all the arguments she'd gone over and over in her head. "I really didn't intend to ask about renting it, but then, once I got it cleaned up and saw just what a nice place it could be, it occurred to me to inquire about renting it."

His smile grew crafty. "All this money of mine you've been spending, you realize the rent's going up, right?"

"Of course. If you'll recall, that was one of the arguments I gave you for fixing it up. You've rented it so cheaply in the past, it's no wonder you've gotten deadbeats and lowlifes as tenants. But if you rent it to me, at a fair market price, I'll be a model tenant. I'll pay on time, every month, no excuses. I'll keep the property in pristine condition. And I'll continue to make improvements, provided you pay for them."

"Like what?"

He hadn't, Grace realized, said no yet.

"The kitchen still needs more work," she pointed out. "Better lighting, especially under the cabinets. There's that big dead space by the back door; I think it could be made into a nice laundry room, with a stacked washer/dryer and a shelf for folding clothes. All the windows need caulking, which should also help make the house more energy-efficient. The garage needs paint; it's a major eyesore. And then there are tons of little things. Like replacing all the nasty old electrical outlets, maybe installing ceiling fans in the bedrooms . . ."

"You love spending other people's money, don't you?" Arthur complained.

She ignored him and went on with her list of improvements. "My friend drew up a wonderful landscape plan for the yard. Did you know there are half a dozen fruit trees in the backyard? Lemon, lime, grapefruit, tangerines. He'll show me how to trim them and fertilize them so they produce again. I'd plant more flowers in the front beds, maybe do away with some of that grass . . ."

"Get rid of grass?" he squawked. "What do you want to do, pave the yard?"

"Not at all," she said calmly. "Maintaining all that grass takes so much time and energy, water and chemicals, my friend thinks flower beds might be a better solution. Oh, and did you know there's a sprinkler system out there?"

"Of course," Arthur said. "Not much good, since it hasn't worked in years and years."

"My friend thinks he can probably get it working again without spending much money," Grace said. "This could be the beauty spot in the neighborhood."

"Not to mention my water bill would go sky-high," he muttered.

"Come on, Arthur," Grace coaxed. "Quit making excuses for why it won't work. Won't you at least consider it?"

He folded the brochures and stuffed them in his back pocket. "I'll give it some thought," he said finally. "Have to discuss it with my wife. She's the real boss, you know."

"That's all I ask," Grace said. "Show her the pictures you took today, tell her my ideas, see what she says."

"Can't promise anything," he warned. "We're busy, getting ready to head up to the mountains."

"That's fine," Grace repeated. "Just let me know. And Arthur?"

"What now?"

"Thanks for the vote of confidence. I'm really thrilled you like what I've done."

Truegrace

One of my favorite old movies is Mr. Blandings Builds His Dream House. *Poor Mr. Blandings (played by Cary Grant) is a harried advertising copywriter living with his happy nuclear family in a cramped city apartment who just wants to build a simple little cottage in the country, but when the dream starts to take on grandiose proportions, Mr. Blandings's sunny version of utopia suddenly turns cloudy. I've thought of that movie a lot lately, as my own home life was dramatically disrupted, and then destroyed. Up until three months ago, I was living in a 6,500-square-foot mansion, that I thought was my own dream house. Now, with the clarity that only hindsight can bring, I realize that dream was mostly spun of high-fructose fantasy.*

These days, I'm finding intense satisfaction in the transformation of a weather-beaten little 1,200-square-foot Florida "cracker cottage" into what I think will be a cozy jewel of a home—maybe even, eventually, my home. I feel a little like Goldilocks, who found one chair too big, another chair too small, but, finally, an exactly-perfect-fit chair that feels "just right." My work on Mandevilla Manor is far from done, but already it's feeling "just right."

44

Nelson Keeler was having one of his good days. "Goddamn it," he roared, when Wyatt told him of his impending doctor's appointment. "I do not have Alzheimer's! I'm fine! That scheming woman . . . you call up that judge, tell him I'll go to the courthouse right now. I'll recite the Declaration of Independence by heart, balance my checkbook, balance his checkbook, and then I'll drop and give him fifty, by God!"

"No, Dad, that's all right," Wyatt protested, but it was too late.

Nelson proceeded to do just that, right there in the living room of the trailer, flattening himself on the floor, doing fifty straight-arm push-ups, counting aloud in a wheezy voice, then sitting up, cross-legged, wiping his perspiring brow with the sleeve of his shirt.

"How many other seventy-four-year-olds you think can do that?"

"None." Wyatt gave his father a hand up. "I know you've got all your marbles. But we've got to prove it to the judge, and to do that, you've got to go see this doctor and get a bunch of tests done. Just remember, you're doing this for Bo, not for Callie."

"Callie!" Nelson spat the name. "Somebody should have knocked some sense into that woman years ago. When this is all over, I'm gonna . . ."

Wyatt steered his father toward the door. "When this is all over, we're gonna laugh about it, but until then, neither of us can afford to do or say anything that might make anyone believe we're a couple of dangerously violent misfits. Right, Dad?"

"If you say so," Nelson muttered.

"One more thing," Wyatt said. "If you're going to convince this doctor, and then the judge, that you're harmless, you've got to keep your temper under check. This means no debating Alex Trebek or the designated-hitter rule. And it especially means no discussion of your bowel movements. Right?"

"Unless the doctor asks," Nelson countered.

"But only if she asks."

It was after six o'clock. Nelson Keeler was sitting upright in a chair in the doctor's office, snoring.

"He's had a really long day," Wyatt told Margaret-Ellen Shank. "He gets up at six, always has, and some nights he doesn't sleep all that well. He usually has a midday nap, but he didn't get that today."

"No need to apologize," Dr. Shank said, her voice soft. "Your dad is quite a guy. I really enjoyed meeting and talking to him today. One thing. What's his diet like?"

Wyatt shrugged. "Dad has a sweet tooth. He likes Pop-Tarts or Twinkies for breakfast. He might eat some canned soup for lunch, and a lot of nights he'll have a frozen chicken potpie for dinner. Or, and I'm not proud of this, a quart of ice cream or some more Twinkies."

Dr. Stark was still making notes. "What did he have for lunch today, do you know?"

"I don't," Wyatt admitted. "I was out in the park working until right before time for his appointment with you."

She frowned and consulted her notes. "Your dad has good balance and coordination, is able to communicate clearly, and his short- and long-term memory seemed to be in an acceptable range for his age. But as the day wore on, his personality changed drastically. I'm not an endocrinologist, but I think there really is a good possibility that your dad might be suffering from diabetes."

Wyatt stared at her. "So . . . you don't think he has Alzheimer's?"

"We'll need to take a look at all the test results, but my initial impression is that he does not. Your Aunt Betsy called him cantankerous, but I'd prefer the word 'spirited.' He clearly adores you and your son and is not an admirer of the boy's mother."

"That's putting it mildly," Wyatt said. "As far as Dad is concerned, Callie is the enemy, because she wants to move to Birmingham and take Bo with her. And, of course, she's now trying to prove that he's senile."

"He's pretty adamant on that subject," Dr. Shank said, smiling. "And I can't blame him. By the way," she added, her eyes twinkling, "I don't agree with him on the subject of Alex Trebek. At all. I think he's every bit as intelligent and talented as Art Fleming."

Wyatt let out a sigh of relief. "We've got to meet with the judge at eleven tomorrow morning. Is there any way you can give us some kind of report?"

She glanced at her watch. "I'll fax over something by ten tomorrow. Will that work?"

"That would be great," Wyatt said, jumping to his feet and pumping her hand. "I can't thank you enough, Dr. Shank. For seeing Dad so quickly and, just, everything. You've been a huge help."

Margaret-Ellen Shank leaned over and tapped Nelson gently on the shoulder. "Mr. Keeler?"

Nelson yawned widely. "What's that?" he asked groggily.

"It's nearly seven o'clock," she told him. She offered her hand; he took it and stood slowly.

"I told Wyatt you need to eat more sensibly," she said, giving him a look of mock disapproval. "No more Pop-Tarts for dinner. Right?"

"Right," he agreed.

45

Grace heard the muffled pinging of an incoming text coming from somewhere beneath the towering pile of merchandise in her shopping cart. She shoved aside the quilt with its vivid orange and green chinoiserie print, the four turquoise and green quilted throw pillows, the green and blue striped dhurrie, and the stack of turquoise and white polka-dotted bath towels.

The pair of green chevron-striped shower curtains she'd bought for the condo's dining room windows slid off the top of the stack and onto the floor. Finally, burrowing deep down into her pocketbook, she brought up the phone.

The text was from Camryn Nobles.

Where r u?

HomeGoods. What's up?

While she waited for a reply, Grace studied the store's furniture selection. Mitzi Stillwell's kitchen had an island crying out for barstools. Here were a pair of barstools with a perfectly acceptable look, clean lines, and a great price, $59.99 a pair. The problem was that they were white. And that was the problem with Mitzi's condo. Every single thing in it was white.

The walls were dead white. The tile floors were white. The sectional sofa in the living room was white, the pair of armchairs facing it was white, the sheer draperies hung from the floor-to-ceiling windows looking out at the sparkling blue Gulf of Mexico were white. In the kitchen, the countertops were white Corian, with a white subway-tile backsplash. The master bedroom had a king-sized bed with an upholstered, tufted white headboard and footboard. The carpet was an off-white flat weave. The guest bedroom featured a pair of twin beds with no headboards at all, just an expanse of white quilted-cotton bedspreads.

Just thinking of all that arctic white made Grace shiver. Maybe, she thought, running a finger over the back of one of the barstools, she could paint the stools a high-gloss tangerine.

Her phone dinged again with a reply from Camryn.

Been digging into Stackpole's financials and hit paydirt. Lunch?

Grace shook her head, annoyed. She had just begun shopping for Mitzi's place. She still needed lamps, bedspreads for the guest bedroom, and a new chandelier to replace the hideous builder-brass one in the dining room—and art. And those was just the accessories. She still needed dining room furniture, dressers for both bedrooms, coffee tables and end tables . . .

Can't it wait til tonight? she typed. With her pocket calculator, she began adding up the tab for the merchandise in her cart. She frowned. She was already at $431.99, not counting the two barstools.

Another ding interrupted her mental mathematics.

Got good stuff. How 'bout meet @Sandbox @2?

Grace shrugged and typed.

See u there.

Cedric Stackpole drummed his fingers on his desktop. He looked down at the faxed report from Dr. Shank, then up at Nelson Keeler. "Mr. Keeler? I understand you are a Vietnam veteran, is that right? In what branch of the service did you serve, sir?"

Was this some kind of trick question? Nelson looked to his son for some kind of signal, but Wyatt remained expressionless.

"That's correct, Judge," Nelson said finally. "I was in the army. Fifth Infantry. Did two tours, managed to get home in one piece. How about you?"

"Er, no," Stackpole said. "I like to think that my time in the judiciary is of some small benefit to my community. But I thank you for your service to this great country."

"You're welcome," Nelson said. "I got drafted, so it wasn't like I had a choice or anything."

Stackpole looked at Nelson over the rim of his glasses. "I understand you had some kind of verbal altercation recently with your daughter-in-law?"

"Altercation's a big word for what we had," Nelson replied calmly.

"Your daughter-in-law is saying that you did use strong language in your conversation with her. In fact, she says you actually threatened her. Did your grandson hear you making threats against his mother, hear you using strong language?"

"I reckon he did," Nelson said, his chin dropping. "I'm ashamed of that, Judge. Ashamed I let her get me riled up like that. And I'm here to promise, I won't let her get my goat again. No sir."

Betsy Entwhistle cleared her voice. "Judge? If I may?"

Stackpole gave her a curt nod.

"I'd just like to point out that Mrs. Keeler is not charging that Nelson Keeler has ever neglected or in any way harmed his grandson. Because he hasn't, and he wouldn't. And if you've read Dr. Shank's report, you can see that Mrs. Keeler's assertion that Nelson is suffering from dementia or the onset of Alzheimer's disease is totally untrue."

Betsy took a deep breath. "Dr. Shank is waiting on the rest of the test results, but she believes Mr. Keeler's occasional, er, bellicosity, could be simply the result of low blood sugar. In fact, she's suggested that Nelson Keeler might be suffering from diabetes, which could be responsible for all these symptoms Mrs. Keeler seems to want to believe are Alzheimer's."

The judge glanced over at Nelson Keeler and considered the old man sitting in the armchair across from him.

Nelson's thinning gray hair was neatly trimmed and combed. He wore a pair of navy dress pants, a white dress shirt that he hadn't donned since his late wife's funeral, and a pair of well-polished black lace-up dress shoes.

"I'm not senile," Nelson volunteered. "There is nothing in the world wrong with me, except maybe a little sugar diabetes, and I told the doctor I'd get that checked out and lay off the Pop-Tarts."

"You do that," Stackpole said finally. He closed the file folder. "I'm going to tell Mrs. Keeler and her lawyer that for now, I agree with your Dr. Shank. It appears to me that you have all your mental faculties and that you pose no threat at all to your grandson."

"Good!" Nelson exclaimed. He pulled himself to a standing position and extended a hand to the judge, who took it, somewhat reluctantly.

"Judge," Betsy said hurriedly. "This is the second time in as many weeks that Mrs. Keeler and her attorney have launched one of these baseless attacks on my client and his father. I hope this will reinforce our argument that it is not in Bo's best interest for you to allow his mother to move her son out of state and away from his father's care."

"You've made your point, Ms. Entwhistle," Stackpole said. "I'll take it under advisement."

Camryn Nobles was sitting at their regular corner table at the Sandbox, with Rochelle seated right across from her, their heads nearly touching, deep in conversation.

Grace dropped down into a chair beside her mother. "I'm starved," she announced. "What's the lunch special?"

"Shrimp burger, tuna melt, gazpacho," Rochelle said.

"Gazpacho?" Grace raised one eyebrow askance.

"My produce supplier gave me a whole bushel of tomatoes with bad spots, for next to nothing," Rochelle said. "Do you have something against gazpacho?"

"I love gazpacho," Camryn said. "Unless it's got green peppers, which don't agree with me."

"This recipe is straight off Grace's Web site," Rochelle said. "No green peppers. Cucumbers, garlic, cilantro . . ."

"You read my blog?"

"When it's interesting, which I occasionally find it is," Rochelle said.

"You bought cilantro?" Grace's second interruption was a clear annoyance to her mother.

"Yes," Rochelle said. "And I peeled the cucumbers, just as your recipe specified, for your information. With, I might add, a garnish of diced avocado and shrimp. Now, is there anything else?"

"No," Grace said, somewhat meekly.

"Would you like a bowl of gazpacho?"

"Yes, please," Grace and Camryn said in unison.

When they'd spooned up the last traces of cold soup and drained their iced tea glasses, Grace and Camryn sat back in their chairs.

"That was pretty damned good," Camryn said with a sigh.

"Better than my original recipe," Grace admitted. "But she'll never tell me how she changed it."

"Mothers," Camryn said, in unspoken agreement.

"Yeah," Grace said. "Now. What kind of dirt did you dig up on Stackpole?"

Camryn reached for her Yves St. Laurent tote bag and extracted a sheaf of computer printouts.

"Judge Cedric N. Stackpole Jr." she said, with a flourish, "is in debt up to his pointy little ears."

Grace rubbed her hands together gleefully. "Oooh. Goody. Do tell."

"This is a list of bank-foreclosed properties I pulled from the county's Web site," Camryn said, tapping a fingernail on the first sheet of paper on the stack. She ran her finger down the columns of tiny print and then jabbed one line, highlighted with a yellow marker.

"See here? 1454 Altadora Way, unit C. Siesta Key." Her finger trailed down the page until it stopped at another yellow-highlighted line of print. "1454 Altadora Way, unit B." Grace's eyes skipped down to the next line, which she read aloud.

"1463 Altadora Circle, unit A. But the mortgage holder is listed as Solomon Holdings," Grace said, squinting at the fine print.

"Solomon, as in, wise King Solomon, biblical judge," Camryn said, deadpan. "I looked it up. C. N. Stackpole is the sole corporate officer of Solomon Holdings. And then I took a ride over to Altadora Commons. It's a development of new town houses not far from his address on Longboat Key. I'll tell you a funny coincidence. I didn't realize it until I pulled up in front of the complex, but I actually looked at one of those town houses with my real estate agent, right after I kicked Dexter out of the house. Prices aren't bad, for Siesta, the unit I looked at was a resale, and they only wanted 575,000 dollars, but it was still way too pricey for my budget, and besides, I didn't like the floorplan."

Camryn leafed through the pages of documents until she found one she wanted, a computer printout of a real estate listing for Altadora Commons. The picture showed a series of tasteful cream stucco two-story town houses with orange stucco barrel-tile roofs, and a not-so-tasteful billboard seemingly mushrooming from a postage-stamp-sized lawn that proclaimed, "Bank Owned. Prestige Homes at Distressed Prices!"

"Wow. And Stackpole owns three of these?"

"Judge Stackpole? Your divorce judge?" Rochelle had come up behind them while they were studying the printouts. She leaned over Camryn's shoulder, staring at the photo of Altadora Commons.

"That's right," Camryn told her. "According to my real estate agent, the original sales price, back in 2007, was between 875,000 and 1.6 million dollars for the biggest units, which were actually two town houses joined together. Then, well, you know what happened to real estate around here. You couldn't give a town house away. Stackpole bought three units from the developer, at what looked like fire-sale prices, in 2010. He paid 420,000 dollars apiece. Which would have been a great deal . . ."

"Except?" Grace asked.

"Except that the county's tax digest was reworked in 2011, and now those units are only appraised at 120,000 apiece," Camryn said, sounding absolutely elated. "He's underwater, in a major way."

"But he can't be broke," Grace objected. "He lives at Longboat Key, and you told us his wife's family has gobs of money."

"The wife's family has money. Stackpole doesn't have squat," Camryn said. "I checked. The house is in her name. And incidentally? It's apparently a lot bigger than it looks from the street. It's on the market for 3.2 million."

Rochelle had eased herself onto a chair. "Bring me up to speed here, Camryn. What does any of this mean to you and Grace?"

"It's just a wild theory we've been tossing back and forth," Grace cautioned.

"It's not a wild theory," Camryn said, tapping the documents on the table. "These printouts prove it. Stackpole's in debt. His wife has money, but he probably can't touch it. He's having an affair with Paula Talbott-Sinclair, and one of them comes up with the idea to mandate women going through his divorce court to seek counseling from Paula, his girlfriend. She gets to soak each of us three hundred dollars per session, for a total of six sessions. There are five people in our group alone, and on the one day I watched her office, I saw three other groups arriving for divorce counseling. Do the math, Grace. They're getting rich off our misery."

"You should do a story about this on the news," Rochelle said excitedly. "Blow the lid off the whole big scam."

"I intend to," Camryn said.

"Isn't it a conflict of interest for you to report on a story you're involved in?" Grace asked.

"It'd be a first-person piece," Camryn said. "And if the story's big enough, I don't see how my station manager can turn it down."

"Look, I'd love it if we could prove those two were in cahoots," Grace said.

"But I talked to Mitzi about this yesterday. Even if you did see all those people going into Paula's office, how do you know they didn't go there of their own free will?"

"Can't you just ask her other patients whether or not Stackpole ordered them to attend therapy with her?" Rochelle asked.

"I wish," Camryn said. "I told you I hung around outside Paula's office last Friday. What I didn't tell you was that she apparently saw me standing there in the parking lot. She came outside and asked me what I was doing! I made up some lame story about looking for a diamond earring I'd dropped Wednesday night but I think she realized there was something fishy going on."

"Mitzi did say she'd take a look at Stackpole's dockets and talk to any attorneys she knows that have had divorce cases before him," Grace said.

"But who knows how long that will take?" Rochelle demanded. "We need action!"

Grace gave her mother the look. "What kind of action would you suggest?"

Rochelle thought. She smiled. She walked away from the table, and when she returned, she brought a handful of flyers, which she offered to Grace.

Come play in the Sandbox. Good for one free appetizer or drink

"I remember these. Dad hired kids to put them on car windshields at the new Publix, right after it opened."

"Until I made him stop, because we were nearly run out of business, giving away all those free drinks and stuffed potato skins," Rochelle said.

"So?" Grace asked. "Am I missing something?"

"I'm not. Rochelle, if you ever get tired of running this bar, you might have a future as an investigative reporter. This," Camryn said admiringly, "is brilliant."

"I still don't get it," Grace said, looking from one woman to the other.

"It's simple," Rochelle said. "Tomorrow morning, I go over to Paula's office. I watch cars pulling up and pay attention to who goes inside. Then, I plaster these coupons all over their windshields. When they bring in the coupons for their freebies, you two swoop in and ask them what you need to know."

"And how do you know they'll use the coupons? Or when they'll use them?" Grace asked.

"I'll just write on the bottom of each coupon that the deal's good for one day only," Rochelle said. "Trust me. Nobody turns down a free drink in this town."

46

Paula Talbott-Sinclair clasped her hands together prayerfully as she stood in the front of the room. She took a deep breath and let it out so s-l-o-w-l-y that the members of the group all subconsciously held their own breaths, wondering what would happen next.

"Hi friends." Her voice was clear and unusually calm. "I want to start our session tonight by talking about personal responsibility." She looked around the room. "All of you are here, in a way, because you were forced to take personal responsibility for some action you took against your partner."

"Ashleigh, you were stalking your husband's new lover. You vandalized her home in what was a very terrifying and thoughtless act of vengeance.

"Wyatt, you punched out the window of your wife's boyfriend's car so violently that you smashed his window and injured your own hand.

"Grace, you deliberately drove your husband's car into a swimming pool and destroyed it.

"Camryn, you discovered a provocative and salacious video of your husband and put it on YouTube, thus exposing him to public ridicule and humiliation."

Paula nodded at Suzanne. "Suzanne, we've all been very patient, waiting for you to admit to us the actions you took that caused you to join this group. Because I'm such a strong believer in personal responsibility, I've been reluctant to force your hand. Up until now."

Suzanne lifted her chin. "I'm ready, Paula. I want to tell the group . . ."

"Are you sure?"

"No," Suzanne said, with a nervous laugh. "I'll never be ready. But I'm willing, and that's the best I can do."

"Did I tell you all that Eric, my husband, is also a professor at Ringling?" Suzanne didn't wait for a reply. "He's in the English department, too. Anyway, I discovered, by accident, that he was sleeping with a co-worker, a woman who'd been my grad assistant last year."

"How'd you figure it out?" Ashleigh asked.

Suzanne's smile was wry. "Modern technology. Eric had gone out for a run. I was doing the laundry and found his phone in the pocket of his pants. As I was putting it on the counter, it pinged, and I saw he'd gotten a text. Darby was at soccer practice, and she was supposed to text one of us to let us know she was on her way home. I just assumed the text would be from her, so I read it. It wasn't from Darby. It was from her."

"The other woman?" Camryn asked.

"Yup. I'll spare you the nitty-gritty. Let's just say she was suggesting a time and place for their next assignation. 'Come horny,' the text said, so that let me know I wasn't overreacting. Just to be sure, I scrolled down the other texts from her. They were all just as graphic, if not more so. And it had been going on for months."

"Did you confront him?" Grace asked.

"No." Suzanne's hands shook as she uncapped the bottle of water she'd been clutching all evening. "I . . . I guess a part of me still didn't want to believe it was true. But another part of me, the cold, analytical researcher, needed data. While I was going through his phone, reading the texts, I found texts from other people, women, but I had no idea who they were."

"He had more than one girlfriend?" Camryn asked. "Just like my cheating husband."

"It gets better, or worse," Suzanne said sadly. "I went online and found something called keystroke software. It's a program you can surreptitiously load onto somebody's computer, and once it's activated, everything that person does on their computer, every e-mail they write or receive, every Web site they visit, you have access to."

"You became your own private detective," Camryn said. "That's so smart!"

"Not really," Suzanne said. "Remember, Camryn, when you said you wished you could take Scopolamine, to forget about your daughter catching Dexter in bed with her roommate? Well, I learned so much about Eric's secret life, I wish the data bank in my head could be wiped clean. But I'm afraid now it's hard-wired into my brain."

She took a sip of water. "Those other women? He was meeting them on Craigslist! For hookups."

"Dear God," Grace muttered.

"Exactly," Suzanne said. "He was meeting strange women in sleazy motel rooms for casual sex. And when he wasn't meeting them in person, they were sexting back and forth. It had been going for years."

"That's just nasty," Ashleigh said. "At least Boyce . . ."

Camryn reached over and grabbed Ashleigh's arm. "Let Suzanne get through this without editorializing. Okay? Otherwise, I will have to pinch your head off of your scrawny little neck." Ashleigh jerked her arm away.

"Camryn?" Paula's voice had a warning note.

Camryn glared at Paula. "I am dead-dog serious. I will hurt her if you do not make her be quiet."

"And I'll help," Grace offered, glaring, in turn, at Ashleigh.

"Everybody?" Suzanne looked amused. "I'm fine. Really. I've been living with this for months and months now. Now? I don't want this slime taking up any more room in my brain. You know?"

They all nodded in unison. They all did know.

"You wouldn't think this could get worse," Suzanne said with a self-conscious laugh. "But it does! Not long after I found out about Eric, I had a regular check-up with my gynecologist, and I had an abnormal pap test."

She looked at Wyatt and blushed. "I'm sorry you have to hear such personal stuff. About my lady parts. But there's just no way to get around this."

"I'll survive," he said, his voice gruff.

Suzanne took a gulp of water. And then the words came tumbling out in an unstoppable torrent. "I had HPV. I didn't even know what it was. My doctor—the same doctor who delivered Darby, who's known me since I was a teenager, had to explain it to me. It was an STD. A sexually transmitted disease."

Grace had to clamp her hand over her mouth to keep from gasping aloud.

"Eric . . . having unprotected sex with those women. He'd given me an STD.

I thought I would die of humiliation, the day my doctor told me. Of course, he was as embarrassed as I was. Long story short, I had cervical cancer.

"I had a total hysterectomy, because my husband gave me a sexually transmitted virus. Which, incidentally, could still come back, as something like anal cancer. My doctor had been quietly urging me to tell Eric what was going on, so he could at least notify the women he'd had sex with. You know, so they could see a doctor. I was so calm on the outside, it was frightening. I scared myself. One day, a week before I was scheduled for surgery, I went on Craigslist. I posted a picture of Eric and advised that any woman who'd ever had a hookup with him should get themselves checked. Because he had an STD. And they were at risk, too."

Suzanne gulped more water. "Then I texted my colleague at the college. I told her I knew about her and Eric. But here was a piece of news she wasn't privy to. And I told her. The day I was scheduled to have my surgery, I told Eric what I'd done. And I told him I wanted him out of our house by the time I got home from the hospital."

"Does Darby know?" Camryn asked. "Why you split up?"

"No," Suzanne said. "I couldn't do that to her. It's bad enough I have this stuff in my head. She's only eighteen. I don't want her hating men for the rest of her life. I don't even want her hating her father."

"But . . ." Ashleigh sputtered. "You let Eric off the hook. He doesn't even have to take responsibility for what he did!"

"He's not off the hook," Suzanne said. "His girlfriend filed a grievance against him with the college, and he was fired. One of the women he met on Craigslist claims he gave her HPV, too, although I don't know how someone who's in the habit of having unprotected sex with strangers can ever figure out how she got an STD. She's hired a lawyer. And so it goes. I think it's safe to say his life is ruined."

"And yours isn't?" Wyatt's face was pink with indignation. "I'm sorry, Suzanne. As a man, I'm sorry. As a husband, I'm sorry." He looked at the others. "We're not all like that. I swear."

"I know you're nothing like that, Wyatt," Suzanne said. "And I don't think every man is like Eric. But you're wrong about one thing. My life isn't ruined. I'm not about to give him that power."

"Right on, sister," Camryn said fiercely.

"Thank you, Suzanne," Paula said quietly. "I can see now why you needed time to find the words to tell your story. We're all full of admiration for your honesty. Right, friends?" She started clapping her hands, slowly, until the others in the semicircle joined in. Paula motioned for Suzanne to stand, and she hugged her. One by one, the others stood and joined the group hug, awkwardly at first, and then, as the moment grew, they stood together, their first real campfire moment.

The members of the group drifted back to their chairs. Paula went on.

"We're in week five of our sessions, and we've got lots of work yet to do before we conclude next week. Tonight, I'm going to ask all of you to think about writing an action plan.

"It's a sort of manifesto for yourselves," Paula explained. "You're all starting a new chapter of your lives. I'd like you to put some thought into how you'll move forward, personally and professionally, physically and emotionally, in a really mindful way."

She glanced at her watch. "This has been pretty intense tonight. Let's take a ten-minute break, and when we come back, we'll talk. Okay?"

Camryn blew her nose. "What's Suzanne's action plan gonna be, Paula? What's she gonna do, grow a new cervix?"

47

Wyatt was the first one to arrive at their table at the Sandbox. He pulled Grace's chair out for her, letting his hand rest, just for a second, on her arm. "Thanks," she said, shooting him a quick, private smile.

Rochelle was at the table in a shot, bringing a pitcher of beer and menus. "Where are the others?"

"They're on their way," Wyatt told her. "I've got a feeling we're going to need a lot of alcohol tonight, Rochelle. In fact, why don't you go ahead and bring Suzanne whatever it is she usually orders?"

"God, yes," Grace said emphatically. "I think she drinks wine spritzers. And I'm gonna need a big old glass of wine myself."

"Why?" Rochelle asked eagerly. "Did something happen tonight? To Suzanne?"

Wyatt's voice was solemn. "Suzanne finally shared tonight. Her husband was having unprotected sex with total strangers he met through Craigslist. He gave her an STD."

"You mean, like venereal disease?"

"Something like that," Grace said. "Only this disease can't be cleared up with penicillin. Suzanne had to have a hysterectomy because of it, and it could still come back."

"Sweet Jesus, Mary, and Joseph!" Rochelle exclaimed. "This really happened to our darling Suzanne?"

"Yes. And she just pulled into the parking lot, so please don't mention it. I mean it, Mom. Not one word."

"I would never," Rochelle said indignantly. She sketched a quick cross on her chest. "So help me."

Suzanne looked from the wine spritzer sitting on the table to Grace. "Thanks." She took a sip. "I needed this."

"You were amazing in group tonight," Ashleigh said, leaning across the table.

"You're our she-roe," Camryn chimed in. "You're like a divorce superhero."

Suzanne sipped her drink. "Not at all. The rest of you spilled your guts that first awful night of group session, when we were all total strangers. It's taken me five weeks to get up the nerve. I'm the biggest wimp in the world."

"No, you're not," Wyatt said. "You're . . . an inspiration."

"Okay, enough," Suzanne said. "You're going to make me start blubbering again. Can we please talk about something else? Anything else?"

Camryn and Grace locked eyes, then looked away. But their expression didn't escape Ashleigh.

"What?" she cried. "You guys know something. Come on, spill. Is it about Paula?"

Grace shrugged. "Camryn found out some stuff about Paula's past."

Suzanne regarded Camryn carefully. "This has something to do with why Paula isn't licensed to practice therapy in Florida, doesn't it?"

"Yeah," Camryn said, surprised. "How'd you know?"

Suzanne hesitated. "Okay, one more thing I've been keeping from you guys. I swear, it's the very last secret. Or, the last one that concerns you. Here it is. Stackpole didn't send me to Paula. I came on my own."

"You mean, you came voluntarily? Why would you do that?" Ashleigh asked.

"After I found out what Eric had done, I was so angry, in such a rage, I scared even myself," Suzanne said. "I had all these awful ideas about how to get my revenge. Fantasies about physically harming him. That's when I knew I had to get help. I went online and googled divorce and therapy and Sarasota, and Paula's name popped up.

"After that first night, I knew there was something off about Paula. Her credentials are actually pretty impressive, but she's very careful not to advertise herself as a therapist or a marriage counselor. She just calls herself a divorce coach. Which got me to wondering."

"Why'd you even keep coming to group after that first night? Or even after the second night, when Paula passed out cold?" Grace asked.

Suzanne looked at the faces sitting around the table. "By then, I knew it wasn't really about her helping me. You all had shared your stories. I knew you were hurting as badly as I was, and I thought maybe you'd help me find a way to deal with this horrible sadness and bitterness that was engulfing me. Turns out, I was right."

"Awwww," Ashleigh said, beaming. "That's so sweet."

"But Paula's helped me, too," Suzanne said. "In her own way. Of course, that doesn't mean I'm not curious about what you discovered, Camryn."

"Okay," Camyrn said. "Here goes."

Rochelle brought another round of drinks, but Suzanne pushed hers away, untouched. "I did wonder if it was something like that. Paula's not a bad person, you know. Just . . . damaged. Like all of us."

Ashleigh was not convinced. "You mean, I'm paying three hundred dollars an hour to get counseling from a convicted drug addict?"

"Recovering drug addict," Grace said. "And remember, Paula doesn't call herself a counselor or a therapist. Just a divorce coach. And who better to coach people through this kind of crap than somebody who's been through it herself?"

"I still think it's a rip-off," Ashleigh insisted. But a moment later, she lowered her voice. "But I don't even care about Paula anymore. I don't even care about that stinker Judge Stackpole. I've got news, y'all. Boyce called! He wants to meet me for lunch next week. And here's the best part. We're meeting at the Ritz!"

"I've never eaten at the Ritz-Carlton," Rochelle said, alighting on an empty chair next to Ashleigh. "Is the food as good as they say?"

"Oh, Rochelle, you're so cute," Ashleigh said, with her tinkling laugh. "Do you know, I've never actually eaten there? As far as I'm concerned, lunch at the Ritz is totally not about the food."

"It's not?" Rochelle looked puzzled.

"Now you're going to make me tell all my naughty secrets," Ashleigh said. She cupped her hands and whispered in Rochelle's ear.

"Ohhh," Rochelle said knowingly. "Now I get it. The Ritz-Carlton is like a high-priced no-tell motel."

"Exactly." Ashleigh giggled.

"Did he say why he wants to have lunch?" Grace asked.

"He didn't have to," Ashleigh said. "It's perfectly clear. He wants me back! I wasn't going to tell y'all this, but since it's kind of a moot point, I will. I saw Suchita, that's his girlfriend, leaving Boyce's office the other day. She's getting fat! And Boyce does not DO fat. He's a plastic surgeon, and appearances have always been important to him." She looked around the table, pausing when she saw Camryn's face.

"And before you say one word, let me just say that I don't intend to let him wriggle off the hook that easily. I mean, please! I do have my pride. I mean to make him pay for what he put me through. Boyce doesn't know it yet, but he's going to be buying a major piece of jewelry to make it up to me."

"Ashleigh," Grace said, "have you really thought this through? You know Boyce was keeping a mistress. You know he cheated on his first wife when he started dating you. What makes you think he won't do it again?"

"Yeah, baby," Camryn said. "I'm sorry, but I do not see this tiger changing his stripes."

"It's different with us," Ashleigh said. "Boyce never loved his first wife. Ever. Their marriage was a joke. I didn't have to break it up. It was already a done deal. So yes, Boyce cheated on me. I've accepted that. Hasn't Paula been yammering for weeks now about acceptance and finding peace?"

Suzanne patted Ashleigh's hand. "We just don't want to see you get hurt again."

"I'm *not* going to get hurt," Ashleigh said. "This is a love story. Plain and simple. Happy ever after. Is that so hard for y'all to believe?"

"It's not that I don't believe it," Camryn said. "It's just that, so far, I've never experienced it."

Ashleigh tossed her hair over one shoulder. "Rochelle, you're on my side, right? And you were married a really long time to Grace's daddy, right? Will you please tell these people that there is such a thing as a happy marriage?"

Rochelle pressed her lips together. "Sorry, honey, that's one thing I wouldn't know about." She looked over Ashleigh's head, her eyes focused on the bar. "Dammit, there's Miller and Bud again, taking up space and hogging the popcorn." She stood. "Next thing you know they'll be having their welfare checks forwarded here. I've gotta go chase them off."

Grace watched her mother hurry away. What was that crack about not knowing anything about happy marriages? She thought back to all the barbed remarks Rochelle had made recently about Butch. At some point, Grace thought, she and Rochelle needed to sit down and really talk about this stuff. Butch had been dead three years now. Was there something about her parents' marriage Rochelle had been keeping from her?

"Grace?" Suzanne waved a hand in front of her face. "Earth to Grace. Come in Grace."

"What?" The others were looking at her expectantly. "Sorry, guess I zoned out for a minute there."

"I was just asking what you thought about Paula's assignment. You know—the action plan?"

"I think it's a good idea," Grace said. "I know for myself, after I walked out on Ben, I was really sort of . . . rudderless, I guess would be the word."

"Paralyzed," Camryn agreed. "After I kicked Dexter to the curb, I couldn't make the simplest decision. And y'all know that is not like me. I pulled through Starbucks one morning, and when the barista asked if I wanted extra sugars, I just burst into tears."

"I already know step one of my action plan," Ashleigh confided. "As soon as I get rid of that Suchita hag, I'm taking my old job back as Boyce's office manager. And let me tell you, I'll be the one doing the meetings with those cute little drug reps from now on."

"I'm sort of undecided," Suzanne said. "Darby's been offered a chance for early enrollment at Elon, a small liberal arts college in North Carolina. Their soccer team was NCAA runner-ups last year, and the head coach personally flew all the way here in the spring to watch Darby play. She turned it down, saying she couldn't imagine missing her senior year of high school, but I think the real reason was that she didn't want to go away and leave me alone so soon after Eric and I split."

"Your daughter sounds like a great kid," Wyatt said.

"I don't know how I got so lucky with her," Suzanne said. "The Elon coach is still calling the house, begging Darby to reconsider. They'd like her to come out right now, to start practicing with the team. Selfishly, I wish she would stay home, finish her senior year, and then go off to college. I want one more year of fixing her breakfast and washing her stinky practice clothes every night! But realistically, there's no reason why she shouldn't do early decision. Darby's a bright kid. She's taken enough Advanced Placement classes at her high school that college work won't be that much of a challenge. This is a terrific opportunity for her."

"Then let her go."

Their heads swung around in unison. Rochelle stood with her hands on the back of Suzanne's chair. "I know, it's none of my business. But it sounds to me like you already know what you should do."

Suzanne swiveled around in her chair. "Thanks, Rochelle. I guess that gives me step one of my plan. Now I just have to persuade Darby that her mother isn't as needy as she thinks."

"I hate to admit that Paula may finally have a good idea," Camryn said. "But what she said tonight does make sense. I've been thinking a lot lately about my career at the station, and where I want it to go."

"You're not thinking of moving are you?" Grace asked.

"You obviously don't know much about the television news business. Women don't move to other markets at my age. At least, not voluntarily. No, this little bit of investigative journalism I've been doing has been a real kick. I've actually been thinking this might be a good time to go off-camera. Maybe consider producing." She grinned widely. "I've always been great at telling other people what to do."

"What about you, Grace?" Ashleigh asked pointedly. "What would be your step one?"

"I've already taken it," Grace said. "I've asked Arthur, the man who owns the house I've been restoring, if he'd let me rent it. If he says yes, I could move in within a week or so."

"You're moving?" Rochelle looked stricken.

"Don't turn my bedroom into an office just yet," Grace warned. "Arthur didn't seem all that wild about the idea, but he didn't say no. He said he'd have to talk it over with his wife. But I'm hopeful."

48

Grace mopped the floor while Rochelle counted down the cash register and bundled up the money for the morning's bank deposit. She double-checked the front door to make sure it was locked and flipped the switch for the neon sign. Then, she went behind the bar, poured herself a glass of wine, and took a seat on the barstool next to Rochelle.

"It's after one," her mother said, looking up from her counting. "I don't mind the company, but you've been getting up and leaving pretty early most mornings lately."

"I'll go to bed in a little while," Grace said. "Can I ask you something?"

"Hmm?" Rochelle was jotting figures in the ledger where she always recorded each day's tally. "This divorce group of yours is good for business. Last year, this same date, we did eighteen hundred dollars. Today, we did twenty-one hundred. And the softball guys didn't even have a game tonight."

Grace closed the book. "Mom, what did you mean earlier, when you said you didn't know anything about happy marriages?"

"Nothing," Rochelle said casually. "You know me, sometimes I run my mouth without thinking."

"Sometimes you do, but I don't think that was the case tonight. Lately, you've been dropping these little . . . I don't know, hints? Is there something about you and Dad's marriage that I don't know?"

"Your dad's dead and buried, Grace. That's all old history."

"I don't think so," Grace said slowly. "Come on, Mom. Be honest with me."

Rochelle took off her reading glasses and buffed them on the hem of her blouse. "Your dad was a good man, Grace. He loved you beyond all reason and was so proud of you and the life you were building. That's what's important for you to know."

"Nuh-uh," Grace said, shaking her head. "There's more to it than that. Ever since I started this divorce-recovery group, you've been hanging around, super interested in everything everybody has to say . . ."

"I'm a nosy old lady," Rochelle said.

"What was going on with you and Dad? Whatever it is, I need to know."

Rochelle let out a long sigh. "Since you insist, I'll tell you. Four years ago, I was ready to divorce your dad. I'd hired a lawyer. I'd even found an apartment to move into. And then we found out he was sick. I couldn't walk out on him like that. He was dying. So I stayed. End of story."

She saw the stunned expression on Grace's face. "I'm sorry, honey. I really never meant for you to hear this, but you asked, and I just couldn't keep dancing around the truth any longer."

Grace felt like she'd had the wind knocked out of her. "Why? What did Dad do? Please don't tell me he had another woman."

Rochelle opened the ledger again. "Some things are best left unsaid, you know? And this is one of them."

"Just tell me, please? So, he had an affair? Was it somebody I knew?"

"It was nobody. A snowbird from Buffalo whose husband used to keep a boat here in the marina during the winter. Her husband died the summer before, and she was down here by herself, and I guess . . . she got lonely."

"Oh, God." Grace felt physically sick. Her father? Butch? The same guy who wore loud Hawaiian shirts and loved country music? The man who gave both Rochelle and Grace the same Whitman Sampler of chocolates every Valentine's Day? Butch had a girlfriend?

"It didn't last very long," Rochelle said quietly. "Your dad was a lousy sneak."

Grace swallowed hard. "How . . . how did you figure it out?"

"He was acting funny. Not like himself. You know how Butch was; he liked his set routine. But that January, he switched barbers. After twenty years of the same haircut, he grows sideburns, for God's sake. He started taking an extra shower, in the middle of the day. You know how I always went to the wholesale house for supplies, right? Well, suddenly, he insisted he should be the one to go pick up our order. He'd be gone two, three hours. One time, he came back without the paper napkins and take-out containers. He had some lame excuse that they were out. Of paper napkins?" She shook her head. "He never did have much of an imagination."

"I don't know what to say," Grace said. "You must have been devastated."

"Mad as hell, more like. Because he'd promised—promised on his mother's grave—he wouldn't put me through that crap again."

"Again? It wasn't the first time?" Grace found herself staring into her own image in the mirror behind the bar, and then at herself, and then at Rochelle, and at Rochelle's image. Who were these strangers?

"No. Not the first time." Rochelle's lips were set in a grim smile. "You were only three the first time he cheated. I found out then, and I left. I took you to my cousin's house in Jacksonville, and we stayed three weeks. Butch was heartbroken. He couldn't stand the idea of not having his baby girl around. He knew he'd messed up. He begged me to take him back, said he'd be a different man. And he was, for a long time."

"I just . . ." Grace swallowed hard. "I don't know what to think. You never said a word. The two of you never fought. My friends' parents were splitting up while we were in high school, and they used to tell me they envied me, because Butch and Rochelle—you know, Butch and Rochelle were solid."

Rochelle reached out and stroked Grace's hair. "Maybe I should have divorced him back then, after the first time. But where would I have gone with a little kid in tow? I had no real job skills; certainly I didn't have any money. And I was too proud to admit to my parents that I'd made a mistake. So I did the easy thing. I went back to Butch. And I stayed."

"All those years? When I thought you guys had the model marriage? That was all a lie? You only stayed together because of me?"

"It wasn't *all* a lie," Rochelle said. "We had some good times. We made a life here, had friends. Had you. I don't want you to think it was a bad life, Grace, which is why I never told any of this to you."

"You could have told me. Especially once I was an adult. I would have understood," Grace said. "It makes me sad to think that you were that unhappy, and I was just . . . oblivious."

"You weren't oblivious. You were busy, spreading your wings, starting a career. A marriage. But now I think, I wonder, if I didn't set you up for failure by giving you unrealistic expectations of your own marriage. Does it make me pathetic, how much vicarious pleasure I got seeing what an amazing woman you were becoming?"

"You've never been pathetic," Grace said. "But what made you finally decide to leave?"

Rochelle fidgeted with her glasses. "Besides Edwina? That was her name. Edwina! I'd say it was just a slow build. One morning, Butch was fussing at me, because I'd bought Chock full o'Nuts instead of Folgers without consulting him."

Grace rolled her eyes. "God. Dad and his coffee."

"I picked up the whole bag of beans and dumped it in the trash. I walked upstairs, packed a bag. When I got downstairs, he looked at me like I'd lost my mind. 'You're leaving over a bag of coffee?' So I looked at him and I said, 'It's not about coffee. It's about Edwina.'"

"Did you think about going to counseling?" Grace asked.

"I went to counseling. Your dad refused to go. He thought it was a waste of his hard-earned money."

"That sounds like Dad," Grace said with a sigh. "I still can't believe you got as far as hiring a divorce lawyer without telling me. Wait a minute. Mitzi? Mitzi was the lawyer you hired?"

Rochelle nodded. "You and Ben hadn't been married that long at the time. You were deliriously happy. I didn't want to upset you. And then, of course, we found out how sick Butch was. I wasn't even gone a week."

"Did he beg you to come back?" Grace asked, teary-eyed now, thinking about her father's last months of life, growing thinner, using a walker, and then, finally, a wheelchair.

"Butch? Never. He didn't have to ask. I knew he needed me, so I came. We never even discussed that week. It was like it never happened." Rochelle got a glint in her eye. She laughed.

"What's so funny?" Grace asked.

"Nothing. I was just thinking about the coffee. When I moved back here, that first morning, I went out to the kitchen to make coffee. There sat a brand-new bag of Chock full o'Nuts. That was Butch's idea of an apology."

Grace laughed until the tears were rolling down her cheeks. "Mom? You know what I remember that last year? When Dad was so sick? You were so strong. You kept the bar running, took him to all his doctor's appointments, to chemo. You bathed him and spoon-fed him when he was too sick to eat, fixed his bed in the living room so he could look out at the water those last few weeks."

Rochelle blinked back her own tears. "He made me promise I wouldn't let him die in the hospital. It was a small enough thing to do."

"So you forgave him?" Grace searched her mother's face for an answer.

"You know? I guess I did," Rochelle said, wonderingly. "At the time, I told myself I was doing it for you—because he was your daddy. But now, I think maybe I did it for me. I hated what Butch did—cheating on me—but I guess at the end, even after everything, I did still love him."

"I'm glad you told me," Grace said. "Thanks for that, Mom."

49

Good morning Grace. Don't know if you'll remember me, but you and I had some dealings a few years ago when I was an assistant to Lily Soo at House Beautiful. *I'm now features editor at* Veranda, *and I've been following your new blog and your new project with such delight. We think our readers would love it, too. Wondering if we might discuss having you write and photograph a monthly feature about your progress at Mandevilla Manor? Can't wait to discuss! All best, Doreen Zelen. P.S. Adore that checkerboard kitchen floor!*

Grace read the e-mail three times, just to make sure it wasn't a figment of her imagination. Then she tucked her laptop under her arm and went running downstairs to the bar.

Rochelle was directing the beer-delivery guy into the storeroom. "Mom!" Grace cried.

Her mother whirled around, knocking her cup of coffee to the floor. "What is it?"

"*Veranda!* They want to hire me to write a series about Mandevilla. Can you believe it? I've subscribed to *Veranda* since forever. And they want me!"

Rochelle grabbed a bar towel and dropped it to the floor, mopping the spilled coffee with her sneaker-clad foot. "Honey, that's fantastic!"

"I know," Grace said. She was hopping up and down with excitement. "*Veranda!* This is a dream assignment."

"How about some breakfast?" Rochelle asked. "You can tell me all the details and I'll cook you some eggs and bacon."

"Can't," Grace said. "I've got to get over to the cottage and get to work. I want to be able to move some furniture in by the end of the week so I'll have some new photographs to show Doreen; she's the *Veranda* editor who e-mailed me. I did a freelance piece for her years ago, when she was at another magazine. I was supposed to stop and pick up Sweetie, but I'm going to text Wyatt and see if he'll drop her off. Talk to you later!"

Arthur Cater was sitting on the front steps of the cottage on Mandevilla when she pulled into the driveway.

"Arthur!" Grace called, as she crossed the lawn. "I'm so glad you're here. Wait 'til I tell you my news."

As soon as she got closer, she saw by the expression on Arthur's face that something was terribly wrong. His face was streaked with what looked like soot, and he suddenly looked like a very, very old man.

"What's wrong?" she asked. "Is it your wife? Is she sick?"

"My wife is fine," Arthur said. "It's the house, Grace. Somebody tried to burn down the house last night."

Grace stood in the living room, staring down at the charred floorboards in the corner closest to the dining room. Soot marks streaked the white walls, and shards of broken glass sparkled from the shattered front windows. She clutched her laptop tightly against her chest and willed herself not to cry.

"The neighbor next door smelled something burning when he got up to let his dog out at six this morning," Arthur said sadly. "He called me, then he called the fire department, then he came over here himself. As soon as he got onto the porch, he saw the flames, right over there. It was just a small blaze, looked like a bundle of rags or something, he said. He broke the window and climbed in. He found the mop bucket you'd been using and doused the fire with water. If he hadn't done that, I don't guess this place would be standing. This house is mostly wood. Heart pine that burns like kindling."

"I don't know what to say," Grace said, her words catching in her throat.

"There's more," Arthur said grimly, jerking his head in the direction of the kitchen. Grace's footsteps echoed in the high-ceilinged empty room. She stood in the doorway of the kitchen, and now she did cry.

Black paint had been spattered all over the kitchen. It oozed down the faces of the new refrigerator and range and trickled down the cabinet faces. Paint pooled on her freshly painted checkerboard floor. "Fuck the Man" had been painted in wobbly black letters across the kitchen window.

"Kids." Arthur spat the word. He pointed at the sink, where an empty plastic half gallon of cheap vodka had been tossed, along with empty cans of Red Bull and assorted brands of beer cans.

"Oh my God." Grace breathed the words. She backed away from the doorway and into the hallway, where half an inch of water sloshed over the floorboards. Wadded up towels littered the floor.

The bathroom door was closed. She was about to open the door when Arthur closed his own gnarled hand over hers. "Don't," he warned. "It's awful bad." He swallowed. "They . . . Grace. They took a dump in the tub and smeared it all over the walls. Then they shoved a towel down the toilet, to back up the plumbing, and did the same thing with the sink. I've shut the water off now, but hadn't had time to clean everything up before you got here."

The bedroom doors were closed, too. Before he could stop her, Grace opened the door to the front bedroom. Day-glo orange paint festooned the walls. The empty paint bucket lay on its side, a river of orange paint spilling onto the newly refinished hardwood floor. More empty beer cans were scattered over the floor, and the room reeked of urine and marijuana smoke.

"Who would do this?" she whispered.

She heard the front door opening then and the sound of boots on the floorboards, and then the skittering of a dog's nails clicking across the floors. "Grace?" Wyatt's voice sounded panicky.

Sweetie came speeding around the corner, and Grace grabbed her up in her arms before the dog could go tracking across the orange paint.

"I'm back here," she called, her voice breaking. A moment later, he was there, by her side. Without another word, he wrapped his arms around both her and the dog, and held them close.

"I'm so sorry," he murmured into her hair. "Are you all right?"

Finally, she sniffed and wiped at her eyes. "I'm okay," she insisted, pulling free.

Arthur stood awkwardly in the middle of the room, brandishing a push broom.

"Wyatt, this is Arthur Cater. He owns the house. Arthur, this is my friend Wyatt, the one I told you about who had the ideas for the garden."

The two men nodded at one another. "What happened here?" Wyatt asked. "I saw the burned places in the living room."

"Somebody broke in and tried to burn it down." Arthur gestured around the bedroom. "But before they got around to that, they did all this. More in the kitchen. The bathroom's worse."

"Who?" Wyatt asked. "Do you have any idea?"

"Kids is my guess," Arthur said. "The neighbor said he noticed a car parked in the driveway last night, around ten. I'd told him about Grace working over here, and he just figured it was her, so he didn't think any more of it. He's the one that called me this morning."

"They had themselves a big ol' party," Grace said bitterly. "You can smell the weed in here. And there are beer cans and a vodka bottle in the kitchen."

"Damned kids," Arthur growled.

"I guess it's too much to hope the neighbor got a description of the car or a license number," Wyatt asked.

"Coulda been blue, coulda been green. It was dark, and he only just glimpsed the car from his own front porch," Arthur said. "Probably doesn't matter. They're long gone by now."

"And nobody heard anything over here?" Grace asked.

"It's been a rental house so long, and we've had so many tenants in and out, the neighbors just started tuning out what goes on over here," Arthur said. "The lady across the street came over this morning when she saw the fire truck to tell me she'd called the police twice on my former tenants, but the cops just issued them a warning. Wish she'd have told me."

"All your hard work," Wyatt said, squeezing Grace's hand. "You had the place looking so good."

"It looked real nice," Arthur agreed. "I'm glad I took those pictures to show my wife, before all of this happened."

Grace dabbed at her eyes with the hem of her oversized T-shirt. "I'll just have to start over, that's all." She picked up the paint can and looked at the label. "At least it's latex. I'll have to repaint the walls, but if I get some rags and get to work on these floors before the paint really hardens, it may be that I won't have to strip the floors again. Thank God this happened after I'd gotten the poly down."

"There's nothing much happening at the park today," Wyatt said. "I'll call my Dad and tell him I'm going to hang around here today and give you a hand. Bo's at his mom's, so I've got the day and the evening free, if you need me."

"Oh no," Grace started to say. Then she shrugged. "Who am I kidding? If you really can spare the time, it would be a lifesaver."

"Sorry, but I won't be much help to you," Arthur said. "I've got a doctor's appointment in an hour, and after that, I've got to take my wife to her doctor. It takes forever to get on his schedule, so I can't change it. Anyway, my bursitis has flared up again. It's hell getting old."

"We'll manage," Grace assured him.

"I'll check back with you later in the day," Arthur said. He looked around at the bedroom walls and shook his head again. "What gets into kids' heads these days? What's the fun of destroying property? Where are their parents? That's what I'd like to know."

He pulled a handkerchief from his pocket and wiped his paint-smeared hands on it. "I took more pictures before you got here," he told Grace. "And the police were here, right after the firemen left. I'll file a claim with the insurance company in between the doctors' visits."

"Thanks, Arthur," Grace said, following him onto the front porch.

He turned just before reaching the door. "You sure you want to bother with doing this all over again? Maybe I should just hire some young fella to come in and clean it up and paint it all and be done with it. Get it rented again and quit worrying."

"No!" Grace said sharply. She smiled sheepishly. "I mean, I wish you wouldn't. I've got so much invested here. I really want to see it through to completion. Besides, I'm still hoping you'll decide to let me rent it when it's done. So I really do have an ulterior motive."

"I'll tackle the kitchen if you want to concentrate on this bedroom," Wyatt offered.

Grace planted a kiss on his chin. "You're a good guy, Wyatt Keeler." Then she went back to work.

It was nearly two o'clock when he poked his head in the bedroom again. She'd managed to mop most of the orange paint off the floors. She'd scraped the dried paint from the window panes and had even put a coat of primer on the walls. The orange paint was so vivid, she was sure it would take at least two coats of primer, plus two coats of the Benjamin Moore. At some point, she'd have to make another trip to the hardware store to buy more paint.

"Looking good," Wyatt said. He held out a white paper sack. "I went and got us some lunch. You ready for a break?"

They sat cross-legged on the front porch to eat their turkey sandwiches. Grace rested her aching back against the wall and took a swig of her Diet Coke. "How's it coming in the kitchen?"

"There's good news and bad news. Which do you want first?"

She made a face. "Tell me the good stuff first."

"I managed to get all the paint off the fridge and stove. We didn't get so lucky with the cupboards. They'll all have to be repainted."

Grace sighed and pushed a strand of sweaty orange-streaked hair off her forehead. "What's the floor looking like?"

Sweetie, who'd been sitting politely on her haunches, stared hungrily at the sandwich wrappings and whined softly. Grace tore off a bit of turkey and tossed it to the dog, who caught it in midair.

"Like a really long night of repainting red and white checkerboards," Wyatt said, grimacing.

Grace groaned and rolled up the legs of her jeans to show him her bruised knees. "I'm still not recovered from the first time I painted that floor. Me and my big ideas."

"I know this is probably a silly question, but couldn't we just paint the whole thing one color?"

"We could—except that I got an e-mail from an editor at *Veranda* magazine this morning. They want me to do a series for them—story and photographs, of my redo of the cottage. And the editor very specifically mentioned that she adores that floor."

"Oh." Wyatt munched on a potato chip. "*Veranda* magazine. That's good?"

"Very good. Especially in my world. It's huge."

"I'd slide over there and give you a congratulatory hug, but I'm too tired."

She smiled. "I'll consider myself hugged. Anyway, who knows if I can get this place cleaned up enough now to even do the story?"

He chewed and thought. "Maybe you could make this"—he swept his hand, indicating the charred porch floor and broken windows—"part of the story. You know, intrepid girl rescues house from fire and paint bomb?"

She raised an eyebrow. "That's actually not a bad idea. Now I wish I'd taken some pictures of the bedroom before I started cleaning it up."

"Could you use the pictures Arthur took?"

"Maybe. I guess they'd have to be scanned or something." She finished off her sandwich and threw a last chunk of turkey to Sweetie, who'd been stealthily creeping closer to the source of the food while she talked.

Wyatt stood and helped her to her feet.

"Guess I'd better grit my teeth and check out the damage in the bathroom," Grace said, making a face. "Arthur wouldn't even let me look in there when I got here this morning. He said it was pretty gross."

"It was," Wyatt said. "Nothing I'd want you to have to deal with. I got the tub and all the walls wiped down with bleach, and I managed to unstop the toilet and mop up most of the water. All I can say is, if I ever get hold of the punks who did all this . . ." He made a fist. "Pow!"

"Yeah," Grace said. "About those punks. I'm not so sure this was the random act of vandalism that Arthur assumes it is."

"Really? Then . . . You're not saying your ex did this, are you?"

"Maybe. Although this—especially the way Arthur described the bathroom—that's not really Ben's style. J'Aimee, on the other hand? I'm not so sure it wasn't her. Or maybe she put somebody else up to it."

"I don't know, Grace," Wyatt said. "What happened here is pretty extreme—even for a pissed-off ex-husband. Besides the fact that the two of them are scum, what makes you think they're behind this?"

"For one thing, the paint. That was a brand-new can of orange paint, and a brand-new can of black paint. I didn't have either of those here in the house, so whoever did it took the trouble to go buy paint and bring it along. So not really a crime of opportunity. Same with the fire. That wasn't just a bunch of rags they used to start the fire in the living room. There were loads of old towels and sheets in the linen closet, but they didn't use them to start it. They brought what looks like a new canvas drop cloth. Because, again, whoever set that fire was quite the little planner. Does that sound like kids to you?"

He stared at her. "Are you sure you haven't been watching too much *CSI*?"

"I've had a lot of time to think while I scrubbed that floor," Grace said. "Shall I tell you what else I think is suspicious?"

"Shoot."

Grace pointed toward the house across the street. The lawn was neatly mowed, and two green recycling bins stood at the curb. "There were three or four different kinds of beer cans in the kitchen sink, plus the Red Bull, plus the vodka. I think whoever did this caper wanted us to think they had a party, so they probably just scooped up some empty bottles and cans along the way. Today was recycling day, so every house on this street had full bins sitting on the curb last night."

"Anything else?" Wyatt asked.

She walked into the living room, and he followed. She kicked at the remains of the charred thing on the floor. "I don't think J'Aimee intended to burn the house down. That's pretty scary, even for her. I think she just wanted to make a little fire. Why else just set fire to something like this? If someone really wanted a fire, they would have poured lighter fluid, or kerosene, or whatever all over the house. But it's just this one little corner of the room that's charred."

"Why would she, or Ben, do any of this?" Wyatt asked. "How do they even know you're working on this house?"

"Trust me, they read TrueGrace every day. J'Aimee steals my pictures and recipes all the time. Both of them have stopped by here. As to why, that's simple. For revenge. The last time J'Aimee lifted one of my blog posts, and the photos and posted them on Gracenotes as her own, I got fed up. It's copyright infringement, pure and simple. I e-mailed all their advertisers to let them know what was going on. I know at least one of their biggest accounts pulled their ads because of that."

"Will you tell the cops?"

"I would if I thought it would do any good," Grace said. "But all I have is a lot of theories. So I'm going to do the one thing that will piss them off the most. I'm going to start all over, and I'm going to make this house fabulous, even if it kills me."

"Okay," he said. "Count me in."

50

Grace stood in the middle of the living room, her hands on her hips, and scowled. Wyatt came in just in time to catch her angry expression. "What now?"

"On top of everything else, she stole my damn iPod," Grace said. "I left it in here the other night. The thing was, like, four years old, but it had all my music; my running music, my painting music, everything. Now it's all gone. Dammit. I need my music to paint by."

"I've got my iPod out in the truck," Wyatt said cautiously. "But it's getting kind of late, isn't it?"

Grace looked out the shattered front window. The sun was hanging low in a bright orange-tinged sky. "Wow, it's almost sunset. What is it, after eight?"

"Five after eight," Wyatt said. "Are you ready to quit yet?"

"Are you?"

"I'll keep working as long as you want to. But you've been at it all day, Grace. Since nine this morning, with only a half-hour break at lunch. Do you really want to keep going?"

"No," she admitted. "As Rochelle would say, my get up and go got up and went. Maybe I'll head home."

"Good idea," Wyatt said.

"Unless . . ." A smile crept over her face.

"Unless what?"

"I was just thinking, you might like to see my other design project."

"I didn't know you had another project."

"It's Mitzi's condo over on Gulf Drive. She's turning it into a furnished vacation rental, and she's hired me to fluff it. The back of my car is actually full of towels and rugs and bedspreads and curtains for the place. I just started shopping for it yesterday."

"Sounds nice," Wyatt said, wondering where this conversation was headed. "But it's getting kind of late for a sightseeing tour. Maybe you could show it to me this weekend?"

"It sits right on the gulf," Grace told him. "The master bedroom has a balcony with a spectacular sunset view. And it has a king-sized bed. And I have the key."

Wyatt's eyes lit up. "Are you propositioning me?"

"Would you think less of me if I were?"

"Not at all," he assured her. "And I promise. I'll still respect you in the morning."

They left Wyatt's truck at Mandevilla Manor and drove to the Publix on Holmes Beach to pick up supplies. While he circled the parking lot, Grace made a sweep of the supermarket. She hummed as she careened through the aisles, tossing a bag of dog food, a bottle of wine, a six-pack of beer, a pound of boiled shrimp, some good cheese, a loaf of French bread, and some grapes into the cart. On her way to the cash register, she caught sight of herself in a mirrored display in the floral department. Ugh! She was a mess. She backtracked through the store and added a bar of scented soap and some shampoo and conditioner to the cart, and then, in a flash of genius, she added a jug of detergent because the condo had a laundry room.

"Get everything we need?" Wyatt asked, pulling alongside her at the entrance to the store.

"I think so," she said, holding up the wine.

When they got to the condo, Wyatt snapped a leash to Sweetie's collar and carried the grocery sacks, and Grace loaded her arms with the linens she'd bought. She juggled the packages while she dug in her pocket for the key. When they entered the apartment, it was already flooded with the dying light of the sunset.

Grace glanced down at her paint-spattered sneakers and kicked them off before stepping onto Mitzi's pristine white carpet, and Wyatt followed suit.

Wyatt dropped the groceries on the kitchen counter and walked back to the living room, standing in front of the sliding glass doors that led out to the balcony. The sky was streaked with brilliant layers of colors, from navy to violet to scarlet, orange, and pink. "Awesome," he breathed. Grace hurried into the bedroom and dropped her packages. By the time she got back to the living room, Wyatt had opened the wine and poured glasses for both of them, and Sweetie was curled up on the rug in front of the television.

"Come here," he said, holding out her glass. She took a sip of the wine. He put his arm around her, and she rested her head against his shoulder.

"Nice place," he said, looking around the room. "Kinda white, though, isn't it?"

"Mitzi's a great lawyer, but, as she herself admits, she sucks at decorating. She gave me a five-thousand-dollar budget and a deadline of two weeks, but otherwise no restrictions."

"Hmm." He was nuzzling her neck. "Is it okay for me to be here?"

Grace chuckled, thinking of her conversation with her lawyer. "I think she'd be okay with it."

He turned her toward him and slid his hands around her waist. "Pardon me for being forward, but didn't you say something about a king-sized bed?"

"Mm-hmm." She gave him a lingering kiss. "What about the sunset?"

"I thought you said the bedroom looked out onto the gulf."

"So I did." She kissed him again, then pulled away.

"Much as I hate to bring up the subject, I am absolutely filthy, and I smell like a goat. I'm just going to jump in the shower, and then maybe we can continue this discussion somewhere else?"

"Okay," he said, running a finger slowly down her arm. "Need anybody to scrub your back?"

"Mmmm. Hold that thought."

The master bedroom had a huge tiled walk-in shower with an adjustable rainforest shower head. Grace hummed as she lathered her entire body, scrubbing at the streaks and specks of orange paint that seemed to coat every inch of her exposed skin. The hot water sluiced down her back and over her chest and her head. She washed and rinsed her hair and wished she'd brought along a razor to shave her legs. The thought struck her that she still had two weeks to work on the condo. She'd make sure and stock the bathroom with a razor—and a toothbrush and toothpaste—after her next shopping trip.

She towel-dried her hair and finger-combed it as best she could, then wrapped herself in another one of the big fluffy towels she'd bought. Then she gathered up the clothes she'd left on the bathroom floor.

Wyatt's voice drifted in from the other room. It sounded like he was on the phone. She hesitated, then pressed her ear to the door.

"Hey Dad." His voice was low. "How're you feeling?

"That's good. Did you have dinner? Did you eat the vegetables I bought you? No Dad, Tater Tots don't count. Yeah. Salad's good. Did you take the new medicine the doctor gave you?"

He sighed. "Yeah, I know you're a grown-up, but I just want to make sure you take your pills. Is that a crime? Okay, great. Callie didn't call, did she? No, Dad, remember? You promised the judge you wouldn't call her that anymore.

"Listen, Dad, I'm, uh, probably not coming home tonight, but I'll be back first thing tomorrow to get the animals fed and open up.

"What? None of your business. I'll see you in the morning."

How sweet is it that he calls his dad to check on him? Grace thought. *This is somebody I could love.*

And then something else occurred to her. She grabbed the jeans she'd dropped on the floor and dug her cell phone out of the pocket. It was Thursday night, which was ten-dollar-pitcher night. Hopefully, Rochelle would be too busy to answer her phone. She really did not want to have a variation of the same conversation Wyatt had just had with his father.

The phone rang once and went right to voice mail. "Hi Mom. Just wanted to let you know I'm not coming home tonight. I've got so much to do, I think I'll just camp over here tonight. See you in the morning." She disconnected hurriedly.

Wyatt was standing by the sliding glass doors in the bedroom when she emerged from the bathroom dressed only in a towel and a smile.

He gave a long, low wolf whistle when he saw her and held his arms open.

Grace padded across the room to him. "Take off your clothes."

He grinned. "If this is your idea of foreplay I can't wait to see what happens next."

"Don't be smutty," Grace said primly. "I bought detergent at Publix, and I'm going to wash our clothes so we have something clean to wear after . . . dinner."

He reached out and grabbed her. "Does this mean we get to have dessert before . . . dinner?"

She kissed him lightly. "We'll see."

He set his wineglass on a table by the window and made a huge production out of stretching and yawning.

"Oh man," he said. "I am soooo tired. I think I'm so tired I'm gonna need you to undress me."

Grace wrapped her arms around his neck. "Is that so?"

"Yes," he said solemnly. "Please."

Grace blushed. "You know I haven't been with another man in a really long time, right?"

He cradled her face between his hands and kissed her again. "It'll come back to you. It's like riding a bike."

She tugged his T-shirt over his head and tossed it to the floor, then ran her hands over the flat plane of his bare chest, resting her fingertips on his nipples. She kissed his ear, then his collarbone, and worked her way to his chest. Wyatt slid his hands around her waist and kissed her hungrily.

Grace slid her hands down lower and felt him inhale sharply. She worked her fingers inside the waistband of his jeans and nimbly unfastened the metal snap before slowly easing the zipper down. She rolled the waistband of his cotton briefs over his slim hips, brushing her hand lightly over his erection.

"Oh God, Grace," he whispered in her ear. She slid her hands around to his rear, cupping her hands on the smooth, cool flesh of his butt, while he kissed her neck, the warm spot at the base of her throat, and then her lips again, parting them with his tongue, both hands entwined in her damp hair.

Grace tugged the waist of his jeans and briefs lower, past his hips, feeling the bulge of his erection pressed against her groin, lower, until she could wrap one bare leg around his and ease the jeans down to his ankles with her toes.

"Nice trick," he murmured in her ear. He released her long enough to kick free of his jeans, then, naked, pulled her to him again.

He flicked the edge of her towel and it dropped to the floor. He took a step backward and gazed at her pale body, silhouetted against the deep-purple sky outside. "You're beautiful," he said. "So beautiful." His hands roamed slowly, lingering on her butt, traveling up her spine and then around her ribs, until he cupped a breast in each hand. His head dipped, nuzzling and suckling each nipple until Grace could hear her own ragged breaths in the still of the darkening room.

She ducked her head and felt the blush starting at the roots of her hair and spreading downward. He pressed a finger under her chin and she looked at him from beneath her lowered lashes.

"I'll take it from here," he said. He took her hand and led her toward the bed.

51

Grace lay on her side, gazing out the sliding glass doors at the deep-blue sky. At some point, Wyatt had opened the doors, and they could hear the waves washing ashore. He was spooned up against her back, his arm draped over her side, with his hand cupped against her breast, his thumb rhythmically brushing against her nipple. He was already aroused again. For that matter, so was she.

She rolled over to face him. "You've got to stop that, or we'll never get any dinner."

Instead, he bent his head and kissed her other nipple. "Would that be such a bad thing?"

"I'm starved," she announced. He caught at her hand, but she neatly slid out of the bed. Still self-conscious, she groped around on the floor for her forgotten bath towel, finally crawling over to where Wyatt had dropped it, several feet from the bed.

As she fastened it, she glanced over her shoulder and saw him, propped up in bed, watching her with amusement.

She gathered up their clothes and went out to the laundry room to load them into the washer. When she'd started the wash, she went to the kitchen and poured herself a glass of the chilled white wine. Through the open bedroom door she heard the sound of the shower starting.

Grace found a large bowl—white pottery, of course, in one of the kitchen cabinets. She dumped in the bag of boiled shrimp, cut up a lemon, and arranged the slices around the edge of the bowl, humming as she worked. She rinsed the green grapes and placed them on a cutting board, next to the loaf of French bread. There was no bread knife in the scarcely appointed drawer of kitchen implements, so she simply tore the bread in hunks and heaped them beside the grapes along with the cheeses she'd picked up in the deli department.

She heard the clicking of nails on the tile floor and looked down. Sweetie jumped up, her front paws scratching at Grace's bare knees.

"Ow," Grace said, leaning down to scratch the little dog's silky ears. "We've got to get you to the groomers to get your nails trimmed. In the meantime, thanks for reminding me. I actually did bring some dinner for you, too."

She poured dog food into one bowl and water into another and set them on the floor, then went back to her preparations, loading all the food, along with the wine bottle and two glasses, onto a large wicker tray.

Wyatt was just emerging from the bathroom as she walked into the bedroom. He had a towel wrapped loosely around his hips, and, with a hand towel, he was rubbing his closely shaven head. His chest was muscled and his abs were not quite male-porn-star tight, but close enough. His skin gleamed darkly tan in contrast to the white towel. She stopped dead in her tracks, forgetting what she'd been about to say.

"You're staring at me," Wyatt pointed out.

"That's not staring. That's lusting." Grace set the tray with the food on the nightstand. She wrapped her arms around his waist and backed him toward the bed.

He laughed, but offered no resistance.

When she had him right where she wanted him, she placed one hand on his chest and toppled him backward.

"You're freaking gorgeous," she said, looking down at him, spread-eagled across the bed. "I thought I liked you best dressed in your little Ranger Rick safari outfit, but that was because I'd never seen you naked. Or in a towel. I definitely like the towel best."

She leaned forward and brushed her fingertips lightly across his chest. Wyatt caught her hand and pulled her down beside him. He pinned her arms to the bed and rolled until he was on top of her.

He frowned down at her. "That is not a Ranger Rick outfit. I'll have you know it's an official Jungle Jerry uniform. My grandmother had them made for everybody who used to work at the park. The one you've seen me wearing is the last one left. The rest are all in tatters, and that one is one rip away from the trash."

She easily worked her hands free from his and ran her palms down his flanks. "You can never throw that uniform away," Grace said sternly. "It's what you were wearing the night we met."

"Minus the parrot poop," he reminded her. "But that wasn't the first time we met. The first time was that day we both went before Stackpole. Remember? I have to confess, I have no idea what you were wearing either time. You looked so angry and intimidating, I was about to flee the premises." He pointed at the tray. "Room service? I like your style."

"There's no dining room furniture yet," she said. "And I still have to buy barstools for the island in the kitchen. And I don't want to eat on that white sofa, not until I have a chance to spray it with a stain repellant. So . . . dinner in bed."

She crawled onto the bed and propped herself up against the padded headboard. Wyatt handed her a glass of wine and took his own. He lightly clinked his glass against hers. "Here's to divorce camp."

An hour later, they'd devoured every morsel of food on the tray and drained the bottle of wine. The towels were scattered about the floor, and after another longer, more leisurely session of lovemaking, they were spooned together on the big bed, Sweetie asleep on the floor beside them, moonlight pouring in through the open doors.

At some point, Grace was vaguely aware of her cell phone, which she'd left on the dresser, dinging softly to indicate an incoming voice mail, and then another, and then another. But she was still too drowsy, too warm and happy and overwhelmingly, bone-deep contented, to rouse herself and see what was going on in the rest of the world.

52

Driving back to the Sandbox the next morning, Sweetie sleeping on the front seat beside her, Grace finally took the time to check the voice mails from the night before.

The first, at 9:45 P.M., was from Rochelle.

"Grace! Those women from the other divorce camp sessions are here. They're on their second round of free drinks. You need to get back here and talk to them."

Shit! She'd totally forgotten her mother's plan to leave free-drink coupons on the windshields of Paula's other divorce campers. She couldn't believe her mother's crazy scheme had actually borne fruit.

The second call, ten minutes later, was also from her mother. "There must be seven or eight of those divorce women in here," Rochelle said, her voice cracking, either from excitement or desperation, Grace didn't know. "What the hell are you doing? Why aren't you here? These women all have hollow legs. They're drinking me broke!"

The third call was from Mitzi Stillwell, and she didn't sound happy. "Grace? It's ten fifteen in the evening. And I have a deposition at 8:00 A.M. I just got a call from your mom, insisting I get over to the Sandbox, to talk to some women she claims have some important information about Stackpole and your therapist. I have a vague idea where you might be right now, but I'm going to claim attorney-client privilege and not divulge that to Rochelle. Instead, I'm going to get out of bed, get dressed, and drive over to that bar to check this out. All I can say is, this had better be good. And he better be good, too."

Rochelle was practically beside herself by the time Grace walked into the bar, shortly before nine.

"Didn't you get any of my messages last night?" her mother demanded. "I kept calling and calling!"

"I'm sorry," Grace said. "Vandals broke into the cottage on Mandevilla sometime Wednesday night. It was a huge mess. They splattered paint all over the place and tried to burn it down. I kind of had my hands full. I had to try to get the paint off the floors and the appliances before it dried, and wash everything down. It was late by the time I got done, and I kind of just collapsed. I didn't get your messages until this morning."

"Vandals?" Rochelle asked. "Did you report it to the police?"

"Arthur did," she replied. "He's dealing with them." She walked around to the back of the bar and poured herself a mug of coffee. She took a sip and seated herself on a barstool. "Did you find out anything from the women who showed up here last night?"

Rochelle took a sip of her own coffee. "I found out a lot of stuff I didn't want to know, that's for sure. Husbands who are cross-dressers. Husbands who like to hang out in public bathrooms and expose themselves to little boys. Husbands who like to watch their wives have sex with strangers . . ."

"Eewww," Grace said. "Stop. I get the picture. I mean, did you find out anything about people who've been referred to Paula by Judge Stackpole?"

"Yup," Rochelle said, looking immensely pleased with herself. She turned to the bar back and pulled a spiral-bound stenographer's notebook from the drawer. "I took notes," she added.

"I must have put twenty or thirty of those coupons in the cars in that therapist's parking lot," she continued. "I didn't get over there 'til nearly eleven yesterday, and by that time, there were five women coming out of her office. I just handed them the coupons, and, since they were watching, I had to put them on the other cars. I got back over there after the lunch hour and hung around an hour, and another group of women, and one man, drove up and went into her office, so I put coupons on their cars. Then this big, burly, scary-looking guy came out of that tattoo place, and he wanted a coupon, so what could I do? I had to give him one. And then . . ."

"Mom," Grace said gently. "You did a great job handing out the coupons. But could you just cut to the chase? How many people actually showed up here last night who said they were in Paula's divorce camp?"

Rochelle didn't like having her story interrupted. "I was getting to that. I guess there were nine women who came in last night over the course of the evening with those free-drink coupons. I was trying not to act too nosy, just, you know, talking them up, asking how their day was going. A couple of them got kind of snotty with me. Just drank their free drink and left, without even leaving me a tip! What kind of woman stiffs a bartender who's giving her free drinks?"

"Probably one whose husband got to keep all the money in the divorce," Grace said.

"Eventually, though, four women sat right here at the bar. I think they were all in the same divorce group, because they were calling each other by their first names and kind of joking about their action plans. One of them said her action plan was to find herself a new sugar daddy. So I kept pouring the free drinks and playing dumb. Finally, I asked the chattiest one, this gal named Ginger, how they all knew each other, and she said they were in the same divorce-recovery group. I told Ginger I was going through a divorce myself, and how did she find out about something like that. And she said it wasn't her idea. The judge in her divorce case told her she *had* to go to a therapist. And not just any therapist. It had to be a therapist named Paula Talbott-Sinclair. That's when I started calling you."

She glared accusingly at her daughter. "And when you didn't call me back, I called Mitzi Stillwell. And she came right away."

"And that's when things started getting really interesting." A woman's dry voice came from behind them. Grace swiveled around on her barstool. "Mitzi! I thought you had an early deposition."

"I did, but when I got to the other attorney's office, he asked if we could reschedule. So here I am."

Rochelle took a mug and filled it with coffee before handing it over to the lawyer.

Mitzi sat down beside Grace. "I'm seriously thinking of hiring your mother as a private investigator. She's *that* good at asking dumb questions and drawing people out without raising their suspicions."

"That's what happens after you've tended bar for thirty years," Rochelle said modestly.

"What did you find out?" Grace begged. "Give me the nitty-gritty, please. I'm dying here."

Mitzi nodded deferentially to Rochelle. "Go ahead."

"All four of those gals, Ginger, Angie, Becky and Harriett, had your judge in their divorces," Rochelle said.

"The Honorable Cedric N. Stackpole Jr." Mitzi put in.

"Right. Harriett Porter, she was the oldest one, probably around my age, her husband owns a Cadillac dealership up north in Indiana, but they live down here full-time now," Rochelle reported. "She discovered her husband was having himself a fling with a male stripper in Tampa. She waited for him outside that club, and when he came outside at two in the morning, she sort of lost her temper and accidentally ran over his Gucci loafers with her SRX Crossover." Rochelle took a sip of coffee. "I'd never heard of such a car, but Harriett says it's sort of a cross between a real Cadillac and an Escalade. Escalades are what all the rappers drive, Harriett says . . ."

"Mom!"

"Right," Rochelle said, without missing a beat. "Stackpole threatened to throw Harriett in jail for aggravated assault, which her lawyer later told her was bullshit, because her husband did not want to have it get in the papers that he'd been run over in the parking lot at Jeepers Peepers. Instead, Stackpole told her she had to attend divorce-recovery group. With Paula."

"And the rest of the women in the group?" Grace asked.

"Different stories, same endings," Rochelle said smugly.

"By the time I got here last night, dear Harriett was fairly intoxicated," Mitzi said. "Lovely lady, but I think she probably needs AA more than she needs divorce recovery. I sat with all the girls for a while; then, I volunteered to make sure Harriett got home safely." She raised an eyebrow. "While she waits for her divorce to get settled, she's living in an enormous rented mansion on Siesta Key. Before I walked her to her door, I casually asked how much she's paying for her divorce-group sessions. Grace, she's paying nine hundred dollars!"

"That's three times as much as the rest of us," Grace said.

"I know," Mitzi said. "I was as stunned as you are. It didn't seem to bother

Harriett. I think she's actually enjoying the sessions with Paula. She apparently hasn't made a lot of friends since moving here. Before I told her good night, I asked for her lawyer's name." Mitzi sighed happily. "It's Carlton Towne. He's senior partner in my old law firm, and a prince of a guy. I put in a call to him first thing this morning."

Rochelle pushed her steno notebook across the bar to Grace. "Here's the name of the other gals in Harriett's group. They even have a name for themselves. The Diva Divorcées. Cute, huh?"

Grace read the names scrawled on the notepad. "Are these their lawyers' names, too?"

"You bet," Rochelle said.

"I only know one of these lawyers personally," Mitzi said, running her finger down the list of names. "And because we have to do this very quietly, with an abundance of caution, I'm not going to call them until absolutely necessary."

Grace nodded. "Just what is it you're planning to do?"

"First, I'm going to call Betsy Entwhistle and chat with her about Wyatt's experience with Stackpole. Then, I'm hoping Carlton Towne will be as frank with me as his client was last night. Then, I think it's time we talked to the other members of your group, Grace, to see what their lawyers have to say. If that goes well, I think we'll probably have enough to file a complaint against Stackpole with the state Judicial Qualifications Committee."

"How long will all that take?" Grace asked. "After next week, we've only got one week of divorce camp left. Then, Stackpole's supposed to rule on my divorce. What if he finds out what we're up to?"

"Leave that to me," Mitzi said. "We're going to gather every bit of documentation possible, and I can be very, very discreet and low-key."

53

Grace, can I speak with you privately for a minute?" Mitzi asked. Rochelle gave them a questioning look but retreated to the kitchen.

Mitzi lowered her voice. "How's the condo coming along?"

Grace blinked. "Good. I went shopping Thursday and picked up a lot of things to bring in some color, since you've got so much white. I don't want it to look too sterile. You're going to have turquoise and lime green, and pops of tangerine . . ."

"How about the bed? I paid nearly two thousand dollars for that mattress, you know."

Grace felt herself blushing and glanced toward the kitchen to make sure her mother was not within earshot. "The mattress is amazing. Totally."

Mitzi smirked. "I just like knowing I've gotten my money's worth."

"Trust me," Grace said. "You did."

Wyatt pulled up in front of Luke Grigsby's house shortly after ten. He'd averted his eyes as he passed his old house, just down the street. It pained him to see the smudged windows, the stack of yellowing plastic-wrapped newspapers at the edge of the driveway, and the forlorn tire swing hanging from a rotted rope tied to a spindly tree in the side yard. Mostly, it pained him to see the "Bank Owned: For Sale" sign in the weed-strewn front yard.

Losing the house to the bank, he realized, was probably more painful than losing Callie.

He glanced at the clock on the truck's dashboard, then at Luke's front door and, as always, felt the same familiar, simmering resentment replace his previously cheerful, even joyous, demeanor.

According to the written agreement they'd hashed out during their separation, Callie was supposed to deliver Bo to Jungle Jerry's on the days Wyatt had custody. In reality, Wyatt usually ended up going to get his son on what he thought of as "hand-off days," because Callie was rarely even remotely on time, which always made Bo anxious and agitated, afraid his mother would change her mind and refuse to allow him to see his father.

Wyatt tapped his fingers impatiently, the back of his wedding ring sounding a *ching-ching-ching* against the hard plastic of the steering wheel. He'd been sitting there for ten, then fifteen minutes. He was reluctant to tap his horn or even go to the front door, because the last person he wanted to see that day was his soon-to-be ex-wife.

He found his mind wandering back to the previous evening, and then this morning. He'd awakened early, as always, shortly after six. It was still dark outside, and Grace was sleeping on her side, faced away from him, moonlight silvering her slumbering form. The quilt had slipped from her bare shoulder. Carefully, he pulled it lower until her back was exposed. He marveled at the elegant curve of her spine, the way her soft brown hair spilled onto the pillow, the way her full hips flowed from her narrow waist. She had a tiny mole on her left shoulder; he could just barely see it. He'd pressed his lips to her shoulder, not really meaning to awaken her, but she'd turned, and seeing his face inches from hers, smiled lazily. He'd thought her beautiful the night before, but finding her like this, tousled and sleep-drunk, he decided she was the most exquisite woman he'd ever known.

The passenger-side door opened abruptly and Bo hopped onto the seat and slammed the door hard. He folded his arms across his chest and grunted. "Let's go."

His son's face was set in anger, his eyes red-rimmed.

"Hey, dude," Wyatt said cheerily. "Something wrong?"

"Mom's really upset," Bo said. "Some guy came over this morning and took her new car, and she's been on the phone hollering and yelling at you know who. Can we just go now?"

What now? Wyatt wondered. Callie's car was a flashy red Mustang convertible. Bo told him Luke had given it to her for her birthday a few months earlier, complete with a vanity tag that read HOTMAMA.

"Is your mom's car not working?"

"No. I mean, yeah, it works good. We were asleep, and then I heard something outside and it was still dark, so I snuck out to the living room window to see if was like a burglar or something, and I saw this guy breaking into Mom's car! I went in and woke her up and told her, and she went and got this like gun out of the dresser. Then she went running outside, but the guy was already inside her car. She was screaming at him to stop, but he just rolled the window down and threw a piece of paper at her, and then he peeled off down the street, going really fast."

Uh-oh. Sounds like the repo man had paid a visit this morning. Mr. Bigshot must have missed a car payment. Or two.

Wyatt would have found it comical, except that witnessing the unpleasant scene had clearly upset the child.

"Well, I'm sure your mom will get it figured out," Wyatt said for lack of anything better to say.

"She's really, really mad at him," Bo said. He gave his father a hopeful look. "Maybe she'll change her mind and they won't get married, and we won't have to move to stinkin' Alabama."

Wyatt was about to pull away from the curb when out of the corner of his eye he saw Luke's front door open. Callie stood in the doorway, dressed only in an oversized T-shirt that barely touched her thighs. Her hair was mussed and rivers of black mascara streamed down her cheeks.

"Wyatt!" she screamed. And then she came running toward the truck in her bare feet.

Bo's eyes were the size of saucers. "Stay here," Wyatt said. He jumped out of the truck and met Callie at the sidewalk. "They repossessed my Mustang," she cried. "It's gone! Luke swears he doesn't know what happened, but I know he's lying. He lied about everything."

Callie threw herself into his arms. He closed them uneasily about her shoulder, turning to see that Bo was still in the truck, his eyes riveted to the unfolding scene.

"Shh," Wyatt said, patting her shoulder. "It's probably just a misunderstanding. Maybe the car payments got posted wrong or something."

"No," she sobbed. "Luke's broke. He's been lying all along. Oh my God, Wyatt. It was all just a big lie. What am I going to do?"

"Hey," he said softly. "We'll figure it out. Look, this is upsetting Bo. Why don't you go inside and get dressed. Let me take him over to the park and get him settled with Dad; then I'll give you a call and we can talk about it. Okay?"

"A call?" Her voice was wobbly. Snot trails dribbled down her face. "Can't you come back here and talk? I could make us some coffee . . ."

"Not here," Wyatt said, his spine stiffening. There was no way he was setting foot inside Luke Grigsby's house again. Not ever.

"Oh," she said. "I get it. Okay. I could come over to the park . . ."

"God no," he replied. "You're not exactly Dad's favorite person these days, Callie."

"That was all Luke's idea," she said quickly. "I never meant anything by it . . ."

Wyatt sighed. "I'll meet you at Starbucks in an hour. Okay? But I can't stay long."

"All right," she said. "Oh my God. This is all such a nightmare."

For once, Wyatt thought bleakly, he'd have to agree with her.

54

Callie had managed a remarkable transformation in the hour since he'd last seen her. Her hair was now clean and shiny and pulled back in a ponytail, she had fresh makeup, and she was dressed in a low-cut pink top and tight white jeans. And, Wyatt noticed, as she clutched the mug of coffee he'd just brought to the table, she wasn't wearing Luke's flashy diamond engagement ring.

"Thanks for coming," she said, her voice low. "I'm sorry I got all hysterical in front of Bo. That was bad. But everything happened so fast . . . I completely lost it."

"He's a sensitive kid," Wyatt said. "I know it's hard to do, but, for his sake, we really have to try to keep things on an even keel."

"I know." Callie nodded and took a sip of coffee. She gazed out the window at the parking lot. When she turned to look at him, her eyes were brimming with fresh tears.

"It's over between me and Luke," she said, her lower lip trembling. "And not just because of the car. Everything he told me? Everything he promised me? It was all just a big fat lie. He lost his job. There is no transfer to Birmingham. He just told me that because he assumed he'd get a new one with another company there. He's known for three weeks now, and he never said a word. Just kept bullshitting me. About everything." She held up her naked left hand. "My ring?

Not real. Not even a good fake. And you know how I found out? I took it to the jewelry store in the mall yesterday, because I wanted to have it sized, and the girl behind the counter actually laughed at me when she saw it. It's a friggin' cubic zirconia."

Wyatt winced. "Did you ask Luke about that?"

"Yes. Of course, he had all these bullshit excuses. He tried to tell me he gave me a fake ring because he was having the real one custom-made, and it wasn't ready yet. He's got lies and excuses for everything."

"Geez. I'm sorry, Callie."

"Not as sorry as me," she said bitterly. "What do I do now? I can't stay with him. I won't. I told him that this morning. I can't marry a liar."

"What'll you do?" he asked.

She shrugged. "I have no idea. I just know I won't stay under the same roof with him. Not another night. I can't have Bo exposed to somebody like that."

"Well, of course, Bo can stay with Dad and me for as long as you need him to. But where will you go?"

"Good question. I don't exactly have a lot of options. Most of my girlfriends? As far as they're concerned, I'm the slut who cheated on her husband. They all made it pretty clear they couldn't stand Luke."

"What about your family?"

"Ha! My parents are barely speaking to me since our breakup. They always thought you walked on water, Wyatt. Anyway, I'm not about to move back to South Carolina. What would I do there? Get a job selling made-in-China sombreros at South of the Border? Anyway, Bo would hate it there. And the schools suck."

You didn't care what Bo thought about Birmingham when you thought you and Luke were moving there, Luke thought.

"What about Kendra?" he asked.

Her lips twisted. "My baby sister is just itching to get a chance to say, 'I told you so.' She never liked Luke, either. Guess maybe I should have polled all my friends and family before falling in love with him and ruining my life, huh?"

Funny how it didn't occur to Callie that she wasn't the only one affected by her affair with Luke Grigsby. She probably just considered her husband and son as collateral damage.

"You've always gotten along with Kendra. Surely she wouldn't turn you away, right? Until you get things figured out?"

"Maybe." Callie didn't sound convinced. She grabbed a paper napkin from the stack Wyatt had brought to the table and used it to blot her eyes.

"Oh God, Wy," she whispered. "How could this have happened? You were the best thing that ever happened to me. And I let you walk away. Can you ever forgive me?"

Wyatt twisted his own paper napkin into a tightly wound ribbon. "What's done is done." *What does she want from me?* he wondered. "You just need to figure out how to get your life back on track, with the least amount of disruption to Bo. He's had more than enough of that in the last year."

"I know, I know," Callie agreed. "I'll call Kendra right now. I can probably stay with her for tonight, at least."

"What about a car?" Wyatt asked.

"That bastard Luke traded my Civic in when he got the Mustang," Callie said. "I drove his old Jeep over here. And he's crazy if he thinks I'll give it back. He owes me. Big-time."

"At least that's something," he said. "Look, Callie. I'm sorry, but I really need to get back to the park. We've got a group of thirty kids coming in with a day camp in an hour, and they're expecting a guided tour and a performance from Cookie."

"I know you're busy," Callie said. "You don't have time for my soap opera. Go on. I'm just going to sit here for a while and try to get my wits about me before I go back to Luke's and start packing up my stuff."

He hesitated. "So . . . we'll plan on keeping Bo at the park, at least through the weekend. Is that okay with you?"

"Sure," she said, shrugging. "What are you going to tell him? About Luke and me?"

"Nothing," Wyatt said. "I'll leave that to you to figure out. You should probably call him later today, when you're calmer. You don't have to tell him the gory details yet. Just let him know you're okay."

Callie reached across the table and squeezed his hand, clinging to him. "I will. And I won't cry anymore. Not in front of him, anyway. Thanks, Wy."

"You're welcome," he said, slowly sliding his hand away from hers. "Good luck with Kendra."

. . .

On Monday, Grace was just unloading the last of her second batch of painting supplies from her car when Arthur's car pulled up to the driveway.

It took him a few minutes to emerge from the car, and when he did, Grace thought he looked tired. Tired and defeated. He walked, stiff-legged, toward where she stood, right outside the front porch.

"Hi, Arthur," she called.

"Hi there, Grace." He looked down at the buckets of paint she'd stacked on the porch steps and sighed and looked away. His shoulders slumped.

"I know, it's a hit to our budget," she said. "But hopefully the insurance will pay for it, right? Anyway, Wyatt and I managed to get all the paint off the floors and the appliances, so I'm just repainting the walls in the bedroom and the kitchen cabinets. And the kitchen floor. Again. That's a pain in the butt, for sure. We'll have to get a floor guy to take a look at the scorched floor in the living room, but maybe that can just be patched."

"Come on inside, Grace. I need to talk to you."

Theirs footsteps echoed in the high-ceilinged rooms. Arthur looked in at the kitchen, and the bedroom and bathroom.

"You've done real good work here, Grace," he said finally. "And I'm gonna pay you for everything you've done. I want to do right by you."

"But?" She dreaded what he was going to say next. It would not be good news, she knew.

"The wife and I had a long talk yesterday. My blood pressure was up pretty high by the time I got to see my doctor, and that got her all upset and worried. And the thing is, at my age, I just don't need the hassle."

"Arthur, once somebody's living here, I seriously doubt you'll have anything like this happen again," Grace said. "Even if you don't rent it to me . . ."

"If we rented it to anybody, it'd be you, Grace. But we're not going to rent it. We talked it over, and what with the money it'll take to put in that central air-conditioning you keep talking about, well, I just don't see putting that much money into the place right now. So we're going to sell it."

"Oh." Grace felt herself sag against the kitchen doorway. "I see."

He swallowed and she saw his Adam's apple bob up and down as he worked through what he was going to say.

"I hate like the dickens to let the place go," he said, running a gnarled hand over the doorframe. "The way you had it looking, just these past couple weeks, my folks would have been proud of that. This was their homeplace, and they always took pride in it. But my wife, she helped me see, the time has come to let it go to somebody else."

Grace couldn't trust herself to speak. She just nodded.

"I've got a real estate agent coming over on Saturday, to look the place over and tell me what she thinks I could sell it for," Arthur said. He looked up at her. "My wife was wondering if maybe you'd be interested in buying it. If you were, we'd try to make you a fair price, taking into consideration how much time you've already put into the house. But we'd need you to make a decision pretty quick, before we go ahead and list it with an agent."

She bit her lip. "If my divorce were final today, and I had the money, I'd love to buy this house," Grace said. "But to be honest with you, I can't say exactly when that's going to happen, or how much of a financial settlement I'm going to get from my ex. The judge in my case . . . well, let's just say he doesn't exactly see things the way my lawyer and I do."

"That's a damn shame," Arthur said. "And that fella, that friend of yours? I don't guess he's in any position . . ."

"He's in almost the same position I am, except he's also got child-support payments," Grace told him. "Anyway, Wyatt and I . . . well, he's a very nice person. But we just started seeing each other. It's way too early to know how that's going to turn out."

"I see. Well, I guess that's that then," he said. "I'm real sorry it had to end like this, Grace. I liked the idea of you fixing up this place, moving in and living here, starting all over again. Don't guess there's any need for you to do any more painting now. I feel bad enough that you put all this time into the place, for nothing."

"Not for nothing," Grace said. "I enjoyed the process. I just hope whoever buys the place will finish the job and do justice to it."

She followed the older man out to the front porch. "I meant to ask you," she said, as he fumbled in his pocket for his car keys. "Did you report the vandalism to the police?"

"Yes. I filed a report. I showed them the pictures I took with my camera. They didn't seem too interested. I guess they see a lot of that type of thing."

"I've got an idea about who might have done it," Grace said slowly. "Would it be okay if I talked to a cop I know?"

He gave her an odd look. "Grace, it's over. I appreciate your wanting to catch whoever did this, but don't you have something better to do with your time?"

"Humor me, will you Arthur? You're probably right. It'll probably come to nothing. But this is personal now. I'd like to see it all the way through, whatever happens."

Arthur patted her shoulder. "You're a stubborn little gal. Guess I should have figured you'd want to get to the bottom of things. All right. Go ahead. And if this cop friend of yours has any questions, have him give me a call."

55

In a pair of frayed jeans with holes at the knees, a Tampa Bay Rays T-shirt, and Wayfarer sunglasses, Pete Strivecky looked nothing like a cop and everything like a too-cool-for-school teenager as he stood on the doorstep of the cottage on Mandevilla, holding his motorcycle helmet under one arm.

"Awesome house," he said when Grace greeted him Tuesday morning. "I'm glad you gave me a call. I've been reading about it on your blog. I even rode my girlfriend over here last weekend so she could take a look at it in person."

"It is an awesome house, or it will be, when whoever buys it gets done," Grace said sadly.

Officer Strivecky stepped inside and immediately walked over to the scorched corner of the living room. "So, you said the fire started here? Looks like it didn't do much damage."

"They poured some kind of lighter fluid or something on a new canvas drop cloth," Grace said. "Fortunately, the neighbor saw the flames through the porch windows, and he was able to put it out before the fire spread."

"Did you happen to save the drop cloth?"

"What was left. I put it out in the garage," Grace said. "Along with the empty paint cans they used in the kitchen and living room."

"Good idea." Strivecky nodded his approval. "Like I told you on the phone,

I'm not a detective, and I'm sure not an arson investigator. But I don't think it would hurt to take a look around."

Strivecky walked through all the rooms in the house while Grace gave her running narrative on all that she'd accomplished in rehabbing the house—and what the vandal did to ruin her handiwork.

When they were done, they sat on the front porch steps, and Grace handed him a bottle of water.

"You really think it's your ex-husband's girlfriend? Why would she do something like that?" he asked.

"Revenge," Grace said succinctly. "She and Ben were blatantly ripping off material from my new blog for Gracenotes. So I e-mailed most of my old advertisers to let them know what was happening. I thought they should know they were spending money with people who have no ethics. At least a couple of them dropped their ads. J'Aimee came over here last week, and she threatened that she'd make me sorry. So yes, I think she's behind this."

"She sounds like a head case," Strivecky said. He took a swig of water. "I can talk to one of our detectives about your suspicions, but I can tell you right now he'll probably say that unless somebody catches her in the act, there's nothing he can do."

"What about if she left fingerprints? On the paint cans, or even in the bathroom, where she did the cute fingerpainting?"

"The bathroom was wiped clean," Strivecky reminded her. "And what if she did leave fingerprints? You said she came over here last week. She could claim she left fingerprints then. But it's not going to get that far, Grace. We already know there's bad blood between you and your ex and this woman. Our detective is going to say this is just another domestic dispute. Nasty, yes. Criminal? Probably not."

Grace kicked at the porch railing with the toe of her sneaker. "This day just keeps getting better and better. Because of *her,* the owner of the house has decided to just sell it, instead of renting it to me. And I can't afford to buy the place myself, because I don't have any money. And now you tell me, even if I could prove it was *her,* there's nothing the police will do."

She glared defiantly at Strivecky. "Now I know why people take the law into their own hands. I feel so powerless—it's infuriating!"

"But you won't do anything to get back at her—right?" Strivecky said. "We didn't have this conversation. Right?"

"Right," she said glumly. "No violence. I'll just have to figure out how to get back at Ben—and her—legally."

Dear Lily: Thanks for your recent e-mail and your kind words about TrueGrace and the cottage on Mandevilla. It was a dream project—while it lasted. Unfortunately, the owner notified me today that he intends to sell the cottage, as is, meaning that my work there will go unfinished. I'd be happy to send you photos of my other current project, although it is not on the same scope as Mandevilla. And I'd love the chance to land an assignment for Veranda. *Regretfully, Grace Davenport, TrueGrace.com*

When she'd sent the e-mail, Grace flopped facedown on her bed and screamed into her pillow. Then she stood up, combed her hair, and called her lawyer.

Nelson Keeler was kitted out in his Jungle Jerry's uniform, khaki safari shirt, khaki slacks (his old khaki shorts no longer fit around his thickened waist), and his battered old safari hat—the leather-lined one that had been handed down to him by his father. He was happily chatting with a half-dozen members of the Hibiscus Garden Club who'd gathered around him in the gift shop after buying their senior-citizen-discounted tickets.

"Now, ladies, we're going to start your tour with a little history of the park," he was saying.

Joyce Barrett, their only other full-time employee, was staring out the glass door leading into the gift shop and ticket area when she saw Callie Keeler briskly approaching.

She was in her eighties and had silver hair she wore in a long braid down her back, and her own Jungle Jerry's costume was immaculately pressed, as always.

"Uh-oh," she whispered under her breath. She glanced back at Nelson, who'd already briefed her on Callie's latest attempt to torpedo Wyatt's happiness. She reached for the walkie-talkie they kept under the ticket counter.

"Wyatt? Office to Wyatt. Storm on the horizon. Repeat. Storm on the horizon."

There was a burst of crackling static. "Shit. Copy that, Joyce. On my way. Be there in five."

Joyce tugged at Nelson's arm. "Er, Nelson?" He looked up, and she jerked her head in the direction of the door just as Callie pushed through it.

Nelson stopped speaking, midsentence. His expression darkened. "What's she doing here?"

"Don't know," Joyce murmured. "But Wyatt's heading back here right now."

"Ladies," Nelson said loudly, turning so that his back was to the door. "Let's head out to the garden now, and I'll fill you in on what's in bloom as we walk." He strode out the double doors to the park without a backward glance.

"Joyce," Callie cooed, when the older woman returned to the ticket counter. "How nice to see you. How are the grandkids?"

"Fine," Joyce said, stone-faced.

"Quite a few cars in the parking lot," Callie said, leaning against the counter. "Business must be picking up, huh?"

"It's all right," Joyce said, her voice a monotone. "We get by."

"Is Wyatt around?" Callie asked, craning her neck to try to see around the bookkeeper.

"He's been out with a group from summer day camp, but he's on his way back now," Joyce said. "Excuse me, Callie. I need to get the snacks ready for those kids. They're always hungry and thirsty when they come back in out of that heat."

She turned to go, but Callie placed a hand on her arm. "Oh, let me help, Joyce. I know where everything is." Callie stepped neatly under the old-fashioned wooden turnstile and bustled into the office.

Two minutes later, when Wyatt hurried into the lobby, followed by thirty clamoring children, Callie was setting juice boxes and plates full of graham crackers and apple slices on the long table in the snack bar.

Bo brought up the rear of the group. He was dressed in a faded and somewhat shrunken Jungle Jerry's T-shirt, and Cookie the parrot was perched on his shoulder. He beamed at the sight of his mother. "Mom!"

"Hey, Bo-Boy," she said, looking up from her task. She met her husband's unsmiling eyes. "Hi, Wy."

"Shots and beer!" the parrot demanded. "Gimme whiskey. Gimme beer."

Callie broke off a piece of graham cracker and held it out for Cookie, who snapped her beak around the cracker—taking with it a sizable chunk of Callie's fingertip.

"Owww," Callie screeched. "Son of a bitch!"

Startled, the parrot squawked and flew crazily around the room, while the day campers alternately screamed, giggled, ducked under tables, and covered their heads with their arms.

After circling the room a couple of times, Cookie finally settled on Wyatt's shoulder. He tried to soothe the agitated bird. "Shhh," he said, stroking the bird's head. "Quiet, Cookie. It's all right."

Callie held her bleeding finger out for inspection. "It is not all right. Look at this! I think I might need stitches."

Bo studied his mother's wound. "Awww, Mom, it's hardly a scratch. Cookie wouldn't really bite you. She just thought your finger was part of the graham cracker."

Callie frowned. Her eyes rolled back. "I think . . . I think I might faint." She looked around the room. "Wyatt! I feel faint!"

Before he could respond, Joyce Barrett swung into action. She bustled to Callie's side and looped an arm around her waist. "Come into the office and let me get you some antiseptic and a Band-Aid." She lowered her voice to a near whisper. "We don't want to upset the children or make them afraid of Cookie, do we?"

Callie scowled but reluctantly allowed herself to be led away. "That bird never did like me."

Later, after he'd loaded the children back on their day-camp bus, returned Cookie to her aviary, and settled Bo in the trailer for a late lunch, Wyatt walked into his office to find Callie seated in the chair in front of his desk.

"There you are," Callie said, holding up her bandaged finger. "See what that stupid bird of yours did to me?"

"Sorry," he said with a shrug. "I think maybe she got a little overexcited with all the kids around. She's never bit Bo or me or Dad before. Did you get yourself set up over at your sister's?"

"Sort of. Kendra's out of town, but she called her next-door neighbor to meet me over there with the key, so I dropped off a load of my stuff there before I stopped off here. At least I don't have to deal with her holier-than-thou crap right now."

"What's Luke have to say about you bailing out on him?"

"Don't know," she said. "He's been calling and texting me all day, but I've been ignoring him. To tell you the truth, I really don't care what that piece of garbage has to say."

Wyatt spread his hands out across his desktop. "What is it you want from me, Callie?"

"Who says I want anything? Can't I just drop by to visit with my son?"

"You've had Bo for the first half of the week. He was with you until a few hours ago. So you'll forgive me if I'm a little suspicious about your motives."

Callie gazed around the office. "God, this place is depressing. When was the last time you painted this room? Or had the floors mopped?"

"I don't have a lot of extra time or money for things like paint jobs these days," he said, struggling to remain civil. "What with legal fees, child support, and the three hundred dollars a week I have to pay for divorce camp."

"Three hundred dollars! Are you serious? That's crazy. That's money your family needs."

"Seriously crazy," Wyatt agreed, his face darkening. "But that's what Judge Stackpole mandated. After your lawyer showed him that video of me smashing Luke's car window. Which the two of you deliberately provoked me into doing."

Callie picked up an old plastic Jungle Jerry's snow globe from the corner of his desk and studied it, deliberately averting her eyes from his.

"That was all Luke's doing," she said, her voice low. "I never thought you'd go crazy and break your hand. I never intended things to go as far as they did."

"You filmed me with your cell phone," Wyatt said. "And then you called the cops. It's a little too convenient to blame everything on Luke, don't you think? You're thirty-six, Callie. Don't you think you bear some responsibility for what happened in our marriage?"

"Some of it," she said, shaking the snow globe, watching the glittering synthetic flakes settle over a tiny plastic replica of the Jungle Jerry's neon sign.

She looked up. "What if I told you I wished none of this had ever happened?"

"But it did happen," he reminded her. "You decided you were in love with somebody else and that you wanted to be with him more than you wanted to be married to me. You chose Luke over me. And our family. That's something I can't just forget."

She turned the snow globe over and picked at the yellowing price sticker with her fingernail. "Sixty-nine cents! How old is this thing?"

"It's ancient," he said. "As old as I feel right now."

Callie looked up. "Bo tells me you have a 'friend.' Is it serious?"

"Maybe. She's a nice woman. Look, Callie. I don't feel comfortable discussing her with you. I'm trying very hard to have a normal life now, to see to it that our son feels loved and safe."

"Is this your way of telling me you're moving on? That you're completely over me?"

Wyatt ran his hands over his head. "Over you? No. I'm trying, but I can't say I'm there yet."

She looked up at him through lowered lashes. "I hope you never get over me. I'm not over you. At all."

56

Grace was the first to arrive at Paula's office. She found the therapist sitting at the desk in the reception area, staring down at something on the computer screen and frowning. There were dark circles under her eyes that even a careful application of concealer couldn't hide.

Paula looked up and immediately clicked to close out the screen. "Hi, Grace," she said. "How's your week going?"

"My week sucks," Grace said flatly. "Thanks for asking."

Paula sighed. "Is there something you'd like to discuss with the group? Is this about your divorce?"

"It's about my life, and right now everything in my life has been screwed up by my divorce, so yeah, I think you could safely say that." Grace felt the tote bag slung over her shoulder move ever so slightly. She started to walk into the inner office.

"Grace?"

She turned to face the therapist.

"Things will get better. I know you think they won't. I know it's hard. But you have to trust me. I've been there," Paula said. "The pain, the rage, the bitterness—if you can find a way to let go of all that, a huge weight will be lifted from your soul."

Grace bit her lip. She wanted to confront Paula with everything she knew or thought she knew about her arrangement with Stackpole. But she'd promised Mitzi to stay quiet until they could absolutely prove their suspicions.

"You've been there?" She couldn't resist. "Through a divorce? Where you lost everything?"

"That's right." Paula's eyes met hers. "I moved here to Florida . . . afterwards. I started over with nothing. Well, next to nothing. It hasn't been easy."

The outer door opened, and Camryn and Suzanne came in. Their conversation came to an abrupt end.

"We'll talk later," Paula said.

"Friends?" Paula gestured around the circle. "We've got so much ground to cover before your completion ceremony next week. But first, I'd like to hear about how your life is going—recovery-wise."

She was met with five blank expressions. "Anybody?"

Nothing.

"All right. I suppose we'll just do this the-old fashioned way. I'll call on you, and you'll share. Camryn?"

"Recovery-wise? Dexter's lawyer called my lawyer this week. He wants his mother's dining room table. Claims it has happy family memories, and it's the only piece of furniture he wants."

"Did you give it to him?" Ashleigh asked.

"Umm-humm," Camryn said, looking pleased with herself. "I hope he can find a good furniture refinisher, though."

Paula looked at her over the top of her wire-framed glasses. "Did you damage the table?"

"Not me," Camryn said, feigning innocence. "But the movers I hired, they were sooooo clumsy. They must have just thrown it into their truck, because when Dexter got it, the top was all scratched up and gouged. I guess it looked pretty bad."

"How bad?" Grace couldn't resist.

Camryn held up her iPhone and scrolled through her photo roll and tapped the screen. She held up the phone for the others to see.

"What's that say?" Suzanne asked. "It looks like writing, on the tabletop, but it's kind of dark."

She handed the phone to Wyatt, who looked, squinted, and laughed. "It's writing. Looks like it says... 'Eat shit and die'? Is that right?" He looked to Camryn for confirmation.

"I was shocked," Camryn said, barely able to concern her merriment.

"Never mind," Paula said, annoyed. "You know, Camryn, if you keep regressing, acting out in these childish and vindictive ways, I'm not going to be able to sign off on your successful completion of these sessions. Truly, you're only hurting yourself."

Camryn muttered something under her breath.

"Ashleigh?" Paula turned to the next person.

"Recovery-wise, I am fantastic," Ashleigh said. "Really. Forgive and forget. I even went out to lunch today with one of the girls in Boyce's office, and I never asked one question about Suchita. I've quit driving by her house, too."

Paula frowned. "I'm glad to hear that, but I wasn't aware you were engaging in such unhealthy, obsessive activities. Remember, Ashleigh, the other woman wasn't the problem in your marriage. She was only a symptom."

"Whatever," Ashleigh said. "I am in a very good place right now. An awesome place."

"Happy to hear it," Paula said. "I wish everybody could move in that direction. Suzanne? Are things going better for you?"

"Maybe a little better," Suzanne admitted. "It's still too painful to talk to Eric, but I finally e-mailed him and told him that Darby has been accepted for early admission to Elon."

Paula beamed at her star patient. "Suzanne! That's a real breakthrough." She looked around the circle. "Friends? Let's give Suzanne our approval."

The others clapped politely.

"Darby's his daughter, too," Suzanne said. "I know she's conflicted—she feels loyalty to me, but she misses seeing him."

"Hmm. Maybe Darby would like to attend one of the 'Daughters of Divorce' seminars I'm going to be giving," Paula suggested. "And I've been thinking that might be helpful for your daughter, too, Camryn."

"No offense, Paula, but right now I can't afford to pay for any more of your sessions," Suzanne said. "Maybe I'll get her some books from the library."

Camryn coughed loudly and looked away.

"Grace? When you came in tonight, you seemed very down about things," Paula said. "Anything specific going on?"

"Very specific," Grace said, biting the words out. She recounted the events of the past few days in vivid detail. "Arthur's going to sell the house. And I'm back where I started."

"That's such a shame," Suzanne said. "I've been following your blog. It was such an adorable house. Do you have any idea who would do such a thing?"

"A very good idea. J'Aimee. My former assistant and my ex's new girlfriend," Grace said. "This is totally her handiwork. And, of course, now the house is out of my reach, because I can't afford to buy a house, because, so far, Judge Stackpole's idea of a property settlement is to give Ben the gold mine and me the shaft. Ben is entitled to everything, and I get nothing. Because he hates women."

"Fucker." Camryn said it quite distinctly.

Paula's face turned pink. "I'm sure that's not the case . . ."

"Not the case?" Ashleigh hooted. "Paula, get a grip! Those pills you've been taking have seriously pickled your punkin'."

The therapist's face paled. "That's very unfair."

"But it's true," Ashleigh insisted. "Nobody else wants to speak out, because they're all soooo afraid Stackpole will screw them even worse than he already has. Not me. I don't care what you or Stackpole say or do. Because after Monday, this is all a moot point anyway. I am so out of here."

She hopped out of her chair. "I'll see y'all later. At the Sandbox. Right?"

"Man, Ashleigh, you knocked Paula for a loop tonight," Camryn said later, with something akin to admiration. "After you left, she was back to her old self. Just going through the motions until eight o'clock rolled around. She didn't even have us read from our journals."

Ashleigh dipped a finger in her margarita and licked it. "I'm not going back for any completion ceremony, y'all." She looked around the table. "This has been kind of fun, in a weird way, but it's not an experience I want to repeat. But hey, if any of y'all ever want a little nip or a tuck, give me a call. I'll make sure Boyce gives you our professional discount."

"What about me?" Wyatt asked.

"What? You think men don't have plastic surgery?" Ashleigh chortled. "Eyelid lifts, chin implants, tummy tucks, breast reductions—honey, you'd be amazed how many men walk into our office. Not to mention all the prescriptions for Rogaine we write." She gazed meaningfully at Wyatt's gleaming dome.

He ran his hand over his head, immediately feeling defensive. "I'm not bald.

I've got plenty of hair. I shave my head because I work outdoors all day. It's cooler. And there's less chance of ticks hiding in my hair."

"Ticks. Eeew." Ashleigh shuddered.

At the other end of the table, Grace waited until the others were engaged in a lively conversation about the cause for Paula's demeanor. She leaned over and spoke in a low voice.

"Camryn? Remember the morning you and your cameraman came to my house? The day after I left Ben?"

"How could I forget?" Camryn said. "Best story of the year."

"I've been wondering. How'd you get past the guard gates?" Grace asked. "None of those other news crews were able to get through security. How'd you do it?"

"Mmm. Trade secret," Camryn said, sipping her drink. "Why do you care?"

"Because I want to go back to the house. And get the rest of my things. But Ben got the security guards to deactivate my key card."

"Gotcha," Camryn said. "Let me call my friend in the morning. See if she can help us out."

"We?"

"You're gonna need a wingman, right?"

Wyatt watched Grace, her head bent close to Camryn's, as they whispered and plotted. He felt an irrational stab of jealousy. All night, he'd tried to catch Grace alone, if only for a moment. He needed to reassure himself that what was between them was real and that they had a future together. But there was always somebody around. He took a sip of his beer, then pushed it aside. He yawned widely, hoping the exaggerated movement would catch her eye.

Finally, she glanced his way, smiling ruefully. He got up and made his way toward the men's bathroom. Grace followed, pausing at the door to the ladies' room. She opened the door, and in the next instant, he'd pushed his way inside, slamming the door and locking it in one fluid movement.

"What are you . . ."

He silenced her with a kiss. "This," he said, his voice muffled.

"And this." His hands slid under the back of her sleeveless cotton top, nimbly unsnapping her bra.

"Also this." He worked his knee between her thighs, her skirt riding up and baring her thighs, pinning her up against the sink vanity. Grace's body arched into his, and he lifted her effortlessly atop the vanity. She leaned back and ran her hand over his cheek. He caught her hand in his and kissed it, then yanked her top over her head in one fluid movement.

She laughed uneasily and crossed her arms over her bare chest. "We can't do this! Everybody's out there. My mother is out there. Somebody's going to notice . . ."

"I've been thinking about you all day, and I have wanted to do this all night," he whispered, cupping one of her breasts and kissing it. She let out a soft, low-pitched moan, then grabbed the waistband of his jeans and traced the zipper's path slowly with her thumb until she heard the sharp intake of his breath against her nipple.

"God, Grace," he breathed. She worked the zipper downward, stroking his erection. His hands fumbled with her skirt. "How does this damned thing come off?"

There was a sharp rap at the door. Grace froze.

"It's occupied," she croaked, hopping down from the vanity and hastily pulling on her top.

Wyatt grabbed for her, but she was too fast for him. He chuckled, despite himself, but she frantically shushed him.

Grace flushed the toilet twice, then groaned loudly and followed that with a remarkably authentic sound effect mimicking violent nausea.

"Come on, already," a girl's annoyed voice came. "I'm about to pee my pants."

"Employee bathroom near kitchen door," Grace called. "Sorry." She gagged violently, for good measure.

"Goddamned amateur," came the girl's parting shot.

When she was sure the girl was gone, Grace collapsed against Wyatt in a fit of giggles. "I'm sorry," she said, turning to the mirror to fix her disheveled clothing and hair. "But we've got to get out of here before we get busted."

She turned and gave him an appraising look, tugging at the hem of his shirt. "I had no idea that the scent of hand sanitizer could be such a turn-on." She opened the door and peeked out. "Okay, coast is clear." She shoved him out. "Go on. Go! I'll wait a minute and then come back to the table."

"Later?" Wyatt asked, kissing her neck. "We need to talk." But somehow, later never arrived that night.

57

Dad?" Bo walked into the kitchen, where Wyatt was shaping hamburger patties. Sweetie followed close on the child's heels, sniffing the air expectantly.

"I know it's late and you're hungry, but dinner's almost ready," Wyatt assured, seasoning the burgers with salt and pepper, stopping to toss a bit of meat to the dog.

"I'm okay." Bo plopped down at his place at the kitchen table. "Can I ask you something?"

"Sure thing." Wyatt put the griddle pan on the burner and turned on the heat. "You want cheese or no on your burger?"

"Cheese," Bo said. "The yellow kind, not the white."

"Got it. What did you want to ask me?"

Bo kicked the table leg. "Do you still hate Mom?"

"Hate her?" Wyatt asked cautiously. "I don't hate your mom, Bo. Is that what you think?"

"Sometimes," the boy said. He helped himself to a handful of potato chips from the bowl on the table and tossed one to Sweetie, who caught it midair. "Mom thinks you hate her. She's pretty sad. Because now she's not gonna marry you know who. And Aunt Kendra is a big bee-yotch." He shoved all the chips in his mouth and chewed furiously.

"You probably shouldn't call your aunt that word, pal," Wyatt said. "It's kind of a bad, grown-up word. So . . . you talked to your mom today?"

"Do we have any onion dip?" Bo asked hopefully.

"Sorry, no. But we've got salad. Did your mom call you today?"

"Yeah," Bo said. "She says we're not gonna live with you know who anymore. Do you think we can get our old house back instead? I kind of miss my room there."

Wyatt sighed. "That's complicated, pal. I wish we could get the old house back, but right now we can't. So I guess you're stuck sharing a room with me. Is that so bad? I mean, I don't snore too loud, do I?"

"Not as loud as Granddad," Bo said, giggling. A moment later, he was serious again. "What about Mom? Where's she going to live?"

Wyatt got up and turned the burner on again. He waited until the eye glowed red, then added the hamburger patties to the grill pan.

Obviously, Callie had unburdened herself to their son at some point during the day. What the hell was she thinking, worrying a six-year-old with this stuff? Did she seriously think she could use Bo to guilt-trip him into taking her back?

"For now, your mom's going to stay with Aunt Kendra," Wyatt said finally. "And then she's going to find a new place to live. And you'll have a new room. Okay? Is that cool with you?"

"I guess," Bo said. He kicked the table leg rhythmically. "But it would be cooler if Mom and me could just live with you. Like we did before." He took another handful of potato chips and shoved them into his mouth and chewed furiously.

Shit. Shit. Shit. Wyatt thought. Callie was really pulling out all the stops. He should have seen this coming.

Wyatt heard the meat sizzling on the cast-iron grill pan. Smoke rose from the stove. He jumped up and flipped the burgers, his mind working furiously to find a way to be honest with the child. Finally, he sat down and reached across the table and took his son's hand in his.

"Look at me, Bo," he said calmly. "Mom and I both love you. More than anything. And that will never change. But she and I, we're probably not ever going to live together again. Not because I hate her, but because we don't love each other the way married people should love each other. I'm sad about that, and I know you're sad about it, too. But that's just the way it has to be. Okay?"

"Okay," Bo said. "Can Sweetie have a hamburger, too?"

"Afraid not," Wyatt said. "Now, go wash your hands and tell Granddad dinner is ready."

Their Friday-night routine seldom varied. Nelson took himself off to bed around nine, and then Wyatt and Bo either watched a movie or played video games, until one or both of them fell asleep. Right now, Bo was sprawled on the floor, scraping the last bit of ice cream from the carton as he watched *The Bad News Bears*—the old Walter Matthau version—for maybe the tenth time since the start of summer. Sweetie was curled up on the floor beside him, her snout resting in his lap.

It had started drizzling shortly after dinner. Now the rain fell steadily, beating a noisy tattoo on the trailer's metal roof and siding.

Wyatt had texted Grace earlier in the afternoon, proposing that they meet somewhere, but discarded that idea after realizing how anxious Bo was about his parents' marital status.

After dinner, he'd managed a furtive phone call while Bo and Nelson did the dishes. "Hey," he'd said, his voice low. "I don't think I can get away tonight after all. Bo is having some issues, and I think I'd better stick close to home."

"Everything okay?" Grace asked. "Your dad's not sick again, is he?"

"Nothing like that," Wyatt said. He knew he should tell Grace what was going on with Callie, but something held him back. All he knew was that he was tired of the tug-of-war. Callie was the past. And Grace was his future. He and Bo deserved a happy future, didn't they?

"I'll call you tomorrow," Wyatt promised. He glanced back toward the kitchen to make sure he couldn't be overheard. "I've got some stuff to tell you. Maybe we could have another sunset viewing at that condo?"

Grace laughed throatily. "I think that could probably be arranged."

He must have dozed off sometime between the end of *The Bad News Bears* and the beginning of *Field of Dreams.* Somebody was banging on the trailer's aluminum storm door. Wyatt jumped up, startled by the noise, but Bo, always a heavy sleeper, didn't move. Sweetie, on the other hand, went on instant alert, running toward the door and barking.

"Wyatt? It's me."

He cursed softly. His midnight caller was Callie. "Shush, Sweetie," Wyatt grumbled. He flipped on the porch light and opened the door.

She was barefoot and rain-soaked, dressed in a low-cut tank top and shorts so tight he could clearly see the outline of her panties. She'd been crying again. And this time, she'd brought baggage. Literally. A large wheeled suitcase rested on the porch, and next to it sat a plastic laundry basket heaped with her belongings.

"Can I come in?" She didn't wait for an answer, picking up the basket of clothes and stepping inside, out of the rain. He hesitated, then grabbed the suitcase, too.

"What's all this?" he asked, gesturing at the luggage.

"My stuff. Can you at least get me a towel so I can dry off before you start yelling at me?"

As she walked past him toward the bathroom, Wyatt detected the smell of alcohol and cigarette smoke. She took her time in the bathroom. He heard water running, and then the sound of a hair-dryer. He waited outside the bathroom door, arms folded across his chest, gathering resolve.

Finally, she emerged, her face pink from heat, hair fluffed, dressed only in his worn terrycloth bathrobe. "You don't mind, right?" Callie asked. "Just until my stuff dries out, okay?"

"You can have the bathrobe," he said, keeping his voice low, "but then you have to leave."

"And go where?" she asked, running her fingers through her hair. "My baby sister kicked me out. You believe that? It's midnight and we're in the middle of a monsoon, and she kicks me out. So for tonight, anyway, you're stuck with me. And I hate to ask, but do you have anything to eat? I didn't get dinner."

He took her by the arm and steered her toward the kitchen. "I'll fix you a sandwich. Keep your voice down," he warned. "Bo's asleep on the living room floor. I don't want him waking up and asking why you're here."

She yanked her arm from his grip and followed him into the kitchen. "We're still married, technically. So why shouldn't I be here?" She looked around the room and frowned. "Unless your new girlfriend is having a sleepover?"

Wyatt took a package of lunch meat from the fridge, along with a jar of mustard. He slapped the meat between two slices of bread, which he slathered with the yellow mustard, then slid the sandwich in front of her.

He decided not to allow Callie to bait him. "What are you doing here, Callie? What did you do to make Kendra kick you out?"

"Nothing!" she said, biting into the sandwich. "Kendra's just a bitch, okay? She resents me. Always has. She was always on your side after we split. And she hated Luke, of course."

She'd knotted the bathrobe loosely around her waist, and it gapped widely at the neck, giving him a too-generous view of her cleavage and a provacative expanse of her bare legs.

The truth was beginning to dawn on him. "Luke came over there tonight, didn't he? That's why Kendra kicked you out. Right?"

"I didn't *invite* him," she said indignantly. "He just showed up. He promised to get my car back for me. So I let him in, but then he started with the same old bullshit, and I called him on it. We were not fighting. It was a *discussion*. But all of a sudden, Kendra goes bat-shit crazy and starts threatening to call the cops on both of us."

"The two of you'd been drinking, right? And don't try to deny it, because you smell like a brewery," Wyatt said.

"What are you, my parole officer? Yes, we had a few beers," Callie said. "But I am not drunk. And anyway, what kind of sister throws somebody out in the middle of a tornado? Kendra wouldn't even listen to me. She literally grabbed my suitcase and pitched it out her window. And she lives on the second floor. I was barely able to grab the basket with the rest of my stuff before she locked me out in the rain."

Callie took another bite of her sandwich, and then another, chewing calmly. "God, I'm hungry. I bet I could eat another sandwich." She looked down at Sweetie, who was crouched on the floor, her liquid brown eyes focused on her.

"Is this the girlfriend's dog?" She tore off a bit of bread and tossed it to the little dog, who caught it in midair. "She's kind of cute, isn't she? What's her name?"

"We're not discussing the dog. And I'm not fixing you another sandwich," Wyatt said. "You can't stay here tonight, Callie."

She raised an eyebrow. "You're kicking me out? Where do you expect me to go at this hour? And don't suggest a motel. You might as well know. I'm flat broke."

"Dammit, Callie!" Wyatt whispered hoarsely. "I'm not going to let you manipulate me like this. I just sent your child-support check."

"And Bo needed new sneakers. And he's outgrown all his clothes," Callie said. "What is the big deal? It's just one night, okay? I'll sleep on the sofa. You won't even know I'm here."

"I will know. More importantly, Bo will know. You've already managed to get him freaked out about where he's going to live now that you and Luke are broken up. I don't want him any more confused than he already is."

But it was too late. They heard light footsteps in the hallway, then the sound of the bathroom door being opened, and then a toilet flushing. A moment later, the sleepy-eyed child rounded the hallway into the kitchen.

"Mom?" he said softly.

She held out her arms and the boy dutifully allowed himself to be folded into an embrace. "Hey, Bo-man," Callie said, hugging him tight. "Are you surprised to see me?"

"Yeah. I mean, no," Bo said, yawning widely. "I thought you were at Aunt Kendra's house."

Callie made a face. "Your Aunt Kendra is a big doo-doo head," she said, laughing as though it were all a joke. "So I came over here to see what you and your dad were up to."

"Are you gonna spend the night?" He shot his father a hopeful look. "Please, Dad? Mom can have my bed. I'll sleep on the sofa."

"Absolutely not!" Callie said. "If anybody gets to sleep on the sofa, it's me." She tousled her son's hair and looked defiantly at Wyatt. "Right, Dad?"

Bo's eyes were pleading. "Okay?"

Wyatt knew when he'd been beaten. "Fine," he said brusquely. "Come on, Bo," he said, holding out his hand for his son. "You're going to bed. I'll get your mom a pillow and a blanket. But this is just for tonight. Tomorrow, she's going to find a new place to live." He glared at his wife. "Right, Mom?"

Callie smiled weakly. "Right."

58

Grace pulled alongside Camryn's car in the Publix shopping center Saturday morning. She hopped into Camryn's car, and moments later the two of them were heading west toward Gulf Vista.

"Nice car," Grace said. She wiped her sweaty palms on her jeans and lightly stroked the Jaguar's sleek leather upholstery.

"It was an anniversary gift from Dexter," Camryn said. "The man does love to buy nice things. Of course, mostly it's to show all his friends how much money he makes and what a big man he is."

"Are you sure your friend is okay with doing this?" Grace asked as they approached the Gulf Vista security gate. "She's not worried Ben might find out?"

"Marissa?" Camryn laughed. "She and LaDarion think your ex is a stuck-up prick. I guess Ben sicced the homeowner's association on them because of Peaches's barking."

"Ben hated that dog," Grace said. "It barked a *lot*. Like, if anybody walked by their house. Or if it was home alone. Which it was, a lot. Plus, your friend and her husband did throw some pretty wild parties. Last year they hired MC Hammer to play at their Fourth of July barbecue. Do you know how many times we heard "Can't Touch This?" Over and over and over . . ."

"MC Hammer?" Camryn snickered. "Seriously? I did not even know that dude was still alive. How did he survive the nineties?"

"I don't know, but I can assure you, he did," Grace said.

There were three cars ahead of them at the visitor's gate to the subdivision. Grace's pulse skipped wildly as they pulled beneath the security shack's portico. "Here goes," Camryn said, under her breath. Grace pulled on a pair of oversized sunglasses.

The Jaguar's driver's-side window rolled down, and the uniformed security guard stepped forward. Grace sucked in her breath and looked away. It was Sheldon, the same guard who'd turned her away the last time she'd attempted to breach the gate at Gulf Vista.

"Morning, ma'am," Sheldon said, leaning in to look at the Jaguar's occupants.

"Good morning," Camryn said. "We're guests of Marissa and LaDarion Banks?"

Sheldon scanned a sheet of paper on his clipboard, running his finger down the lines of type.

"Ms. Nobles?" he asked, peering into the car's interior. Grace held her breath.

"That's correct," Camryn said.

The guard handed her a guest pass. "Leave that on your dashboard, if you would please, ma'am," he said, and waved her through.

"Nice digs," Camryn said admiringly, as they rolled slowly past the house on Sand Dollar Lane. "What did this place set you back, a million, million and a half?"

"I'm not sure," Grace admitted. "Ben handled all that. This was one of the model homes. He cut a deal with the developer, and then cut more deals with the contractors who put in the landscaping and the pool and the media room. A lot of the extras, we got at cost, or less, in return for advertising and editorial mention on Gracenotes."

"And you walked away from all that."

"'Ran away' would be a more accurate way to describe my departure," Grace said.

"And now you're living above a bar on Cortez," Camryn said. "Girlfriend, that is a big change, and I'm not just talking about zip codes."

"Want to know something?" Grace gestured out the window, at the velvety green lawns and lush beds of blooming tropical flowers and palm trees, behind which loomed glimpses of red barrel-tile roofs and white stucco homes. "None of this seems real to me. I lived in this neighborhood for two years. I went to parties, gave parties here, but I haven't heard from a single person since the night I put Ben's car in the pool."

"Mm-hmm," Camryn said. "You broke the rules. Acted ugly, made a mess. Got the law involved." She flipped up her own sunglasses, and grinned. "Welcome to the real world, Grace Davenport."

She turned the corner and pulled into the driveway of a house that dwarfed all the other houses in the subdivision. A wrought-iron gate with curlicued flourishes identified the mansion as Villa Marissa. Camryn opened her window, leaned out, and looked up at the small security camera mounted on the stucco gatepost. "Marissa? It's Camryn. Open sesame!"

The gates swung open noiselessly, and they followed the driveway around to the front of the mansion, an enormous, vaguely Tuscan villa, where a petite woman with long jet-black hair and a complexion the shade of caffe latte waited in a gleaming black golf cart.

"Ladies!" Marissa Banks beamed. She was dressed in a sleeveless hot-pink Nike tank top and matching pink golf shorts, along with pink and white golf cleats. She clapped her hands excitedly. "Welcome to my house."

"Marissa, this is my friend Grace, but I think you've probably already met, right?"

Grace reached out and shook the other woman's hand. "Thanks so much for doing this. You're really sure you want to get involved in my drama?"

"Of course," Marissa said. "You can only get your nails and hair done so many times in one week. I'm dying of boredom. This is going to be fun. Like old times, right, Cammie? Remember that time we snuck onto the grounds at Doral so you could try to interview Tiger Woods?"

"And you distracted the security guards with a phony wardrobe malfunction? How could I ever forget that?" Camryn asked, shaking her head at the memory. "Does LeDarion know you've flashed boob to half the men in South Florida, just to get exclusive interviews?"

"How do you think we met in the first place?" Marissa laughed. "Of course, he thinks he's the only one who ever got a sneak peek. And we're gonna keep it that way, right?"

"Just between us girls," Camryn said. She glanced at Grace. "Are you ready?"

Grace let out a long, shaky breath. "As ready as I'm gonna be. I want this over with. Marissa, are you sure the coast is clear? Ben has a standing golf game at the club Saturday mornings, but you just never know . . ."

"I've been watching the place since eight. He left about eight thirty, and his little girlfriend left maybe fifteen minutes after that." Marissa rolled her eyes. "What a skank! You know she sunbathes nude most of the time, right? Every pool guy and maintenance man in the neighborhood has had a look at her goodies."

"Let's do it," Camryn said.

After Marissa dropped them off in the golf cart, promising to return as soon as they texted her, Grace and Camryn walked briskly to the rear of the house, where Grace unlocked the kitchen door.

"Wowsers," Camryn said, eyeing the gleaming expanse of black granite countertops, the stainless steel commercial stove, and the glass-front refrigerator. "This kitchen is immaculate. She's a pretty good housekeeper."

Grace glared.

"For a skank, that is," Camryn added.

"Oh, please. J'Aimee doesn't know how to cook," Grace said. "They probably eat at the club every night—or order out for pizza or Chinese."

She went into the dining room and pulled open the top drawer of the mahogany Empire buffet, pausing to run an appreciative finger over her sterling flatware. "Looks like it's all here," she said, after doing a quick count. Grace trotted out to the laundry room and came back with a king-sized pillowcase, into which she unceremoniously dumped all the silver.

"Let's stack everything by the back door," Camryn said, holding up a heavily decorated silver teapot. "That's what professional burglars do. So they can make a quick getaway."

"We're not burglars," Grace said sharply. She took the teapot from Camryn's hand and set it back on the top of the buffet. "I'm not taking anything that isn't mine. The tea service was Ben's grandmother's. The flatware is mine."

When she'd loaded in all the silver, Camryn placed it in the kitchen, near the door.

Grace walked quickly up the back staircase with Camryn following close behind. "How many bedrooms?" Camryn asked.

"Um, six, but we only had furniture in three of them," Grace said. She breezed down the second floor hallway toward the master wing, while Camryn opened every door they passed to gaze inside.

"Enough with the sightseeing," Grace urged. "I don't want to stick around here any longer than absolutely necessary. Let's just get the rest of my stuff and go, okay?"

She pushed open the door to the master bedroom. The king-sized bed was unmade, and clothes and shoes and towels littered nearly every flat surface.

"Uh-huh." Camryn nodded, taking in the disarray. "Now we see the girl's true colors."

"Ironic," Grace said. "Ben is a total neat nut. He even colorizes his sock drawer."

"You could put my whole downstairs in this bedroom," Camryn said, slowly doing a 360-degree turn to take it all in. She sat on the bed and fingered the rumpled top sheet. "Are these Pratesi?"

"Yup," Grace said. "We did a giveaway with them."

"Think the skank would notice if I borrowed a set of 'em?"

"In here." Grace jerked her head in the direction of her home office. She opened one of the custom cabinets and began loading her photographic equipment into a black duffel bag she'd brought along for that purpose. Her Nikon camera bodies, her lenses—all of it went into the bag. She scanned the bookshelves holding the hundreds of design books she'd lovingly collected and cataloged over the years, pulling out her favorites and adding them to the duffel bag.

She dragged the duffel bag into the bedroom and dumped it before heading into her dressing room, where Camryn stood, looking bug-eyed at the clothing. She held out the sleeve of a gaudy tie-dyed dress. "This doesn't look like your style."

Grace wrinkled her nose. "None of this stuff is mine. It's all hers." She opened one of the drawers in the built-in center cupboard and, with her pinkie, held up a hot-pink scrap of lace. "Totally not mine."

She continued rifling through the clothing in the closet. "Damn! This is all J'Aimee's crap. If she threw my clothes out . . ."

"Hey!" Camryn stood in the doorway. "I think I found your stuff. It's in the room next door."

. . .

Nearly every item of clothing Grace owned had been dumped on the bedroom floor. Dresses and blouses still on hangers, folding clothes, shoes, handbags—all of it tossed in the corner. Grace stood with her hands on her hips, looking around the room, a lump rising in her throat.

"What a pretty room," Camryn said, looking around.

Grace had spent weeks choosing just the right shade of pale seafoam green for the walls of the bedroom. She'd chosen a natural linen fabric for drapes with a narrow turquoise ribbon trim. The dresser was an old one she'd found at an estate sale in Bradenton, a battered oak chest of drawers that she'd painted a soft white, distressed, then waxed. The only other furniture in the room was an antique wicker rocking chair. She'd reupholstered it herself with a turquoise gingham cushion.

"Where's the bed?" Camryn asked.

"Never got around to buying one," Grace said. Her smile was tight. "This was going to be the nursery."

"Oh." Camryn put an arm around Grace's shoulder. "You wanted kids?"

"Yeah. I had started taking fertility meds, but then . . ." She shrugged. "So it's just as well. I see the crap Wyatt is going through with his ex, and, well, a divorce is tough enough for grown-ups without putting a little kid through all that."

Grace picked out a few items of clothing, a couple pair of jeans, her favorite little black dress, and a battered leather bomber jacket she'd owned since high school days. "Let's go," she said, turning toward the door.

"That's all you're taking?" Camryn gestured at the mound of clothes and accessories. "You're just going to leave all this stuff here?" She picked up a hot-pink linen dress. "Girl, this is Tory Burch." She added a black-and-white striped patent leather purse. "And this is Kate Spade. You don't walk away from Kate and Tory."

"Take them if you want," Grace said. She looked around the room, searching for an empty suitcase, but found only a lumpy black plastic trash bag. She dumped the contents of the bag onto the floor.

But this clothing wasn't hers. There was a pair of denim shorts, two sizes smaller than Grace wore, a sleeveless black T-shirt, and a pair of new-looking tennis shoes. Everything in the bag was spattered with paint. Bright orange paint. The same memorable hue that had been splashed across the walls at Mandevilla Manor.

"I knew it," Grace said softly, picking up the T-shirt and holding it out for Camryn to see. "I knew it was her."

She heard footsteps on the stairs and froze. A moment later, Ben walked into the room. "What the hell do you think you're doing?"

The two women stared at him. Ben's face was already tanned, but now it was flushed red with anger.

Camryn looked at her in a state of panic. Grace swallowed hard, and then she recalled her mission, and her motive.

"I came to pick up some of my belongings," she said.

"You're burglarizing my home," Ben said. He held up his cell phone. "Sheldon spotted you when you came through the gate, and he called me to ask if I knew you were in the neighborhood. I've got to remember to tip him better at Christmas this year."

"It's still my home, too," Grace said, glaring at him. "And I'm not taking anything that doesn't belong to me."

He pointed at the duffel bag at her feet. "What's in there?"

"My cameras, some of my design books. Nothing of yours."

"I should call the cops on you," Ben said. He picked up the duffel bag and withdrew her macro lens. "This doesn't belong to you."

She snatched it out of his hands. "My dad gave me this for my birthday the last year he was alive. And I'll be damned if I'll let the two of you have it."

"Take it and get out then," Ben said. He glanced at Camryn. "I know you. Camryn Nobles, News Four You. Does your station manager know you're in the habit of breaking and entering?"

Grace shook the paint-spattered T-shirt at Ben. "Do your blog advertisers know you and the slut are in the habit of breaking and entering and vandalizing private property?"

Ben looked at the T-shirt with disinterest. "What's that supposed to be?"

"Your girlfriend was wearing this the other night when she trashed the house I've been working on over on Mandevilla. And don't even try to deny it. This is the same orange paint she splashed all over the kitchen walls. She read my blog posts on TrueGrace, saw that I had a new project, and decided to ruin it for me."

"Ridiculous," Ben said. But he suddenly looked uncomfortable.

"Were you there, too?" Grace asked, her voice rising. "Did you help her break in? I bet you did."

"You're crazy," Ben said. "J'Aimee doesn't even know where that house is."

"Sure she does. Anybody who reads my blog would know it's on Mandevilla. J'Aimee showed up there just last week. To warn me that if I contacted any more of your advertisers, she'd get even with me. And that's just what she did."

"I'm telling you you're wrong. J'Aimee wouldn't do anything like that," Ben insisted.

Grace shoved the T-shirt in his face. "She did it, Ben! And here's the proof. Orange paint. She got it all over her clothes."

He pushed her hand away.

"You really didn't know what she was up to, Ben, did you? She was hiding this stuff from you."

"Take your crap and get out," Ben said, sounding weary.

They heard a door slam from downstairs, and then footsteps.

"Ben?" J'Aimee's voice was shrill, panicky. "Where are you? Call the police! We've been robbed." She was practically running up the stairs.

"I'm in here," Ben called. "And it's not burglars. It's Grace."

59

What's she doing here?" J'Aimee looked from Ben to Grace, eyes narrowed with suspicion.

"Picking up some of my belongings," Grace said. She held up the black T-shirt. "But I think you mixed up some of your stuff with mine."

J'Aimee pushed a strand of black hair behind one ear. She was dressed in chic lime-green cropped Lululemon yoga pants and a midriff-baring sports bra, and she was barefoot. She flicked the fabric of the T-shirt. "That's not mine." She gestured around the room. "All this crap is yours. You might as well take the rest of it when you go, because I'm getting ready to redecorate in here."

A shadow passed briefly over Grace's face. J'Aimee knew she'd been planning on using this room as a nursery. She'd even volunteered to help paint it, not even six months ago, shortly after she'd become Grace's assistant.

She swallowed her grief over what might have been and channeled it into anger over what had actually occurred.

"These clothes are yours and you know it," Grace said. She dropped the T-shirt and picked up the paint-spotted sneakers. "These shoes are a size six. And I wear an eight. Notice the paint? It's the exact same color as the orange you tossed all over the house on Mandevilla."

"I don't know what you're talking about," J'Aimee said, turning to leave.

"Ben? I'm gonna hit the shower. Could you make sure she doesn't take anything of mine?"

Grace reached out and snagged the stretchy shoulder strap of J'Aimee's top. The younger woman tried to tug loose of Grace's grip, but she held tight.

"Oh, don't go just yet, J'Aimee. Don't you want to tell Ben about the rest of the sweet stunts you pulled at that house? I mean, besides the paint? Don't you want to brag about how you actually pooped in the bathtub, and then wrote obscenities on the wall with your own excrement?"

"Classy," Camryn muttered.

Ben's face registered revulsion. "Come on, Grace."

"I'm betting you didn't share that happy little story," Grace said. "Fortunately, I've got pictures to prove it," She reached for her cell phone. She didn't, actually, but she knew Ben wouldn't look at them, even if she did have pictures.

"Gross," J'Aimee said, trying to inch away. But Grace pulled her back, keeping a firm hold on J'Aimee's top.

"You should know," Grace retorted. "How about the fire? Did you tell Ben you also set a fire in the living room? If it hadn't been for the neighbor, who saw the flames shortly after you tried to torch the place, it probably would have burned to the ground."

"I didn't!" J'Aimee said stubbornly. She grabbed Grace's hands and wrenched herself loose.

Camryn had been standing quietly on the sidelines, but now she stepped forward. She took one of the sneakers and sniffed it delicately.

"Yup," she said succinctly. "Lighter fluid." She carefully placed both shoes in her oversized pocketbook. "The fire marshall is going to want to take a look at these." She glanced over at Grace. "Let's take the shirt and pants, too. I'll bet they've got traces of lighter fluid, too. It doesn't even take a crime lab."

"Who the hell are you?" J'Aimee demanded.

"Just a friend," Camryn said lightly. "Who happens to be an investigative reporter."

"She's from channel four," Ben said, sounding uneasy. "The same reporter who snuck in after Grace left."

"How did they get in here today?" J'Aimee demanded. "I thought you left instructions at the gate."

Camryn struck a pose and held up the sneaker like an imaginary microphone, saying sotto voce, "News Four You has learned that a local lifestyles blogger, J'Aimee . . ."

She turned to Grace. "What's her last name?"

"Scoggins," Grace said.

"Lifestyle blogger J'Aimee Scoggins is under investigation for breaking and entering, destruction of private property, and arson after she allegedly broke into a residence on Anna Maria Island being redecorated by rival blogger Grace Davenport. Davenport, thirty-four . . ."

"I'm actually thirty-eight," Grace corrected.

"Davenport, thirty-eight, is the estranged wife of local businessman Ben Stanton. Sources tell me that J'Aimee Scoggins and Stanton are romantically involved," Camryn said.

"Very funny," Ben said. He pointed toward the door. "Now, leave. Or I will call the cops."

Grace gathered up the rest of the paint-spattered clothing and slid it into the plastic sack, which she gripped tightly.

"You still haven't asked her if she did it," she said. "But maybe you already know the answer."

Ben turned suddenly and stared at J'Aimee. "Tell me you didn't do any of this. Please."

J'Aimee took a step backward. "She's bluffing. She can't prove those clothes are mine. She probably put them here herself."

"J'Aimee?" Ben's deep voice was chilly. "Yes or no?"

"Yes! Okay?" J'Aimee said defiantly. "It was just a little joke. God! You people need to lighten up. I didn't mean to break the glass. I was opening the window, which was unlocked, and it just cracked. You can't break into a place that isn't even really locked up."

"What about the paint?" Ben asked.

"Big deal. A little orange paint. The place is a dump. Anyway, she had it coming, writing to my advertisers, telling them I was stealing from her . . . We lost our Kohler ads because of her."

Ben swore softly, under his breath. "And what she said? About the bathroom? Dear God, tell me you didn't actually . . ."

"It was just a joke!" J'Aimee exclaimed. "Okay, maybe it did get a little out of hand. I took a bunch of empty beer cans over there, to make it look like it was kids, and I had a couple of wine coolers of my own, so maybe that wasn't really a cool thing to do." She glanced at Grace. "I'm sorry, okay? Is that what you want to hear?"

"No," Grace snapped. "Sorry doesn't cut it anymore. You could have burned that house to the ground. It belongs to a sweet old man who was getting ready to rent it to me. But after you vandalized the place, he just wants to sell it and be done with it. You and I both know you weren't joking around when you went over there the other night. You wanted to send me a message. Well, you did that, all right. I got the message loud and clear."

Ben was shaking his head. "I can't believe you pulled a stupid stunt like this. Arson! Really? They put people in jail for that, J'Aimee."

"I'm sorry! I told you I was sorry," J'Aimee said, her voice pleading. "Ben . . ."

"Go take your shower," Ben said wearily. "I can't deal with you right now."

J'Aimee turned and slunk out of the room. A moment later, they heard the bedroom door slam.

Camryn edged toward the door, too. "I'll just, uh, be waiting outside. Whenever you're ready."

Ben watched her go. He sighed loudly. "Look, Grace, you have to believe me. I did not put J'Aimee up to this. I would never . . . I mean, we've had our differences." He swallowed and looked away. "The stuff with Gracenotes, that's business. It's not personal."

"It's very personal to me," Grace said. "You and J'Aimee have done your best to put me out of business. You say it wasn't your idea to have her vandalize that house, but you and I both know J'Aimee's never had an original idea in her life. She took her cues from you. Maybe you didn't light that fire, but you sure as hell showed her where the matches were."

He rubbed his jaw. "You're not serious about going to the police with this, are you? J'Aimee's just a kid. Yeah, she did it to get back at you. Because you intimidate her. No matter what, in a weird way, you're still her idol. You heard her. As far as she knew, this was just a prank that got out of hand."

"I'm her idol? That's a laugh."

"It's true," Ben insisted. "She reads every word you write, goes back over your old posts, trying to copy your style. I keep trying to tell her, she's got her own style, which she should develop, but for some reason she's fixated on you, on being bigger, better than you. I guess maybe I should have seen the potential for what happened, should have reined her in before it came to this."

"Ya think?" Grace shot back.

"I'm asking you, please. Don't make a federal case out of this. I'll have a serious talk with J'Aimee. And I'll do whatever it takes to make it right. I'll pay for all the damages, reimburse you for your lost time. I'll fix it. I promise."

"You'll fix it," Grace said, laughing bitterly. "There's that expression of yours again. You just love the idea of covering things up, of pretending they never happened, don't you, Ben?"

"I'm a pragmatist. A businessman," he said calmly. "So, do we have a deal?"

She crossed her arms and gave him a long, hard look. "It's not up to me. It's Arthur's house. I'll tell him about your offer."

"And you'll suggest we settle this without the police getting involved?" he persisted.

Grace saw an opening, and she went for it. "I'll suggest he accept your offer. On one condition."

Ben rolled his eyes. "Here it comes. The blackmail."

"You can call it whatever you like," Grace said. "Here's the deal. You tell your lawyer that you want to settle things fairly with me. I'm not looking to gouge you, Ben. But it's totally unfair that I should have to walk away from this marriage with not a dime to my name. We built a business together, and by rights half of the proceeds from it should be mine. That's what I want. No more, no less."

"And if I don't give you what you want?"

Grace held the garbage bag aloft. "There's always this. And remember, Camryn was standing right here when J'Aimee confessed. I wouldn't put it past her to have recorded the whole thing. You know how sneaky these journalism types are."

60

By the time Grace emerged from the house, Marissa and Camryn were waiting for her in the golf cart. Camryn held the pillowcase with the wedding silver in her lap. Grace placed the duffel bag with her books and camera equipment on the floor of the backseat and climbed onto the seat, tightly clutching the black garbage bag.

"Let's go," Grace said, glancing back toward the house, half expecting J'Aimee to follow in hot pursuit.

Marissa steered the cart down the driveway and around the corner toward her own house.

Camryn turned around in her seat, one eyebrow raised in question. "So?"

"Mission accomplished," Grace said. "I got what I came for. And more." Marissa turned around, too, and the three women high-fived each other.

"I'm afraid I blew it, though," Marissa said apologetically. "I just went in the house for a minute. They must have slipped right past me. But I hear you got the goods on that little bitch."

"We'll see," Grace said. "The big thing is, we managed to rattle Ben. He's really worried I might go to the cops."

"How worried?" Camryn asked.

"Worried enough that he agreed to talk financial settlement."

"That's great," Camryn said. "You must have done some major cage rattling after I hightailed it out of there."

"I might have mentioned that you were probably secretly taping J'Aimee's confession," Grace admitted.

Camryn smirked, then pulled her iPhone from her pocket, held it up, and tapped an icon. J'Aimee's high-pitched voice floated in the air. "It was a joke," she screeched. Camryn tapped the button and the phone went silent.

"Never underestimate a woman," she advised. "Especially one who's been jerked around the way you and I have."

The two high-fived each other one more time.

"Where's my father?"

Wyatt stood staring down at Callie, still half asleep on the sofa.

She stretched and yawned. "What?"

"Dad. He's not here. Where'd he go?"

Callie sat up slowly. "How should I know?"

"Did he see you here this morning?" Wyatt demanded. "Come on, Callie. This is important. Did he say anything?"

"No. Well, yeah. I mean, he came out of his room, and I heard him banging pots and pans around in the kitchen, making coffee. I went out and asked him if I could have a cup, and he just stared at me. He put the coffeepot down and walked out the door. God! I'm telling you, there is something wrong with that old man. And I'm not talking about diabetes, Wyatt. He's seriously senile."

"Shit," Wyatt said softly. "He's not senile! He can't stand the sight of you, if you want to know the truth. He probably saw you here, dressed in my robe, and got the wrong idea. Which way did he go, did you see?"

"You know how I am before I get my coffee in the morning. He left. That's all I know."

"Hey, Mom."

Callie and Wyatt turned to see their young son, standing in the doorway to the living room, dressed in his Lightning McQueen pajama bottoms.

"Good morning, Bo-Bo," Callie said, her pout turning instantly to a sunny smile. "Come give your mama some sugar."

Bo allowed himself to be cuddled, but only for a moment. Pulling away, he looked at his father's troubled countenance.

"Is Granddad missing again?"

"Not really missing," Wyatt said hastily. "He went out for a walk early this morning, and I'm a little worried, because I don't know whether he remembered to eat some breakfast or take his medicine. I'm going to hop on the cart and take a spin around the park to pick him up. You want to help me track him?"

"Sure!" Bo looked hesitantly at his mother. "I'll be right back, Mom, okay?"

"Take all the time you need," Callie said, yawning again. "I'll be around when you get back."

Grace tried calling Wyatt from the Publix parking lot, but her call went directly to voice mail. It was just as well, she thought, because she really wanted to tell him firsthand how her visit to Gulf Vista played out.

She drove around to the back entrance to Jungle Jerry's and found the nearly hidden driveway that led to Wyatt's trailer. His truck was parked under the carport, in front of a vehicle she'd never seen before, a battered and rust-spotted Jeep.

She tapped lightly at the aluminum storm door. "Wyatt?" she called, and was rewarded with the sound of Sweetie's answering bark, followed by a frantic scratching at the door. She waited another minute. Maybe he was in the shower? Or out in the park, on the golf cart? Grace tapped again, and Sweetie gave another answering bark.

She tried the door. It was unlocked. She pushed the door open and stepped inside. Sweetie threw herself joyously at Grace's ankle, yipping excitedly.

"Hi, little girl," Grace said, scooping the dog up into her arms. "Where are the guys? Huh? Are you the only one home?"

"Not quite."

Grace looked up, startled.

Callie Keeler stood in the doorway from the kitchen, eating from an oversized bowl of cereal. She was barefoot, dressed only in a short, faded bathrobe, loosely belted around her waist.

"If you're looking for my husband, you just missed him," Callie said. "He and Bo are out in the park, looking for Nelson."

"Oh."

Grace's chest constricted. She hugged Sweetie close and blinked. She felt her face growing hot.

Callie laughed at her obvious discomfort and took another bite of cereal. A bit of milk trickled down her chin, and she dabbed at it with her sleeve, revealing, in the process, that she was naked under the robe.

"Awkward moment, huh? I'm guessing you must be the girlfriend Bo's been telling me about. It's Grace, right?"

"Yes," Grace managed to say.

Callie held out the bowl. "You want some cereal? It's Cocoa Puffs. I swear, you're never too old for Cocoa Puffs."

"No thanks," Grace said. She turned and left.

"Don't go on my account," Callie called, chuckling to herself. "I'll tell Wyatt you dropped by."

"Dumb, dumb, dumb." Grace banged her head on the steering wheel with each exclamation. Sweetie whined and crawled onto her lap, licking her chin as a consolation prize.

She started the car and headed down the sandy driveway toward the street. She blinked back tears as she navigated through the thick foliage that lined both sides of the narrow one-way drive.

It was after ten o'clock in the morning, and there stood Callie Keeler, dressed only in Wyatt's robe, calmly eating cereal. Obviously, she'd spent the night there. "You just missed my husband," she'd said. Not "ex-husband," not "Wyatt," but "husband," letting Grace know she'd reclaimed him.

"You can have him," Grace muttered.

No wonder he'd begged off seeing her last night. He'd had a much better offer from his wayward wife. And why should that come as a surprise? Wyatt had made it clear right from the start that his first commitment was to his son's happiness. And like any six-year-old, Bo wanted his parents back together.

How could she have believed he wanted to start a new life with her? How could she let herself get sucked into a relationship on the rebound? Double rebound, if you wanted to be technical, since both she and Wyatt were coming out of ruined marriages. And with a guy she'd met in a divorce-recovery group!

"Stupid, stupid, stupid," she chanted, slapping the dashboard for emphasis.

Sweetie looked up at her with huge, uncomprehending brown eyes.

"Never trust a man, Sweetie," Grace told the dog. "They all lie. Every damn one of them is a liar."

Her cell phone rang. She grabbed it and looked at the caller ID. It was Wyatt.

"This is the liar calling right now," Grace told Sweetie. "Can you believe it?"

She tossed the phone onto the seat, and the little dog sniffed it. The phone rang again. She knew without looking it would be him. And he'd probably keep calling. Why postpone the inevitable? She snatched up the phone and tapped the CONNECT button.

"What?"

"Grace, I just got back to the trailer. Callie told me you came by."

"How nice of her." Grace sneered. "She's a great hostess, Wyatt. She even offered me some of her Cocoa Puffs. I'm sure you two will be very happy. Again."

"Look, it's not like you think," Wyatt said. "I don't care what she told you; we are not back together. We are not getting back together."

"So, last night—was that just a one-night stand? And you think that doesn't count?"

"She slept on the sofa! She broke up with Luke last week, and she called me, hoping I'd let her stay here, but I told her there was no way. So she went to her sister's house, but Luke showed up over there, and they were drinking, so Kendra kicked her out in the middle of the night. You know what it was like last night—it was raining. And then Bo woke up and saw her, so what was I gonna do, kick her out into the rain, with my son standing there, begging me to let her stay?"

"Let me ask you a question," Grace said, her voice oddly cold. "You say this all started last week? Did it ever occur to you to mention to me that your wife was trying to move back in with you? Especially after you told me you couldn't see me last night, because of Bo?"

"That was a mistake on my part, and I know that now," he said, his words tumbling together. "But I didn't tell you because I knew you'd get the wrong idea," Wyatt said. "Which you did. I never had any intention of taking Callie back. It's over between us. And I've told her that. Repeatedly."

"And yet there she was this morning, all cozied up at your place. Was that your robe she was wearing? Or has she already started to unpack?"

"Dammit, Grace," Wyatt said hoarsely. "She slept on the sofa. And she's gone now. I told her she can't come back. And if you don't believe me, you can ask Dad. That's where I was when you came by, out looking for him. He saw

Callie asleep on the sofa this morning, and he was so pissed, he just took off, because he can't stand to be under the same roof with her. Or ask Bo. He's in the other room, sulking, because he didn't want his mother to go. But she has. Okay? It is over between Callie and me."

Grace bit her lip. She pulled out of the driveway and into traffic. "You just think it's over," she told him. "But she's not going to let you go, and Bo's not going to let her go. I can't do this, Wyatt. I can't hang around, wondering what will happen with Callie's next crisis. You need to figure all this stuff out by yourself. You're not ready for a new relationship. Not with me, anyway."

"Grace?" His voice was pleading. "I care about you Grace. Don't hang up, please. Just meet me someplace, okay, and let's talk about this. What about Gus's? That doughnut place? Can you just at least talk to me face-to-face?"

"I don't think so," she said sadly. "Not even for doughnuts."

61

Grace unlocked the door to Mitzi's condo and gently set Sweetie down on the floor. She sank down onto the white sofa and stared out the sliding glass doors at the jade-green surf below. The giddy euphoria she'd experienced earlier in the day, after finally forcing Ben to agree to a financial settlement, was forgotten. Now she felt the gray mist of depression settling over her, like a suffocating woolen blanket.

The bright, buttery-hued sunlight pouring into the apartment was a cruel intrusion. She covered her eyes with one of the colorful throw pillows she'd bought only days earlier and flounced facedown on the sofa.

She heard the muffled sound of her cell phone ringing and ignored it. She let two more calls go directly to voice mail. Time passed. Grace was vaguely aware of the warmth of Sweetie, who'd curled up on the sofa alongside her. She heard the waves rolling ashore outside, and the distant sound of seagulls, and the occasional slamming of a car door.

But the sound of a key turning in the condo's door jolted her back to consciousness. She rolled over and saw the front door swing open, but she did not bother to sit up.

"There you are," Mitzi Stillwell exclaimed. "I've been looking all over town for you. Why didn't you answer my calls? Or your mother's?"

"I just . . . didn't want to deal with anything," Grace said dully. "Why? What's going on?"

Mitzi walked over and sat on the edge of the club chair. "What's wrong with you? Are you sick?"

"I'm okay," Grace said. "Relatively speaking."

Her lawyer gave her an appraising look. "You had a fight with Wyatt, didn't you?"

"It's over," Grace said.

Mitzi groaned. "Oh no. Don't tell me. He's gone back to his wife?"

"Not yet, but he probably will," Grace said. "She broke up with her boyfriend, and she spent the night at his place last night. Which he didn't feel the need to tell me. So it's only a matter of time."

"Did he tell you he wants her back?"

"No," Grace admitted. "He says she slept on the sofa, and the only reason he let her stay was because it was raining so hard last night, and Bo begged him to. He swears they're through, but I don't believe it."

Mitzi patted her arm. "I'm sorry, Grace. I see this all the time in my line of work. Couples go through the worst kind of traumas, file for divorce, then, at some point, they begin to think maybe they ought to give it another try. You especially see it in families with young children."

"No kid wants to see his parents split up," Grace said, thinking about her own reaction to Rochelle's recent disturbing revelation about her marriage to Grace's father.

Mitzi sighed. "Well, that's not exactly true. There are kids who've seen too much—too much violence, hostility, aggression in their parents' marriage. Those kids crave normality; they crave peace. And the smart ones know that's only possible if a toxic marriage does break up."

"I'm just thankful Ben and I didn't have kids," Grace said.

"Speaking of Ben," Mitzi said, raising an eyebrow. "Dickie Murphree called me out of the blue a little while ago, to say they're ready to talk settlement."

"Good," Grace said.

"Good? That's all you can say? Come on, Grace, snap out of it! This is huge. For months now, they've totally stonewalled us. And now, suddenly, they finally want to settle. Any idea what caused this new development?"

"I went over to the house this morning, to get some of my things. And in the process, I found pretty solid proof that J'Aimee really did vandalize Mandevilla Manor."

"How the hell did you get past security?" Mitzi asked. "Please don't tell me you burglarized the place."

"Camryn—my friend from divorce-recovery group? She's friends with the woman who lives directly behind our house, Marissa. She's married to LaDarion Banks, the baseball player. Marissa called the gate and told them she was expecting Camryn as her guest. And I didn't have to break into the house. I still have my key. Easy-peasy."

"And at some point during your unauthorized visit, Ben just agreed to a fair and equitable settlement with you?"

"Ben doesn't want J'Aimee charged with the vandalism—and arson—at Mandevilla Manor. I told him I'd let Arthur know what I'd discovered but that I'd suggest Arthur allow Ben to pay for all the damages and make restitution, without getting the cops involved. Naturally, Ben was grateful," Grace said.

"Naturally," Mitzi said wryly. "I've got news on another front, too. I had a long chat yesterday with Carlton Towne concerning the experience of his client, Harriett, with Judge Stackpole."

"And?" Grace was determined not to get her hopes built up. She'd had enough of an emotional roller-coaster ride for one day. For one year, even.

"Carlton is very old-school. He's been practicing law in this county for more than forty years, and he doesn't like to rock the boat."

"So, that's that," Grace said. "It was worth a try, though."

"Would you stop being so negative! Carlton may be adverse to rocking the boat, but on the other hand, he is also a stickler on the matter of rules and ethics. And he was enraged when I told him how Stackpole has been ordering divorcing parties into therapy—and then steering those same parties to a woman with whom he's romantically involved. He agrees with me that we should file a formal complaint with the JQC."

"Remind me what the JQC actually is?" Grace said.

"Judicial Qualifications Committee. It's the state agency that governs and disciplines judges," Mitzi said. "So that's our next step. First, we document every single instance we know of where Stackpole made attending therapy mandatory for divorcing parties. Then, we assemble an exhaustingly thorough and compelling complaint and take it to the JQC. And if all goes well, they take Stackpole to the woodshed. Metaphorically speaking."

Grace scratched Sweetie's ears absentmindedly. "And you really think this JQC will believe us? And they'll do what?"

"They can do anything from a reprimand to a fine to a suspension from office to removing him from office," Mitzi said. "He could also be 'involuntarily retired due to illness,' although I doubt it would come to that."

"And what do you need from me?" Grace asked.

"We need Paula Talbott-Sinclair on our side. We need her to tell the JQC about her involvement with Judge Stackpole."

"Is that all?" Grace shook her head. "Mitzi, how am I supposed to make that happen? What makes you think I can get Paula to turn on her sugar daddy?"

Mitzi gave her an appraising look. "You're a woman of many talents, Grace, not the least of which is charm. So you do your thing, and I'll do mine. Deal?"

Grace stared out the window for a while. "I'll give it a shot," she said finally.

"Good," Mitzi said briskly. She reached out and patted Sweetie's head. "What'll you do about the dog? I mean, will you still split custody with Wyatt at night?"

"Gaaaawd," Grace said, flopping backward onto the sofa again. "I hadn't even thought about that. I won't take her back to Wyatt's. And I can't take her to my mom's place."

"Well," Mitzi said, looking around the condo. "I guess it wouldn't hurt if the two of you stayed here for a couple weeks. It's really coming along, Grace. I love the bright colors, and the lamps and things. I never would have thought of doing any of this."

"I couldn't just squat here," Grace said uneasily. "It wouldn't be right."

"Why not? You've still got more work to do here, and I'm too busy to use it for the next month or so anyway. The complex is pet-friendly." Mitzi picked up her oversized pocketbook and went to the door.

"I think you should stay," she said, her hand on the doorknob. "You've been through a rough patch. Spend some time here alone, you and Sweetie. If all goes well, Ben will cough up an equitable settlement; we'll get Stackpole out of our hair, if not off the bench; and then you can figure out the next chapter in the Grace Davenport story."

Grace gave her lawyer a rueful smile. "Next chapter? Right now, I can't even figure out the next five minutes."

62

Grace lolled on the sofa, flipping through channels with the remote control. She paused when she got to *The Real Housewives of Atlanta*. Rochelle watched the show religiously, but Grace had never really seen it. But tonight, she thought, as she dipped a plastic fork into the paper carton of take-out kung pao chicken, and only tonight, she would watch trashy TV reruns and wallow in self-pity.

Her cell phone rang. She picked it up and looked at the caller ID. It was Camryn.

"Where are you and what are you doing?" Camryn demanded.

"I'm at a client's condo, watching *The Real Housewives of Atlanta*," she said warily. "Can I ask you a question? Who are these women? Why do they have their own television show?"

"Girlfriend, I do not have the time to explain RHOA to you. Anyway, you need to turn on channel eight. Now. Because, honey, this is priceless."

Sweetie was sitting directly on top of the remote control. Grace gently slid it out from under the dog's butt and pointed the remote at Mitzi's forty-eight-inch flat screen. She was rewarded by fuzzy footage of what looked like two well-dressed women who appeared to be pelting each other with . . . dinner rolls? They were both screeching at the top of their lungs.

"A food fight? On the ten o'clock news? This is why you called?" Grace asked.

"Keep watching," Camryn said, chuckling. "It gets better."

A man's deep voice cut through the shrill din. "Eileen! What the hell?"

"Did you get that?" Camryn asked. "Recognize that voice?"

Grace leaned forward and stared intently at the television, but the camera kept jerking back and forth between the two women. The older of the two, a brunette, lunged toward the other, clawing at her face. Now, a man was tugging at her arm, vainly attempting to fend her off. His back was to the camera, but, once, Grace glimpsed a vaguely familiar profile.

The younger woman, a strikingly attractive African-American woman with short, platinum-blond hair was batting away the other woman's blows. "Get her off of me," she hollered. "Cedric, do something."

Cedric?

"It can't be," Grace whispered, dropping onto the floor, crawling closer to the television until her face was only inches from the screen. The man glanced over his shoulder at the camera, then flung his hand across his face. "Are you filming this? Stop that! Get that thing away from me." He whirled around, and for a moment, just a moment, Grace saw the angry countenance of the Honorable Cedric N. Stackpole Jr.

"Hey, man," another male voice protested. "You can't do that." And then the camera jerked violently, and the footage ended.

"Oh. My. God." Grace was clutching her hand to her chest. "Did I really just see what I think I saw?"

"In living color," Camryn said. "Merry Christmas to us."

"What? I mean, how . . ." Grace sputtered. "What exactly did I just watch?"

"That, Gracie dear, was footage taken last night at a restaurant in Sarasota by an alert diner, who just happened to be talking to a friend on his cell phone, when Eileen Stackpole walked into the restaurant and caught her husband having a tête-à-tête with a pretty young thing."

"I think I've seen her before," Grace said. "The PYT, I mean."

"Mm-hmm," Camryn said. "We have all seen that girl. She's a twenty-three-year-old bailiff assigned to Stackpole's courtroom. Her name is Monique Massey. And I guarantee you the two of them were not discussing tort reform in a cozy little booth in a pricey French bistro at ten o'clock last night."

Grace could hardly take it all in. "How did this end up on the news? What's it all mean?"

"It got on the news because Stackpole flipped his shit when he realized the other diner was filming the whole thing. He knocked the cell phone out of the guy's hand and took a swing at him. One of the waiters pulled the judge off the guy, but, in the meantime, the cell-phone guy's dinner companion called the cops."

"Tell me they arrested Stackpole," Grace begged.

"No such luck," Camryn said. "Stackpole paid his bill and hustled lil Monique outta there before the po-po arrived. And Eileen took a powder, too. The restaurant manager smoothed things over by offering everybody in the place a free drink and dessert. By the time the cops arrived, all was calm. But at some point, the waiter pulled the cell-phone guy aside and whispered to him the identity of his assailant. Apparently, Stackpole is a regular there—and a lousy tipper. Now the cell-phone guy says he's going to sue Stackpole for assault and battery."

"How do you happen to know so much about all this?" Grace asked. "And why isn't this story on *your* station?"

Camryn sighed heavily. "The cell-phone guy e-mailed the footage to me first. But because of my, er, prior history with Stackpole, my news director doesn't want anything to do with the story. I begged and pleaded and threatened, but he won't budge. So I might have tipped off a friend at our rival station. Anonymously, of course. At least the story is out there, and it's hugely embarrassing to Stackpole. So for once, I don't even mind being scooped."

"What else do you know?" Grace asked. "Did Mrs. Stackpole just happen to bump into the judge and this bailiff, or did she know they'd been seeing each other? And what happens now? Will she divorce him? And what about the guy with the camera?"

Before Camryn could answer her barrage of questions, Grace's phone beeped to alert her that she had another incoming call. "Sorry," Grace said. "I better take this. It's my lawyer."

"I'm thinking this calls for a celebration," Camryn said hastily. "Tomorrow night, eight, at the Sandbox. I'll call everybody else. You're in, right?"

"Absolutely," Grace said.

. . .

"Did you just see the news on channel eight?" Mitzi asked gleefully.

"Camryn, one of the girls in my divorce group, called to tell me about it," Grace said. "I could just watch it over and over; it's so delicious."

"You totally can. It was on at six o'clock, too. They've already posted the footage on the station's Web site," Mitzi told her. "I've watched it four times, and it gets better with every viewing."

"Better for us," Grace said. "But how would you like to be Eileen Stackpole? Can you imagine the humiliation?"

"I can't imagine marrying the man in the first place. Yeechhh. What a worm! Of course, there's got to be a lot more to the story than what they put on the air tonight," Mitzi speculated. "And the rumors are already flying all over town. Right before I called you, I heard from one of the other lawyers who's tried divorces before Stackpole. She heard Eileen Stackpole didn't just stumble into that restaurant last night. She'd supposedly hired a private investigator. He's the one who let her know Stackpole was playing footsie with his bailiff."

"A twenty-three-year-old!" Grace exclaimed. "And I definitely remember her being in the courtroom that first time we went before Stackpole. Remember, she shushed us?"

"So that's where I've seen her," Mitzi said. She laughed. "Oh, my. Cedric has been a very naughty boy, hasn't he?"

"But is all of this anything that would get him in trouble with your JQC?" Grace asked. "I mean, is being a slimeball enough to get you kicked off the bench?"

"Good question," Mitzi said. "Having your wife attack your girlfriend in a very public place might not be grounds for discipline by the JQC. Although the fact that he's involved with an employee of the court seems unethical. But I wonder how it would sit with Paula? I wonder if she knows Stackpole has *another* other woman—besides her?"

"I guess I'll have to ask her how she feels about it," Grace said, wincing.

"You do that. And let me know what you find out," Mitzi said.

63

Grace arrived at Paula Sinclair-Talbott's office at eight o'clock on that already-steamy Monday morning, determined that she would be Paula's first client of the day.

She watched idly as the strip shopping center slowly came to life. At nine, a woman wearing a brilliant orange silk sari unlocked the doors at the Diaper Depot. At 9:30 two middle-aged Hispanic women arrived together at the door to the hearing-aid center.

Twice, her phone rang. Both times it was Wyatt. The second time, she was tempted to answer, just to hear his voice, hear him tell her he missed her and wanted her back. She had to grip the steering wheel with both hands to keep from picking up. This was for the best, she told herself.

Finally, at ten 'til ten, she watched as the VW bug zipped into a parking space three cars away. Paula Talbott-Sinclair walked briskly to her office door, unlocked it, and disappeared inside.

Paula was standing in the reception area, staring down at the computer terminal, when Grace walked inside.

"Grace?" Paula looked up and frowned. Her blond curls were mussed and there were dark circles under her unmade-up eyes. She wore a faded, shapeless black jersey dress that hung limply on her slender frame and cheap red rubber flip-flops. There were no tinkly earrings or ankle bracelets this morning. It didn't look like she'd had a fun weekend.

That makes two of us, Grace thought.

"This is a surprise," Paula said. "Is there something urgent you need to discuss?"

Grace cleared her throat. "Uh, yes, actually, there is something kind of important I'd like to talk to you about. That's okay, right? I mean, in the beginning, you told us we could call you about anything."

"Well . . . I suppose I have time," Paula said, hesitantly. "My first group doesn't start until ten thirty. Come on inside."

Grace followed the therapist into the inner office. The heat was stifling. She watched while Paula switched on the lights and then a small window-air-conditioning unit. "Sit down," Paula said, grabbing one of the folding chairs from the semicircle and dragging it over to a position in front of her desk.

"I'm going to make some tea," Paula said. "Would you like a cup?"

What she'd like, Grace thought nervously, was a Xanax, or at least a stiff cocktail. "No thanks," she said politely.

Paula drifted around the room, putting a kettle on a hot plate, rearranging the circle of chairs, and then, finally, when the tea kettle whistled, pouring the water into a lumpy pottery mug.

"Now," she said, settling into the chair behind her desk. "What's happening in your world today, Grace?"

"Um." Grace fidgeted with the strap of her purse. She'd rehearsed her speech half a dozen times at home and in the car this morning, but there was no way she could make this an easy discussion.

"The thing is, Paula," she started. "I think there's something happening in *your* world that we need to discuss."

"Oh?" Paula cautiously sipped her tea. "And how is anything in my world relevant to you?"

Grace felt her face grow warm. "I've been attending your divorce-recovery sessions—for six weeks now—because Judge Stackpole basically made it a condition of granting my divorce. And the others in my group—Camryn, Ashleigh, and Wyatt—Judge Stackpole sent them to you, too."

"That's correct," Paula said. "The judge has been a wonderful advocate for my healing work."

"He's been your lover, too," Grace blurted. "Right?"

Paula looked like she'd been slapped. "I beg your pardon?"

Grace took a deep breath, and the words came tumbling out. "We saw you together! That night the judge dropped in on our session. Wyatt and I came back here to your office. We saw you getting out of his car. You'd obviously had a big fight. You were yelling at him, and then you got out of his car and kicked his tires. You were crying and really upset."

"You're mistaken," Paula said, her voice low.

"We both saw you, Paula," Grace insisted. "And we know it was Judge Stackpole, because after he left you, we followed him back to his house on Longboat Key."

Bright pink splotches of color bloomed on Paula's long pale face. "The judge is . . . a friend. We had a misunderstanding that night. That's all."

"I don't think so. We all noticed how you were around him that night. You were absolutely . . . giddy. Come on, Paula. You're always after all of us about honesty. Why don't you be honest with me? Admit you're having an affair with Stackpole."

Paula's hands shook so violently she had to set the mug of tea on the desktop. "Therapists never discuss their personal life with their patients. This is highly inappropriate, Grace." Her voice was stern, but Grace noticed that Paula was now clasping her hands tightly together in her lap—probably to stop the shaking.

Grace was shaking, too. But now the fear was gone, replaced by anger.

"Inappropriate? Do you want to talk about appropriate behavior, Paula? Because that's a subject I'd love to discuss with you. What would you say about a prominent judge—who, by the way, is married—having an affair with a therapist? Would you say it's appropriate for that judge to *require* parties in divorces in his court to attend therapy with his mistress?"

"Mistress!" Paula yelped. "How dare you?"

Paula's outrage only fueled Grace's refusal to back down.

"Mistress—it's a nasty word, isn't it, Paula? But that's what you are. You're sleeping with him, and in return he sends all these shell-shocked divorce disasters right here to your office, where they pay handsomely for the privilege of listening to your hypocrisy. The five people in my group are forking over fifteen hundred dollars a week for this bullshit," Grace said. "How much of that do you have to kick to Stackpole, Paula? Half? Or does he even let you keep that much?"

"You've got no right to talk to me like this," Paula said, pushing back from her desk, looking wildly around the room for an escape hatch.

"What are you gonna do, Paula? Rat me out to the judge? Flunk me out of divorce camp? I have every right to call you out. But what I want to know is, When do you call him out? Huh, Paula? When do you quit being his victim?"

Paula's eyes flared. "You don't know what you're talking about."

"Sure I do. You moved here from Oregon after your life went up in flames—a bad divorce, a nasty little pill habit, then the arrest and then rehab. You moved to Florida to start over again, right? But you can't get licensed to call yourself a therapist here, can you? And then you meet Stackpole, and the two of you cook up this little 'divorce recovery' racket."

"It's not a racket," Paula said fiercely. "I care deeply about my patients. I counsel them and do my damnedest to help them . . ." Her voice trailed off, and her shoulders slumped.

"Avoid what happened to you?" Grace finished it for her. "How are you going to help us, Paula, when you're still so messed up yourself?"

Tears welled up in the therapist's eyes. "That's not fair. I'm sober again. I had a relapse, yes, but that's over now. And it's because of all I've gone through that I can be effective with my patients. I can use my experiences to help them get through their pain and sense of loss."

"Keep telling yourself that, Paula," Grace said. "Maybe part of it's true. But what about the rest of it? You're conspiring with Stackpole. He funnels patients to you—and we don't have any choice in the matter. If we want to get on with our lives, you have to sign off on our therapy. It's fraud."

Paula clasped and unclasped her hands. "I am a *good* therapist. I can help people; I really can. But how was I going to start a new practice? Rent office space, establish myself in the therapeutic community here? Everywhere I looked, I had people slamming doors in my face. After my divorce—it was so humiliating. And unfair. He's the one who slept with a patient and violated his professional oath. But I'm the one who lost everything. He gets to start over with a new life and a new wife, and I get . . ." She looked around the room, with its worn and stained carpet, cheap furniture, and depressing, institutional green walls. "I get this."

Grace sighed. "Yeah, well, welcome to my world. The same thing happened to me—thanks to your boyfriend, the Honorable Cedric N. Stackpole."

Paula lifted her chin defiantly. "You're in a better place now because of me,

Grace. I know you don't believe it, but you are. Everybody in your group has made remarkable progress. Look at Suzanne. She's not the same person she was when she walked into this office seven weeks ago."

"Okay," Grace said. "I'll give you that one. Suzanne might be the poster girl for divorce recovery. But that doesn't give you a pass where Stackpole is concerned. He's a creep, Paula. He's a crook and a fraud and a cheater. He cheats on his wife, and he cheats on you. Did you happen to catch the news last night?"

Paula bit her lip but said nothing.

"Did you?"

"I saw," she said, her voice barely above a whisper. "Oh my God. It's all so ugly."

Grace felt sorry for Paula. She felt sorry for Eileen Stackpole, and she felt sorry for herself and everybody in her divorce group. But sorry wouldn't begin to fix what Stackpole had done.

"She's twenty-three, did you know that?" Grace asked. "That girl? The one he was cheating on you with? She's a bailiff in his courtroom. Her name is Monique Massey."

"He was mentoring her," Paula said, her chin quivering as she said it.

"Is that what he told you?" Grace asked. "What a crock! She's a county employee. He's a judge! You don't discuss your career in an expensive restaurant at ten o'clock at night. You talk about it over a cup of coffee in the break room. Or at lunch at the meat and three downtown by the courthouse. Even you couldn't believe a load of bullshit like that."

Paula sprang from her chair. "I have patients coming. You have to go, Grace."

Grace stayed seated. "It's all starting to come apart now, Paula. My lawyer and I have talked to your other patients—and their lawyers. We're going to file a complaint with the state Judicial Qualifications Committee. We can prove Stackpole's bias against women. Wyatt's your only male divorce-recovery patient—right? We know Stackpole had some kind of an unethical arrangement with you. And now we know about the affair with his bailiff."

Paula opened the door to the outer office. "You need to leave. Right now. I won't listen to any more of this."

Finally, Grace got up. "I'll leave," she said, standing just inside the doorway. "But I won't shut up. This isn't going to go away." She studied the therapist's face, looking for some opening, some sense that Paula might switch sides.

"I think you really do care about your patients, Paula. I don't know how you got mixed up with a sleazeball like Stackpole, but you have to know he's been using you. He's betrayed his oath of office, and he's betrayed you. Maybe you should take some of your own advice. Take an honest look at what's happened in your life since you hooked up with Stackpole. Come up with an action plan."

The bell on the outer office door tinkled and a middle-aged woman stepped inside. "Hello, Rachel!" Paula called out. "I'll be right with you."

She lowered her voice to a whisper. "You have to go!"

Grace touched the therapist's wrist. "Think about it, Paula. We need your help. We *are* going to file a complaint against him. There will be an investigation. Questions are going to be asked."

The door opened and another woman stepped inside. Paula looked frantically from Grace to the two women standing in her waiting room.

"Almost done here," Paula called cheerily.

"I'm going to have my lawyer call you," Grace said quietly. "Her name is Mitzi Stillwell. She's a nice person. Will you at least talk to her?"

"Go!" Paula said fiercely.

64

The members of the Lady Slipper Garden Circle asked endless questions about Jungle Jerry's unusual bromeliad and orchid collection, and Wyatt patiently answered each and every one. By noon he'd marshaled the eleven women through the park and returned them to the gift shop, where they ate their box lunches and listened to the patented garden-club talk his grandfather had written forty years earlier.

Finally, shortly after two, Joyce ushered the last garden clubber out the door and into the parking lot.

Wyatt collapsed onto his desk chair and drained the bottle of cold water Joyce brought him. "How was I?" he asked, as she sat in the chair opposite his.

"You were terrific," Joyce said. "You always are. Every single one of them wanted to adopt you and take you home and feed you. A couple of the younger ones? I think they had better plans."

Wyatt laughed and blushed.

"When is she leaving?" Joyce asked.

"Who?"

"Callie. You know I don't normally poke my nose into your business, but I have to be honest with you, Wyatt. If she's here for good, I'm leaving."

Wyatt's jaw tightened. "She leaves today. In fact, I told her this morning she had to be gone by lunchtime."

"She's still here. She took Bo over to Scout's house and she was gone for a couple hours, but now she's back again, and your dad is furious. He won't stay in your place while she's there, so he's been out cleaning the bird cages for hours now, and I don't think it's good for him to be out in the heat this time of day."

"Thanks, Joyce. I'll deal with it. Would you please lock up here, then go fetch Nelson and tell him the coast is about to be clear?"

Joyce smiled. "I'll be happy to."

He found Callie in the trailer's kitchen. She was barefoot, humming happily, and stirring something on top of the stove.

"What do you think you're doing?" he demanded.

"What's it look like I'm doing?" She didn't look up. "I'm fixing my spaghetti sauce for dinner tonight. It's Bo's favorite."

"Leave it," Wyatt said.

Now, she turned from the stove, still holding the spoon she'd been using on the sauce. "Oh, for Pete's sake, Wyatt. You know I don't have any place to stay. Why are you being such a complete dick about this?"

He pried the wooden spoon from her hand and dropped it in the sink. "We're getting divorced, Callie. That's what you wanted, and that's what you're getting. Despite your best efforts, I've managed to rebuild my life. Without you. I've tried to be nice, but nice doesn't work with you. So now, I need you to get your stuff and put it in your vehicle and leave."

"And go where?" she said, already pouting.

"I don't care where you go from here," he said, amazed at the fact that he really didn't. "Go back to your sister's, to a motel, whatever. But you're not staying here."

Wyatt reached into his pocket and peeled off four hundred-dollar bills. "This is all the cash I've got. And it's all you're getting until next month, so don't think you can come back here again for more."

She just stared at him. "You're really serious."

He took her hand, pressed the bills into her palm, and closed her fingers over them. "Serious as a heart attack."

"If Bo comes home from Scout's and I'm not here, he'll be heartbroken. I promised him spaghetti and garlic bread tonight . . ."

"Bo's used to you breaking your promises," Wyatt pointed out. "He'll get over it. You can call him after you find a place to stay."

Callie held up the crumpled bills. "And what am I supposed to do when this is gone? Sleep on a park bench? Eat at a shelter?"

Wyatt shrugged. "You might think about a job. But again, not my problem."

It took her two trips to pack her stuff into the Jeep. She banged the screen door as hard as she could both times. Finally, he heard the car's engine sputter and stall, and roar to life again. He heard the spin of her tires on the crushed-shell driveway as she sped down the road and out of his life. For now.

Monday was delivery day at the Sandbox. Grace found Rochelle standing in the dining room, clipboard in hand, as the Budweiser driver unloaded cases of beer and trundled them into the kitchen.

"I was wondering where you'd been," she said as Grace came around the bar to fix herself a cold drink.

"I've been everywhere... and nowhere," Grace replied. "I spent the weekend at Mitzi's condo." She gave her mother an apologetic smile. "Guess I should have called, huh?"

"Would have been nice," Rochelle said. "But you're an adult. I get that you need your privacy." She looked up from her invoices. "If you want to talk about what's going on with you, I'm happy to just listen."

"I'll give you the condensed version. Saturday, I went over to the house and found proof that J'Aimee really did vandalize and set fire to Arthur's house. Then I blackmailed Ben into agreeing to a financial settlement. I broke up with Wyatt. Did you see the news last night? Stackpole's wife caught him with another other woman at a restaurant in Sarasota, and it made the news last night. And then this morning, I dropped in on Paula and tried to convince her she should help us get Stackpole thrown off the bench. It's been a busy time, Mom."

"That's quite a list of accomplishments. Did I hear you say you broke up with Wyatt?"

"Yes," Grace said.

Rochelle sighed and patted her daughter's hand. "Oh, Gracie. Why?"

"His wife wants him back," Grace said. "Bo wants his parents back together." She shrugged. "It was probably inevitable."

"Doesn't Wyatt get a say in any of this?"

"He says he and Callie are never getting back together and that he wants to make a life with me, but..."

"But you're ready to give him up anyway?" Rochelle shook her head. "God, Grace. I could have sworn you were born with a backbone."

"This is not about standing up for myself! It's about reality, Mom. Callie will do whatever it takes to get her claws into Wyatt. She spent the night over there Friday, after she'd broken up with her boyfriend, and Wyatt wasn't even going to tell me. In fact, she told me—after I showed up at his place to pick up Sweetie. She met me at the door dressed in his bathrobe. And she made sure I noticed she wasn't wearing anything underneath."

"Do you actually think Wyatt slept with her? Or that he even wanted to?"

Grace took her time answering, slowly peeling the paper wrapper from a drinking straw. "No," she said finally. "But the point is . . ."

Rochelle waved her off. "The point is you don't trust the man. You don't trust his feelings for you. You don't trust his ability to see through his ex. And you don't trust yourself to work through any of this stuff in order to be with him," Rochelle said. "And that's a damned shame."

"I can't have this conversation with you," Grace said, twisting the straw wrapper into a tight spiral. "I appreciate that you like Wyatt, and you want us to be together, but I have to do what's right for me."

"And if I didn't love you so much, I would agree with you and let you alone," Rochelle said. "But I love you too much to watch while you let happiness slip right through your fingers. You walked away from Ben when you found out he was a cheater. And I supported you on that. One hundred percent. But honey, Wyatt's not Ben. Wyatt is good and loyal and true, and when I see the way he looks at you, and the way you look at him when you think nobody is watching, I know he's the one. I think you know it, too."

Grace pushed her drink away. "I don't know anything. That's the problem. Yeah, I think I love him. And I thought he loved me. But look what happened with Ben. I had no clue Ben was sleeping with J'Aimee, and they were literally doing it right under my nose. So how can I be sure Wyatt is the one? We only met two months ago."

"Just trust your feelings for him," Rochelle said gently. "And remember, nothing in this life is ever going to be one hundred percent for certain. But you can't just hide out, never risk getting hurt again. What kind of life would that be?"

"A safe one," Grace said.

"No." Rochelle shook her head vehemently. "Not safe. Boring. Sad. A total waste."

. . .

Grace sat on the bench on Coquina Beach and hugged Sweetie to her chest. The tide was out and a lone gray heron was stalking something in the calm shallow water. It was the same bench she'd sat on with Wyatt only a few days earlier. Sweetie wriggled in her arms, lifted her chin, and licked Grace's chin. She glanced down at the cell phone on the picnic table, for the tenth time in the past hour. Wyatt had called twice that morning and texted her half an hour ago.

His message was short and to the point. *She's gone. I'm not taking her back. You're what I want.*

He seemed so sure. Why couldn't she be like that?

Because, Grace thought. *Because you're the girl who painted her first apartment six different shades of white the first week you were living there. Because you dated Ben for two years and lived with him for another two before finally deciding to marry him.*

She'd waited and waffled after meeting Ben, and still she'd made a mistake. Maybe her mother was right. Maybe mistakes were inevitable. But maybe this time, she really had found *the* one. There was only one way to find out for sure.

Grace snatched up the phone and tapped the icon beside Wyatt's name. She wouldn't give herself any more time to think, wouldn't have second thoughts. This time around, she would just go with her heart.

"Grace?" Wyatt answered on the first ring.

"Don't talk," Grace said hurriedly. "Just tell me where you want to meet."

"Anywhere you want," Wyatt said. "Can it wait 'til I close up the park at five? Bo is at Scout's house. Dad can stay with him after I bring him back here. Are we all still meeting at the Sandbox tonight?"

"Yes, and yes," Grace said. "I'll be at Mitzi's condo."

65

Grace paced back and forth in the small living room, stopping every five minutes to look out the window at the parking lot, to adjust the drapes, fluff a pillow, or check her makeup in the mirror. She hadn't been this nervous about meeting a man since her first real car date at the age of fifteen. Her palms were actually sweaty.

She'd taken pains with her makeup and had actually changed outfits three times—not that she had that many changes of clothes to begin with—before settling on a pair of blue seersucker capris and a sleeveless white blouse. God help her—she'd even painted her toenails a vivid crimson shade called Sassy Lassie.

Sweetie lay on a throw pillow on the sofa, looking perplexed by Grace's nervous energy.

Grace was midway through her third circuit of the condo when her phone rang. She leapt to grab it, but paused when she saw the caller ID.

Ashleigh Hartounian. Probably, Grace thought, she was calling to ask about that night's get-together at the bar.

"Hi, Ashleigh," she said.

"Graaaace." Ashleigh was sobbing.

"Are you all right?"

"Nooooo," Ashleigh wailed. "I'm not okay. I'll never be okay."

"What is it?" Grace asked. "What's wrong?"

"It's . . . it's . . . Boyce."

Now Grace remembered: today was the day Ashleigh's ex-husband had invited her out to lunch. This was the day Ashleigh expected to win him back and return to her fairy-tale existence as the doctor's wife. Obviously, things hadn't gone as Ashleigh had anticipated.

"Do you want to talk?" Grace asked, hoping she didn't. She was standing in front of the window, craning her neck to see out to the parking lot, watching for Wyatt's car. It was after five.

"No! I'm so upset, I feel like my head is gonna explode."

"Well . . ." Grace started.

"That bitch Suchita!" Ashleigh said. "I should have expected she'd pull a stunt like this. That's all it is, a stunt, to try to trap Boyce."

"Suchita?" Grace was drawing a blank. A truck pulled into the complex's parking lot, but it wasn't Wyatt's.

"You know, Suchita. That little slut drug rep he's been sleeping with. She's the one who got me in trouble with Stackpole in the first place."

"Ohhh," Grace said. "The woman whose house you painted. Now I remember. What's she done to trap Boyce?" As soon as the words were out of her mouth, Grace had a sinking feeling she knew just what Suchita had done.

"She got herself knocked up! Or so she says. It's the oldest trick in the book, but Boyce is such a dummy he never saw it coming. Do you believe this shit?"

"Does this mean he didn't take you to lunch to get back with you?" *Dumb question,* Grace thought.

"He says they're getting married!" Ashleigh screeched. "As soon as our divorce is final. He only took me to lunch because he said he wanted to tell me himself, before one of the girls in the office spilled the beans. Do you believe that?"

Ashleigh was crying again, her wails so loud that Grace had to hold the phone a couple inches from her ear.

"That bitch!" Ashleigh said. "She's five months pregnant. That explains why she looked so fat when I saw her leaving his office last week. And it's a boy! Boyce is ecstatic. It was all he could talk about, the bastard. I wanted to slug him—I was so upset."

"I'm so sorry," Grace said.

"She's the one who's going to be sorry," Ashleigh said. "I'm not gonna let that bitch ruin my life."

"Ashleigh!" Grace said. "Get a grip. If she's pregnant and Boyce intends to marry her, there's nothing you can do."

"That's what you think. There's plenty I can do. And I will."

"Leave it alone, Ashleigh," Grace warned. "Do not do anything you'll regret. I know you're upset right now, but it's probably for the best."

"You don't know a damned thing, Grace," Ashleigh said, her voice suddenly harsh. "Just because you walked away from your marriage doesn't mean I'm ready to walk away from mine. I should have known better than to expect you to understand what I'm going through. I have no intention of letting that little home wrecker steal my husband."

Grace felt a chill go down her spine.

"Ashleigh, where are you right now?" she asked quietly. "I don't think you should be alone. Let's talk this through. I've been there, too, remember."

"Thanks anyway, but I'm not really in the mood for a chat right now," Ashleigh said.

"You're coming to the Sandbox tonight, right?"

"What's the point?" Ashleigh asked. "I told you last week I wasn't coming back to group sessions."

"Didn't you see the news the other night?" Grace asked. "Stackpole's wife caught him with another woman and raised a ruckus in a restaurant in Sarasota."

"Was the other woman Paula?" Ashleigh asked.

"No, that's what makes it all so deliciously sleazy. He was with a twenty-three-year-old woman who is one of the bailiffs in his courtroom. Highly unethical, of course."

"Does Paula know?" Ashleigh asked.

"Yup," Grace said. "I had a long talk with her this morning. I think she's this close to helping us file a formal complaint against Stackpole with the Judicial Qualifications Committee."

"And why would she do that?" Ashleigh asked.

"I think she knows he's been using her by referring all these divorcing women to her for therapy group and then forcing her to pay him kickbacks."

"Hah! Can you prove it?"

"Not yet," Grace admitted. "Just come hang out with us tonight at the Sandbox. I'll tell you the whole story then."

"I don't care about any of that," Ashleigh said abruptly. "That's somebody else's problem. Look, Grace, I gotta go now."

"Go where?" Grace asked. "Ashleigh, where are you? Are you at home? Is there somebody you could call to come over and stay with you for a while?"

"I'm in the car," Ashleigh said. "I've been driving around for hours. And I don't need a babysitter. I just wanted to talk to somebody. But I've made up my mind what I need to do."

"Ashleigh?"

The line went dead.

Grace cursed and tapped the redial button.

The phone rang twice.

"Leave me alone, Grace," Ashleigh said. "This is between me and her."

"Her?"

"You know exactly who I mean. Suchita. I'm gonna take care of business. Do what I should have done months ago, before things got out of hand."

"Ashleigh, stay away from that girl. You're angry and upset, but stalking her is not the answer. You'll only get yourself in more trouble."

"I don't care," Ashleigh insisted. "I don't care about anything. Except Boyce. He's all I have. He's the only thing in this world I give a damn about."

"Come on," Grace said. "That's not really true. You have family; you have friends . . ."

"What friends? You mean all those losers in group? Get real. None of y'all give a damn about me."

"We do," Grace said. "We all care about you. I care. You must know that, or you wouldn't have called me."

Silence.

"Ashleigh? Are you still there?"

"I'm here," Ashleigh said. She was crying again. "That's sweet, Grace. Really sweet. I'm sorry. I didn't mean to call you a loser. You're not like the others."

"You're upset," Grace said soothingly. She was looking out the window again, wondering what time it was.

"You said you're in the car. Where are you? Do you want to meet? We could get a cup of coffee and talk."

"I'm . . . oh, hell. I've just been driving around. I guess I'm at Bradenton Beach. But I don't want any coffee. A drink, maybe. Yeah, another margarita."

"Another? You've already had a margarita, and you're driving?"

"Just a couple. But they were little ones, and mostly ice. If you're gonna lecture me about drinking and driving, I'll hang up right now."

"No lecture," Grace said quickly. "Look, why don't you pull into the next gas station you see and call me back. I'm not far away at all. I'll come and meet you. How does that sound?"

"If you want to," Ashleigh said. "But I'm warning you. It won't change my mind."

"Call me right back," Grace said. "I'll meet you, wherever you are."

She left Sweetie napping in the condo and called Wyatt on the fly.

"Grace, hi," he said, sounding out of breath. "I know I'm late, but I had to go through the drive-through at Wendy's to get dinner for Bo. I'll only be another thirty minutes. Promise."

"Actually, that'll be fine," Grace said. "Ashleigh just called me. Today was the day her ex invited her to go to lunch. But instead of asking her to come back to him, he announced that his girlfriend is five months pregnant, and he's going to marry her as soon as their divorce is final."

"Oh, wow," Wyatt said. "And she was so sure he was going to get back with her. How'd she take the news?"

"About like you'd expect," Grace said. "She's obsessed with getting Boyce back, or at least keeping that girl from marrying him. She's been driving around, drinking margaritas, plotting some kind of revenge. I'm really worried she'll do something drastic. I'm going to go meet her and try and talk some sense into her."

"Is that a good idea?" Wyatt asked. "If she's been drinking?"

"I don't know what else to do," Grace said. "She's talking crazy. I'm afraid she might hurt herself—or somebody else."

"Please don't go meet her by yourself," Wyatt said. "Just wait thirty minutes, okay? I'll take Bo straight home, and then come by and pick you up. We can go together. She might listen if we both ganged up on her."

"Maybe," Grace said reluctantly. "But I promised I'd come right away, as soon as she pulls into a gas station. I'll try and stall her. But hurry, can you?"

"I'm ten minutes from home and another fifteen from the condo," Wyatt said. "Stay right there."

66

Okay, I'm here," Ashleigh said, without bothering with a greeting. "So, are you coming, or what?"

"Here, where?" Grace asked.

"Um, it's a Hess station on Manatee, but you better get here fast, because I do not like the looks of this place. It's definitely in the hood. The bathroom was so nasty I had to pee standing up."

"I'm trying to think where that is," Grace said slowly. "Like, what block of Manatee is that?"

"How should I know?" Ashleigh snapped. "I don't even know why I agreed to meet you. You can't change my mind, you know. That bitch Suchita is history. She's toast."

"Please don't talk like that," Grace begged. She hesitated, wondering if she should mention that Wyatt would be joining them. Stall her, he'd suggested. But that was no easy feat.

She gazed around the room and spotted Sweetie, who'd hopped off the sofa and was now sitting in front of the sliding glass doors facing the gulf.

"Look, Ashleigh, I just need to let Sweetie out for a potty break before I leave her alone," Grace said.

"Who's Sweetie?"

"My dog. She's a rescue, and I've got her over at a client's condo, but I don't dare leave her alone unless I take her out. Just give me fifteen minutes, okay?"

"You want me to hang around here for fifteen minutes? No way! You said you'd meet me right away. Hell, if I hang around here for another fifteen minutes, I could be carjacked. Shiiiiit," Ashleigh swore softly. "I knew this was a bad idea. Thanks anyway, Grace, but I gotta be moving on."

"No, don't leave there," Grace said hastily. "I'll come right now. You said you're at Manatee, but what's close by? What's the intersection and which corner? Give me a landmark, Ashleigh. I'm not really familiar with that part of town."

"For God's sake. I don't know. Let's see . . . um, yeah, there's a strip shopping center with a Bealls outlet right across from the Hess station."

"If you're worried about the gas station, drive over there," Grace suggested. "You can just go inside and wait until I pull up. Nobody's going to carjack you at a Bealls."

"Maybe." The other woman sounded unconvinced. "Or maybe I'll stay here and get a wine cooler while I wait."

"I really don't think you should have anything else to drink," Grace said.

"And I don't give a flying fuck what you think," Ashleigh retorted. "It's five forty-five right now. If you're not here by six, I'm history."

"I'm coming," Grace said hurriedly. "Stay right there."

Grace called Wyatt from her car. "Sorry, but I can't wait for you," she told him. "I'm meeting Ashleigh at the Hess station on Manatee. She's so antsy, I really couldn't stall her any longer. She's already talking about buying a wine cooler. I'll keep her there as long as I can, and hopefully you can meet us there."

Wyatt sighed loudly. "I don't like this Grace. If she's been drinking like you say she has, I don't think you're going to be able to reason with her. I think maybe you should call the cops and let them handle it."

"Ashleigh respects me. She'll listen to me," Grace said. "Don't worry. I'm just going to talk to her, calm her down, and persuade her to leave her car there and let me drive her home. She's not a maniac, Wyatt. She's upset, and she's talking smack, but I honestly don't think she's capable of really harming somebody—other than herself."

"I hope you're right," Wyatt said. "I just dropped Bo off with my dad. I'll be there in ten minutes. Okay?"

"Hurry," Grace said. And she disconnected.

She spotted the red BMW as soon as she pulled into the gas station. Ashleigh tooted her horn and waved. Grace parked in one of the slots in front of the convenience store and trotted over to Ashleigh's car.

The BMW's engine was running, and when the electric window slid down noiselessly and Grace bent down to talk to her friend, a blast of cold air hit her face. Grace's heart sank when she saw two empty wine-cooler bottles tossed in the passenger seat.

"Hey, Grace," Ashleigh said. Her face was pale and her usually flawless makeup was smeared and tear-streaked. "You know this is a waste of time, right?"

"I don't mind wasting my time," Grace said lightly. "Why don't we go over and sit in my car and talk?"

"Nuh-uh," Ashleigh said, shaking her head vigorously. "I like my car just fine." She patted the leather-upholstered passenger seat. "You can sit here." She reached down to the floor and pulled up a full key-lime-flavored wine cooler. "Look, I bought one for you. We can have a party. A pity party, right?"

"Um, I'm not really thirsty," Grace said. "Come on, Ashleigh. You've had too much to drink to be driving. Let's go sit in my car, and I'll drive you home. You can plot revenge against Suchita tomorrow."

"No effin' way," Ashleigh said. "Tonight's the night. That bitch is going down!" She tossed her blond hair defiantly over her shoulder. "And if you're gonna be such a buzzkiller, you can just go on to your divorce meeting. Because I've got stuff to do. See ya around, Grace." She rolled the window up.

"Wait!" Grace said, pounding the BMW's roof. She looked over her shoulder, hoping against hope to see Wyatt's truck. Ashleigh was definitely drunk, and in no mood to be reasoned with.

The window slid down again. "You comin' or not?" Ashleigh held up the wine cooler. Grace sighed and took it, crossing to the passenger seat.

Ashleigh popped the lock and Grace moved the empties aside before sliding into the passenger seat.

Ashleigh watched her expectantly. Grace uncapped the bottle and took a sip of the ultrasweet cooler.

"That's more like it." Ashleigh cackled. "Par-tay! Woo-hoo!" She threw the car into reverse and just as quickly into drive.

"Wait," Grace said, the back of her head slamming against the headrest. "Ashleigh, no! You're in no condition to drive."

"Don't be such a nag. I'm fine!" Ashleigh countered. She looked both ways, then zipped out of the parking lot and onto the highway, narrowly avoiding a collision with an oncoming white sedan before crossing the median into the far westbound lane.

Grace glanced over at Ashleigh, who looked back and laughed. "See? I told you. I'm fine. Those wine coolers have almost no alcohol in 'em, and anyway, I've got a really high tolerance. I can drink, like, half a dozen margaritas and not feel a thing. We're just a couple of girls, out cruisin', just like in high school. Didn't you and your girlfriends ever get a little buzzed and go cruisin'?"

"You're not fine," Grace said, groping for her seat belt. "And we're not in high school, and you're past being buzzed. Anyway, I thought we were just going to talk. Ashleigh, if you want to drive drunk, that's your decision, but I do not want to go along for the ride."

"Too bad," Ashleigh said. "I keep telling you I'm not drunk. Okay? You wanted to talk, let's talk."

Ashleigh wove the BMW in and out of traffic, twice coming so close to clipping another car, Grace finally just squeezed her eyes tightly and prayed, because she was too nervous to watch where Ashleigh was going.

"I want you to turn around and take me back to that gas station," Grace said through gritted teeth. "Or just pull over and drop me off. This isn't funny, you know."

"You're right; it's not funny. It's fuckin' tragic is what it is," Ashleigh said. Her eyes brimmed over with tears. "I tried calling Boyce while I was waiting for you. The number I had was disconnected. He just called me on it, like this morning. She did that. I just know it. One of her spies probably told her Boyce took me to lunch today. But what she doesn't know is—I've got spies of my own."

She fumbled in the center console of the car and came up with her cell phone. "Here. Grab the steering wheel," she told Grace.

Grace reached over and took the steering wheel with her left hand, grateful that the heavy flow of traffic on Manatee meant that Ashleigh was only doing about thirty miles per hour.

Ashleigh was squinting down at the list of contacts on her phone, scrolling down, looking for something.

"Who are you calling?" Grace asked.

"Here it is!" Ashleigh said triumphantly. She tapped the number and waited, and then frowned. "The bitch won't pick up. I bet Boyce told her not to talk to me."

"Suchiiiiita." Ashleigh's voice was low and spooky. "Pick up the phone, little mama. I've got a message for you. No? You don't wanna talk to me? That's okay. Cuz I'm coming for you, bitch. Remember? I know exactly where you live. And guess what? You can run, but you can't hide."

She disconnected the phone, dropped it into her lap, and took the steering wheel again.

Grace's mouth felt dry, and she felt beads of perspiration popping up on her forehead, despite the chill from the BMW's air conditioner. She glanced in the rearview mirror, but there was no sign of Wyatt's truck. She felt in the pocket of her shorts for her phone, found it, and slid it into her lap.

She had to call Wyatt, try to let him know what Ashleigh intended. Maybe he could call Boyce Hartounian and warn him that Ashleigh was on a rampage. She glanced over at Ashleigh, who seemed to be watching the road. She managed to thumb down her recent calls and tap Wyatt's number, but then the BMW suddenly swerved into the far left lane and, seconds later, without signal or warning, made a sharp left turn, crossing two lanes of oncoming traffic, earning her a blast of horns from the cars she narrowly avoided T-boning. Grace's phone flew out of her hand and slid down between the seats.

"Ashleigh!" Grace cried. "What the hell are you doing?"

The driver shrugged. "Sorry. Guess I cut it a little close, huh?"

"You nearly got me killed," Grace said angrily. "If you want to kill yourself, that's your business, but I want out of this car, right now. Pull over, dammit."

With her left hand, she tried groping the area beneath her seat, but the small phone eluded her grasp.

Ashleigh laughed. "Don't be such a chickenshit, Grace. Look, I'm barely doing thirty now."

It was true. They'd turned onto a quiet, treelined residential street. It was narrow, and cars were parked along the curbs on both sides, dictating a slower speed. Grace wondered if she'd managed to connect the call to Wyatt, wondered if he could hear them right now. She prayed it was so.

"What is this neighborhood?" she asked loudly.

"It's Newtown," Ashleigh said. "The bitch lives right around here, but I can't remember the name of the street. I'll know it when I see it, though."

She was scanning both sides of the street, looking ahead at the street signs.

They were going just slow enough, Grace realized, that she could escape the car without risking her life. She snaked her right hand over toward the passenger door, her fingers clasping the handle.

Click. Grace tugged at the handle, but it was too late.

Ashleigh laughed. "Childproof locks. Great invention, huh? Come on, Grace. Why do you wanna jump ship? I thought you were gonna be my wingman on this mission."

"I don't want anything to do with this," Grace said. "You're scaring me now, Ashleigh. Just pull over and let me out, okay? Or let me drive. You're in no condition to be behind the wheel. You're going to do something stupid and dangerous and end up in real trouble."

"Trouble?" Ashleigh glanced over at her. "What? Stackpole is gonna put me in remedial divorce counseling? Sentence me to community service again? You don't get it, Grace, do you? I don't give a rat's ass about any of that. I just want to give that bitch what she deserves. Once she's out of the picture, Boyce will realize what he's been missing."

Grace clamped her lips together. Finally, the reality of the situation dawned on her. Nothing she could say would sway Ashleigh's resolve. She glanced again in the rearview mirror. Was that a flash of red, a block back? Wyatt's truck? She said another silent prayer.

Ashleigh drove one block, turned right, drove two more blocks, and turned left. The truck sped up and seemed to be closing the gap between it and the BMW, but then it was forced to come to a halt as an enormous SUV backed slowly down a driveway and into the street, totally blocking it.

Come on, come on, come on, Grace chanted silently.

"This is her street!" Ashleigh muttered. "I knew it was around here." She made a sharp left and slowed the BMW to a crawl, craning her neck to see the numbers on the mailboxes.

If she hadn't been so thoroughly terrified, Grace might have been craning her neck, too. The street was lined with moss-draped oak trees, lawns with thick green grass, and neatly tended beds of flowers. The homes were cozy stucco and wood-frame bungalows built in the twenties and thirties, with welcoming porches and gabled roofs.

It was a storybook street, but Grace had a feeling that this story would not have a happy ending.

"Oh, yeah," Ashleigh said softly. "This is the right block." She glanced over at Grace. "You see this neighborhood? I checked—the cheapest house on this street sold for 377,000 dollars. And I'm living in a dump condo that rents for eleven hundred a month. Ask yourself how a twenty-eight-year-old drug rep affords a house here. I'll tell you how—she hooks up with a rich plastic surgeon and makes him her baby daddy."

She pointed to a house at the end of the street. "That's it. That's her place."

"What . . . what are you planning to do?" Grace checked the rearview mirror. No sign of the truck.

"I'm just going to talk to her, that's all," Ashleigh said, her voice singsongy. "Make her see that she needs to step away."

But as they were talking, they saw a silver Audi back swiftly down the driveway. They were three houses away. As soon as the Audi was on the street, it accelerated so quickly that the tires screeched on the pavement.

"That's her!" Ashleigh said. She sped up, but the Audi zipped through the next intersection without slowing down.

"She knows what my car looks like," Ashleigh muttered. She accelerated, closing the gap between the two cars.

The Audi made two quick turns, and Ashleigh stayed close, flying through stop signs. The Audi managed to stay two car lengths ahead, and never slowed down before making a left.

They were back on Manatee again, heading west. The Audi sped through the thinning traffic, darting in and out of lanes, but Ashleigh gripped the steering wheel and kept on the car's tail. They were doing sixty miles an hour now, somehow managing to make all the green lights. Grace kept looking in the rearview mirror, and when she glimpsed the red truck again, she began daring to hope. Wyatt was there, not far behind. He would think of some way to stop this crazy race.

The Audi sped up again, and Ashleigh did the same. They were only a car length behind now, and the BMW's speedometer was inching over seventy miles per hour.

The GULF BEACHES sign flashed by. "She's headed for Boyce's beach house on Anna Maria," Ashleigh said. "Like he can hide her. Dumb bitch."

Grace saw the fringe of Australian pines, white sands, and the glint of sunlight on the sparkling water of Palma Sola Bay. The Audi was still a car length ahead, but Ashleigh stomped on the accelerator, and the speedometer needle jumped. They were doing eighty-five now. The Audi wove in and out of traffic, and the BMW stayed right with it. They flew over the first causeway, and Grace held her breath, terrified Ashleigh might somehow send them both flying over the concrete bridge embankment and into the waters below. Her fears eased momentarily when they were over the bridge and into another stretch of causeway, lined on both sides by sandy beaches and the shallow waters of the bay, but not for long.

A lumbering dump truck loomed ahead of them in the right-hand lane, forcing the Audi to slow considerably. Ashleigh veered into the left lane and passed the dump truck. She slowed, waiting for the truck to pass on the right, and laughed triumphantly when she came alongside the Audi.

Grace glimpsed the driver as they pulled alongside the Audi—a long curtain of dark hair, and when the woman looked over and saw who was beside her, her face mirrored the look of shock and horror in Grace's own face.

"Gotcha!" Ashleigh screamed. She jerked the BMW's steering wheel hard to the right, but just as she did so, Grace heard the squeal of the Audi's brakes. The BMW veered off the road.

Grace had the sensation of time slowing. She heard screams—her own, Ashleigh's? She'd never be sure. She was aware of the car slamming through an expanse of corrugated metal fencing, of the windshield shattering, of the splintering of wood on metal as they glanced off a pine tree, and, moments later, of the rush of water.

And then it was quiet.

67

Wyatt pushed the old truck's accelerator all the way to the floor once he heard the one-sided conversation on Grace's call. He shuddered at the sound of Ashleigh's slurred speech. She was drunk, deranged, out of control. And Grace was strapped into the passenger seat right beside her, helpless.

As he closed the gap between the racing cars and his own, he saw Ashleigh's frenzied pursuit of the silver Audi, guessing the driver was Suchita, Ashleigh's romantic rival. He didn't have a clear idea of what he'd do if and when he caught up to the women, but he knew he would have to do something. He wondered, fleetingly, if Ashleigh had a gun. The only gun Wyatt owned was Nelson's old service pistol—but it was kept under lock and key in the file cabinet in the office. And what if he did have the gun? How would he use it? Shoot out the tires of a moving vehicle? Ridiculous.

A dozen awful scenarios flashed through his mind as he struggled to keep pace.

He wondered if the same scenarios occurred to Grace. Her voice sounded so calm, so cool on the other end of the phone. "Keep trying, Grace," he murmured.

They crossed the first bay bridge, and he managed to catch up to within two car lengths when a lumbering old dump truck forced everybody to slow down.

But in the blink of an eye, everything changed. He saw the BMW switch lanes, saw it pull alongside the Audi, and then deliberately try and sideswipe the other car.

The Audi's driver slammed on the brakes, and seconds later, to his horror, he saw the BMW veer off the road and plow through the metal fencing. He saw the cloud of sand spewed by the spinning tires, heard the crunch of metal on metal, and, worst of all, heard the hair-raising chorus of screams from inside the BMW.

And then nothing, except the pounding of his own blood in his ears, as he saw the car skimming into the jade green waters of Palma Sola Bay.

Wyatt was out of the truck almost before it stopped, with the only tool he had at hand, the heavy Maglite flashlight he kept under the front seat. He ran through the jagged opening in the fencing left by the BMW and waded into the warm, shallow water. The BMW was immersed up to its hood ornament. He cursed himself for not removing the thick-soled leather work boots that made his trek to the car take what seemed like hours.

Finally, he reached the car. The windshield was shattered, and water was seeping in. He could see that the air bags had deployed and were already deflated. He splashed over to the passenger side, and his heart leapt when he saw Grace's brown hair. He yanked furiously at the door, until he remembered that Ashleigh had locked it.

"Grace!" he shouted. "Grace. Are you all right?" She turned her head slightly to the right, and he could see a thin trickle of blood oozing down her face.

"Turn your head away," he shouted, and began hammering at the center of the window with the butt of the flashlight. He slammed it against the glass again and again, until finally the window seemed to crinkle into a million pieces and fall away.

"Give me your arms," he told her, but she stared at him, dazed or in shock; he wasn't quite sure. "Your arms!" he repeated. "I'm going to pull you out. Come on, Grace. I need to get you out of this water."

"I can't," she said, her voice weak. Wyatt grabbed her by the shoulder. "Come on, honey. You can do this."

She shook her head violently, fumbling with something in her lap. Wyatt stuck his head in the window and saw that her seat belt was still fastened and that water had reached her knees. He leaned in until his torso was in the car and, with shaking fingers, managed to unbuckle it.

"Okay," he said. "Okay. You're good now. Let's go, Gracie. Let's get you out."

Finally, she nodded, turned, and knelt on the seat, reaching her arms for him. He wrapped his own arms under hers. "Put your arms around my neck," he urged. He tugged while she wriggled, and, finally, she came free of the car, collapsing against him in the waist-deep water.

Wyatt stood there for a moment, holding her tightly against his chest, unwilling to let her go. "Are you hurt?" he asked. "Your head, legs, arms, anything?"

"I'm okay," she said shakily. And then, unbelievably, she laughed a little, whispering in his ear. "But I think maybe I peed my pants." He laughed, too, then. "Don't tell anybody, but I might have peed mine, too. Just a little, when I saw the car go airborne."

"Ashleigh," she said urgently. "Get Ashleigh out."

"I need to get you to the shore," he said, starting for the beach, but she pulled away.

"No. I can walk by myself. Get Ashleigh. Please, Wyatt."

He nodded grimly and turned back toward the BMW.

Ashleigh was slumped over in the driver's seat. He broke the window out with his flashlight, calling her name. "Ashleigh? Ashleigh? Talk to me. Come on, Ashleigh. It's Wyatt. Talk to me."

He reached in and touched the base of her neck. She was warm, and he could feel a pulse, but her breathing was shallow. Water was up to her lap and streaming in through the windshield and the passenger window. He wriggled halfway through the window and saw that, unlike Grace, Ashleigh hadn't fastened her seat belt. Which shouldn't have come as a surprise. He grasped the unmoving woman under the arms, in the same way he had grabbed Grace, but she was a dead weight. He backed out a little, trying for the door handle, already knowing it wouldn't open.

The water was still rising. It was chest-high. He grabbed Ashleigh again and tugged, inching her body in an agonizingly slow process. At some point, he was aware of the sound of sirens, of voices coming from the beach.

Finally, a rough arm grasped his. "We got this, buddy."

He turned and saw a pair of uniformed paramedics. "She's breathing, but she's unconscious."

"Thanks," one of them said. "You can step away now."

. . .

He found Grace sitting on the tailgate of the ambulance, wrapped in a blanket. A Band-Aid had been applied to the cut over her eyebrow. Sitting beside her, also wrapped in a blanket, despite the August heat, was a stunning brunette, who was shaking and crying uncontrollably.

It was Suchita, the driver of the Audi.

A female EMT had fastened a blood-pressure cuff to Suchita's upper arm. "You're all right," the woman said in a soothing voice. "Your blood pressure's a little high, but not off the charts. And your baby should be fine, too. But we can transport you to the hospital, if you'd like to get checked out."

"No!" Suchita said. "I want to wait for my fiancé. Boyce is on the way. He should be here soon. He's a doctor; he'll take care of me."

Wyatt nodded in Grace's direction, catching the EMT's eye. "Is she all right? Nothing broken?"

"She's good," the EMT said. "You're gonna want to watch her overnight, make sure she's not concussed, but otherwise the cut over her eye is the only thing. She was damned lucky."

Suchita turned and stared at Grace. "You're her friend? Why? Why did you let her come after me? She tried to kill me. She wanted to kill me and my baby."

"I didn't," Grace said, her voice a whisper. "I tried to stop her. But she'd been drinking . . ."

"She's crazy," Suchita said flatly. "I told Boyce she was dangerous. After she painted my house? I wouldn't stay there again. Not by myself. But she wouldn't leave me alone. She followed me, watched us if we went out together. And then she got my phone number, and she started leaving me messages. I told Boyce. I played him the voice mail messages she's been leaving me. He thought she was just trying to intimidate me. He said she wasn't dangerous." She shivered. "I only went home today to pick up my mail. And that's when she showed up."

Grace looked up at Wyatt. "Is Ashleigh . . . ?"

"She's breathing, but she's unconscious," Wyatt said. "She wasn't wearing her seat belt. I think maybe she hit her head."

"It all happened so fast," Grace said. "And I was so scared. I kept looking back, hoping you were there."

"I got there as quick as I could," Wyatt said. "But that damned SUV had the street blocked, and then, once she got out on Manatee and she was speeding, my old truck couldn't keep up. The whole thing starts to shimmy and rattle after I hit sixty."

"It doesn't matter," Grace said, clutching his hand. "You got here. You got me out of the car. You're here now. That's all that matters."

"I'm here, and I'm staying," Wyatt said, his voice choking with emotion. He looked over at the EMT. "Okay if I take her home now?"

Just then, a short, balding, middle-aged man came rushing up to the ambulance. Wyatt stepped back, but the EMT put out a hand to stop him from coming any closer.

"I'm a physician," he said, puffing out his chest. "Dr. Hartounian. This is my fiancée. Have you checked her vital signs? Did she tell you she's five months pregnant?"

"She checked out perfect," the EMT said. "Not a scratch on her. Physically, anyway." And she stepped aside.

"Suchita? My God! Are you all right?" Hartounian gestured toward the pair of EMTs who were bundling a stretcher into the second ambulance. "Is that really Ashleigh?"

"I'm . . . I'm . . ." Suchita's voice trailed and broke off into sobs as she threw herself into Boyce Hartounian's arms.

"It's okay, baby. I'm here. Boyce is here," he crooned tenderly, rubbing her back and arms. She was two inches taller than he, but his arms were tanned and muscular. He glanced over at Grace and his eyes narrowed.

"Who are you?" he asked, all business. "You're Ashleigh's friend? I just spoke to one of the police officers. They say the two of you had been drinking. What the hell were you thinking letting her get behind the wheel of a car? If anything happens to our child . . ."

"My name is Grace Davenport," Grace said, feeling her temper flare. "I wasn't the one who was drinking. That was all Ashleigh. And I didn't let her drive. In fact, I was trying to talk her into letting me take her home. She called me earlier, upset after your lunch with her . . ."

Suchita looked up. "You took her to *lunch*? Without telling me?"

Wyatt took Grace's arm and gently steered her away from the ambulance. He meant to take her home, get her in some dry clothes, let the shock wear off. But two uniformed police officers stood beside his truck, waiting for answers.

. . .

An hour later, after giving her statement to the cops—and agreeing to a Breathalyzer test to prove she hadn't been responsible for any of the half dozen empty wine-cooler bottles found in the BMW, Grace finally climbed into the front seat of Wyatt's truck.

He'd changed into the spare clothes he kept in a gym bag in the truck—his Manasota Maulers coaches' shirt, shorts, and a pair of baseball cleats.

"What do you think will happen to Ashleigh?" she asked, as Wyatt pulled slowly back onto the roadway.

Wyatt shrugged. "I know you feel sorry for her, but at this point, I hope they throw the book at her. Ashleigh very nearly killed three people today—four if you count Suchita's baby. She'll be charged with drunk driving, for sure. And it sounds like if Boyce Hartounian has his way, I guess they could add attempted homicide, or whatever you call it."

Grace grimaced at the mention of Hartounian. "What a pompous jerk!"

"He must have something the ladies love," Wyatt observed. "To have two hotties like Ashleigh and Suchita fighting over him."

"What he has is a nice big bank account," Grace countered. She closed her eyes and rested her head on the back of the seat. A moment later, she sat up again. "What time is it?"

"Nearly seven," Wyatt said. He closed his hand over hers. "Just rest, okay? I'm going to take you to the condo, let you get changed and showered. I called your mom, just to let her know what happened, so she won't be worried. And I talked to Nelson, to let him know I won't be coming home tonight. The EMTs told me you need to have somebody checking you through the night."

"No!" Grace said. "I mean, that's sweet and all that you want to take care of me. But everybody's meeting at the Sandbox tonight. Mitzi's coming, too. They're expecting me."

"Not a good idea," Wyatt said. "Why don't you just call your mom back and tell her to let everybody know you're not coming?"

"I can't call anybody. Remember? My cell phone is still in what's left of Ashleigh's car. Anyway, I have to go, and you need to be there, too. This is important, Wyatt. If we're going to file a complaint against Stackpole with the JQC, we need everybody to give Mitzi a statement. She's bringing women from Paula's other groups, too. And there's an outside chance Paula herself might show up."

"You think Paula's going to turn against her boyfriend?" Wyatt scoffed. "Now I know you've got a head injury."

Grace proceeded to fill Wyatt in on the Honorable Cedric N. Stackpole's not-so-honorable but very complicated love life.

"I told Paula about the meeting tonight, about what we're doing," Grace said. "She's really conflicted. But I think maybe she's tired of being victimized by him. I think there's an outside chance she'll show up and help us."

"Doubtful," Wyatt said, unconvinced.

"I don't care. Let's go straight to the Sandbox. I can shower and change there." She flashed a smile. "Please? I need you on my team."

He shrugged. "Team Grace? Okay. Sign me up."

68

Rochelle was carrying a tray of drinks and food to a table of softball players at the back of the room when her bedraggled daughter came scuttling through the side door of the Sandbox, trying not to be noticed.

She dropped the tray on the table, sloshing beer on the shortstop's cheeseburger and sending the catcher's order of hot wings sailing off the plate and into the second baseman's lap.

"Sorry." Rochelle tossed a dry bar towel to the coach, who was, thankfully, a regular.

"Jesus H!" she exclaimed, hurrying over to Grace's side. She hugged her daughter fiercely. "You look awful! Are you sure you don't need to go to the emergency room?"

"I look worse than I feel," Grace said. "I'll be fine after I get a shower." She looked over her mother's shoulder at the table in the corner, where a dozen women chattered away. "Is everybody here?"

"Everybody except you two—and Ashleigh. If that girl's not dead already, I'll kill her myself," Rochelle said.

"Did you tell the others what happened?" Grace asked.

"Just that there'd been an accident and that you were okay and Ashleigh was taken to the hospital," Rochelle said. "I'll let you fill 'em in. If you're sure you feel like it."

"Wyatt can do it while I get cleaned up." Grace leaned over and planted a kiss on Wyatt's cheek. He blushed, then kissed her back.

"I take it you two patched things up?" Rochelle asked as they watched Grace depart.

"I think so," Wyatt said. "I hope so. I can't go through another day like today. When I realized she was in that car with Ashleigh—the kind of danger she was in . . ."

He ducked his head and swallowed. "If something had happened to her? I honestly don't know what I'd do, Rochelle. I know it's crazy—falling in love with somebody you meet in divorce therapy? But I did. And I think she did, too. And when this is all over, I want us to get married."

Rochelle raised one eyebrow. "You're asking my permission?"

Wyatt laughed and blushed again. "I guess not. Just maybe for your approval. I know I'm not the best financial risk. She'd be going from that mansion she lived in with her ex to a trailer—literally. But I promise you, I love Grace, and I'll never hurt her. I'll spend the rest of my life taking care of her."

"Grace can actually take care of herself," Rochelle said. "Just make her laugh and smile and enjoy life like she used to. Be good to each other. The rest will work itself out."

Mitzi Stillwell dabbed at the beer rings on the tabletop with a paper napkin, then placed a thick file folder on it.

She looked at the eleven women arrayed around the two tables Rochelle had pushed together in a quiet corner of the bar. Camryn Nobles trained a small handheld video camera on Mitzi, then panned around at the other women.

Suzanne passed around the documents Mitzi had prepared: disclaimers, giving Camryn the right to film the women telling their stories and attesting that they were giving their statements of their own free will.

Harriett Porter cleared her throat nervously. Camryn gave her an encouraging nod. "Just pretend you're talking to a friend," she prompted.

Harriett licked her lips and began speaking. "We had our first hearing before Judge Stackpole back in December. I, er, did something I now regret, and Judge Stackpole was very, very angry with me."

"What exactly did you do that made him so angry?" Camryn asked.

"Well, I found out that my husband was having an affair with a stripper . . ." She looked at Camryn. "Is it okay to say it was a male stripper?"

Camryn laughed and nodded.

"Okay, so it was this guy. Named Anubis. I guess that was his stripper name. Anyway, Daryl, that's my husband, was putting tens of thousands of dollars on our American Express card at this place in Tampa called Jeepers-Peepers. I was getting our tax stuff ready for the accountant, which is how I found the AmEx bills. And, well, I, uh, um, I went over to that place one Thursday afternoon, Jeepers-Peepers, and I saw him—Daryl, that is, standing in the parking lot, and he was stuffing money into this guy's—what do you call it? Not a G-string, if it's a man, right? It was sort of a sequined jockstrap."

"Actually?" Thea, an attractive woman in her early fifties raised her hand. "Technically, it's not a jockstrap. It's called a codpiece. I know because I'm from New Orleans."

"Thanks, hon," Harriett said. "He was stuffing fifty-dollar bills into this stripper's codpiece. Right there in broad daylight! And it made me so mad, I lost it. Literally. One minute I was trying to take pictures of Daryl and his boyfriend with my phone, and the next minute I had crashed the car into a Dumpster. The police said I ran over Daryl's foot. I don't remember that part. I do remember he was wearing the four-hundred-dollar Italian loafers I bought him for Father's Day."

Camryn's chest was heaving with silent laughter, and tears were rolling down her face. Harriett was too caught up in her story to notice the reporter's reaction.

"Judge Stackpole called me a renegade!" she said angrily. "My lawyer said I should get half of Daryl's pension plan—I never worked after we married, because he wanted me to stay home with our children. But Stackpole told me I was an able-bodied woman and I should get a job and stop being a leech. And then he told me he wouldn't sign off on our divorce until I completed this divorce-recovery counseling. With a woman named Paula Talbott-Sinclair. Who I later found out isn't even licensed to practice therapy in this state!"

"Did the judge give you the option of seeking treatment with any therapist? Or did he specify Ms. Talbott-Sinclair?" Camryn asked.

"He handed me her business card, right there in the courtroom," Harriett said. "And he said she would have to notify him that I'd completed six weeks of sessions before he would grant our divorce."

Harriett's face was pink with indignation. "She charged me nine hundred dollars a session. Later, after I talked to some other women in the group and we began comparing notes, I found out they were only paying a third of that! And the thing is, I'm still pissed off at Daryl. I haven't recovered from our divorce at all. I don't know if I ever will."

"Thank you, Harriett," Camryn said soberly. She put the camera down and beamed at the women around the table.

"That was great. Who's next?"

Suzanne took a deep breath and a sip of her iced tea. She was wearing a bright orange top and a flattering new shade of lipstick, and she'd had her hair cut and colored.

"Shall I go?" she asked.

"Oh my God," Grace whispered. She was seated, facing the door, when a slender woman with unruly blond curls opened the door of the Sandbox and looked around hesitantly. She stood in the doorway, scanning the room, looking for something.

Grace jumped up and waved. "Paula! We're over here."

Conversation at the table came to an abrupt halt as Paula Talbott-Sinclair timidly approached the table. She stopped a few feet away, looking at Grace for guidance.

"What's she doing here?" one of the women said angrily, jumping up from her seat and snatching up her pocketbook. "Spying on us for Stackpole?"

Paula's already-pale face blanched.

"I invited her," Grace said, standing. She reached out a hand for the therapist. "Paula? There's an empty seat right here, beside mine."

Paula's lower lip trembled. "I don't want to intrude. Maybe it would be better if I didn't stay."

"No," Camryn said. "Stay."

"Please," Suzanne said.

When she was finally seated, Rochelle hurried over to take the newcomer's order.

"Mom?" Grace said politely. "This is Paula. Paula, this is my mom, Rochelle."

"The therapist?" Rochelle looked from Paula to Grace to Wyatt. "You're the therapist?"

"Counselor," Paula corrected. "And I'll just have iced tea, please. Green, if you have it." She lowered her voice and leaned in closer to Grace.

"How's Ashleigh? Have you heard anything?"

"You know about Ashleigh? Already? Has it been on the news?"

Paula shook her head. "Ashleigh called me this afternoon. I guess it must have been before you went to meet her. And then a detective called me just before I came over here. The police retrieved Ashleigh's cell phone, and they were following up on all her recent calls. They wouldn't tell me much—just that she'd made an attempt on another woman's life and nearly killed herself in the process."

Grace stared at the therapist. "Let me get this straight. Ashleigh called you? Today?"

"She called me at the office, and I just happened to pick up. She'd obviously been drinking. She was ranting and raving about getting revenge against—what's the other woman's name?"

"Suchita."

"Right. Suchita. Ashleigh was manic. It was hard to get a word in edgewise. I begged her to come to the office, to talk things over, but she wouldn't hear of it. She was cursing and making all kinds of wild threats. She talked about setting fire to her ex's house or somehow poisoning the woman."

Paula shook her head. "Ashleigh was in a very dark place."

"I still don't understand why she called *you*," Grace said. "No offense, Paula, but she thought you were a quack."

"I'm well aware," Paula said. "She told me that several times today. But I think Ashleigh knew she was spinning out of control. She was desperate for help." Paula looked around the table, recognizing all the faces arrayed around it.

"I failed Ashleigh. And I failed all of these women." She glanced over at Wyatt, who was sitting on the other side of Grace. "And I failed you, too."

Paula squared her shoulders and addressed Grace. "You said your lawyer would be at this meeting. Is she here?"

Mitzi raised her hand. "Mitzi Stillwell, attorney at law."

Paula motioned to Camryn. "You can turn on that camera now. I'm ready to tell my story. All of it. If you're ready to hear it."

"I met Cedric at a cocktail party, soon after I moved down here. We struck up a conversation. He seemed interested in my work—I told him about the seminars

I'd done out west and about the book. And—I guess I rattled on a little too long about the end of my marriage. He was sympathetic, and it was clear he was attracted to me . . ."

Paula looked directly into the camera. "I know this sounds incredibly lame—but at the time I had no idea he was married. If I'd known then—I would never have started an affair. Not after the way my own marriage ended. That's no excuse, I know. I should have made it my business to ask more questions, when he never wanted to meet me in public, insisted on meeting at my place. Maybe I didn't really want to know. Cedric is the first man I've been intimate with since my divorce.

"Maybe a month after we'd started seeing each other, he confessed he was married. I was shocked, tried to break it off, but he seemed committed to ending his marriage and being with me. I gave him my book and suggested he read it. Not long after that, he suggested that he should refer clients to me—clients whose divorces he was presiding over.

"It didn't occur to me that this was a breach of ethics. I was flattered and delighted that a distinguished judge thought I could assist these people."

"Oh for God's sake," Camryn said, pausing the video. "Paula, are you trying to tell us that it never occurred to you that you'd hit the motherlode with Stackpole making these counseling sessions mandatory? Come on! You were making fifteen hundred dollars a week just from the people in my little group."

Paula bit her lip and looked away. Rochelle brought her iced tea. She took a long sip. "I'll answer that on camera, if you like."

"When I moved here, I was very nearly destitute. I'd been in rehab and lost my license to practice in Oregon. When my husband and I divorced, we sold our home there at the very bottom of the market, for what amounted to pennies on the dollar, and, of course, he got half of that. I moved to Florida with my clothes, my car, and very little else. I was living in a motel room and working part-time as a social worker in a nursing home when I met Cedric.

"Cedric thought I should go into private practice again. He suggested I could get around Florida's tough licensing laws by not calling myself a therapist or a marriage counselor. He loaned me the money to rent my office space and buy a computer and some secondhand office furniture. Start-up funding, he called it.

He was hearing so many divorce cases. He said there was a real need for the kind of therapy I offer. And he said it could very lucrative."

"I'll say it was lucrative," Harriett put in. Camryn swung around in her seat and focused the camera on her. "With what I paid you alone in the past six months, you could have bought a nice midsized sedan. And yet you're still driving that dinky little toy car and operating out of that dump office. What happened to all the money? We heard you had a drug problem. Is that where it all went?"

Camryn chuckled, as did several other women at the table, although not Grace and not Suzanne.

Paula winced.

"That's a fair question, Harriett. I'm guessing by mentioning my drug problem you're referring to my arrest for forging prescriptions for tranquilizers in Oregon. I completed my court-ordered rehab out there, and I was doing reasonably well until I got involved with Cedric. And then . . . well, I can't sugarcoat it, can I? I had a relapse. Obtaining drugs is much easier in Florida. I went to a storefront clinic, got a script, and I was in business again.

"You want to know where the money went? Not to drugs. I'm clean again. Most of it went to Cedric. Right off the bat, he told me my fee schedule was a joke. He said the patients he was referring to me were screwed up and desperate to get out of their lousy marriages. Why shouldn't they pay, and why shouldn't he be compensated for all those referrals? Especially since he'd already 'loaned' me all the money to get on my feet again."

"Kickbacks," Mitzi said succinctly. "You were paying him kickbacks? How much?"

"I can't give you a precise figure," Paula said. "But I only kept roughly a third of my fees. The rest I handed over to Cedric."

"How did you pay him?" Mitzi asked. "Cash, check? Do you have any records?"

Paula looked puzzled. "You mean receipts? Don't be absurd. Remember, Cedric was a lawyer before he was a judge. He's really quite brilliant."

"Then, how did you pay him?" Camryn asked from down the table. "If we're going to be able to make charges stick against Stackpole, Mitzi here is going to need some proof."

"I understand," Paula said. "I was getting to that, Camryn, if you'll just be patient."

"Sorry." Camryn flashed a grin and started filming again.

"Cedric's wife kept all their household accounts. He said she watched every penny he earned or spent. I know she was pretty wealthy in her own right, and he resented that—she didn't work, but she controlled the purse strings. He was very careful. He set up a janitorial business called Clean Sweep. All the money I paid him, I wrote out the checks to Clean Sweep. It was supposed to be for nightly cleaning and paper supplies, things like that."

"But it was a dummy corporation?" Mitzi asked.

"As far as I know, I was Clean Sweep's only client," Paula said. "And I never got any janitorial services. I cleaned the office myself."

"Sounds like you got taken to the cleaners yourself, girlfriend," Thea chimed in.

Paula sighed. "He said he loved me. But he'd signed a prenup before marrying his wife. If he left, he'd be living on a judge's salary. Peanuts, he called it. The money I gave him, he called it our nest egg. We were going to buy a cottage on Anna Maria. I was going to work on getting my licensing back. He'd leave the bench, start his own law firm. We'd give our own version of my old divorce diversion seminars and travel all over. We'd write a book together. He even had a title: *De-Toxing After Divorce*."

"Damn!" Camryn said. "That's a fabulous title. I'd buy a book called that. You know, if it was written by somebody other than Stackpole."

"And me," Paula said. She shrugged. "That's all I came to say, really. I'm sorry I allowed all of this to happen. Sorry I was a party to Cedric's scheme. Sorry I failed all of you. Could you turn the camera off now, please, Camryn?"

Camryn set the camera down carefully on the tabletop.

"Thank you, Paula," Grace said. "I mean it. Your coming here tonight and telling your story, that took a lot of courage. We all appreciate it, don't we, ladies?" She looked around the table, but the women returned only blank stares.

Suzanne stood up. She clapped her hands together. Slowly. Grace nodded and stood, too, and began clapping, as did Wyatt. They looked expectantly at Camryn, who nodded, stood, and joined in. Slowly, one by one, all the women at the table stood and joined in the polite applause.

69

Wyatt tiptoed into the bedroom and set the teacup on the nightstand. He hurried to the windows to draw the curtains. The EMTs had versed him in postconcussion rules—no bright sunlight, sharp noises, or too much physical activity. Plenty of sleep, plenty of fluids, plenty of watchfulness. Grace had fallen asleep in the truck the previous night, just minutes after they'd left the Sandbox.

He'd hurried her into bed, and spent the night on the armchair beside it, waking occasionally, to listen to her soft, steady breathing, gently touch her hair, and to reassure himself that she was here and she was safe.

It was nearly ten now. Sweetie trotted into the room and sat expectantly at his feet. He tossed her a treat, and she chewed noisily.

"Shh," he cautioned.

Grace turned on her side and sat up slowly. "Oh, stop tiptoeing around! I'm awake, and I'm fine." She patted the bed and Sweetie jumped up, did a quick circle, and then settled herself into a nest just under Grace's arm.

Wyatt dropped a kiss on Grace's forehead and sat down on the few inches of bed the little dog hadn't claimed.

"How's the head?"

"A little achey, but better than it felt last night." She glanced at the clock on the nightstand. "It's ten already! Why didn't you wake me?"

"You needed to sleep," he said. "And the EMTs told me you should take it easy for the next few days."

"But I don't need a babysitter. And you need to get to work. So move along, mister," she ordered.

He held four fingers in front of her face. "How many?"

"Four."

"How did you get hurt?"

She rolled her eyes.

"Humor me," Wyatt said. "I'm supposed to test your memory."

"I was in a speeding car driven by a maniac. We went off the road and into the bay. Things get a little blurry after we hit the water. I do know you pulled me out and saved my life."

"And then you promised to love me forever and be my sex slave," Wyatt prompted.

"That part I don't remember," Grace said.

He shrugged. "It was worth a shot."

Wyatt pulled a bottle of Tylenol from his pocket and gestured to the tea. "Drink that and take two of these. And then drink some more. You're supposed to stay quiet today. I've already walked Sweetie, and there's some cereal and fruit in the kitchen. I've got to get over to the park now, but your mom will be by after the lunch rush is over."

"Run along now," Grace said. "You're sweet, but I really don't need babysitting and I hate being fussed over."

"Humor me," he said. "I nearly lost you yesterday." He thumped his chest meaningfully. "I love you, Grace. Really, deeply, truly."

"I know it." She yawned and her eyelids drooped. "I think I love you, too. But I think I need another nap."

70

Grace slept. And then she slept some more. Despite her protests and much to her annoyance, Wyatt and Rochelle continued to cosset her.

After a week had gone by she'd had enough. When Wyatt showed up at the condo after work that Friday afternoon, he found her fully dressed, tapping away at her laptop at the dining room table.

"Hey you," he said, unsnapping Sweetie's leash and setting down the bag of take-out Chinese. "What's that?"

"My blog. I haven't written a word in nearly two weeks. I'm afraid my readers will think I'm dead."

He tried to read over her shoulder, but she shielded the screen with both hands. "It's not ready for public consumption yet. My writing has gotten sort of . . . rusty. I'll let you read it after I've cleaned it up and edited a little."

"Okay." He opened one of the white paper sacks. "Which do you want for dinner? Kung pao or sizzling shrimp?"

"Neither, thanks," Grace told him. "I've been stuck here for what feels like forever. Let's go out. I don't care where, just as long as I'm not staring at these four walls and eating Tylenol."

Wyatt nodded at the view out the French doors. "You're bored looking at the Gulf of Mexico?"

"I don't want to *look* at it anymore," Grace said. "I want to walk in it, splash in it, get wet, sweaty, sandy—anything but safe and sleepy, which is what I've been all week long."

"You're sure you feel like that?" Wyatt looked at her anxiously. "No headaches? Funny smells?"

"I am absolutely symptom-free and bored to tears. And I am truly grateful for all the loving care you and my mom have given me this week. I know you must have been neglecting Bo and your dad, not to mention work."

"We aren't exactly swamped at Jungle Jerry's this time of year," Wyatt said. "Yesterday we did exactly sixty-two dollars in admissions. Anyway, Dad understands, and Bo's just happy he's gotten to spend so much time with Sweetie. In fact, he sent you this."

Wyatt reached into the pocket of his shorts and handed her a carefully folded sheet of paper.

"Awww," Grace said softly. It was a crayon masterpiece, vividly rendered in black and orange and green and red, with spiky objects erupting from what looked like either a garbage can or a spaceship. Written in exuberant red letters across the bottom was a caption reading, "GRACE, GET BETTER SOON. Luv, Your Freind Bo."

"We're working on the spelling thing," Wyatt said. "But you'll notice he spelled your name correctly. And his, too."

Grace outlined the drawing with her fingertip. "I love it. What's it supposed to be?"

"Silly girl," he chided her. "That's a bouquet of red roses. He wanted to buy you some from the QuikTrip, but since they were plastic, which I assumed would offend your sensibilities, I suggested he draw you some instead."

"I'm going to have this framed and keep it forever. He really is the sweetest, most thoughtful boy."

"He gets that from me," Wyatt said modestly. "And lest the son outshine the father, I brought you a present from me, too." From the other pocket he produced her cell phone.

"My iPhone!" She touched the ON button and the screen lit up. "It works! How did you manage this?"

"The cops told me where Ashleigh's car was towed, and Tuesday morning, after I left you, I bribed, er, tipped the salvage guy twenty bucks to let me retrieve it."

"But it must have gotten wet. It was ruined."

"It did get wet. But I went online and read some stuff about how to save it. Turns out, if you don't turn the thing on, which I didn't, and just put it in a plastic bag full of uncooked rice and let it sit for a couple days, to let the rice absorb the moisture, there's a good chance it might still work."

Grace turned the phone over and over. "It's ridiculous how much I missed this thing. I've felt like I was in solitary confinement without it."

Wyatt looked a little guilty. "I actually powered it up yesterday. I couldn't help but notice, you had some missed calls. And some voice messages."

Grace scrolled down her call log. Lots of missed calls. One from Paula Talbott-Sinclair, one from Arthur Cater, some out-of-area numbers she didn't recognize—and three calls from Ben, and two voice mails. She gave Wyatt a questioning look.

"I didn't listen to any of them, I swear. Although I'll admit I was tempted. If you want to listen now, or call anybody, I can come back in a little while."

Part of her was tempted to send him away, to hunker down with the phone, catch up with the world—and find out why her soon-to-be ex had called her more times in the past week than he had in the previous three months. And then she glanced out the window, at the sun sparkling on the water, at a handful of late-afternoon beach strollers.

"It can wait," she said, tucking the phone into the pocket of her shorts. She whistled for Sweetie. "Let's go."

They picked up grouper sandwiches and a couple of $1.50 beers at the Rod and Reel Pier, eating them on the lower deck, watching the fishermen, and chatting about life. Sweetie sat expectantly at their feet, waiting for her share of their dinner.

"Betsy called me today to say a new judge has been assigned to my divorce," Wyatt told her. "Charlie Davis. She says he's fairly young but has a good reputation. And he's speedy. His nickname is Rocket Docket Davis. She thinks it'll only be a matter of weeks now."

"That's good," Grace said, trying to sound noncommittal. "Mitzi dropped by earlier today. She says we finally got the luck of the draw with Catherine Chandler. She's the senior judge—and what Mitzi calls a card-carrying feminist. She expects Dickie Murphree and Ben will squawk about it, but there's not a damned thing they can do about it." While she spoke, her hand hovered unconsciously over the pocket with her cell phone.

"Go ahead and listen to your messages and voice mails," Wyatt said. "I know the suspense is killing you. I'm gonna go back upstairs and get a slice of key lime pie. Text me when you're done, and we can go for that walk I promised."

"You sure?" Grace flashed him a grateful smile.

"Grace?" Arthur Cater seemed to be shouting into the phone. "Are you there? Listen, I had a visit from your, uh, husband. I guess he's still your husband? Anyway, he straightened me out on a couple of things, and afterward, the wife and I got to talking. She's got her heart set on you finishing up your work on the house on Mandevilla. The upshot is, we'd like to sell you the place if you're still interested. You better call me quick, though, before I list it with an agent."

"Yippee!" Heads turned as Grace stood and did a modified happy dance, right there in the middle of the Rod and Reel Pier.

She took a swallow of beer and hit the call-back button.

"That you, Grace?" Arthur was still shouting. "I was beginning to think maybe you'd found another project for yourself."

"Not at all, Arthur! My phone and I were out of commission for a few days, so I just now got your message. I would absolutely love to talk to you about buying Mandevilla." Her heart was racing—she was so excited—but she knew she had to ask the hard question. "Do you have any idea how much you'd want for it?"

"What I want and what I'll take are two different matters," he said, chuckling. He named his price, and Grace's pulse blipped and her mouth went dry.

"You still there?" he hollered.

"I'm here, Arthur. But you must know, the house is worth at least fifty thousand more than that."

"It's probably worth seventy-five thousand more than that," he corrected her. "But my accountant says if we make too big a profit, I'm gonna get screwed over at tax time. More importantly, my wife swears she'll nag me into the grave unless I see to it that you finish what you started with that little old cracker house."

"I really want to meet your wife, Arthur," Grace said.

"That can be arranged. So . . . what do you say?"

She chose her words carefully. "I want to say you've got a deal. Right now. But to be honest, my divorce settlement is still up in the air. We've got a new judge, though, and my lawyer thinks everything should be settled pretty soon."

"Fair enough. You call me when it's all settled, then, will you?"

"The minute I know something, I'll call. And thanks, Arthur. Really. Thanks."

Grace took another sip of her beer and stared out at the water. A school of fingerling mullet slashed just below the surface of the green water, and a couple of screeching gulls swooped in to pick off a few.

Arthur said Ben had paid him a visit. Whatever he'd told the old man, it had been enough to change his mind about selling her the house. She wondered if her own mostly idle threats to tell the police about J'Aimee's involvement in vandalizing the house had prompted the visit to Arthur.

She turned the phone over and over in her hand. Part of her was dying of curiosity, part of her dreaded hearing Ben's voice. There was only one way to find out what he wanted. She listened to the first voice mail he'd left—which had been Monday evening.

"Hey, uh, it's me. Give me a call."

Tuesday morning, he'd left another message.

"Okay, Grace, if you're trying to be coy, it's not working. Call me, okay? I've, uh, got a proposition for you."

A proposition? Did she even want to know? Yes. She did want to know exactly what Ben was up to. Without giving it much more thought, she touched the redial.

"Grace?" Ben sounded . . . different. "Listen, I didn't know about the accident. Your lawyer just called Dickie about getting together to finalize the settlement, and she mentioned you'd had a head injury. What a hell of a thing. Are you all right?"

"I am now. Are we finalizing a financial settlement? Is that the reason you called?"

"It's one of the reasons. Uh, there have been some changes around here, and I thought I should let you know about them. Before it's final and everything."

"Oh-kayyy," she said slowly. Where was this going? Why was he being so civil? Maybe he'd been hit on the head, too?

"First off, I'm getting ready to list the house and move," he said briskly. "Dickie informs me that the new judge will probably make me split the proceeds with you, so he says I have to let you know, in case you have any interest in buying out my half."

"You're moving? Where? Why?"

"It's time," he said. "I've had a job offer from a big-time agency in New York. They're opening a new media division, and it's too good an opportunity to pass up. But they want me up and running right after Labor Day, which doesn't give me a lot of time to sell the house and find a new place."

Her mind was racing. "What about the blog? What about J'Aimee? Will she move with you?"

There was a long stretch of dead silence on the other end of the phone.

"No. J'Aimee is not part of the new package," Ben said. "If you must know, she's gone. As for the blog, well, that was another reason for my reaching out to you."

"I see."

"If you've been following it, you probably noticed that our sponsorships were down, and the numbers had stagnated. I won't get into the reasons for that."

A smile played across Grace's lips. Of course Ben wouldn't get into the reasons why Gracenotes had tanked. It had tanked because it was Graceless. Not that she'd rub that in his face.

"I still think it's a good business model," Ben was saying. "For the right person. Somebody like you. Anyway, if you want it back, it's yours. I'll send you the new passwords and the contact info for the current advertisers. We can work out a payment schedule as we go."

Was that a compliment he was sneaking in under the radar?

"Where is all this going, Ben?" she asked.

"Shit." He sighed.

"Ben?"

"What? You want me to grovel? Beg for forgiveness? Not my style, Grace, and you know it."

"You sure know how to charm a girl," Grace said, her tone acidic.

He sighed. "Sorry. This isn't easy for me. A lot's happened, Grace. Do I regret what happened? Yeah. I do. J'Aimee was a mistake. Huge mistake. And I take responsibility for that. I'd like to think I'm a better man than that."

"You used to be a better man than that," Grace said quietly. "But there's a lot I regret, too. Drowning your car was not one of my finer moments."

He laughed. "Nor mine. But I guess I probably had it coming."

"So. Where does this leave us?" she asked.

"I guess you don't want to buy out my share of the house?"

She shuddered. The fact that Ben had just given her the closest thing to an apology she'd ever get from him didn't mean she ever intended to spend another night in the house where he'd betrayed her.

"No thanks."

"Didn't think so. I'll e-mail you the listing agreement. You can let me know if you think the asking price is realistic. I'd like to get out from under it as quickly as possible."

"Whatever you want," Grace said. "The faster it sells, the faster I can buy a house for myself."

"Yeah. About that. I went to see the old man over there on Mandevilla."

"Arthur. He told me. And he offered to sell it to me for a price I can't pass up."

"Good," Ben said gruffly. "You should have a house of your own. And that place suits you, Grace."

She was touched. "Thank you, Ben. That's the nicest thing you've said to me in a really long time."

"See? I'm not a jerk one hundred percent of the time."

"I know you're not."

"You might share that thought with Rochelle. She doesn't have a very high opinion of me."

"Mom? Have you talked to her recently?"

"Saw her today, as a matter of fact. After Dickie told me you'd been in an accident, I took flowers for you over to the Sandbox. She told me you weren't there, but she wouldn't say where you were staying. I'm guessing you've moved in with the new guy?"

Was that a note of jealousy she detected?

"No, I'm not living with Wyatt," she said.

"None of my business, but are things pretty serious between the two of you?"

She couldn't resist. "I'll answer that if you'll tell me what happened to J'Aimee. You said she's gone? Did she leave before or after you accepted the new job?"

"You first," Ben said.

"Yes, things are fairly serious between us. But his divorce isn't final yet, either, and he has a young son, and there are complications with his ex. All that aside, he's a great guy, and I think we have a future together. Now, you."

"Christ," he grumbled. "J'Aimee's moved to California. End of story."

"Nuh-uh, you don't get off that easy," Grace chided. "What's she doing in California?"

"Auditioning for some crazy reality show she read about on the Internet. Look, Grace, I gotta go."

"Not before you tell me what kind of a reality show," Grace said. "You owe me at least that much, Ben."

He mumbled something incoherent.

"What's that?"

He mumbled again.

"I can't make out what you're saying, Ben."

"It's called *Homewreckers.* Got that? I came home from golf last week and she'd packed her crap and loaded up her car and announced she was going to Hollywood to get a part in a reality show about women who sleep with married men. In other words, home wreckers."

Grace laughed so hard, she couldn't catch her breath.

"Glad you're amused," Ben groused.

"Sorry," she said, gasping for air. "Very sorry. Good-bye Ben."

Wyatt came back and shared his key lime pie with her, and it was so good, she made him buy her a second slice. Then they got in the truck and drove up the beach. They didn't discuss it, but Grace had a feeling she knew where they were headed.

He parked the car at Coquina Beach. "We're still not supposed to have a dog on this beach," Grace pointed out, nodding at Sweetie, who was perched in her lap.

Wyatt opened his door and then came around and opened hers. "I won't tell if you won't tell."

They left their shoes on the soft carpet of pine needles and walked down to the water's edge. Grace stood still and let her toes sink into the pale gray sand. She looked down at the warm water swirling around her ankles, at the foam frosting the waves as they lapped at the shore. A lifetime ago, she'd felt a suffocating panic, strapped into Ashleigh's car, with the water rising around her knees. Now, with Wyatt's hand clasped in hers, she felt as light as the gull's feather that floated past.

She inhaled and exhaled. "This is good. This is what I needed."

They walked for nearly an hour, until the brilliant orange sun hovered just above the tops of the Australian pines. Then they found a picnic bench and settled in to watch the show.

"I talked to Ben," she said, with Wyatt's arm thrown casually around her shoulders.

"Oh?"

"He's ready to settle. I think his lawyer saw the handwriting on the wall. Anyway, it turns out he's accepted a new job in New York. He's moving immediately, and he wanted to know if I wanted to buy out his share of the house."

"The mansion?"

"Whatever. There's nothing there for me now."

"Is the girlfriend going with him?"

"No. She's gone to seek her fame and fortune in Hollywood. Ben didn't sound too heartbroken about it. In fact, I think he was relieved."

Wyatt turned to look at her. "How about you? Are you relieved? To have her out of the picture?"

She shrugged. "Funny you should ask. I find myself curiously apathetic about J'Aimee. Guess I've let go of the anger. I wonder what Paula would say about that."

"I think she'd say you've had a growth moment," Wyatt said, making two-fingered quote marks in the air.

"Maybe I have," Grace mused. "I'll have to write about that in my journal." She reached over and laced her fingers through his. "How 'bout you? Had any growth moments of your own lately?"

"As a matter of fact, I have. A couple of them, actually."

"Wanna share?" She kept her tone light.

"Dad and I had some long talks this week. Turns out, he's not opposed to my selling Jungle Jerry's to the state for a park."

"Really? So . . . it's a done deal?"

"We're dealing with the state of Florida, Grace. Everything works at a snail's pace with them. But it turns out they've got some kind of federal grant to develop what they call urban parklands. Smaller parks, under fifty acres, like ours, where the emphasis will be on community education rather than recreation. We'd keep the original gardens, get rid of the old playground equipment, and, in its place, develop demonstration gardens for heirloom Florida fruits, vegetables, and flowers. The guy with the state seems to think there's a good chance I'd be offered the job as park superintendent, or whatever they call them these days."

"That's great, Wyatt!" she said, beaming. "It sounds perfect for you."

"I know. If I had to write my dream-job description, this would be it."

Sweetie perked up her ears and gave a low growl. They both looked up and saw an elderly man inching slowly down the beach toward them. He was shirtless and his sun-browned skin gleamed in the dying sunlight. Baggy black shorts hung from his hips to just above mahogany-colored knobby knees. Below these he wore what looked like white surgical stockings and thick-soled black rubber sandals. He didn't appear to see or hear them—or Sweetie.

The old man wore a pair of enormous earphones connected to an unwieldy metal detector, and his eyes were glued to the sand as he waved the detector's wand back and forth over a three-foot-wide swath of sand.

Grace nodded in his direction. "You think he ever finds anything valuable? From the looks of him, he must spend hours and hours with that thing."

"He probably finds lots of bottle caps and pennies. Maybe the occasional set of keys or a piece of jewelry. Probably just enough to keep him in gas and beer," Wyatt said.

"But he never gives up. And he walks for miles. I've seen him every day this week, on the beach outside Mitzi's condo. I guess it gives him something to do," Grace said.

"You said you had a couple growth moments this week?" Grace asked idly, her eyes following the treasure seeker's progress. "What was the other one?"

"Mm-hmm," Wyatt said. He rested his lips briefly against her right temple. "Callie showed up at the park again yesterday, begging me to give her a job. And another chance."

Grace half stood and tried to pull away, but Wyatt gently tugged her back down beside him.

"I told her no," he said, placing his hand on her cheek. "Hell, no. What you said just now—that there's nothing there for you—back at your old house, with Ben. That's how it is with me and Callie. I wish her well, for Bo's sake, but that's it."

"You're sure?" Grace held her breath.

"Never surer," Wyatt said. "It's you and me now, kid, if you'll have me." Slowly, he slid off the thick gold band on his left ring finger. He stood up, cocked his throwing arm back, and made his pitch.

"This is me, letting go," he said.

The wedding band spiraled and looped, the dull gold catching glints of the fading sunlight. It landed fifty feet away, in the soft sand, maybe twenty yards in front of the old man, who seemed not to see it.

"Good arm, huh?" Wyatt said, admiring his own prowess.

Grace wrapped her arms around his neck and kissed her approval. "Good arm, good man," she murmured. "Good everything."

Epilogue

True Grace, Feb. 14

The old rules of etiquette for second marriages were stern and absolute. In her starchy 1957 Complete Book of Etiquette: A Guide to Gracious Living, *Amy Vanderbilt opined that the second-time ceremony must be small, and that the "mature" bride should never wear white or a veil, or, heaven forbid, expect wedding gifts. She cautioned, too, that many ministers would actually refuse to perform a second wedding in a church! Invitations should not be engraved, as with a formal first wedding, but a handwritten note would be acceptable.*

Thankfully, wedding rules these days have been relaxed, or sometimes, totally discarded. Although I'm a traditionalist at heart, for our own second wedding, my intended and I wanted something intimate and meaningful, with just a few close friends and family members.

We actually didn't tell our guests that they were coming to a wedding at all. Instead, we invited them to what we simply billed as a garden party. Of course, we have the good fortune to have access to one of the most beautiful settings I can imagine, Wyatt's family's small but charming botanical park, here on Florida's Gulf Coast.

The party was to be the last private family party at Jungle Jerry's, an old-timey Florida tourist attraction founded by Wyatt's grandparents shortly after World War II, before the park is turned over to the state of Florida.

Our guests arrived at the park's front gate at dusk and were ferried to the party site by golf carts. When they reached the small enclosed butterfly garden, they were greeted with glasses of pink champagne, iced tea, or locally brewed beer.

Wyatt and I mingled with our guests and enjoyed the food he and I prepared together from local farms and fishermen—stone crab "martinis," chilled shrimp and avocado gazpacho, and crab beignets with pineapple-mango salsa. All the food was set out on rustic wooden picnic tables that were hand-built years ago by Wyatt's grandfather, with centerpieces of hibiscus, lilies, orchids, and other flowers picked right from the gardens.

Shortly before sunset, a small string quartet arrived and began to play classical music. At that point, we invited everybody to be seated in a semicircle of battered vintage lawn chairs and proceeded to the surprise event of the evening—our wedding!

The minister, a family friend who happens to be a regular at my mother's bar, stepped in front of a weathered wooden trellis, which was lit by hundreds of tiny white fairy lights and blooming with pale pink New Dawn roses.

When the wedding march started, I joined Wyatt in front of the makeshift altar.

Amy Vanderbilt says that for a second-time-around wedding, the attendants should be limited to one each for the bride and groom and should be the bride and groom's age. But, since Amy's long gone, we broke the rules—just a little.

The bride (that's me!) wore a 1960s vintage lace-over-silk minidress dyed the same exact hue as the roses. My bouquet was one made for me by Wyatt, from flowers he grew at the park, including hot-pink lilies, deep-violet hydrangeas, and my favorites—heavenly white gardenias. No other flowers were necessary, since the scent of the orange blossoms from the citrus gardens blanketed the late-afternoon air.

I promised Wyatt I wouldn't ask him to get too dressed up, so he chose his own khaki slacks, a nice white dress shirt—and in a major concession to the importance of the occasion, a navy blue blazer, which he promptly ditched right after the ceremony. He also wore a boutonniere—of rosemary and white phlox clipped from the garden at our tiny newly restored cottage.

Since my own father is deceased, Wyatt's dad, Nelson, agreed to give me away. Wyatt chose his six-year-old son Bo as his best man. Nelson wore his best (and only) good gray suit, and Bo was heartbreakingly adorable in his own khakis and blue blazer.

I'd begged my mother to be my maid of honor, but she gracefully declined with the excuse that she didn't want anybody to mistake her for a maiden. As if!

Instead, my friend Camryn agreed to be my attendant. Camryn loves fashion, so she wore a chic one-shouldered deep-violet silk dress by a designer so trendy I'd never heard of her. And spike heels—Camryn says she feels barefoot unless she's wearing at least four-inch heels—even during a garden wedding in February.

Amy Vanderbilt probably never considered the idea of including a pet in a wedding party, but since our little rescue dog, Sweetie, is such an important part of our blended family, she had to have a role in our big day. Bo was proud and happy to walk her down the aisle, although he did state loudly that he thought the pink tulle ruffle I fastened around her neck was "disgusting."

After we said our vows, my mother revealed her masterpiece—a three-tiered lemon pound cake with strawberry cream cheese frosting—topped with an ingenious bride and groom crafted by Bo—from Legos.

We cut the cake, had some toasts, and, when it got dark and chilly, we all repaired to the after party at the Sandbox, my mother's bar in nearby Cortez.

I don't know what Amy Vanderbilt would have thought of our second-time-around wedding, but I know, for us, it was definitely an affair to remember.

Grace was rushing around the bar, greeting guests, when she spotted a newcomer out of the corner of her eye. She threw her arms around the woman.

"Suzanne! You came back. I'm so happy to see you."

"There's no way I would have missed your garden party—and then to sneak in a wedding, well, what can I say? It was beautiful, unexpected, and so romantic, Grace. Like something out of a fairy tale."

"Thanks," Grace said, beaming. She gestured to the willowy young woman at Suzanne's side. "And this must be Darby."

"It is. Darby, meet our beautiful, blushing bride, Grace."

Wyatt wandered up and wrapped an arm around Suzanne's and Grace's waists. "And don't forget the blushing bridegroom."

Darby was a slender brunette, two inches taller than her mother, but with the same striking olive-green eyes. "Congratulations," she said shyly. "Mom's told me all about you, and the rest of the group."

"Look who's here," Camryn shrieked, enveloping Suzanne in a hug before standing back to critique her appearance. "You look amazing," Camryn said. "How's life in North Carolina? And the new job?"

"It's good," Suzanne said. "I'm slowly getting used to winter. And snow! I had to actually go out and buy a wool coat and boots. The job is good." She glanced at Darby, who'd drifted off and was chatting with Camryn's daughter, Jana. "Elon is a good fit. For both of us."

Camryn leaned in, her eyes dancing with a mischevious glint. "And what about men? Are you getting any action?"

Suzanne blushed violently. "I've actually had a couple real dates. The men's soccer coach. He's a good bit younger, but . . ."

"Ooh, Suzanne. You're a cougar!" Camryn linked her arm through Suzanne's and Grace's. "Look at us now, y'all. Grace and Wyatt married. Suzanne moved off and prowling around up there in North Carolina . . ."

"What about you?" Suzanne asked. "Grace says you left News Four You."

"I sure did," Camryn said. "There was a senior producer's slot open, but I got passed over, so I up and left. I'm producing the six o'clock news at channel two. The money's not quite as good, but I get to sleep in for the first time in twenty years. And I sub-in on camera when somebody's out sick or on vacation."

"Men?" Suzanne raised a quizzical eyebrow.

"I was seeing somebody, but it didn't work out," Camryn said. "That's one thing I learned from my divorce. If it's not right, it's not right. Cut your losses and move on."

"Has anybody heard from Ashleigh?" Suzanne asked, looking around the room.

"Oh, sure," Camryn said. "You can't keep that girl down. She did some work-release thing as part of her sentence for trying to kill her ex's baby mama. She's working for another plastic surgeon and living down in Naples. She has to wear one of those electronic-monitoring bracelet things, which she hates, 'cuz she says it makes her ankles look fat, so she has to wear pants and can't show off her legs anymore."

"Ashleigh would have been here today, except the idea of being around all the party stuff—you know, with liquor and everything, made her a little anxious," Grace said. "She's been clean and sober for six months now."

"Really?" Suzanne looked taken aback. "I mean, you two are on speaking terms? After everything that happened?"

"Grace has a much more forgiving heart than I do," Wyatt said. "I'm good with Ashleigh now, although Grace is banned from ever getting in a car with her again."

Grace laughed. "She's changed a lot since that day. I think it was a turning point for her."

"You'll never guess who Ashleigh's AA sponsor was," Camryn said.

"Who?" Suzanne was still scanning the room, looking for familiar faces.

"None other than Paula Talbott-Sinclair," Camryn said.

"I wondered what happened to Paula," Suzanne admitted. "I know you all might disagree, but I really think she did eventually help all of us in our group."

Wyatt pulled Grace into his arms. "I, for one, am eternally grateful to Paula. Without her, I might never have met the love of my life."

Grace rewarded her new husband with a kiss, then looked at her friends. "He's a sweet-talking fool, but he's right about Paula. If she did nothing else, she brought us all together, at the lowest point in our lives, and forced us to look at our attitudes and expectations about love."

"Don't forget what we did for *her*," Camryn chimed in. "She might still be mixed up with that parasite Cedric Stackpole if we hadn't exposed him for the scum-sucking dog he really is. I bet she never would have had the nerve to rat him out to the state if it hadn't been for us. And she damn sure wouldn't have been able to reinvent herself like she has without me."

"Paula reinvented herself?" Suzanne looked puzzled. "How? And what did you have to do with that?"

"Paula is now a certified laughter coach," Camryn said. "She works with people dealing with depression, terminal illness, and severe emotional problems. I did a feature story on her before I left News Four, and now she's got her own syndicated radio show."

"Any news about dear old Stackpole?" Suzanne asked.

"He's actually been in the news a good bit recently," Grace said, not bothering to suppress her glee. "The feds raided his new law office and seized all his tax records. My lawyer says the IRS is going after him big-time for falsifying tax records and tax evasion, among other things."

"That's one story I would have loved to have been in on," Camryn said. "What I wouldn't give to stick a live microphone in his sorry face."

"Just his face?" Wyatt asked. "And don't forget, Stackpole still has to deal with the lawsuit filed by that guy who filmed his wife and girlfriend's hair-pulling match in Sarasota. Couldn't happen to a nicer guy, huh?"

As they chatted and caught up on each other's lives, music began to filter into the room. Chairs scraped against the wooden floor as they were cleared out of the way, and guests began to edge onto the makeshift dance floor.

"You hired a DJ?" Suzanne asked, looking around the room.

"Better," Rochelle said, joining the group. "When Grace was making me clean up the place, I finally got rid of Butch's old Ms. Pac-Man game. It was broken, and I couldn't get anybody to fix it. Instead, I found an old jukebox at the flea market and had it restored. I put in all the records he and I used to dance to."

"And even some music from the last half century," Wyatt teased.

Grace tugged at his arm. "Okay, enough talk, mister. This is our wedding night, and you are going to dance with me, and that's final."

"Gladly," Wyatt said, leading her into the middle of the cramped floor.

Suzanne looked at Camryn. "Dance?"

"Damn straight," Camryn said. "But just so you know, I always lead."

The party was still in full swing at ten o'clock, when the two grizzled barflies known as Miller and Bud approached the Sandbox door. Miller pushed on the door, but it didn't move.

"Hey," he said, puzzled. "The lights are on, but it's locked. What's up with that?"

Bud pointed to a small hand-lettered note taped to the door.

CLOSED DUE TO PRIVATE PARTY

"They can't do that to us," Miller protested. "It's Sunday night. We always watch the games on Sundays."

Bud pressed his bulbous pink nose against the glass door and peered inside. "Man! They got all kind of food on the tables, and balloons and decorations and shit, and some kind of fancy pink drinks in martini glasses."

Miller shoved him aside and took a gander for himself. "They're dancing!" He turned to Bud in astonishment. "They're actually dancing in there." He frowned. "I see a couple guys—there's an old dude in a suit, and a younger guy dancing with Rochelle's daughter, and some little kid—hey, the kid is dancing with Rochelle."

"Lemme see." Bud elbowed him out of the way. He looked disgusted. "It's mostly women in there. And they're not even watching the game."

"Must be a ladies' night thing," Miller concluded sadly as he turned away from the door. "Looks like we're gonna have to find ourselves someplace new, Bud."

Acknowledgments

Gale H. Moore of Largo, Florida, and Jean Higham of St. Petersburg, Florida, as well as Beth Fleishman of Raleigh, North Carolina, gave me good legal advice for the research for this book—but in the interest of fiction and plotting, I kept some of what they gave me and made up my own rules of law where needed, so don't blame them if you don't think my plot is plausible! Many women were generous with tales of their own divorce wars, but Martha Woodham and Melita Easters was especially gracious with their time. On the homefront, Grace Quinn was as essential and good-natured as always—in the face of looming disasters and tax deadlines. The women of Weymouth—where this book was initially conceived and eventually delivered, were amazing, and I owe them all—Alexandra Sokoloff, Bren Witchger, Diane Chamberlain, Katy Munger, Margaret Maron, and Sarah Shaber, a huge debt of gratitude. Thanks also to the amazing team at St. Martin's Press, including but not limited to Sally Richardson and Matthew Shear, my fabulous editor Jennifer Enderlin, publicist John Karle, and many more, including Michael Storrings, who always gives me such a delicious book jacket. Meg Walker at Tandem Literary gets huge thanks for her marketing genius and great Facebook advice. I am so blessed to have the best damn literary agent in the business—Stuart Krichevsky, and to him and the folks at SKLA, including Shana and Ross, I send hugs and kisses—and virtual pound cakes. Lastly but never last, the biggest thanks go to my family,

Tom, Katie and Mark, Andy, Molly and Griffin, who make everything possible. I may write about divorce and heartache, but in real life, my champion, my hero, my best friend, Mr. MKA, aka Tom Trocheck, is the inspiration for every good guy in every book.

Save the Date

This book is dedicated with love
to Tom, my starter husband, lover, partner,
and best friend, who truly did save the date this time around.

Acknowledgments

The author wishes to thank the fabulous Meg Reggie of Meg Reggie PR in Atlanta for accidentally giving me the idea for *Save the Date,* as well as for throwing a damn good launch party. Also thanks to Julie Driscoll of Garden on The Square in Savannah, for allowing me to hang out and ask dumb questions. Genius wedding stylist Elizabeth Demos of Savannah answered every question I threw at her, and offered amazingly good plot twists. Tybee Island and Savannah friends Susan Kelleher, Diane Kaufman, Carolyn Stillwell, and Polly Powers Stramm made great sounding boards.

The members of the Weymouth Seven writers group: Alex Sokoloff, Brenda Witchger, Diane Chamberlain, Margaret Maron, Katy Munger, and Sarah Shaber were, as always, invaluable midwives who helped me deliver this baby.

The professionalism, encouragement, and tender loving care given to me and my work by my agent, Stuart Krichevsky, and the team at SKLA, Shana Cohen and Ross Harris, mean more to me than I can say. I am so very blessed to have them along for the ride! And speaking of teams, Meghan Walker of Tandem Literary and Jennifer Romanello are the world's best and most talented at marketing and public relations.

Huge thanks, as always, go to the entire St. Martin's Press gang, but especially to wonder-editor-adviser-lifesaver Jennifer Enderlin, whose patience and wise counsel helped shape and complete this book. Thanks, too, to publisher Sally Richardson and the rest of the Flatiron Building team, including but not limited to John Karle, Matt Baldacci, Jeanne-Marie Hudson, AnneMarie Tallberg, Jeff Dodes, Stephanie Davis, and Michael Storrings, who gave me another great cover.

My family keeps me grounded and sane—and feeling loved. Thanks and love to the home team, Tom, Katie, Mark, and Andy—and my precious babies Molly and Griffin.

Last but certainly not least, thanks to you, dear readers—wherever you are—for allowing my childhood dream of becoming a writer to come true.

1

Something was off. Cara Kryzik was no psychic, but the minute her bare feet hit the floor that morning, she sensed it.

She sniffed the air apprehensively and was met with the sweet perfume from the tiny nosegay of gardenias—her favorites—that she'd placed in a sterling bud vase on her dresser the night before.

Had she overslept? No. The big bells of St. John the Baptist cathedral were ringing the eight-o'clock hour as she descended the stairs from her apartment to her shop one floor below.

Cara shuffled down the narrow hallway to the front of the darkened flower shop. She flicked on the wall switch, and the multitude of thrift-shop chandeliers she'd hung at varying heights from the tall-ceilinged room twinkled to light, their images reflecting from all the mirrors staged around the space. It was a small room, but she thought the chandeliers and mirrors expanded the space visually.

See? She scoffed at her own foolish sense of foreboding. All was well.

She pulled up the shades over the front windows and smiled. It was a bright, sunny Friday morning, and within seconds, her puppy, Poppy, had her nose pressed against the glass-paneled front door, watching a pair of squirrels scamper past on the sidewalk outside on Jones Street.

The message-waiting light was blinking on the shop's answering machine. She gave the machine a fond pat. Business had been slow. But it was May. Mother's Day was next Sunday, it was prom season, and wedding season, too. Things were already picking up.

And then? She felt a single bead of perspiration trickle down her back. She frowned. Why was it so hot in the shop? Even for Savannah the room seemed stuffy and overheated. Cara went to the thermostat on the wall and squinted, trying to see the reading.

She'd turned the thermostat up before bed last night, just to 81, hoping to save a little on her always spiraling electricity bill. The air-conditioning unit was temperamental at best, and her landlord was never prompt when it came to making repairs. She had a string of appointments in the shop today, and it wouldn't do to have brides and their mamas stewing in their own juices.

She fiddled with the control for a moment, holding her breath, waiting to hear the compressor click to life. When it did, she exhaled. *See? All is well.*

Before she could sit down to check her emails, the shop phone rang.

She'd known who the caller would be. "Good morning, Lillian," Cara chirped. "How's our bride today? Is she getting jittery?"

"She's still asleep, thank God," Lillian Fanning said. Never one to waste time on pleasantries, Lillian got right down to business. "Listen, Cara, I've been thinking. I know we said white candles for the altar, but with an early-evening wedding, I really believe ivory or ecru would be much more effective."

Cara crossed her eyes in exasperation. She'd already special-ordered two dozen hand-dipped organic soy *white* candles for Torie Fanning's wedding tomorrow. But it was useless to tell the mother of the bride that it was impossible to get the candles in a different color at this late date.

She heard the bell on the front door jingle and looked up to see her assistant, Bert, let himself in, a large coffee in one hand and his bicycle helmet in the other.

"Lillian Fanning?" He mouthed the words, and Cara nodded. For the past two weeks, Lillian had called Bloom at least twice a day, every day.

"I'll see what I can do," Cara said, being deliberately vague.

"Ecru or ivory, *not* white," Lillian repeated.

Cara sighed. "Of course."

"What about the flowers? Did everything get delivered? And you've got Torie's grandmother's epergne polished for the bride's table?"

"Everything is absolutely under control," Cara assured Lillian. "I've got all the bridesmaids' bouquets finished, and I'll start on Torie's this afternoon, so it will be absolutely the freshest possible. And Lillian? I have to say the two of you have made the most exquisite flower choices I've ever seen in this town."

"I should hope so, for what this wedding is costing us," Lillian Fanning said. "I'll see you at the church tomorrow."

Cara hung up and stuck out her tongue at the phone.

"Is it hot in here, or is it just me?" Bert asked, standing in front of the thermostat and fanning himself with an envelope he grabbed off a stack of bills on her desk.

"I turned it up last night before I went to bed, but I think it's starting to cool down now," Cara said.

"Well, I'm roasting," Bert declared. He looked at her closely. "You're not having chills again, are you?"

"No! I'm fine. I took the last of those darned antibiotics on Tuesday. I can't afford to get sick ever again."

Cara took Bert's hand and placed it on her own forehead. "See? Cool as a cucumber. No fever, no temp, no problem."

But Bert wasn't paying attention. He was staring at the glass door of their flower cooler. Even through the door, beaded as it was with condensation, it was a grim sight.

"Uh-oh."

Cara flung the door of the cooler open. "Oh, God."

She couldn't believe her eyes. All the flowers in all the buckets in the cooler were limp, dead, dying. Torie Fanning's bridesmaids' bouquets, so carefully wrapped in their silk-satin binding, were toast. She glanced at the thermometer hanging from the top shelf and felt like weeping. It had been at 35 degrees last night, before she'd gone upstairs. But now it was at 86.

She let the door close and pressed her face against the glass. The reassuring hum of the compressor motor was silent.

"The cooler is dead," she said. "And so are the flowers. The motor must have conked out sometime overnight."

Bert reached for the Rolodex on the desk. "I'll call the repairman. Didn't he just fix this thing like six weeks ago?"

Cara nodded glumly. "He did. To the tune of three hundred dollars. But he warned me then, he didn't know how long it would keep running. When I opened the shop I bought it off a guy whose pizza place had gone out of business. Turns out this thing is so old, you can't find new parts for it. My guy had to jerry-rig it with secondhand parts he had lying around his shop."

"What are we gonna do?"

Cara closed her eyes, hoping for inspiration. "I have no idea. All I know is, Lillian Fanning will shit a brick if she finds out about this. You heard me, I just promised her we had everything under control. The most demanding bride I've ever worked with—and this had to happen today."

She opened the cooler door again and grabbed the nearest bucket. Three dozen long-stemmed white iceberg roses were crammed into it, and their heads drooped like so many sleepy toddlers.

"Dead." She dropped a handful of roses into the trash and reached for the next bucket, and the next, repeating the diagnosis—and throwing them away.

When she was done, the big plastic trash bin was full and all that was left on the counter was one bucketful of leatherleaf ferns—"You can't kill these things, even if you tried," Cara noted—and a raggedy assortment of single blossoms that had somehow managed to survive.

Bert grabbed one of the pale blue mophead hydrangea blossoms and with his secateurs snipped off the end of the stem. He turned on the faucet in the worktable sink, let the water heat up, then filled an empty bucket with hot water. He plunged the first hydrangea in, and reached for another.

"We can save these," he said. "I'll reprocess all of them, strip the leaves, trim the stems. Put some Floralife in the water. They're not all a total loss. I bet they'll perk right back up."

Cara kicked at the trash can with the toe of her sandal, wincing in pain as soon as she'd done it. "That's twelve thousand dollars' worth of flowers, gone. Even if we save some of them, there's no way we can even put together a boutonniere out of this mess, let alone enough flowers for Torie, eight bridesmaids, and all the flowers for the church and the reception. And it's too late to get more flowers shipped from California in time for tomorrow."

Bert looked around the room, as though a new shipment of flowers might magically appear from thin air.

"What about the wholesale house? Can't you call them? Or we could run over there and see what they've got."

"Breitmueller's? On a Friday morning in May? With all the weddings and proms going on around town? They'll be picked clean by now. Anyway, they don't carry the kinds of flowers we promised Torie. Lilies of the valley? Ranunculus? Casablanca lilies? Peonies? "

"What about Lamar?" Bert asked. "I know we usually see him on Thursdays, but maybe, if you called and told him what happened . . ."

Cara blinked back tears. "Lamar's clear up in Atlanta, Bert. He's not gonna come all the way down here just to save my bacon. . . ."

Bert pointed at the phone. "C'mon, Cara. That old man loves you. He might make a special trip, if you explained what was at stake."

Cara shrugged and reached for her Rolodex. But before she could flip to Lamar's card, the shop phone rang.

She picked up the phone and looked at the caller ID, and her hand froze. The area code was one she knew by heart: 614 for Columbus, Ohio. And, of course, the caller was one she knew all too well, too.

She should let the call roll over to voicemail. Ignore it. He'd only call back, and keep calling until she picked up. Her day couldn't get much worse now. So why put off the inevitable?

Cara swallowed hard and tapped the receive button.

"Hi, Dad."

. . .

"Cara? Are you all right?" Her father's voice boomed so loudly she had to hold the phone several inches from her ear. Lieutenant Colonel Paul Kryzik's idea of a whisper was more like a shout to most people.

"Fine, Dad. How are you?"

Cara felt a knot forming in the pit of her stomach. She knew exactly why the Colonel was calling; had, in fact, been expecting this call for weeks now.

"Look, Dad, I know I'm kinda late with my payment..."

"I haven't had a phone call, much less a check from you, in three months now," he said. "What's going on down there?"

She swallowed hard. "We're just coming into my busiest season. Remember, I told you that? I've got a spring and summer full of weddings booked. But I've had all kinds of expenses. Buying the van, getting my website designed, finishing out the shop and buying equipment..."

"Our agreement was that you'd start making payments on the loan in February. You should have had plenty of money from Valentine's Day business, right?"

She felt a stabbing pain between her eyes. "We actually had a pretty good Valentine's Day. But all the profits went back into the shop. My computer died, and I had to buy a new one..."

"Not my problem," her father shot back. "If you'd prepared a detailed business plan, as I'd suggested, you could have anticipated that a five-year-old computer would need to be replaced. It's called a contingency plan. These things are a cost of doing business, Cara."

"I know, but..."

"If you've got business coming into the shop, I'd think you'd be in a position to start repaying at least the interest on your loan," he went on.

"Dad, if you'd just let me explain," Cara started.

But the Colonel wasn't interested in explanations. Not from her.

"I should have known something like this would happen. It's never a good idea to loan money to family, especially since you didn't even have a sound business plan for this shop of yours."

"That's not true," Cara said sharply. "I drew up a business plan. I did cost projections, market studies, I researched rent and utilities, I did everything I could. But how could I anticipate something like having to replace a computer? Or a deadbeat innkeeper who refuses to pay me for three months' worth of arrangements? Just this morning, I came downstairs, and my flower cooler had died. Along with twelve thousand dollars' worth of inventory I need for a wedding tomorrow. Some things are just out of my control, Dad. You of all people know that."

"Water under the bridge," he said, interrupting. "The fact is, if you can't even begin repaying the interest on a loan, after six months, your business has no hope of success. Even you can see that, right?"

"No! I can't see it. My business is building every week. We've got new clients, a few new commercial accounts. I just need a little more time to get things up and running. This wedding tomorrow, Dad? It's a ten-thousand-dollar deal." Cara hated the pleading note she heard creeping into her voice.

"For which you just admitted you don't have any flowers," the Colonel shot back. "Look, Cara. This just proves my point. You're a smart girl, and a hard worker, I'll give you that. But somebody like you has no business running a business. Take that innkeeper. You think I would have given three months of credit to a new account? Not on your life!"

Cara felt her left eye twitching, and her headache was taking on a new life of its own. She opened the drawer of her desk, found the bottle of aspirin, popped three into her mouth, and choked them down with a swallow of now-cold coffee.

She had to end this call before her head exploded.

"Dad? I'm sorry, but I really need to go now. We've got to replace those flowers I lost, and I've got another bride coming in for an appointment. I'll send you a check by the end of next week. Swear to God. And after that, I'll catch up. Monthly payments, just like we agreed. Okay?"

"No. Not okay," he said. "I know this is painful for you, Cara, but admit it, this florist thing of yours hasn't worked out. Just like your marriage. And frankly, I'm out of patience with pretending everything is okay. I'm not some ATM machine, you know. Two years from now, I'm retiring from the community college. I have to start thinking about my own welfare. Twenty thousand dollars is a lot of money at my age. I'm sorry, but I'm pulling the plug on this little enterprise of yours."

Cara's eyes widened, and her jaw dropped. "Pull the plug? What's that supposed to mean?"

"Just what it sounds like. It's over, Cara. No more stalling, no more excuses. I'm calling your loan. It's still the first week of May. Close up the shop. Call your landlord, let her know you're breaking your lease. Maybe if you give her plenty of advance notice, she'll prorate your rent."

"Break the lease?" Cara's mouth went dry. Her hands clutched the phone so hard her fingertips turned white. "Close the shop?"

From across the room, Bert, who'd given up any pretense of not listening in, looked as shocked as she felt.

"There's no reason for you to stay down there in Savannah any longer," her father continued, as though everything were settled, just like that, because he said so. "You've no ties, there, really. Leo's not taking you back, and anyway . . ."

"Leo?" Cara screeched. "Dad, I left Leo, not the other way around."

"A technicality," the Colonel said calmly. "Let's not split hairs. I think it would be better if you got a little place of your own. I could probably talk to somebody here at the school about a job, but if you think you still want to fool around with flowers, you can probably find something around town. . . ."

"Dad!" Cara shouted into the phone. "Stop. Just stop!"

"There's no need to scream, young lady," the Colonel said sternly. "I'm not deaf."

You might as well be, Cara thought. *You never hear a word I say. You never have. I'm thirty-six years old, as you dearly love to point out, and you've never really listened to me. Not in my whole life.*

"I can't discuss this right now," she managed.

There was an extended silence on the other end of the phone. And then a dial tone. Even when he wasn't speaking to her, the Colonel always managed to get in the last word. Or nonword.

Cara flung the phone onto the counter. The shop was quiet, except for the slow drip of the faucet in the sink. Bert tiptoed over, stood behind her, and placed his long, strong fingertips on her shoulders. Wordlessly, he began methodically kneading the knotted-up muscles. Poppy crept over, from her hiding place under the worktable, and tentatively placed her front paws on Cara's knees.

At least, she thought wryly, she now knew what was off. Everything. Everything was off. "I'm screwed," she whispered.

2

Cara bit her lip and did her best to blink back the tears of frustration that inevitably followed a conversation with her father. She looked over at the sad pile of flowers on the worktable. Without thinking, she reached for one of the few surviving roses. She clipped the stem end, then stripped off the remaining leaves, then added it to the hydrangeas rehydrating in the bucket.

She glanced around the shop. It was only three hundred square feet, but it was hers now. What was it the Colonel had called it? Her "little enterprise"? Not that he'd ever seen the shop. Her father had visited only once in the five years she'd been living in Savannah, and that had been shortly after she and Leo moved down from Ohio.

This was before she'd taken a job three years ago, answering the phone at Flowers by Norma. Her boss, a feisty octogenarian named Norma Poole, had been in business for thirty years. Norma's specialty was funeral and hospital flowers. Her arrangements were as tightly structured as her trademark bright orange bouffant hairdo. A cantankerous chain-smoker, Norma had nonetheless taken a shine to her young protégé, and before she knew it, Cara was not only delivering bouquets, she was actually creating them.

Not two and a half years ago, Norma had walked into the shop and plunked a set of keys onto the same worktable Cara was now using.

"Today's the day, Cara Mia," Norma said in that raspy voice of hers.

"What day is that, Norma?"

"My last day. Your first."

"Huh?" Cara gave the older woman a searching look.

"It's all yours," Norma said, gesturing expansively. "All three hundred square feet of it." She tapped her chest. "Just came from the doctor's office. He has some X-rays of my lungs that don't look so good."

"Oh, Norma!" Cara clutched the old lady's arm. "Is it . . . ?"

"Yup." Norma shrugged. "He wants me to do chemo, but I'm eighty-two, for cryin' out loud. I told him, 'No way, José.' My baby sister has a nice two-bedroom condo down in Sarasota." She smiled. "Always wanted to be able to say I was spending my last days wintering in Florida."

Cara swallowed hard. "Surely not your last days?"

"Close enough," Norma said cheerfully.

"I'm so, so sorry," Cara started. "What can I do? Help pack up the shop?"

"Why would you do that?" Norma asked. "I'm giving it to you, hon. Well, not the building. Bernice and Sylvia Bradley own that. But my lease has another year to run on it. It's October now, and the rent's paid up till January. All the equipment, and the inventory, such as it is, is paid for. And you're welcome to it, if you want the headache."

"Seriously?" Cara couldn't believe what she was hearing. She knew Norma liked her well enough—but to just give her this business?

Norma coughed for a moment, and sat down to catch her breath. "I don't have the energy to pack the place up. And it'd be a pain in the ass to try to hang around and sell everything. Not that it's worth all that much. The delivery van? The odometer quit at two hundred thousand miles, and it's a piece of crap, if you want the truth. But it's a paid-for piece of crap. If you want it, I'll get my lawyer to handle everything, get you the deed to the car, and we'll do a bill of sale for everything else."

"Uh, Norma?" She hated to broach the subject of money, but the fact was, she didn't have much money of her own. Leo handled all their finances, and he considered her job at Flowers by Norma as more of a hobby than a career.

Norma must have read her mind. "I was thinking a dollar. Would that work for you?"

"A dollar? Are you kidding? Norma, this business is worth thousands and thousands of dollars."

"And what would I do with that kind of money?" Norma's pale blue eyes peered over the rim of her sparkly-framed glasses. "The doctor says I'll be gone in a few months. My kid sister is the only family I've got left. She's fixed fine, got more dough than I ever thought about having."

"You could leave it to a charity."

"Charity!" Norma made a face and coughed again. "Charity begins at home," she said, when she'd caught her breath. "I don't have much, but I don't feel like giving what I do have to strangers." She tapped Cara's shoulder. "So. Looks like you're an instant heiress. Kind of."

Cara took a deep breath, and then another. Bert was hovering nearby, an anxious expression on his face.

"Everything okay?" he asked.

"Ask me later." She picked up the telephone and made the call she'd been about to make—right before the Colonel decided to ruin her week.

Lamar Boudreau was Cara's secret weapon. She'd met him at an industry trade show in Atlanta, not long after she'd transformed Norma's into Bloom. Every week Lamar drove his refrigerated van to a wholesale warehouse adjacent to the Atlanta airport, and filled his "bucket truck" with choice imported flowers in unusual colors and varieties not stocked by her Savannah wholesaler—tulips, lilies, gerbera daisies, freesias, and snapdragons from Holland; roses, delphiniums, and asters from Ecuador; and spray chrysanthemums and alstroemeria from Colombia. From there, he made deliveries to fewer than a dozen florists around the state.

Under normal circumstances, Lamar and his bucket truck arrived in Savannah on Wednesdays. As far as Cara knew, she was his only local customer, and she intended to keep it that way. These days most of her brides didn't want to settle for their mother's same-old carnations and sweetheart roses. They wanted the trendy flowers spotted in their favorite high-end glossy wedding magazines and, increasingly, on Pinterest. And that's where Lamar Boudreau came in.

"Lamar? It's Cara, in Savannah."

"How you doin', girl?"

"Not too good," she admitted. "My cooler conked out on me overnight, and most of those flowers you delivered Wednesday are DOA. I've got a huge wedding tomorrow. Can you help me out?"

"Aww, Cara," he moaned. "I can't be coming all the way back down there today. I got other customers besides you, ya know."

"I know, Lamar, but none you love as much as me."

From across the room Bert rolled his eyes.

"That's true," Lamar said, with a chuckle. "But don't you be telling my wife 'bout us."

"What about it? Pretty please? This is a big order, so I'll make it worth your while."

"You know how much gas my van burns up when I make a trip clear down there to the coast? Anyway, much as I wish I could help, I can't do it today."

"How far south are you coming?" Cara persisted.

"On my way to Macon next," Lamar said. "Last call of the day."

"Perfect! I'll meet you anyplace you say. I'm working with the pickiest bride on the planet, and her mother's even worse, so make sure you save the good stuff for me, okay?"

"Don't I always?" Lamar said. "I'll see you at the Cracker Barrel on Riverside Drive at two."

After tracking down the repairman and issuing dire threats about what would happen if he didn't return to the shop to get her cooler up and running again,

Cara sent Bert to the wholesale house to try to buy more stock, and spent the rest of the morning fielding phone calls and dealing with appointments and brides.

When Bert returned to Bloom at noon, Cara was waiting by the door. “I’m headed to Macon to meet Lamar,” she informed him. She glanced over at Poppy, who was lounging nearby, watching her every move. “Can you do me a favor and watch you-know-who? I’d take her with me, but you know she gets carsick after more than fifteen or twenty minutes, and I haven’t had enough advance time to give her the meds.”

“That’s cool,” Bert said easily.

“And if Lillian Fanning calls again, and she will call, lie through your teeth and tell her we’ve got her friggin’ ecru candles.”

“Got it,” he said.

3

After working all night on Torie Fanning's *second* set of wedding arrangements, by Saturday morning Cara was operating on Red Bull and desperation. She would have given anything for an hour of sleep. But this was May, and she'd sleep, she promised herself, when wedding season was over.

Right now, she had a ten-o'clock appointment. She took another covert sip of Red Bull and poured two flutes of orange juice, topping it off with Sam's Club champagne.

She set the silver tray down carefully on the big worktable in the shop and beamed at today's couple, Michelle and Hank.

"All right then, you two," she said, hoping she sounded cheerful. "Let's talk about your big day!"

Michelle pushed her iPad across the zinc top of the worktable. She poised one pink polished fingertip on the screen. "This is my board for the altar centerpieces. As you can see, I'm looking for something loose and relaxed, in the blue and purple range, with greenery that's a softer silver, gray. For the containers, I'd like big ironstone pitchers like these." She tapped one picture on the screen, then slid her fingertip across the screen.

"Now. Here's what I'm thinking for my bouquet and the bridesmaids. White tea roses, white Stargazer lilies, pale, pale yellow stephanotis. Hand-dyed ribbons in the colors of the girl's dresses."

She slid over to the next board. "These are the girl's dresses. I'm having ten attendants. I would have kept it at eight, but *his* mother"—she cut her eyes sideways at her fiancé, a budget analyst named Hank—"is having a cat fit and insisting I have his sisters—and I'm sorry, honey, but Geneva is clinically obese, and LeAnne has that unfortunate red hair, so I can't have anything pink. . . ."

She sighed heavily, then clasped her fiancé's hand and wrinkled her pert button nose. "You agree, don't you, Hank?"

Hank's hair was also what Cara thought of as an unfortunate shade of red, but he nodded agreement. "Geneva's thinking about gastric bypass. If she goes in this summer, I think we can count on her being a size sixteen by October. Anyway, pink does nothing for Michelle's coloring. So that's why we're thinking mostly blues, purples, some silver and gray for everything at the church."

"Right," Michelle agreed. "Then, at the reception, which will be in the Westin's ballroom, we'll segue into deeper, more dramatic colors."

"Show her the tablecloths," Hank urged. "Ombré! Michelle got an unbelievable deal on the fabric at this online store."

Michelle slid her fingertip and a new Pinterest board popped up. This one was labeled "Ideas for wedding receptions."

Cara Kryzik nodded and jotted down notes. "Got it. Blues, silvers, purples. No pink. Loose arrangements. Mostly white for the bridesmaids. Are we doing anything else at the church? Pew bows, anything like that? You did say it's at St. John's, right?"

"No pew bows," Hank said emphatically. "That's just so . . . nineties."

Michelle snapped the cover of the iPad. "So I guess that's it for now. You'll put together a mood board for me? And a proposal? By, say . . . Wednesday?"

"Wednesday will be fine," Cara said. She glanced at Bert, who'd also been taking notes throughout the two-hour meeting. "I'll email it, and then we can talk."

Bride and groom stood and left, holding hands.

The bells on the shop door jingled merrily as the couple left.

Cara rolled her eyes. "Cute couple. Controlling bride. Passive-aggressive groom. I give them three years, tops."

"Mmm-hmm," Bert said, still jotting down notes. "Less than that if she wises up and figures out she's married a raging homosexual."

Cara Kryzik raised one eyebrow. "You think?"

"Takes one to know one," Bert said.

May and June were always a blur for Bloom, but this year, Cara thought, might be the year that topped all years. If those talking-head economists wanted a real signal that the recession was over, they had only to look at her upcoming wedding calendar.

May was already manic, and it was just the first Saturday of the month. June would be even busier. Her calendar was full with showers, rehearsal dinners, and weddings.

But busy didn't necessarily mean profitable. If she could just avoid any more equipment-related disasters, she might, just might, be able to put together enough money to send the Colonel a big fat check by the end of the month.

This morning she'd delivered the centerpieces for a bridesmaids' brunch at nine, met with Michelle and Hank, and by one she was already behind schedule finishing up the flowers for the most demanding bride she'd ever worked with.

Cara wrapped a single white rose with green floral tape and inserted it into the already over-the-top centerpiece of white ranunculus, orange parrot tulips, and green and blue hydrangeas that were spilling out of an heirloom Georgian silver soup tureen destined for the buffet table.

"What do you think?" she asked, turning to her assistant.

Bert put down his scissors and gazed over the top of his wire-rimmed granny glasses at the towering arrangement.

"Baudy, gawdy, and fabulous," he decreed. "But you know our little bride Torie. More is always more with that girl."

"I know," Cara said with a sigh, selecting another flower from the dwindling bucket on the floor. "Half these flowers would be a showstopper, but I can't make Torie see that. She is determined to have the most ostentatious wedding in the history of Savannah. It's too bad we have to waste all this effort and beauty on a girl who doesn't know a pansy from a petunia."

"As though Torie Fanning would ever deign to sniff anything as incredibly middle-class as either a pansy or a petunia," Bert said.

The shop phone rang and Cara glanced over at the caller-ID screen. "Speaking of which, there's the smother of the bride now." Her hand hovered over the receiver. "I swear, if Lillian calls me with one more demand, I am going to go stark, raving bonkers."

"Think of the invoice we're going to present when this whole circus is over," Bert advised.

"No. I'm thinking of the look on the Colonel's face when he opens the envelope with his check," Cara corrected.

"Exactly," he said, nodding. "Just hold your nose and smile pretty."

The phone kept ringing.

"Brides!" Cara muttered. "If I ever even entertain the idea of getting married again, Bert, you are authorized to smack me upside the head and have me committed."

"Never say never," Bert warned.

"I'm serious," Cara said. She looked across the workroom. "Here Poppy," she called.

The curly-haired goldendoodle puppy raced over to her side and propped her front paws on Cara's knees. Cara bent down to let the puppy lick her chin. "Puppy love. That's all I need. No more men, and definitely no more weddings."

Bert pointed at the phone, which was still ringing. "Really. Don't you think you'd better get that?"

"I'm not answering," Cara said defiantly. She got up from her stool and stretched. "And I am not stuffing any more flowers in this centerpiece. The wedding is in less than five hours. We've got to get these arrangements loaded in the van and get them out to Isle of Hope before three. Whatever Lillian wants, it'll just have to . . ."

Before she could finish the sentence, they heard the tinkling of bells coming from the front of the shop. Poppy pricked up her ears and started toward the sound.

"Close the door!" Cara hollered. "Don't let the dog get . . ."

But it was too late. Sensing an opening, the seven-month-old goldendoodle, Poppy, streaked toward daylight.

"Grab her," Cara called to the startled stranger who's just entered Bloom. He paused for only a split second, pivoted, and lunged toward Poppy, managing to grab on to her collar. But Poppy, an obedience-school dropout who was as determined as she was undisciplined, easily wriggled out of the collar and was out the door in a flash, joyously running full-tilt down West Jones Street.

"Shit!" Cara cried.

"Not again," Bert echoed. "Not today."

"Sorry," the stranger said, turning from Cara to Bert, still holding the collar in his right hand. "I wanted to get some flowers sent to my sister in the hospital . . ."

"Can you help him?" Cara gave Bert a pleading look. "I'll go after Poppy. If I'm not back in fifteen minutes, start loading the van without me."

Cara sprinted out of Bloom without looking back.

"Poppy!" she called, cupping her hands over her mouth as a makeshift megaphone. "Poppy, come back!"

She passed the restored nineteenth-century town houses and elegant storefronts in her block, and dashed across Barnard Street, dodging cars as she ran.

Three tourists with cameras strung around their necks and unfolded street maps stood on the corner, arguing loudly about where to have lunch.

"No more barbecue," snapped a twenty-something girl in a tie-dyed shirt and white shorts.

"Did you see a dog run past just now?" Cara interrupted. "Curly white hair, maybe thirty pounds?"

"That way." The girl's middle-aged father pointed east. "She sure can run."

Cara continued east down Jones. She paused by the line of people still queued up for lunch outside Mrs. Wilkes' boardinghouse. "Did you see a dog run past here?" she asked breathlessly.

"Thataway," volunteered a bespectacled senior citizen with a plastic tour-company lanyard around her neck.

Cara ran on, crossing Whitaker, Bull, Drayton, and Abercorn. Her thin-soled sandals flapped against the steaming concrete sidewalks. Her face was sheened with sweat, her T-shirt glued to her chest.

"See a dog?" she asked, pausing beside a college kid locking his bike to a utility pole in front of a classroom building on the art-college campus.

"Huh?"

Twenty minutes had passed. But nobody else had spotted the puppy. Reluctantly, she started jogging back toward Bloom, breathing heavily and sweating profusely.

Bert had the van pulled around to the front of the shop by the time she got back. "Anything?"

"No," Cara said, near tears. "Look, just wait here. I'm going to take the van and see if I can spot her."

"Cara? Lillian has called back twice, and now Torie's started calling. And her wedding director wants to know why we aren't already out at the church. You know it'll take us thirty minutes to get out to Isle of Hope."

"Stall 'em," Cara said. "I can't let Poppy just wander around downtown. She'll get hit by one of those tour buses, or run over by one of the horse-drawn carriages. And even if somebody does find her, they won't know who she is, because she's not wearing her collar. Please, Bert?"

Bert shrugged and went back inside the shop to try to mollify their clients.

Cara drove east and north this time, trolling the side streets, leaning out the window of the pink-and-white-striped van, calling her puppy's name, straining for a familiar glimpse of curly white fur, but to no avail. While she cruised, her cell phone rang and pinged and buzzed, with incoming calls, texts, and emails, all of which she ignored.

She was backtracking toward the shop, turning up Habersham at East Charlton, when she saw a tall, bare-chested man dressed in nylon running shorts and expensive-looking running shoes, tugging a medium-sized, furry white dog by a piece of rope. He was walking down the lane behind Charlton.

"Poppy!" Cara cried. She veered left and into the lane.

"Hey!" she called to the man. She leaned out the open window of the van. "Excuse me, that's my dog."

He was in his mid thirties—the man, not the dog. His dark hair was pushed back from his forehead and his chest gleamed with perspiration. Even in her extreme distress, Cara noted that he was seriously ripped. The man glanced down at the puppy, then back up at Cara.

He frowned. "The hell it is. This is *my* dog."

"No." Cara put the van in park. "Honestly. That's Poppy. My goldendoodle."

"No," he said impatiently, starting to walk away. "This is Shaz. Unfortunately, this is *my* goldendoodle."

Cara climbed down out of the van and hurried after him. "That's impossible. There aren't that many dogs like this in Savannah. I had to go all the way to Atlanta to find mine. And that one *is* mine." She searched in the pocket of her shorts and held out one of the doggie treats she always carried. "Here Poppy."

The puppy looked up at Cara and wagged enthusiastically.

"Shaz!" the man said loudly. The puppy looked at him and wagged her tail even harder.

"See?"

"She does that with everybody," Cara said, desperation creeping into her voice. "She's never met a stranger."

"If she's yours, where's her dog tag?" the man demanded.

"Back at my flower shop, on West Jones. A customer came in, and he tried to grab Poppy as she made a break for the door, but Poppy managed to wriggle out of her collar." She waved the treat under the dog's nose. "Here Poppy," she coaxed. "Come to Mama."

The puppy's ears pricked up, and she lunged toward Cara, but the man pulled her back.

"See?" Cara said triumphantly. "That's Poppy."

"No," he said, wedging the now wriggling puppy firmly between his calves. "That's a cheap trick. And this is Shaz. She'd kill her grandma for a dog treat."

"If that's your dog, where's its collar?

"In my truck, back at my house. I was just taking her to the groomer, whom she hates, and the truck window was open, and she jumped out the window and took off. Come on, Shaz." He started walking away, and the puppy trotted obediently at his heels.

"Poppy," Cara called, near tears. "Come here, girl. Time to go home."

"Nice try," the man said, glancing back over his shoulder. "But I don't have time for this. Good luck finding your dog."

The puppy gave one backward look, but the man was jogging again, and the dog followed right on his heels.

Cara jumped back behind the wheel of the van. "Hey," she hollered out the open window. She beeped the horn. "Come back here."

The man jogged on down the lane, and she crept along right behind him, honking her horn every few minutes, and hollering out the window. "Stop! Come here, Poppy." She knew she looked like a lunatic, and she just didn't care.

Poppy, the little traitor, seemed quite content to follow along behind her new friend, never straying or yanking at the makeshift leash as she sometimes did when Cara took her for her morning walk.

Finally, they reached a block on Macon Street. The houses here were simpler than the grand brick and stucco townhomes farther west in the historic district. Mostly single-story wood-frame homes, they were known as freedman's cottages because they'd originally been built after the Civil War by newly emancipated slaves.

The runner paused in front of one of the least distinguished cottages on the block. Paint was peeling from the dingy white clapboards, a shutter at the window was missing several slats, and the faded aqua door seemed to be held together with duct tape. There was a wooden window box beneath the double window, but the plants were dried up and shriveled beyond recognition. The man propped his foot on the top step of the stoop and retrieved a key from a pocket in the tongue of his running shoe.

That's when he looked over and spotted Cara, parked at the curb, the van's motor idling.

"Beat it," he called.

She held her cell phone up for him to see. "Give me back my dog or I'll call the cops."

"Get away from my house or I'll call the cops myself," he retorted. He picked Poppy up in his arms and climbed the rest of the steps to the doorway. He unlocked the door. Cara jumped from the truck and ran for the minuscule porch, but he was too quick. He stepped inside and slammed the door in her face. A moment later, she heard a deadbolt lock slide into place.

"Dognapper!" Cara pounded on the door with her fist. "Give me back my dog!"

"Crazy stalker woman, go away," came the muffled reply.

She banged on the door, and looked around to ring the doorbell, but it was defunct, dangling by a single frayed wire from the dry-rotted doorframe.

Cara gave the door an ineffective kick, resulting only in a badly stubbed big toe.

"I'm calling the cops," she screamed, her lips plastered against the doorframe.

"I already called 'em," came back his voice.

She paced back and forth in front of the cottage, waiting for the police. Bert called, and she instructed him to load as many of the flowers as he could into his own car, and start ferrying them over to the church. Torie and Lillian Fanning called, too, but she let those calls go to voicemail.

While she paced, Cara studied the house, hoping the runner would somehow relent and release Poppy. The cottage was a puzzle. It sported a jaunty new-looking red tin roof, but there were cracks in the wavy glass of the front windows, and she could see that two or three of the clapboards were perilously close to falling off the house.

Cara called the police again. This time, a bored-sounding dispatcher informed her that the police had actual crimes to solve, and that an officer might not show up for another hour.

"But he's got my dog," Cara protested. "And he won't even open the door or listen to reason."

"Ma'am?" the dispatcher said. "Try to work it out like adults, why don't you?"

She disconnected and walked back over to the house. She climbed onto the front stoop and peered in through the dust-caked window. The room inside held a battered leather sofa and a flat-screen television squatting on a sheet of plywood stretched across sawhorses. The room was littered with stacks of lumber, tools, and paint buckets. There was no sign of Poppy. She would have cried, but she had a wedding to get to.

4

Did you find Poppy?" Bert asked, as she raced back into the shop.

"He's still got her locked up," Cara said. "And the police were no help at all." She was pulling her sweat-soaked T-shirt over her head as she raced for the back stairs to her second-floor apartment above the shop.

"Never mind," Bert called up after her. "I've already taken the altar arrangements, the pew bows and centerpieces out there. But we've still got the bouquets and boutonnieres and the buffet arrangements here, so hurry! I'll get the van loaded. After the wedding, I'll help you get Poppy back."

Ten minutes later, she was back downstairs, her still-damp butterscotch-colored hair pulled into a careless French knot, dressed in a floaty vintage flower-sprigged pink silk garden-party dress, and pink cowboy boots.

The ride out Skidaway Road to the Isle of Hope was a nail-biter, but they pulled up to the quaint, white wood-framed Methodist church at exactly five o'clock, with only an hour to spare before the wedding.

Cara toted the cardboard carton with the bride's flowers into the back of the church, where she was met by Lillian Fanning, her carefully made-up face contorted with anger and anxiety.

"Finally!" Lillian snapped, snatching the box of flowers from Cara's hands. "I've been having heart palpitations for the last hour. Where on earth have you been? Didn't you get any of my calls or texts?"

"So sorry," Cara responded. "The battery ran down on my cell phone. But we're here now. Bert's taking the rest of the arrangements over to the reception. Honestly, Lillian. We have it all under control."

"Mama? Is that Cara with my damn flowers?" A willowy brunette in a stunning strapless cream satin Vera Wang gown poked her head out the door of the bride's room.

"It's me, Torie," Cara said. "I was just telling your mom, everything's good."

A small, nervous woman in a pale blue dress fluttered out of the room. "Whatever you do, don't upset her any more," Ellie Lewis, the wedding planner, whispered in Cara's ear. "She's already threatened to strangle one of the flower girls."

"I'm coming," Cara said, scuttling into the room with the box of flowers held before her like a peace offering.

Torie Fanning was a gorgeous mess. Her glossy black updo was coming unpinned, and the tight-fitting bodice of her gown gaped in the back where the last half-dozen tiny satin-covered buttons refused to fasten. The dress fit snugly over her hips—a little too snugly, Cara thought—then flared out with multiple layers of spangly tulle that made the bride look like a mermaid. An overwrought, undermedicated mermaid.

"It's about damned time," Torie said.

"Sorry, sorry, sorry," Cara said. She moved behind the bride and began fastening the buttons. "You look amazing, Torie," she said, her voice low and soothing. It was the same voice she used to coax Poppy to take her heartworm meds. It usually worked well on dogs and neurotics.

"Truly. You're my most beautiful bride ever," Cara said.

"The dress isn't too tight? I think that fuckin' seamstress took it in too much." Torie inhaled sharply as Cara tugged at the last satin button, praying that it would close the gap.

"Oh my God. I can't breathe," Torie croaked.

"Perfect," Cara assured her. "You don't have to breathe. You just have to look amazing. And you do."

She placed her hands lightly on Torie's shoulders and spun her slowly around. She lifted the bouquet from its nest of tissue and handed it to her.

"Now. Isn't this worth the wait?" Cara crossed her fingers, waiting for Torie's reaction.

She'd chosen the most spectacular flowers from Lamar's bucket truck, all in Torie's wedding palette of purples, greens, blues, and pale coral. Hydrangeas, tea roses, and tiny white lilies of the valley and stephanotis made a dinner-plate-sized bouquet, wrapped in hand-dyed watery lavender silk ribbons, fastened with an exquisite platinum brooch with diamond and pearl lilies of the valley.

The bride's expression softened. The shadow of a smile appeared. Torie turned the bouquet this way and that. She touched the delicate tracery of the antique brooch with her finger. "This is pretty. Where did it come from?"

"It was Ryan's grandmother's," Cara said. "And yes, the diamonds and pearls are real. It's a signed Cartier piece. He thought of it all by himself, and he told me it was perfect—the sweetest flower for the sweetest girl in the world."

Which was a big, stinking lie, of course. One of Cara's trademark touches was to include a piece of family jewelry—a little surprise from the groom to the bride—in every bridal bouquet. She'd called Ryan weeks before the wedding to ask him to find a suitable jewel to gift Torie. And she had to admit, he'd come up with a winner.

Torie burst into tears. "That's so like him. He is so thoughtful. And I'm such a bitch! I don't deserve somebody as wonderful as Ryan."

The wedding planner's right eye twitched three times in rapid succession. She patted Torie on the shoulder. "Come on, dear, don't cry. You'll ruin your makeup."

Cara gave Torie a fond pat on the arm. "You're not a bitch. You're just a little emotional. Perfectly natural."

Another lie. Well, it was an occupational hazard. Lying to brides and their mothers.

Cara tucked a stray lock of raven's-wing hair behind Torie's ear. "All right. You're ready. Take a deep breath and try to relax. I've got to go get the rest of the flowers handed out and check on the church. You're calm now, right?"

Torie sniffed and nodded.

"Your bridesmaids' flowers are all right there too," Cara said, pointing at the box she'd put on a nearby tabletop. "Is everybody here?"

"They're here," the wedding planner volunteered. "They're just in the bathroom, touching up their makeup. I'll give them their bouquets."

"Great," Cara said. "I just want to run through the church and check on everything."

She hurried through the side door to the church and took a deep breath. The sanctuary was cool and quiet—and blessedly still for the moment. Her altar arrangements looked magnificent, spilling out of the church's own tall chased-silver urns. The candles in the Fanning family candelabras were definitely white, but she could only hope Lillian would not notice the difference. Cara buzzed up and down the aisles, straightening pew bows and picking up errant rose petals from the white satin runner.

After picking up the box with the boutonnieres, she knocked on the door of the vestry.

"It's open," a male voice called.

The scene here was the opposite of the one in the bride's room. Half a dozen men were attired in tuxes, but with vests unbuttoned and ties untied. They were puffing on cigars and handing around a silver flask, and from the slightly glazed eyes of the assembled company, it was evident that everybody had already had more than a sip of Knob Creek.

"Hey Cara, how's it goin'?" Ryan Finnerty was as calm and laid-back as his bride was overwrought. He was tall with a blocky build, with strawberry-blond hair and the Tom Sawyer freckles that went with hair that color, and a square jaw and an easy, gap-toothed grin. Ryan wasn't classically handsome, but Cara had developed just the teensiest crush on him during all the pre-wedding planning. He was friendly, down-to-earth, impossible to dislike. She wondered if he knew what, exactly, he was getting into with a high-maintenance girl like Torie.

"Goin' good, Ryan," Cara said. She handed the boutonnieres around to all the groomsmen.

"How's Torie?" Ryan stubbed out his cigar and began fastening the flower to the lapel of his jacket.

"Fine," she lied. "Excited that the big day is finally here. How are things going in here? Everybody present and accounted for?"

"We're good," Ryan drawled. "But we're waiting on my lame-ass best man to show up."

"Oh?" Cara tried not to sound alarmed. But it was getting close to show-time. "Has anybody heard from him this morning?"

The door to the vestry opened and a dark-haired man in jeans and a T-shirt strolled in.

"About damn time, Jack," one of the other groomsmen muttered.

"Aw, chill out," the newcomer said. "We got plenty of time."

Cara gasped. "You!"

He turned and his expression darkened. "You! Did you follow me out here?"

Ryan looked from Cara to the latest arrival. "You two know each other?"

"She's been stalking me all afternoon," Jack said, shaking his head.

"He stole my dog," Cara countered. "He's a dognapper."

"Ignore her," Jack said, pulling his T-shirt over his head. "She's clearly deranged."

"Dude," Ryan said. "You're late."

"Yeah, sorry about that," Jack said, looking around the cramped room. He pointed to a garment bag hanging from the back of the door. "Is that mine?"

"Hell yeah," Ryan said, glancing at his watch. "And you better get into it too. You guys are going to start hauling people down the aisle pretty soon. You're getting Mom and Grandma, right?"

"Taken care of," Jack said. He had kicked off his Topsiders and was pushing his arms through the sleeves of the starched white shirt.

The door opened again and the wedding planner coughed and waved aside the smoke. "Um, gentlemen, we've got guests arriving."

Ryan waved them out of the room. "Come on, guys. Get going. We don't need any hitches today. You know how Torie gets."

Cara saw two of the groomsmen roll their eyes, and she grinned despite herself.

If you only knew.

As the men filed past her, she checked and adjusted their ties and boutonnieres. Then she turned to the best man. He was tall and rangy, with the weather-beaten look of a man who spent a lot of time outdoors. His hazel eyes had flecks of gold beneath thick brows, which at this moment were drawn into an uncompromising frown.

"You mind?" he said pointedly, fastening the studs on his tux shirt. "I'm trying to get dressed here."

"And I'm trying to get my dog back," Cara said. "I'm not leaving this room until you agree to hand over Poppy."

"Suit yourself," he said. He unzipped his jeans and nimbly stepped out of them.

Cara blushed and looked away quickly, but the impression was made and it caused an involuntary fluttering in her chest. The starched shirttails hung just low enough to reveal an inch or two of black briefs and tanned, well-muscled thighs. This dognapper was a very, um, well-proportioned man.

"See anything you like?" Jack asked. He turned and reached for his pants, and Cara's face grew hotter as she appreciated the back view almost as much as the front. She mentally chastised herself. *Stop leering at this man. He has your dog!*

He turned around and with deliberate leisure stepped into his pants, pulling the suspenders over his shoulders, leaving the fly unzipped, she was sure, in a deliberate attempt to embarrass her. His eyes met hers, and she forced herself not to look away as he finally zipped up. Cara blushed even deeper, but stood her ground. "Please give me back my dog."

"I don't have your dog."

Restrained organ music floated from the direction of the sanctuary. Cara clenched her fists on her hips and stared at him.

He stared right back, his jaw clenched tightly. He was smooth-shaven now, his dark wavy hair brushed back from a high forehead.

"Looks like a stalemate," he said, his hazel eyes unblinking. He picked up the cummerbund, buckled it, then slid the buckle to the back.

There was a brief knock at the door. "C'mon, Jack," Ryan called impatiently. "Don't make me send Mom in there after you."

"Gotta go," Jack said, gesturing toward the door. "There'll be hell to pay if I screw up this wedding. I'm already on the bride's shit list for keeping little brother out all night at the bachelor party."

"Wait. Did you say Ryan's your brother?"

He looped the bowtie under his collar. Cara felt an irresistible urge to reach up and tie it for him, even though all she really wanted to do was strangle him with it.

"Ryan is two years younger than me. He's the nice one. I'm the asshole."

The door opened and an older woman in a floor-length peach-colored gown stuck her head in the door. "Jack! For God's sake—get a move on! Everybody's waiting on us."

Jack plucked his tux jacket off the hanger. "Keep your shirt on, Mom."

The woman gave Cara an appraising look. "Who's this?"

"The owner of the dog your son stole from me earlier today," Cara said. After a moment of hesitation, she held out her hand. "I'm Cara Kryzik."

The woman's dark hair was flecked with streaks of gray, and her head barely met her son's shoulder. Her hazel eyes crinkled in amusement. "So nice to meet you. I'm Frannie Finnerty. But why on earth would Jack steal your dog? He has a dog of his own."

"Ignore her. She's just the florist. And she's crazier than a shit-house rat," Jack said. He tucked his mother's arm through his own and steered her nimbly toward the door.

"Wait!" Cara called.

He wheeled around. "Now what?"

She grasped the ends of his bowtie and quickly tied it. The top of her head barely reached his chin, and he smelled like Irish Spring soap. Magically delicious? Or was that Lucky Charms? Make that maddeningly delicious. Then she plucked the last boutonniere from the cardboard box, grabbed the black satin lapel of his jacket, and jabbed at it violently with the long pearl-headed pin.

"Ow!" He jerked away, opened his jacket, and looked with disbelief at the tiny spot of blood blooming on his starched white shirtfront. "You did that on purpose."

"Serves you right," Cara said, jabbing again, until the flower was securely fastened to his coat.

"Jack!" His mother tugged at his arm. "Come on. Everybody else has been seated. Torie's bridesmaids are all lined up. We have to go!"

Jack narrowed his eyes and gave the florist his long-practiced stink-eye. It was wasted on her, he knew. She was a head shorter than he, but she stood her ground without flinching. Her hair wasn't quite blond and wasn't quite brown, more of an in-between caramel color, he decided. She had large, liquid brown eyes with surprisingly dark lashes that dominated her heart-shaped face. He was pretty sure she was wearing no more makeup than a little pink lipstick, and even that was wasted, since she was scowling up at him, returning his stink-eye measure for measure.

Finally, she took a step backward. "This isn't over," she said softly, under her breath.

"That's what you think," he said. And then he allowed his mother to drag him out of the vestry and into the wedding melee.

5

Cara didn't stick around the church to watch Torie Fanning pledge her troth to Ryan Finnerty. She rarely did. Weddings were her business, not her pleasure, she told herself.

Instead, she raced for the van, pausing only to give the sky an anxious look. She and Ellie Lewis, the wedding planner, had done their best to talk Torie out of an outdoor reception. It was already hot in Savannah, and tornado season to boot. Cara had witnessed way too many weather-related wedding disasters, including one memorable reception where a sudden lightning storm had pinned seventy-five black-tie and cocktail-gowned guests huddled together in terror under the Victorian wooden gazebo in Whitfield Square.

But Torie was determined to have her reception at home, on the back lawn at the Shutters, her parents' gracious old home on the bluff at the Isle of Hope, facing the Skidaway River. And amazingly, it looked as though the weather was going to cooperate. A fresh breeze was blowing in off the river, and the humidity was actually bearable.

Cara pulled the van into the long driveway at the gray-shingled Fanning house, relieved to see Bert's car already tucked beside the carriage house, in front of the caterer's trucks. The brilliant blue sky had faded to a pale lavender—one of Torie's wedding colors, of course. The setting sun sparkled on the pale green water (also one of Torie's colors) lapping at the long dock opposite the Shutters.

The Fannings' dockhouse had been torn down and rebuilt just for the wedding, and now green-and-white-striped canvas drapes fluttered from its open corners, and a large wrought-iron chandelier hung from its peaked ceiling. This was where the guests would mingle and sip cocktails to watch the sunset while waiting for the wedding party to arrive from the church.

Cara hurried across the wide expanse of front lawn, her boot heels sinking into the grass. She crossed the road and found Bert standing in the dockhouse, directing a helper who was fastening baskets of flowers to the tiki torches dotting the corners of the dock.

"Well?" he asked, turning to face her. "Is the deed done?"

"The soloist was just starting when I left. Everything at the church looked great. And Torie actually cried when I handed her the bouquet with Ryan's pin. I'd say we have twenty more minutes before the first guests arrive."

Bert nodded. "You didn't try to talk the groom into making a run for it?"

"Hah! And foul up my biggest wedding of this season? No way. Anyway, even if I had, Ryan wouldn't have run. The poor guy is totally koo-koo for Cocoa Puffs over Torie."

Bert wrinkled his nose. "No accounting for taste. So . . . what do you think?"

"I think they might just have a shot at making it for the long haul," Cara admitted. "But only because Ryan Finnerty is a total teddy bear. You?"

He shrugged. "I give them six years. Although, if she gets knocked up sooner, I could be wrong."

Cara giggled. "I've got news for you, sport. She's *already* preggers. That gown fit her with room to spare when it was delivered in March."

Bert's eyes widened. "You think?"

"I know," she assured him. "At the rehearsal dinner? She stuck to iced tea all night. And did you see the way her boobs were about to fall out of the dress? I promise you, we'll be doing baby-shower balloon bouquets for her by fall."

Cara took a brisk walk around the dockhouse, straightening tablecloths on the caterer's highboy tabletops, brushing at the stray fern frond or fallen petal. Technically, this was the wedding planner's job, but Cara Kryzik never left anything to chance.

"I'm going to head back over to the reception tent," she told Bert. "All the flowers in the baskets here have water?"

"Check," Bert said.

"And you've misted the ferns with water?"

"Not my first rodeo, boss lady."

She patted his shoulder. "I think I'll keep you."

The first thing she checked at the reception tent was the compressor for the rented air conditioner. It was humming along, she noted with relief. The only thing worse than bad weather for an outdoor function in Savannah was a nonfunctioning air conditioner—or even a heater. Again, the tent and the air-conditioning were not her responsibility, but you couldn't tell that to a finicky bride who was prone to pitch a fit over the slightest flaw in her plans.

Cara stood quietly in the entrance to the tent, taking it all in. The temperature had cooled down nicely, and her flowers, she thought, not immodestly, looked sensational.

She'd commissioned a local glassblower to create three-foot-tall vases for the centerpieces, and these were placed in the center of each of the thirty round tables in the room. The tables themselves were covered in sea-foam-colored linen flounced cloths. Spilling from each vase were arrangements of coral tea roses, blue hydrangeas, variegated Swedish ivy, and marguerite daisies. Hanging from the metal support beams of the tent, she'd rigged up five enormous ivy-covered ten-arm wire chandeliers fitted with battery-operated candles. She pulled a small remote-control pad from her pocket, clicked a button, and the candles began to flicker in the dim light of the tent.

White-coated waiters moved efficiently about the tent, polishing water and wine glasses at each place setting, adjusting and straightening the thick silver place settings and gold-rimmed dinner plates.

"Cara, hi!" Torie's caterer, Layne Pelletier, hurried to her side.

"You've outdone yourself this time, girlfriend," Layne said, gesturing around the tent.

Cara sighed. "Let's just hope our bride agrees with you."

"How can she not? It's perfection. I've been snapping pictures of the tables to put up on my own website. Your flowers plus my food—it's going to be the party of the year."

"Hope so," Cara said. "The Fannings move in some pretty lofty circles. This little clambake of Torie's could be a real rainmaker if all goes well."

"It will," Layne assured her. "Were you at the church just now? Any idea how long before everbody will start arriving?"

They heard the sound of car doors closing. "About now," Cara said. "Showtime!"

Normally, the wedding party's arrival would signal Cara's departure. If she left now, maybe she could drive back to the dognapper's house on Macon Street. Maybe there was a backyard. She could cruise down the lane and steal her dog back while Jack Finnerty was still at the wedding. Cara was heading for her van when she heard her name being called.

"Cara . . . so glad you're still here." It was Ellie Lewis, the wedding planner.

"Just leaving," Cara said. "I've checked everything in both tents, and it's all good. By the way, thanks again for referring me to the Fannings."

Ellie's face was shiny pink with perspiration. "Don't thank me yet," she warned. "The photographer wants to get some candid shots of the wedding party down at the dock, and Torie is insistent that you should be there to style things."

"I'm not a photo stylist," Cara protested. "And honestly, Ellie, I'm whipped. I've been on my feet for nearly twenty-four hours. All I want right now is a shower and a cocktail—and my bed." *And my dog,* she thought.

Ellie nodded glumly. "I don't blame you. I've had a bellyful of Torie and Mommy Dearest these past few weeks. I'd leave too, if I could. But you know how it goes—I'll be here till the bitter end tonight."

She turned and began to trudge back across the lawn.

Cara had her hand on the van's door handle, but when she saw the dejected droop of her colleague's shoulders, she just didn't have the heart to abandon ship.

"Ellie," she called.

"Yes?"

"Wait for me, dammit."

By eight o'clock, the big reception tent vibrated with life. Dinner service for three hundred guests was winding down and the eight-piece orchestra was just starting to tune up. Cara made a few last-minute adjustments to the flowers on the cake table and tiptoed toward the door.

"Cara!"

Torie's voice rose above the din of the crowd. Her mermaid skirts rustled as she cut a swath through the crowd. The bride reached out and grasped Cara's hands in hers. "You're not leaving already! The party's just starting to crank up."

"Well, yes, I was," she said, a little taken aback by Torie's sudden show of friendliness.

"But, you can't," Torie said. "I mean, of course, you don't have to stay, but Ryan and I really, really wish you would stay. You've been such a big part of all the planning for the wedding, and it would really, really mean a lot to us if you would stay and help us celebrate."

Huh?

"Well, uh," she stammered.

A large hand clamped down on her shoulder. Cara looked up to see Ryan standing beside her, his freckled face beaming with happiness—and maybe just a little extra Knob Creek bonhomie.

"What's this?" he asked.

"Honey, tell Cara she needs to stay and celebrate with us," Torie cooed.

"I was just fixin' to tell her that," Ryan said. He gestured around the tent.

"You made everything so awesome for us—now you need to stay and enjoy it for a while."

"Oh no, I really couldn't," Cara demurred. "You're very sweet to invite me, but honestly, my job is done here. And I wouldn't dream of imposing. . . ."

"It's not imposing," Ryan said. He pointed across the room. "Look. Layne's gonna hang around and party."

Layne Pelletier had shed her chef's jacket and was bellied up to the bar with a long-necked bottle of Sweetwater in her right hand. She saw Cara looking, and raised it in a salute.

"But Layne has to stay and make sure the dessert service and after-dinner drinks and the cake cutting go off," Cara protested. "That's nothing to do with me."

"That's just it," Torie admitted. "Mama and I would love it if you'd *at least* stay for the cake cutting. The photographer wants us all to have our flowers around the cake, just so . . . and nobody can make things look the way you can. . . ."

So . . . it wasn't *really* about having her stay to enjoy the party, Cara realized. It was just one more task Torie had assigned her florist. Resistance, she knew, was futile.

"Okay," she said wearily.

She fetched herself a glass of white wine from the bar, then sank down into a vacant seat at a table near the back of the tent, and watched as the party swirled around her.

Torie and Ryan's friends and family were a fun-loving bunch. They crowded the dance floor for every song, only thinning out long enough to allow Torie and Bill Fanning to have their traditional father-daughter spotlight dance to "The Way You Look Tonight."

It was nearly nine o'clock when Cara's rumbling stomach reminded her that she'd eaten nothing since breakfast. The orchestra had packed up and departed, and now a disc jockey was playing from the makeshift wooden bandstand. While the party went on, there was still a chance she could steal her dog back. Bert could just as easily style the flowers for the cake cutting.

She worked her way around the perimeter of the tent and was headed for the spot where Bert stood when Ryan spotted her.

He grabbed her by the hand and started dragging her toward the dance floor. "C'mon, Cara. They're playing our song."

"Ryan, you're sweet, but I'm the help. And the help doesn't dance at weddings."

"Sure they do," he said—just as Layne Pelletier boogied past with one of her waiters.

"Their" song was apparently KC and the Sunshine Band's "Shake Your Booty," and the next thing she knew, Cara had joined the line dance snaking its way across the dance floor, sliding, popping, and locking with the whole sweaty ensemble.

Finally, the song wound down and she began edging her way back toward Bert, but Ryan caught her by the waist.

"One more dance," he urged. The record was Harry Connick Jr.'s version of "It Had to Be You." "How're you not gonna dance to this?"

"Where's Torie?" Cara asked. "This is a song for the two of you."

"Nah. She's sitting out the next few numbers." Ryan looked around, then whispered, "She's uh, kind of, uh . . ."

"Pregnant?" Cara whispered back.

His grin lit up his face. "Yeah. It's pretty cool. She told you, huh?"

"She didn't have to," Cara said. "Congratulations."

For a guy who was built like a linebacker, Ryan was a surprisingly smooth dancer. He hummed along with the first few bars of the music.

"I wanted to thank you for everything you've done for us," he said, as they glided across the floor. "I know Torie's been kind of wound up these past few days. So thanks for putting up with all of us."

"All part of my job," Cara assured him.

"You mind me asking what's up with you and my brother?" Ryan asked. "He seemed pretty ticked off at you, back at the church."

"He stole my dog earlier today," Cara said.

"Yeah. You keep saying that. But that doesn't sound like Jack."

"Well, he did. Poppy ran away from the shop today, and when I went looking for her, I caught him dragging her down Jones Street. Now he's got Poppy, and he won't give her back."

"Why would Jack steal your dog? He's got a dog."

"He claims his dog ran away, and he spotted mine and so he stole her. But I know Poppy. There's not another dog in this town who looks like her. And he won't give her back."

"If you gave him half a chance he'd probably give you Shaz too. He's always complaining how much time she takes away from his work."

"What's your brother do for a living? Aside from stealing dogs?"

"Torie didn't tell you? Jack works with me, restoring historic properties. We're business partners."

"I saw the *historic property* he lives in on Macon Street today," Cara said, with a dismissive sniff. "No offense, but that place looks like a dump."

Ryan frowned. "Yeah, well, he sort of lost his momentum when Zoey left. Anyway, we've been working night and day to get my new house in Ardsley Park finished before Torie movies in. Jack does all the carpentry work. He's really a master craftsman."

"Who's Zoey? Not that I care."

"His ex-girlfriend," Ryan said. He was about to say more, but the song ended, and the DJ was moving through the crowd with a cordless mike.

"Torie Fanning Finnerty," he boomed. "Calling Torie and her bridesmaids. And I need all the single ladies here tonight. Single ladies—to the dance floor!"

"Thanks for the dance, Ryan." Cara managed a tight smile and began to head back to her table. But the groom grabbed her hand. "Not so fast. You heard the man. All the single ladies. That means you."

"Noooo," she wailed. "It's really not appropriate. . . ."

But her protest fell on deaf ears. Torie and her bridesmaids, eight strong, and at least sixty other women poured onto the dance floor, sweeping Cara along with them.

"Come on, Cara," Layne Pelletier coaxed, handing her an icy long-necked beer. "Time to cut loose!"

"What the hell," Cara said, taking a long swig of the beer. It went down good. Really good. And so it was that that she found herself doing her best Beyoncé moves, chanting along at the top of her lungs, "Ya shoulda put a ring on it. . . ."

When that song was winding down, Bert found her and handed her a glass of white wine. A recovering alcoholic, Bert didn't drink, but he'd apparently decided to join the fun, too, because he'd shed his staid blue blazer and tie, not to mention his shoes, and in just another minute she and Bert were breaking it down to "Brick House."

At some point, maybe after one of the other groomsmen—his name was Matt, or at least she thought his name was Matt—slow-danced with her to Ben E. King's "Stand By Me," it dawned on Cara that she was just a tiny bit buzzed.

She didn't hesitate when Ryan pulled her into the line dance for the Electric Slide. She slid and clapped and tapped and rocked and threw herself into the rhythm of the song. The dance was almost over. She was doing a pivot-turn when she came face-to-face with none other than Jack, the dognapper. She turned again, abruptly, and stumbled badly.

As luck would have it, the dance ended, and Ryan helped steady her.

"Having fun?" he asked.

Her face was flushed and her damp hair stuck to her forehead. "I am, but it still doesn't feel right. . . ."

But Ryan nimbly swung her into the next dance. The lights in the tent dimmed, and she heard Louis Armstrong's raspy version of "What a Wonderful World."

"You're a really good dancer," he said.

"Thanks, I used to . . ."

Before she knew it, Ryan was handing her off to another partner. His brother Jack.

"You!" Cara said, starting to pull away.

"Yes, me," Jack retorted. He clamped a hand around her waist, took her right hand in his, and pulled her close to his chest.

She wouldn't give him the satisfaction of breaking away. Right after this dance, she would sneak over to his place and liberate her puppy. For now, though, she floated along to the music. It was a nice song, after all, a nice sentiment, for a nice wedding. She closed her eyes and almost managed to forget her partner's identity.

Almost. But she was all too aware of his proximity. His hand in hers was deeply callused. He was an even better dancer than his brother. One time, she raised her lashes just enough to see his face. When he wasn't scowling at her, he was downright good-looking.

The song wound down, but he kept his hand on her waist. She looked up in surprise.

"My mother's watching," he murmured. "She says I'm antisocial. Do me a favor and pretend like you're enjoying yourself, okay? For just another three minutes?"

Cara shrugged. Maybe, if she played nice, he'd relent and release her dog.

She heard a few bars of music, took a couple of tentative steps. But Jack stopped abruptly. "What the hell? Jimmy Buffett? Whose idea of a joke is this?" His spine stiffened. He dropped her hand, shook his head. "Sorry."

Without another word, he stalked off, leaving her alone, in the middle of the dance floor.

She stood in disbelief, watching him go.

6

Jack hurried out of the tent, hoping to avoid the ever-watchful eyes of Torie—and his mother. By the time he made it to his truck, he'd stripped off the tux jacket, unknotted the tie, and ditched the cummerbund. He unlocked the door, slung the clothes inside, then slid onto the seat and kicked off those gawdawful shiny black lace-up shoes.

Once he was on the Skidaway Road, headed back toward town, he opened the truck windows and cranked up the radio. What a night! He'd only had one beer, but his head was throbbing. Weddings.

Shit.

All day Ryan had walked around with that goofy-ass grin on his face. And why? He'd just promised to love and obey a girl who would run his butt ragged for the rest of his life. So okay, even he had to admit Torie Fanning was one hot chick. But Ryan had dated lots of women just as hot as Torie, hotter even. Why this one?

Jack didn't get it. Never would. But then, his own history with the ladies wasn't exactly stellar.

Exhibit A: Zoey Ackerman. They'd met at a wedding. Jack had been a groomsman, Zoey was the bride's cousin. His face darkened at the memory of it. Nothing good ever happened at weddings. He'd been standing at the bar, waiting for a beer. A tall blonde sidled up, introduced herself. She was new in town, had just taken a job as a Pilates instructor at the Downtown Athletic Club, where Jack was a member at the time.

It had started as a little harmless flirtation. The next thing he knew, she'd moved into the Macon Street cottage with him. The one closet in the house was jammed with her stuff—not that Jack was exactly a snappy dresser, but it would have been good to have a hanger for his one decent pair of khakis and dress shirt.

In the beginning, it had all been good times. Zoey was great to look at, fun to be with, and yeah, the sex wasn't bad either. She termed the Macon Street cottage "adorable."

Two months in, though, everything began to change. Nothing pleased her. She hated his friends, his family, especially hated his job.

He'd come home late at night, covered in sawdust, his hair and face streaked with paint, and she'd make not-so-subtle cracks about manual labor. He had a college degree in business management, didn't he? Why couldn't he work at a nine-to-five desk job, with normal hours and sick days and profit sharing and vacation?

Nobody else had to work Saturdays or Sundays, or evenings—why did he?

He'd taken her to a job site—exactly once—to try to show her what it was he did for a living.

It had been one of those huge old Victorian mansions facing Forsyth Park. The place had been chopped up into ten apartments for college students in the 1980s, but the new owners, two retired doctors from Michigan, wanted it restored—to the standards that would qualify it for historic-preservation tax credits. He and Ryan spent six months totally rehabbing the place, gutting it down to the studs, installing all new, up-to-date plumbing, wiring, heat and air systems—then restoring the original horsehair-and-plaster walls, hardwood floors, everything.

Over the years, most of the original moldings and millwork had been destroyed, so Jack had spent hours and hours poring over photographs of houses from the same era, drawing up plans for the new moldings and woodwork, then painstakingly re-creating them. The crown moldings in the dining room, for example, included five different profiles.

Zoey had walked in with him that Saturday morning, sniffed, and wrinkled her nose. “Rat poop!”

She’d retreated to the truck and refused to ever set foot on one of his job sites again.

Maybe that’s when he should have seen the handwriting on the wall. Instead, they’d hung on together for nearly a year. He probably wasn’t the ideal boyfriend. He worked all the time, and when he wasn’t working, he wanted to just chill at home, or maybe out at the beach. Zoey, on the other hand, wanted to go clubbing, or out to dinner, or maybe up to Atlanta to visit friends. He hated Atlanta, and he wasn’t crazy about her friends, either. They’d nearly split up the night she brought home the dog.

It was January. He’d been busting his ass between two different job sites, including Ryan’s house. He’d come home near midnight, to find Zoey sitting up in bed cuddling with what looked to him like a Muppets version of a dog.

“What’s this?” he’d asked, eyeing the dog suspiciously.

“This is Princess Scheherazade of Betancourt,” she’d trilled. “She’s a purebred goldendoodle. Is she not the most precious thing you’ve ever seen?”

“Yeah, precious. What’s she doing in my bed?”

In retrospect, this might not have been the ideal question to ask of a woman who was already deeply infatuated with a new puppy.

“She’s mine. I mean, ours,” Zoey said. Her pale blue eyes filled with tears. “I thought you loved dogs.”

Christ!

“I love dogs. I think they’re great. For people who have the time to spend with them. But I’m working fourteen-hour days and six-day weeks, and you’re at the club all day. Who’s gonna take care of her while we’re at work?”

“I’ll take care of her, of course, if you’re going to be like that about it. But, I mean, you own the business, right? Why couldn’t she go to work with you? She’s great company.” Zoey buried her face in the dog’s fluffy coat. “Aren’t you an angel? Aren’t you good company?”

The dog lavished Zoey’s face with a big sloppy kiss. Then it turned its big black button eyes toward Jack—and he could swear the damn thing grinned at him.

After that, the dog slept every night in the bed with them. Every night, she wedged her hot, hairy body in between him and Zoey. Every morning, he awoke to hot doggy breath in his face.

To be perfectly honest, they were at that point in the relationship where the only thing that was working was the sex. After Shaz? They didn't even have that.

Shaz. He glanced at his watch. She'd been locked up in the cottage all night. He was dead tired, but he'd need to take her out for a run as soon as he got home. It would feel good to get out of this damned monkey suit, lace up his running shoes, and work up an honest sweat.

He unlocked the front door, walked in, and stepped directly in what looked like a fresh piddle puddle.

He was shocked. Zoey had actually managed to housebreak the dog before she pulled her disappearing act. Shaz hadn't had an accident in months. And now this?

He fetched a wet rag from the kitchen and mopped up the mess. He'd sanded and stained the heart-pine floors back in the fall, but he'd never actually gotten around to sealing them. Which was a shame, because now he'd have to sand them down all over again.

"Shaz!" He glanced around the room. Kind of a depressing sight, reflected in the flickering blue light of the big screen. He'd turned on the television before leaving, something to give the dog company. He was pretty sure she liked ESPN and Animal Planet.

No sign of the dog. His stomach clenched. Had she somehow managed to get out? He'd locked all the doors earlier. He was really not in the mood tonight to go hunting for a runaway dog.

"Shaz?" He walked through the combination living-dining room, through the short hallway. He turned on the light in the bedroom. She was stretched out across the bed, with her head nesting on his pillow.

The dog lifted her muzzle and gave him a long, disdainful stare.

"Shaz!" His voice was sharp. "Come!"

Her tail thumped on the bedding, but she didn't budge.

He walked over to the bed and grabbed her by her collar. "Come on girl. Off the bed. You know the rules. No dogs in my bed."

It was a new rule, one he'd instituted as soon as Zoey walked out. Shaz had a big, oversized beanbag bed in the corner of the bedroom, and most nights, she was content to sleep there.

"Shaz?" His voice was stern. "Off!"

Thump. Thump. Thump.

"Did you pee on the floor, Shaz?"

Thump. Thump. Thump. She seemed downright proud of it.

He sighed, changed into a clean T-shirt and shorts, and laced up his running shoes. "C'mon, girl. Let's go work the kinks out."

Shaz blinked. She yawned. But she didn't budge.

Bert glanced over at Cara, who leaned against the window on the passenger side of the van.

"I'd say the wedding was an unqualified success, wouldn't you?"

"Mmm-hmm," Cara said, her eyes half closed. "Thanks for being my designated driver. I'll take you back out to the Fannings' in the morning for your car."

"Lillian actually hugged me tonight. So did Torie."

"Mmm-hmm."

"I gave out a bunch of our business cards at the wedding. Three of Torie's bridesmaids are engaged."

That got her attention. She sat up straight for a moment. "Really? Which ones?"

"Alison? The little blonde. And the taller blonde? The one they call Chatty? Oh, and Brenna, the supertanned brunette. She actually got engaged tonight, to one of Ryan's fraternity brothers."

"That's great," Cara said. "Anybody mention actual wedding dates?"

"Not to me," Bert said. "But all three of them swore they want you to do their flowers."

"I just hope they call," Cara said. "We don't have a lot lined up for the fall."

"We will," Bert said, ever loyal. "You always get panicky this time of year, and we always have more work than we can handle, come fall."

"You never can tell, though," Cara cautioned him. "Remember how dead it was last October?"

"And then we had weddings booked every weekend in November, through May," Bert said. "Can't you just relax a little? Everything is going to work out."

"I can't afford to relax," Cara said. "I owe the Colonel twenty thousand dollars. And on top of that, I checked my email back at the wedding, while you were out breaking it down on the dance floor. Bernice Bradley emailed me to let me know she wants to renew our lease. I've been going month to month for a while now—and when we renew, our rent is going up to nearly double what we pay now."

"What? That's crap! The Bradleys haven't touched the place in years. Your ceiling leaks upstairs, and the plumbing keeps backing up. . . ."

"I know," Cara said, shaking her head. "But they've got me by the short hairs. They know it's a great location. Where else am I going to find that much square footage downtown—and with its own parking space? And with the apartment upstairs, it's perfect for me."

"I think you should call their bluff," Bert said, steering the van down Skidaway Road. "Call your real-estate agent, ask her to put out some feelers for another location. Let the Bradleys get wind of that. Look at all the improvements you've made to their property. You're probably the best tenant they've ever had. I bet they'd hate to lose you."

"But I'd hate it even more—if I have to move. It's perfect visibility—so close to the biggest downtown churches."

"What about that storefront on Bull? Where the antique shop used to be? Now, that's a great location. Tons of traffic."

"And no parking. I looked at that space the last time it became vacant. There's a reason why no business stays there longer than a year. If my brides can't find a place to park, they'll drive right on up the road to another florist shop."

"Never," Bert said. "These girls want a Bloom wedding. You've got the look they love, Cara."

"Today," she muttered. "But all that can change in the blink of an eye. These brides are all incredibly fickle. Everybody wants the next cool, hip look. And if I don't stay right on top of my game, I'll be yesterday's news."

She'd dozed off. It was nearly midnight. Bert parked the van in the space in back of the shop, then reached over and gently shook her shoulder.

"Cara? We're home."

She yawned and looked out the window at the poorly lit lane. "God. For a minute there, I almost forgot about Poppy. That horrible man still has her."

Bert cocked one eyebrow. "You seemed to be having a nice time dancing with that horrible man, earlier this evening. You two were getting pretty close, it looked like to me."

"He's a lunatic," Cara said. "Did you see what he did? Left me standing in the middle of the dance floor! One minute we were dancing—and the next, he just stopped cold. Walked off and left, after mumbling something about Jimmy fucking Buffett."

"I did see him leave. I figured you'd picked a fight with him," Bert said.

"I never said a word. I thought he might relent and hand Poppy over to me if I played nice. Dumb idea."

"What can you do now? I mean, if he won't give her back?"

"I'll take her back," Cara said, yawning. "He stole her from me, so I'll steal her back from him."

"How exactly do you steal your own dog?" Bert asked.

"Not sure," she admitted. "But I'm going over there to case the joint. Just as soon as I chug a Red Bull."

"Right now? It's midnight, Cara. What if he calls the cops?"

"He won't. And they won't come anyway. Remember, I tried to get them involved earlier, and they flat refused."

"I think you'd better wait till morning. I know that block. It's kind of sketchy at night. And what if his neighbors see you and think you're trying to break in? You'd be the one getting hauled off to the pokey."

"You could go with me. Ride shotgun?"

"Sorry. No can do. I've got plans tonight."

Cara gave him an appraising look. "What kind of plans?"

"I'm meeting somebody for a drink."

"Somebody. As in a guy?"

"Maybe."

"Bert Rosen! Are you hooking up with somebody you just met tonight? At the wedding?"

He looked insulted. "It's not a hookup. It's just a drink. An innocent drink."

"Who is he? Do I know him? Did I meet him?"

"You don't actually know him, but you did meet. He's actually one of Ryan's fraternity brothers."

"You're kidding." Cara giggled despite her weariness. "You're telling me one of Ryan Finnerty's frat-tastic macho buddies is actually gay?"

"Shh. He's not officially out. At least not to Ryan."

Cara opened her door and climbed down out of the van. "If you won't go with me, I guess I'll have to wait until tomorrow morning. But I'm telling you right now, if he doesn't hand over Poppy—I might do something radical."

"Go get some sleep," Bert advised. "I'll go over there with you myself in the morning before we go get my car and we'll storm the castle together."

It was the first night she'd spent alone in her apartment without Poppy, and now the apartment was eerily quiet without her.

Cara undressed quickly. She washed her face and pulled on a well-worn oversized T-shirt and climbed into bed. It had been a long, busy day, and she was exhausted, but she couldn't sleep. The bed seemed too big without Poppy stretched out on the other side of it. So she got up and arranged herself on the sofa in her combination living-dining room.

The living room's big bay window looked out on the street. She heard cars driving slowly down the brick street, heard doors opening and closing, her neighbors, two SCAD art students, laughing and talking as they came home from one of their customary late nights.

Finally, she drifted off to sleep, maybe around three? She wasn't sure.

Sunday. It was the one day of the week Jack Finnerty allowed himself the luxury of sleeping in. He was asleep, in a near-coma stage, when his cell phone rang. Blindly, he reached toward the packing-crate nightstand. The phone fell to the floor, but it kept ringing.

Jack leaned over the edge of the bed and groped around on the floor. Finally, his fingers closed on the phone. He thumbed the On button. Three-thirty in the friggin' morning. The number on the caller ID wasn't familiar. A wrong number at three-thirty in the morning? He tossed the phone back onto the nightstand, turned over, and tried to go back to sleep.

But the phone was ringing again. He snatched it up, prepared to give this loser an earful. He wasn't prepared for what he got instead.

It was Zoey.

"Dammit, Jack," she cried. "What the hell are you thinking?"

"I'm thinking it's nearly four in the fuckin' morning," Jack said, his voice thick with sleep. "What do you want, Zoey?"

"I want to know why you didn't let me know you managed to lose Scheherazade," Zoey demanded.

Jack rose up on one elbow and looked over at the dog asleep on her bed, not far from his own. Well, really his bed was nothing more than a mattress and boxspring. But still.

"Shaz is right here," he said, yawning. "Have you and Jiminy Cricket been getting into some of that California weed?"

"His name is Jamey, and for your information, just because he's a musician, does not mean that he is a dope fiend, not that it's any of your business," she retorted. "And I'd just love to know how my dog can be in two places at one time."

"I still don't know what you're talking about," Jack said, flopping backward onto the bed.

"I got a call earlier tonight from Dr. Katz's office, telling me that somebody found Shaz running loose on Victory Drive. Thank heavens, some good Samaritan picked her up and took her to the vet's office. They recognized her immediately, of course, but then they checked the microchip just to be sure, and they called me."

That got his attention. He sat straight up in the bed and turned on the lamp. Now the dog was awake, too. Her ears pricked up, and her nose was quivering, as though she knew she was being discussed.

"Zoey? Are you telling me that the dog sitting right here in this bedroom is not Shaz?" He buried his head in his hands. The dog edged closer and licked his ear.

Her voice was shrill. "I don't have any idea who or what you've got in your bedroom, Jack Finnerty, but yes, I am telling you that Scheherazade is being boarded at Dr. Katz's office tonight. The vet tech said it's a miracle she didn't get hit by a car, crossing all that traffic on Abercorn Street. No thanks to you."

"You're saying Shaz is at the vet's office?"

"Jack! Have you heard a single word I've said? Yes! I am telling you Dr. Katz has Shaz. See? You never listen to me, Jack. This is just one more example. . . ."

He turned his head and was staring directly into the dog's unblinking eyes.

"Poppy?"

The dog tilted its head and thumped its tail on the scarred wooden floor.

"Christ," Jack moaned. "You really are Poppy."

"Have you got a woman there, Jack?" Zoey asked.

As if.

"None of your damned business," he growled.

"Scheherazade is a very valuable dog, Jack," Zoey went on. "The breeder said once she's old enough to breed, her puppies could fetch as much as two thousand dollars. So I don't appreciate your letting her wander around town without so much as a collar."

"I didn't let her *do* anything," Jack said. "I was taking her to that groomer of yours, who she detests, by the way, and she jumped out the window of my truck. I went looking for her and found another goldendoodle wandering down the lane behind West Charlton. I naturally assumed she was Shaz, so I tied a rope around her neck and walked her back home. What I didn't know, since you couldn't be bothered to tell me, was that I'd actually dognapped somebody else's dog. A very angry somebody, who tried to sic the cops on me."

"Not my problem," Zoey said airily.

"Actually, it is your problem, since Shaz is your dog," Jack pointed out.

That shut her up. At least momentarily. Any other woman would have been feeling painfully guilty by now, for abandoning her lover and her seven-month-old puppy, to run off to California the day after hooking up with a Jimmy Buffett impersonator she'd just met at a bar on River Street. A guy who called himself Jamey Buttons, for God's sake.

But Zoey was not just any other woman.

"You told me you wanted a dog," Zoey said accusingly.

"And you told me you loved me and wanted to have my children someday," Jack said. "And just for the record? The dog I wanted was a black lab, not some funny-looking designer dog."

"I'm not going to let you put a big guilt trip on me, Jack," Zoey said. "I actually wanted to let you know that Jamey has a gig playing on a cruise ship out of Fort Lauderdale for the next three months, and I've signed on to be the ship's Pilates instructor. I'll send for Scheherazade when we get back. Probably in August."

"Yippee," Jack said bitterly. "Bye, Zoey."

"Wait, Jack," she said quickly. "Don't forget, you've got to pick Shaz up by noon, or pay an extra day's boarding fee. As it is, you already owe them seventy dollars."

7

Jack tried, but couldn't get back to sleep. Poppy was no help. She rested her muzzle on the edge of the mattress, watching him with her big, sad puppy eyes. He turned away, facing the wall, but he could feel Poppy's warm breath on his neck.

Finally, he relented. He flipped back over and scratched under her chin. "There. Okay? Now can we get some sleep around here?"

Maybe he couldn't sleep because he was dreading the coming morning. And seeing Poppy's owner again.

The woman was a pistol, for sure. Her name was Cara Kryzik, Ryan told him. She wasn't bad-looking, if you went for that kind of look. Which he didn't. He'd always enjoyed blondes: tall, cool, athletic blondes. Like Zoey.

This Cara person, on the other hand, was the opposite of his type. She had shoulder-length, flyaway not-quite-brown, not-quite-blond hair. Big brown eyes that glittered dangerously when she was pissed off, a heart-shaped face, high cheekbones, and full, pink, lips that reminded him of overblown roses.

She dressed funny, too. That night, at the wedding, she'd worn an old-fashioned-looking pink silk rig that looked more like a nightgown, with its lacy inset bodice. She'd somehow managed to look sexy and demure at the same time, although he totally didn't get how that look worked with pink cowboy boots.

Every time he'd turned around at the reception, she'd been right there in his face, telling him off, demanding that he return her dog.

His lamebrain brother, Ryan, found the whole scenario highly entertaining. But then, Ryan had notoriously eccentric taste in women. Take Torie, for instance.

"She's worth the trouble," Ryan said, when Jack pointed out the differences in their personalities. "I like a woman with fire." Especially, he'd added, "in bed."

It had been Ryan who'd coaxed Cara into dancing, despite her protests. His brother was a consummate party animal. He'd danced with almost all the women at the reception, including the seven-year-old flower girl, most of the bridesmaids, and their arthritic aunt Betty.

And he'd forced Jack onto the dance floor, too.

"You're my best man," he'd informed Jack, who would have preferred to melt into the woodwork. "It's on the list of duties. Right up there with planning the bachelor party and making the first toast."

So Jack had danced with their mother, he'd danced with Aunt Betty, he'd danced with Torie, and he'd even, at one point, been tricked into dancing with Cara Kryzik.

Torie had dragged him from the safety of the bar to do some stupid line dance, and he'd somehow ended up right beside Cara, who glowered at him with undisguised venom. Two dances later, Ryan shoved him into Cara's clutches.

It was a slow dance. She was a decent dancer, and she actually felt pretty good in his arms, with his hand sliding over the smooth pink silk, and the warm, sun-browned skin of her back and bare arms. Her figure was full and rounded in the right places. She wore the lightest of perfumes and her hair smelled faintly of cherries.

But then it happened. Louie Armstrong's wonderful world ended, and the DJ was playing "Come Monday."

He felt his face flush and his feet grow leaden. She'd looked up at him in shock. And that was that. Jimmy fuckin' Buffett. He'd fled like a thief in the night.

Smooth move, he told himself now, reliving that moment. Real smooth move, Ace.

So, just to recap. He'd stolen this woman's dog. Called the cops on her, accused her of stalking, insulted her, and then abandoned her in the middle of a dance.

She, in turn, had called him a jerk and a liar. She was moody and dressed weird, and according to Ryan, she was just coming off a lousy divorce and seemed to hate all men, with the exception of her gay assistant.

He flopped over on his other side, facing away from the still-vigilant Poppy. Tomorrow morning, first thing, he would have to return the dog and face her wrath.

8

Cara heard a buzzing from somewhere far away. Still dead asleep, she flung an arm in the general vicinity of the nightstand, searching for the alarm, to shut it off. She slapped wildly in the direction of the clock, but the buzzing wouldn't stop.

Annoyed, she flopped over, opened one eye, and stared at the clock. It wasn't buzzing. And she hadn't set it. But something, somewhere, was buzzing. And at eight o'clock on a Sunday morning. Her doorbell?

Cara jumped out of bed, wide-eyed and startled. Who would be ringing her bell that early on a Sunday?

She stumbled over to the window and looked down at the street below. A man stood by the recessed entry to the apartment. He had a big, fluffy white dog on a leash.

Poppy!

Cara flew down the wooden staircase, barefoot, dressed only in her sleep shirt. She unlatched the chain guard and flipped the deadbolt.

Jack Finnerty stood on the street just outside her door. He wore paint-spattered jeans, a faded T-shirt, and a look that could best be described as sheepish.

"Uh, well, here's your dog."

"Poppy!"

The dog stood up on her hind legs, put her front paws on Cara's hips, and shook all over with joy. Cara wrapped her arms around the dog. "I missed you! You bad, bad girl. I missed you so much. I hardly slept last night, worrying about you."

"Yeah, uh, she didn't get much sleep either," Jack volunteered. "Look, I'm really sorry about this. I've been a jerk. I should have listened to you yesterday."

"Yes," Cara said severely. "You should have. And yes, you were a jerk. And worse."

"You're right," he said, staring down at his shoes. "And I apologize."

"Where's your dog?" she asked, sticking her head out the door and looking around.

"At home. Now. After she jumped out of my truck yesterday, she made it all the way to Victory Drive and Abercorn. A woman managed to corral her and she took her to the vet, and they recognized her. Shaz is chipped, so they read the chip, just to be sure, and called the owner."

"You," she said accusingly.

Jack winced. "My ex. Shaz technically belongs to her. But she's out in California, so Shaz is mine. Sorta. The vet called Zoey yesterday to let her know Shaz had been found. But Zoey, being Zoey, decided to torture me by not calling me until three this morning."

Cara looked him over. His hair was mussed and there were dark circles under his eyes, so it was apparent he'd gotten about as much sleep as she had.

"Look." Jack's voice was low. "I really am sorry. Truly. Your dog looks almost exactly like Shaz. But if I hadn't been such a prick, I would have looked closer and realized I had the wrong dog. Especially since when I got home last night, I discovered she'd peed all over my hardwood floors. Shaz is housebroken. Your dog, on the other hand, is fairly neurotic, but I guess you already know that."

"Neurotic! She is not," Cara said sharply. "And Poppy is housebroken. She never pees at home. She was probably traumatized by being dognapped. And then left alone in a strange house for hours and hours."

"Whatever," Jack said. "I better get back to Shaz. She's been penned up in a crate at the vet's office all night, and right now she's probably not too happy with me either."

"Thank you for bringing Poppy back," Cara said coolly. "She's home now, and that's all that matters."

"Have you had her microchipped?" Jack asked.

"No. I keep meaning to, but running my own business . . ."

"You should do it right away, especially since she seems to be such an escape artist," he suggested.

"I know how to take care of my own dog," Cara said, bristling. "Maybe you should do a better job of taking care of your own, especially since she got all the way to Abercorn and Victory."

"Riiight." Jack's lips were clamped tightly in anger. "Anyway, see ya."

She took great satisfaction in slamming the door in his face. "Not if I see you first, jerk," she muttered. Poppy whined, and Cara knelt down on the floor and hugged her tightly. "Don't ever do that again, you hear me?"

Still kneeling, she gazed out the sidelights as Jack walked rapidly down Jones Street.

"Horrible man," she told Poppy. "I feel sorry for his real dog. No wonder she ran away from home."

She sniffed the top of Poppy's head and scratched under her chin. In addition to her puppy smell and the special rose-scented dog shampoo Cara bathed her with, there was a whiff of something else. Cara sniffed again, and recognized the scent.

"Sawdust?" she said, wrinkling her nose and holding Poppy at arm's length. "Really?"

9

There were days when Cara hated Savannah. No matter its lofty ambitions of being the Paris of the South, Savannah was still a very small town. Everybody who counted in the town's complicated social structure knew everybody else—and their business.

She chafed at Savannah's insularity, its petty small-town politics, and its collective suspicion of anything or anybody new or "from away." She'd tried hard to lose what she thought was only a faint Midwestern accent, but whenever she spoke to a local they invariably demanded to know where she was from.

On the other hand, sometimes that economy of scale worked in her favor. It had taken months for word of mouth to spread about Cara's flowers, and even then, it had only happened courtesy of a timid little bride named Kristin Marie Manley.

Somehow, Kristin had stumbled across Cara's cluttered little flower shop, back when she was still transitioning from Flowers by Norma. She hadn't even put up her pink and white awning, or changed the sign, so as far as the world knew, good old Norma Poole was still turning out big, bunchy arrangements of gladiolus and leatherleaf ferns.

Kristin was newly engaged to the son of a prominent Savannah banker. She'd been raised by her widower father, and the two of them were clueless about what was involved in putting on a big society wedding. So Cara had taken her in hand, spent hours and hours with her, and with a laughably spare budget had still managed to pull off one of the prettiest, most meaningful weddings she had ever planned.

As luck would have it, Kristin's new mother-in-law, Vicki Cooper, loved the flowers she'd done for her son's wedding, and absolutely adored Cara. Vicki was on the board of half a dozen Savannah charities and foundations, and within a year of Kristin's wedding to Cason Cooper, thanks to Vicki, Bloom was finally, slowly, starting to blossom.

Vicki, bless her generous, loudmouthed soul, was the gift that kept on giving.

Torie Fanning had been a Vicki connection—and on this steamy Monday morning in May, Cara had an appointment with yet another of Vicki's acquaintances.

Cara had heard from Vicki just the previous week. As usual, Vicki was on her way to yet another of her endless meetings.

"Listen, Cara, sugar, you're going to be hearing from a dear friend of mine, and I just want to give you a heads-up. Marie Trapnell's daughter Brooke just got engaged to the oldest Strayhorn boy, Harris. You know the Strayhorns, right?"

"Mmm, the name is familiar. Do they have something to do with shipping?"

"You could say that. Honey, Mitchell Strayhorn *is* Strayhorn Shipping. And of course, the Trapnells have been around Savannah since forever. I adore Marie Trapnell, and I know you'll be extra nice to her, 'cause she's goin' through kind of a hard time right now. Okay? Gotta scoot. Stay sweet, you hear?"

Cara fixed a pitcher of geranium-scented iced tea, filled two tumblers with ice, and arranged a few sugar cookies on a silver tray on her worktable. She placed her photo album on the table, then went over to the cooler and grabbed a handful of flowers—some daisies, a sprig of blue verbena, and some red bee balm.

These she clipped and stuffed in the sterling bud vase that had been her grandmother's.

The bells on the shop door tinkled, and a pale, nervous-looking woman stood looking uncertainly around the room.

"Mrs. Trapnell?" Cara hurried toward her, but Poppy bounded into the room, nearly knocking the poor woman on her butt.

"Poppy, down!" Cara cried. "Bad girl!"

"Oh, she's all right," the woman said, her voice soft. She stroked Poppy's ears and looked up at Cara. "What a beautiful dog. What breed is she?"

"She's a goldendoodle. A very disobedient, undisciplined cross between what's called a cream English golden retriever and a standard poodle," Cara said. "But please don't judge the breed by Poppy. I'm afraid I haven't been very effective at training her."

"She's just high-spirited, is all." The woman extended her hand. "I'm Marie Trapnell. Vicki Cooper's friend? And you're Cara—how do I pronounce your last name?"

" 'Krizzik'—the 'y' is soft," Cara said. "It's always good to meet one of Vicki's friends, Mrs. Trapnell. She seems to know everybody in Savannah, doesn't she?"

"Please, call me Marie. Yes, Vicki does know an astonishing number of people. I don't know how she juggles all her charitable and social commitments. I get exhausted just looking at one week of her calendar."

Cara guided Marie Trapnell to the worktable, seated her, and poured two glasses of iced tea.

"So," she said, once Marie seemed comfortable. "Vicki tells me your daughter just got engaged. What an exciting time for you."

Marie's face flushed softly with happiness. Now that she was sitting across the table from her, Cara realized the mother of the bride was probably much younger than she'd initially estimated. She was fair-complected, with intelligent brown eyes, a short, straight nose, and poker-straight shoulder-length graying brown hair pushed back from her high forehead with a tortoiseshell hair band. Her clothes were obviously expensive—a little nothing sleeveless cotton shift in a sedate pastel print, low-heeled pumps, and a Ferragamo handbag. She wore pearl stud earrings, but no other jewelry.

"Brooke wanted to come with me to meet you, but she had a client meeting she couldn't get out of. She's a second-year associate at Farrell Wynant Hanrahan," Marie said.

"Have they set the wedding date?" Cara asked, opening her day planner.

"Oh yes," Marie said. "And that's what's giving me heart palpitations. They're getting married in less than eight weeks."

"Oh my," Cara said. "That doesn't give us much time, does it?"

"It gives me *no* time," Marie agreed. "I've tried and tried to get Brooke and Harris to move the date at least to October, but Harris is adamant. July sixth it is, and he refuses to discuss any other date."

"Well . . ." Cara turned to the July page of her calendar. She had weddings every Saturday of the month, and several big debutante parties later that month. But a big black X had been drawn through the notes she'd scribbled there.

"Ahh, yes," Cara said, tapping the X with a fingertip. "I did have a wedding scheduled on the sixth, but I'm afraid it's been called off."

"Oh." Marie looked startled. "Oh, how sad."

Marie would never know just how sad Cara was about that canceled wedding. Hannah Draper's daddy had major bucks, and only one daughter. But just two weeks earlier, Hannah had come home from her senior year at Wellesley and announced a change of plans. Hannah, it seemed, had discovered her true sexual leanings, and was deliriously in love with her field-hockey coach.

Thank God, Cara was thinking, she'd been firm about that nonrefundable fifty percent deposit on the flowers. And thank God, again, that this new bride wanted the only open Saturday she had for July.

"Was your daughter able to book a church on such short notice?" Cara knew that all the big downtown churches, Christ Church, Independent Presbyterian, St. John's Episcopal, Wesley Monumental, First Baptist, and the Cathedral of St. John the Baptist, were all always booked up for summer weddings as far as two years in advance. She knew of at least one bride, Leigh-Anne

Grady, whose mother had booked her wedding at Christ Church two months before dear Leigh-Anne had actually gotten engaged.

Marie fiddled with one of her pearl earrings. "The church isn't the problem. We're actually going to have the ceremony and the reception at Cabin Creek—the Strayhorns' plantation in South Carolina."

"Ahh," Cara said, trying to contain her excitement. She'd seen photos of Cabin Creek in numerous magazines. It was a working rice plantation on twelve hundred acres, just across the river from Savannah. From the photographs it looked like the main house would make Tara look like a bait shack.

In her mind, Cara was already designing the flower arrangements for Cabin Creek's high-ceilinged entrance hall. She'd have to meet the bride very soon, to discover her flower and color preferences. Was she a brunette like her mother?

"Um, Cara?"

"Oh, sorry. Marie, I've got so many questions. When do you think Brooke will be available to meet with me? And what about Harris? And his mother? Since it's their home, will they want to be consulted?"

"Harris?" Marie looked blank. "Do you usually talk to the grooms? I guess it didn't occur to me. . . ."

"It just depends on the couple. Some grooms like to be consulted on every detail of the event, while with others—and I will say this is the majority—all they care about is what kind of beer is served at the reception."

"Well, uh, Harris probably falls into the latter group," Marie said. "Anyway, he travels a good bit for business, and according to Brooke, all he cares about is that everything is tasteful. Libba Strayhorn, that's Harris's mother, has already said she's happy for me to plan everything." She gave Cara a dubious shrug. "Libba is very horsey. According to Harris, she'd live in the stables at Cabin Creek if she could."

"I have to admit, it's sort of overwhelming," Marie went on. "I've never had to plan a wedding before. I eloped, you see. Anyway, I'd really hoped Brooke could join us this morning. To tell you the truth, I didn't even know where to begin. I was just talking to Vicki about that last week—we're both on the literacy-council board, and she insisted that you would be the perfect person to help us."

"Vicki has been very kind to me," Cara said. "I've done weddings for several of her friends in town."

"That's what she said. In fact, I was at Torie Fanning's wedding Saturday night. I thought everything was absolutely beautiful."

"I'm glad," Cara said. "Maybe we could start there. Was there anything in particular at Torie's wedding that you liked—or even disliked?"

"Well . . . I loved all those hydrangeas. So old-fashioned. But Brooke is a very modern girl. I'm not sure she'd share my opinion."

Cara flipped open the cover of her photo album. "These are photos of some of my weddings over the past few years. Most of these are in my portfolio on my website, so hopefully, you and Brooke could look through it and see if there are any flowers or styles or colors that speak to you."

Marie nodded. "That sounds like a good idea. All I have to do is manage to get Brooke to slow down for an hour or so to think about the wedding."

"What about her gown?" Cara asked. "It would be helpful if I had a photo of it—and also of her bridesmaids' gowns."

"Her gown." Marie said it like a sigh. "She hasn't bought one yet."

"Really?" Cara raised one eyebrow. "Is she aware that it can take as long as three months to order a gown, get it delivered and fitted?"

"How well I know," Marie said. "This daughter of mine—she can be unbelievably stubborn. She's looked in magazines, shopped in Atlanta, tried on dozens and dozens of gowns, but so far she says the dress—the magic dress, she calls it—hasn't grabbed her. I want to grab *her*—around the throat," she said apologetically.

"Can she wear a dress off the rack?" Cara asked, which was a tactful way of asking if the MIA bride was a standard size.

"She's a size six, so I don't think it will be too hard to fit her," Marie said. "But I'd feel so much better if she could just choose something . . . anything."

Cara scribbled a note to herself on her notepad, then looked back at Marie. "Bridesmaids? How many?"

"One. Just one maid of honor. Harris's sister Holly."

"Does Holly have a dress? Do we know what color?"

Marie rolled her eyes. "Brown. For a July wedding. It seems all wrong to me. Does a brown dress sound as awful to you as it does to me?"

"Wellll . . ." Cara flipped a couple of pages of the photo album. "It depends on how brown the brown dress is. For instance, the right shade can be flattering—and brown is a wonderful foil for pale pink flowers." She tapped a fingertip on a photo of a wedding she'd done the previous October. "See?"

Marie opened the gold clasp of her pocketbook, pulled out a pair of horn-rimmed reading glasses, and peered down at the photo. "Oh. Hmm. But this was a fall wedding, wasn't it? And the girl—the bridesmaid—she was a blond. Holly is a strawberry blond."

"You've got a point there," Cara said. "But can you talk Brooke and Holly out of a brown dress for a July wedding?"

"Probably not."

"Then we'll figure out a way to make it work."

Marie smiled and closed the book. "Vicki was right. I do like you." She bit her lip and looked out the window of the shop.

"But?" Cara asked, waiting for the other shoe to drop.

"It's not up to me. Not completely."

"Of course, I understand totally," Cara said. "When do you think Brooke can make time to meet with me?"

"Not Brooke," Marie said quietly. "Her father."

10

Marie Trapnell was flipping the pages of the wedding photo album, avoiding Cara's eyes.

"Gordon—my ex-husband—has been very clear that he wants to be completely involved in the planning of Brooke's wedding."

"That's very . . . sweet," Cara said, trying to tread carefully. "I guess he and Brooke must be very close?"

"At one time Brooke was an absolute daddy's girl. Since the divorce, well, Brooke is conflicted. She feels loyalty to me, I think, and she's still angry at her father. And her new stepmother."

Marie's eyes flickered with something resembling emotion. "We are *all* still angry at Gordon. Nevertheless, Gordon is adamant that if he is to pay for this wedding he has to have complete veto power."

"I see." Cara had done lots of weddings for brides and grooms with divorced parents. It was never particularly easy, but the upcoming Trapnell-Strayhorn nuptials were already sounding like a major pain in the posterior.

"Would your ex-husband like to meet with me? Or would he prefer to wait until we come up with some kind of a proposal and a budget?"

Marie was fidgeting with her other earring now. "I should warn you,

Gordon is interviewing other florists. He seems to think that's how you plan a wedding. Brooke has tried to reason with him, but, well, Gordon does things his own way."

"I appreciate your letting me know that." Cara closed the photo album. "To be honest, Marie, I have a pretty busy summer coming up. I appreciate your honesty, and your interest in working with me, but if your ex wants to hire somebody else, well, maybe I'm not the right person for you."

"No!" Marie's voice was sharp. "You're the exact right florist for our wedding. Please don't bow out. I've seen your photo album, I was at Torie's wedding. I know you'll give Brooke something lovely and memorable. I'll have Brooke look at your website, but I know she'll love your work. And then, maybe she can talk some sense into her daddy. If he'll listen to anybody, he'll listen to her."

"Of course," Cara said. "Talk it over with Brooke. Have her look at my portfolio. But do keep in mind that time is really running very short for a July wedding. If I'm going to do a good job, I'll need some kind of a commitment from you—by the end of the week. Does that sound reasonable?"

"Very reasonable." Marie stood and straightened the nonexistent wrinkles in her dress.

Cara nodded. "Just out of curiosity—do you happen to know what other florists your ex-husband is interviewing?"

Marie chewed her bottom lip. "It's just one florist. Somebody Patricia met at a wedding in Charleston. I don't actually know his name. Just that he's very well known, and considered very chic. I believe he's just opened a shop here in Savannah. I think he and Patricia have become bosom buddies."

"And Patricia is?"

Marie's brown eyes narrowed. "Gordon's new wife."

As soon as the would-be new client left, Bert popped his head out of the back room, where he'd been getting hospital orders ready for delivery. He rubbed his hands together in the manner of a cartoon villain. "Oooh. Drama."

Cara laughed. "Which I don't especially need in my life right now."

Poppy edged over to Bert and rubbed up against his legs.

"Hello, Miss Thang," Bert said, obligingly scratching the dog's ears. "When did you come home?"

"Yesterday morning. It seems her captor discovered his own dog at his vet's office. He showed up here at eight yesterday morning, looking pretty embarrassed."

"Good for him," Bert said. "Poppy doesn't seem any worse for the wear, right?"

"Guess not," she admitted. "I had to give her a bath just to get rid of the smell of sawdust. And I don't ever want to go through a night like that again."

"Tell me about our new client. Obviously, I was eavesdropping from the back room. But I came in late. Who is she, and where did she come from?"

"Another of Vicki Cooper's friends. Her name is Marie Trapnell, and her daughter is marrying one of the Strayhorns."

"Big money marrying big money. Me likey," Bert said. "But the ex-husband has to approve you? And he's interviewing another florist? What is up with that?"

"Sounds like another control freak. Which I would just as soon avoid. Marie seems like a very nice person, but I honestly won't mind when they choose somebody else."

"Wait just a second," Bert protested. "Why wouldn't they choose you?"

"You heard the woman, right? The daddy wants some hotshot florist from Charleston. I guess this guy just decided to expand into Savannah."

Bert moved over to the laptop, and his long, tanned fingers began to fly over the keyboard. "Hang on, I'm Googling."

A moment later he looked up. "Well, his name is Cullen Kane, and from the look of his website, he has quite the business. Big-ass shop on Tradd Street, and he's had lots of events published—*Town and Country, Charleston Magazine, Garden and Gun*, and on and on. He just expanded to Savannah last month. Opened a little outpost on Habersham Street."

Cara's curiosity got the better of her. "Let me see that thing." She peered over Bert's shoulder at the website. The opening page was an extreme closeup of a mouthwateringly beautiful all-white bride's bouquet, featuring velvety magnolia blossoms, crinum lilies, orange blossoms, and stephanotis.

She paged over to Cullen Kane's portfolio, which featured dozens of achingly gorgeous photographs of his flowers showcased in all kinds of settings.

Bert clicked the mouse on the About Us tab of the website, and read his bio aloud in a deeply accented Southern cartoon voice that made him sound like Foghorn Leghorn.

> Cullen Kane is a native Charlestonian. He received his undergraduate degree in English Literature from the College of Charleston. Cullen spent his senior year abroad in England, where he met and studied floral design for three years under famed horticulturist Rosemary Verey. Returning to the States, Cullen settled in Napa Valley, California, where he became the in-house floral designer for Valleyview House, the largest private event venue in Napa. In 2008, Cullen returned home to Charleston, where he opened Cullen Kane Floral Design Studio.

"Here's a photo of him," Bert said, tapping the laptop screen.

"Oh shit," Cara said.

The photo of Cullen Kane showed him lounging in an artistically weathered Adirondack chair, with a stretch of the low-country marsh in the background. He was dressed in an open-necked white dress shirt, with a celadon-green sweater knotted casually over his shoulders. His glossy blond hair was worn stylishly long, he had a small goatee, and his hand rested lightly on a Cavalier King Charles spaniel in his lap. He was a candy-coated cinematic version of everything a Southern gentleman should look like.

"I'd hire him if I weren't me," Cara said glumly.

"He's certainly yummy-looking," Bert agreed. "You know, if you go in for that kind of screamingly effeminate, highly overqualified overachieving type. But if he's such a hotshot in Charleston, why would he want to open shop in Savannah?"

"To make my life a living hell," she said.

Bert laughed. "That's right, Cara. Cullen Kane hasn't even met you and he's already conspiring to put you out of business and ruin your life. Are we feeling just the teeniest bit paranoid this morning?"

Monday was technically Cara's day off, but she hadn't hesitated to schedule the appointment with Marie Trapnell.

Now Poppy was standing by the door, scratching to go out.

"I'll take her if you like," Bert offered.

"Thanks, but it'll do me good to stretch my legs," Cara said. She grabbed Poppy's leash and clipped it to her collar, which she'd already shortened by a notch.

"Now listen," she told the puppy, who was already straining at her leash as they exited the shop. "Slow down. Heel. We've really got to work on this obedience thing, you know."

It was a spectacular late-spring morning. The sky was blue, and a slight breeze stirred the Spanish moss draping the live-oak trees.. She gave Poppy a little slack in her leash and the dog gamboled along happily down the street. Cara heard feet approaching rapidly from behind.

"On your left," a gruff voice called out. She stepped to the right just in time to avoid being mowed down by a sweaty male jogger wearing a white T-shirt and red running shorts. He had a familiar-looking puppy on a leash.

Poppy gave an excited yelp of recognition and lunged for the puppy and the jogger, nearly yanking Cara off her feet.

"Poppy, heel!" Cara exclaimd. "Sit!"

But Poppy did no such thing. She strained at her leash, whining her disappointment at being kept from joining the jogger.

It was him! Jack the dog thief. She watched as he and his dog sped away down the street, without so much as a backward glance. It had all happened so fast she'd nearly missed it. But yes, the other puppy did bear a resemblance to Poppy. She was certainly a goldendoodle, and she shared Poppy's creamy coloring and curly coat.

"Come on, girl," Cara said, giving her dog an affectionate ear scratch. "Let's get a move on before it gets too hot."

She and Poppy continued their stroll, walking down Jones to Whitaker, and then south on Whitaker, where she happily window-shopped at the half-dozen little boutiques and antique shops that were some of her favorite local haunts. They continued on Whitaker, crossing over at Gaston Street when they got close to Forsyth Park.

It was late, nearly ten, but the park was still full of joggers, dog walkers, and young mothers with babies in strollers and toddlers in tow. Cara greeted several young mothers who'd been her brides not so long ago. She and Poppy did one circuit of the park, then walked over to the Sentient Bean, where she treated herself to a cold bottle of water and an orange cranberry scone and Poppy to a vegan dog biscuit.

When they were within a block of home, Poppy, already a creature of habit at seven months, did her business in her own dainty way, squatting in her customary spot between two huge camellia bushes, as though she required absolute privacy from prying eyes. Cara cleaned up after her pet, and walked back to the shop, keeping a wary eye out for joggers with goldendoodles.

Bert was finishing up a staid hospital arrangement of daisies and carnations.

"You're not going to believe it," he said, after she'd unclipped Poppy and washed her hands. "I just got off the phone with Lillian Fanning."

"And what was her complaint? Honestly, Bert, Torie's wedding was truly as close to perfection as I've ever gotten. And yet she still finds something to bitch about? I give up!"

"Not so fast," Bert said. "She wasn't calling to complain. Actually she was calling to thank you for making Torie's day so amazing. Her phone's been ringing off the hook from calls from all her friends, wanting to know who did Torie's flowers."

"Really? Lillian was actually pleased about something? That's a first."

" 'Tickled pink' were her exact words. And," he added, then paused for drama. "She also wanted to ask a huge favor."

"Such as?"

"She's giving a baby-shower luncheon for Torie's cousin Lindsay at the golf club tomorrow, and it just occurred to her that she'd love for us to whip up a few 'teensy' little centerpieces, and a corsage. I told her no, of course. There's no way we can do something like that with no lead time."

"Why would you do that? We can't turn down business, especially from somebody like Lillian Fanning."

Bert gestured toward the shop's glass-fronted flower cooler. "Look in there. We're cleaned out. I used the last pathetic little carnations for this hospital arrangement that just came in. All we've got left is some sad yellow spider mums and a few sprigs of baby's breath. Which we both know will never satisfy Lillian. She wouldn't have spider mums and baby's breath for her worst enemy's funeral. And Lamar won't be back here until day after tomorrow."

"Oh." Cara stood in front of the cooler and peered inside. Bert had a point. The dozen buckets of water in the cooler were nearly empty.

"Dadgummit. I hate giving up that kind of business. Was Lillian talking about the smaller eight-tops at the golf club?"

"Yes," Bert said. "but it doesn't matter. We don't have any flowers. You're a floral designer, Cara. Not a magician."

"How many tables?" Cara asked, reaching for her phone with one hand and her supplier's catalogue with the other.

"Eight," Bert said. "What are you thinking?"

"What color scheme?" Cara asked, rapidly flipping the pages of the catalogue.

"She didn't specify. Just something pretty and springish. You're not seriously thinking of taking this party on, are you?"

"Is the baby a girl or boy?"

"Girl," Bert said.

"Call Lillian Fanning," she told Bert. "And let her know there's been a change of plans."

Cara had her Savannah wholesaler, Breitmueller's, on speed dial.

"Wendy? This is Cara over at Bloom. How are you?"

"Fine," Wendy Breitmueller said cautiously. "What do you need, Cara?"

"Pink and white," Cara said. "Springy, youthful. With maybe some silvery gray foliage? And I need something feminine and pretty for corsages, but no gigantic orchids. Maybe some pink spray roses?"

"Mmm-hmm," Cara said, jotting down notes as Wendy listed what was available. "That sounds good. Love the idea of the tulips and the pink stocks and the foxgloves. And I'll take all the pink gerberas you've got. Can you put everything aside for me? I'll come over right away to pick everything up."

She hung up the phone and grabbed her car keys.

"Lillian is thrilled you'll do her flowers. But I think you're crazy," Bert said disapprovingly. "It's supposed to be your day off, remember? And when was the last time you actually took any time for yourself?"

"I know exactly how long it's been," Cara said ruefully. "I haven't had a real day off since the Monday before Valentine's Day last year."

Valentine's Day the previous year had been memorable, for sure, but for all the wrong reasons. It was her birthday, but because of the business she was in, Cara rarely had time to celebrate.

That year had been crazier than usual. She'd been forced to rent a second van just to get the flower deliveries covered. And when her second driver slipped and fell and broke his ankle on the third delivery of the afternoon, Cara had gotten behind the wheel of the van in his place.

She was making the last delivery of the afternoon, to a dentist's office on the south side of town: two dozen long-stemmed American Beauty roses to the dentist's wife, who ran the office, for her husband, Dr. Pratt, one of Cara's regular customers.

While Nancy Pratt was oohing and aahing over the roses from her husband in the reception area, another florist's delivery driver had walked into the office, with a huge vase of lilacs.

Lilacs? Who ordered lilacs in Savannah? Only one man Cara knew of. Her husband, Leo.

As soon as she saw the lilacs, Mrs. Pratt opened the door to the back office. "Cyndi! Flowers from your mystery man again."

Cara heard a chorus of giggles from the girls in the office—the receptionists and billing clerks and hygienists. "Our Cyndi has a mysterious beau who sends her gorgeous flowers every month," Mrs. Pratt confided.

A petite redhead in a tight-fitting white lab coat unbuttoned just enough to reveal her double-D décolletage burst through the door.

"Oh my God, is he is the sweetest thing ever?" She reached for the card stuck among the lilacs. Then she saw Cara, standing there beside Mrs. Pratt and her American Beauty roses, and Cyndi froze. She snatched the vase and disappeared into the back office.

Cara had seen enough. When she got home she picked up the huge vase of lilacs that had been left on her doorstep, and set them on the kitchen counter. She listened to the message Leo left on her voicemail. "Late meeting tonight. Sorry babe. I know you'll be dead on your feet by the time you get this, so we'll celebrate your birthday tomorrow night. 'Kay? Love you."

Leo's message had a strangely energizing effect on Cara. She went into his home office, and using a nail file, pried open the desk drawer where he kept their financial records. It was easy to find the statements for the new Visa card he'd procured for himself, easier still to find the monthly flower deliveries to Cyndi Snodgrass and the biweekly check-ins at the Airport Courtyard Marriott, visits that neatly coincided with Leo's supposed sales meetings in Atlanta.

Cara left the Visa statements on top of the desk. She dumped the lilacs onto the middle of their bed. She packed her clothes and her books and called Bert on the way over to his apartment to ask if she could stay in his guest room for a few nights.

She'd hired a lawyer and started divorce proceedings the next day, and within two weeks she'd rented the apartment over Bloom. And she'd worked every day since then, with the exception of the day after this Valentine's Day, when she'd gone to visit the breeder in Atlanta to pick out her own birthday present, her new roommate, Poppy.

"You're going to burn yourself out," Bert chided her now. "Do you realize we've got weddings every Saturday for the next six weeks, not to mention the Mandelbaums' golden anniversary party and those two huge banquets at the Westin? Plus the deb parties . . ."

"We can't afford to turn down Lillian Fanning," Cara said firmly. "Between Lillian and Vicki Cooper—if this keeps up we'll have more business than we can handle."

"We *already* have more business than we can deal with," Bert grumped.

"We can handle it," Cara said.

"Yeah, if we don't want to have a life. Which I do," he added.

"Are you referring to your new frat friend? Or the fireman?" Cara asked.

Bert winked. "You could say things are heating up with my love life." He put an arm around her shoulders. "And what about you? It's been what, a year and a half since you left Leo? You have got to stop burying yourself in work, Cara."

"Stop and smell the roses, you mean?"

"Something like that. Not all men are like Leo, you know. Some of us are actually faithful and caring and thoughtful. And fun to be around."

"All the men I know who fit that description in this town are gay," Cara pointed out.

"You never meet any new men. All you ever do is work. And you'll never meet anybody nice again if you keep up like this," Bert said.

"Has it occurred to you that I don't want to meet anybody new?" Cara tried to keep her voice light. "I'm done with men." She reached down and scooped the wriggling Poppy into her arms, burying her nose in the dog's rose-scented curls.

"I've got a dog now," she informed her assistant. "She never steals the covers. Never lies. And she would never, ever sleep with some skanky dental hygienist with short arms and big boobs. Plus, Poppy loves me unconditionally."

"Except when she runs away," Bert said.

"That reminds me," Cara said. "When I was out walking Poppy earlier, the jerk ran right past me—with his real dog in tow."

"But he did go to all the trouble to track you down here and bring her back yesterday," Bert said. "So he can't be that big a jerk."

"You don't know him like I do," Cara said. "Look, Bert. I've got to get moving if I'm going to get over to Breitmueller's for Lillian's flowers. Will you keep an eye on Poppy?"

"That's cool," Bert said. He looked down at Poppy, who was standing by the window, wagging her tail as she watched a woman walk by with a pair of dachshunds on leash. "But maybe you should think about getting Poppy microchipped. Just in case she gets out again. Right?"

"All right, all right, I will," Cara said. "The very next time I have a day off."

11

On Tuesday, Cara used one hip to bump open the door at the Savannah Golf Club at 10:45 a.m. Her face was beaded with perspiration and she was well aware that she looked a hot mess.

The previous day's pickup from Breitmueller's had been a failure.

She'd arrived at the wholesaler shortly before noon. But the buckets of flowers holding her order were nothing like what she'd been promised.

Gaudy hot pink dyed carnations, some sad-looking cream spray roses, a few Stargazer lilies, and loads of stiff yellowish baby's breath.

She marched over to the office, where Wendy Breitmueller was typing away on her computer terminal.

"Oh, hi, Cara," Wendy said, not looking up. "We pulled your order, it's back out in the warehouse."

"That's not what I ordered, Wendy," Cara said sharply. "Come on! Baby's breath? And those yucky dyed carnations? Where are my tulips? My pink spray roses? My gerberas?"

Wendy sighed. "Look, it's not my fault. Allen took a big phone order just before I talked to you, and he'd already promised all the stuff you wanted to another client. You know how it goes. This is our busy season, and unless you call up a week ahead of time and let us know what you need, you take what you get. First come, first served."

"But you promised *me*," Cara reminded her. "Not less than an hour ago. I've got a baby shower tomorrow for one of my regular clients, and there is no way I can show up at the golf club with that mess out there."

"You're welcome to walk around in the warehouse and pick out whatever else looks good," Wendy said with a shrug. Reluctantly, she got up from her computer and led Cara back into the chilled air of the warehouse.

Cara saw a huge cluster of buckets lined up near the loading-dock doors, holding what looked like a whole greenhouse full of blooms: peonies, tulips, hydrangeas, orchids, roses, ranunculus, lilies, and more.

"That!" Cara said, pointing. "That's what you promised me."

"Sorry, like I told you, it's all spoken for. Allen's new customer."

"Wow. All that for one client?"

"He's got two shops. Been open in Charleston for a while, and now he's moved over to Savannah too. And he's just as particular about his flowers as you."

Cara felt a twinge of jealousy. "Are all these flowers for Cullen Kane?"

"Sure," Wendy said. "You know him?"

"Just of him," she said. "I guess he has some pretty fancy clients."

"I'd say so," Wendy said.

Cara was still looking at all those flowers by the loading dock. "Wait a minute, Wendy. He's got *tons* of pink tulips. But I didn't get any. And I specifically ordered three dozen."

Wendy shrugged. "Nothing I can do about it, Cara."

"Since when?" Cara asked. "You're the owner. Come on, Wendy. You know this isn't right. I might not order as many flowers as this new guy, but I've been a good customer. You can't just short me like this. At least split the order with me."

"Oh, Cara," Wendy sighed.

Cara could sense she was softening.

"Wendy? Don't do me like this. Please? I need those tulips."

She shook her head, then gestured toward the buckets of flowers, looking furtively around the warehouse. "I can spare a dozen of these pink tulips."

"Two dozen," Cara said, not too proud to beg. "I've got all these tabletops at the golf club."

"Eighteen," Wendy said. "Take 'em, but be quick about it. I don't want Allen to catch me raiding his customer's order. I'll adjust your bill. Now shoo, before I change my mind."

Cara spent all Tuesday morning scrounging up enough greenery to fill in for the missing flowers for her centerpieces—snipping asparagus ferns from one friend's garden in Ardsley Park, Meyer lemon leaves from a client's courtyard, and silvery-gray lamb's ears from the hip-pocket-sized container garden she tended behind the shop. She made a trip over to Whole Foods and bought four fat pots of pink hydrangeas, wincing at the cash register while she paid retail prices for the flowers.

She'd even made a quick trip out to Wilmington Island, where she knew of a thick patch of blue plumbago growing in the Publix shopping center parking lot. She'd parked her car right by the patch, snipped a big batch, then fled like a thief in the night. It wasn't really stealing, she'd told herself. The plumbago needed trimming.

All that foraging put her behind schedule—she'd intended to get to the golf club by ten. She had her arms full—a huge cardboard box containing eight square glass centerpieces, plus the corsages in their clear plastic clamshell boxes. She looked around the nearly empty lobby, wondering where the party was being held.

Lillian Fanning hurried toward her. She wore a sleeveless coral sheath, matching sling-back heels, and a necklace of twined turquoise, coral, and seed pearls. "Cara!" she called. "We're back here, in the grill." Lillian looked pointedly down at the thin gold watch on her wrist.

"Hi, Lillian," Cara said. "Sorry to be a little late."

Lillian glanced over at the box. "Those look nice," she said. "I'm so glad you could do this. I know it was short notice, but after seeing all the beautiful centerpieces you did for Torie, I just couldn't settle for those dreary little half-dead flower sprigs the club puts out for luncheons."

"Happy to do it," Cara said, struggling to keep up in Lillian's wake.

The tables in the grill had already been set for luncheon. Pale pink cloths covered the rounds, and somebody, Lillian, she assumed, had placed tiny wrapped boxes at each place setting. Cara hurried around the room, depositing the centerpieces where Lillian directed.

They heard voices coming from the doorway. "Oh good," Lillian said, turning to see the first arrivals. "That's Lindsay."

"Then I'll just get out of your hair," Cara said. She unloaded the corsages onto a chair and made a beeline for the door.

She was streaking across the lobby when she heard a familiar voice call her name.

"Cara! Yoo-hoo!"

Vicki Cooper and a woman Cara didn't recognize were walking toward her.

Cara pasted a smile on her face and wiped her palms on the seat of her capris. She was sweaty and her clothes were smudged with specks of mud from her morning of greenery wrangling, and she should have stopped back at the shop to change her clothes before delivering the flowers to the club, but time had been her enemy all morning.

Vicki Cooper, on the other hand, looked fresh as a daisy in a sleeveless black silk dress, silver wedge sandals, and chunky silver bracelets and hoop earrings. Vicki's shimmery white hair hung to her shoulders. Her deep blue eyes were lightly made up and she wore a peach-colored lipstick. At sixty, Vicki looked like what Cara wanted to be when she grew up.

"Pretend you don't see me," Cara told Vicki, giving her a quick hug. "I've been playing in the dirt all morning, and I'm a big mess."

"You look fine! Cara, I want you to meet Faith McCurdy. Faith, this is our favorite florist in town, Cara Kryzik. She did all the flowers for our son's wedding, and she's an absolute genius."

The other woman was in her early sixties, dressed in a tidy shirtwaist dress, heels, and hose. "So nice to meet you," she murmured.

"Faith's nephew Tyler Carver is married to Lindsay Fanning," Vicki said. "Is that what you're doing here? Flowers for the baby shower?"

"Just delivered them," Cara said. She looked around the lobby and saw several groups of women walking toward the entrance to the grill. "And I better move along."

"Oh, don't run off just yet," Vicki protested, catching Cara by the arm. "Faith, you go ahead on. I'll be along in a minute. I just want to chat with Cara for a moment."

Vicki drew Cara to an alcove on the far side of the lobby, gesturing for her to sit on a settee looking out on the golf course.

"I won't take a minute of your time," Vicki started. "Just wanted to check. Did you hear from Marie Trapnell?"

"I met with her yesterday. Thanks so much for the referral."

"Well?" Vicki raised an eyebrow expectantly.

"It's . . . complicated," Cara said. "Marie is very nice, and we hit it off immediately. But it sounds as though her ex-husband is the one who is really running the show. She says he's got another florist in town he's very interested in working with. I told her I understand . . ."

"What?" Vicki's voice echoed through the high-ceilinged room. "Are you telling me Gordon Trapnell now fancies himself as an event planner?"

Cara looked around the room, uneasy at discussing a client's private life, even if the client might not even turn out to be her client.

"According to Marie, Mr. Trapnell wants to be involved in every aspect of his daughter's wedding."

"Oh, puh-leez," Vicki drawled. "Gordon doesn't care a thing in the world about this wedding. He just wants to make a big show of being the adoring daddy to his darling Brookie, because he's eaten up with guilt over his shabby treatment of poor Marie. Which he should be. But Brooke's a smart girl. She has no illusions about Daddy Rat."

"This doesn't sound like something I need to get in the middle of," Cara demurred.

"What exactly did Marie tell you—about the circumstances of her divorce?" Vicki asked, leaning forward. "Come on, you can tell me. It's not like it's a secret."

Cara shrugged. "She didn't get into the details. She just said she thinks Brooke feels torn—between loyalty to her mother, and anger at her father. Something about the second wife?"

"Patricia," Vicki said. "Or Patti, as she used to be called before she decided to reinvent herself. Patricia Showalter Linencamp Trapnell. Do you know her?"

"No."

"You haven't missed much," Vicki said. "What a remorseless little tramp she is. And when I think about how she had all of us fooled . . ."

Cara twisted around in her chair. She really needed to get back to the shop. And she didn't want to be seen slinging mud with Vicki Cooper right in the middle of the golf-club lobby. It just didn't look right.

"I know, I know, you think this is all just petty gossip," Vicki said. "But you know me, Cara. I never gossip."

Cara struggled to keep a straight face.

"How did you leave it with Marie?" Vicki asked.

"I just asked if she could let me know by Friday whether or not her ex had decided to hire this other florist his new wife, Patricia, knows."

"Oh yes, Cullen Kane, boy wonder. Patricia's new best friend. I hear they're practically joined at the hip these days. And that's who Gordon wants to hire to do the flowers for Brooke's wedding?"

"I think so," Cara said. "Although Marie did say her ex might want to interview me."

"Absurd!" Vicki said. "Gordon doesn't know the first thing about flowers. This is all Patricia's doing."

"I might just go ahead and bow out," Cara said. "After all, if they really want Cullen Kane . . ."

"Don't you dare!" Vicki said sharply. "This is all just a control issue. Gordon wants to prove that he still has Marie under his big fat thumb, that's all."

"Still, if he's paying for his daughter's wedding, you can't blame him for wanting to be consulted."

"Marie doesn't need Gordon's money to pay for Brooke's wedding. She inherited more money than he'll ever think about having, from her grandfather when he passed away last year," Vicki confided.

"I've known Gordon for years and years," Vicki said now. "Patricia too, for that matter. And I hate what the two of them have done to Marie. She's a shell of her former self, Cara. Would you believe, she used to be a senior vice president at one of the biggest ad agencies in New York? She's twice as smart as Gordon ever hoped to be, but gave up her career after she married that goober. Even after she had Brooke, Marie was a powerhouse. Headed up the development committee for Brooke's school that raised a five-million-dollar endowment fund, was on the board of the library, she helped get the book festival started here, chaired the United Way campaign . . ."

"Really?" It was hard for Cara to reconcile the image of a powerful business executive with the nervous, uncertain woman she'd met the previous day.

"The divorce shook her to the core," Vicki confided. She made a face. "When I think of that weasel Patricia, pretending to be Marie's dear friend all those years—it literally makes me sick. You think you know somebody, right? And then they turn out to be a devious, backstabbing bitch."

"You were friends with this Patricia?"

"Honey, we all ran around in the same crowd. Brooke and my Cason started preschool together. Patricia's twins from her first marriage were a year older, and anyway, after Patricia split with Billy, her second husband, she shipped the boys off to military school and that was the last we saw of them. I never liked Patricia, her pretensions were always a little much as far as I was concerned—but our husbands were business associates and golf buddies. You know how that works in this town."

Cara did know.

"When Patricia snaked Gordon away from Marie, she did more than just wreck a marriage. She broke up our supper club—couples were taking sides, of course, and it wasn't fun anymore. Our book club dissolved—Marie was the glue, and after she quit coming, because of Patricia, we never got back on track. I know it's selfish of me, considering what Marie has been through, but really, even though it's been four or five years, I'm still so mad about book club I could spit!"

As she talked, Vicki was idly watching the flow of traffic in the country-club lobby. Men in golf and tennis togs filtered in, heading for the men's card room; young mothers with small children in swimsuits came in from the pool. Vicki's eyes widened.

"Well I'll be damned," she said, her voice low. "Speak of the devil."

Cara casually glanced to her left. Two women were walking in, their heads bent together in conversation. They headed toward the main dining room.

"The blonde? With the face transplant? That's Patricia," Vicki murmured. "I don't know the gal she's with. Probably one of her new friends from Charleston. She pretty much burned all her bridges here, so she had to go trawling up there for some new besties."

Patricia Trapnell was scanning the room as she walked. She spotted Vicki Cooper, gave her a bright smile and a finger wave, then turned back toward her friend.

"She knows better than to try to speak to me," Vicki said bitterly.

Cara saw an opening and went for it. "Thanks for the backgrounder on the Trapnells, Vicki. It's probably a good thing to get the whole story before I meet with the husband. But I have a feeling this is all going to be moot, if Patricia is that close to Cullen Kane."

She stood up to leave, but Vicki seized her by the arm.

"Look, Cara. I know you don't want to get involved in some messy intramarital showdown. All I'm saying is, don't back down just yet. I'm thinking Marie is about to get fed up with Gordon's dictatorial bullshit. And when she does, she's going to want Brooke's wedding to be everything that girl has dreamed of since she was in pigtails. You're the one who can give her that. Right?"

"Maybe," Cara conceded. "Guess I'll just have to wait and see how the interview goes."

12

The courtyard garden behind the little shop on Jones Street was what convinced her not to leave when Cara was considering moving the shop after she inherited it from Norma.

Cara told herself that she stayed out of convenience. Plus, there was the space itself—high-ceilinged and airy, with a wide front window looking out on the street, a serviceable office nook, and a nice-sized workroom that could be curtained off from her showroom. There was space in the showroom for her flower cooler, and shelves that held the various unusual and vintage containers and knickknacks she sold in addition to her flower arrangements. There was a dedicated parking space out back for the delivery van. And the block itself was a good one, on tree-shaded West Jones Street, surrounded by private residences as well as a handful of discreet businesses: a trendy women's boutique, a gift and card shop, and a pair of antique shops.

On the downside, she'd had to put hours and hours of sweat equity into transforming the place from Norma's to Bloom: sanding and refinishing the floors, painting the exposed brick walls, and having display shelves and tables built. It was only when her costs began to mount up that she'd had to go to her father, hat in hand, to beg for a loan.

She might have been okay after that, if life hadn't happened. If the van hadn't needed a whole new suspension. If the computer hadn't died, if she hadn't had to pay for expensive photography to showcase her portfolio on her website. If. If. If.

Still, most days, she was at peace with the decision to stay on Jones Street and live above the shop. And the thing that that made her heart really sing about her new home was that pocket-sized courtyard garden. It was surrounded by a high wall of aged Savannah gray bricks, and the design was simple, two narrow rectangular planting beds outlined with more brick and a border of dwarf boxwoods.

A brick walkway bisected the space, and there was a small brick-paved patio.

When she'd inherited the lease from Norma, the beds were overgrown with chickweed, privet, wild onions, and morning glories that spilled over the borders and onto the basketweave brick walkway. A ginormous wisteria vine with a trunk the size of her waist had taken up occupancy in the right rear corner of the courtyard, and its tendrils had wound their way clear around the brick walls and up a neighbor's two-story-high camellia.

Busy with remodeling the downstairs, she'd had no time to spend on that garden, until her marriage crumbled and she'd retreated to the apartment on the top floor of the building.

Cara had barely unpacked her clothes before starting her assault on the garden. Every morning at daylight she had donned jeans and work gloves and headed out to the courtyard to do battle for a couple of hours before going to work in the shop. She hacked down most of the wisteria and weeded the borders for what seemed like weeks. Her hands were left blistered, and callused, and every night when she soaked in the claw-foot bathtub in her upstairs apartment, she got a kind of grim satisfaction from viewing what she saw as the battle scars from a failed marriage.

Leo called. He texted. But when he dropped by the shop, Bert gave him the cold shoulder and glared at him with undisguised loathing. Leo suggested counseling. That's when Cara suggested he get their house listed and sold, because she needed her share of the equity to grow her business.

Leo gazed at her with his round blue eyes—the ones she'd gazed into on her wedding day, when he'd promise to love her forever. "It was a mistake. All right? How many ways can I tell you I'm sorry? Didn't you ever make a mistake you came to deeply regret?"

"Yes," Cara said gravely. "Marrying you. Believing you would be faithful was a mistake. That's my big regret."

When she'd cleared out the invaders in her courtyard, she'd been thrilled to find the bones of a lovely old garden. Hiding in the shadow of the wisteria she found a beautifully mottled marble birdbath with a bowl shaped like a sunflower. With Bert's help, she'd dragged it into the center of the courtyard and dug out a circular bed and planted lavender, rosemary, creeping thyme, and three different varieties of scented geraniums at its base.

As the weather warmed up and spring arrived in Savannah, she was thrilled when an unnamed heirloom rose she'd pruned back sprouted new canes and brought forth a froth of delicate white blossoms with orange-tipped centers.

When one of her elderly spinster Jones Street neighbors died, Cara went to the estate sale and bought two huge old terra-cotta pots, which she dragged home in a rusty little red wagon she'd found in a trash pile down the lane. She dumped out the hideous cast-iron plants that had filled those pots for decades, and in their place she planted a pair of lemon trees.

She planted banana trees in the far corner of the beds and underplanted them with hostas, ferns, and ruffly bicolored caladiums.

Leo called one day to tell her the house was under contract. The next day, when she knew he'd be at work, she drove the van over to the house, and let herself into the back gate. With Bert's help, she loaded up the only furniture she really wanted from her previous life, a pair of teak Luytens benches that had been a wedding gift from her father.

She doubted Leo would notice they were missing. The only time he went into their backyard was to mow the grass or practice his backswing.

Cara searched the Savannah Craigslist ads for weeks before she finally found a square teak outdoor table. She added a market umbrella and placed her benches on either side of it.

When spring came, even if it was raining or storming, Cara stole away to her courtyard garden for an hour or two. She'd light one of the red-currant candles she sold in the shop and then have her dinner sitting at the table. She sipped wine while she plucked weeds or snipped herbs, or just sat, with Poppy at her feet, watching the stars, listening to the rustle of the birds in the treetops.

Sometimes Bert would join her. He'd donated a pair of weather-beaten Adirondack chairs to the garden. They would sit back on the chairs, not talking. Cara would sip her pinot grigio and Bert, a recovering alcoholic, would occasionally sneak a joint—although this was not something she actually approved of.

"Gimme a break," Bert would say, closing his eyes, tilting his head skyward and blowing smoke through his nostrils. "I quit drinking. You can't make me give up all my vices."

Thursday night, after putting together dozens of Mother's Day arrangements for delivery, Cara and Bert were sitting in the courtyard garden. Bert slapped at a mosquito and sighed. "Here it comes. Skeeter season. Makes me want to move to Maine. I hate those little fuckers."

"They have stinging black flies in Maine, Bert," Cara pointed out. "And mud. Months and months of mud. Not to mention snow."

"Never mind," he said lazily. "So—did I hear right? You're actually going to interview for the privilege of doing that Trapnell wedding?"

"Yessss," she said, already regretting what she thought of as her capitulation. "I really like Marie Trapnell. And Vicki Cooper tracked me down at the golf club Tuesday and begged me to at least consider taking the job if they offer it. Brooke's father, Gordon, called me today to set up an appointment for 'a chat.' He wants me to see the Strayhorns' plantation house, so I can get an idea of where the wedding is being held. So yes, I'm going over to Cabin Creek tomorrow, hat in hand, to present my ideas for the wedding."

"Want me to tag along?"

"Normally, I'd love to have you accompany me. It looks pretty fancy, don't you think, to introduce you as my assistant and have you carry my photo book and bow and scrape like a minion?"

"Bowing and scraping? Not in my job description."

"Anyway, I need you at the shop tomorrow to finish up with the Mother's Day orders. And don't forget, we've got Laurie-Beth Winship's wedding Saturday. But don't worry, I promise to bring back a full description."

13

Somebody, at some point in the Strayhorn family history, had a puckish sense of humor. Cabin Creek? Cara drove slowly down the bumpy crushed oyster-shell drive. Age-blackened live oaks dripping with thick curtains of Spanish moss shaded both sides of the roadway, their trunks dotted with clumps of dark green Resurrection ferns, and the trees were underplanted with hedges of azaleas, past blooming, but still lovely. A rail fence separated the drive from a vast green pasture, and a trio of horses grazed outside a weathered barn. At the end of the quarter-mile drive, a weathered cypress sign was nailed to one of the trees.

SLOW DOWN. SMALL CHILDREN. LARGE DOGS. OLD MEN.

The house loomed ahead. Cara had read up on Cabin Creek in a book about low-country plantation homes. The property had been a land grant from King George III, but the original homeplace, described as a two-story wood-frame cabin, had burned in the early 1800s, and the Strayhorns, who'd done well with cotton, rice, and indigo, built themselves a showplace to display all that wealth.

Cabin Creek was no longer a cabin. Not by any stretch of the imagination. The main house was a three-story Greek Revival beauty, with a two-story-tall portico supported by four thick Doric columns. A widow's walk topped the portico. Large wings sprouted from each side of the main house, and the estate was set on an expanse of deep green lawn, with foundation plantings of carefully clipped boxwoods.

Cara followed the drive around to the right side of the house, as Gordon Trapnell had instructed, where she found a gravel car park adjoining a low three-bay garage. She parked her own car next to a sleek silver Jaguar, and walked around to a smaller side entrance marked by a pair of miniature versions of the front columns.

Before she could ring the doorbell, the door opened. A stocky middle-aged woman dressed in faded blue jeans and a grubby T-shirt pushed open the screen door. An army-green ballcap with an embroidered Cabin Creek logo shaded the woman's round, ruddy face.

"Are you the florist?" she asked.

"Uh yes," Cara said, taken aback. Funny way for a butler to dress.

The woman extended her hand and opened the door wider. "Great! So glad to meet you. I'm Libba Strayhorn. Come on in. I was just getting ready to go out to the stables, but Gordon and Patricia are inside. I'll show you the way, then let you all talk."

They were in what was obviously used as a mudroom by the Strayhorn family. It was high-ceilinged, with a marble floor, but simple wooden benches lined each side, and wall-mounted hooks held jackets and coats. Muddy boots were lined up beneath the benches, and a pair of shotguns rested casually in one corner.

Libba walked quickly, the soles of her riding boots clacking against the marble floor. Cara followed her through a pair of double doors into a formal parlor with an immense fireplace mounted by a fancy gilt-framed mirror. Stiff brocade-covered Empire-era settees and armchairs faced the fireplace. Libba didn't slow. Instead she led Cara through yet another doorway, into a cypress-paneled library.

Gordon Trapnell and his wife were sitting at a felt-topped game table near the fireplace. "Cara?" he asked, standing to shake her hand.

He was short, maybe only an inch or two taller than Cara, with thinning dark hair, carefully combed across his high-domed head, and a neatly clipped mustache. He wore silver wire-rimmed glasses, a pale pink logoed Polo shirt, and dark dress slacks.

"Yes, hello, Mr. Trapnell."

"Call me Gordon." He turned toward the woman seated to his right and beamed. "And this is Patricia, my wife."

Cara had only caught a glimpse of Patricia Trapnell at the golf club earlier in the week, just a blur of blond hair and cheekbones.

Patricia's silicone-plumped lips widened into what she probably thought was a smile. But her skin was stretched so tightly over the high cheekbones, it really resembled more of a grimace. Her pale blue eyes had an almost Asian tilt. Her face was skillfully made up, and her blond hair gleamed in the low light of the library. She was dressed in a cobalt-blue silk blouse.

"Hello, Cara," she said, her voice husky. "We've heard so much about your work. And of course, we loved what you did for Torie Fanning's wedding last week. Please sit, and tell us about your ideas for Brooke and Harris."

"I'm going to leave you experts to it then," Libba Strayhorn said, and she hurried out of the room.

Cara took a deep breath and opened her iPad. "These are a few ideas I came up with for the church, and the reception," she said, tapping an icon on the screen that read "Trapnell Wedding."

"Of course, everything is very preliminary," she said. "I was able to find pictures on the internet of the ballroom and the chapel here at Cabin Creek, but it would still be helpful for me to see them in person, just to get a sense of the scale of the spaces."

"Of course," Gordon Trapnell said. "We can walk around and show you the layout after we chat. Libba has graciously given us the run of the place."

"I forgot to ask Marie—how many guests?"

Patricia sighed deeply. "That's been a matter of controversy. Brooke and her mother have some quaint notion about a small, intimate affair. But they totally overlook the fact that with Gordon's and my extensive social and business contacts, not to mention the Strayhorns,' we're talking about three hundred people minimum—and that's cutting the guest list right to the bone."

"To the bone," Gordon said, nodding agreement.

"And do you have a budget in mind?" Cara asked.

"Not really," Patricia said. She gave Gordon a warm smile, then reached over and squeezed her husband's hand. "How do you put a price tag on a father's love for his only daughter?"

"Exactly," Cara replied.

Really? This is about demonstrating love for Brooke? Not about showing your "extensive business and social contacts" just how much money you have to throw around on an overblown wedding your kid doesn't even really want?

Cara tapped an icon marked "Centerpieces." "Since it's a July wedding, I thought we might stick to cooler colors, blues, greens, white, cream, maybe some lavenders and silvers." She glanced from Brooke to Gordon. "Are those colors Brooke likes?"

Gordon glanced at his wife for guidance. Patricia rolled her eyes. "Brooke doesn't really have much of a sense of color at all, bless her heart. Or style, for that matter. As far as I can tell, she wears navy blue or black suits to work, and she lives in running clothes on the weekend."

"Oh."

"*We* thought, that is, Gordon and I thought, it might be exciting to do something really dramatic with the tables. We were at a wedding in Charleston last month, that was simply *stunning.* The designer had spent time in India, and he designed these amazing pierced brass vessels and low tables, with piles and piles of cushions and Oriental rugs, and there were no flowers at all, just flickering lights, and piles of exotic fruits, pomegranates and what have you, and the tablecloths were embroidered, with mirrors . . ."

"No flowers?" Cara said blankly.

Then what the hell am I doing here?

"But we wouldn't want to copy that look, not exactly," Patricia added hastily. "And anyway, that was just to give you an idea of the kind of emotions we'd like to elicit with our event."

It's a wedding, Cara thought. *And it's not actually your wedding. It's Brooke's and Harris's.*

"What we're looking for, Cara, is something absolutely original," Gordon said.

"Something that hasn't been done in Savannah. None of those tired old post-deb looks you see all the time," Patricia added. "And to be perfectly honest, Cara, we have looked at a presentation by another designer which was beyond amazing. So I guess what Gordon is asking from you, is to be amazing."

Cara looked down at her iPad. *Screw this. Be amazing? That's your design mandate?*

She willed herself to smile. "Would you like to look at some of my ideas now?"

Patricia scrolled rapidly through the photos and sketches Cara had assembled, and five minutes later, handed the iPad back.

"Interesting," she said. "Lots of silver vases and such. Very traditional though, wouldn't you say?"

"Well, yes. I assumed that since the wedding and reception were being held in a historic home, you'd want the flowers to fit in with the setting. But I'm not necessarily tied to any one look. We do lots of cutting-edge weddings. In fact, tomorrow, we're doing the décor for a wedding in an old cotton warehouse down on River Street, and the bride requested an industrial, steampunk look, with some goth elements mixed in."

"Goth?" Gordon looked to his wife for interpretation.

"Oh, you know, Gordie. Those kids who wander around with their faces made up with white powder and black-lined eyes and lips, like something out of a Halloween fright show."

"People do that at weddings? Adults?" He shook his head. "Thank God Brooke was never into that sort of thing."

Cara couldn't help herself. There was no way these people were going to hire her, so why not have a little fun with them? "Instead of tablecloths, we're topping the tables with long sheets of rusted corrugated tin, from old farmhouses. And we're doing centerpieces with all black flowers, and animal skulls."

Patricia's pale eyes bugged out slightly. "Not . . . real animal skulls."

"Oh sure," Cara said cheerfully. "The groom is a big hunter, so he's collected things over the years from his own kills and walks in the woods. I've managed to incorporate rattlesnake rattles in the bride's bouquet, strung on strips of deer rawhide. Plus, I've been buying additional skulls and antlers online for months now."

"Dear God," Patricia said faintly. She looked a little ill.

"And we're having a tattoo booth," Cara added. "I've designed a custom tattoo that combines the bride's and groom's initials and their wedding date. It's the first one I've designed, and I'm really very proud of how it turned out."

"Who in hell *are* these people?" Gordon demanded.

"Laurie-Beth Winship?" Cara said. "She's marrying Payton Jelks."

"That's not Frank and Elizabeth Winship's child, is it?" Patricia asked. "I know they have a daughter, but Laurie-Beth was in Brooke's debutante class. Surely they wouldn't sanction something like that. . . ."

"It is," Cara said. "Do you know the Winships? I just love them. So adventurous. Elizabeth has already promised that she'll get tattooed tomorrow night, but I think Frank is a little squeamish about needles, so he's just going to do the henna thing. You wouldn't think a radiologist would be, would you? Squeamish, I mean."

"Dear God." This time Gordon and Patricia said it as a duet.

14

Cara climbed uneasily to the top of the scaffolding, eight feet off the ground. She aimed the can of black spray paint at the age-blackened brick wall and began writing, in big, looping letters.

LUV WILL KEEP US 2-GETHER.

She looked down at Bert, who was holding the piece of paper that acted as their script. Bert, it turned out, was afraid of heights. The next time she hired an assistant, she vowed, she would have to ask prospects about their phobias. But for now, it was what it was. "What next?"

"Mmm. Says here 'Laurie-Beth (heart) Payton.' "

Cara walked a few paces down the catwalk, and clambered up to the next level, the paint can tucked into the waistband of her jeans. She painted the next phrase, walked four feet to the left, and looked down. "Next?"

Bert had to crane his neck to see her. He cupped his hands to form a make-shift megaphone. " 'You are the sunshine of my life.' "

She remembered that one. It was the title of Laurie-Beth's parents' favorite song from their own courtship. She sprayed the phrase on the wall, using the last little bit of the spray paint. She tossed the can to the ground and began the slow climb down.

Bert still had his eyes tightly closed when she reached the concrete floor. "You can look now," she said, touching his arm.

He did. The two of them walked around the cavernous warehouse, surveying their handiwork.

"Fanfuckintastic," Bert said.

And Cara, despite all her initial misgivings, had to agree.

Laurie-Beth Winship had read one too many wedding magazines, stayed too long on Pinterest. Despite her mother's tearful pleas for a nice, traditional reception at the Oglethorpe Club, or the Chatham City Club, Laura-Beth had proclaimed she wanted a "real" venue for her wedding.

Unable to find a wedding planner willing to execute her vision, Laurie-Beth had appointed Cara her de facto "imagineer."

This cotton warehouse belonged to one of Elizabeth Winship's great-uncles, but it hadn't been used in at least thirty years. They'd had to hire a commercial cleaning crew to come in and steam-clean the brick walls and pressure-wash the grease-soaked floors. After that, the one existing bathroom, which consisted of nothing more than a urinal and a sink, had to be gutted and rebuilt into a proper unisex facility—while still keeping to Laurie-Beth's "industrial" look.

It would have been cheaper, Cara thought, to just build a new warehouse. But she kept that thought to herself, and gamely soldiered on, buoyed by the thought of the handsome fee the Winships were paying her.

So here they were, on the Friday night before the Winship-Jelks wedding. It was nearly midnight, and she and Bert had been working all evening. They'd hung miles of safety lights, spray-painted graffiti on everything that didn't move, and strung canvas painters' dropcloths from those rusty steel girders to form a backdrop for the newly built bandstand constructed of old wooden pallets Cara had liberated from the back of a nearby building supply.

The oversized wooden cable spools that would act as cocktail tables had been wheeled into place, and tables, improvised from corrugated metal spread over sawhorses, were arrayed around the dance floor.

"You really think the flowers are okay?" Cara asked Bert.

He shrugged. They'd cleaned out two local feed and seed stores of every galvanized bucket, tub, and horse trough in stock. These were now filled with leafless branches that had been spray-painted black, and strung with white lights and chains made of beer-can pop-tops. On every tree, Cara had wired bunches of carnations, dip-dyed in bloodred and black.

More dyed black flowers filled recycled aluminum cans on the tabletops, which were interspersed with Cara's carefully curated assortment of animal skulls.

"It's sure as hell original," Bert said. "And that's what she wanted, right?"

"If Tim Burton married Alice Cooper, I think this is what their wedding would look like," Cara muttered. She yawned. "Let's go. I'm dead on my feet, and we've got another loooong day tomorrow."

She pulled the van to the curb in front of Bert's apartment on St. Julian Street. "See you in the morning."

"Hey. You never told me how your meeting with the Trapnells went," Bert said, his hand on the passenger door.

"It went. The plantation? Cabin Creek—it's unbelievable. If it weren't for the bride's father and stepmother, I'd love to design a wedding in that house. But those two? Gordon and Patricia?" She made a face. "It's the first time I've ever hoped *not* to get hired."

"Then why bother to talk to them?" Bert asked. "We're not exactly hurting for work, Cara."

"I know, I know. I keep telling myself that. But I really liked Marie, the mom."

"That's your problem, Cara," Bert said, interrupting. "You like *everybody*. You get sucked into their dramas, become a part of their family, and then get stuck in the middle of their shit. You're a florist, honey, not a family therapist!"

"You're wrong. I absolutely don't like Gordon, and it took me about five seconds to decide I detest Patricia. But Marie—she's a different story. She's sort of a lost soul, and I just get the feeling Patricia will totally mow her and Brooke down, if I don't get the job. But don't worry. They are so *not* going to hire me. I told them about everything we had planned for Laurie-Beth's wedding and they were really and truly appalled. Anyway, Patricia is totally gaga over this Cullen Kane guy from Charleston."

"Oh yeah, *him*," Bert said, with a sneer. "Just what Savannah needs. Another flower fairy."

Cara laughed and gave his shoulder a gentle shove. "Go on, get out. We've both got to get our beauty rest. See you in the morning."

15

Cara caught sight of the stranger just as she was finishing the last details of the elaborate arch she'd constructed out of fallen tree branches, Spanish moss, deer antlers, grouse feathers, ivy, and dried hydrangeas. Since it was where Laurie-Beth and Payton would stand to say their vows she wanted to make sure an errant antler wouldn't fall off and bonk the couple on the head. Concussions were never fun at a wedding.

She'd arrived at the cotton warehouse late Saturday afternoon, already behind schedule.

He was standing just inside the propped-open door of the warehouse, his arms crossed over his chest, and a late-afternoon ray of sunlight seemed to catch and illuminate his blond tresses, almost like a halo. He wasn't a guest; the wedding wasn't for another two hours, and anyway, he was dressed casually, in designer jeans—7 For All Mankind, she was sure, a silky black T-shirt, and black motorcycle boots. He had deliberate beard stubble, piercing green eyes, and he was tall enough and slender enough to be a runway model.

But she knew he wasn't. The hair was the giveaway. She'd seen it on his website.

He was watching her, spying on the competition, and he didn't care if she knew. Should she confront him, ask him to leave? But that would make him think she had something to hide. She decided to ignore him, for now anyway.

Cara stood on the top rung of her stepladder, and steadied herself with both hands on the side supports of the arch. She made another pass with the picture wire, looping it around and around Payton Jelks's prized ten-point antlers, which she'd secured to the top of the arch, then tying it off on the backside of the arch, where it wouldn't be seen.

She reached into the bag of extra feathers and dried flowers she'd slung over her left shoulder, pulled her glue gun from the holster she'd rigged on her belt, and went to add another cluster of dried hydrangea blooms, leaning ever-so-slightly to the right. Which was a mistake. It was like a slow-motion cartoon. She tried to counteract the wobble, inching to the left, but she overcorrected, and it was too late. She grabbed for the right tree branch. Also a mistake. It came away in her hand, and she tumbled to the concrete floor.

And her arch, her gorgeous, forest-fantasy arch, came tumbling right down around her.

She fell flat on her ass, but instinctively shielded her head with her arms, as antlers and branches and feathers rained down around her. She felt a sear on her calf, felt the hot glue gun ricocheting onto the floor.

"Shit!"

He was at her side in a moment, kneeling down beside her, pulling her to a sitting position.

"Hey! Are you okay?" He brushed feathers and moss and dried hydrangea petals from her hair and shoulders.

"Shit!" she repeated, looking around at the ruins. "Shit. Damn. Hell. Piss."

He laughed, throwing his head back, displaying a set of perfect white teeth in contrast to his perfect golden tan. Actually, he was prettier than a runway model. He looked like something off the cover of a paperback romance novel. Biker boots and all.

"At least you didn't get impaled in the throat with an antler."

"At least," she said sourly.

"Can you stand?" he asked, extending a hand to help her up.

"Guess I'd better, if I'm gonna get this thing rebuilt before seven." She took his hand and managed to stand. Her tailbone was already starting to throb, her right shin was bleeding, and she could see a bruise blooming on her right elbow, where she'd tried to break her fall.

"Thanks," she said.

"I'm sorry about your arch," he said. "It was really looking pretty kick-ass."

"I know," Cara said. "Was."

He hesitated for a moment. "I could help you put it back together. You know, if you want."

Did she? Did she want his help?

"I'm Cullen Kane," he said. "The new kid in town."

"I know," she said.

"And you're Cara Kryzik," he said. "Bloom. I'm a big fan of your work."

"Thanks," she said, feeling her face redden. Was he being facetious? How would he know what her work looked like? Unlike him, she'd never had a wedding published.

"I was a guest at that wedding you did last weekend. Lillian Fanning's sister-in-law used to be married to my cousin."

"Really?" She hadn't noticed him at the Fanning wedding, but then, she'd been so distracted, what with Poppy and the creep who'd dognapped her, that that shouldn't have been a big surprise. Cara arched an eyebrow. "I'm surprised Lillian didn't ask *you* to do Torie's flowers."

"Gawd forbid," he drawled. "I've known Torie since she was in diapers, and she was hell on wheels even back then."

Cara wasn't sure whether to agree or take the high road. "Torie was a . . . challenge," she allowed.

He smiled. "Tactful and talented. Anyway, I really did love what you did at their wedding. I'm sure Torie and Lillian were insisting on some blown-out Versailles-style designs. You did a nice job of reining them in, but still giving them what they thought they wanted."

"Well . . . thanks. Thanks very much. I appreciate the compliment, coming from somebody in the field."

"Not at all." He gestured at the pile of branches. "I really would be happy to help you resurrect your arch. I'm pretty handy with a cordless drill and a glue gun."

"Oh, I couldn't," she tried to demur. But the minutes were ticking away. It had taken both her and Bert an entire day to build the damn thing back at the shop.

"Professional courtesy," he said, bowing from the waist. "I insist."

True to his word, Cullen Kane was a whiz with power tools. With the extra set of hands, they were able to get the branch structure rebuilt in only thirty minutes. This time, though, at his suggestion, they added bracing with some extra branches she'd brought along. He tugged hard on both sides, and then at the top of the arch, and this time around, there wasn't the slightest wobble.

He was so tall he didn't even really need the stepladder to wire the antlers to the top of the arch. So Cara worked on the side supports, attaching the antlers and feathers and flowers, while he positioned the ten-point antlers precisely at the top of the arch, adding sprays of dried flowers and feathers in a carefully contrived medallion shape, even fashioning a rough bow with a long strand of ivy, before applying more festoons of Spanish moss.

"Dammit," Cara muttered under her breath, looking up at his composition.

"Too much?" He stood back.

"No. Much better. Dammit."

"It was your vision," he said. "All I did was follow directions."

He was really insufferable. She should hate him. And she kind of did hate him, making her grateful for his help.

She glanced at her watch. "Oh! I've gotta get out of here. Gotta get home and shower and change before the wedding party starts arriving." She held out her hand. "Thanks for helping out. You were a lifesaver."

He shrugged. "It was the least I could do, after you caught me spying ."

She took a half step backward. "I suppose Patricia Trapnell told you they'd interviewed me for Brooke's wedding."

"She did. That's Patricia. She loves intrigue. Loves to pit one person against the other."

"I'm really not your competition," Cara told him. "I think they only interviewed me as a courtesy to Brooke's mother. Our styles seem . . . very different."

"Not so different," Cullen said, flashing those beautiful teeth again. "We're both perfectionists."

"There is that," Cara admitted. She grabbed a broom and started sweeping up the stray bits of moss and flower petals.

"Good luck with the wedding," Cullen said, realizing he'd been dismissed.

"Thanks," Cara said. "And good luck with yours."

He arched one eyebrow in an implied challenge. "We'll see, won't we?"

16

The wedding party looked to Cara like a group of trick-or-treaters who'd gotten lost on their way to Halloween. The bridesmaids wore matching short black spandex dresses that resembled overgrown tube tops, over black fishnet hose and short black bootees. The groomsmen wore black leather pants, and T-shirts with custom screen-printed designs featuring snarling befanged monsters.

The bridegroom was dressed in black leather pants, too, but instead of a screen-printed shirt he wore a metal-studded black leather vest over his bare chest. And he'd shaved his head for the occasion.

Laurie-Beth Winship's choice of a wedding gown was equally quirky—she'd designed it herself, with a bodice made of her grandmother's tightly laced 1950s corset, and a skirt made of layers of another grandmother's Irish lace curtains—but somehow, the wacky creation totally suited her pale complexion and long red hair.

It was a remarkably relaxed group. There were no hysterics, no panic attacks, no death threats issued. Even Payton, the edgy investment banker/punk rocker groom, seemed to be having a good time, as he and Laurie-Beth held their two-year-old son, Levi, between them as they swayed to "Brown-Eyed Girl."

Best of all, the wedding arch stood firm throughout the ceremony, even when little Levi managed to yank off one of the deer antlers while his parents were saying their vows.

It was actually a very original party, Cara decided, happy that she'd made a deal with the wedding photographer to document everything for her lookbook at the shop. Although most of her Savannah brides still clung tightly to tradition, the Winship-Jelks wedding would show that she could deliver the goods no matter how outrageous the request. She was getting positively misty-eyed, sipping her second glass of blanc-de-blanc champagne, leaning against one of the steel support columns, watching the swirl of black-clad guests, as they laughed and danced and table-hopped around the cavernous warehouse, the multiple bloodred candles sending their shadows dancing across the rustic walls.

"I notice you're not wearing black tonight," came a low voice in her ear. "Even though the bride decreed an all-black dress code for her guests."

Cara recognized the voice at once. She didn't bother to turn and address him face-to-face. "I'm not a guest. I'm just the florist."

He stood so close she could smell his pine-scented soap, feel the tickle of his beard on her bare shoulder, which sent a delicious shiver down her spine, which she instantly regretted.

"And yet, here you are. What color would you call that dress of yours?"

She looked down at the vintage orangish-pink silk cocktail dress she'd found on eBay. It was an old favorite that she'd worn to half a dozen weddings since buying it. It was obviously homemade, with sweet pinked seams, a metal zipper sewn into the side seam that dated it to the sixties, thin spaghetti straps, and hand-appliquéd daisies around the hem of the frothing full skirt.

"Hmm. I guess I'd call this coral."

"Kinda pretty," he said grudgingly.

"Kinda?" Now she did turn around. What she saw made her raise one questioning eyebrow. Jack Finnerty had ignored Laurie-Beth's blackout edict, too. Instead, he wore a blue seersucker suit, a pale yellow button-down shirt, no tie, and battered brown Topsiders on his sockless feet. "You sweet-tongued devil, you."

He was sipping a Moon River pale ale from a plastic cup. "I gather you did all these, uh, arrangements tonight. Mind if I ask what's with all the black flowers and skulls and heavy metal?"

Her smile was tight. "The bride and groom tell me their dreams. I make it happen."

She sipped her champagne and wished he'd go away.

"Do you do all the flowers for all the weddings in Savannah?"

"Just the cool ones. Do you come to all the weddings in Savannah?" she countered.

"Not all of 'em," Jack said. "I guess I get around. It just happens I went to school with Laurie-Beth's older brother. And Laurie-Beth and I went out a couple times. You know, way back in the day before she met Payton."

"You went to school with Austin?" Cara asked.

"Technically. He was a couple years ahead of me in school, so we never hung out together much."

"I see," Cara said, gazing across the room at the brother in mention, Austin Winship, a towering six-foot-five presence, who at that moment seemed to be in danger of teetering facedown onto the grits bar the caterer had set up in the far corner.

Jack followed her eyes. "Ol' Austin seems to have gotten pretty caught up in the spirit of the wedding festivities. Is he actually a real justice of the peace or something?"

"Oh, no," Cara assured him. "Payton was dead set on not having a real minister for the wedding, so Austin got himself ordained into some nondenominational denomination, just for tonight."

"Is this one of those peyote-eating churches, by any chance?" Jack asked. "Because even a casual observer, like myself, can tell that Austin seems to have ingested some kind of pharmacologically enhanced substance."

That did make Cara laugh. "He showed up pretty glassy-eyed tonight. And

I'm assuming that high-pitched giggle that he kept breaking into during the ceremony isn't part of his day-to-day persona?"

"As I said, we weren't really friends," Jack said. "Austin missed his senior year at Country Day because his parents enrolled him in what was billed as an 'alternative school' out in Oregon."

"Rehab," Cara said.

"Exactly," Jack agreed.

There was an uneasy lull in the conversation. Cara found herself wishing he'd go away and simultaneously hoping he wouldn't.

Jack Finnerty made her nervous. He'd made her nervous every time she looked out the window of the shop over the past week and caught a glimpse of him running past, with Shaz trotting alongside. It made her nervous to realize how much time she spent gazing out that same window, hoping for a glance of him. And it made her desperately anxious when she found herself driving past his hovel on Macon Street, telling herself she was simply taking a shortcut to the Kroger, which was actually not a shortcut to the grocery store.

Jack Finnerty was taking up way too much space in her head. He'd looked so remotely elegant and reserved—and unbearably snotty—in his tuxedo the previous Saturday. And then when she'd opened her door Sunday and found him all sweaty and buff, standing on her doorstep with that look of chagrin on his face.

And now, damn him, he'd turned up here tonight, in his stinking seersucker suit, striking just the right note between hopelessly preppy and effortlessly casual. He was just a guy, one of these obnoxious Savannah guys who knew everybody and fit in everywhere without even trying.

He had to know the effect he was having on her, standing so close she swore she could see a bit of sawdust clinging to the lapel of his jacket. It was all she could do to keep herself from reaching out to dust it off. She could even see a place on his chin where he'd nicked himself shaving, a tiny dot of dried blood standing out from the dark stubble. She clasped her hands behind her back, just in case.

"How's the dog?" Jack finally asked.

"Poppy? She's fine. Happy to be home."

"Any more accidents?"

He was being deliberately annoying. Cara frowned. "I told you, she's housebroken."

Which wasn't completely true. If Cara left her alone for more than a few hours, Poppy would sometimes stand by the door, waiting for her to come home, even though there was a dog door that would let her out into the courtyard. Sometimes, Bert told her, Poppy would lie down in front of the shop door, staring at it, as though willing her to come back through it. Cara believed Poppy peed on the floor as revenge, or out of separation anxiety.

Was she really raising a neurotic puppy?

She gave Jack a sharp look. "How about your dog. Shaz? I'm guessing she hasn't run away lately?"

"No," Jack said. He leaned in even closer, his breath tickling her face. She took a half step backward. "Listen. Let me ask you something about Poppy. Would you say she's moody?"

"Moody? No." Cara laughed. "Why, is your dog moody?"

"She's just not very . . . peppy. I thought all puppies were kinda bouncy and off the wall and crazy. But that's not Shaz. She's pretty quiet. Seems to sleep most of the day. And when I come home from work, she kind of looks at me. Like, 'What? You're back? Who cares?' When I get ready to go out for a run, I almost have to drag her out the door. I was thinking maybe it has something to do with the breed."

For just a moment, she was tempted to suggest that maybe it had something to do with *him*. But no. He seemed seriously worried about Shaz, and she was touched by his concern.

"I don't think goldendoodles are particularly moody. I mean, yeah, Poppy sometimes lets me know she misses me when I'm working late, or not paying her proper attention, but mostly, she's a happy camper. And if I don't walk her at least twice every day, she lets me know I'm being a slacker."

"Hmm," he said.

"Is there a chance Shaz is depressed? I mean, has anything changed in her routine that would make her want to run away?"

. . .

Jack took a long swig of his beer. Hell yeah, he wanted to tell her. Everything had changed in Shaz's routine. His, too. The minute Zoey walked out the door, it had all changed. He would have liked to have left, too. But he had bills to pay, and obligations to his brother, and their business. Anyway, where would he have gone?

It wasn't that he actually missed Zoey that much. They hadn't gotten along for months before she left. They quarreled constantly. Zoey couldn't understand why they couldn't travel, cut loose, have some fun. Couldn't he get a real job in a real office, instead of coming home late every night, dirty and sweaty, his hands and hair spattered with paint, his clothes leaking sawdust with every step he took?

He couldn't really blame her for resenting him. He'd had a good job as an insurance broker when they met a year previously. He drove a new BMW 750, had a sleek glass and chrome loft in a new development down by the river. He'd walked away from all of it, only two months after Zoey moved in, selling the loft to buy the crappy little freedman's cottage on Macon Street, trading in the Beemer for a used F-150 pickup, leaving behind his slick suits for painter's pants and a tool belt when he and Ryan started their historic-restoration business.

Jack had bedgrudgingly accepted Zoey's crazy designer dog, christened with a name he couldn't even spell. And then she'd taken off, leaving him and Shaz trying to figure out where it had all gone so wrong.

He glanced over at Cara's empty glass, deciding to save her the dismal details of his dismal home life. "Is that champagne? Can I get you another? Or maybe you wanna dance?" He hoped he didn't sound too eager. In fact, he halfway hoped she'd tell him no. Then he'd have an excuse to go home and drink some real liquor. Maybe he'd even think about hanging some doors, or finishing the tile in the hall bathroom.

"After Torie's wedding, I didn't think you liked to dance," Cara said.

"Oh." He looked away, his hands in his pockets, looking bored. "I'm okay with dancing. It was just that song. It's stupid, I know. . . ."

"Torie told me," she said, her voice gentle. "About your girlfriend."

"Torie talks too much," he snapped. "How about that drink?"

But now the bride and groom were making their way to the cake table. Laurie-Beth had commissioned a sculptor friend to make figurines of her and Payton, authentic down to the tiniest real flowers in her bouquet, for a cake topper. The caterer had asked Cara to stick around for the cake-cutting ceremony so she could help remove the sculpture before it came under attack from the Confederate-era sword Payton planned to use.

"Sorry, can't," Cara said, giving him a smile he hoped was full of regret. "I'm still on duty."

She hurried off in the direction of the bride and groom, leaving Jack Finnerty staring at her back, at her bare shoulders, and her neck. She really did dress oddly, and yet, he thought she was by far the prettiest girl in the room that night, with her windblown butterscotch curls tied up with a pink satin ribbon. Her pink-orange skirt billowed out from around her tightly belted waist, and she reminded him of a tropical hibiscus blossom. Begging to be picked.

17

Bert was lounging on a low brick wall outside the warehouse, smoking a questionable substance with Austin Winship. When they saw Cara approaching, they giggled in unison, threw down the butts and stamped them flat. Austin drifted down the cobblestoned walkway toward River Street, where yet another party beckoned.

"Heeyyyy, Cara," Bert said, in a singsongy voice. "Is the reception over already?"

"It is for me," she told him. "Do you want a lift back to your place?"

Bert looked off toward the river, where they could hear faint strains of loud rock music, and laughter, but Austin had already disappeared.

"I guess," he said.

She left the van's windows down for the short ride back to Bert's apartment on St. Julian Street, which was only a few blocks away from her own place.

"I saw you talking to your favorite person," Bert said, giving her a sly sideways look.

"Jack Finnerty? He's not so bad."

"Certainly not bad-looking," he said. "Kind of a coincidence that he'd show up at two weddings you were working, two weeks in a row, don't you think?"

"He knows a lot of people," Cara said. "He went to school with Laurie-Beth's brother. And he knows Payton's brother too."

"Interesting," Bert said. "What were you two chatting about?"

"Nothing, really. Our dogs. He thinks his dog is depressed."

Bert giggled. "Maybe his dog needs some puppy uppers."

She rolled her eyes in the dark.

"So. Is he married? Seeing somebody?"

"Not married. Had a bad breakup with his girlfriend a few months ago. And before you start, Bert, I am *not* interested."

He feigned a look of innocence. "I'm not saying a word."

"You were thinking it," Cara said. "I could hear you loud and clear."

"Would it hurt you to have a life after Leo? To start seeing a nice, good-looking guy, who also happens to have a dog?"

"Yes," Cara said crisply. "It would. Now let's drop it, shall we?"

He waved his hands wearily. "Whatever. You're the boss."

She pulled the van alongside the curb outside his apartment. Bert got out and walked unsteadily over to the driver's-side window and leaned in.

He lightly touched her shoulder. "Don't be mad at me, okay?"

"I'm not mad. But you're wasted. Why don't you get some sleep?"

"I am *not* wasted. A little buzzed maybe, but definitely not wasted. So, I just want to tell you one more thing. And it's going to make you mad at me, but I'm telling you anyway. The guy was watching you. All night. But not in a creepy way. I saw him looking around, during the ceremony, and when he finally spotted you, he got this dippy smile on his face."

"You're imagining things," she told him. "Go to bed, okay?"

"Oh-kay. But remember, you heard it here first."

She was a block away from Bert's apartment, humming along to the radio, when she realized, much to her chagrin, that she had a big dippy smile on her own face.

18

Cara was on the phone with a customer when she heard the shop door open. It was only 8:30 a.m., but Bert was out on a delivery, so she was manning the store by herself. She placed a hand over the receiver and addressed the visitor. "Be with you in a minute."

While her phone customer droned on and on about the exact right shade of red she wanted for the roses she was sending her recuperating granny, Cara sized up her visitor, who was wandering around the shop, examining some of the "make and take" arrangements in the walk-in cooler.

She was a bride, obviously. In her late twenties, tall and slender, with skin so pale it was nearly opaque, and fine, dark hair gathered into a hastily styled ponytail tied with a scrunchy. A scrunchy? Cara didn't even know those still existed. The bride wore very little makeup and was dressed in a navy-blue suit and white silk blouse that fairly screamed job interview. The earpiece from her phone dangled from one ear, and she clutched a briefcase under one arm. Every once in a while, she glanced furtively down at her watch. The diamond solitaire on her left ring finger was impressive, at least two carats, Cara thought, and her pulse quickened. She needed to finish up with the sixty-dollar red rose order and get with this bride.

When she'd finally managed to persuade her caller that she'd only use the very freshest, loveliest, long-stemmed roses for her arrangement, she put the phone down with a sense of relief.

"Good morning," she said, hurrying around from behind her worktable. "Is there anything special I can help you with?"

"No. Well, yes, I mean, are you the owner? Cara? I think my mother's already been in to see you. I'm getting married in July, and we thought, I mean, well Vicki Cooper raved about the flowers you did for their wedding and . . ."

"I'm Cara. And you must be Brooke Trapnell. Is that right? Marie's daughter?"

"That's right." Brooke nodded. A faint blush crept over her face. "I understand you met with my father and stepmother too?"

"Yes," Cara said. "Just last week. I met them over at Cabin Creek. What a beautiful spot for a wedding. You must be very excited."

Brooke was busy looking around the shop. She traced the tip of a white phalaenopsis orchid with her fingertip. "This is so pretty. What kind of flower is it?"

"It's a phalaenopsis," Cara said. "Do you like orchids?"

The girl was still concentrating on the orchid. "Hmm?" She looked up at Cara. "I'm sorry. What were you saying before?"

"Just that you must be getting excited. With your wedding only a few weeks away."

The girl nodded, her face serious. "Patricia printed out this timeline thing from one of the wedding websites, and according to it, I'm already hopelessly behind schedule. On top of everything else, I've got a big trial scheduled a week before the wedding. I'm actually starting to feel pretty panicky."

"Oh, no. Don't be panicky," Cara said. "That's my job. Your job is to look beautiful and enjoy your special day."

Brooke gave her a dubious look. "Half the girls I know have gotten married this past year. I've been a bridesmaid six times just since September, and it's been hell. Every single time. Have you ever seen a bride who wasn't panicky?"

"Well, there was this one girl this past weekend," Cara admitted. "But she was probably the exception to the rule. "

"One of my friends, Melanie Eaves? Maybe you know her? Her caterer went out of business two weeks before the wedding. Mel got so stressed her hair was falling out in big clumps. She lost so much weight they finally put a feeding tube in her stomach."

"Oh my."

"And this other girl? She was a year ahead of me in law school at Georgia? Samantha Epstein? She ended up going so far over budget, her parents were fighting like cats and dogs, and they ended up filing for divorce. Like, the week before Samantha's wedding. Her father refused to go the reception."

"That's too bad," Cara said.

"Yes, well, at least that won't happen with my parents. Patricia already took care of that, didn't she?"

"Ummm," Cara said, stalling.

"Anyway." Brooke stole another glance at her watch. "Oh, God, look at the time. I promised my mom I'd come by and see you. About the flowers. She said you'd need to talk to me?"

"Yes," Cara said. "Usually I like to spend some time with the bride, to talk about what type flowers you like, color preferences, style. Maybe you have a Pinterest board, or some pictures from the wedding magazines you've been clipping, something like that?"

Brooke shrugged. "Not really. I guess I'm not much into that kind of stuff. Whatever you and Mom come up with, I'm sure I'll like."

This was a first for Cara. A bride who didn't have pages and pages of carefully clipped or pinned wedding photoraphs. Earlier in the spring, she'd done flowers for a bride who'd actually been scrapbooking her future wedding since the age of twelve.

"No favorite color or flower?"

Brooke flicked the phalaenopsis blossom. "This is pretty."

"That's a start," Cara said. "We can do some really pretty arrangments with orchids. Probably not just orchids though, right? I'm thinking maybe something very simple and natural-looking?"

Brooke nodded vigorously. "Yes. Definitely simple. I don't want anything too . . ." She waved her hands in the air. "Too fluffy. Or show-offy. Do you know what I mean?"

Yes, Cara thought, *I do: the exact opposite of what your father and stepmother are envisioning.*

"Anything else?" Cara asked. "Besides orchids for your bouquet? What about your attendants? And the groom and groomsmen? Any particular flower your fiancé likes—or hates?"

"Harris?" Brooke shrugged. "He's a guy." Her face softened. "A sweetie, but he's probably even more clueless than me when it comes to something like this. As far as Harris Strayhorn is concerned, as long as we have an open bar and some kind of barbecue at the reception, he'll be happy."

"Like a lot of grooms," Cara said, laughing. "I can help you figure out the boutonnieres—maybe in Harris's school colors or something? And we'll need to talk about flowers for the reception, as well as the chapel at Cabin Creek. Patricia showed me the dining room, which is lovely. But Patricia wasn't clear on whether you'll be doing a seated dinner or a buffet, so that's something we'll need to talk about. . . ."

"All that?" Brooke twisted the solitaire on her ring finger with her right hand. Around and around, looking down at it and then back up at Cara. "Just, I mean, can't you make all the flowers sort of all look like the same thing?"

Cara heard a faint ringing coming from the vicinity of Brooke's jacket pocket, prompting the girl to start patting all the pockets of her jacket, searching for her phone.

"Oh geez. I have to take this. It's the office. Hello?" Brooke's eyebrows drew together, her narrow shoulders hunched over. "Right. Yes. Absolutely. I'm on my way in right now. I can do a conference call in ten minutes. Will that work?"

She was heading for the door, already immersed in business.

Cara cleared her throat, and Brooke turned.

"Look. Just talk to my mom, would you? The two of you can work it out much better than I could."

"What about your father?" Cara asked. "I think he and your stepmother have some ideas. . . ."

"No!" Brooke said sharply. "Patricia already took over my dad. She doesn't get to take over my wedding too. I won't let her."

"Well okay," Cara said. "But they have another florist in mind. I'm actually not certain they plan to hire me."

"It's my damned wedding," Brooke said, her jaw clenched. "And my mother and I am hiring you. Period."

She threw open the shop door and hurried down the sidewalk.

19

The siege by Trapnells descended upon Cara Kryzik at 6 p.m. on Wednesday, right at closing time.

Brooke and Marie Trapnell arrived at the door, just as she was wheeling in the old-fashioned wooden garden cart full of potted plants from the sidewalk.

Brooke wore a black lady lawyer dress with a black-and-white-striped jacket, and an expression of pure misery. Her mother was dressed more casually, but the expression was almost identical to Brooke's.

"Brooke, Marie, uh, well, how nice to see you," Cara stammered. She heard a car door slam then, and glancing over, saw Patricia Trapnell step out of the silver Jaguar parked in a no-parking slot at the curb.

Her head whipped from the stepmother to the mother and daughter.

"Hi, Patricia," Cara said. She felt her scalp prickle, and wondered if this was what the sensation of fight-or-flight was like.

"You're about to close, aren't you?" Brooke said. Brooke glared at Patricia, who'd joined them on the sidewalk. "I *told* you, she closes at six."

"But not for you," Cara said quickly.

"Of course not," Patricia said, her voice silky, as she neatly sidestepped Marie and Brooke. "We're so sorry to catch you like this, on the spur of the moment, but as I was just explaining to Brooke, if we're going to pull off this wedding, we simply have to start nailing down the details. Now."

Patricia reached into the large buff-colored calfskin bag that dangled from her shoulder. Cara, who told herself she only read *In Style* magazine to keep up with wedding trends, recognized the handbag as the $3,500 Fendi bag she'd drooled over in a recent issue.

"Here," Patricia said, thrusting a document into her hands. "This is the game plan we've finally managed to hammer out."

"Game plan?" Cara said dumbly, glancing down at the multipage dossier.

"For our wedding, of course," Patricia said.

"*My* wedding. Mine and Harris's," Brooke said.

"Which her father and I are paying for," Patricia added.

Marie coughed quietly.

"And her mother, of course," Patricia said, giving Marie a curt nod.

"Does this mean you want me to do the flowers?" Cara looked directly at Brooke.

"Yes," Brooke said, nodding vigorously. "And everything else, too. Flowers, food, all that stuff. Can you?"

"Brooke, I'm flattered to be asked, but, I'm not a wedding planner—I can give you the name of several people locally who'd do a wonderful job. I work with most of them. . . ."

"That's what I suggested," Patricia said. "What we need is a professional planner to pull together all our vendors, the photographer, the caterer, the cake baker, the band, the valet-parking people . . ."

"I want Cara," Brooke said. She crossed slim, freckled arms over her chest, and in that moment, Cara found new admiration for this bride who'd suddenly acquired a backbone. "She's done tons of weddings for lots of girls I know, right?"

"Well, flowers for the weddings," Cara said cautiously.

In fact, she'd been a de facto wedding planner lots of times, mostly for small weddings, as a favor to her budget-minded brides. And she'd complained, privately, to Bert, that she might as well have charged for the service, though she never had.

"See!" Patricia said. "Brooke, we're not talking about some little cake and punch affair at the American Legion hall. Your father has budgeted two hundred and fifty thousand dollars."

Cara was about to agree with Patricia. Why get in over her head?

But then the figure she'd just mentioned floated before Cara's eyes. A budget of $250,000. Not just a measly $10,000 for flowers. A quarter of a million smackers. Of which she, as the wedding planner, could expect to be paid twenty percent.

Suddenly, dollar signs danced merrily in the humid afternoon air. That much money could wipe out her debt to the Colonel. No more phone calls, emails, or terse text messages. No more ramen-noodle dinners. She could buy a new cooler for the shop, get a reliable car. Her mind swirled with all the possibilities.

Why shouldn't she plan Brooke's wedding?

"Look," Cara said, "we don't have to stand out here in the heat, debating this. Why don't you all come inside and sit down? I'll make us some iced tea—or we can even have a glass of wine, if you like, and we can discuss the pros and cons."

Cara found the pitcher of peach iced tea in the fridge, glancing longingly at the bottle of pinot grigio on the rack in the door. When this ambush was over, she promised herself, that bottle would be empty.

While the ladies sipped their tea, Cara skimmed over the "game plan." Brooke jiggled her foot impatiently and pulled out her phone, texting a mile a minute.

The first line of the document was a surprise. "Two hundred fifty guests? Really?"

"I know," Brooke said, not bothering to look up from her phone. "Crazy, right? And you should see the list. People I've never met. People I haven't seen since, like, ever. If it were up to me, we'd have fifty, tops."

"It's not up to you, though, is it?" Patricia set her tea glass down on the tabletop with a clatter.

Marie looked up at the ceiling and hummed under her breath. This discussion, Cara sensed, had been going on for hours, if not days.

"Apparently, not," Brooke muttered.

Cara read on. "Passed appetizers during cocktail hour. Seated dinner.... Will the dining room at Cabin Creek hold two hundred fifty people?"

"Easily." Patricia said. "According to Libba Strayhorn, they can open up the doors between the dining room and the twin parlors and entrance hall and easily accommodate that many."

"It'll be awful," Brooke said. "A mass of hot, sweaty, hungry, overdressed social climbers, all pawing at me and grabbing for the last piece of shrimp."

"Brooke..." Marie gave her daughter a warning look.

"So..." Cara did some quick math. "Maybe do cocktails and apps in the entry hall as people are entering. We'll have scattered high-top tables around the perimeter of the room. For flowers—maybe just some bud vases on the high-tops?"

"Whatever." Brooke was texting again. Marie reached over and gently took the phone from her daughter's hand.

"Do you have a caterer in mind?" Cara asked, directing the question at Marie.

"Well..."

"Simple Elegance does all the best events in town," Patricia put in. "They did an amazing job for a dinner for us a few years ago."

"Your wedding dinner?" Brooke shot her stepmother a malicious smirk.

Patricia had the grace to blush. "Well, yes, as a matter of fact."

"They're *not* doing *my* wedding reception," Brooke said.

"We've got lots of fabulous caterers in Savannah," Cara said, desperate to fill that awkward moment. "I work with Layne Pelletier of Fete Accompli a lot. In fact, she did Torie Fanning's wedding."

"That food at Torie's wedding was wonderful," Marie said. "Especially that salmon tartare thingy on the corncakes."

"Harris adores salmon," Brooke said. "Let's go with Layne."

"She's good, I suppose," Patricia allowed. "I know the Fannings were pleased with what she did."

Cara looked back at the "game plan." "Okay, well, this does look like a fairly ambitious event. Full bar with premium brands, wine service with dinner . . ."

"*My* friends all drink beer," Brooke said pointedly. "But, whatever. . . ."

"Dancing after dinner," Cara went on. "Disc jockey?"

Patricia's waxen face took on something close to a look of pain. "An orchestra," she said. "If the kids want to have a DJ, they can do that at the after-party."

"We might be hard-pressed to book an orchestra at this late date," Cara warned. "In fact, it might be tricky to get the best vendors, working this close to the date, especially Layne. She usually stays booked up months and months ahead of time."

Patricia reached back into her Fendi bag for her phone. She tapped a button, looked up at the others. "I'm calling Carlos at Simple Elegance. We have a relationship. I'm sure if the others are busy, he'd be willing to accommodate us."

"Patricia!" Brooke glared at her stepmother. "Cara is our wedding planner. Can't you just let her figure this out?"

The older woman sighed, shrugged, put the phone away.

"I'll start making calls right away," Cara said. "If we can't get Layne, I do know Carlos at Simple Elegance, as well as several other people. But again, no promises."

Marie glanced over at Brooke. "Honey, couldn't we could just wait until fall, October, say?"

"No." Brooke shook her head vehemently. "I've got another huge civil trial coming up this fall. Harris has a conference in San Francisco. It's July or nothing." She glanced from Marie to Patricia. "July sixth. It's the anniversary of our first date."

"Impossible," Patricia muttered.

"I'll make it work. Somehow," Cara said. She sounded more positive than she felt. A big-budget wedding in six weeks? Was she nuts to think she could pull it off?

"Great," Brooke said. She took a last sip of iced tea, draining her glass, and stood. "I'm meeting Harris for dinner in ten minutes. I'll let all of you deal with the rest of the details." She put her hand lightly on Marie's shoulder. "Okay, Mom?"

"Wait!"

The others looked at Cara in surprise.

"Your wedding dress? You've ordered one, right? I really need to take a look at it, and I definitely need to talk about your preferences for flowers for your bouquet and the reception."

Patricia gave a derisive snort.

"She actually did buy a dress," Marie said quietly. "It's lovely. Very simple, very flattering for Brooke's figure."

"Do you have a photo?" Cara asked.

Brooke frowned. "No photos. But the dress is out in Mom's car."

"You bought a wedding gown off the rack?" Patricia shuddered. "Do I dare ask where you got it?"

"Some bride place in Atlanta," Brooke said carelessly. "Mom can show you." She started for the door.

"Brooke, honestly!' Marie called after her. "Cara really needs to get these things settled. Can't you call Harris and tell him you'll be a little late?"

"You can deal with all that stuff," Brooke said. "You know what I like, Mom. Just no orange. Or purple. Or red. Or yellow."

With that, she stepped out of her black pumps, slipped on a fair of flats, and was out the door, striding down the sidewalk without a backward look.

Which left Marie and Patricia sitting at the worktable in Cara's shop, separated only by a space of about three feet. Things got very quiet. Too quiet.

Cara jumped up. "Wine anybody?"

"Definitely," Marie said.

"Unless you've got the makings for a dry martini," Patricia said hopefully.

20

By Friday morning, she'd not only gotten the signed contract for the Trapnell wedding, she had a $12,500 deposit check in her hot little hand.

"Awesome," Bert said, when Cara showed him the check. "So, now you're a full-fledged wedding planner?"

"As far as the Trapnells are concerned, I am."

"We're rich," Bert said. "Wanna take your favorite assistant out to lunch?"

"You can have half my tuna sandwich if you like. We're not rich. We're not even solvent. Yet." She nodded toward the pile of bills on her desk. "It took six hundred dollars to replace the compressor on the cooler. I spent close to five thousand dollars replacing the flowers for Torie's wedding, which ate up half my profit from that wedding. And if I don't pay my phone bill by two p.m. today, they're going to cut off our service."

"And then there's the Colonel," Bert said.

"There's always the Colonel," Cara agreed. "He gets paid first—ten thousand right off the top."

"I thought he told you he wanted the whole magilla—twenty thousand," Bert said.

"I don't *have* the whole magilla," she reminded her assistant. "But I get the rest of the Trapnell deposit two weeks before the wedding. If the sky doesn't fall on my head between now and then—I should be able to fork over the rest of his money."

"Sounds like a plan," Bert said. "Speaking of—are we okay for Maya's wedding tonight? She's not one of our usual angsty brides, but she did text me this morning and ask if everything was okay."

Maya Gaines wasn't her typical Bloom bride. She was just out of design school at SCAD, and her flower budget was nearly nonexistent. Cara had agreed to take the job as a favor to Bert, who'd known the bride since elementary school. But also because Maya was hip and cute—and just plain nice. The ceremony—and the reception—would be at the Knights of Columbus hall just a few blocks away on Liberty Street.

"We should be fine," Cara said. She pointed to the buckets in the cooler, which she'd filled with inexpensive "filler" flowers she'd picked up earlier in the morning at Sam's Club.

"That's all the stuff you'll need for the boutonnieres," she said. "Get started on those, and I'll run over to Breitmueller's to pick up the rest of Maya's order. You can make the bouquets when I get back, and I'll start on the table arrangements." She looked around the workroom. "Did you pick up the Mason jars?"

"And the raffia, and the Twizzlers," Bert said. "So, you're really going to plunk red licorice sticks in those flower arrangements?"

"Along with red striped Pixy Stix," Cara said. "They're the bride and groom's favorite candies. They're Maya's colors. And they're cheap."

"I guess," Bert said, looking dubious.

"You mark my word. By tomorrow morning, those Mason-jar arrangements with Twizzlers and Pixy Stix are going to be all over Instagram and Pinterest."

Cara was at the wholesale house, watching her sales rep total her tab, carefully adding up each item with her pocket calculator. Even an innocent ten-dollar overcharge could throw Maya's tiny budget out of whack.

Without warning, Cullen Kane sidled over. He was wearing a loose-fitting blue linen shirt and white jeans, with a cluster of silver and leather bracelets on his right wrist. Cara, on the other hand, was wearing a faded orange sundress and rubber flip-flops.

He stood a little too close, invading her personal space.

"Hi there," Cara said, taking a half step backward. "How are you?"

"Fine. But not as fine as you, apparently. Congratulations. I hear you're doing the Trapnell wedding."

She blinked. "Where'd you hear that? I just signed the contract last night."

"Patricia's a dear friend," Cullen said. "We talk every night. I don't mind telling you I was a little surprised. She felt badly about it, but it's not as if I need the work."

"Of course not," Cara said.

Cullen came even closer. He smelled like Clinique moisturizer. He was so close she could see that he was actually wearing guyliner. Skillfully applied, yes, but it was still eyeliner.

"Any guesses why Brooke got her way and hired you?" he asked.

"Because it's her wedding, and I'm good at what I do?"

"Don't be naïve," he snapped. "Brookie is still pissed off that Gordon left Marie for Patricia. She can't get it into her head that after years of being trapped in a loveless marriage, Gordon actually had the balls to be with a real woman."

"A real woman named Patricia."

"Exactly. Yes, Patricia. Who in no way broke up that marriage. Anyway, it's been ages, but Marie still can't deal, which means that her daughter can't deal. And Brookie, PS, doesn't actually give a rat's ass about flowers, or any of this. So she's torturing Gordon with all this wedding crap, just to get back at him. It's all about retaliation with that girl."

"Thanks for the backgrounder," Cara said. "Or, at least, your theory of the background."

"And I hear you've now signed on as wedding planner too. Quite a coup. Let me ask. Have you ever actually planned an entire wedding before?"

She felt her face grow hot. "Obviously."

"A wedding with a two-hundred-and-fifty-thousand-dollar budget? With a high-profile client like the Trapnells and Strayhorns? Were you aware that Patricia's been in contact with *Town and Country* to have the wedding covered by them?"

Cara's mouth went dry. Patricia hadn't bothered to mention she was angling for a glossy society-magazine story about her stepdaughter's wedding, but she shouldn't have been surprised. The woman was dying for attention.

"As far as I'm concerned, all my weddings are high-profile," Cara said. "All my brides are incredibly special to me, and I try to give each one exactly the day of their dreams. No matter what the budget."

"How sweet," Cullen purred. He glanced over at the table where her order had been assembled.

Cara's buckets held bunches of cheerful Shasta daisies, red zinnias, yellow gerbera daisies, and Queen Anne's lace. A grand total of $867, by her calculator.

"Looks like you're doing a children's birthday party," he observed. "Let me guess. Circus theme?"

She chose to ignore the taunt. Instead she pointed at the masses of flowers covering the counter next to hers. It was piled high with exotic flowers, all in vivid tropical shades of orange, purples, hot pinks, and lime green.

"Gypsy wedding?" she asked.

He smiled blandly. "Just a dinner party Patricia is throwing tonight for Alexandra Skouras. Do you know her? She's the new head of marketing for General Mills. She and her husband Creighton just bought a second home over at Palmetto Bluff."

"Never met them," Cara admitted. Or heard of them, she wanted to say.

Her sales rep had finished tallying her order, and silently handed her the receipt.

Ignoring Cullen Kane, Cara checked the total on the receipt against the one on her calculator.

"Looks fine," she told the young woman, whom she hadn't worked with before. "Just put it on my account, please."

"Name?"

"Cara Kryzik. It should be under Bloom."

The clerk tapped her keyboard, found Cara's name in the system, but frowned.

"Um. It looks like there's a hold on your account."

Cara felt the blood drain from her face.

"Ouch," Cullen said, under his breath. He gave Cara a mock sympathetic smile, and finally moved back to his own side of the counter. But Cara knew he was watching. And listening intently.

"That's got to be a mistake," Cara said quietly.

The girl shook her head. "I only know what's in the system. This says you've got an outstanding balance."

"Look," Cara whispered. "I paid that bill yesterday. In full."

"But it's not been entered into the system," the girl said.

"I get that," Cara said, losing patience. "But the check is probably in your accounting office right now. Maybe it hasn't been posted yet."

"Probably not." The girl shrugged and looked meaningfully over Cara's shoulder, at another florist, who was hovering nearby with a bucketful of pink and white carnations.

"Okay. So what are we gonna do?" Cara asked. "I'd just write you another check, but I didn't bring my checkbook with me. I literally just ran over here to get these flowers for the wedding I'm doing tonight. I can come back later. All right?"

"Nope," the girl said. "Sorry. New policy. I can't let you take any product out of here until that hold is lifted."

"This is crazy," Cara moaned. "I've never had this happen before. And I need these flowers."

"Sorry," the girl said, but clearly, she wasn't sorry. She wasn't even terribly interested in Cara, or her credit hold. "Next."

The florist with the carnations stepped around Cara, giving her a quick, pitying look, the kind you'd give a crazy bag lady with a shopping cart full of recycling.

But Cara wasn't budging, and she wasn't leaving Breitmueller's without her damn flowers.

"Call Wendy," she told the girl. "Please."

. . .

Thirty minutes later, they found Cara's check in a stack of unopened mail on the bookkeeper's desk.

"Cara, I'm so sorry," Wendy Breitmueller said. They were sitting in her glass-walled office, located on a catwalk overlooking the warehouse. "Obviously, Janet didn't handle that very tactfully."

"No," Cara said, remembering the looks of pity and contempt she'd been given by the other customers in the warehouse. "She didn't. I was mortified."

"She's new," Wendy said. "But I've explained to her that that's not how we handle credit issues. You have my promise, it won't happen again."

"Hope not," Cara said, standing. She looked down at her phone. Two texts from Bert had popped up while she was dealing with this latest snafu.

WHERE R U?

And then, *NEED THOSE DAMN FLOWERS.*

Wendy followed her to the office door. "I hear business is looking up. You're doing the Trapnell wedding?"

"Damn!" Cara said. "Word travels fast."

"It's a small town," Wendy said with a smile. "People talk."

"People like Cullen Kane?"

"I think he's jealous of you," Wendy told her.

"Me? I'm no threat to him."

"Anybody who gets what he thinks he wants is a threat to somebody like Cullen Kane," Wendy advised. "Remember that."

21

Bert was standing at the worktable, fastening sprigs of rosemary and daisies together with floral tape. He looked up as Cara came in the door, weighed down with the flowers.

"Thought maybe you'd been abducted by aliens," he said, putting down the boutonniere he'd been working on. "Everything okay?"

"Grrr" was her only answer. "Ask me later. I've got to get moving with these bouquets and arrangements."

Fortunately, Maya had chosen only two attendants for her wedding. Cara went to work first on the most important bouquet. And as she bunched together the sunny reds, whites, and yellows for the bride's bouquet, snipping their stems and stripping the lower leaves, she felt her anger and frustration melt away. She reached into the cooler and brought out a handful of lemon leaves she'd trimmed from the tree in the courtyard garden, and tucked the glossy leaves in and around the flowers, turning the bouquet in her hand as she worked, studying it to make sure it worked from all angles.

She put the bouquet down in a Mason jar of water on the worktable, stepped back, and thought. It needed a touch of drama, she decided. After another moment, she walked out the back door into the garden, and stood there, hands on her hips, surveying what she had in bloom.

Finally, she spied the happy green and yellow zebra-striped leaves of the canna plant that had been left behind by a long-ago gardener. Cara wasn't normally a fan of the lowly canna, but she'd loved this zany striped foliage the moment she spotted it among the weeds and underbrush in the courtyard. With her scissors, she cut two of the long, straplike leaves and brought them back inside.

Bert watched while she split the leaves in half lengthwise, then wound them around and around the bouquet stem, like so much living ribbon, finally fastening the ends together with a large vintage enameled daisy brooch from the 1960s.

"Ohmygod, that's awesome," he laughed, when she held the bouquet up for inspection. "It's so Maya! She'll love it."

Maya Gaines knew what suited her. She was Amerasian, petite, just over five feet tall, with a mop of shiny dark curls. Her wedding dress was a short, pale yellow eyelet frock with spaghetti straps and a yellow satin bow at the waist. Her shoes were red ankle-strap heels, and instead of a veil she wore a narrow-brimmed straw fedora trimmed with yellow ribbon and a jaunty red fabric daisy.

She hopped up and down and hugged Cara when she walked into the K of C hall and saw the tables, with their white paper toppers and centerpieces of flowers and candy. Hanging from the ceiling at random heights were oversized red, yellow, and white tissue-paper flowers Cara had assigned for Maya and her sisters to create.

"I love it," Maya exclaimed, twirling around and touching the Mason jars. "It's what I dreamed about, only better. Twizzlers! And Pixy Stix! Wait until Jared sees these."

Cara laughed. "I really don't think Jared is going to get all that excited about Twizzlers on his wedding day."

"You don't know Jared," Maya replied. "He's a total candyholic."

. . .

The ceremony was brief, but sweet. Standing before a beaming white-haired Asian man, who Cara later learned was the bride's maternal grandfather, Maya and Jared pledged to love each other and play nice, and hold hands through every adventure life would bring them.

When they'd exchanged rings and kissed, the crowd of around a hundred in the hall roared their approval and clapped and whistled.

Cara and Bert, who'd stayed for the ceremony, exchanged a look. "What do you think?" Cara whispered.

"They'll make it," Bert said solemnly. "She's a sweetheart, and Jared's the first non-asshole she's dated. I mean, they've lived together for three years, the whole time Maya was in school."

Cara raised one eyebrow. "Forever? Really?"

Bert nodded vigorously. "Yeah. A hundred percent. I mean, I wouldn't want to jinx them, but if anybody can make a marriage work, it's those two zanies."

Cara was in line at the buffet, about to serve herself a pig in a blanket from the steam tray, when for some reason, a couple on the dance floor caught her eye. She had to look again.

Jack Finnerty! He wore a dress shirt with rolled-up sleeves, khaki slacks, and a straw fedora not too unlike the one the bride wore. In fact, most of the men and many of the women at the wedding wore hats. It was the new hipster thing, Bert had informed her. He himself was sporting a straw boater.

The girl Jack was with was nearly his height, with long light brown hair. She wore a strapless navy-blue sundress, and she danced effortlessly with Jack, laughing and chattering away as they moved through the crowd on the dance floor.

Bert stood beside her in the line and saw what she was watching. "Hey. Isn't that the dognapper? Who let him in here?"

Cara shrugged. "He literally knows everybody in Savannah. I don't know how the man has time to work, in between going to weddings every weekend."

They found a table near the back of the room; Cara sipped a glass of pinot grigio, and Bert ate what she estimated was his weight in boiled shrimp, pigs in a blanket, and Buffalo chicken drumettes.

"How do you eat like that and never gain weight?" she asked. "I bet you've eaten like, twelve thousand calories, just while I've been sitting here."

Her assistant was as tall and gangly as a strand of sea oats, six foot three, weighing maybe 140 on his version of a fat day. He'd died his blond hair purple in honor of his best friend's wedding, and he wore skinny white jeans, a red shirt, and a narrow yellow tie, loosened at the neck. Bert patted the vicinity of his belly. "I don't know. I just like food. I guess I like it as much as I used to like Scotch. So now, I eat instead of booze."

"You're an exoskeleton, I swear," she countered.

They stayed until the bride and groom cut the wedding cake, which in their case was actually a huge Key lime pie, and then Cara tried to leave. She'd already stayed longer than she'd planned, lingering only because she was enjoying attending a wedding with a happy, carefree bride and groom—a rarity in her business.

"C'mon," Bert protested. "Stay awhile. You haven't even danced with me."

"You dance? With women?"

He looked around the room. "Sometimes. When there are no other attractive options."

"Am I supposed to be flattered?"

Still, she allowed him to lead her onto the dance floor, where she tried, mostly unsuccessfully, to match the rhythm of the weird technopunk song the disc jockey was playing.

"I give up," she said finally, after the third time her sandal-clad foot had been thrashed by another dancer.

She was headed back to her table when a hand touched her elbow. "Quitter."

Cara turned and found herself facing Jack Finnerty, who was suddenly solo.

"It's this music," she said. "I'm only thirty-six, but I totally don't get it. There's no beat, no rhythm."

"There probably is," he corrected her. "But I think it's like high-pitched tones only dogs can hear. You have to be under thirty to appreciate this music."

She gave him a rueful smile. "Your date seems to get it."

"Date?" He looked around.

"Your dance partner? The girl you were with earlier?"

As soon as she opened her mouth she regretted it. Now he'd think she was watching him. Which she had been, of course.

"The pretty girl in the blue dress?"

"Meghan? You thought Meghan was my date?" He chuckled. "Wow. That really makes me feel like a dirty old man."

"Aren't you?" She was making a beeline for the table, intent on getting her handbag and going home.

"Meghan's my little sister," Jack said. "Wait until I tell her you thought I was with her, like with her."

Cara narrowed her eyes. "You're telling me you have a sister? She wasn't at Ryan and Torie's wedding. I know, because she's so striking, I would have noticed her."

"She was still in school. She just finished a semester abroad in Scotland," Jack said, amused. "Had finals the week of the wedding."

"I see," Cara said, looking around to try to spy the girl again.

"Also?" He lowered his voice conspiratorially. "Meghan and Torie aren't what you would call best friends."

"Do I dare ask what you're doing here tonight?" Cara asked. He'd followed her to the table and was standing by her side, obviously not in a hurry to leave.

"You want a beer?" he asked, deflecting her question. He snapped his fingers. "No. Wait. You drink wine. Pinot, right?"

"Riiight. But I was just leaving."

"Why? The night's young."

"But I'm not. Remember? I stayed longer than I planned as it is. I've got to be back here in the morning to clear out the flowers and things, and then I've got an early appointment over in South Carolina. Besides, since I've already owned up to being a geezer, I gotta tell you, this music is giving me a headache."

He smiled. "Grab your purse and follow me."

Bert was dancing with the bride. She managed to catch his eye and gave him a signal indicating her exit.

She followed Jack as he threaded his way through the swirl of thrashing dancers out the door and onto the street outside.

It was cooler there, and a cluster of partygoers stood around on the sidewalk, smoking and talking quietly.

"Better?"

She nodded.

"What about that drink?" he asked.

"What about your little sister?"

He shrugged. "Meghan won't mind. She didn't want to show up at Maya's wedding without a date, but now that the party's revved up, she'll never miss me."

"So she's a friend of Maya's? Or Jared's?"

"Both. Maya used to babysit her. And Jared used to work for Ryan and me."

Cara shrugged. It was only nine o'clock. "Where did you have in mind?"

"How about Doyle's? It's just down the block. We can walk if you want."

"All right," she agreed.

Doyle's Pub was a fairly new place, near the DeSoto Hilton on Liberty Street.. It was busy, but the hostess led them to a booth in the far reaches of the room and a waitress came and took their drink orders.

Sliding onto the bench opposite hers, Jack looked around the room appreciatively. "I remember when this was the old Shamrock Shop. My grandmother always bought all her birthday cards here." He pointed to the far wall, where the bar was located. "And that was the candy counter. All the St. Vincent's girls would come in here to buy candy and Cokes after school. Which meant the BC guys showed up too. It was a happening place."

"Still happening," Cara said, looking around. "I know they've been open at least a year, but this is actually the first time I've been in."

"Did you ever come in here, back in the day? Where'd you go to high school?"

"Not here," Cara said. "I'm an Air Force brat. I went to six different schools between elementary and high school, but I finished up in Columbus, Ohio."

"I figured." He nodded. "Not much of a Southern accent."

"I'm working on it. I've learned to say 'fixin' to' and 'crank the car' and 'carry me to the store,' but that's as far as I've gotten."

"You should hang around my aunt Betty," Jack said. "Born and raised here, never lived anyplace other than Savannah. Half the time, even I can't understand what she's saying."

The drinks came then. He seemed to be studying her, waiting for something. It was making her nervous. *He* made her nervous. Fidgety.

Say something, she told herself. "How's your . . ."

"How's your dog?" he blurted out, at the exact same time.

They both laughed.

"You start," he said. "How is Poppy? Over her trauma?"

"She's good," Cara said. "How about Shaz?"

"Not as depressed. I've started taking her to job sites with me now, and she's kinda into that. Although Torie's not crazy about having her at the house—she thinks Shaz intimidates Benji."

"Benji?"

"Torie's dog. Some kinda purse puppy. I don't know what kind of dog he is. Ryan calls him a shih tzu."

"But not in front of Torie."

"No."

"I'm lucky Poppy can just come downstairs to the shop with me most of the time. When I'm not there—is it weird that I leave the television on for her to watch?"

"Don't ask me. I leave the Animal Planet on for Shaz. Or Sports South."

"Poppy loves that too," she confided. "That and Disney."

They sipped their drinks. Cara decided it was her turn to study him. See if she could make him feel as fidgety as she felt.

He was easy to look at. Intelligent hazel eyes with crinkle lines at the corners, that made her think he laughed a lot when he wasn't around her. He had the dry, weather-beaten skin of somebody who worked outside, a trace of five-o'clock shadow on his strong jawline. He'd taken off his hat, and his dark hair was a little matted, but he wasn't the kind of guy who'd be self-conscious about that. His hands, clamped around his beer stein, were strong, sun-browned, callused.

Ryan told her that Jack was getting over a bad breakup. Torie had told her about the Jimmy Buffett impersonator. *Why would anybody leave somebody who looks like Jack Finnerty?*

"Kinda weird our dogs look so much alike," Jack said. "I've been wondering about that."

"You don't see that many goldendoodles in Savannah," she agreed. "I had to go to Atlanta to find Poppy's breeder. Where'd you get Shaz?"

"I think Zoey got her in Atlanta."

"You think?"

"We'd talked about getting a dog, in kind of an abstract way. Like, we were running in the park one day, and she said, 'We should get a dog.' And I said, 'Yeah.' And a few weeks later, I come home, and there's Shaz. Don't get me wrong. I like dogs. I love 'em. But it would have been nice if she'd discussed it with me."

He sipped his beer. "It wasn't the best time to bring a puppy into the mix. Relationship-wise. We weren't really getting along anyway. So I was pissed at her, and she was pissed at me for being pissed about the dog. And we were both pissed when Shaz pissed on the floor, which totally wasn't the dog's fault. She was a puppy! It went like that. Anyway, we split up. Probably just as well."

"If it was her dog, I'm surprised she didn't take Shaz."

"Not as surprised as me." They both laughed at that. "She was with one of her girlfriends at a bar on River Street, she met this guy, he was playing there. I guess they hooked up right away. . . ."

His face darkened at the telling. "He's a Jimmy Buffett impersonator, for God's sake."

"Oh my."

"That was a Friday night," he went on. "It was late March. Ryan and I were working crazy hours, trying to finish this Victorian house on Huntingdon Street. A total gut job. So I worked all day Saturday and Sunday too. When I got home that night, we had this big blowout of a fight about it. And again, in hindsight, I know now it wasn't about the dog, and it wasn't really about me working too much. At some point, I realized I needed to cool off. So I got in the truck, and I went back to the job site, and I actually slept in the truck that night, because I was too pissed off to go home. . . ."

"And that was it?" Cara asked.

"Yeah. How lame is this? I go back home the next morning, to shower, and she's gone. Packed up most of her clothes and crap, and just headed out on the road with this character, who calls himself . . . get this . . . Jamey Buttons."

Cara groaned. "And she left Shaz behind."

"And me. Now I'm like the opposite of what the song says. Come Monday, *nothin'* was all right."

22

There was a votive candle in a jar on their table, and the small flame lit Cara's face in shades of pinks and peach as she leaned in, listening to him tell the end of the Jack and Zoey story. She had large, expressive brown eyes, and her nose had a weird little indent at the very tip, and her hair, which she'd worn up, was falling down, strands lightly touching the bare skin on her shoulders. Her lips were the color of ripe peaches. Or was that just the candlelight? She was wearing the same orangey-pink dress she'd had on the night of Ryan's wedding.

Why am I telling her all this? Why does she care? Why do I care?

He cared because he'd been deserted, left behind. Because Zoey had found somebody else. Somebody better. And let's face it, he cared because she'd beat him to the punch, leaving him before he could leave her.

But why should Cara Kryzik care about any of this? Maybe . . . because she'd been hurt, too. At least, that's what Ryan had said. She was a good listener. Zoey never listened worth a damn. You'd start telling her something, and she'd interrupt, stepping all over your sentences, making you forget what you were talking about, turning everything around, until, inevitably, whatever you were about to say was somehow about her. Her day. Her crappy job. Her. Her. Her.

"Do you miss her?" Cara was asking.

"Who? Zoey?" He would have shrugged off the question, but there was something about this girl that made him speak the truth, even when it was painful.

"Maybe. Yeah, okay. Sometimes. And then she pulls some stunt, like letting hours go by before letting me know that Shaz has been turned in to the vet's office, and I've abducted somebody else's dog."

She nodded.

"What about you?" he asked softly. "Ryan tells me you're divorced. Pretty recently?"

Cara bit her lip and looked out the window. "Last April. Hard to believe it's been a year."

"Miss him?"

"No." She fairly spat the word.

"Really? Never? How long were you married?"

"It would have been five years, but we split last year on Valentine's Day."

Jack grimaced. "Brutal."

"It was also my birthday."

"Shit," he said softly.

"Exactly. He was a shit. Which is why I now have a dog."

"A female dog," Jack observed.

Cara took a long sip of wine and then a deep breath. "Hate to say it, but I'd better start thinking about heading home."

"Really?"

Jack could have kicked himself. He'd struck a nerve, asking about her ex. What was he thinking? Never, ever, ask a girl about an ex. Was he that out of practice?

He put some money on the tabletop and stood, holding out a hand to steady her, as she pulled herself from the narrow booth. Her hand was small and warm, but her fingers were long, like an artist's.

When she was standing, he released her hand, but rested his own, lightly, on the small of her back, as they made their way to the door. Doyle's was packed now, with a din that drowned out anything they could have said, until they were back outside on the sidewalk again.

"Can I give you a ride home? My truck's just parked over on Liberty."

"Thanks, but I've got the shop van parked in the lane behind the K of C."

"Oh."

His face fell, and Cara was secretly glad. They'd had a drink together. Just one. But she was starting to like him. Okay, she'd started liking him the day he brought Poppy back home, and apologized. And she thought just maybe, he kind of liked her.

"You could walk me back over to the van," she offered. "I'm no fraidycat, but I definitely don't like walking in these dark downtown lanes at night."

"Good thinking," he said. "You never can tell what kind of lowlifes are wandering around down here on a Friday night." As they moved down the sidewalk, she hesitated, but then reached over and tucked her hand through his arm. "For safety," she said gravely. "Because you really never can tell."

He squeezed her hand, and gave her a sideways glance, and her smile was warm, as though they both shared some exciting new secret.

He could have covered the two blocks to the K of C hall in less than five minutes. Instead, he took his own sweet time. He *strolled*. It was a typical May night in Savannah, in the mid-eighties, and the scent of her light, flowery perfume wafted in the warm evening air.

She was walking slowly, too. "I'm a house voyeur," she confessed, as they passed a stately town house. "I love walking around downtown, peeking in the lit windows. I want to see what kind of furniture people have, the pictures hanging on their walls, their wallpaper. My ex used to accuse me of being a peeping Tom. You ever do that?"

"No. Okay, occasionally. But I'm trying to see the molding profile, the staircase details, the old hardware, and the window casings."

"I'm even worse when it comes to gardens. I'm forever riding down lanes, hoping for a glimpse into somebody's courtyard. Someday, somebody's probably going to see me peeking through their fence and sic the cops on me."

"Like I tried to do after you followed me home a couple weeks ago?"

"I guess it's lucky for both of us the cops had better things to do that night," Cara said. They walked past Liberty Street and entered the lane that ran behind the Knights of Columbus hall. Jack took the opportunity to put a protective arm around Cara's shoulder. Just in case.

"This is me." The pale pink striped Bloom van was parked near the K of C's back door. They heard music from inside. A group of men were standing just down the lane, talking loudly, their lit cigarettes making an arc in the inky night. They heard a loud metallic clatter, as something was tossed against a battered trash can.

"Party's still going," Jack said, nodding in that direction. "I think I recognize a couple of those guys from the wedding. Tommy Hart, the guy in the black fedora? He used to date Meghan."

"I hope Bert's gone home by now," Cara said. "He's been sober two years now, and I shouldn't worry about him, I know, but it can't be easy for him, being around parties and booze all the time, every time we do a wedding."

"Want me to go inside and check on him?" Jack offered.

"No. He's a grown-up. I don't want him to think I don't trust him. What about you, will you go back inside, to find your sister?"

Instead of answering, he pulled his phone from his pocket and showed her the screen. There was a text message—

Gone out with the girlz. Don't tell Mom.

He grinned. "That's Meghan for you."

Cara reached in her bag for her keys, and he moved closer beside her, with his hand on her arm, and she realized, with a start, that he was probably going to kiss her. A little frizzle of electricity shot up her spine, as she realized she hoped he would.

She found the key and fit it in the lock. His hand touched her cheek, lightly, and he leaned down.

"Hey, asshole!" A man's voice echoed in the lane. They heard glass splintering against concrete, and more voices.

"Drunks," Jack said, shrugging.

"What the fuck? Man, that's not cool!"

Jack jerked his head around to see what was happening.

More glass shattering. Shouts.

A door opened from a town house at the entrance to the lane, spilling light into the lane. They could see four men, clumped together, and a fifth man, sprawled on his back on the broken asphalt.

A shrill woman's voice called from the back of the house. "Whoever's out there I'm calling the cops. I mean it, I'm calling them right now!"

"Fuck you, bitch." Coarse laughter. But the men slunk off into the darkness, like so many feral cats. All but the one, who was still on the ground, clutching his black fedora, curled up now in a fetal position. Even from where they stood, they could hear his groans of pain.

Jack sighed. "I better see if he's all right."

"Tommy?" Jack crouched over the fallen man. "You okay?"

Dumb question. Tommy Hart was definitely not okay. His nose was already a bloody, swollen pulp, and his left eye was closed, a ring of purple already blooming.

He helped the younger man to a sitting position.

Tommy held both hands to his face. "I'm fuuuucked up."

"I see that," Jack said. "Did they hit you anywhere else?"

"No maan. Just my faaace." The words were slurred. "I think my nose is broke."

They heard the loud wail of a police siren.

"Will he be okay?"

Jack turned, and was surprised to see Cara, kneeling on the filthy, glass-strewn asphalt, at his side.

"His nose is probably broken," Jack said succinctly.

Before he could say anything else, Tommy Hart, improbably, staggered to his feet. “I gotta go, man.” He swayed, and it looked, for a moment, that he might fall down again. Blood dripped down the front of his face, onto his white shirt.

“Whoa,” Jack said. He wrapped an arm around Tommy’s shoulder. “You need to get your nose looked at.”

“Yeah. Later.” Tommy tried to pull away, but Jack held his ground.

“Where do you think you’re going?”

“I got to go,” Tommy insisted. He glanced toward the end of the lane. “Cops. I don’t need to be messing with the po-po.” He tried again to free himself from Jack’s grasp. “Come on, Jack. I’m okay.”

“You’re not okay,” Jack repeated. “You’re shitfaced. You can’t drive like this.”

The sirens were growing closer.

Tommy moaned. “I can’t get another MIP. They’ll pull my driver’s license. I’ll lose my freakin’ job. My old man will kill me.”

“Come on, then,” Jack said. “Let’s walk.” With his arm around Tommy’s shoulder, he force-marched him in the direction of the K of C hall.

Cara followed, unsure of her next move. She hesitated, then picked up the battered black felt fedora she found lying on the ground.

Jack banged hard on the K of C’s kitchen door, and a frightened-looking Hispanic man yanked the door open a few inches.

“Incoming,” Jack said. Silently, the porter held the door open wide enough for them to pass.

Jack shoved Tommy onto a rickety kitchen stool, went to the commercial ice machine, and scooped up a handful of ice, which he wrapped in a white terry dishcloth.

“Jesus!” Tommy yelped, as Jack held the cloth to his battered nose.

“How’d you get here tonight?” Jack asked.

“Huh?”

“Do you have a car here?”

“Yeah. Of course. I’m parked on the square.” Tommy looked up at him through his good eye. “I can drive.”

"Nuh-uh," Jack said. "You can't hardly walk. No way I'm letting you get behind the wheel of a car. You still living at your mom's place? On Wilmington Island?"

"I ain't saying."

"Fine," Jack said. "I'll just drop you off at the ER at Memorial. Let them deal with you."

"No! Okay. We're still in the same rathole in Spinnaker Cove."

"That's better. You ready to roll?"

Tommy shot Jack a hopeful look. "I could use a drink. For pain."

"You could use a kick to the head," Jack said. "You're underage, probably got, what, a couple minor-in-possession citations already? And you think I'm gonna pour you another beer?" He pulled the boy to his feet. "Let's go."

Tommy stood, unsteadily.

"Keys?" Jack held out his hand.

"Fuuuuck." Tommy dug them out of his pants pocket and handed them over.

Cara followed them to the front of the hall. It was nearly ten, but the party raged on. In the middle of the dance floor, Maya and Jared danced alone, bodies pressed close together, performing what Cara thought was a fairly credible tango.

On the sidewalk, Jack turned and gave her an apologetic smile. "Sorry. But this kid's mom is an old family friend. Tommy's not a bad guy, but he seems to attract trouble. I better get him loaded up. Want me to drive you around to your van?"

She looked over at Tommy, who'd draped himself over a parking meter, head resting on his chest. He seemed to be humming something.

"No need. Now that the bad guys are gone. What about you? You're driving him all the way out to Wilmington Island? I could follow you out, give you a ride back."

"Thanks, but no," he said. "I'll catch a ride back to town."

"You're sure?"

He touched her cheek lightly, his voice full of regret. "No. But that's another story."

Suddenly, with no warning, he pulled her close, his arms wrapped around her waist. He kissed her quickly. She'd had exactly two glasses of wine, but she felt dizzy, so she pulled him closer. His tongue slipped through her lips . . .

"Bllllleeeechhh."

Tommy was crouched on the curb, his head between his knees. "Blllecchh."

Jack released her, reluctantly. He shrugged. "Kids. Okay if I give you a call next week?"

She gave him another quick kiss. "You better."

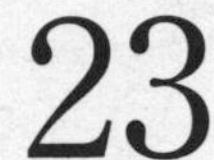

The South Carolina low country was a sea of green and gold, contrasted against a pure blue sky. Wildflowers bloomed in muddy ditches, and carpets of red clover paved the higher ground along the roadway.

As always, in her mind, Cara was composing arrangements. She could see a small jelly glass filled with those lowly ditch daisies, wild violets, and red clovers, with slender stalks of sweet grass spiking and spilling over the sides of the glass.

Brooke Trapnell had professed no real interest in flowers, but she did have definite color biases. With her dark hair and fair skin, tones of silvers, blues, pinks, and lavender might be nice. She'd nixed purple, but lavender wasn't really purple. When she got back to the shop, Cara decided, she'd put some flowers together, snap a picture, and text it to Brooke. Texts, she'd already discovered, were the best way to communicate with this busy bride.

So much to get done for this wedding, in such a short time span. Thankfully, she'd already gotten commitments from Layne at Fete Accompli to cater, and found two of her favorite photography studios that had openings for July 6. She'd emailed links to both photographers' websites to all parties, and as soon as Brooke, or more likely, Marie, got back to her, she'd get that nailed down.

Patricia Trapnell had already sent audio clips from the orchestra she was determined to hire, and since there was no obvious reason to veto them, Brooke had reluctantly agreed, so Cara had called the orchestra's booking agent that morning, and their contract was sitting on her desk back at the shop.

It was a forty-five-minute drive from Savannah to Cabin Creek, and for the rest of the journey, Cara puzzled not over flowers or canapés, but the more interesting and confusing topic of Jack Finnerty and his behavior the night before.

She really didn't know what to make of this man.

He could have left his sister's old friend in that alley the previous night. Could have walked away with Cara, maybe sweet-talked his way into her apartment, and who knows, eventually her bed. Yes, she'd fantasized about that. He could have allowed the underage drunk to get picked up by the police. It would have saved a lot of time and trouble if he'd just walked away. But he hadn't.

Leaving his own truck where it was, Jack had cleaned the kid up as best he could, loaded him into his beat-up Camry, and driven him all the way home. And then—he'd texted Cara to make sure *she'd* gotten home all right.

What kind of guy did something as kind and caring as that? Her brow furrowed. Was he really that sweet, or was he just trying to impress her?

Libba Strayhorn was standing in front of the magnificent plantation house, an incongruous figure in her faded ball cap, brown riding pants, blue work shirt, and scuffed leather riding boots. She had a black and white dog at her heels as she walked back and forth among the boxwood borders, leaning down to pull up weeds.

She waved as Cara drove around to the car park, and walked around to meet her.

"Hey there!" Libba greeted her. "I hear you're the one who's going to make this whole wedding happen. Congratulations!"

She leaned in and stage-whispered. "Just between you and me and Rowdy here, I'm glad it's you. That other fella was just a little too fancy for my tastes."

"I'm glad you're glad," Cara said. "And thanks again for agreeing to let me come out today and walk through the house again. Are you sure you have time to do this with me?"

"Plenty of time," Libba assured her. "The horses are exercised, and I've got the whole day free for this. Mitch is out of town on business, but as he likes to say, his only role in this wedding is to smile and nod and stay sober."

They walked through the front door, into the high-ceilinged entry foyer, with its hand-painted Chinese-motif wallpaper and black-and-white-checkerboard marble floor. A spectacular antique gold-leafed Chippendale mirror took up most of one wall of the foyer, and Cara eyed it apprehensively.

"You know, Libba, the plan is to have cocktails and passed appetizers in here as the guests arrive. I think we're expecting about two hundred and fifty people. It could be quite a crush. I know this mirror must be an old family piece, and I'm a little worried somebody could accidentally jostle and damage it. Do you think that's something you might want to move to storage during the reception?"

"I don't see why," Libba said, giving the mirror a fond pat. "This thing's been in this hall for at least a hundred and fifty years. It withstood Union forces, who camped out here during the war, and even worse, all those generations of rambunctious Strayhorn boys, including Mitch and Harris. Anyway, we couldn't move it if we wanted to. It's bolted to that wall."

"Great," Cara said. "It's so stunning, I'd hate to lose it. I was thinking we could leave a big silver bowl on that console table for guests to drop cards and gifts."

"Okay," Libba said. "You're the boss. What else do you want in here?"

"Nothing, really. We'll bring in rented high-top tables and scatter them against the walls, so people will have a place to rest their drink glasses."

She and Libba passed from the hallway into the double parlors, and discussed the placement of tables and chairs, and the bride and groom's table.

They went into the kitchen, which was huge, but surprisingly modest for a house of Cabin Creek's grandeur. The cabinets were vintage forties, metal, with tiny patches of rust beginning to show through at the edges, the countertops yellow formica, and the floors were worn yellow linoleum tile.

"Mitch is all het up about ripping this old stuff out and putting in a completely new kitchen with all the modern bells and whistles. He's the cook in the family," Libba confided. "He's got his eye on an eight-burner restaurant range and one of those double-door glass-front fridges, marble countertops, the works."

"Sounds like a dream," said Cara enviously. "The kitchen in my tiny apartment downtown would fit inside your pantry."

Libba shrugged. "Personally, I don't see the point. Holly has her own apartment in Savannah, and Harris and Brooke have their own place there too. It's just Mitch and me here most nights, and this old stuff has worked fine for the forty years we've lived here, but then again, someday, we hope, Harris and Brooke will be living here, with a passel of kids, and they'll appreciate a kitchen like that."

"You wouldn't try to do the kitchen before the wedding, right?" Cara asked.

"Oh no," Libba assured her. "Maybe in the fall, when things quiet down."

"Good. You've got a lot of counter space, which is great, because our caterer is going to need every inch of it. Layne is going to want to run over here to take a look at the space too, but she's already said she may want to bring in an extra fridge, and maybe even an extra cooktop, but I think there'd be room for that if we move out the table and chairs in your eating nook. Would that be okay?"

"Sure," Libba said. "As long as we have a place to get a cup of coffee and a bowl of cereal in the morning, Mitch and I are fine."

As they moved through the house, Cara marveled to herself at the good nature and calm radiated by this mother of the groom. In less than five weeks, her home would be invaded by a huge, lavish wedding complete with 250 guests, but she seemed totally unfazed by any and all requests Cara made.

"Can we take another look at the ballroom?" Cara asked, as they neared the back of the house.

Libba nodded. "Hasn't been used since Harris's twenty-first-birthday party. I guess you've noticed Mitch and I aren't really big on entertaining. We enjoy it when we do it, but mostly, we're out here in the country, keeping to ourselves with the horses and dogs. Or, I am. Mitch is happy as long as he's got his big-screen TV, twenty-four-hour cable sports, and an easy ride to the airport when he needs to travel, which he does a lot for his business."

The ballroom was another grand, high-ceilinged room in a wing that had been added on to Cabin Creek, Libba told her, in the 1950s. "Mitch's grandparents had it built for his parents' wedding. Back then, there was nothing around here where you could have a big party, no country clubs or hotel ballrooms, nothing like that."

"It's lovely," Cara said. Floor-to-ceiling windows ran down both sides of the long room, and there was a low platform at the far end. "Perfect for the orchestra," Cara said.

Libba rolled her eyes. "They sure are getting grand with this wedding. I wouldn't even know where to start to look for something like that."

"It's a lot," Cara agreed. "But Patricia has tracked down a ten-piece orchestra out of Charleston. I've heard some clips of their work, and seen some YouTube videos. They play all the standards, great dance music, all the way up to the nineties."

"What's Brooke think about all this fuss?"

Cara studied the other woman. "I can tell she's not crazy about it. And to tell you the truth, I don't understand why she bowed to Gordon and Patricia in all this."

"I can tell you. Because her daddy bribed her," Libba said with a snort. "Offered to pay off her law-school loans if she'd agree to a big to-do."

"Ahhh. That explains a lot. Don't get me wrong, I'm thrilled to have the work, Libba, but the last time I was out here meeting with the Trapnells, I got the distinct impression that Patricia was planning on hiring Cullen Kane."

"She was. But then Brooke dug in her heels and insisted they hire you instead. I think it was all about tweaking her stepmother—although you didn't hear me say that."

"What's Harris think about all the wedding plans?" Cara asked. "Do you know, I haven't even met him yet?"

"Those kids stay so darned busy, I don't know how they even had time to get engaged," Libba said. "Harris is pretty easygoing. He does love a party, though. I think whatever Brooke decides will be fine with him."

Cara looked around the ballroom. Although the architectural details were good, it was apparent that the room hadn't been used in years. The white paint on the walls was yellowing, and the wood trim on all the window casings was peeling. The highly polished oak floor was scuffed, and the fussy crystal chandeliers were coated with dust and grime.

Libba noticed Cara's appraisal. "Needs some spiffing up in here, that's for sure. I'm gonna have the painters in, and we'll have the floors stripped and buffed. Guess I'm gonna have to bribe my housekeeper to see about those old chandeliers."

"Some freshening up, and it'll be glorious," Cara assured her.

"What were you thinking about parking all the cars?" Cara asked, as they walked back toward the front door. "We'll have valet-parking people, of course, but we'll need to figure out where to put the cars without trampling all your landscaping."

In answer, Libba flung the front door open and pointed to a pasture on the west side of the house. "Plenty of room over there. It's higher ground than the east side of the property, so even if it does rain that night, it should drain quickly."

As they crossed to the pasture, Cara was glad she'd dressed casually for the trip, in jeans and tennis shoes. Already, she'd sidestepped one horse plop.

The two women leaned over the barbed-wire pasture fence. Two horses, one black, one brown, grazed nearby in the tall grass.

Libba whistled softly, and both horses raised their heads, then ambled over, to accept their owner's head pats and soft praises.

"We'll move these guys over to the other pasture the week before the wedding," Libba said. "And don't worry, I'll get one of the men to make sure the pasture is thoroughly shoveled out and the grass mown. Don't want Patricia ruining her Jimmy Choos on the big day."

Cara pointed at a weathered silver barn at the far end of the pasture. "Is that your stable?"

"Not anymore," Libba said. "That building down the pathway from where you parked the car, that's the new stable. Mitch had it built as a fiftieth-birthday present for me. Those horses live better than we do now," she said proudly.

Cara had a glimmer of an idea. "What do you keep in the old barn, then?"

"Random crap," Libba said, grinning. "Why do you ask?"

"Well . . . sometimes, especially with a big, formal wedding, brides and grooms like to have an after-party, for the guests of their own generation. Sort of a place everybody can cut loose. We bring in a DJ, and the bride and groom usually change into casual clothes. Sometimes, we do a midnight buffet. Just something fun. We've done wienie roasts, barbecues, in cold weather I've seen couples have bonfires with spiked hot chocolate and s'mores . . ."

"We could probably do something like that in the barn," Libba said slowly. "Want to take a look?"

It took both women tugging on the old barn doors to yank them open, their rusted hinges squealing in protest.

Cara's eyes took a moment to adjust to the dimness. The barn was redolent of mildew, leather, old hay, older manure, but somehow it was a rich, pleasant, promising scent. She craned her head and stared up at the high, peaked ceiling, where pinpricks of daylight shone through the rusted tin roof.

It looked like the barn had become home to anything and everything the Strayhorns owned that was too broken to use but too valued to discard. Cardboard boxes were stacked in corners, there was a profusion of tools, tires, old saddles, unidentified agricultural machinery, discarded appliances, broken furniture, and even a faded red Mustang, sans tires, perched on jacks. Everything was coated with a thick film of dust, and the overhead corners were festooned with cobwebs.

"That's Mitch's first car," Libba said, pointing at the Mustang. "He swears he's going to restore it someday. Maybe when he retires. We'll see. The man doesn't know the first thing about cars or engines." She turned slowly and pointed out other family mementos. "Harris's crib. The first dryer I ever owned. My mother-in-law's favorite riding lawn mower." She turned to Cara with a sheepish grin. "See? Random crap. Living this far out in the country, it's easier to just stick stuff in the barn than it is to have it hauled off to the dump.

"Mitch would love to have everything in here cleared out. Except the Mustang. That's the holy of holies. But everything else?" She shrugged. "Time to let go of all of it."

"Except Harris's crib," Cara guessed.

"Precisely."

Libba was walking around the barn, examining the walls. "Don't know how long this thing has been standing. Mitch's mom said it was here when she moved to Cabin Creek. And we did keep the horses here for years." She glanced up at the glints of daylight.

"Have to get a new roof. Otherwise, I think this thing could probably stand another seventy-five years."

It was a big barn, and roofs, Cara knew, were expensive.

"Is that something you'd want to undertake? With all the other expenses with the wedding?"

"We'd have to do it sooner or later, if we want the barn to keep standing," Libba said. "Which we do. Only problem is, getting somebody reliable over here to do the work. With the economy like it's been, you'd think people would be eager for a job, but that's not how it is out here. The last work we had done here? I wanted to rip out the old tub in our master bath and put in a nice big glass-walled shower. Like you see in all the magazines." She snorted in disgust. "The jacklegs we hired took six months, screwed it up so bad, Mitch kicked 'em out before the tile was even grouted. We still can't use that shower."

"I might have an idea," Cara said slowly. "I know a contractor in Savannah . . . all they do is historic-restoration work. I suppose that would include roofs. . . ."

"I'd love to talk to them. Maybe they could take care of the other stuff we want to do before the wedding too. See about those leaky windows in the ballroom, get the barn fixed up."

"It's the Finnerty brothers," Cara said. "I just did a wedding for Ryan Finnerty, the younger of the two brothers. He married Torie Fanning."

"Finnerty? From Savannah? We know the Finnertys. Been knowing 'em for years. I didn't realize they were contractors."

"I can get you their number. They haven't done any work for me personally, but I'm sure it would be easy enough to check their references."

"I wouldn't worry about references with those boys," Libba said. She nodded emphatically. "I'll call their mom tonight." She looked pleased with herself. "Yes sir. Fix this place up nice."

"Would you keep horses here again?" Cara asked.

"No. We've got the new stables for them." Libba's face took on a wistful quality. "This old barn has a lot of good memories for our family. Holly and her friends played house up in the loft. Harris and his buddies would play out here, on rainy days. It was their secret clubhouse, their army fort. He was in a kind of garage band in high school. They were awful! I wouldn't let 'em play in the house, so they practiced out here. Mitch said he and his brothers did the same thing when they were kids." She turned to Cara.

"Someday, I hope, we'll move Harris's crib back into the big house. And this barn will be full of my grandbabies, playing hide-and-go-seek, and pirate and bad garage rock.

"That is," she said, pulling a face, "if Harris and Brooke can slow down enough eventually to give me those grandbabies while I'm still young enough to enjoy them."

Cara reached out and squeezed Libba's hand. "I hope they will."

Libba sighed, and the two women picked their way through debris toward the door.

By now, both their faces were coated with a sheen of perspiration.

Libba mopped her forehead with a blue bandanna. "You can see how hot it is in here right now, and it's only May. How are we gonna get this place cooled down enough come July?"

"It's actually not that difficult," Cara said. "We do tons of weddings in tents and all kinds of outbuildings these days. We'll rent generators and big air-conditioning units."

"Really?" Libba looked impressed. "You can air-condition a barn?"

"I did the flowers for a wedding in an airplane hangar last August," Cara assured her. "With enough money, you can do just about anything."

"One thing we know," Libba said with a laugh. "Gordon Trapnell has more than enough money. And he's bound and determined to spend it on this wedding. But you know what? I don't want to rent air conditioners. Let's just buy us a new system. That way we don't have to give it back. And I don't have to feel beholden to Gordon or Patricia."

24

Jack ran past the town house on Jones Street three times the following Sunday morning before he finally worked up the nerve to stop.

"This is stupid," he muttered, slowing to a walk, as he approached the house. He looked down at Shaz, who was panting heavily. "I could just tell her you need a drink. She might turn me down, but she would never turn away a thirsty dog."

Shaz seemed to agree. In fact, as soon as they got in front of the stoop leading up to the shop, she abruptly sat, and refused to be moved, no matter how hard Jack pulled on her leash.

He wound the leash around the wrought-iron window box beside the door and rang the bell, shifting nervously from one foot to the other as he waited.

"We'll just act like we were passing by, and decided to stop on the spur of the moment."

Five minutes passed. He looked down at Shaz, who didn't seem perturbed by the delay. "Maybe she's at church."

Shaz gave him a baleful stare.

"She could have gone out to brunch. Like a date or something. Or out of town for the weekend. " They heard a short, excited bark then, coming from the other side of the door. Shaz stood now, her ears pricked in excitement.

Finally, the paper shade on the glass shop door was pulled up. Cara Kryzik looked out at them, bemused. She wore shorts and a tank top and her hair was wrapped in a towel.

"Or maybe she was in the shower," Cara said, opening the door. Poppy stood directly behind her, peering around her legs.

Jack felt his face redden. "You heard, huh?"

She pointed upward. He took a step back, off the stoop, and saw the open window directly above the stoop. "My bedroom. When that window's open, I can hear everything out on the street. It can make for some pretty interesting nights."

"You don't have air-conditioning?" It was the best comeback he could think of.

"Not right at the moment," Cara said. "It's on the blink, which is not at all unusual. I've been calling the landlord for two days, but she hasn't called back. If I don't hear from her by tonight, I swear, I'm gonna buy myself a window unit and deduct the cost from my rent."

"You should," Jack agreed. "It was in the high eighties last night."

"It was in the low nineties upstairs," Cara said. "Did I hear you say something about some water for Shaz? And how about you? I could fix us some iced coffee?"

As she'd promised, the interior of the shop was steamy. While Cara disappeared into a small kitchenette, he looked around.

It was a small room, no bigger than his living room on Macon Street. But she'd hung a dozen old mirrors on the exposed brick walls, and they made the room look larger. There was a large zinc-topped worktable, a small antique table with three chairs in a bay near the front window, a glass countertop with a cash register, and a large glass-doored cooler full of buckets holding flowers.

An alcove hid behind a half-opened curtain, and he could see a desk stacked with papers, a computer, and a phone.

"How's your friend Tommy?" Cara called from the kitchen.

"Alive."

"Thanks to you."

"He was passed out cold by the time I got him home. It was all I could do to unload him from that Camry and dump him on a lawn chair under the carport. He left a pretty sheepish message on my answering machine the next day. I think the experience might have helped him sober up—and grow up—a little."

"And how did you get back to town to your truck?"

"I texted Ryan and he gave me a ride."

Cara came out of the kitchenette holding two tall frosted glasses of iced coffee. "Let's take the drinks and the dogs out to the courtyard garden. I've got dog bowls out there, so Shaz can have that water you promised."

He followed her down a narrow hallway, passing a stairway that led to the upstairs apartment, and a closed door that he guessed held a bathroom.

The garden was a surprise. There were a pair of tall palm trees at the back of the garden, and these were underplanted with lush banana trees, hydrangeas, hostas, ivy, ferns, and a dozen more plants whose names he didn't know. A walkway of mottled Savannah gray bricks bisected the planting beds. She set the drinks down on a teak table shaded by a large market umbrella, and motioned for him to take a bench opposite the one she sat on.

"Nice," he said appreciatively. "But I guess it makes sense you'd have a great garden, you being a florist."

"It's my escape hatch from reality," she said. Poppy found a place in the shade of the umbrella, while Shaz roamed around, sniffing the plants, until finally spotting the aluminum bowl of water near the hose bib.

Jack took a sip of the coffee, but he was still studying her garden. There was something different about it, and it took a moment before it dawned on him.

"No color," he said, nodding slowly. "Except white. It's all white and green. And a little bit of yellow."

"That's right. I'm around color all day. I love it, but when I get away from work, my eyes need to rest. I find green and white really soothing."

"Very soothing," he agreed. "And it feels a lot cooler than I'd expect."

"That's the plan."

He cleared his throat. "I had a call from Libba Strayhorn yesterday. She wants to talk to us about doing some work over at their place in South Carolina. I guess I have you to thank for that."

"She's a nice lady, and they've had some bad luck with contractors."

"So I heard. My family's known Mitch and Libba for a long time, you know. From when they lived in Ardsley Park. Harris was two years behind me in school, and Holly must be in her mid-twenties by now. I'd lost track of them, after they sold the house in town and moved over there full-time."

"Have you been to Cabin Creek?"

"Not in years, since we were little kids. She said something about fixing up the old barn?"

"That's right. Their son's wedding is July sixth, and the hope is that we can have the after-party in the barn."

He wrinkled his nose. "A wedding? In a barn? In July?"

"They moved the horses to a new stable several years ago, and once they clear out all the junk that's accumulated there over the years, and you get the roof patched up, it'll be great," Cara said.

"Kinda hot." Jack fanned his face with his hand.

"We'll bring in air conditioners."

"Ryan and I are going over there tomorrow to check it out," he told her.

"Speaking of weddings." Her eyes twinkled with mischief. "Where were you last night?"

"Last night? I dunno. Home, I guess. We worked late, finishing up at Ryan's house. Why?"

"I did the flowers for a wedding—and you weren't there. I thought you went to every wedding in Savannah."

"Who got married?"

"Emily Braswell and Rob Mabry."

He shook his head. "Never heard of 'em. They must be new in town."

"As a matter of fact, her father was just transferred here last year by the Army Corps of Engineers. And the groom is from Macon."

"Then that explains it. Nice wedding?"

Cara leaned over and picked a dead frond from a fern, crumbling the browning leaf between her fingertips. "It was okay. Bert and I give them about a fifty-fifty chance."

"Of what?"

"Surviving." She shrugged, and one of the skinny straps of her tank top slipped off her shoulder. She left it there, and it distracted him for a moment, affording him a tantalizing glimpse of the pale skin of her upper breast.

He looked away, and then back, and by then, she'd adjusted it. Too bad. It was a nice view. Nicer even than all these cool green and white flowers. Now, what had he been about to say? Oh yeah.

"You rate their marriage chances? That seems pretty cynical."

"You see as many couples as I do, work with as many crazy brides and overbearing moms as me, you'd be cynical too," she said calmly. "I've only been in business for myself two and a half years here, and I can't tell you how many couples don't even make it to their first anniversary."

Poppy stirred, getting to her feet and staring intently at the brick wall running along the back of the courtyard. A squirrel paused there. Shaz saw the squirrel, too, and both the dogs went bounding toward their intended quarry. Instead of scampering away, though, the squirrel held its ground, chattering angrily at the two dogs four feet below, who were now balancing on their hind legs, whimpering and pawing ineffectively at the brick.

"Shaz!" Jack called. "Down!" The dog ignored him.

"Poppy! Leave that squirrel alone," Cara added. "I swear, it's the same squirrel. He does this every day, just to torment poor Poppy."

After a moment, the squirrel, bored with the contest, took off again, and the dogs, defeated, ambled over to the water bowl, where they took turns drinking, until the empty water bowl clanged loudly against the brick walkway.

"Just out of curiosity, why do you refer to the squirrel as a he? Did you see something I didn't see?"

"Oh, for Pete's sake," Cara said crossly. "Isn't it obvious? I'm a man-hater.

That's why I think all marriages will inevitably fail, and why all annoying squirrels must be male."

Jack laughed despite himself. "What was wrong with yesterday's couple? Why are they doomed?"

"For one thing, the groom was unbelievably domineering. He had to have a say in every detail. He even picked out Emily's gown."

"That's unusual?"

She stared at him as though he'd grown a third eye in the middle of his forehead.

"Are you kidding? Yes, it's unusual. There's an old superstition that says it's bad luck for a groom to see the bride's dress before the wedding."

"Or?"

"Or his testicles will turn black and fall off. I don't know, Jack. I just know this guy was controlling and domineering, and it doesn't bode well for the marriage."

"I see. Anything else? So, he's the only one at fault?"

"No, of course not. After all, Emily allows him to boss her around about all this stuff. When she gets fed up, she sulks and then cries. Buckets and buckets of tears."

"Oooh." Jack grimaced. "I hate a crier."

"Me too!" she exclaimed. "But it's an occupational hazard with my job. Now that I think of it, I've only done flowers for one wedding that that didn't involve at least one tearfest or temper tantrum."

"And that was?"

"Last Friday night's wedding, as a matter of fact. Maya and Jared."

He nodded. "I don't know Jared that well. He only worked for us a year or so. But Maya's always been pretty chill. So, how did you guys rate their chances?"

"Mmm. Bert and Maya have been best friends, forever. He gives them a hundred percent. Says he's positive they'll make it."

Jack studied her face. "But you're not so sure."

"Shit happens. People change. What seems like a sure bet, suddenly turns into a sucker bet."

"Is that what happened to you?"

Cara didn't answer. She got up, turned on the hose, and refilled the water bowl. On the way back to the table, she paused to right a flowerpot one of the dogs had upended.

"Cara?" He said it gently.

25

Her glass was nearly empty. She stared down into it, wondering if she should make an excuse, get up, offer a refill, hope he'd forget the topic while she was away. Somehow, she doubted it. She hadn't known Jack Finnerty long, but she could tell he was very focused when he wanted to be.

"Why do you want to know about my marriage?" she asked finally.

He stared, apparently taken aback. "Is it still painful to talk about?"

"It's not my favorite topic, no. But I'm over him, as I told you before."

"Yes. You did say that." He waited.

Cara sighed. "He cheated on me, okay? He had a little girlfriend, and they'd have their twosomes every other week, at a motel out by the airport, when he was supposed to be at a sales meeting in Atlanta. I was too dumb to realize what was going on. When I found out, I ended it. I moved out, stayed a while with Bert, then rented this apartment, upstairs over the shop."

"And that was it? No counseling, no attempt at a reconciliation?"

"Now you sound like Leo," she said. "Why would I want a reconciliation? Or need counseling? He was quite clearly in love with somebody else. No need to prolong the inevitable."

Did she sound bitter? she wondered. Maybe that was because she was bitter.

Jack had gotten quiet again. He sat back on the bench and took a sip of the iced coffee. All the ice had melted. She should really ask if he'd like another. But did she even want him to stay? What was the point of all this?

"The woman he cheated with. Are they still together?"

She felt her face go pink. "He says not. But then, he's a liar. And a liar will tell you whatever they think you want to hear."

"I'm not on his side, you know. I never even met the guy."

"His name is Leo," she said. "Leo Giardinella. He's in sales with Great South Office Products. He plays golf with an eight handicap, and he's an Auburn fan, even though he never went to Auburn, and you'd probably like him a lot. Everybody likes Leo a lot. You never met anybody who didn't like Leo. He could totally sell ice to Eskimos. My dad? The Colonel? He still thinks it's somehow my fault our marriage broke up."

"What about your mom? What did she think of him?"

Cara shrugged. "She died while I was a freshman in college. But knowing her, she would have loved Leo too."

She was suddenly close to tears now, and he'd just told her he hated a crier. So maybe now he'd leave, and she was pretty sure she didn't care if he did.

"For the record, I went to Georgia Tech," Jack said evenly. "I tried golf, but I don't have the patience to chase a little white ball around all day. I run, and sometimes I play tennis. And Leo? Your ex? He sounds like an asshole."

"He was," she said, sniffing.

Jack got up and came around the table and sat down on the bench beside her. With his little finger, he wiped away the huge tear that was welling up in her right eye. And then he leaned in, and he very gently kissed her.

"You wanna get some lunch?" he asked.

The Firefly Café was on Habersham Street near Troup Square. They leashed up the dogs and walked over, sitting at a café table outside. Cara ordered a crab salad and Jack had the patty melt and fries, and they sat in the sunshine, eating and talking about not much of anything.

Shaz and Poppy lolled in the shade under their table, strategically positioned for stray bits of food.

As usual, Jack seemed to know half the people who walked past, or were seated nearby.

Cara sat, a look of amusement on her face as he chatted with two elderly ladies still in their church clothes, at a table nearby.

"What?" he said, when he turned back to her. "They play bridge with my aunt Betty. Irene O'Conner, the one with the pink hair? Her daughter is Meghan's godmother."

"Do you ever go anyplace where you don't know somebody?"

"I've lived here all my life, and my parents and grandparents did too. Is that a crime? Don't you know a lot of people in—where'd you say you grew up? Akron?"

"Columbus. And I know some people, but nothing like you. Anyway, I only finished high school there. Went away to college, met Leo, and eventually we moved down here to Savannah."

"Why Savannah?"

"Leo had a job offer. It was a promotion and a pay raise, and it seemed like a good idea. I didn't have much of a career going in Columbus, so there was no reason for me not to move. Even though I didn't know a soul down here. "

"And no reason to move back up there after your divorce?"

"The Colonel, my father, wanted me to move back. But by then I had the shop, and I was determined to make it work."

"And just as determined not to let the Colonel boss you around?"

She helped herself to a French fry from the paper basket that held his sandwich. "Look. I love my dad. I really do. He's tried to be supportive, in his own way. After Norma, the former owner, moved away and left me the business, the Colonel loaned me the money to make the improvements to the building and buy my equipment. I'm the creative type, not a finance genius, but he sent me books about drawing up a business plan, and bookkeeping, and all that."

"I sense a but."

Cara looked away. "Sometimes I think he wants me to fail. Things haven't been going so great. I've had a lot of capital expenditures—car problems, computer problems, equipment problems. Everything costs more than it should, and it's all stuff I didn't anticipate. And it took a long time for the business to start coming in."

"I don't know anything about flowers, but I've seen a lot of yours at all these weddings lately, and they looked pretty damn impressive to me. And I do know Torie, and Lillian Fanning. They wouldn't have hired you for Torie's wedding if they thought you were no good."

"I *am* good at what I do," Cara said. "But I'm an outsider in Savannah. These girls here, it's like a closed society. If you didn't go to Country Day or Savannah Christian or St. Vincent's you might as well be from Mars."

"But you did Torie's wedding. And that bizarro wedding for the Winships. And Maya's. And it sounds like this clambake the Trapnells and Strayhorns are planning is pretty extreme."

That stopped her cold. She was whining. And God knows she hated a whiner, almost as much as she hated a crier.

"You're right," she said, straightening her shoulders. "You're absolutely right. It's just that it's taken so long, and I'm still not really in the black. And stuff keeps happening to me. . . ."

She filled Jack in on the broken cooler and the spoiled flowers, and all the rest of her financial woes.

He listened calmly, nodding, not judging.

"My dad wants his money back," Cara said, taking a deep breath. "And I can't blame him. When I borrowed it, the deal was that I'd start making payments in February. But I haven't. I couldn't. Not while keeping the lights on in the shop."

"And you explained that to him?"

"I tried. But the Colonel is the Colonel. He hears what he wants. And what he wants to hear is that I give up. He wants me to admit defeat, move back home, and be a dutiful daughter."

Cara felt her fists clench and unclench. "But I can't. I just can't!"

"Then don't," he said lightly. "Look, I know starting a new business is hard. Especially in a new town, where, as you say, you don't really know anybody. Ryan and I have been here all our lives, and it's been an uphill battle for us."

"Really?" It was hard to imagine anything was difficult for this charming Irishman, who'd apparently never met a stranger.

"Hell yeah," Jack said. "For one thing, our timing sucked. I quit my job, put all my savings into buying tools, equipment, all of it, everything it takes to start a new business. Our plan was to do high-end historic-restoration projects. And it would have been a good plan, except the economy was still stalled. People who'd bought an old house in the historic district had paid top-of-the-market prices and now, planning to renovate, they find out they're already underwater on their mortgages. That hundred-thousand-dollar kitchen we were supposed to build for them? Forget about it. New master suite? Not in the master plan anymore. It wouldn't have been so bad, if it had just been me. But I'd talked Ryan into coming in with me. And we had guys. Masons, carpenters, electricians. We had to let everybody go. Everybody who was expecting a paycheck, counting on us, we had to let go."

She leaned closer across the table. "How'd you survive?"

"We lived lean. Took whatever crappy jobs we could get. Our family's friends felt sorry for us, so they'd hire us to hang some Sheetrock, build a garage, replace a deck. I sold my condo downtown and bought the place over on Macon Street. It was a foreclosure. Ryan, he's actually got a teaching degree. He did some substitute teaching, hired on as an after-school soccer coach at the Y. And we just kept at it."

"And you're okay now."

"Finally. People are feeling better about the economy. The people we did those little jobs for, they were happy with the work. They're calling us back for bigger projects. And they've told their friends."

"So, a happy ending. You've got a good business, friends, a house, a dog."

"But in the meantime, Zoey left me. She got tired of hanging around, waiting for me to come home from work, to make her my number-one priority."

"You've still got the dog," Cara said, looking away.

"And I've got high hopes for everything else," Jack said. "There's this girl I keep running into at weddings . . ." And then he did it. He actually winked at her.

"You make me actually feel like I'm not a hopeless cause," Cara said, sitting back in her chair, feeling herself actually relax.

"You're a work in progress, darlin'," Jack said. "Same as me."

26

It was nearly 10 a.m. when Bert finally walked through the front door at Bloom. He dropped the morning newspaper on the worktable and headed straight to the coffeepot, ignoring Cara's pointed stares.

When he sat down at the worktable, he sipped from his mug and began leafing through the morning's phone orders. His hair was mussed, his beard unshaven, and it looked as though he'd slept in his clothes—either that, or he'd been rolled by a mugger.

He caught her watching him. "What?"

"Late night last night?"

"Maybe," he said, running his hands through his hair, which only made it worse. He stared her down. "And no. I haven't been drinking. Because I know that's what you're thinking. But I haven't."

He had her there. She had wondered. He'd worked so hard for his sobriety. She knew too well how it was with an alcoholic, though. They were always just one drink away from a fall.

"Would have been nice if you'd called to let me know you'd be in late." She kept her voice deliberately mild. It was unlike Bert to be late, or to fail to let her know he'd be late.

"Sorry," he said, looking contrite. "It won't happen again."

He mopped his forehead with one of the pink message slips. "Jesus, it's hot in here. What's going on with the air-conditioning?"

"It's been out since Friday night. I had to sleep with all the windows open over the weekend. I've left half a dozen voicemails for the Bradleys, but they haven't bothered to return any of them. I'm thinking of running over to their house. In fact, I was waiting for you to get here so I could go."

"Oh," Bert said. "Oh, crap. I forget you don't get the paper. Um, there's actually a pretty good reason you haven't heard back from Bernice."

"Such as?"

Bert flipped the *Savannah Morning News* open to the obituary page, and trailed a bony finger down the listings until he came to a block of type.

"Oh damn," Cara said. "That's awful. I didn't even know she was sick."

> Bradley, Bernice, 91, of Savannah. Joined the band of heavenly angels Friday, after a brief illness. Predeceased by husband Alvin P. Bradley. Survived by faithful daughter Sylvia Bradley, 73, of Savannah. Funeral services, Tuesday, at Fox & Weeks Hodgson funeral chapel.

"Now I feel just terrible. I've been cussing Bernice all weekend. The last message I left on their machine, I even threatened to buy a window unit and subtract it from next month's rent."

"You shouldn't feel bad about that," Bert said. "That old biddy was so cheap she squeaked when she walked. And her daughter's just as bad. There's a reason Sylvia's a dried-up old maid. She's just as mean and stingy as her mama. The two of them have been living in that big house on Forty-fourth Street in Ardsley Park for decades, and even though everybody knows they're rolling in the dough, the place looks like it's falling to pieces."

"Still, it's not nice to talk bad of the dead," Cara insisted. She was still reading Bernice Bradley's obituary, the details of her membership in the United Daughters of the Confederacy, the Eastern Star, her thirty-year employment with J. C. Penney's.

"Bernice was my landlady, not a friend. I mean, I don't even think she liked me," Cara mused. "So I think it would be bad taste to show up at the service. We'll send a nice arrangement instead. One of those old-timey ones on stands. Do we have any of those metal easel thingies left in the back, from Norma's?"

Bert got up to check the stockroom, but then Cara read the last line of the funeral notice. Out loud.

"'In lieu of flowers, memorials may be made to charity.'"

"Hold it," she said, grabbing Bert's shirtsleeve as he passed. "That nasty old bat! In lieu of flowers, my ass!"

"She's dead, and she's still managing to give you the finger," Bert laughed.

By late afternoon, Cara had Bloom's front and back doors propped open and a large box fan positioned in the doorway, both as a ventilation aid and to keep Poppy from making another escape.

She printed out a photo she'd taken of Brooke's wedding dress, and had it taped to the wall just above her computer, while she leafed through online catalogues and sketched out ideas for the bride's bouquet and the other arrangements for the wedding and reception.

"That's Brooke's dress?"

"Yes. Thank God she finally went to Atlanta and bought one before her mother and stepmother took matters into their own hands."

"Pretty plain," Bert said, a note of disdain in his voice.

The gown, of heavy duchesse ivory satin, *was* simple. Sleeveless, with a deep V-neck, it was fitted close to the body, flaring out into soft folds just below the knees. Cara pointed a finger at the detail at the waist. "This is antique lace, reembroidered with seed pearls. No other lace, no sequins or flounces, or any of that. Brooke's a natural beauty, with a great figure. She doesn't need anything more than this. No veil either. I'm just going to make a hair ornament with flowers, and she'll use that to pin her hair back behind one ear."

The shop phone rang; she glanced over at the caller ID, and made a face before answering.

"Hi, Patricia."

"Hi Cara. I just thought I'd touch base and make sure that you've got things well in hand for the wedding. Is the caterer a definite, because if not, I've got Carlos on notice to hold the date for me."

"Yes," Cara said. "Fete Accompli is a done deal. Layne's signed the contract, and I'll send it over to you and Gordon for your signature. And when that's done, you'll need to put down a deposit."

"I understand," Patricia said. "When can we schedule a tasting, for the menu for the reception? Cullen says he always suggests the bride's family have a tasting at least a month before the wedding, so they can tweak anything they don't like."

Cara found herself grinding her back molars. Patricia Trapnell was determined to micromanage this wedding, whether Brooke wanted her to or not.

"Cara?" Patricia's voice was sharp. "Are you still there?"

"I'll talk to Layne about that, and get a couple possible dates, and we'll set that up based on Brooke's availability."

"Brooke's availability. That might be never," Patricia huffed.

"I'll ask her mother to let her know it's a priority," Cara said, unable to resist getting in a dig.

Which apparently went right over Patricia's head.

"Libba Strayhorn tells me that they're thinking of having the old barn redone to have the after-party out there," Patricia said. "Is that a good idea? I mean, a barn? Where horses have been?"

"I toured the barn with Libba," Cara said. "The horses haven't been kept there in years. And Libba's going to have it completely cleaned out and restored. We've done flowers for parties in barns and all kinds of unique settings in the past couple years. It's actually not all that unusual an idea. And this will give Brooke and Harris an opportunity to relax and mingle with their friends in a much more casual atmosphere."

"Couldn't they just as well do that in the house? Where there's air-conditioning and running water?"

Now it was Patricia's turn to get in a dig. Which Cara, in turn, decided to ignore.

"Was there anything else, Patricia?"

"Hmm. Just going down my list. I assume you've gotten a firm commitment from the photographer? Cullen says she stays booked for months and months in advance. I know we'll want to give her a list of shots we want taken, before and after the wedding. And Gordon is hoping to have Brooke sit for a portrait in her wedding gown."

"Yes. Meredith has assured me she has us on her books for July sixth. I'll let her know about your request for a portrait, but that's something you'll need to take up with Brooke, since I'm assuming it needs to be done well before the actual wedding day."

"I'll do that," Patricia said. "Or rather, I'll have Gordon do it. Brooke somehow doesn't seem to receive any of my phone calls, emails, or texts."

Big surprise, Cara thought.

"All right then," Cara said briskly. "I'll just get back to my flowers. Thanks for calling, Patricia."

After she'd disconnected from the call, Cara looked at the phone with distaste. This, she thought, was what she was in for, over the next five weeks. Weekly, if not daily, contact with Patricia Trapnell. When all was said and done, Cara was sure, she would have more than earned her wedding-planning fee for this event.

Cara went back to her catalogue and her sketches for the Trapnell wedding, and Bert worked efficiently through the phone orders, putting together hospital and birthday arrangements, answering the phone, and then going through their flower stock, to see what needed reordering.

The room grew warmer and warmer. They drank what seemed like gallons of water, and Cara silently checked online, pricing room-sized window air conditioners—one for the shop, and one for her apartment.

When the phone rang around three in the afternoon, Bert glanced over, crossed his eyes, and ignored it.

"Lillian Fanning," he told Cara. "If she's paid her bills, I don't see why we have to talk to her again."

"Maybe she wants us to do flowers for another event," Cara said crisply, reaching for the phone. "Which is why I don't want us screening calls. You never know . . ."

"I know that woman, and with her, it's never pleasant," he shot back.

"Lillian," Cara said, her voice radiating warmth she didn't actually feel. "So good to hear from you again. Are you all rested up from the wedding excitement yet?"

"Mostly. Bill and I just got back from two weeks in Bermuda. The weather was nice, but the service! I can't think why anybody would go there a second time. . . ."

"Have the wedding proofs come back yet?" Cara asked. She really wasn't in the mood to listen to one of Lillian's rants this afternoon. "Please be sure to let me know when I can see them. I'd love to use some of them on my website. That photo of you and Torie, together on the dock, just at sunset, has to be great."

"The proofs aren't back, which is just so annoying," Lillian started. "I can't even get into that right now. Listen, Cara, I'm calling about the silver."

"Silver?" Cara was hot and tired. And her mind was a blank.

"My silver. The things you used for the wedding. The candlesticks, the bud vases, the punch bowl, and the epergne. They were all supposed to be returned to me after the wedding."

Cara noted that Lillian referred to the silver as things "*you* used." They had, of course, used the Fanning family silver at the mother of the bride's insistence.

She closed her eyes and tried to think back, to the night of Torie's wedding, and the Sunday afterward. She remembered rounding up all the pieces and checking them off against the inventory she'd taken, as she always did, when they used a client's own pieces for an event. She'd done it the morning after the wedding.

And she even remembered loading them into a large plastic bin lined with towels, to keep the pieces from being scratched. She could see the bin in the back of the van. But what she could not remember was taking the bin back to the Fannings' home.

"Hang on a minute, Lillian, please," she said. "Let me just check something."

She put Lillian Fanning on hold and turned to Bert.

"I heard," he said. "Her silver."

"Did we return it?" Cara asked, her voice urgent. "I guess maybe I was a little buzzed that night. I remember packing it up and putting it in the van, but that's it. Please tell me we returned it all to her."

"I tried," Bert said, already defensive. "I've been over there three different times in the last month, while I was out on deliveries. But nobody was home, and I definitely wasn't gonna just leave it sitting on their doorstep."

"They were in Bermuda for two weeks.."

He was unmoved. "Tell Lillian to take a chill pill. The silver is all still out in the van."

"The van?" Cara cried. "Half a dozen cars on this block have been broken into over the past six months. Why wouldn't you bring it in here, where it would be safe?"

"Here, where?" He gestured around the tiny, cluttered workshop.

Without another word, she got up, hurrying toward the back of the shop, to where the van was parked. "Please let it be therepleasepleaseplease." She felt acid rising in her throat. She unlocked the wrought-iron courtyard gate and stepped into the lane. The van was in its parking slot, which was boldly marked PRIVATE PARKING FOR BLOOM FLORAL.

Her fingers were trembling so badly she had to hold the key with both hands to unlock the back tailgate. Finally, she flung the doors open, and with her heart in her mouth, shoved aside a packing blanket to uncover the plastic bin, filled with the Fanning family silver.

Cara sank down on the tailgate to catch her breath, then jumped up quickly, the heat from the bumper searing the exposed flesh on her thighs. She grabbed the heavy bin, relocked the van, and went back inside.

She picked up the phone. "Lillian?"

"What on earth!" The older woman's tone seared almost as much as that overheated bumper. "I was just about to hang up and call back."

"I am so, so sorry," Cara exclaimed. "The silver is all right here at the shop."

No need to tell Lillian that her priceless family heirlooms had been riding around in her van since the wedding.

"We did try to return it to you, after the wedding, but nobody was home, so we just decided to leave it here, for safekeeping, until we heard from you."

"You're hearing from me now," Lillian said pointedly.

"And I'll bring the silver back to you immediately. I'll deliver it myself. Is now a good time?"

"Now's fine," Lillian said.

27

I'll go." Bert jumped up from his seat at the worktable. He pointed at the finished flower arrangements in the cooler. "It's my fault Lillian's pissed at you."

"I'll do the drops at Candler and Memorial. There's a funeral arrangement to go to Gamble Funeral Home too. Then we've got a delivery on the south side. I'll head out to Isle of Hope after that, and personally deliver Lillian's treasure right to her door."

"No, that's okay. Just take care of the other deliveries. I'll use my own car and take the silver back. Ultimately, it's my responsibility."

"Please?" He gave her his winningest smile. "I want to. You were right. I should have at least brought that bin into the shop and let you decide what to do with it. It was pure laziness on my part."

"Well . . . if you really want to . . ."

The phone rang and they both reached for it. And stopped, when they saw Lillian Fanning's name on the caller ID screen again.

"Now what?" Cara murmured.

"Hi Lillian. We were just heading your way."

"Change of plans," Lillian said, skipping a greeting. "I'm meeting a friend for drinks at the club. But I'll leave a key to the back door. It'll be under the lid of the gas grill on the patio. Just put the silver in the kitchen and leave the key where you found it afterward."

"We can do that," Cara said, grateful that neither of them would have to experience their client's wrath face-to-face.

She quickly put together a small nosegay of pink roses to fit inside one of Lillian's silver bud vases. Then she helped load the flower arrangements into the built-in racks in the van while Bert put the bin of silver in the front seat.

"There's a key under the gas grill lid on the patio around the back of the Fannings' house," she told her assistant. "Put the little nosegay in the middle of the kitchen table, will you? Leave the rest of the silver in the bin, on the kitchen counter. And for God's sake, be sure you've locked up tight when you leave."

He nodded and hopped into the driver's seat. Then he stuck his head out the open window. "Okay if I keep the van and use it tonight, Mom?" He cocked his head to the side. "I promise to put gas in it. Pretty please?"

Cara laughed despite herself. She could never stay mad at Bert for long, and he damned well knew it. And it wasn't an unusual request. His own car was an unreliable seventeen-year-old Honda, which was why he mostly relied on his bike for transportation around town.

"Okay, but make sure all your homework's done first! And no riding around town picking up strange girls."

"No problemo," Bert said. He backed up the van and drove slowly down the lane.

28

Shaz was sprawled on the floor in front the air-conditioning vent in the living room. When Jack came out of the bedroom Sunday morning, dressed in running clothes and holding her leash, she regarded him with total disinterest.

"Up, Shaz," he said. She yawned and stayed put.

"Come on Shaz. Be a good girl. Let's go for a run before it gets too hot."

He clipped the leash to her collar and tugged gently. "It'll be fun," he lied.

It was nearly nine o'clock and the temperatures were already in the high eighties. But he'd worked long hours all week, returning home just at dark most nights, too worn out to do much more than take the puppy for a quick stroll around the block. A run, he decided, would be good for both of them.

Most days, he took Shaz with him over to South Carolina and Cabin Creek, where he and Ryan had started work on the old barn. After only a week, they'd already worked out a routine. He and Ryan would leave Savannah while it was still dark, and by dawn the two men would be up on the roof, ripping off the old tin, exposing multiple layers of brittle tar, and then finally the wooden subroof.

Shaz was happy to start the mornings romping around the pasture, sniffing the horses, but otherwise keeping a cautious distance. The rest of those hot days, she found a place in the cool dim of one of the old horse stalls, leaving only occasionally to drink from her bowl of water, or to investigate strange new smells and sights outside.

During the worst heat of the day, Jack and Ryan loaded up the truck with the Strayhorn family's decades of junk and hauled it off to the nearby dump. It was hot, exhausting work, but they had a deadline, so they kept up the pace, only taking a day off on Sunday—and then only at Torie's insistence.

Jack tugged again at Shaz's leash now, and she reluctantly stood up and allowed herself to be led outside.

They took their usual route, loping easily north down Habersham. The street was Sunday-morning quiet. They passed Broughton, Savannah's version of Main Street, and ran through Warren Square, where a homeless man napped on a bench, and on to Bay Street.

An early-morning breakfast crowd milled outside around the door at B. Matthew's, and Shaz stopped abruptly, sniffing the aroma of bacon when the restaurant door was opened.

"Later," Jack said, tugging again. They continued west on Bay Street, where tourists stood in groups on street corners, consulting their maps, or aiming cameras at the photo-ready moss-draped oaks on the far side of the street.

After only a mile, Shaz was panting, and Jack's shirt was drenched with sweat. He slowed to a walk, crossed Bay at Bull, and escorted Shaz to the shade under an oak, where he bought a bottle of water from a street vendor, uncapped it, and let Shaz refresh herself, laughing as she eagerly lapped the glugging water. He poured the last few drops of the water into his palms and splashed it onto his face, and they set off again.

Man and dog ran up Whitaker Street, past the chic boutiques and home-furnishing stores, until they got to Forsyth Park. It was shadier here, and the sidewalks were already crowded with other runners, walkers, and skateboarders. After two laps around the park, he stopped and bought another bottle of water to share with Shaz.

He set off north again on Whitaker, telling himself it would be natural for their route home to pass by the red-brick building on West Jones Street. And if Cara and her dog happened to be out for a Sunday walk, well, that would be just fine.

As it happened, Cara and Poppy weren't out for a walk. But they were sitting on the stoop in front of Bloom. Or rather, Cara was sitting on the stoop. Poppy was sitting at the base of a crepe myrtle tree located in a planting bed of ivy in the middle of the sidewalk. The goldendoodle was staring intently up at the tree branches, where a large gray squirrel chattered indignantly.

Cara had her hair tied up in a sloppy topknot, and she was wearing the least amount of clothing she could get away with in public, a short periwinkle-blue cotton sundress, and matching cheap blue flip-flops.

The shop door was propped open with a box window fan, which she'd turned on in an effort to cool herself. Pages of the Sunday *New York Times* fluttered in the listless warm breeze from the fan, held down with a tall plastic tumbler of iced tea.

She spotted the familiar figure of Jack Finnerty and his dog as soon as they turned onto her block, and she felt a little shiver of excitement, followed quickly by the dismaying fact of her appearance.

Unable to sleep in the suffocating heat of the apartment, she'd been up since six. She'd fed Poppy, forced herself to eat a container of Greek yogurt and some strawberries for breakfast, and walked over to the coffee shop and newsstand on Liberty Street, where she picked up the iced tea and the Sunday paper.

She'd tried reading out in the back garden, but swarms of gnats and mosquitoes forced her inside. The courtyard was cooler, but at least out here on the stoop she could use the window fan to keep the biting bugs at bay.

Despite the fan, her face was sheened with perspiration, and her arms were slicked with a combination of sweat and insect repellent. Her hair was a hot, damp mess, and of course, she wore no makeup.

"Hey!" Jack called. Poppy turned to see where the voice was coming from, and bounded over to greet her old friend and his dog.

"Poppy!" Cara called anxiously. But the dog was content to give Jack's outstretched hand a lick of acknowledgment, falling quickly in step with the pair as they approached the stoop.

It was too late to run inside and try to clean up. Instead, she smiled up at him. "Good run?"

"Hot. Shaz wasn't really too much into it, so we just kind of took it easy this morning."

Cara leaned down and patted Shaz's head. "Let me get you guys something cold to drink," she offered.

"That'd be great," Jack said. She moved aside the box fan to allow her guests to enter the shop.

"Sorry about the heat," she said, turning from the refrigerator in the shop's kitchenette. She held out a bottle of cold water, and went to the sink to run water into a bowl for Shaz.

"Trying to save money on the electric bill?" Jack asked. He'd been in the shop for less than five minutes, and sweat was already dripping from his face. He held the bottle of water to the back of his neck, wiped his brow with a paper towel Cara handed him.

She made a face. "The air conditioner's not working. Again."

"Geez," he said. "How long has it been like this?"

Cara set the bowl on the floor, and Shaz and Poppy both crowded around it, lapping water as fast as they could.

"More than a week," she said. "It's been hell."

"What does your landlord say?" he asked. "Didn't they send somebody over to fix it?"

"My landlady passed away week before last. I'd been calling even before that, and I've been trying to reach her daughter,, but so far, no call back. This is typical of them. Worst. Landlords. Ever."

"That's bullshit," Jack said angrily. "You can't live like this, with no air."

"Tell me about it. I've got two or three box fans, like the one I've got in the doorway, but all they really do is move the hot air around. Pretty miserable."

"Where's your thermostat?" Jack asked. "I'm no HVAC guy, but I can at least take a look."

She pointed down the hall, toward the staircase. "On the wall, there."

Cara followed Jack down the hall. He stood in front of the small metal box mounted on the plaster wall. He punched the Cool button, but did not hear the unit switch on.

"Okay," he shrugged. "Fuse box? It's an old house, I'm guessing maybe the electrical hasn't been updated in a while?"

"Probably not in at least thirty years," Cara agreed. "Sometimes if I'm using my hair dryer or iron, it shorts out a circuit. The fuse box is back there, near the back door to the courtyard."

He flipped open the fuse box and studied the row of breakers and fuses. "Doesn't look like any of the breakers have been flipped. Do you change the filters pretty often?" he asked.

She nodded. "Every month."

"Is the unit outside?" Jack asked, his hand on the doorknob.

"In the courtyard."

"Got a screwdriver?"

The unit, a rust-speckled gray cube, sat on a wooden platform in a corner of the courtyard garden. Jack unscrewed the back panel of the unit and peered at the exposed machinery.

"What are you looking for?" Cara asked, looking over his shoulder.

"Just anything that looks obviously wrong. I was hoping maybe it was something simple, like a slipped or broken blower belt. Or maybe that the condenser was iced over, but that doesn't seem to be the case."

He fetched the garden hose from a large terra-cotta pot where it was coiled nearby. Turning on the spigot, he sprayed it over the box, in a deliberate back and forth pattern.

"What's that for?" Cara asked, swatting at a mosquito on her neck.

"Rinsing off the coils," he explained. "They can get blocked with all the pollen and dust and leaves and crud, and then you don't get cooling."

She nodded, acting as though she understood.

"I turned the controls off before we came out. Would you go inside and flip it on and see if we get lucky and it starts up?"

Cara crossed her fingers, flipped the thermostat on, and prayed for the dull thump that signaled the unit coming to life. Nothing. She ran her hand in front of the air register. More nothing.

"Sorry," Jack said, meeting her at the back door. "I looked at the manufacturer's plate on the back of it—it was installed in '82. The average life span of a central-air unit is supposed to be ten or fifteen years. I think that thing is DOA."

"Crap." She leaned her forehead against the wall beside the thermostat. "I don't think I can go on like this."

"You shouldn't have to. Tomorrow, first thing, send the landlord a registered letter, telling her you plan to have the unit repaired or replaced, and that you'll deduct whatever costs you incur from your rent."

"And what do I do in the meantime?" she asked. "I looked at the weather report this morning. This heat wave isn't going to let up. We don't even have any rain in the forecast. And anyway, I don't have the money to buy a central-air-conditioning unit like that. It's probably at least three or four thousand dollars."

"Can you open some windows? At least get some air circulating? These old houses were built to catch cross currents."

"I've tried, believe me. They're all painted shut. I hacked at the window in my bedroom with a screwdriver and even a steak knife, but I couldn't get it to budge. Every window in this house is like that."

He glanced toward the stairs. "Want me to give it a try?"

"Be my guest."

The staircase opened into a hallway that was the twin to the one on the first floor. The second floor, as she'd warned, was stifling. What had probably originally been a bedroom was now a combination living/dining room, visible through an arched entryway that Jack estimated had been installed sometime around the turn of the 1900s.

A large bay window looked out on the courtyard garden, and there were double banks of windows on the side walls, overlooking the sliver of side garden that separated this building from the ones next door.

A faded Oriental rug in muted blues, greens, and roses covered the wood floors, and a pair of overstuffed white slipcovered sofas faced each other, separated by an old painted trunk that was used as a coffee table. Bookcases flanked the windows. In the dining area, a round oak table was surrounded by a set of four mismatched high-backed chairs painted a soft fern green. A matte-green vase in the center of the table held a bouquet of wilted daisies. A small side table held another box fan, humming ineffectively in the corner.

He'd seen some of the finest, most elegant parlors in the historic district, spaces filled with valuable antiques, priceless art, silver, first-edition books, and designer trappings. But none of them looked as welcoming as Cara Kryzik's living room.

This room looked to Jack like a room where you could sit and sip a glass of wine, read a book, or just be. There were paintings scattered about, on the walls and propped on the bookshelves, watercolors and oils, all of them either landscapes or still lifes with flowers. He was no art expert, but he thought these were probably the works of gifted amateurs—flea-market finds, most likely. There was also a laughably small flat-screen television nearly hidden on the bookshelves among the books.

He thought of the living room in his own cottage on Macon Street, cluttered with bins of his clothing, books, and detritus. At least when Zoey lived with him, the place was clean. There was a ratty leather sofa, now covered in dog hair, a lumpy brown leather recliner where he fell asleep more nights than he'd like to admit, this facing his prized sixty-four-inch high-definition surround-sound television propped on a pair of sawhorses. No pictures hung on his walls, no rugs softened his floors. It occurred to him that although he owned his own house, he had never taken the time to make it a home.

"Where's the kitchen?" he asked, turning toward her. Cara stepped into the hallway and pushed aside a flowered green and white curtain that concealed what he'd assumed was probably a closet or bathroom.

At one time, it had probably been another small bedroom. But now the space was fitted with a set of 1950s-era flesh-pink metal kitchen cabinets, a small two-burner stove, with a cherry-red teakettle on the back burner, a stained porcelain sink barely big enough to hold a medium-sized saucepan, and the skinniest refrigerator he'd ever seen. There was a single window over the sink, and it held a jelly jar with a cluster of faded pink flowers. A flowered mug in the sink held a teaspoon.

"You cook in here?" he asked.

"All the time," Cara said with a laugh. "It's tiny, but it does the job."

They continued down the hallway, and Cara pointed through the open door. "My boudoir."

Cara's bedroom was a large, high-ceilinged room, with wide coved crown molding at the ceiling, and high baseboard molding, all painted a yellowing white. The wallpaper was old and age-speckled, but the pattern of ivy and white roses against a pale aqua background made the room look like the inside of a garden.

The ceiling was painted a soft aqua, and there was a large Victorian brass gaslight that had been electrified, hanging from the middle of an ornate plaster medallion. The scarred heart-pine floors were bare, with the exception of some scattered braided rugs in muted colors. An elaborately carved and gingerbread-decked mantel on one wall held a small coal-burning fireplace.

Her bed, a white-painted four-poster, was unmade, its crocheted bedspread tossed aside, the pillows and sheets rumpled.

"You caught me," Cara said lightly. "I usually make my bed, but last night was so miserable, and it's so hot, I couldn't stand being up here one more second."

"I'm shocked," Jack said, with a laugh.

"Nice room," he said, looking around. "All original woodwork and plaster and wallpaper. Even the fireplace. I guess that's the upside of having a cheapskate landlord. They left everything alone. You'd be surprised how many downtown houses from this era I see that have been carved up or stripped of everything original."

"Oh, it's all original," Cara said ruefully. "Right down to the ancient plumbing, the leaky roof, and the crappy wiring."

He went over to the double set of windows facing the street, took the screwdriver she'd given him earlier, and ran it across the windowsill. Paint shavings fell onto the floor, but the window stayed shut.

He went around the room, examining the other windows, but they were all in the same condition, as Cara warned, painted shut with years and years' worth of layers.

"Okay," he said, turning to her. "I'm gonna run home, get my truck and some tools, and I'll be back in about half an hour."

"Really?" Her face lit up. "It's your day off, and I know you do this for a living and I hate to ask . . . but if there's any way you can cool this place down—even a little—you would totally be my hero for life."

"No big thing," he said lightly, heading for the stairs.

"Just leave Shaz here with me and Poppy," Cara called. "They can stay out in the garden where it's a little cooler."

29

Half an hour later, Jack eased his pickup truck into the lane behind Cara's town house. Back at home he'd taken a quick shower, and grinned at himself in the bathroom mirror as he shaved for the first time that weekend. Wouldn't hurt to not look like like a Yeti, he decided. He changed into jeans, a T-shirt, and work boots, then went outside to load what he needed.

He went around to the bed of the truck, grabbed his tool belt, and fastened it around his waist.

Cara met him at the gate from the courtyard, unlocking it so he could enter. She eyed the tool belt, then looked over his shoulder at the truck. "Ladders?"

"Yup. I'm thinking I'll probably need to unseal the windows from the outside as well as the inside. No telling what all they did to paint those windows shut."

"I had no idea this was going to be such a production," Cara fretted.

Like those of many homes and shops in the historic district, Bloom's front windows were covered with decorative and functional wrought-iron burglar bars. Jack attacked these with his cordless screwdriver. Cara helped him lift off the bars, and set them aside, along with the flower boxes she'd planted with ferns and Nikko Blue hydrangeas.

He pulled a lethal-looking tool from his belt. It had a spade-shaped head with wicked serrated edges, and he ran it along the edge where the windowsill met the bottom of the lower window sash.

"What the heck is that thing?" Cara asked.

He held it up for her to examine. "It's called a window zipper. We have to use them on almost every historic restoration we do downtown."

"Gotta get me one of those," she nodded.

He performed the same operation on the top of the window sash, then ran the tool along the sides of the sash.

"Now we move inside," Jack told her.

He used the zipper on the interior of the front window, and then, with an X-Acto knife, removed globs of old paint from the sash lock before he could finally flip it open. Then he examined the window jambs. "If we're lucky, these babies will still have the sash cords and sash weights."

He took a small pry bar and worked it cautiously under the edge of the jamb, popping off the molding and exposing the channel, where he pointed at the cotton sash cord. "Good news."

He pushed hard on the bottom sash, but it didn't budge.

"Uh-oh," Cara said glumly.

"I'm not done yet." Now he took a slender putty knife, inserted it between the windowsill and the bottom sash, and lightly tapped it with a hammer, working the knife from side to side along the sash. He did the same thing on the top of the sash.

This time, when he pushed, the window slowly slid open.

Cara threw her arms around Jack. "My hero!"

He grinned. "And it only took what? About forty-five minutes?" He poked his head out the open window. "I'll put the burglar bars back up—but you're definitely gonna need some window screens, or you'll get eaten alive in here. Do you happen to know if there are any still around?"

"I think I remember seeing some screens in the toolshed," Cara said, with a shudder.

"What?"

"The last time I opened the shed, I saw a rat. I haven't been out there since."

"Does that mean you want *me* to rummage around in the shed?"

"Yes, please," she said meekly.

Twenty minutes later, he was back, with an armload of wood-framed window screens. His shirt and pants were streaked with dirt, and a bit of cobweb hung from his hair. She silently picked it off.

"See any rats?"

"Mmm. Not the rats. But evidence that they've been there. You might want to put some poison out there. I also found more sets of burglar bars, probably for the second-story windows. I'm thinking I'll need to put those up if we can get those windows open."

"Absolutely."

After he'd worked his way around to the back of the house, unsealing the windows, Jack got out the extension ladder and clambered up to work on the second-story windows.

Declaring herself his assistant, Cara did what she could to help, rinsing off the window screens with the hose, wielding the window zipper on the inside windows, breaking the painted seals with the putty knife and hammer the way he'd shown her, fetching tools from his truck, and even ferrying the newly cleaned window screens up the ladder.

Overhead, the sun blazed down. It was hot, sweaty work. But by six that evening, Cara had enough open windows—with screens and burglar bars in place—to admit what little hot breeze existed.

After loading the ladder and the last of his tools into the truck, Jack came into the town house.

"Up here," Cara called down. He found her in the kitchen alcove. She handed him a cold long-neck bottle of beer before uncapping her own.

"Just what the doctor ordered," he said. "Thanks." They clinked bottles and he drank thirstily.

"Are you kidding? You just spent your whole day—your day off—doing what you get paid thousands of dollars to do."

"Wait'll you get my bill."

Her face fell.

"Kidding. Really. I was happy to be able to help out. I just wish I could have resuscitated your air conditioner. Getting the windows open is only a temporary fix, you know. You're gonna have to make your landlady install a new air unit."

"I'm calling Sylvia first thing in the morning, and I'm going to keep on calling, and I'll send her a registered letter, like you suggested. But in the meantime, I am so, so grateful to you, Jack. Let me at least take you out to dinner, as partial payment. Okay?"

He gestured down at his grimy clothes. "Like this?"

"Okay. I'll cook here. What do you like?"

She opened the refrigerator, and stood in front of the door, letting the cold air wash over her. "Ahh."

Jack leaned against the doorjamb, appreciating the view.

"I like you," he said.

And he did. Her topknot had mostly come undone, and loose strands of her butterscotch hair fell over one eye and around her exposed collarbone. Her face was pink and sunburned, and her chest, arms, and legs were dirt-smudged. She was barefoot, and he noticed that her toenails were painted sort of a coral color. Her cotton sundress was thin and faded, and in the dim light of the kitchen he could see her body clearly silhouetted through the light from the refrigerator.

She had worked as hard as he had today, without complaint, eager to learn the skills he took for granted. Now she was as grimy as he, but she was totally unself-conscious and unapologetic about her appearance.

"Me?"

He put his hands around her waist and drew her to him. "You," he said, and kissed her deeply.

She kissed him back, without hesitation. They stood there like that, with the cool refrigerated air washing over them. His lips traveled to her earlobes, and then to the nape of her neck and her collarbone. Her skin tasted warm and sweat-salty, but she still smelled faintly sweet, like floral shampoo.

"I could make us a salad," she whispered, as she worked her hands up the back of his shirt.

"Mmm. Salad's good."

Her dress had skinny little straps that tied in a bow. He took the end of one of the stringlike things between his teeth and pulled, and it easily came undone. He kissed the bare spot, nibbling it just a little.

She inhaled sharply, but there was no protest, so he kissed his way, slowly, across her collarbone, pausing at the hollow just below her chin, where he felt her pulse quicken. Her head was thrown back, eyes closed, but her hands were busy on his back, massaging his shoulder blades, running down his back, then around, to his chest, her thumbs brushing his nipples. He detoured for a moment, burying his hands in her thick hair, and then he was kissing her again, their tongues darting in and out of each other's parted lips. Her hands roamed down to his hips, and then back to his chest again.

She was saying something, but he'd lost his concentration. "Hmm?"

"I said, what kind of dressing?"

But before he could answer, not that he had an answer, she'd gathered the hem of his T-shirt in her fists, and abruptly jerked it upward. Helpfully, he crossed his arms over his head, and allowed her to pull it all the way off.

She took a half step backward, and assessed him lazily, through lowered eyelashes. Jack felt the blast of cold air on his bare chest. Caught her chin in his hand. "Did you say dressing, or undressing?"

Cara had drunk exactly one-half of a beer. So why did she feel so dizzy, intoxicated, and totally unlike herself?

It was all Jack Finnerty's fault. She was not the kind of woman who noticed men's bodies, ogled the way their jeans fit, obsessed about their muscled physiques, or fantasized about their romantic prowess.

So why had that been not far from her mind? All. Damn. Day. Why had she paused at the foot of that ladder, gazing up at his butt with an unexpected heat that seemed centered somewhere south of decent? Why had she obsessed about that thin-cotton T-shirt, sweat-soaked, clinging to his chest and his belly, wishing he'd just rip it off? And when the weight of his tool belt dragged his jeans down, and she'd glimpsed his navel and a downward-pointing arrow of dark hair, why had she been forced to go inside and slap cold water on her neck and face? Why?

Maybe it was inevitable that they would end up like this. After all, the second time she locked eyes with Jack, he'd dropped his trousers in front of her with absolutely no hesitation.

Jack kissed her again, and worked his knee between her legs.

"I could grill us a steak," she whispered.

Dinner was the last thing on Jack's mind. "Hmm?" His lips were working their way toward her left shoulder. He took the other thin strip of fabric between his teeth, pulled, and performed the same cheap trick as before. The strap fell away, and he nuzzled her bare, salty shoulder. Like a pretzel. Only way better. With his thumbs, he leisurely worked the dress downward, until he found her breasts, and her nipples, lowering his head to kiss them each, in turn.

Another brief gasp.

For a moment, he debated about the proper way to do this. The top of her dress had some kind of elastic. Should he pull it over her head, as she'd done with his shirt, or downward? Such a delicious dilemma.

"Steak." She'd plunged her own hands into the waist of his jeans, her fingertips easing lower, digging into the flesh of his backside, at the same time, pressing her torso against his. He was already hard.

He nudged her backward, until she was pressed against the refrigerator shelves.

"I like steak."

Down was the way to go, Jack decided. While his lips concentrated on her breasts, he skimmed his hands over her hips, pausing there. He found the hem of the dress, and in one easy movement, tugged it downward, past her hips and then her knees. From there, the dress fell to the floor, puddling around her bare ankles. Cara stood on her tiptoes, and with her right foot, delicately swept the discarded dress to one side.

The one remaining, infinitesimal rational part of her brain not subsumed with crazed lust told Cara that this current situation was insane, indecent, and yet, weirdly intoxicating. She was naked, except for her panties, which weren't all that substantial, with her tushie pushed up against the cold metal shelves of her refrigerator. It was broad daylight outside. Her front door wasn't even locked. What was she thinking?

Right now, the contents of her fridge, not all that exciting—the past-expiration-date quart of milk, half-head of Romaine lettuce, containers of no-fat Greek yogurt and assorted Tupperware containers of leftover roast chicken, steamed broccoli and molding strawberries, not to mention the pickles, mustard and Paul Newman balsamic vinaigrette—were getting the show of their lives. What was she thinking?

She didn't care. And she definitely didn't want to think.

Cara smoothed her hands over Jack's flat belly, hooked her fingertips into the waistline of his jeans, pushed them down to his narrow hips, appreciating the hollow of his hipbones. She let the palm of her right hand drift leisurely down to his crotch, pausing there. Now it was his turn to gasp. She glanced down, and just the tiniest smile played across her lips as she saw his erection straining against the denim fabric. She grasped his waistband and nimbly unbuttoned his jeans.

She stopped then, and ran her hands back up his chest, feeling the rough texture of hair, of muscle and bone. And something else. She opened her eyes, frowned. Tiny black flecks of some hardened substance dotted his chest. With her fingernail, she scraped off a fleck and held it up for him to see.

"Roofing tar."

"Oh."

"From the barn at Cabin Creek. So it's all your fault."

"We'll have to work on that," Cara said. She lowered her head, and with her tongue and teeth, gently teased his nipples as her hands slowly inched downward, down toward the waistband of his jeans. With her thumbnail, she raked the metal tines of his fly. Down. Up. Down again. She cupped him with the same hand. He moaned into her hair. "You're killin' me here."

She was naked, except for that languorous smile and a tiny pair of panties.

Pink, with flowers. Naturally. He rolled them easily past her hips, her thighs and knees. And then gravity did the rest. She stepped daintily out of them and kicked them in the direction of the dress.

He kissed her and pulled away, finally able to feast on the sight of her—naked, just the way he'd imagined her since the first time he'd spotted her in that pink dress at his brother's wedding. Only much, much better.

Her hair tumbled down around her shoulders, and her chest was lightly freckled, her full breasts flushed pink. She had a narrow waist that belled out to full hips and a delicious, rounded butt.

Cara didn't have the taut, angular physique of Zoey, who spent most of her waking hours at the gym, and the rest of them obsessively weighing herself and measuring every morsel, every calorie of food she ingested.

This was a woman's body, the body of somebody with an appetite for the good things in life. This was a body he could spend a long time exploring.

Only now, her lips were slightly blue, and her skin was pebbled with goose bumps. And those shivers he'd felt, when he'd pressed himself urgently against her?

"Are you cold?"

"G-G-G-God y-e-s-s-s."

30

What about the dogs?" Cara asked, as he pulled her down the hallway, toward the bedroom. She was glad he had his back to her, convinced her frostbitten butt was probably permanently imprinted with the Frigidaire logo.

"They're on their own." Jack plopped down on the edge of her bed, unknotting the laces of his work boots, kicking one free, then the other. He pulled her down beside him.

Suddenly shy about her state of undress, she clutched for the quilt draped over the foot of the bed, pulling it across her exposed breasts. "Maybe we should check on them. They're awfully quiet out there. I hope Poppy isn't showing Shaz how to dig up my peonies."

He yanked the quilt off. "I'll buy you a carload of peonies. Later."

Cara crossed her arms across her exposed breasts. Was she actually going to go through with this? She hadn't been with a man since leaving Leo, had only slept with two other men before marrying Leo. And what about birth control?

Too late. Jack scooted backward onto the pile of pillows at the head of her bed, tugging at her hand. "C'mere."

She was stretched out beside him. He turned toward her, gave her a lazy smile. He ran his hands down her side, all the way down, and then back up. One hand slid between her thighs and paused there. Cara gripped his shoulders.

"Um, Jack?"

His tongue was making slow, excruciating circles around her nipple. Her body curled into his as he stroked and nipped and kissed, and she knew she could lose her mind—and self-control—any minute now.

"Hmm?"

He rolled away from her, just a few inches. "Don't worry. I've got something in my pocket."

Cara looked down. "So I see."

"Dirty girl." He flopped onto his back, waiting.

She hesitated only a moment. Propping herself up on one elbow, she pressed the flat of her hand lightly against the bulge of his jeans. "Here?"

He was touching her again, his gaze locked with hers.

Cara worked the metal zipper down half an inch at a time, stroking as she did so. "Here?" she whispered.

"You're getting warm."

Cara laughed. "You don't even know. . . ."

She had the zipper all the way down now, and could see the waistband of his gray knit briefs, the erection straining against it. She let her fingertips trail across him.

"Warmer."

Cara rolled onto her knees and grasped his jeans and the waistband of the briefs with both hands, sliding them lower. He stuck one leg between hers, so that she was directly over him. He ran his hands down her flank, and then around, and upward, suckling one breast, and then the other.

She nearly lost her concentration. The jeans were down around his hips now, and he thoughtfully thrust his hips upward, off the bed, so that she could tug them down, past his thighs. As her hands explored all the possible hiding spots for what she was seeking, as well as potential pleasure points, she felt the small square packet in his right front pocket.

She took her right foot, swung it over his leg and down, sliding the jeans all the way to his ankles.

Cara sat up with the jeans in hands, reached in, and extracted the foil-wrapped condom. "Got it," she exclaimed.

"You win," Jack said, reaching for her.

If she'd been cold standing in front of the Frigidaire, she was on fire now. At some point, Jack dragged a second box fan into the bedroom, placed it on a chair, and angled it toward the bed. The fan blades whirred ineffectively, but at least, she thought, remembering her open windows, they would have prevented anybody on the sidewalk below from hearing what was going on up here.

Their lovemaking started out slowly. She wanted him badly, but was too shy to tell him how badly. But Jack Finnerty seemed to know what she wanted, and what she needed. Eventually, whatever inhibitions she'd initially felt disappeared. She lost herself in the joy of pleasing him and letting him please her.

"You're beautiful, you know that?" He was lying on his side, facing her, their bodies slicked with sex and sweat.

"I'm a hot mess and we both know it," Cara retorted. "I can't believe I let you take me to bed as filthy as I was. And I really can't believe I let you into my bed as filthy as you were!"

"Who took who to bed? You were the one who asked me what I liked?"

"I was referring to dinner options," she said, trying in vain to sound prim.

"So now I know. You like your men dirty. And you like your sex dirty." Jack chuckled as he leaned forward and gave her a lingering kiss.

"No. Really. This was lovely. But now, I have *got* to have a shower." Cara sat up and swung her legs over the edge of the bed, reaching for the quilt to wrap around herself.

He sat up too, in time to grab the edge of the quilt and pull it away from her.

Cara crossed her arms over her bare chest, then shrugged. They'd spent the last hour and a half naked. He'd explored every inch of her body, and she his. It was too late to play shy.

"Wait up," he said, standing. "I could use a shower myself. No use in wasting water." He gave her a hopeful grin.

She opened her bathroom door and gestured inside. The room was tiled in pale pink, with a burgundy tile border. There was a pink toilet, a pink sink, and the smallest pink bathtub he'd ever seen—and he'd seen a lot of bathtubs in his job.

"Is that a Barbie dream tub?" he asked, pushing aside the flowered shower curtain to look down at it. It was barely big enough for one adult, let alone two.

Cara stepped around him, turned on the faucets, and stepped in. "Don't worry, I'll save you some hot water."

She emerged from the shower wrapped in a thick white terry bath sheet, with her damp hair wrapped in another towel. He was standing, bemused, and stitch-stark naked, leaning against the doorway outside the bathroom.

Jack Finnerty had to be the least inhibited man she'd ever met, Cara decided. She handed him a clean towel and a washcloth. "Your turn. Listen, while you're in the shower, I'm going to run to the store for a couple things."

"More condoms?" He waggled his eyebrows in a comic leer. "Whipped cream?"

"Steak," she said. "And a couple baking potatoes. Where are your clothes?"

He hooked a finger inside the edge of her towel and pulled her toward him. Good God, he was already aroused again.

"Why, you wanna hide 'em so you can keep me here as your love slave?"

"Dream on." She kissed his nose. "I'll throw 'em in the wash. Rapid cycle. You don't want to put on those grubby jeans again after a shower, right?"

"Not really. It would be great if you'd go ahead and wash 'em, but I always keep a spare pair of jeans and a shirt in the truck."

"Okay. I'll check on the dogs on my way out."

He'd seen her grill on his various trips in and out of the courtyard earlier. "I'll start the grill, if you tell me where you keep the charcoal."

"There's a big galvanized trash can just outside the back door. The charcoal's inside it and the lighter fluid should be sitting right beside it."

When he got out of the shower, Jack wrapped the towel around his waist and wandered into her living room. The room was like her, he decided, and he approved. Lots of books. Novels. She had eclectic taste, from classics to recent best-sellers, heavy on mystery with some girly-looking romance novels mixed in. There were three whole shelves of gardening and interior-design books. And one devoted to nonfiction. Some history, some pop culture.

He'd never seen Zoey read anything heavier than *Us* magazine.

There were also half a dozen self-help books with dreary, depressing-sounding titles on Cara's bookshelves. These, he decided, would be classified as "relationship books." *When Love Dies. Divorce: Getting Over It, Getting Through It.*

And then there was his favorite: *Putting Back the Pieces: Post-Divorce Recovery.*

He pulled it from the shelves and leafed through it, noting several pages that she'd dog-eared. The author photo of this little gem showed a grim-faced Slavic-looking woman, who, according to her bio, had a thriving marital therapy practice in New York. The author, a Dr. Jankovic, reminded him of Frau Blücher from *Young Frankenstein.*

For a moment, he felt a spasm of guilt, for invading Cara's privacy. But that didn't stop him from skimming down one of the pages, and when he saw a passage heavily underlined in ink, he read it aloud.

> Over and over again in my thirty years of practice, I find a recurring pattern among patients whose marriages have failed. After careful examination, we discover that all too many of them have been attracted to a partner, in part because something in that spouse's family life supplies that which was lacking in a person's own life. Children of failed marriages often choose a partner from an intact home, in the mistaken belief that marital happiness can be genetically transferable.

What was that about? All Jack knew about Cara's parents was that her father was a strict, controlling military type and her mother was dead. And of the ex, Leo, he knew even less, except that the guy was a shit.

And he also knew that no matter what she said, the divorce had left Cara emotionally fragile.

He found the stacked washer-dryer unit in a closet just off the kitchen, and transferred his clothes into the dryer. Then he padded outside, with the towel wrapped loosely around his hips, to get the grill started.

As soon as he opened the back door, Poppy and Shaz bounded over to greet him, tails wagging. He winced when he saw the havoc they'd wrought in Cara's garden. Flowerpots were upended, plants matted down, and yes, it looked like one or both of the dogs had been digging up the beds. He'd have to make good on the peony IOU.

He dumped charcoal in the grill, added lighter fluid, and looked around for matches. Finding none, Jack went inside, found his truck keys on a small table in the hall, and went through the garden gate, into the lane where his truck was parked.

Stepping carefully to avoid broken glass and worse on the lane's crumbling asphalt paving, he unlocked the truck and reached under the front seat, pulling out the rolled-up jeans and clean T-shirt he kept there. He stretched across the seat, opened the glove box, and scrabbled around until he found a box of kitchen matches.

He was just locking the truck again when a shiny black Lexus rolled slowly down the lane. The car's windshield was tinted, so he couldn't see the driver, until he stopped right beside Jack and the electric window slid down.

The driver was a white guy, late thirties, with blond hair and a deeply tanned face. Despite the tinted windows, he wore a pair of Ray-Bans.

Jack didn't know the guy. He tucked the clean clothes under his arm and started back toward the gate.

"Hey man," the stranger called out.

Jack turned around, but said nothing.

"What's goin' on?"

Jack shrugged, and the towel settled lower on his hips. He retucked it. "Not much." He turned to go again.

"Some kinda party goin' on in there?" The blond jerked his chin in the direction of the courtyard and the town house beyond and smirked.

"Nope." Was the guy trying to proposition him? The historic district had a vibrant gay community, and it was well known that people sometimes trolled the quieter lanes and parks looking for a casual hookup. It wouldn't be the first time he'd been approached. And after all, Jack was standing in the lane, barefoot and dressed only in a towel.

"See ya," Jack said, and he motored back inside, being careful to lock and padlock the gate behind him. The Lexus rolled on down the lane, and he went inside to get dressed.

While he was grilling the steaks, Cara put the potatoes in the oven and threw together a salad, slicing fat, ripe red tomatoes she'd bought at the Saturday farmers' market in Forsyth Park, and crumbling locally made goat cheese into a vinaigrette dressing. She went out to the garden to snip some dill and chives from her herb patch, and handed Jack a cold Moon River.

He gave her an appreciative kiss, and wrapped his arms around her waist. "You smell nice," he murmured, nuzzling her hair.

"So do you. Hey—did you use my shampoo and conditioner?"

"Sure. If that's a problem, next time, I'll bring my own."

"What makes you think there's gonna be a next time?" She stifled a giggle.

He ran his hands up under her T-shirt. "There will be. You can't get enough of me, right? You're insatiable, right?"

Cara pushed him away lightly. "Don't burn my steak, wise guy."

The mosquitoes and gnats swarmed the garden right at dusk, so they ate at the dining-room table, moving the box fans from the bedroom into the living area.

Jack sipped the last of the wine she'd poured him, and pushed back from the table.

"That was great," he said. "I guess I could cook if I took the trouble, but living alone, hell, most of the time when I get home from work, I have a microwave burrito or something like that. Having a real steak, and salad, all of it, that's a treat." He turned and flipped a bit of steak to Shaz, who had spent the past hour crouched by his feet, hoping for a treat.

"The books say you shouldn't give dogs table scraps," Cara said. She looked down at Poppy, who'd also been hanging around, hoping for a handout.

"You always go by what the books say?"

"No. But Poppy's breeder said the same thing."

He grunted something noncommittal, then sighed. "I'll get these dishes cleaned up, then I better get on down the road. Early day out at Cabin Creek tomorrow."

She nodded, and helped carry their dishes into the kitchen. He ran soapy water in her sink, carefully washed and rinsed everything while she dried. When the kitchen was cleaned up, he whistled for Shaz.

"Let's go girl," he called. The dog stood slowly.

Cara followed them downstairs. "Oh. I almost forgot. Your clothes." She moved toward the washer-dryer, but Jack caught her by the hand. "Why don't I leave 'em here? You know, just in case?"

"You mean for next time? You're not very subtle, you know." She put her arms around his neck and kissed him.

"Subtle no. Smooth yes." He kissed her deeply and sighed.

"Hmm?" Cara inhaled his scent, and halfway wished he'd stay.

"Today was fun," Jack said. "I mean it. It wasn't like work at all. We make a good team, you know. And then dinner was awesome—the only time I get a real Sunday dinner is if I drop by my mom's house."

Cara raised one amused eyebrow. "And before dinner?"

"I was pretty amazing, wasn't I?"

She swatted his arm.

"Okay. You were amazing too."

She grinned. "Wait'll you get the bill."

31

Monday morning hadn't started well. It was hot. And sticky, and the box fans at Bloom did little more than circulate more hot, sticky air. At eight o'clock, Cara called Sylvia Bradley and left a message on her phone.

"Sylvia? This is Cara Kryzik calling again about the broken air-conditioning over here on Jones Street. I'm sorry about your mother, but I really, really need you to get somebody over here to see about replacing our unit. Please call me."

At nine, she called again.

"Sylvia? Cara. It is eighty-eight degrees in my shop. Eighty-eight degrees! Upstairs it's in the nineties. This is totally unacceptable. Please call and let me know when I can expect to have a new unit."

Slamming the phone down, Cara got up and walked over to the fan, pulling her damp tank top away from her chest. She had a million things to do today, but the heat had already drained her of energy.

She was in the kitchenette, fetching another bottle of cold water, when she heard the shop bell tinkle.

"Cara?"

Crap. She knew that voice. Why today, of all days?

Forcing a smile, she walked into the front room. "Lillian! So nice to see you. And what a beautiful tan from Bermuda!"

Lillian Fanning did not return her smile. Actually, her narrow, carefully made-up face was more pink than tan, and Cara had a feeling it wasn't just from the heat.

"What's going on?" Lillian demanded, pointing at the dueling window fans. "It feels like a third-world country in here."

"Our air-conditioning is broken. I've called our landlady but . . ."

"Appalling. Look, Cara," Lillian interrupted. "This isn't a social call. My epergne? Where is it?"

"Epergne?"

"Yes. My grandmother's silver epergne that you used at Brooke's reception."

"Isn't it with the rest of the silver? I mean, Bert delivered that silver to you Friday afternoon, didn't he?"

"The rest of the silver, yes. It was in the kitchen when I got home late Friday. But not the epergne. The most valuable piece I own. Is it still here, Cara?"

Cara felt a familiar knot of fear and panic in the pit of her stomach. She tried to think, tried to remember if she'd actually seen the epergne in with the rest of the Fannings' pieces.

"I . . . I don't know, Lillian. I put the bin of silver in the back of the van Friday afternoon, and I guess I just assumed it was in there. You're sure it's not at your house?"

"Of course I'm sure! Sunday morning, I unpacked all of it. I wanted to polish everything before putting the pieces back in the tarnish-proof bags I keep them in. But the epergne wasn't there."

Cara's mind raced. "Maybe it fell out of the bin. I can check in the back of the van."

"You do that." Lillian's voice was steely. She crossed her arms over her chest. "I'll wait right here."

"The thing is, I can't. Bert, my assistant, is driving the van. He's uh . . . out on a delivery."

The truth of the matter was, her assistant was MIA again this morning. Along with the van, which he'd had over the weekend.

"Can you call him? Ask him to check to see if it's there?"

"Of course." Cara gestured toward the chair closest to the window and the fan. "Please sit. I'll get you a bottle of water. . . ."

"I'm not thirsty." She lifted her hair from the nape of her neck and exhaled noisily. "How do you stand this?"

"Be right back," Cara said. She fled into the hallway with her cell phone and punched in Bert's cell-phone number, which immediately went to voicemail.

"Bert! Where the hell are you? Lillian Fanning is standing in the shop with smoke coming out of her ears. Her epergne was missing from that bin of silver you dropped off Friday. I need you to check in the van to see if it fell out. Call me immediately, either way. Like right now!"

Cara reluctantly retraced her sheps to the front of the shop.

"Well?" Lillian Fanning hadn't moved. "What did he say? Did he find it?"

Cara's throat was so dry she thought she might spit cotton. "Um, actually I couldn't reach him. He's probably out on Wilmington Island. There's a dead zone there, do you know the spot? Right on Johnny Mercer? My cell calls always get dropped there."

"Did you leave him a message? Does he understand how important this is?"

"I did, and we both understand how important this is. I promise, Lillian, as soon as he calls me, I'll call you. I feel sure the epergne probably just spilled out of the bin in the back of the van, and Bert didn't notice it."

"I hope that's the case," Lillian said huffily. "That epergne is a family heirloom. It was made by a Savannah silversmith in the eighteenth century, and of course, it's a museum-quality piece, which means it's irreplaceable."

All she could do was nod and walk Lillian to the door.

"I'll call," Cara promised, yet again.

After Lillian's departure, Cara called Torie's wedding photographer.

"Billy? It's Cara. Can you do me a huge favor? I know you haven't delivered the proof book from the Fanning wedding yet, but I've got a problem. Can you look through your shots of the reception and see if you've got one of the table for gifts and cards? I'm looking for a shot of this silver epergne we used to hold cards. It's gone missing, and if it doesn't turn up, I'm in a shitload of trouble."

"Damn, Cara," Billy Shook said. "Was it Lillian's?"

"Unfortunately."

"Damn. I don't ever want to deal with that woman again. I feel your pain, Cara. Pretty sure I've got at least one shot like that. I'll look right now and email you whatever I find."

Half an hour and two more panicky phone calls later, she heard the van pull into the lane in back of the shop. It was nearly ten o'clock.

Cara did a slow burn while she waited to confront her assistant.

He strolled in through the back door, whistling. His damp hair was slicked back from his forehead, still bearing comb marks. He carried two grande iced macchiatos, one of which he handed to Cara, with his most ingratiating smile.

"I know I'm a little late. Before you say anything, I'm sorry. Okay? Whew—it's hot in here. What's going on with Sylvia Bradley? Are they gonna fix the air, or what?"

"We'll get to that," Cara said. "First off, why haven't you returned any of my phone calls?"

His face went blank. "Calls?" He reached into the pocket of his black skinny jeans and pulled out his phone. "Oh man. My battery's dead. Sorry. I didn't even realize. I left my charger at home."

"Second—this is the second Monday in a row that you've been over an hour late. And not a word to give me a heads-up. I'm running a business here, Bert. We've got orders to fill, deliveries to get out, work to do. What's going on with you?"

He shrugged and stared down at the floor. "Nothing. Hey, I said I was sorry. . . ."

"And last week you said the same thing, and that it wouldn't happen again. This isn't like you, Bert. As your employer—and your friend—I think I deserve some kind of explanation."

"It's nothing. I went out of town for the weekend, and we were delayed getting back this morning, and like I said, I left my phone charger at home."

"'We'? This is a new boyfriend?"

"Maybe," he said, his expression sullen. "Since when does my private life become any of your business?"

Cara felt her spine stiffen and her temples start to pound. "You make it my business when your private life interferes with your ability to do your job. Which is what's been happening the past two weeks. I wasn't going to say anything, because I was happy for you. But you leave me no choice. You disappear for hours at a time, slack off, ignore phone calls, come in late . . . and now this thing with Lillian's silver epergne . . ."

"What about the silver? C'mon, Cara. I told you I took the damned silver back to that bitch. . . ."

"There's a piece missing. Lillian Fanning showed up here this morning, loaded for bear, and I can't say I blame her. Which is what I was *trying* to call you about. I wanted you to check to see if maybe it had fallen out of the bin and was in the back of the van. But you couldn't be bothered to keep your phone charged. Or to come to work on time."

Bert shook his head obstinately. "*Why* are you making such a federal case out of this? I'll go look right now."

"Fine," Cara said. "Go look."

He hesitated. "What the fuck is an epergne anyway?"

She pulled out the photo of the Fanning epergne that Billy Shook had emailed, and that she'd printed out.

"It's a centerpiece thingy. Multiple arms that can hold little fruits or candies or flowers. We used it in the tent at the wedding, to hold gift cards. Lillian's is an eighteenth-century family heirloom. And she says it's irreplaceable."

They took the delivery van apart. Removed the racks for flower arrangements, lifted the bed liner, but there was no sign of the aforementioned epergne.

Cara dragged herself back into the shop and held her head under the faucet in the kitchenette, letting cold water sluice over her face and hair. The thought occurred to her that this would be a handy way to drown herself.

When she turned around, Bert stood in the doorway, shifting nervously from foot to foot. Beneath all the pouting and bravado, he obviously knew he'd messed up. "Now what?"

She sighed. "I've got a menu tasting with Brooke Trapnell and her fiancé at the caterers in exactly forty-five minutes. So I've got to get myself presentable for that. In the meantime, I need you to take the van, and retrace—exactly—the route you took last Friday out to Isle of Hope and the Fannings' house. Every stop—the hospital, any house you made a delivery to—every stop, Bert. You go in, and show them the photo of the epergne, and you ask if they've seen it."

He rolled his eyes dramatically. "Like that's gonna work."

"Just do it," she exploded. "And get yourself another charger for your phone. "

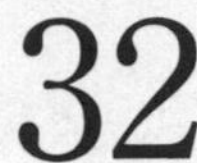

32

Delicious smells assaulted her nostrils as Cara pushed through the door at Fete Accompli. Layne Pelletier stood at attention just inside the door, hands clasped behind her back. She wore the traditional black and white checked slacks, clogs, and a white kerchief tied over her hair. Her white chef's smock was spotless, her name embroidered in script over her left breast.

Her face fell when she saw that Cara was alone. "The bride's not with you?"

"No. She and Harris called right before I left the shop and said they were running late. They're supposed to meet me here."

"You don't think they'll stand us up, right? I've spent a small fortune fixing all this food."

"No, no, they're coming," Cara assured the caterer. "Marie made Brooke swear she had it on her calendar."

Cara followed her nose into the shop's small dining area. A long wooden table held a starched white cloth and a small floral arrangement of lilies, roses, and hypericum berries she'd had Bert drop by earlier on his way to track down the missing epergne.

"I'm so hungry, I could faint," Cara confided. A small round of roast beef stood on a carving stand under a red heat lamp, a pool of juices \radiating out from it. Silver chafing dishes held a dozen other hot dishes. Shallow bowls filled with finely crushed ice held arrays of boiled shrimp, oysters, and stone-crab claws. A smoked salmon fillet was sprinkled with capers, finely diced hard-boiled eggs, and lemon slices.

Wordlessly, Layne handed Cara a napkin, and loaded it with boiled shrimp.

Cara walked down to the far end of the table. A silver tiered stand held half a dozen iced cupcakes. She turned to Layne. "Cupcakes? Cute, but that doesn't seem like something the Trapnells are going to think is impressive."

"We won't serve cupcakes. These are just all the different options for cake flavors and icings I can do. It's not cost-effective for me to bake six whole wedding cakes for just a menu tasting," Layne explained.

The shop door opened, and Marie Trapnell stepped in. "Hi. Sorry to be late."

Cara introduced Layne and Marie, and Marie looked at her watch and frowned. "I can't believe the kids aren't here yet. Brooke texted me they were leaving her office fifteen minutes ago." A faint chirp sounded from the direction of Marie's pocketbook. She dug it out, read the text message, smiled, and held it up for the other women to see.

On way. There in 5.

"Wow!" Marie walked over to the buffet table. "This looks wonderful. Are we really going to have all this?"

Layne glanced at Cara for an answer.

"Not necessarily all of it. When I talked to your husband . . ."

"Ex-husband, actually," Marie said quietly.

"Oh. Right. Sorry, of course. Anyway, Mr. Trapnell said he and his wife wanted to sample everything we offer, so they could get . . ."

Marie's face paled. "Are you saying that Gordon's coming today? And Patricia too?"

This was news to Cara. And not happy news.

"Um, well, I think that was the plan. Isn't that the plan?" Layne asked Cara.

Uh-oh, Cara thought. Once again, Patricia Trapnell had managed an end run around her.

"When I set up the tasting with Layne today, I was under the impression that it was just going to be the bride and groom and mother of the bride." Cara chose her words carefully.

The door opened again, and Brooke Trapnell rushed in, a tall strawberry-blond man right behind. "Hi everybody. Sorry to be late!"

Brooke Trapnell wore pearls, white running shoes, and a crisp seersucker power suit, straight out of a Brooks Brothers catalogue. Her fiancé was dressed more casually, in khakis and a blue button-down dress shirt.

Marie gave her daughter an exasperated hug. "I was afraid you weren't coming."

"I tried, Marie," Brooke's fiancé said ruefully. "I even fibbed and told her we were supposed to be here half an hour earlier. . . ."

"Sweet boy!" Marie Trapnell beamed her approval, then kissed him on the cheek and turned to Cara.

"Cara Kryzik, this is my future son-in-law, Harris Strayhorn."

"Hey there." Harris's handshake was firm, his smile genuine. He looked a lot like his mother, with fair hair, blue eyes, and the same ruddy complexion. But he was half a head taller than Brooke, long-limbed and gangly, like a colt whose legs had outgrown the rest of his body.

Harris's eyes widened as he took in the food table. "Oh man, is that all for us? Awesome!" He turned to Brooke, tugging at her sleeve. "Honey, check out this spread!"

Brooke laughed. "He is always hungry. Always. You wouldn't believe he just came from a breakfast meeting, right?"

"I happen to enjoy good food," Harris said. "Is that a crime?"

"It's a good thing you know how to cook," Marie said. "Because if it's up to Brooke, you might starve to death."

"That's not true. I can fix oatmeal, and scrambled eggs, and grits, of course," Brooke protested.

"Do you ever eat any of that yourself?" Layne asked dubiously, taking in the bride's slender figure.

"No," Marie said, frowning now at the way Brooke's jacket hung loosely from her shoulders.

"I eat," Brooke said.

Harris raised one eyebrow. "What? What have you eaten today?"

"Well . . . nothing, but that's just because I knew we would be pigging out at this tasting, and I didn't want to spoil my appetite."

"She has no appetite," Marie said flatly. "Except for work."

"And me," Harris said, wrapping an arm around his fiancée's waist.

Obviously ready to change the subject, Brooke pointed at the food table. "Okay so can we get started? This all looks great, but I've got a two-o'clock meeting back at the office."

Layne gave Cara a questioning glance.

"Yes. Let's go ahead and start tasting and comparing notes," Cara said. "I gather we're expecting Gordon and Patricia to join us, but I don't want to hold you two up."

Brooke had picked up a slice of roast beef from the carving station, but she dropped the fork now, with a clatter.

"Mom?" She stared at Marie. "You didn't tell me Dad and Patricia were coming."

"I didn't know myself, until just now. It's fine though. Really. I can deal. Let's just go ahead and begin."

Harris stepped over to the table and began loading a plate with food. He popped a shrimp in his mouth and chewed, nodding his head in approval.

"Can we have the shrimp? What, are they cooked in beer or something?"

"Boiled in beer, actually," Layne volunteered.

Harris dropped one on Brooke's empty plate. "Try this. We gotta have this for the wedding."

But Brooke ignored the food. "I can't believe she just invited herself today. I *told* Daddy she keeps trying to run things. . . ."

Marie put her hand on Brooke's sleeve. "Let's just let it go for today, okay? Layne has fixed all this beautiful food for us to try. You can have another discussion with your dad later."

"It's so not okay," Brooke said, stony-faced.

"Honey?" Harris said, soothingly. "C'mon. Just eat something."

. . .

They worked their way around the table. For as skinny as he was, Harris Strayhorn's appetite and enthusiasm knew no bounds. He was every mother's dream, every caterer's dream. He loved it all.

For her part, Brooke merely picked at the offerings, despite her mother's urging.

Marie was busily taking notes and conferring with Layne. "I love the little new potatoes with the caviar and sour cream. Brooke?"

"I'm not really into fish eggs, but if you like them, that's fine," Brooke said.

They were ten minutes into the tasting when the shop door opened and Patricia Trapnell swept in.

"Shit," Brooke said under her breath. Marie shot her a warning look.

Patricia didn't offer a greeting, or an excuse for her lateness. "You've started already?" She glared accusingly at Cara.

"Yes. We did, Patricia. Harris and I have jobs. We can't wait around all day for you." Brooke glowered at her stepmother. "Where's Daddy?"

"Something came up." Patricia picked up a plate and started down the line, but frowned when she saw the roast beef.

"Layne? I thought we discussed tenderloin, not steamship round. It'll be so hot that day, and honestly, I think that presentation is so passé. It reminds people of being on a second-rate cruise ship."

"Well," Layne began.

"I asked for this cut," Brooke said. "It's Harris's favorite. His dad's too. And it's not passé, but even if it were, nobody but you would care."

"Fine." Patricia's lips pursed and she moved on to the next dish. She pointed with her fork at one of the chafing dishes.

"What's that supposed to be?"

Layne dabbed a bead of perspiration from her forehead. "That's the roast asparagus you requested."

"But it's wrapped in bacon," Patricia said, her nostrils quivering. "We're supposed to have prosciutto. Cold-smoked prosciutto. Don't think I don't know the difference."

"For the reception, we'll use prosciutto," Layne assured her. "But I have to special-order it from my supplier, and he only delivers on Tuesdays and Thursdays."

"We're going to want to taste the prosciutto before the wedding," Patricia warned. "It's an entirely different taste."

Brooke snorted, and this time, Patricia decided not to let it pass. She whirled around to confront the bride.

"You may not care about these things, Brooke Trapnell, but I can assure you your father and I do care. We're paying eighty dollars a plate for this reception. And that does not include the bar. So please excuse me if I happen to object when somebody expects me to pay for prosciutto when it's clearly only bacon. Is that too much to ask?"

Marie hesitated, then stepped between her daughter and Patricia.

"We all want a beautiful wedding, don't we, Brooke?"

Brooke rolled her eyes, then looked away.

"Hey, honey?" It was Harris's turn to referee now. He had a smear of chocolate icing on his upper lip, and a glob of coconut on his shirt collar. He grabbed her hand and towed her toward the opposite end of the table. "Come down here and check out the desserts. Cupcakes! I freakin' love 'em."

"Cupcakes?" Patricia's surgically stretched face registered her horror. She stalked down to the dessert offerings. "Are we having a 4-H picnic, Layne? Really?"

"No!" Layne hurried over. "These are just all the different cake types and frostings and fillings we do. I thought Brooke and Harris could taste everything and decide, and then, of course, we'll do a proper cake. . . ."

"Forget it," Brooke said, her eyes blazing. "Just let Patricia decide. After all, she's the one running this show."

Brooke reached over and snatched the lemon-iced cupcake he'd just bitten into from Harris's hand. She set it down on the table.

"Aww, man . . ." he groaned.

"We've got to get back to work," Brooke announced. She turned and walked rapidly toward the door.

"Harris! I'm leaving."

Harris looked at Layne, then at Cara, then at Marie. He shrugged. “Sorry. Gotta go.”

He was halfway to the door when he turned, returned to the table, picked up his cupcake, and hurried back to the side of his one true love.

Somehow, after Brooke had gone, the women managed to work out a menu that suited Patricia as well as Marie. When everybody was gone, Layne went to the door of Fete Accompli and locked the deadbolt. Wordlessly, she went to the big walk-in cooler in her catering kitchen. She took out a half-open bottle of chardonnay, tipped it to her lips, and swigged for at least a minute. Then she handed it to Cara. “Be my guest.”

33

Bert met her at the door of the shop, and the look on his face telegraphed the bad news. "I've looked everywhere," Bert said, rubbing a hand wearily over his face. "Honest to God, Cara. Every single stop I made Friday, I retraced. I showed everybody the picture of the epergne. I even crawled around in the grass and the bushes at the Shutters. Since it was low tide, I even looked around that dock, thinking maybe somebody got drunk and chunked it in the water for a joke. But nothing. It ain't there."

"Oh God." Cara thumped her forehead on her desk. First Lillian Fanning, then Patricia Trapnell. Now this. What was wrong with her karma?

"What now? Will you call her and tell her?"

Cara popped three aspirin in her mouth and dry-swallowed them.

"I can't deal with Lillian right now. I think I might have heat stroke." She pulled her sticky shirt away from her chest.

"Did you call Sylvia Bradley again?" Bert asked.

"Yes, I called her. She doesn't pick up the phone, because she doesn't want to deal with me. I've sent her a registered letter, too." Cara reached into her desk drawer and got her pocketbook.

"Let's go," she told Bert.

"Where to?"

"To wherever they sell air conditioners. I can't spend one more hour living like this."

The salesman at Lowe's carefully explained the merits and options of all the room-size air conditioners the store carried.

"Which one is the next to cheapest?"

The salesman looked startled. "Next to cheapest?"

"My father taught me never to buy the cheapest model of anything. Or the most expensive," Cara explained. "I sure can't afford the next to most expensive, so I guess I'm buying the next to cheapest."

"Most affordable," the salesman said gently.

"Whatever. As long as you have it in stock and we can walk out of here with it in the next ten minutes."

She handed over her credit card and held her breath waiting to see if the transaction would go through. She'd maxed out most of her cards, but this one, a Visa that had come through the mail months ago, was one she'd activated but never used. She thought of it as her Plan B card. And she reflected, grimly, that there was no Plan C.

Cara had sent the Colonel a check for $15,000 the minute Gordon Trapnell had paid the deposit for his daughter's wedding. It meant letting her other past-due bills ripen a little longer, but at least, she thought, it would forestall her father for another few weeks.

But there would be no more stalling on purchasing an air conditioner. She couldn't have brides entering a shop that felt like a sauna. And she couldn't deal with all the crap life was throwing at her, working in those conditions after spending another sleepless night upstairs.

She and Bert carried the precious new air-conditioning unit into the shop and unboxed it immediately, fitting it into one of the front windows. Cara held out the thin plastic remote control, took a deep breath, and clicked the On button. The air conditioner's motor hummed to life, and a stream of chilled air wafted into the room.

"Sweet blessed baby Jesus," Cara murmured, standing in front of the unit. She ducked her head and let it blow her sweat-soaked hair, then turned around, lifted the back of her skirt, and let the cold air billow up it like a balloon.

"I should have done this ten days ago," she said finally.

"Yeah, you should have," Bert said. "Maybe you wouldn't be in such a pissy mood all the time if it wasn't so friggin' hot in here."

Cara clamped a hand on his shoulder. "Listen, my friend. My expecting you to be a prompt, reliable, responsible employee does not constitute pissininess."

"Gawwwwd," he exclaimed. "You act like it's my fault that damned epergne is missing. You're totally gonna throw me under the bus on this, aren't you?"

"I'm not blaming anything on you," she said, trying to keep her tone even. "I'm going to call Lillian right now, and let her know we couldn't find it. I own this business, and I'm taking responsibility for it."

"Great," he said.

"Bert?"

"Yeah?"

"In the meantime, you need to change your attitude and your performance. Or you can just find yourself another job."

He looked her in the eye. "Are we done? I've got the afternoon deliveries to get out."

"We're done. After you finish the deliveries, bring the van back here for the night, please."

He laughed unpleasantly. "So, what? You're grounding me? I'm twenty-nine years old, Cara."

"And you act like a fifteen-year-old. If I could lock you in time-out too, I'd do it."

After he'd gone, she closed the rest of the shop windows and sat at her desk for a moment, trying to enjoy the calm before the storm.

What, she wondered, was going on with Bert? He'd been working for her for two years. They'd never had a real argument, or even a disagreement. He had a real talent for floral arranging, and when he'd come to her, directly out of alcohol rehab, he'd been so grateful to have a job, he was like a puppy, desperate for love and attention.

But these past two weeks, he'd changed. He swore he wasn't drinking, but what else could she think, given his most recent disappearance?

Her halfhearted suggestion that she might fire him hadn't had the effect she'd hoped for. He'd merely stared her down. The thing was, she genuinely cared about Bert. He'd been a sounding board throughout her breakup with Leo, had even given her shelter on his sofa for the first week after she'd left Leo. He was funny, generous, and mostly even-keeled.

Cara didn't want to hire a new assistant. She wanted her old one back.

She was gazing out the shop window, trying to get up the nerve to call Lillian Fanning, when she saw a white Mercedes zoom up to the curb outside Bloom and park in the loading zone.

Her right eye twitched and she reached for the aspirin bottle again. Perfect. Speak of the devil.

Lillian was dressed in tennis whites, but not a hair on her immaculately coiffed head was mussed.

She pushed the shop door open and planted herself in front of the worktable where Cara sat. "Well?" She raised one eyebrow, expectantly.

"I'm so sorry, Lillian. Bert and I took the van apart. He retraced every stop he made last week, on his way out to Isle of Hope when he was returning the silver. It didn't turn up." Cara felt tears prick her eyes. She swallowed hard. "I don't know what to say. I feel terrible about this."

"Unbelievable!" Lillian exploded. "You feel terrible? You lose the single most valuable family heirloom I own, and that's the best you can do? Feel terrible? Is that supposed to mean something to me?"

"N-n-n-no," Cara squeaked.

"What do you intend to do about it?" Lillian demanded.

"What would you like me to do?"

"Have you called the police?"

"The police? Why would I call the police?"

"Because obviously, it's been stolen." Lillian looked around the shop. "Did you ask your assistant if he'd seen it?"

"Yes! He spent most of the afternoon looking for it."

"And you believe him?"

Cara felt her scalp prickle. "Yes. I believe him. Bert has worked for me for two years. Why would he lie about something like this?"

"Why wouldn't he? That epergne is worth thousands and thousands of dollars. What do you pay the man? Minimum wage?"

"I pay Bert a living wage," Cara said, struggling to keep her temper. "He's not a thief, Lillian. Or a liar. And neither am I. In fact, I resent your implying otherwise."

"What do you really know about him, Cara? Do you run a criminal-record check before you hire these people?"

"I know that Bert Rosen is a decent, honest, hardworking person."

"And how did you come to hire this decent, honest, hardworking person? Did he come to you with references?"

No, Cara thought. *He came to me right out of rehab. And I hired him because I believe he deserved a second chance. And he still does.*

Lillian took a step closer to Cara, and then another step. "I don't give a good goddamn what you resent. You and your assistant are responsible for the loss of that epergne. It didn't just get up and run away. It was stolen! And if you won't file a police report, I will."

"And then what?" Cara asked. She refused to take Lillian's bait. "Is the epergne insured?"

"I'll have to call our agent," Lillian said. "And our lawyer."

Cara felt first her right eye twitch, and then her left. Lawyer?

"Let me know what you find out," she said finally. "Of course, if the epergne isn't insured, I fully intend to pay for its replacement."

Lillian gave her a pitying look. "How sweet. And how do you plan to come up with that kind of money?"

Cara chewed the inside of her mouth. She felt bile rising in her throat. She searched for some clever, searing retort to Lillian's patronizing sneer. But she had nothing. Except that throbbing pain in her temple.

"Let me worry about that," she said finally.

34

Cara was creating her sixth new-baby arrangement of the morning. It wasn't a terribly creative endeavor—pink carnations, multicolored gerbera daisies, and white for mothers of baby girls, blue hydrangeas, daisies, and white carnations for those who'd delivered boys. Sometimes, she did dish gardens, with themed flowers tucked in. But she loved putting them together, loved the thought of new moms, smiling down at their own new creations, and then up at the candy stripers delivering their flowers.

She also loved the fact that few of the recipients of those arrangements had the time or energy to call up and bitch at her about misplaced epergnes or tacky-looking cupcakes.

True to her word, Lillian had reported the epergne as stolen to the police. On Tuesday, an apologetic Savannah police detective called to make an appointment to discuss the incident.

The missing epergne—combined with the hot sticky climate in her upstairs apartment—had kept her awake for two nights in a row. Finally, Wednesday night, Cara dragged a sofa cushion, pillow, and quilt downstairs and slept in the blissful cool of the workroom.

And Thursday morning, in the middle of all those happy baby flower arrangements, the detective arrived. She was a middle-aged black woman, who introduced herself as Zarah Peebles. "Zarah, like Sarah with a 'Z,'" she said, handing Cara her business card.

She showed Cara a photo of Lillian Fanning's missing family heirloom.

"Yes," Cara sighed. "That's the epergne. As I told Lillian, the last time I remember specifically seeing it was Sunday morning, when we went back to Isle of Hope to finish taking down everything used in the reception. It was placed in a bin in the back of my delivery van."

"If the wedding was held at the Fannings' home, why didn't you just take it back into the house?" Detective Peebles asked.

"It was the morning after their daughter's wedding, they'd had a late night, and I didn't want to disturb their rest. Anyway, I wanted to take everything back to the shop, and make sure it was cleaned up before I returned everything. The candlesticks still had wax on them, and some of the bowls had been used for flower arrangements."

"And did you bring everything back here and clean it up, as you'd planned?"

"No," Cara admitted. "We had an incredibly busy week, another huge wedding, and time . . . just got away from me. To tell you the truth, I'd forgotten we even still had the silver, until Lillian called on Friday to ask about it."

"So . . . where was this bin of silver during that next week?"

"In the van."

"And who had access to the van?"

"Just me. And Bert, my assistant."

Detective Peebles frowned. "Where is the van usually parked?"

"Sometimes, if there's a parking space out front, we park it on Jones. But usually we park in my dedicated slot in the lane."

"Lot of break-ins in this neighborhood," Detective Peebles observed. "Probably not the best idea to have a boxful of valuable silver in a van parked in a lane where any wandering crackhead could check it out."

Cara sighed. "No, it wasn't. I can't tell you how much I regret that. But the bin was at the very back of the van, and there are no windows there, so a thief wouldn't have known it was there. And the van was locked."

"All the time? You're sure about that?"

"Reasonably sure."

Detective Peebles was scribbling notes.

"Can I take a look at the van?"

"Right now, my assistant is out making deliveries. I can call him and ask him to head back here as soon as he's done. But I can tell you right now, the van hadn't been broken into. And all the rest of the Fannings' silver was there. Why would somebody take just that one piece, and not the rest of it?"

"Because it was the most valuable piece?"

"Was it?"

The detective flipped some pages in her notebook. "Mrs. Fanning says she had it appraised at the Telfair Museum a couple years ago, and it's valued at a hundred and thirty-five thousand dollars."

"What?" Cara felt her jaw drop. "Lillian never told me it was that valuable. I never would have used it at the reception. And I certainly wouldn't have just piled it in a bin with those other pieces. Or left it in the back of the van for a week."

"Hindsight," Detective Peebles said. "I looked at the picture she gave me of that epergne. Am I saying it right?"

"I think it's pronounced 'ay-purn,'" Cara said.

"Not my kind of thing at all. Kinda ugly if you ask me. But from what Mrs. Fanning says, that doohickey is worth more than my house and car put together."

"And mine."

"Okay," the detective said. "That's about all I needed to ask you. Oh yeah, your assistant's full name?"

"Bert Rosen. Hubert, actually." Cara hesitated. "Look, Detective. I know Lillian probably told you she thinks Bert stole the epergne. She said as much to me when she came in here Monday. But I know him. He's not a thief. He wouldn't do that."

"How long have you known him?"

"Two and a half years, and nothing like this has ever happened. Ever."

"What do you know about his background? How'd you come to hire this Bert Rosen?"

Cara bit her lip. "He was referred to me through an organization called the Step-Up Society. They work with men and women who've been through alcohol and drug rehab. Bert is a recovering alcoholic."

"You hired somebody right out of rehab? Kinda risky, don't you think?"

"His counselor at Step-Up is somebody I know. He vouched for Bert. I met him, we liked each other, so I hired him on a trial basis, and it worked out. It worked out great."

"Pretty generous of you," Detective Peebles said. She looked around the shop, taking it all in. "How about you? Have you gone through rehab? Is that why you're sympathetic to somebody like your assistant?"

"No. I've not been through rehab. I'm strictly a social drinker. But I grew up with an alcoholic. I know the struggles they face to keep sober."

"Your dad?" the detective asked.

"My mom," Cara said.

She was still brooding about her police interview when the shop phone rang. She picked up the receiver, not even checking the caller-ID screen. "Bloom Floral Design," she said, trying to sound perkier than she felt.

"Hello?"

Cara was so surprised, she nearly dropped the phone. The thready, high-pitched voice on the other end sounded just like her recently deceased landlady.

"Bernice?"

"Who the hell is this?" the voice on the other end demanded. "Is this some kind of joke?"

"Uh, no. I'm sorry. This is Cara Kryzik. Is this Sylvia?" Come to think of it, Cara had never actually spoken to Bernice Bradley's daughter. She'd always dealt with the older of the two women.

"Yes, it's Sylvia."

Sylvia Bradley sounded eerily like her mother.

"Um, well, Sylvia, I wanted to tell you how very sorry I am about your loss. Your mother was a remarkable woman." It was the nicest thing Cara could say on the spur of the moment. "I'm sure she'll be greatly missed."

"Thank you," Sylvia said curtly. "I see you've been calling to complain about the air conditioner on Jones Street? Again and again? Don't you think it's pretty indecent to be hounding me like this, with my mother not even dead a week?"

"Um, I'm sorry. Truly, very sorry," Cara heard herself stammering. And then she remembered what Bert had pointed out. The Bradleys were the worst kinds of landlords. She paid a premium price for the town house on Jones Street, and had never been even a day late with her rent. The least she should expect from her landlady was a livable building. And when temperatures were in the nineties, that was definitely not livable. Not for a home, or a business.

Cara was emboldened by that thought.

"The thing is, my air conditioner is broken again. It's the third time this spring. It's been broken for ten days, and you know how hot it's been. It's bad enough that I have to try to sleep with no air-conditioning. But it's embarrassing when I have clients, including brides, come into the shop, only to find it's like an oven. It's starting to affect my business, Sylvia. So I would really appreciate if you could get somebody over here to fix it. Today."

"That's not going to happen," Sylvia said flatly. "Even if I could get somebody on such short notice, which I can't. I have a lot of business to tend to, getting Mother's estate taken care of."

Cara's fuse snapped. "No disrespect, Sylvia, but that's not good enough. I've called you repeatedly, with no response, and I even sent a registered letter, so I know you've been notified. This week, I couldn't take the heat another minute. I bought a window unit and installed it downstairs in the shop. And unless you send somebody over here to replace the central unit, I'm going to buy a second unit to allow me to sleep upstairs."

"You do that," Sylvia said.

"And I'm going to attach the receipts and deduct them from my rent next month," Cara added.

There was a prolonged silence at the other end of the phone. *Gotcha*, Cara thought.

She heard paper rustling in the void. And another long pause.

"Maybe there won't be a next month," Sylvia said finally, with a dry, raspy chuckle.

"What's that supposed to mean?" Could she be hearing correctly? Was this shrew actually threatening her?

"Your lease expired in March," Sylvia pointed out.

"I know that," Cara said, trying to sound more confident than she felt. "But I had an agreement with Bernice. She was fine with me going month to month until June. Then she was going to have a new lease prepared. She'd talked about raising my rent, and I'd agreed, in theory, as long as she got the plumbing looked at and the air-conditioning problems resolved."

"Mother never said anything about that to me," Sylvia said. "Not that it really matters now. I was going to wait and notify you after the closing, but I reckon now's as good a time as any."

Cara felt her scalp prickle. "Closing?"

"I'm about sick and tired of dealing with whiny tenants and their piddly problems," Sylvia said. "Mama might have put up with that mess, but she's dead now. Jones Street is sold. As of June thirtieth. You got a problem, take it up with the new owner."

"Wait!'" Cara cried. "You sold my building? Without even telling me?"

"Sure did," Sylvia said.

"What if I wanted to buy the building? You didn't even give me right of first refusal."

"Didn't have to," Sylvia said. "Anyway, the way I hear it, you're just barely hanging on over there as it is. Where would you get the money to buy a valuable property like that?"

"What!" Cara exploded. "Where did you hear something like that? That's a lie! My business is solid, and growing. Who did you sell it to anyway? You owe me that much."

"I don't owe you one sorry thing," Sylvia Bradley said. "I reckon you'll be hearing from the new owner soon enough. Here's a word of advice to you though. Start packing. I think he's got plans for that building that don't include you."

. . .

After leaving half a dozen voicemail messages for her lawyer, Cara finally got a callback, shortly before five.

"Hi Cara," Melinda Ennis said cheerfully. "How's the flower business?"

Melinda had been another gift from Vicki Cooper, a smart, savvy young Emory Law School grad who wanted a champagne wedding on a beer budget. Cara had managed to pull it off, and in return, the grateful bride had handled Cara's divorce pro bono.

"It *was* picking up," Cara said. "But after today, I just don't know. It's like the universe is conspiring to grind its heel in my face."

"What's going on?"

Cara quickly filled the lawyer in on the conversation she'd had with Sylvia Bradley.

"She won't even tell me who the new owner is," Cara said, a note of desperation in her voice. "Can she do that—legally?"

"Well, morally and ethically, it sucks," Melinda said carefully. "But since you no longer have a lease in effect, legally, your landlord is correct. She's under no obligation to you whatsoever."

"But that's not right! I've been in this building for over two years, and I've never even been a day late with my rent. I've spent thousands of dollars of my own money fixing it up. And the Bradleys did nothing—nothing to keep up the property. The plumbing, the electrical, the wiring, even the roof, all need work."

"Maybe the new owner will be more responsive," Melinda said soothingly. "It sounds like you've been a model tenant. So hopefully, he'll want to work something out and keep you happy."

"I doubt it. Sylvia said the new owner has plans for my building that don't include me. She actually suggested I should start packing."

"What a hateful old bitch," Melinda said with a sigh. "I wish there was something I could do to help here, but I guess you'll just have to wait until you hear from the new landlord."

"Isn't there any way I can find out right now? Some kind of court records you could look up?"

"Once the property's closed and the deed is registered, it'll be public information," Melinda said. "But not until then. Sylvia actually told you the closing isn't till the end of the month?"

"The thirtieth," Cara confirmed. "Three weeks from now. What if this new owner really does kick me out? How am I gonna find a new place I can afford, pack up and move in the middle of my busiest time of the year?"

"We're just going to have to be proactive," Melinda said. "You know what Savannah's like. Everybody talks about everything. Especially real-estate transactions. Tell you what. I'll go over to the courthouse tomorrow, do some poking around. I'll get Andy to tap into his old-boy network too. We'll figure out who the owner is, come up with an offer you can afford, and approach him before he has time to shop around for new tenants."

"You really think that could work?" Cara asked. She had serious doubts.

"It's worth a try," Melinda said. "But Cara? I don't want to scare you or anything, but in the meantime, just in case, maybe you'd better start looking around for a new address."

Cara looked around her tiny shop, and thought of the comfortable aerie she'd fashioned for herself upstairs. Her budget was stretched to the max already. A new address?

She wondered what her brides would think of a florist who lived and worked out of a petal-pink van.

35

When the going got tough, Cara headed for the shower. She didn't know when she'd started treating the shower like a combination confessional and therapist's couch.

Maybe it had started when she'd first moved to Savannah. Leo was the kind of man who made friends effortlessly. Within a month of their move, he was having drinks after work with clients, weaseled his way into a golf foursome, was on a first-name basis with all their neighbors.

"Never met a stranger, that boy!" the Colonel liked to say of her ex.

It was harder for Cara. Every time she opened her mouth, people would stare at her and ask, "Where are you *from*?" And when she said Ohio they looked at her with pity. Nobody could pronounce her name—"Kryzike? Kris-shick? What kind of name is that?"

"Krizz-ick," she'd say patiently. "It's a Croatian name."

To which they'd look even more puzzled. "Croatia? That's a country?"

She had little in common with the neighbors in their subdivision, most of whom were young mothers, who already had their own friends—their own play groups, their own supper clubs, their own girlfriends. They never came right out and said it, but the situation was clear. Nobody was currently taking applications for new friends.

Once, that first fall after they moved in, out of desperation, she'd written out invitations to a soup supper and slipped them into the mailboxes of all eight houses on their end of the block.

She'd fixed a huge pot of Italian wedding soup, a salad, and an apple streusel pie, and set everything out on the dining room table, along with a gorgeous arrangement of fall flowers she'd placed in a hollowed-out pumpkin. Exactly one couple—Arnie and Sheila Jenkins, retirees who lived at the head of the street—came. They'd eaten their soup hurriedly, made lame excuses for why nobody else had come—"Georgia has a home game tomorrow"—and rushed off without even touching dessert. She would never forget the look of pity on their faces.

Cara had thrown the whole pie in the trash and retreated to the shower to weep and curse.

Friday nights during the spring were the worst. She'd come home from work, and see women standing in knots in the cul-de-sac, chatting, sipping from plastic wineglasses, while their children circled on bikes or scooters. She'd smell the charcoal drifting from backyard grills, see couples hurrying to each other's houses with covered casserole dishes, or coolers tucked under their arms.

Cara would retreat to the shower. She'd stand under the shower and cry while she washed her hair. She'd curse the snobby neighbors and call them crackers and ignorant rednecks while she shaved her legs. While she was rubbing conditioner into her scalp she'd tell herself it wasn't her—it was them. She'd had friends back home. Lots of friends.

When her marriage to Leo crumbled, Cara hid in the shower. She could still remember that night—that awful Valentine's Day night—when she'd figured out he was having a fling with the dental hygienist. She'd locked herself in the bathroom and stayed in the shower for two hours, only emerging after the hot water ran out. Then she'd packed her bags and run away from home. And cursed again, when she realized she'd left a nearly new bottle of expensive shampoo in her old shower. Would the dental hygienist use it?

Now, two years later, just when she'd thought maybe her luck was changing, just when she'd managed to feather a new nest for herself, the tiny pink bathtub in her downtown apartment—the one Jack referred to as the Barbie dream tub—became her solace once again. Her building sold? Where would she go? Where would she get the money to start over? Not from her father, she knew. She already had a missed call from the Colonel this morning. He always called on the shop phone, thank goodness.

The old lead pipes in the town house knocked and shuddered when she turned on the spigot, and normally the hot-water heater took a full fifteen minutes to heat up, and would run out before she'd finished crying—or rinsing her hair. But today she was taking a cool bath.

Somehow, this time, when she stepped onto the bath mat, she felt a little better. Maybe Sylvia Bradley was mistaken. Any landlord would be an improvement over the Bradleys. Maybe the new owner would finally fix up the building and allow her to stay. And if not? This was not the only house in the historic district. Nearly every block had at least one "for lease" sign in a front window. She'd call her real-estate agent and start looking. At least, she thought, she had the Trapnell wedding coming up. She'd have to postpone paying off her debt to the Colonel. She'd just have to make him understand. He was her father—he'd *have* to understand.

The one good thing about sleeping on the shop floor was that she was up early every morning. By eight o'clock, she'd already finished making the four bridesmaids' bouquets for Saturday's wedding. She'd pulled incoming orders off their internet server, and written up the phone orders so that Bert could get started on them when he got in at nine. She frowned, remembering the earlier confrontation with her assistant. He'd *better* get in at nine.

At 8:45, she was wheeling the vintage garden cart out to the sidewalk when she saw Jack's big black truck come down the block. She felt a little tug in her chest. It was pathetic and needy, but yes, she'd wondered if and when he'd call again.

He parked across the street and jumped out of the truck. He was dressed for work, blue jeans, clean white T-shirt, work boots. She found herself studying him, measuring him against Leo, Leo in his expensive sport coats and silk ties and spit-polished shoes. Leo with his salesman's smoothness. No. Make that slickness.

Jack Finnerty wasn't polished and he wasn't smooth, and his jeans were faded and ragged at the knee, and he looked so good right now she got a little weak in the knees as he crossed the street, bounded onto the curb, and grabbed her around the waist for a kiss.

"Some welcoming committee," he said, when he let her go.

"What are you doing in town?" Cara asked, smiling up at him. "I thought you were working out at Cabin Creek all week."

"Ryan's over there now, waiting on a lumber delivery," he said. "We found some old-growth heart pine that came out of a closed-up textile mill in Greenville, South Carolina, for the new floor for the barn." He hesitated, then frowned.

"You're not gonna like what I've got to tell you."

She sighed. "I guess you've heard. Probably Torie told Ryan and Ryan told you, right? Well, it's true. Somehow, I managed to lose Lillian Fanning's heirloom silver epergne. She's called the police, and now it's a whole big thing."

"Epergne? No, I don't know anything about that," Jack said, running a hand through his hair. "But hell, that's bad enough. Lillian's not saying you stole it, right?"

"Not me. No. She's convinced Bert is a thief."

Jack rolled his eyes. "She probably misplaced it herself. It'll turn up."

"I hope you're right," Cara said. "Because the thing is worth like a hundred and twenty-five thousand dollars."

His eyes widened. "Holy crap."

"I know. So, what is it you have to tell me that I'm not gonna like? You're married? Carrying an STD? Come on, Jack, just spit it out and get it over with."

He picked a bloom from a potted gardenia on the garden cart and handed it to her. A consolation prize? "I'm here because your new landlord wants an estimate of what it's gonna cost to renovate your building."

"Well, at least you're not married, and you haven't given me a venereal disease," Cara said, making a weak joke.

"Did you have any idea your landlady was selling the place?" he asked.

"None. Sylvia finally returned my calls yesterday, and while I was in the middle of chewing her out about the air-conditioning, she dropped the bomb. Said it didn't matter because she'd sold the building. Without even telling me! And then she basically told me I should start packing, because the new landlord has plans that don't include me."

Jack nodded sympathetically. "It sucks. Big-time."

She grabbed the front of his T-shirt. "So who hired you? Who bought the building? Sylvia wouldn't even give me the satisfaction of telling me. I guess maybe she's afraid I'll call the guy and tell him everything that's wrong with the building before the sale closes."

"He hasn't hired us yet. But I get the feeling the guy already knows what all's wrong with the building. He's been in it a couple times, from what he told me."

"What?" Cara's fists clenched and unclenched. "She let somebody in the building when I wasn't home? She didn't even have the decency to call me? Who is it?"

"You know a guy named Cullen Kane? Another florist in town? He's the guy."

Cara's jaw dropped. She was well and truly flummoxed. "No. That can't be. Not him. Anybody but him."

"You know him?"

She nodded dumbly. "I think he wants to put me out of business. And this is step one in his Kill Cara Kryzik campaign."

They went inside the shop and he sat at the worktable while she recounted how she'd unwittingly managed to become Cullen Kane's business rival.

"It's not like I went after Brooke Trapnell to get her to hire me. But she did, and this wedding is too big a deal for me to pass up. It's the biggest budget I've ever worked with, and I'll make enough money from it to finally pay back my dad—maybe even get a decent delivery van."

Jack still wasn't convinced. "You really think Cullen Kane bought this building out of revenge? That's pretty far-fetched, Cara."

"I know," she admitted. "I'm really not normally this paranoid. But you didn't see the look on his face when I ran into him at the wholesale house. It's like I've taken his favorite toy and he'll do anything to get it back."

Jack drummed his fingertips on the table. "Okay. If that's his game, I don't have to work for him. I'm pretty sure he's getting bids from other contractors. I'll tell him I've got too much work on my plate right now. Which is actually kind of true."

"Thanks." Cara gave his hand a grateful squeeze.

"I'm not the only contractor in town though," he reminded her. "It won't be hard to find somebody who will give him an estimate, and do the work, when it comes right down to it."

"I know." She sighed. "Just out of curiosity, what did Kane say when he called you?"

"He told me his name, that he was in the process of buying a building on Jones Street. That it had retail space on the ground floor—currently occupied by a florist shop."

"Currently," Cara said bitterly. "But not for long."

"He said there was an apartment on the second floor, and that the top floor was currently not occupied."

"That's true," Cara said. "What else did he say? Did he tell you his plans for the building?"

"Not really. He said it looked like the previous owners had been pretty slack on maintenance. He'd seen the water stains on your apartment ceiling, so he wanted the roof and chimneys checked, and was concerned about the air-conditioning unit after seeing how hot it was on the second floor. I think he must have been up there in the past week, now that I think about it."

"Oh my God." Cara shuddered. "It gives me the creeps, knowing he was sneaking around, looking at my stuff, checking everything out, and I had no idea he was even here."

"Yeah. It sucks your landlady didn't even have the decency to let you know she'd let him in to check it out," Jack said.

"Did you tell him you know me?" Cara asked.

"I didn't see any reason to tell him, especially since I figured you'd be pretty upset about all this anyway."

" 'Upset' is putting it mildly."

"Have you ever been up to the top floor?" Jack asked.

"No. There's stairway access through a door at the end of my hallway, but that door was locked when I rented the place. I just figured the Bradleys were too cheap to get it redone. And I was glad to have the building all to myself."

"Did you say the Bradleys were your landlords? Do you mean Bernice and Sylvia Bradley?"

"They're the ones. So, you know them?"

"They live a couple streets over from my parents. Couple of old tightwads," Jack said. He held up a key. "I got the impression Cullen Kane plans to open up the third floor and get it redone. We could take a look—if you're curious."

"I am curious. But I've got too much work to get done this morning. I'm already behind schedule—and we're not even officially open." She glanced up at the clock on the wall. "Bert's got five minutes to get here, and if he's late again today, I might have to start looking for a new assistant as well as a new address."

Jack stood up. "I'll leave you to it then. But if you don't mind, I think I'll run upstairs and take a look at that third floor."

"Suit yourself," Cara said.

He went down the hallway toward the stairs, then thought better of it.

"Hey. Whose wedding are you doing tomorrow? Not Lindsay Crawford and Will Becket by any chance?"

"No way," Cara said. "What? Are you the best man?"

He grinned. "Nah. Just an old friend from high school."

"Does that mean I'll see you there tomorrow night?"

"I wasn't gonna go," Jack said. "Ryan and I are working tomorrow. But now that you mention it . . . maybe I'll change my plans. Especially if you're gonna wear that pink dress of yours."

"Oh geez. That's right. You've seen me in that same dress now what? Three times? How embarrassing."

"I love that dress," Jack said enthusiastically, remembering how it swished about her knees when she danced, and the view of her cleavage. "You were wearing that dress the night we met."

"And I was wearing a dirty T-shirt and grubby shorts earlier that day when you stole my dog," she reminded him.

"Wear the pink dress, okay?" He waggled his eyebrows in that comic way of his. "For me."

36

At the stroke of nine, Bert walked in the back door. He held only one coffee cup in his hand, which he emphatically set down on the worktable before beginning to leaf through the day's phone orders.

"Hello," Cara said pointedly.

"Hey." He got up and went to the walk-in cooler, plucked an armful of roses, carnations, and ferns from the buckets, and slammed the cooler door. In another moment, he was whacking away at the flowers, stripping leaves, snipping stems in a flurry of barely contained violence.

She debated asking Bert why he was pissed—because his body language told her he was. And then she decided she didn't care why he was pissed. Some days it was better not to poke the bear. Was that an expression her father used, or was it one of her grandmother's?

After another fifteen minutes of silent sulking, Bert abruptly slammed down his clippers.

"That police detective? Did you know she showed up at my apartment? That bitch Lillian Fanning told her I stole that epergne!"

"I knew Detective Peebles wanted to talk to you," Cara said quietly.

"Yeah. She basically called me a thief. What the hell would I want with that hideous piece of crap?"

"Just calm down, okay?" Cara was startled to realize she sounded just like her father. "It turns out that hideous piece-of-crap epergne is worth about a hundred and twenty-five thousand dollars. And I told the detective you're not a thief."

Bert's eyes narrowed. "You also told her I was a drunk."

"She asked me what I knew about your background and how I came to hire you. I wasn't going to lie about it, Bert. So yes, I told her you'd been in rehab. I also told her you've been sober for two years and that I trust you completely."

"Except that you don't. Do you?"

Before she could ponder that question, the shop phone rang. Bert snatched up the receiver, listened for a moment, then handed her the phone, his face an expressionless mask.

"It's the Colonel."

Bert was really, really pissed at her.

"Hi Dad," Cara said cautiously. "I was just getting ready to call you. Did you get the check?"

"I got it," the Colonel said. "But it's not what I was expecting. Only half of what you owe?"

She crossed her eyes and glanced over at Bert, whose job it was to make her laugh during ordeals like this. Nothing. He stared studiously down at a handful of pink carnations as if they were the most fascinating things he'd ever seen.

"I know, Dad. But it's the best I can do right now." She took a deep breath. How to make her father understand the financial pressures she was under, without making it sound like she was broke and desperate—especially when she actually was broke and desperate?

"I have a huge wedding coming up July sixth, and in a couple weeks I'll get paid the balance of my fees, and then I'll try to send you the rest."

"Not good enough, young lady," her father said.

"Dad. If you'd just listen . . ."

He wouldn't, of course.

"I'm just glad your mother's not alive to see what's become of you," the Colonel said. "She'd be so disappointed."

Cara blinked. The Colonel invoked her late mother' name rarely, if at all. This was unfair, a sneak attack. What did her mother have to do with her failures at business?

As a child, Cara sensed there was something different about Barbara Kryzik. Her mother loved books and reading, and painting. Maybe that's where Cara had gotten her artistic talents.

Wherever the military sent them, Barbara Kryzik always managed to find an art studio, where she could work on her paintings, mostly dreamy abstract pastels, and a group of bored officers' wives who liked to play cards and day drink. Somehow, it had managed to escape Cara's notice that her mother had quietly become a lush.

In her freshman year of college, second semester, a neighbor had called Cara's dorm room, to register concern that Barbara seemed to have lost an alarming amount of weight. Cara had skipped class and driven home to see for herself. She'd been horrified at her mother's appearance. Her mother had always prided herself on her svelte figure, but now Barbara was gaunt, a withered human coat hanger. Her skin was pale and waxy, her once-lustrous dark hair so thinned that Cara could see patches of scalp.

She'd somehow managed to bundle her mother into the front seat of her car and driven her directly to the emergency room.

The young resident in the emergency room had run a battery of tests on Barbara, and then called Cara aside for a chat.

He was very young, that doctor, young enough and cute enough so that, to her enduring shame, the first thing that crossed Cara's mind was not what he would tell her about her mother, but whether or not he was married—or looking.

"Your mom tells me your dad is stationed overseas?" he'd said. The doctor had blue-green eyes. So light, they reminded her of the water at Panama City Beach, where she'd spent spring break just a few weeks earlier.

"Yes. Turkey right now. Air Force."

"When was the last time he saw your mother?"

Cara had to stop and think. "Maybe a year. A little more? Look. Is it cancer? Do I need to call him and get him home?"

"It's not cancer, and it's not life-threatening. Unless she ignores my advice and keeps on drinking."

Cara still remembered that sensation—that she'd been kicked in the stomach.

"Drinking?" she'd said stupidly. "My mom doesn't drink. I mean, not that much. Maybe some wine at dinner."

"Are you sure?" His voice was so gentle, almost a whisper. "Aren't you away at college?"

"Yes, but . . ."

"She's drunk right now," the doctor had said. "It's a good thing you drove, because her blood alcohol is sky high. Her liver function, everything, points to acute alcoholism. The weight loss—that's a side effect. She's malnourished. And dehydrated. We're giving her fluids, and we'll keep her overnight."

Cara was mesmerized by those sea-green eyes. "And then what?" she heard herself ask.

"That's up to you and your father," the doctor said. "But if it were my mom, I'd want her to go to rehab. Because if she doesn't stop drinking, she really will kill herself."

The colonel had come home from Turkey, and Barbara had cried and apologized and begged for forgiveness, and willingly gone to a very expensive private facility in Florida that her father insisted on calling "the hospital." He'd somehow managed a transfer, and gone right back to work at the base an hour from "the hospital."

Her mother had emerged from rehab proclaiming herself a new woman. And then she'd died six months later from liver failure.

Sometimes Cara wondered if, had her mother lived, she and the Colonel would have stayed married. She wondered whether her father's attitude toward his only child would have somehow softened. Sometimes, and these were the times she was most ashamed of, she wondered what life would have been like if her father had died and her mother were the survivor.

She'd returned to college after her mother's funeral, and at a roommate's insistence, had seen a therapist for grief counseling.

When Cara mentioned her father's career in the military, the therapist had frowned. "If you're looking for your father to fill the hole your mother's death has left in your life, you're going to be disappointed. To say that all career military men are distant and forbidding is a cliché, but from what you've told me about your father, in this case, the cliché fits."

Despite the therapist's warning, Cara had hoped her mother's death would bring her closer to her father. And just as predicted, she'd been disappointed. And her father, in turn, had been disappointed in her. Continually, it seemed, since the day Cara announced she'd left Leo.

Now, it appeared, the Colonel was out of patience with her, and her numerous failings.

"Here's the point that seems to be escaping you," he said irritably. "Your business is not a success. I'm sorry to be blunt, but since you refuse to face facts, I will. I know you've worked hard, but nevertheless, you've run up debts, and it's admirable that you want to pay them off, but there comes a time when it's foolish to sink good money into a bad idea. That's what I want you to realize. I don't intend to let you keep running away from the truth. I can't keep underwriting a doomed enterprise like this flower shop of yours. I think now would be a good time for you to face the truth."

"And come home," she said dully.

"Exactly," the Colonel said.

"Dad?" Cara's temples were throbbing. "My business is not a bad idea. I'll send you the rest of your money as soon as I have it."

She hung up and placed her phone facedown on the tabletop.

37

Bert swiveled around in his chair to face her. "The Colonel really wants his money, huh?"

"He wants me to throw in the towel and admit that I'm a failure," Cara said. She shook her head, as if by shaking it she could shake loose the image of her mother, and her real or imagined disappointments.

From a file folder on her desk Cara picked up her notes about tomorrow's bride, Lindsay Crawford.

She studied the photo of Lindsay's gown. It was the look of choice this season, strapless, of course, with a heavily beaded bodice, asymmetrical shirring at the waist, and a long fishtail train.

Cara held up the photo of the dress for Bert to see. "This dress? I know for a fact Lindsay paid six thousand dollars for it. Six thousand dollars! For a dress she'll wear for what? Four hours, tops? I've had at least five other brides this year with this dress. That's thirty thousand dollars. Do you know what I could do with that kind of money?"

"Tell me about it," Bert said. "And I don't even like their chances that much. She hates his mother, and the word on the street is that he's got a wandering eye. I'm thinking less than a fifty percent chance for those two."

"You're probably right," Cara said. She went to the cooler and gathered the flowers she needed for Lindsay's bouquet: orange tulips, red and yellow roses, and yellow stocks.

Cara gathered all the flowers in her left hand, held them up, then snipped all the stems to the same length.

"Sounds like things got a little tense back there when you were on the phone with your dad," Bert said.

Cara shot him a look. She found a length of the white satin ribbon Lindsay had chosen, measured off three yards, and cut it.

"Yeah. He as much as told me it's a good thing my mom is dead, since I'm such a big disappointment and all."

Cara began stripping the soft, velvety leaves of the stocks. "He never mentions my mom. Well, hardly ever. So today he brought out the big guilt guns. That's how the Colonel plays the game. Pile on the guilt. Your mother's dead, and I'm all alone. You're a failure. At marriage and at business. You're a bad daughter. And a lousy credit risk."

Cara picked up her scissors and carefully trimmed the bright orange stamens from the Stargazer lilies, sweeping them off the tabletop and into the trash can at her feet. She selected four stems of glossy green lemon leaves, arranging them around the perimeter of the bouquet, like a ruff.

Blinking back tears, she picked up the ribbon. Twirling the bouquet with her left hand, she began wrapping the ribbon around the flowers. She felt a sharp stab on her right thumb and looked down to see a single huge droplet of crimson blood drip down onto the flawless white satin of Lindsay Crawford's bouquet.

Cara tossed the ruined bouquet onto the worktable. She'd forgotten to trim the rose thorns. The Colonel was right. She was a hopeless fuckup.

Bert busied himself with the altar flowers, stuffing long stems of gladiolus, ferns, roses, and lilies into the trumpet-shaped vases provided by Lindsay's church.

He glanced over at Cara.

"What are you going to do about the damned epergne? I mean, Lillian can't prove anything. Maybe she lost it herself."

Cara shrugged. "The problem is, it was my responsibility. And I can't prove we didn't lose it."

"In other words, you're saying it's my fault."

Cara stood up from her chair. Her head was throbbing, her back hurt, and she was about sick of her assistant's attitude.

"For the last time, I do not think that you're a thief. Okay? But something is going on with you, and it's affecting your work. You won't tell me what it is, so what am I supposed to think?"

"It's just some personal stuff I'm dealing with."

"You've got personal stuff? Seriously? Look around you, Bert. This shop? I'm about to lose it. Literally. Yeah. Sylvia Bradley sold the building right out from under me. And the new owner is already breathing down my neck to get me out. So I don't give a hairy rat's ass about your personal stuff. Just do your job, okay?"

He got up, shaking his head. He put the altar arrangement on the bottom shelf of the cooler and slammed the door.

"I'm taking lunch. Back in an hour."

"You just got here."

"Dock my pay. I'm gone."

Cara watched through the front window as Bert strode quickly down the sidewalk. She wished she could run away, too. Instead, she picked up Lindsay's bouquet and began cutting away the blood-spattered ribbon.

38

Bert was giving her the silent treatment. And Cara was slinging it right back at him. Throughout the day the phone rang, customers walked in and out of Bloom, and they conducted business. But commerce was the only conversation that day. If she asked Bert a question he answered in clipped monosyllables.

Their normal easy work rhythm was out of sync, and as the day wore on, Cara's anxiety increased. Arrangments for delivery backed up, and without Bert's cooperation, she realized she'd have a long night of work ahead.

Even Poppy sensed the tension in the shop. The dog stayed directly beneath Cara's feet while she worked, moving only to follow her owner every time Cara moved.

At five on the dot, Bert stood up. "I'm gone." Cara glanced over at him, and then at the cooler, where only one of the six boutonnieres for the next day's wedding was completed. She had to bite her tongue to keep from suggesting that if he left for the day, he should stay gone.

"See you," she said.

. . .

At six, her cell phone rang, but she didn't bother to see who was calling. She still had Lindsay's bridesmaids' bouquets to make, the boutonnieres, and two large table arrangements for the buffet table at the reception. Poppy paced around the shop, but there was no time to take the dog for a walk.

Her phone rang three more times over the next two hours, and she let it roll over to voicemail, all the while cursing her absent assistant, and also cursing herself for letting him get away with slacking off.

She was so lost in her work the first soft knock at the shop door barely registered. At the second knock, she frowned. "We're closed!" she called out.

"Cara, it's Jack."

He had a huge brown paper bag with grease spots in one arm, and Shaz's leash looped around his wrist.

"What's this?" Cara asked, as he walked in and set the bag down on the worktable.

"Dinner. I've been calling and calling, but you didn't answer. I rode by an hour ago to see if you were here, and I could see you working through the window, so I figured the only way I was going to see you tonight was if I brought dinner to you."

She sniffed the bag. "Chinese?"

"I wasn't sure what you liked, so I kinda got a variety. Moo shu pork, shrimp with lobster sauce, chicken with snow peas, beef and broccolis, egg drop soup . . ."

Cara's stomach growled loudly, and she opened the bag and began parceling out the white boxes. "You are a lovely man, Jack Finnerty. I just now realized I haven't eaten anything today since a banana at seven this morning."

"Busy day?"

"Busy and horrible. I'd tell you about it, but it would just spoil your appetite. And I'm still not done. Will you hate me if we just eat down here?"

"I could never hate you," he said.

"Hang on and I'll go get some forks and paper plates."

"Plates? I thought that's what those little white boxes were for?"

"Only if you're a lonely old maid," Cara said, heading for the kitchenette. She glanced at the back door and saw a puddle.

"Oh, Poppy," she said with a sigh.

The dog hung her head. Cara felt flooded with guilt. She hadn't taken the dog for a walk, hadn't paid her the least attention all day.

"Not your fault, girl," she muttered, fetching paper towels and spray cleaner.

Cara had to force herself not to scarf down every morsel of fried rice and moo shu pork. He'd brought a six-pack of Tsingtao beer, and Jack sipped his beer and watched with obvious amusement as she made quick work of dinner.

Finally, she set her fork down with a sigh of happiness. "Thank you for that. I feel better already. But how was your day? How's it going out at the Strayhorns'?"

"Good. We got the roof finished. Galvalume standing-seam tin, and it looks awesome. Once we finished that, Libba decided she wanted some windows to lighten the place up. We've ordered those. And we got the ductwork installed for the HVAC. We power-washed all the walls inside and out and now we've also got the floors down. Wait till you see them. We were gonna re-mill them, because of all the gouges and stains from oil and machinery, but once we took a look, we decided to leave them as is. Even Libba loved the character. We just gave the floor a light sanding, and it brought out the most amazing color, a soft gray-brown. . . ."

"Mouse ear," Cara said.

"Huh?"

"Oh, it's a paint color I saw once. I think it's supposed to describe the color of the inside of a mouse's ear, but I like to think of it as that soft gray-brown you just described."

Jack leaned over and with the tip of his little finger removed a grain of rice from the corner of her mouth before kissing her lightly. "Mouse ear? As I remember, you're not too fond of rodents."

"No. Hate rats. And mice." She kissed him back. "But you? I kinda like you."

"Thanks. The feeling is mutual."

Jack followed her into the kitchenette and they cleaned up the dinner dishes together.

"How much more work do you have to do on the barn?" Cara asked.

"The new windows should get shipped this week, and we'll get them installed. And then Libba decided she wanted a powder room, and a kitchen, so we've stubbed in the plumbing for that. . . ."

"A kitchen and a powder room?" Cara frowned. "I had no idea they were doing that too. This is getting pretty expensive, huh?"

"Just materials, so far? We've spent around sixty thousand dollars, and that's not including our labor."

She shook her head. "All that money just for an after-party. Don't get me wrong, I'm glad it turned out to be a good job for you and Ryan, but it just seems like a crazy expense—and all for an after-party. Not even the reception. And why? Brooke Trapnell doesn't even really care about most of this stuff."

"Libba cares," Jack assured her. "She's really stoked about getting that old barn fixed up. She's got all kinds of plans for the place."

"I know. Grandkids. Libba is such a sweet lady. I hope she gets her wish."

"Why wouldn't she? What? You don't think Brooke and Harris want kids?"

"Honestly? I'm not sure Brooke knows what she wants."

"Harris seems like a decent guy. I guess I was expecting some snotty, stuck-up punk. The Strayhorns have more money than God. But he's okay. He came out to the farm yesterday and helped us unload some materials. He asked a lot of questions. He's really interested in the old building."

"He's nice," Cara agreed.

"What? You don't like their chances either?"

Cara shugged. "Doesn't matter. It's not like I'm an expert."

"You seem pretty down tonight."

"Just a little tired. Want to go upstairs?"

He grinned. "I thought you'd never ask."

Their lovemaking had a different edge this time, but neither of them could have said why.

Afterward, Cara lay with her chin on Jack's chest, and with his fingertip he traced slow circles on her bare back. "Want to talk about your day? I'm happy to listen. Are you still worried about your building being sold?"

"It's just been an all-around sucky day. And not just that. I haven't even really had time to think about calling my real-estate agent."

"Why don't you just go see this Cullen Kane? Put your cards on the table. Let him know you want to stay."

She hesitated. "The thing is—maybe I shouldn't stay."

"Hey!" He cupped his hand under her chin. "What's that mean?"

"The Colonel—my father, called this morning. He wants his money back, which is not new, but now he's taken things to an entirely new level of guilt inducement. He actually told me it was a good thing my mom was dead—so she can't see what a disappointment I've become."

She forced a brittle smile. "He never says he misses her. But I know he does, and I guess his pressuring me to come home is his screwed-up way of saying he misses me too."

Jack wrapped both arms around her. "Oh God, honey. I'm sorry. No wonder you're so on edge tonight. So . . . what? You're saying maybe you should close up the shop and go home to be with your dad? I get that. But if you're not sure?"

"No," Cara cut him off. "I don't want to go home. Ohio's his home, not mine. It's the last place I want to be right now. Which pretty much makes me the worst daughter ever. I'm a horrible person, you know."

She gave him a sad smile. "Run away, Jack Finnerty. You're much too nice for a selfish, rotten person like me."

"I'm not going anywhere," he said firmly. "If you don't want to go back to Ohio, you must have your reasons. And you're not a horrible person."

"Maybe not. But I'm pretty screwed up." She gave him a condensed version of her parents' toxic marriage. "I can't remember a time when either of them seemed happy together. When my dad was stationed overseas, my mom resented his being gone. I guess that's when the drinking started. But when he was home, it was even worse. When I was away at college, I used to look for any excuse not to go home to see them. Freshman year, I even went skiing with a friend in Tahoe, just so I wouldn't have to spend Christmas listening to them snipe at each other. I went away for spring break too, and as soon as I got back, that's when she got really sick. Six months later, she was dead."

"Why do you think they stayed together all that time?" Jack asked.

She gave a rueful laugh. "I've asked myself that same question a hundred times. I don't know. Maybe they were so used to miserable they didn't know there were any other possibilities."

Jack squeezed her shoulder.

"In a way, I think maybe that's why when Leo asked me to marry him, I said yes."

"Just so you could get away from home?"

"That was part of it. But a big part of it was Leo's family. They are absolutely the nicest, most normal people you ever met. His parents have been married forever. They ran a business together, and they're retired now, but they still do everything together. They hold hands in the grocery store, and his dad calls his mom his bride. And he has this sweet grandmother—everybody calls her Grannie Annie. Leo has two younger brothers and a sister, who was like my best friend, until the divorce. I think I convinced myself that if I married Leo, we would have the same kind of marriage his parents had."

"If he comes from such a great family, how come Leo turned out so bad?"

"I wish I knew. Sometimes, I wonder if things would have been different if we'd stayed up in Ohio, you know, around his family, instead of moving down here to Savannah."

"No," Jack said succinctly. "He would have had an affair with an Ohio secretary or an Ohio babysitter. Your ex sounds like a player, darlin', and a player is always gonna play."

Cara smiled up at him. "Did you just call me darlin'?"

"I dunno. Did I? Did you like that?"

"Say it again."

"Maybe later. Something I've been wondering. Why were things so bad here for you? Is it the town? Do you hate Savannah?"

"Not really. Well, at first maybe I did. It's just that—this is pathetic. I still sometimes feel like an alien down here. I guess part of it's that I sound like a Yankee."

"Not all the time."

"You're just saying that so you can get in my pants," Cara teased.

"It worked, didn't it?"

"Leo? As soon as we moved down here, he was in his element. He was here a week and he was already saying 'fixin' to,' and 'hey y'all' and 'bless your heart.' He just fit right in."

"Like a pig in slop," Jack said.

"Huh?"

"It's a Southern thing, darlin'. And you're saying you didn't fit in?"

"Not really. After I left Leo, I didn't even have a girlfriend I could call up to help me move. I only had Bert, who, come to think of it, is my only girlfriend in Savannah."

Cara sighed deeply. "That's why I'm so bugged by how he's been acting lately. He's apparently got some new boyfriend he won't talk about. Which is not like Bert at all. Usually, he wants to spill all the tawdry little details of his latest conquest. I don't know. Maybe I'm just jealous."

"It sounds like you've got good reason to be upset with him, if he's not doing his job," Jack pointed out.

"The thing is, if he keeps up this way, I won't have any other choice but to fire him. And I don't want that. I want to keep him, as my assistant, and my friend."

Jack kissed her shoulder and ran his hands down her back, lingering on her butt. "I'll be your friend." He pulled her closer and nudged a knee between her thighs. "I'm a really awesome friend."

"Mmm," Cara said slowly. "But can you fix flowers?"

39

In the morning, Cara sat up and marveled at the man in bed beside her. Sunlight splashed across his shoulders, so brown against her white sheets. His dark hair was tousled and his cheek was stubbled. His breathing was deep and even. She could have watched him like that all morning, he was that nice to wake up to.

It had rained hard overnight, and with the windows open, there was still somewhat of a cooling breeze.

They'd closed the bedroom door the night before, and now she heard a soft scratching at the door. Poppy? Or Shaz? She swung her legs over the side of the bed, but before she could move, a dark arm snaked around her waist.

She glanced over her shoulder. "Don't go," Jack mumbled.

"Gotta let the dogs out. Go back to sleep."

"Mmm. Come back to bed."

Cara pulled on a pair of drawstring cotton boxer shorts and a cami and slid her feet into flip-flops. The dogs raced each other down the stairs, and out into the courtyard garden.

She went into the kitchenette and started the coffeepot. Did she have any food in the house for breakfast? There was nothing in the kitchenette fridge, except a pint of half-and-half, some bottles of water, two cans of Red Bull, and a jar of pickles. And two cardboard cartons of leftover Chinese takeout. Shrimp with lobster sauce for breakfast? She shuddered.

When the coffee was ready, she fixed two mugs. Realized she didn't know how the man she'd just slept with took his coffee. She shrugged. She knew the most important things there were to know about Jack Finnerty. He was kind and thoughtful. He snored, but softly. Unlike other men she'd been with, he didn't fall asleep instantly after lovemaking. She smiled, thinking back to last night. He'd been the only good thing about Friday.

Upstairs, she brushed her teeth quickly and finger-combed her messy hair. She set a mug on the nightstand and stood looking down at Jack.

Without warning he reached out, grabbed her hand, and pulled her back onto the bed.

"Hey," she protested. "I thought you were sleeping."

He rolled over on his side to face her and ran his hands up under her camisole, brushing her nipples with his thumbs. He kissed her deeply, and she tasted toothpaste. "You weren't asleep at all!"

"It's called playin' possum," he chuckled.

Their coffee got cold. Eventually, she made another pot. Jack leashed up the dogs and walked them over to Parker's on Drayton Street, bringing back two sausage biscuits—for him—and a blueberry muffin—for her.

While he was gone, Cara showered and dressed quickly in shorts and a tank top. Not even nine o'clock yet, and it was already getting hot and sticky upstairs.

They took their coffee and breakfast out into the courtyard garden. Jack pointed out a suspicious mound of dirt beneath one of the crepe myrtles. "Looks like Shaz was trying to tunnel out of here this morning. Sorry about that."

"It could just as well have been Poppy," Cara said.

She'd propped open the back door to the shop so the dogs could come and go, and now they heard a loud knocking at the front door.

"Ignore that," Cara told Jack. "Probably some guy desperate to buy flowers for a forgotten anniversary."

The knocking continued.

"Sounds pretty desperate," Jack said. "Maybe you should take pity on the poor guy and bail him out."

Cara rolled her eyes, but she stood up and went to the front door, where the knocking continued.

"Hang on," she called. "I'm coming."

She pulled up the shade and stared out at her desperate customer. Only it was no customer. It was Leo. Her ex.

Her first instinct was to pull the shade back down and run the other way. But it was too late for that. He'd already seen her.

He was dressed for work: sport coat, tie, slacks, polished loafers. His Ray-Bans hung from a band around his neck. He looked good, like the kind of cute guy you'd flirt with if you stood next to him in line at Starbucks. Which, come to think of it, was how they'd met all those years ago. Incredibly, he held a huge bunch of lilacs in his right hand, and a box of cheap drugstore chocolates in the other.

She unlocked the door and opened it.

"Cara!" His eyes lit up. "I didn't, I mean, I wasn't sure you'd be here. Or, if you were, if you'd open the door."

"I'm here, Leo," she said, forcing herself to look stern. "What do you want?"

"Here." He thrust the flowers and chocolates toward her. His sandy blond hair flopped into his eyes. In another minute, if she wasn't careful, she'd push his hair back, straighten his tie. Old habits died hard. Instead, she kept her hands at her side, fists clenched tightly.

"What's this?" she asked.

"It's an anniversary present. Happy anniversary Cara."

Anniversary? She frowned. And then it dawned on her. Seven years ago today, she'd made the biggest mistake of her life.

"Leo, we're divorced. We don't have an anniversary anymore."

"Sure we do. Just because you signed a piece of paper, that doesn't change the fact that we got married." He leaned in and touched her cheek. "I've missed you, baby."

She batted his hand away.

"Really? You missed me? Why's that? Did your girlfriend find herself another married man to fool around with?"

He rocked back on his heels a bit, eyes wide in surprise. He wasn't used to this attitude. Not from her. She'd been sweet as pie most of her life. Fun-loving, easygoing, eager to please. It had been Leo's idea to move to Savannah, a year after their marriage. A great job opportunity, he said. Unlimited chance for advancement in his sales career.

So she'd smiled and nodded, then packed up her life in Columbus, Ohio. Waved good-bye to family and friends. She'd quit the job she loved, managing a vintage clothing store near the university. And she'd moved to the South—a place she'd never even visited, except for a couple of spring break trips to Florida—to Savannah, a place where she didn't know a single living soul.

That Cara was gone now, she told herself. Never to return.

Leo, a born salesman, never met a deal he couldn't close.

"Aww, Cara," he said, his voice low, mouth turned down. A textbook picture of contrition.

"That's all over with. It was over as soon as it began. I was such a jerk. I can't believe what I put you through. And for what? For nothing. Swear to God, you were always the only girl for me. The only girl I ever loved. My mom calls me every Sunday and wants to know when we're getting back together."

Her face hardened. "Tell her we're not getting back together. Tell her you cheated on me."

"Grannie Annie had a stroke last month. Did you know that? Dad fixed her up an apartment in the garage at our place. She still has our wedding picture on her dresser."

She sighed. "Don't do this to me, Leo. Please?" She had her hand on the door, was about to close it. But he was too quick for her. Always had been.

He lowered his head, put his lips next to her ears before she could jerk away. "Cara Mia, why?"

It was a line from the song, the stupid song her mother named her for. In another minute, if she let him, he'd be warbling "Must we say good-bye?"

"This won't work, Leo," she said, shaking her head sadly.

"Just let me take you out to dinner. No strings, just a nice dinner with a nice bottle of wine. Please? It's killing me, to think of you alone on our anniversary."

"I won't be alone," Cara said. "And as it happens, I already have plans tonight."

"Oh yeah. Right. Saturday, and it's wedding season so you're probably working. But what about after? A late dinner? I know the maître d' at the new place on Orleans Square. . . ."

Just then, Poppy trotted over to see what her owner was doing. She nudged the back of Cara's knees with her head.

Leo looked stunned. "A dog? You got a dog?"

He knelt down and tugged at Poppy's collar, until she was halfway out the door. "Hey, fella," Leo crooned, scratching her nose, then her ears. "What a good fella. What a good dog!" He looked up at Cara. "I never saw a dog like this before. What kind is he?"

"*She* is a golden doodle—a cross between an English golden retriever and a standard poodle."

"Beautiful animal," Leo said. Poppy, the shameless little slut, fell hard for him, flopping onto the ground and rolling over so he could scratch her belly. If she'd had a telephone number, she would have given it to him.

"What's her name?"

"Poppy," Cara said.

"Figures. A flower name for a flower girl's dog." He stood up. "I always thought we'd get a dog. Pick one out together. Take it for a run in the park."

He gave her that crooked little grin that always used to work, back in the day. "Another thing to add to my list of regrets. You went and got a dog without me."

Enough, she thought.

"Look, Leo. I have to go. I actually do have a wedding tonight, and every second I stand here with you puts me that much further behind."

"I know, I know," he said. "Tick tock, right? You're quite the career girl these days, from what I hear." He leaned in again, and before she could stop him, he was kissing her, a lingering brush on the lips.

"Happy anniversary, Cara Mia mine. I'll call you."

She was just about to close the door.

"Cara?" Jack stood in the hallway entrance to the shop. He strode to her side and glared at Leo.

"What the hell?"

Leo glared right back, then pointed at Jack. "You. The guy in the towel. Last week."

"Yeah. That was me. And you were the guy in the truck, cruising down the lane."

Cara looked from Jack to Leo. "You two know each other?"

Leo shook his head. "What? You're sleeping with this guy?"

Jack put an arm across her shoulder. "*This* is your ex? The dude is stalking you, Cara. He drove down the lane twice last week while you were gone. Hell, the way he stared at me, I thought he was getting ready to proposition me."

"In your dreams, towel boy," Leo sneered.

"That's enough, kids," Cara said. She gave her ex-husband a not-so-gentle backward shove. Then she closed and locked the door. And pulled down the shade.

"What was that he called you?" Jack asked.

"Cara Mia. Mia is my middle name," Cara said. "What's your middle name?"

"Joseph. John Joseph. But back to you. So, your name is Cara Mia, like the song?"

"Yep. Jay and the Americans. My mom was a big fan."

"Mine too," Jack said. He jerked his head in the direction of the front door. "What did he want? Besides to suck face with you?"

"He seems to think it's our anniversary." She looked down and realized she was still holding the flowers and candy he'd thrust into her hands. Cara walked over to the trash can and dropped them in.

"He's a tool," Jack said. "And the next time I catch him driving by here, I'm gonna take my pry bar and put a big ol' dent in that pretty-boy Lexus of his."

"Ooh. Drama," Cara said. But she was smiling when she said it.

40

It had taken Cara two weeks of calling, emailing, and texting, but she'd finally gotten Brooke and Harris to agree to meet for lunch and go over wedding plans.

But when Brooke arrived in the lobby at Johnny Harris, the iconic barbecue restaurant on Victory Drive in midtown, she was alone. She was dressed in a black and white herringbone checked suit, with black pumps and a pink silk blouse, and to Cara's shock, the bride's long, lustrous dark hair had been chopped off at chin length.

"Harris's flight from New York didn't come in," Brooke said. "Anyway, he pretty much said he's fine with whatever we decide." She caught Cara staring at her hair, and she pushed a strand behind one ear.

"You don't like it, do you?"

"It's just . . . different," Cara said. "Usually my brides are trying to grow their hair out before the wedding."

Brooke shrugged. "It's been so hot. And long hair is such a pain. Blowing it dry and everything, I just don't have the time. . . ."

The bride looked pointedly down at her watch, and then at the vacant hostess stand. It was a Monday, and the restaurant was already crowded. "Should we have made a reservation? I only have an hour before I need to get back to the office."

"The hostess will be back in a minute. A party of twelve came in right before you did," Cara assured her. She couldn't get over Brooke's hair. It was not a flattering cut, emphasizing the sharp planes of her hollow cheeks.

"What does Harris think of it?"

"He says he loves it, but I'm not so sure. Mom would never say anything critical—at least to my face. And of course, Patricia and my dad are appalled. Which kind of makes it fun."

"Brooke? Brooke Trapnell?"

A tall slender man with sun-streaked shoulder-length brown hair broke away from the group of men with whom he'd just entered the lobby. He wore a forest-green golf shirt with an embroidered logo, khaki cargo shorts, and Topsider deck shoes.

Brooke turned to see who was addressing her. For a moment, she looked puzzled, but then her face lit up. "Petey!" She flung her arms around the newcomer's neck. They hugged tightly.

Brooke pulled back a little, beaming up at his face. "Oh my God, Pete. I can't believe it's really you. Where have you been? What are you doing here?"

"Well, you know, I've been out west, Montana and Colorado, working for the Park Service. And I've just transferred here a couple months ago."

"Here? You're back in Savannah? That's awesome."

"Actually, no. I'm working on Cumberland Island. I'm just up here today for some meetings with our regional director." He gestured toward the group of men who were drifting toward the dining room. "What about you? Are you still living here in town? I heard you graduated from law school, so what, you're a lady lawyer now?"

Brooke's laugh was almost giddy. "I don't know about the lady part, but yeah, I'm a second-year associate. I do mostly corporate law."

"Cool." He snapped his fingers. "Hey. Didn't your folks used to have a place down on Cumberland?"

"My mom's family does. Loblolly. I can't believe you remember that after all these years."

"Do you ever go down there?"

"Hey, Pete." One of the park-service men was standing at the hostess stand, gesturing toward him. "Our table's ready."

"Coming."

Pete turned back to Brooke. "Gotta go. But we need to catch up. Wait. Let me give you my card."

He dug in the pocket of his cargo shorts, but came out empty-handed. "Damn. Wouldn't you know? I didn't bring any with me."

Brooke reached into her pocketbook and brought out a sterling silver case. She withdrew a thick vellum square and handed it to him. "Here's mine."

"Pete!"

"Coming!"

When they were seated and the waitress had taken their orders, Cara brought out her iPad, and they got down to business.

"So. Here's the reception menu we came up with after you had to leave the other day. . . ."

"You mean after Patricia took over the whole thing?" Brooke scanned the screen, nodding. "Sure. This looks okay. But it seems like a lot of food to me."

"We're doing a seated dinner," Cara reminded her. With her fingertip, she scrolled over to the next page. "These are the appetizers that will be passed during cocktail hour. . . ."

Brooke wrinkled her nose. "Fried calamari? Gross. Let me guess. Patricia's idea?"

"Layne's version is really lightly battered. If you want, I can set it up for you and Harris to taste that, and the rest of the appetizers."

"Never mind." Brooke took a bite of her salad and looked around the big, dome-ceilinged dining room, her eyes lingering on the men taking up a table at the far end of the room.

"Pete? Was that his name? An old friend?" Cara asked.

"Hmm?" Brooke's face flushed. "Yeah. Pete Haynes. We uh, I guess we sort of had a thing, the summer before I left for college. But then I went away, to

University of Virginia, and he was already a sophomore at Georgia. You know how that goes."

"And this was the first time you've seen him since then?"

Brooke stabbed a piece of chicken with her fork. "Um. Not really." She looked away, then down at her plate, then leaned forward across the table. "My parents totally don't know anything about this. Okay? In fact, none of my friends know it."

Cara waited.

"Summer after I graduated from UVA, my dad got me this big-deal internship with our congressman. In Washington." Brooke rolled her eyes. "What a blowhard that guy was. Typical, right? Anyway, Pete was living there too that summer, he'd graduated with a degree in marine biology, and he'd gotten a desk job working for some government agency. Something to do with endangered species? And we kind of, you know. Got together."

"Dated?" Cara laughed. "Brooke, you're almost thirty. Why does that have to be a secret from your parents? Or your friends?"

Brooke's face colored. "Because at the time, Harris and I were unofficially engaged."

"Oh."

"Yeah. It's like that." She smiled sadly. "Technically, I was sleeping with two guys. Which is *not* who I am. In August, Pete had a job offer, with the Park Service, out in Montana. His dream job. And he wanted me to go with him." Brooke fiddled with a strand of her hair.

"But you said no."

"I was supposed to start law school at Emory. Harris was already there, starting on his MBA. He'd rented a house for us. And right around then, that's when the shit hit the fan with my parents. My dad moved out, and moved in with Patricia. My mom was a mess. . . ."

"Bad timing," Cara said sympathetically.

"The worst." Brooke stared down at her half-eaten salad. She picked up a cellophane-wrapped package of saltines and crumbled it between her fingertips.

"It's probably a good thing Mom couldn't come today." Brooke looked around the dining room, its dark paneling and leatherette booths, at the domed blue-painted ceiling with twinkling lights. "This was their place. Hers and dad's. Back in the seventies, when they were dating, it was kind of a big deal to come to dinner here."

"Really?" To Cara, Johnny Harris was just a barbecue restaurant. She liked their barbecue sauce, but it was hard for her to imagine the place as a hot nightspot.

"Yeah. They'd get all dressed up. I remember we used to have a photo album, with a picture of them sitting at one of those booths over there." Brooke pointed to the opposite end of the room. "You can't really tell from here, but there were curtains you could draw, for privacy, and you could push a little button to summon your waiter. The buttons are still there. Anyway, if you can believe it, Dad had this bushy hair, and big ol' sideburns and a kind of handlebar mustache. He looked like a porn star! And Mom's hair was really long and straight, and she wore dangly earrings. And she's sitting right beside Dad, with his arm around her shoulders and he's totally looking right down her cleavage!"

Brooke got a sudden fit of giggles, which were over nearly as soon as they'd begun. "After they split up, I thought Mom probably burned all those old pictures. But the last time I was home, I was in her bedroom, and she'd told me I could borrow her pearls, for this stupid engagement party, and I found that picture in the bottom of her jewelry box."

"You think your mom's still not over him?"

"Not really. She tries to put on a good show around me, but I think she's still really sad. And hurt."

"Does she date?"

"My mom? No. I wish she would though."

Brooke's gaze had returned to the table where Pete Haynes was sitting.

"How about you?" Cara asked. "And your friend Pete? After your breakup, he was okay?"

"Yeah. . . ." Brooke's voice trailed off. "Pete—he knew how my parents were. Well, my dad, anyway. Snobby, right? Pete wasn't from the wrong side of the tracks, not at all, but he went to public high school, that kind of thing."

"Did Pete know about you and Harris?"

Brooke's eyes widened. "Oh God, no. That summer, it was just such an odd thing for me. It was like the first time I realized I was an adult, and I didn't have to be under my dad's thumb for the rest of my life."

"A summer of rebellion," Cara said. "I get that. My dad was career military. He still expects everybody to stand at attention and salute."

"Rebellion. Exactly. But at some point, even a rebel has to figure out what to do with their life. And for me, law school and Emory made sense. I've always wanted to be a lawyer. And Harris made sense. He's sweet and loyal and smart."

"Harris is a good guy," Cara said.

Brooke twisted her engagement ring. "The absolute best. He loves me. I don't know why, or how I got this lucky, but Harris loves me. Pete was cool with whatever I wanted to do. He probably only asked me to move out there with him because he thought he *should* ask."

"And you didn't keep in touch after that? At all?"

Brooke colored again.

"Facebook?" Cara guessed.

"He doesn't know it's me," Brooke said. "I made up a name, said I was a friend of a friend of a friend of his who likes whitewater rafting."

"Did you know he'd moved back to Georgia?" Cara asked.

"No! Pete's hardly ever on Facebook. Occasionally he posts a picture of his puppy, or a sunset or something. Nothing personal."

Cara arched one eyebrow. She'd done enough Facebook stalking of her own to know how this worked.

"You're telling me you don't check his status?"

"Not in a relationship," Brooke said, her voice barely a whisper. "Anyway, what else do we need to discuss? About the wedding? Patricia texts me every day, asking for a status report. She's making me nuts."

"Right. Okay. Did you get a chance to look at the photographers' websites that I sent you? Any preferences?"

"Yeah, but I thought Patricia already hired some photographer."

"Meredith. She only does portraits. This photographer is for the actual wedding."

"Geez. Does everything have to be so complicated? Anyway, yeah, I liked them both. Mom really liked the woman—what's her name?"

"Rita McCall. I think Rita really has a nice way with candids and black-and-white. And she's so good at capturing the mood of the event."

"Fine. Then let's go with Rita McCall," Brooke said. "What else? I've only got a few more minutes."

"Hmm. We really need to discuss table markers and favors. I've some ideas. Since the Strayhorns are in shipping, I thought we could do these miniature shipping containers, stencil your name and Harris's on one side . . ."

"Great."

"I've got a great artisanal chocolatier in town, he'll come up with a signature chocolate filling for us—do you like milk chocolate or dark chocolate?"

"Dark, I guess. I don't actually eat a lot of sweets."

Not surprising, Cara thought, looking at the bride's picked-over salad.

"I thought we could do maybe six or eight pieces of chocolate in each container."

"Okay."

"Now," Cara said, taking a deep breath. "The seating chart. It's going to get complicated, it always is when there's been a divorce in the family. You've got the list of people who've already responded, so if you would, maybe give me your thoughts on who should be seated where."

"My thoughts?" Brooke shook her head impatiently. "I look at the list, and I don't know most of these people. Maybe Harris does, but I don't. Here's all I want, Cara. Just don't put Patricia anywhere near me. Or my mom. Or actually, if you could just not put her in the same room with us, that would be good."

"Be real, please Brooke," Cara said sharply. She scrolled back over to the seating chart she'd made up—circles and rectangles drawn to scale and arrayed around the ballroom at Cabin Creek. "Just take a look, please, this is important, if not to you, to your parents and the Strayhorns. . . ."

Brooke frowned, but bent her head and studied the chart. A shadow fell over the iPad and they both looked up. Pete Haynes cleared his throat, as though he were about to make a speech.

"Listen, Brooke. I've got to get on the road if I'm going to make the afternoon ferry from St. Marys over to Cumberland." He handed her a scrap of paper. "That's my email. Cell-phone service on the island is pretty crappy. And I don't get up to Savannah that much because of the project I'm working on. With the wild horses. But if you're coming down there anytime, I was thinking it'd be great to get together. . . ."

Brooke looked at the slip of paper, then placed it on the tabletop. She looked over at Cara. "Pete, this is Cara Kryzik."

"Hi," he said, shaking Cara's hand politely. "I'm an old friend of Brooke's. Pete Haynes. Sorry to interrupt your lunch."

"Not at all," Cara murmured.

"The thing is, Pete, Cara's my wedding planner. I'm getting married next month."

"July the sixth," Cara said helpfully.

If he was stunned, he didn't show it. "You're engaged?"

Brooke held up her left hand, where Harris Strayhorn's diamond solitaire twinkled from her slender ring finger. "I am."

"Oh." He shifted from one foot to the other as the news sunk in. "That's great. Good for you. Congratulations."

"Thanks," Brooke said. She gave him a bright smile. "How about you? Is there a wife down there on Cumberland Island?"

"No," he said, pressing his lips together. "Nothing like that. Anyway, I gotta get going. It was nice to see you again, Brooke. And uh, good luck with the wedding and everything. I hope you'll, uh, be very happy."

"I'm sure we will be," Brooke said. Cara watched Brooke watching him weave his way through the crowded tables to the dining room exit. The waitress came over, and dropped the leatherette folder with the bill on the table, but Brooke picked it up before Cara could.

"My treat," Brooke said. She tucked some bills in the envelope. They both stood to leave.

"You'll go over the seating chart?" Cara prompted.

"I swear. Email it to me again, and I'll let you know," Brooke promised.

"Today?"

"Absolutely."

Cara stood and took her pocketbook from the back of the chair. She couldn't help but notice that the slip of paper with Pete Haynes's email address was right where Brooke had left it.

41

Cara was headed back to the shop when her cell phone rang.

"Hi Brooke. Did you have a chance to look at the seating chart this quickly?"

"Sorry, not yet. Cara?"

"Yes?"

"About what I said. Earlier, in the restaurant. About me and Pete. You probably think I'm awful. A total slut."

"I don't think that," Cara said. "Anyway, it was a long time ago. You said yourself, until today you hadn't seen the guy in years."

"It's been five years. I'm not trying to excuse what I did, but you have to understand. That summer? Before I moved to Atlanta and started law school, it was like I was in this little bubble, and the only reality was me and Pete. I still can't explain it. I loved Harris, and I knew we would get married eventually. But he was in Atlanta, and I was in DC. And Pete was right there. And we had so much fun together, it was like we were kids back in high school again."

"Brooke. Why are you telling me all this? I'm not judging you."

"I know," Brooke said, sighing. "Maybe I'm trying to explain it to myself. The thing is, at the time, it didn't seem wrong. As long as Harris didn't know about Pete, and Pete didn't know about Harris, I thought nobody could get hurt. And they didn't. It was just that one summer."

"Five years ago," Cara said.

"And it's over," Brooke said. "Okay. This was weird. Forget I called. Forget I told you any of it."

"Any of what?"

"Thanks, Cara," Brooke said.

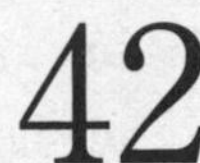

42

The bride leaned across Cara's desk and stabbed a long pearly pink fingernail at page 72 of the March 2009 issue of *Martha Stewart Weddings*. The page was dog-eared, and the rest of the magazine bristled with pink Post-it notes.

"This one. This is the exact bouquet I want. I've saved this magazine since I was eighteen years old. I picked out my wedding dress because I knew it would go with this bouquet."

Cara groaned inwardly. How well she knew this particular wedding bouquet. She was sure it was the most-pinned item on every single bride's Pinterest page in the universe. She wanted to rip page 72 out of this magazine, ball it up, and burn it.

Instead, she did what she always did. She picked up a pencil and pointed it at each flower in the bouquet.

"Heather, these flowers here? They are Casablanca lilies. They wholesale at thirty dollars a stem. I count five stems in this bouquet—so that's a hundred and fifty dollars right there. These pretty ruffly flowers? Like overblown roses? These are premium peonies. This size bunch wholesales at about seventy-five dollars."

"What?" Heather drew back as though she'd been slapped. "Thirty dollars for one lily?"

"Yes. Although one stem will have multiple blossoms. They're imported." Cara pointed at the petite bell-shaped flowers edging the infamous Martha Stewart bouquet. "Now these—these are the budget killers."

"Yes. Lilies of the valley," Heather said eagerly. "Kate Middleton's whole bouquet was made of them."

"Yes," Cara said. "I'm aware." Which was the understatement of the year. Ever since the royal wedding of Prince William and Kate Middleton, she'd been besieged with brides insisting upon having lilies of the valley.

"Here's the thing, Heather. Lilies of the valley are so tiny, you need a lot of them to make any impact at all. One tiny bunch, which is ten skinny stems, is ninety dollars. I'd say there are at least six bunches in this bouquet. That's three hundred and sixty dollars."

Heather's mother had been sitting beside the bride, frowning. But now the MOB's eyes bugged out. "That must be a mistake. We didn't spend three hundred and sixty dollars for her older sister's whole flower budget."

Heather rolled her eyes. "Mama, Jessica got married eight years ago! She only had one bridesmaid, and we had the reception at your house."

"It was still a lovely wedding," the mother insisted. "And I can tell you right now, your daddy is not going to pay five hundred and forty dollars for some itty-bitty flowers just because some English princess had them."

"Also? Besides being expensive, Lilies of the valley are extremely fragile. Your wedding is in August. In summer months, our suppliers won't even guarantee what kind of condition they'll be in when they arrive here." Cara gave the MOB an apologetic shrug.

"No lilies," the mother shot back.

Cara reached over and gently closed the March 2009 issue of *Martha Stewart Weddings*. "Heather, the bouquet you're looking at costs roughly twelve hundred dollars."

"No way," Heather breathed.

"Way. And what did you say your flower budget was for this wedding? With, what? Six bridesmaids?"

Heather looked at her mother for guidance. "Two thousand. And not a penny more."

"Okay," Cara said. Heather looked like a sweet girl. And her mother, as far as MOBs went, seemed nice, too. But with their budget, they could not afford a full-scale Bloom wedding. And with Cara's current cash-flow situation, she couldn't afford to take them on pro bono.

"Let's do this. Let's think about a nice, simple bouquet for you, Heather. I can make you up something very pretty, with white hydrangeas, tea roses, and white hypericum berries, for around a hundred and fifty. It won't be anywhere as big or showy as the bouquet in your magazine, but it will still be lovely with your dress."

Heather's nose wrinkled. "Hydrangeas? Like my meemaw grows in her yard?"

"Yes. Hydrangeas." Cara shoved Heather's magazine aside and snapped open her iPad. She scrolled through the photos of weddings she'd done until she came to what she privately called "Bargain Basement Bouquet."

"We can get these in all white, in a pale green, shades of pinks, blues, creams, and purples," Cara said.

"That's beautiful." Heather's mother nodded emphatically.

"It is kind of pretty," the bride begrudgingly admitted. "What do we do about the bridesmaids' bouquets?"

"You go minimalist," Cara said. "One or two stems of hydrangeas, and you do a ruffle of hydrangea leaves to fill it out."

"Wait. Are you saying you want me to make the bridesmaids' bouquets?"

"If you do them, you can get away with spending around fifteen dollars apiece, and that includes a pretty white satin ribbon binding, which you can buy at Michael's. You can find lots of tutorials online that show you how to make a simple bouquet. If I do them, I have to charge markup and labor, and that's going to bring the price of each of those bouquets to sixty dollars," Cara explained.

"I never heard of such a thing," the MOB said. "Anyway, we still need flowers for the church and the reception. Who's going to do them?"

Heather's eyes were pleading. Her mother was glaring at both of them.

"All right," Cara relented. "I'll do your bouquet and the church flowers, for two thousand dollars. But the altar flowers will also have to be carried over to your church parlor for the reception. You'll need to deputize one of your bridesmaids or girlfriends to be in charge of that."

"I'll ask Jessica to do it," Heather said.

"Two thousand is a really tight budget," Cara warned. "I need you to understand that you won't have exotic or imported flowers. We can do a lot with hydrangeas and carnations and glads and spray roses and local foliage. Do you have any friends with pretty gardens? We can use hosta leaves and ivy and ferns for greenery and that will save you a lot of money."

"My sister is in a garden club," Heather's mom said. "She'll let us cut whatever we need."

"Wonderful," Cara said. She stood up, as a signal that their meeting was over. "One more thing? The way this works is, you pay me half today, and the other half is due two weeks before the wedding."

"A thousand dollars? Today?" The MOB clutched her pocketbook to her chest, as though Cara might make a lunge for it at any moment.

"Yes," Cara said firmly. Some things were not negotiable.

"Mama?" Heather put an arm around her mother's shoulders. "We agreed, right? Two thousand for flowers."

"But I thought we'd just look at pictures, and discuss," the mother said.

Cara felt her patience wearing thin. In reality, her patience was flat gone. She gave the two women a bright smile. "You're welcome to check around with other florists, but this is standard in our business. I really can't give you any more of a consultation without receiving a deposit check. Today."

Let them walk, Cara thought. *I can't afford this kind of charity. I might not even still be in business in August.*

"Mama?" Heather was opening her own pocketbook, taking out her checkbook. She wrote the check, ripped it from the book, and handed it to Cara.

"Thank you," Heather said fervently. "Thank you so much."

. . .

Bert had been sitting at his side of the worktable, putting together hospital bouquets, listening throughout the consultation. When mother and daughter were gone, he slapped his scissors on the table.

"Looorrrrd," he drawled. "When I looked out the window and saw those two pull up in that tired old Ford Fiesta I almost told them they'd come to the wrong place. What I don't get is why you didn't just tell them you can't do a Bloom wedding for two thousand dollars. Why didn't you just tell them to take their sad little selves out to Sam's Club? They can get a whole lot of wilted chrysanthemums and daisies and carnations for two thousand dollars over there."

"Cut it out, Bert," Cara said sharply. "I can't blame the girl for wanting something nice. Most girls dream about their wedding day their whole life. It's not Heather's fault all those magazines and websites love to feature fairytale weddings—but never explain what the price tags are."

"You're not doing her any favor indulging in her little fantasy world," Bert said. "She'll never find even a half-assed photographer or a caterer with the kind of piddly budget she's talking about. She should just get her sourpuss mama to give her the money she'd spend on a tacky wedding and then elope. Spend the money on a trip to South of the Border, or a down payment on a double-wide."

"Fun is fun, but now that's just mean," Cara said. "When did you get to be such a bitch?"

"And when did you get so high-minded and holier-than-thou?" he shot back. "Come on, Cara, lighten up, will you? We always used to have such fun around here, but lately, you're so serious. Everything is so dire. Frankly, it's depressing."

Bert's phone, which he'd placed on the worktable beside him, buzzed to signal an incoming text. He looked down, read it, then scrambled down off his high-backed stool. "I'm going to lunch."

"You just got back from a coffee run that took thirty minutes," Cara said. "And you came in thirty minutes late this morning. You've been pulling this same disappearing act all week. I warned you earlier, Bert. We've got Mary

Payne's ninetieth-birthday party tonight, and the bar association dinner at the Chatham Club tomorrow night, not to mention the phone orders we need to get done and delivered. I can't get it all done by myself. And I shouldn't have to."

"Are you telling me I can't take a lunch hour? That's probably against the law, you know."

"I'm telling you you've already taken a lunch hour," she shot back. "If you're really hungry, I'll go upstairs and fix you a sandwich, or we can get a pizza delivered. But we both know that's not the case. We both know that text you just got is a booty call from your new boyfriend."

"Screw you!" Bert said angrily. "Just because you've got no life and live like a nun, doesn't mean I have to." He picked up his phone and walked deliberately toward the door.

"I mean it, Bert," Cara said, clenching and unclenching her fists. "If you walk out that door now, you're done. Don't bother coming back."

He had his hand on the doorknob. He hesitated, then strode back toward the worktable.

Relief flooded Cara's body. She didn't want this. But he'd pushed her right to the edge.

Bert opened the drawer on his side of the worktable. He picked up the backpack he'd slung over his chair and tossed in a paperback book, his favorite scissors, and a coffee mug. Then he reached up to the shelf behind the table, took his iPod station and iPod, and threw them into the bag with the rest of his belongings.

"I'm not giving you a reference for another job," Cara called, just as he reached the shop door.

"I don't need one." He slammed the door. Hard.

43

Poppy stood at the front window, watching the squirrel in the tree outside, and waiting, Cara felt sure, for her friend Bert to change his mind and come back.

"He's gone," Cara said, getting up to scratch the dog's ears and toss her a conciliatory puppy treat. "Anyway, he's just a man. They come and they go, girl, and when one decides to leave, all you can do is get out of the way."

Poppy gave her a baleful look, then concentrated on chewing her treat. In the meantime, a battered white pickup truck pulled up to the curb outside, parking in the loading zone. A youngish man in paint-spattered overalls and a green John Deere tractor cap got out of the truck and stood on the sidewalk. He pulled a smart phone from the bib of his overalls, stepped backward and began taking photos. He trotted across the street and snapped more photos as Cara stood, watching.

The man recrossed and walked past the shop window and out of her line of sight. Cara opened the door and peered out, just in time to see him rounding the corner and turning south on Whitaker.

"Here, Poppy!" Cara locked the front door and headed for the rear of the shop and the door into the courtyard. Poppy bounded out into the garden and gave a short, surprised yelp as the stranger stepped into the garden through the door from the lane.

"Hey!" Cara called, her voice sharp. "What do you think you're doing?"

Poppy barked loudly, and lunged forward, but Cara caught her by her collar.

"Uh, the landlord sent me over." Seeing him up close, she could see he was probably in his mid-twenties, with brown hair sticking out from the back of his cap, and a string of tattoos on both forearms. He took a half step backward.

"Which landlord?"

He looked confused. "The one who owns this building, I guess. Wanted me to give him some estimates for doing all the work needs doing."

"Him? The last I heard, Sylvia Bradley still owns this building. Was she the one who called you?"

"Look, ma'am, I don't want any trouble. I'm just doing my job. The guy called me, gave me this address, said he was looking to restore an old building on West Jones Street."

Cara felt her face go hot with anger. "You're talking about Cullen Kane?"

"Yeah."

"Did he give you the key to get through that gate just now?"

"Sure."

"You can't just come in here like this. I live here. This is my business. My rent is paid up until the end of the month."

"Hey, all I know is, the guy said it's okay. He has keys to the place, he sent me over to look around. I'm not gonna bother you or nothin'. . . ."

He took a step toward Cara, and Poppy let out a deep-throated warning growl, the likes of which Cara had never heard before from the people-loving puppy. She grasped the collar tighter. Her unwanted visitor looked uneasily around, as though he might need a weapon to fend off this fluffy white killer guard dog.

"What's your name?" Cara asked.

"Ricky Ucinski."

"Ricky, no offense, but I'm not letting you in my house."

"Geez," he said. "What do I tell Mr. Kane?"

"Tell him the crazy woman who lives here set her dog on you when you unlocked the back gate. And tell him if he sends any more contractors over here again, I'll do the same thing to them."

Ricky Ucinski looked distinctly uncomfortable with this message. "You wouldn't really set that dog on me, would you?"

Poppy growled again, as if on cue.

Cara gave a grim smile. "I really don't think you want to find that out, Ricky."

Apprentice floral-designer needed. Owner-operated floral design studio in downtown historic area seeks assistant/apprentice with artistic flair, design skills, working knowledge of flowers helpful, but not mandatory. Ideal candidate must be responsible, reliable, self-starter. Duties also include some clerical work and flower delivery. Must have valid driver's license and immediate availability.

Cara looked down at the Craigslist help-wanted ad and thought for a moment before rapidly typing the most important addition to the ad:

Whiners, sulkers, and self-involved slackers need not apply.

She added her contact information and hit the Send button. It was nearly four o'clock. She'd loaded the van with the afternoon's deliveries, and taken Poppy on a brief walk. But she had one pressing piece of business to attend to before anything else.

Cullen Kane Floral Design Studio was located in a former Piggly Wiggly grocery store on Habersham Street in midtown Savannah. As far as Cara knew, nearly everything in Savannah was located in a building that used to be something else, and everybody knew what that something was. In her case, she only knew it because she'd spent ten minutes staring at Kane's website, which trumpeted that his studio was located "in a sensitively upcycled circa-1946 Piggly Wiggly."

The old red-brick building had been painted charcoal gray, and now sported crisp red-and-white-striped awnings over the plate-glass windows. Huge terra-cotta pots on either side of the front door had palm trees underplanted with white lobelia and asparagus ferns, and the front door itself was painted a gloss red, with wrought-iron inserts featuring the intertwined CK logo, which was also painted in four-foot-high letters on the side of the building.

She parked the van in the lot beside his shop, trying to ignore the stabbing envy in her gut. Kane had at least sixteen spaces in his own dedicated lot, where more palm trees were planted in oversized wooden tubs. A gleaming black Mercedes box truck emblazoned with the CK logo was parked near the door. If a truck could look chic, this one did.

Cara took a deep breath and pushed the door open. The air inside the shop was lightly perfumed and deliciously cooled. The ceiling was open to exposed wooden roof rafters, and dropped ceiling fans whirred soundlessly overhead. A reception area had been screened off from the rest of the building with a red latticework partition, and in front of it, at a black midcentury modern desk, sat a familiar figure—Bert Rosen, dressed in an unfamiliar tight-fitting black T-shirt with the scrolling CK logo.

He was talking on the phone and tapping notes into the laptop computer on the desk and didn't notice her at first, which allowed Cara time to feel the full extent of the rage and jealousy boiling up from her gut.

Suddenly, it all fell into place. The no-shows, the long weekends, the long lunch hours and mystery text messages. Her assistant's phantom boyfriend had finally been unmasked.

Bert clicked off the phone, but kept typing. Without looking up he parroted the greeting, which he'd already mastered. "Welcome to Cullen Kane Design. I'll be with you in a moment."

"I can wait."

That got his attention.

"Cara?" His pale face bloomed a bright shade of red that exactly matched the screen behind his desk.

"Bert." She gestured around the shop. "You seem to have had a pretty busy lunch hour."

"You fired me," he said. "What was I supposed to do? Go on welfare?"

"I fired you four hours ago. You seem to have had a remarkably fast recovery. Or were you already working here—and I'm the last to know?"

He shrugged. "Whatever."

"Where is he?"

"Who?"

"Your boss," Cara said. "I need to see him. Right now."

"I'll call back to the workroom and see if he's available. What's this in reference to?"

Cara reached over and grabbed the neckline of Bert's black T-shirt, in the process knocking over a heavy crystal vase holding an arrangement of bamboo leaves and spiky red bird-of-paradise blooms. "This is in reference to him sabotaging my life, buying my building out from under me, and seducing a formerly valuable employee."

"Owww." Bert slapped ineffectively at Cara's hand. "Cut it out."

She abruptly released the shirt and he snapped backward like a limp rubber band.

A stream of water flowed across the desk and into his lap. "Look what you did!"

"Never mind calling. I'll find him myself."

She charged around the screen. Directly behind it was an informal seating area, with a pair of low white leather tufted sofas facing each other across from a chunky Lucite coffee table.

Behind that Cara saw six workstations, occupied by designers clad in signature black CK Design T-shirts, who were busily assembling what looked like enough extravagant flower arrangements to fill Savannah's largest cathedral.

She kept going. At the back of the open space she spied a glass-enclosed office. Cullen Kane sat at another midcentury modern desk. He was on the phone, his back turned away from the workroom, so he never even saw her coming.

Cara yanked the door of his office open. He spun around in his chair. "I've got to go," he told his caller. "We'll talk later."

Kane hung up the phone. If he was surprised to see her, he didn't show it. "Hi there. To what do I owe the pleasure?"

"We need to talk," Cara hissed.

"Love to," Kane said. He gestured to the chair facing his desk. "Please sit. Can I get you something to drink? What would you like? Perrier, some champagne? I'll get Bert to bring us something."

Cara bristled. "Nothing. I want nothing from you. Except my life back."

"Oh, please." Kane gave an airy wave. "You're upset that I bought your building?"

"Bought it out from under me," Cara said. Her face felt stiff and unnatural, and the anger, fizzing just below the surface, felt like a fast-moving rash. "To put me out of business."

"Not at all," he said pleasantly. "This was a good investment. That's all. What? You think I've cooked up some grand conspiracy against you?"

"Haven't you? You spread nasty rumors around town about my finances. You buy my building and then start sending contractors over to look at it—while I'm still living there. You poison my employee's relationship toward me. . . ."

Kane leaned back in his chair and studied her thoughtfully. "How long have you been harboring these paranoid delusions of yours? Really, Cara. First of all, yes, I bought your building. Jones Street is the most beautiful street in the historic district, and your block is one of the most desirable. I would have been crazy to pass it up."

"You don't need another shop," Cara cried. "This place has four times the space Bloom has. You've obviously spent a fortune redoing this. You've got parking, location, everything."

He shrugged. "I happen to like your building. It's quaint. I like real estate, and it was a good buy."

"It's a dump and you know it. The Bradleys haven't spent one nickel on it in probably twenty years."

"I know. That's what makes it so delicious. The possibilities are endless."

Cara swallowed the bile rising up in her throat. Swallowed her pride. "I want to stay in my building. I want a new lease. So. How much?"

"No telling," he said lightly. "You've turned away the two contractors I sent over there to get estimates."

"You walked the building before you signed the contract with Sylvia. While

I was gone. You went through it, went through my apartment. And you didn't even have the decency to ask my permission."

"Your landlord isn't obligated to ask for your permission to show the property. You don't even have a lease."

"How much?" Cara persisted. "I want to stay in my building. I don't want to move."

"Sorry. That's impossible. I'm planning a total restoration. Down to the studs. New roof, all new electric, plumbing, HVAC. After I'm done, well, we both know you won't be able to afford to stay."

"Why don't you let me worry about that?" Cara could hear her own breaths, coming fast and shallow. Was she about to hyperventilate?

He leaned across the desk. She could see the bleached blond highlights in his hair, the ghost of five-o'clock shadow on his cheeks. The skin over his cheeks and forehead was pulled unnaturally taut. Maybe he and Patricia Trapnell shared the same surgeon. He wore some kind of gold medallion on a fine chain around his neck. This close, she could see that he wore blue-tinted contacts.

"You're not listening to me," he said, his voice low and deadly serious. "You have two weeks to vacate the premises. You and your dog and the rest of your stuff? I want all of it out of there. Two weeks. If you're not gone, I call the sheriff."

Cara rocked backward on her heels, singed by the intensity of his animosity toward her.

"Why?" she whispered. "Why are you doing this to me?"

Kane's phone rang. He picked it up immediately. "Cullen Kane," he said smoothly. He looked over at Cara—his glance telegraphing just what an insignificant nuisance he regarded her as.

"It's nothing personal." He swiveled his chair around so that she was facing his back.

She stalked back to the reception area, where Bert was wearing a telephone headset, typing away at the computer. He didn't look up, although she knew he'd seen her coming.

She reached down and yanked off the headset. That got his attention.

"What now?"

"Answer me one question," Cara said. Her voice quavered so much that she could barely trust herself to say more. "How did he know my building was on the market, when I didn't even know?"

"Huh?"

"Don't play dumb, Bert. I asked you how Cullen Kane knew that Sylvia Bradley might be interested in selling Jones Street. Did you tell him?"

"I don't . . . what are you saying? Are you saying Cullen is the one who bought your building?"

"You know he bought it," Cara said angrily. "And the only way he could have known it was available was from you. Pillow talk, huh?"

"No!" Bert protested. "I mean, he could have seen old Mrs. Bradley's obituary. It was in the paper. That's how we found out."

"Yeah, but we knew who my landlady was. There was nothing in the obituary about that. So how would Cullen Kane figure out? You told him, right?"

Bert's right eye twitched. "I told him the old bat died, and her daughter wouldn't fix the air-conditioning, and the place was like a furnace. Yes! Okay? Big deal. I had no idea he'd go out and buy the place. I swear, I didn't know he'd bought it until you just told me."

"Did you also tell Cullen I owed my father a lot of money, and that he was bugging me to repay him? Did you tell your new boyfriend I was in dire straits—until Brooke Trapnell decided to hire me to plan her wedding?"

"He already knew you were broke," Bert said. "He was at Breitmueller's the day they put a hold on your credit, remember?"

"But you told him the other stuff, didn't you?"

Bert looked down at his computer terminal, and then out the window, anywhere but at Cara. "I might have mentioned it. In passing."

Cara grasped the edge of his desk with both hands. "How could you? I trusted you, Bert. I thought you were my friend. It's bad enough that you snuck around behind my back, sleeping with somebody we both know wants to put me out of business. He's kicking me out of my building in two weeks. Did he tell you that? Then you go blabbing my personal financial information to him. I just . . . I just can't believe you'd betray me this way. And for what? A hookup? A job answering his phone? A free Cullen Kane T-shirt? That's all this is, Bert, I guarantee it. He's using you to destroy me. And when he's done, he'll toss you aside, the same way he mowed me down."

Bert's face hardened. "You don't know what you're talking about, Cara. Cullen and I . . . you don't know anything about him. Or us."

The front door opened then, and a young couple walked in, holding hands. "You need to go, Cara," Bert said. He looked over her head, dismissing her the same way his lover had earlier.

"Hello! Welcome to Cullen Kane Floral Design Studio. You must be Kimberly and Stephen. Can I get you a Perrier? Some champagne?"

44

—*I am very innerested in you job. I like flowers. Can start immediately. What is pay?*

Cara stared down at the flood of responses to her Craigslist ad. She'd placed it six hours ago, and her inbox was jammed.

Dear Sir: I am the person for this situation. I don't know much about flowers, but that's cool. I learn fast and at the job I'm at now, people say I am an all-around awesome worker. Your ad said something about a driver's license. The thing is, I should get mine back in three months. Is that cool?

She shook her head. Not cool.

Hello! I am currently working as a floral designer in Indiana, but am looking to relocate to your area. I have 28 years experience as a florist. Am seeking a top-notch opportunity with an industry leader. My salary requirements are as follows: $70K annual minimum salary with bonus incentives, and company vehicle. I would also expect to be reimbursed for moving expenses. When can I expect to hear from you?

"Never," Cara muttered, hitting the Delete button.

She scrolled down the other responses and felt her spirits sink. She counted seventy-four emails. Two-thirds of the respondents either couldn't spell or apparently did not actually speak English.

Hey my name is Tiki and I seen your ad on Craigslist and I am very interested in the job. I feel like I would be good at this job because I like to drive and talk on the phone. Please give me a call, okay?

Greetings! My name is Evangeline Brody! I am ready to become your new assistant! Everybody says I have a bubbly personality and I really like flowers! I know a lot about computers too, so you should definitely give me a call so we can talk about how I can be an asset to your company!

Cara felt exhausted just reading Evangeline's email. She deleted it, and the next three responses, too. But the next response? Hmm.

Good afternoon. I have been a stay-at-home mom for the past seven years, but prior to that I worked as an in-house floral designer at Publix in Atlanta. I have basic computer skills, but am willing to learn any programs you need. I have a valid driver's license, and although my work references are a little out of date, I can offer character references from my neighbors and my pastor. I hope to hear from you soon. Best wishes, Ginny Best.

Cara typed as fast as she could.

Hi Ginny. Would love to meet you for interview. Can you be here tomorrow morning at 9 a.m.? She added the shop's address and phone number.

45

Jack and Ryan Finnerty sat on the tailgate of Jack's truck, finishing off their lunch of convenience-store heat-'n'-eat burritos and iced tea. Jack kicked the dust from his work boots and loudly crunched the ice from his cup.

"Hey, bro, what's with you?" Ryan asked, balling up the paper burrito wrapper and tossing it into the back of the truck along with the rest of the day's trash.

"Nothin'. Why?"

"You're all, like, happy and stuff. Right now, you're sitting there with this shit-eating grin on your face. And I know it's not because of the excellent cuisine we just consumed."

"Probably just gas," Jack said, thumping his chest with his fist and summoning up a belch on command, a talent he'd possessed since kindergarten.

Ryan matched his belch.

"Mom would be so proud," Jack said.

"So, back to why you're in such a great mood lately. Like the best mood you've been in since, like, a long time."

"Since Zoey left you mean?"

"Well, yeah. You heard from her?"

"Nope."

"You seeing somebody new?" Ryan studied his brother with deepening suspicion. "Wait a minute. I know that look. You're not just seeing somebody. You're sleeping with somebody."

"I don't know what you're talking about," Jack said, tossing his burrito wrapper at the trash heap.

"Sure you do. You were moping around, moody and grouchy as hell, for weeks after Zoey took off. All during the wedding, you were a total sad bastard. But now, this past couple weeks, you're Mister Happy Face. Mister Happy Face who's getting laid on a regular basis. Even Torie's noticed you were acting different."

Jack hopped down off the tailgate. "Enough chitchat. Let's go finish sanding that floor so we can get the first layer of stain put down before we knock off tonight. I told Libba we'd put down the first coat of poly tomorrow morning. The wedding's less than three weeks away."

"I'll get back to work as soon as you tell me who the lucky lady is that you're getting lucky with." Ryan leaned back on his elbows and watched his older brother rebuckling his tool belt. "Is it somebody I know?"

Jack tried to look indignant. "I would never kiss and tell."

"Sure you would. Come on, gimme something here. Some vicarious enjoyment."

"What's that supposed to mean? You're the one who's still on his honeymoon."

"Tell that to my bride. When Torie's not barfing up her breakfast she's locked herself in the bedroom crying about how fat her ass is getting."

"Morning sickness? How long is that supposed to go on?"

"According to the stack of books on her bedside table, it's usually for the first trimester. But we're heading into week thirteen right now, and I don't mind telling you, it's been a long dry spell, if you know what I mean."

Jack nodded sympathetically. "I feel for you."

"Just gimme some details. It somehow makes my situation more bearable if I at least know my big brother is getting some."

"Anybody ever tell you you're a pig?"

"All the time. Who is she?"

"I haven't even said I'm seeing somebody."

"You don't have to. I know the signs when I see 'em. Anyway, good for you. I was almost on the verge of agreeing to let Torie fix you up with one of her girlfriends."

"Thanks, but no thanks."

At the end of the day the two brothers climbed into Jack's truck and steered it back across the Talmadge Memorial Bridge, home to Savannah. Their skin and clothes were coated with a thick dusting of sawdust, their clothes damp with sweat.

They listened to the radio and discussed the plan for the next day's work.

"Other than not too much going on in the bedroom, how's everything else going with you guys?" Jack asked.

"Good," Ryan said. "I promised Torie we could go pick out a crib for the nursery this weekend. Which reminds me, I'll drive myself tomorrow. I'm supposed to meet her at the doctor's office at three. We're going to see an ultrasound of the baby."

"Cool. So you'll know if it's a boy or a girl?"

"That's what they tell me."

"I got five bucks says it's a girl," Jack said.

"That's what Mom says too," Ryan said. "I don't care either way. Boy, girl, just so it's healthy—and looks like her but has my temperament."

"I heard that," Jack said. "Do you guys see much of Torie's folks?

"Not as much as they'd like. Torie talks to Lillian all the time. I try to keep my distance. Her old man's all right—but Lillian? What a mouth that woman has on her. Swear to God, she wakes up every day and has a beef with somebody."

"Like who?" Jack asked, trying to sound indifferent.

"Anybody. Everybody. The dry cleaner who melted a button on her favorite jacket, the neighbor whose cat keeps crapping in her garden. Oh yeah, her current obsession is with some silver piece she claims our wedding florist stole."

"For real?"

"Yeah. It's crazy. Remember Cara, from our wedding? Real cute gal. You danced with her at the reception."

"I think I remember her," Jack said vaguely.

"Anyway, after the reception was over, Torie's folks went to the Bahamas for a getaway. When she got back, Cara returned all the silver they used at the reception. Except this one antique doohickey went missing. Apparently it's pretty old, belonged to her grandmother or somebody. Lillian went ballistic. She went over there, accused Cara of stealing it, called the cops and everything."

"Wow. That's pretty radical."

"Torie told Lillian that Cara wouldn't do anything like that. You met Cara. She's no thief. But once Lillian gets something in her head, she's like a damn bulldog, keeps chewing and tussling, and nobody can call her off."

"So what happens now? After she called in the cops?"

Ryan shrugged and wiped the sweat from his dust-caked forehead. "Some detective came over to talk to Lillian, then went to see Cara. They've talked to the assistant too. And I guess they're checking pawn shops around town to see if it turns up."

"But the cops aren't gonna arrest the florist, right? I mean, they can't prove she stole the thing, like you said."

"For all we know, somebody took the damn thing home from the wedding with 'em. You were there, everybody was blitzed. In the meantime, Lillian is bad-mouthing poor Cara all over town."

"Seems like a shame," Jack said. "Can't Torie do anything to calm Lillian down?"

"She's tried. In fact, they had a big fight over it last weekend. Now Lillian's not talking to Torie, which is fine by me."

"In-laws."

Jack turned the truck onto East Forty-sixth Street and pulled alongside the curb in front of his brother's Craftsman bungalow. "Porch railing looks good," he said, nodding toward the house.

"Yeah, it worked out okay," Ryan said. He gathered his tools and stepped out of the truck. "See you in the morning. Remember, I don't need you to pick me up."

As soon as he'd dropped his brother off, Jack headed north, toward downtown. He found himself smiling, and whistling. Mister Happy Face, Ryan had called him. Maybe he was. Maybe he had something to smile about these days.

He found himself cruising slowly past Bloom, on West Jones Street. It was nearly seven, but Cara hadn't brought in the garden cart full of plants she kept outside the shop. He halfway considered stopping and offering to help her bring it in, then, glancing down at himself, thought better of it. Maybe he'd go home, shower, then call and ask her out to dinner. Between all the weddings she always had on weekends, and his amped-up timetable for the Strayhorn project, they still hadn't had what he considered a real date.

He picked up his cell phone and tapped her number. It rang three times, and then went to voicemail. Jack frowned. She must be working on something. He knew she had a wedding over the weekend, and that her assistant was slacking off.

"Hey, it's me," he said. "I just rolled past your place and it looks like you're working. How about I take you out to dinner tonight? I'm headed home to shower. Call me, okay?"

Jack thought about the matter that had put a smile on his face earlier in the afternoon. He'd almost confided in Ryan. He and his brother were close, best friends, if you got right down to it. But then he'd decided it wouldn't be fair to Cara.

He hesitated, then tapped her number.

"Me again," he said ruefully. "Listen, I've got a proposition for you. Maybe we can talk about it over dinner."

When he got to his block of Macon Street, he pounded the steering wheel in frustration. A pair of bright yellow sawhorses were pulled across the street, and city work crews were busily tearing up the pavement.

"What the hell?" he muttered, taking a left turn down the lane. He had a single narrow parking space in back of his cottage, but he preferred parking on the well-lit street out front, since he still hadn't taken the time to install a motion-activated light in the backyard as a deterrent to thieves.

Grumbling, he shoehorned the truck into his allotted space between two sets of garbage cans. He got out of the truck, locked it, then went around to fetch his heavy tool kit. No way he'd leave it in the truck for any passing thugs to steal.

He had to set the toolbox down while he sorted through the keys on his ring to find the small one that fit the back-gate padlock. Finding it, he unlocked the gate, stepped into his ill-kempt back garden, and locked it again, tugging hard on the padlock to make sure it was secure. He wasn't taking any chances on Shaz making any more great escapes.

Although, come to think of it, the last time she'd gotten out, things had worked out okay.

"Shaz!" He looked around the yard, expecting to see the big white furball come bounding full-speed at him. He wasn't the only one at this address whose mood had improved lately.

Since he'd started taking her on regular walks, and even out to the job site some days, Shaz was a different dog. She was lively, playful, energetic, what you expected from a puppy.

But where the hell was she? He'd put her out in the yard before leaving this morning, being careful to make sure she had fresh water in her bowl, food, and chew toys. He'd bought a dog door that would allow Shaz access to the kitchen when he was gone, but hadn't had time to install it yet.

He peered around the yard, checking to see if she was nestled in the shade beneath the garden's only tree, a large water oak that desperately needed limbing up. No Shaz.

"Shaz!" Jack was starting to worry. Had she somehow managed to get out some other way? He scanned the fence line, but there was no sign that she'd managed to burrow beneath it, and there was no way she could have jumped the six-foot-high stockade fence.

His pulse raced as he considered the alternatives. Could somebody have broken in and taken the dog? How? The gate had been locked. He hurried to the back porch and tried the door. Locked. He turned the key and stepped into the kitchen, hoping, against logic, that Shaz had magically figured out a way to get inside.

"Shaz!"

"Wowf!" The dog raced into the kitchen and planted her paws on his chest, her tail wagging a mile a minute.

"Damn, girl, you scared me. How the hell did you get in here?"

"Jack?"

For a moment, he could have sworn his heart nearly stopped from a combination of shock and fright.

A woman's voice. Faint, but distinct, and it was coming from the front of the house.

"Jack, is that you?"

46

She was curled up on the sofa, dressed only in a bra and panties, drinking one of his Dos Equis beers. Her blond hair was lank and she wore no makeup, and there were dark circles under her eyes. A pair of battered Mexican leather sandals sat on the floor, along with her oversized pocketbook.

"Surprise!"

Shaz jumped up on the sofa and laid across her mistress's lap. Reunited at last.

Jack just stared.

"Zoey? What are you doing here?"

She offered him a weak smile. "I came back."

"So I see. Why?"

Zoey put the beer down on the floor. "What do you mean, why? I came back because I missed you." She kissed the top of Shaz's head, and the adoring puppy rewarded her with a lavish lick on the chin.

"What about Jiminy Cricket? Won't you be missing him?"

Her lips were dried and cracked, but she still managed to form her signature Zoey Ackerman pout.

"Jesus H. Christ, Jack. For the millionth time, his name is Jamey. Jamey Buttons. And for your information, that's all over."

"I thought you were on a cruise ship. For like six weeks. What'd you do? Swim back to shore?"

"In case you haven't noticed, I happen to be pretty damn sick. Ever hear of a thing called norovirus?"

"What? That's the name of your boyfriend's new band?"

"Ha ha. Don't you ever watch the news? Norovirus is a highly contagious virus that's like, the scourge of cruise ships. We were just off Raritan on our last trip when people started getting sick. I was teaching a Pilates class on the sunset deck when all of a sudden, I just, well, I barely made it to the bathroom. And the next thing I know, everybody else in my class is barfing and . . . you know."

"Diarrhea?"

She shuddered. "I barely made it back to my cabin in time. Ten minutes later, here comes Jamey—and now he's sick!"

"Too bad," Jack said.

"Have you ever seen one of the bathrooms on those cruise ships? They're like the size of a telephone booth. And we had to share it!"

"Poor you."

She narrowed her eyes. "You think it's funny, don't you? I thought I was dying. For two whole days, I couldn't leave our cabin. And neither could he. It was beyond disgusting. And there was like, nobody to help us. Almost everybody on the whole ship was sick. I kept ringing for the steward, but he was sick too. Finally, somebody brought some Gatorade and some saltines, but I couldn't keep anything down. I lost six pounds in three days."

"But you lived," Jack said.

"No thanks to that jerk Jamey." She sighed dramatically. "We are so over, it's not even real. I guess you never really know somebody till you're locked up in a shoebox-sized room with them with raging diarrhea and nausea, huh?"

"Words of wisdom," Jack said. "Very sage. But you still haven't told me how you ended up back here."

"They had to turn the ship around and go back to port in Lauderdale two days early," Zoey said. "They gave all the passengers discount vouchers for another trip and stuff, and the cruise line wanted me to stay on, and work on another of their ships, because now they have to completely sanitize the one we were on, but I was like, no effin' way. I hope I never see another cruise ship as long as I live. Or Jamey. I got off the boat Wednesday, but I was too sick and weak to travel, so I got a room near the port. Then, this morning, I drove straight here."

"To my place."

It took a moment for that to sink in. "Our place. I live here, Jack."

He squatted on the floor beside the sofa so that he could be at eye level. "Zoey, you left me. You said you were in love with another guy, so you packed up your clothes, and you left."

Huge tears welled up in Zoey's blue eyes. "It was a mistake," she whispered. "I, I can't explain it. That thing they say about women, going for musicians? It's true! He had like a spell on me. But it wasn't real. I figured that out. The whole time I was sick, I just kept thinking, if I get off this boat alive, I'm going back to Jack, and I'll never leave him again."

She grabbed his hand and clutched it to her chest. "I missed you so much, Jackie."

His cell phone rang. He stood, awkwardly, and pulled it from his pocket, checking the caller ID. It was Cara.

"Jackie?" Zoey looked up at him expectantly.

"I gotta take this call," he said, his voice brusque. He turned and strode back into the kitchen.

"Hey, you," Cara said. "I just heard your message. I'd love some dinner, if it's not too late."

He paused and glanced back over his shoulder. Zoey now stood in the doorway from the living room, glaring at him. Her skin was deeply tanned, but she looked gaunt.

"Uh," he stammered. "I just got in myself, and I haven't even showered yet."

"I can wait," Cara said. "What, thirty minutes?"

"The thing is, there's been kind of an unexpected development here."

"Shaz didn't run off again, did she?"

"No, nothing like that," Jack said. "I've got some out-of-town company, is all. Sort of out of the blue."

Zoey frowned. "Since when am I company? Who are you talking to? Is that a woman?"

"Jack?" Cara said. "What kind of company?"

Shaz trotted into the kitchen and rubbed up against his legs. He looked helplessly from Zoey to the dog to the back door. If he left right now, he could make it over to Cara's house, explain everything in person. And maybe Zoey would dematerialize.

"Hey!" Zoey called loudly. "Whoever is on the phone? Jack can't talk right now. Because his girlfriend is back. And he needs to take care of her. So just hang up, okay?"

He covered the phone with his hand. "Shut the fuck up," he said hoarsely, slamming the kitchen door in Zoey's face.

"Cara?"

There was a long pause.

"Oh," Cara said. "Was that really Zoey?"

"Yeah," he said slowly. "When I got home from work a little while ago, she was here. That cruise ship she was on? Everybody got some kind of stomach virus. She said they got back to port yesterday, and she drove here today. Out of the clear blue."

"*Siren of the Seas*? I heard about that on the news. That's the ship she was on?"

"I don't know and I don't care," Jack said, wearily rubbing his hand across his face, staring at his own grubby reflection in the kitchen window. "You gotta believe me, Cara. I had no idea she was coming back. I don't want her here. We're through. I was just trying to tell her that when you called."

"What's she want from you? What happened to the Jimmy Buffett impersonator?"

"She says they broke up. I guess she thinks she can just show up here and I'll take her back. But she's dead wrong."

"What'll you do?"

"Tell her to leave," Jack said. "She sure as hell can't stay here with me."

"Is she still sick?"

"Zoey? She's fine! Okay, it looks like she lost a little weight. But she was well enough to drive seven hours straight from Fort Lauderdale, so as far as I'm concerned, she can just keep driving."

"That seems awfully mean," Cara said. "The people on that ship were really sick. Some of them are still in the hospital."

He snorted. "You don't know Zoey. She's like a cockroach. No matter how many times you stomp on her, she just gets up and keeps going. Look. Are we still on for dinner? Let me grab a shower and I'll be over there in fifteen."

"Are you sure?"

"Positive. What do you feel like for dinner?"

"Doesn't matter. After the day I've had, I'll just be happy to see a friendly face."

"I can do friendly," Jack said. "Very friendly."

He stalked back into the living room. Zoey was stretched out on the sofa, with Shaz perched at her feet. She gave Jack a playful wink. "Was that your new squeeze? Did you tell her about me?"

"None of your business," he said, looking around the room. "By the way, where the hell are your clothes?"

She wrinkled her nose. "Gross. The health department people who met us at the port told us we should make sure and like, sanitize everything. So we don't spread the virus. Or get it again. God forbid. As soon as I got here, I threw everything into the washing machine."

"Everything? What were you planning to wear in the meantime?"

She arched one eyebrow. "I wasn't planning to wear anything. Actually, you kind of spoiled my surprise, coming in the back door the way you did. I had this big welcome back to Jack all planned out."

"Yeah. I remember the last surprise you planned for me. I came home to an empty house, and a puppy who'd peed all over the floor. I'm pretty much over your surprises, Zoey."

She stood up, stretched, and reached her arms out toward him. "It's different this time, Jackie."

"Forget it," he said, deftly stepping sideways. "Not interested."

Zoey was not to be deterred. "I'm not contagious."

"No," Jack said, deadpan. "You're not. Whatever you've got, I'm finally immune to it. I'm gonna take a shower now, then I'm going out for a while. While I'm gone, I suggest you finish up your laundry, get dressed, and move along down the road."

"What? You're kicking me out? Just like that?"

"Just like that," he agreed. He headed for the shower. "Why don't you check the washing machine? I bet your stuff is clean by now."

He'd just stepped into the shower when he heard the bathroom doorknob turn. And then turn again. Jack chuckled and turned his face up to the nozzle, letting the water stream over his face.

Zoey pounded on the door. "You locked the door?" she hollered. "Asshole! What if I need to pee?"

"Take it outside," he called back. He reached for the soap and frowned when he saw the familiar silver and pink bottles of shampoo and conditioner on the window ledge. She'd already begun the process of moving in again. This time, though, the process would stop. Tonight.

When he'd toweled off and put on clean clothes, he walked out to the living room to find Zoey still reclining on the leather sofa. Thankfully, she'd gotten dressed, and was wearing an oversized blue-and-white-striped shirt and jeans. She'd combed her hair and twisted it back from her face and was looking semihuman again.

"Is that my shirt?" he asked.

She shrugged. "You never wear this shirt, so I didn't think you'd mind. My stuff's still in the dryer. I found a pair of my old jeans in the laundry room. You look nice. Where are you off to?"

"Out."

"Like, out to dinner? Not that you've asked, but I haven't had anything to eat. Not in hours and hours. And there's nothing in the fridge. I checked."

"Maybe you should go find yourself something then. Right after you pack up your stuff. I'm not taking you to dinner. And you can't stay here, Zoey."

"Where would you suggest I go? This was my home too, Jack. I can't believe you're being like this."

"Believe it," he said. "Call up one of your girlfriends. Or go to a motel."

She sat up then and crossed one long, lithe leg over the other. "The thing is, I'm sort of short of funds right at the minute. We only get paid every two weeks. I gave the cruise line this address, and they're supposed to forward my final check week after next."

Zoey gave him a sad little smile. "See? You just have to put up with me for two more weeks. Then I'll get out of your hair. If that's what you really want."

"Oh no." He shook his head emphatically. "Oh, hell, to the no. You're not pulling that broke and helpless crap on me again. You've been living on a cruise ship for what, three, four months? Your room and food was free, you had no living expenses. If you're broke, that's your problem. Not mine."

She turned on the tears again. "I can't believe you're being like this. I told you I was sorry."

"Actually, you never once said you were sorry," he pointed out. "Not that I care. Here's the deal, Zoey. I'm leaving now." He reached into his pocket, pulled out a money clip, and peeled off five twenty-dollar bills. "This is my parting gift to you. Buy yourself some dinner, get a room somewhere, whatever. Just make sure you're gone by the time I get back here tonight."

Zoey looked at the bills with obvious disbelief. "A hundred lousy bucks? That's it?"

"Yup." He grabbed the leash from the hook by the front door and whistled. "Shaz! Come."

The dog looked up at Zoey, and then at Jack.

"Shaz!"

She trotted over and Jack hooked the leash to her collar. "Let's go girl." He picked up his truck keys and headed for the back door.

"You can't take my dog," Zoey said, running after him. "I bought her. She's mine. You didn't even want a puppy."

Jack kept walking. "She grew on me. Anyway, possession is nine-tenths of the law."

"You can't keep her," Zoey called. "As soon as I get my check, I'm taking her with me."

Jack stopped dead in his tracks and turned around. "That reminds me." He held out his hand, palm side up.

"What?" she said sullenly.

"My house key. I'd like it back. You can just push the thumb lock when you leave."

She stalked out of the room and returned a minute later. She flipped the key, and he caught it in midair.

He was almost out the back door when, out of the corner of his eye, he saw a beer can go sailing past his head before banging against the wall. Beer dripped down the door casing. He needed to paint anyway.

"Asshole!" she screamed.

47

Cara stepped out the front door just as Jack was pressing the doorbell.

"I brought Shaz. I thought she and Poppy could hang out together," Jack said.

"Good idea." They took Shaz outside, where Poppy seemed ecstatic at the prospect of company, and made sure both dogs had water and toys before heading back out to the street.

"You look nice," Cara said, as Jack leaned in to kiss her. "And you smell nice too."

"You clean up pretty good yourself," he said, his lips lingering on hers. "And you smell way better than me."

"Girls are supposed to smell better than boys," she said, then gestured down at her own capris and sheer cotton flower-printed tunic. "Am I underdressed? Where are we going?"

"You're not underdressed at all. I thought we'd go to Guale, over on Drayton Street. Does that sound all right?"

"I've seen Guale written up in magazines, but I've never been. Isn't it pretty fancy?"

"Not really. The food's great, but I've gone in there wearing jeans before, and nobody even looks twice. Parking's a pain though. Is it too hot to walk over there?"

"Walking's good." She lifted her right foot to show off her Kelly-green sandals. "I've even got on flats."

It was dusk now, and the streetlights had come on, and the faintest damp breeze ruffled the fronds of a palm tree on the corner. As they were crossing Whitaker Street, Jack casually reached over and clasped Cara's hand. And he didn't let go when they'd reached the other side. She flashed him a smile and kept walking.

"What?" he asked.

"Nothing."

"Tell me."

"You'll think I'm being ridiculous."

"Probably. Tell me anyway?"

"I don't know. This just . . . it feels so nice. And normal. Walking down the street holding hands with a cute boy . . ."

"A boy? You make it sound like we're teenagers."

"All of a sudden, I feel like a teenager. I've truly had the most appalling day in a most appalling week, and then Jack Finnerty shows up at my door, wearing a starched dress shirt and polished loafers, and smelling like aftershave. And he's taking me to dinner . . . and for a few minutes there, it made me forget my troubles. It made me remember what it's like to have somebody to care about." She blushed. "I told you it was silly."

"C'mere," Jack said. He pulled her into the darkened lane between Charlton and Jones and pressed her back against the wall of a pink stucco town house. "I'll make you feel like a teenager." He ran his hands beneath her shirt and slipped his tongue in her mouth.

Cara gave a very small, very feeble squeak of protest. She kissed him back, twined her arms around his neck, pulled him closer. Emboldened, he worked his thumbs under the band of her bra, teasing her nipples until she gasped and gave him a gentle backward shove.

"I am *not* having sex with you in an alley," she said, smoothing down her rumpled tunic.

He chuckled and kissed her again. "We don't call them alleys in Savannah. We call them lanes. Anyway, you're the one who said you liked feeling like a teenager."

"I didn't say I liked being felt up like a teenager in public," Cara countered. "There's a time and a place for everything."

Jack sighed and straightened his own shirt. "Same old story I used to get in high school."

They'd just given the waiter their dinner order when Jack's cell phone buzzed. He took it from his pocket, read the text message, and gave a loud grunt of exasperation before putting it away again.

Cara raised a questioning eyebrow.

"Zoey. I'm not answering her because I don't want to encourage her."

"Just out of curiosity, what does she want?"

"She claims her car won't start. Wants me to come give her a jump. Okay, poor choice of words. Her battery is dead. Or so she claims. It's all a ruse."

Cara leaned forward. "Can I ask you something? What's Zoey like? How did the two of you end up together in the first place?"

"How does anybody end up together? Dumb luck. I was dumb, she was lucky. Or the other way around. How about we talk about something else? Anything else? You said you'd had a bad day? Tell me about that."

Cara looked around the dining room. She was glad they had come here tonight. This was good. A nice distraction. The tablecloth was pale yellow linen. There was a candle in a glass jar, and a small clear bud vase held a stem of pink alstroemeria that was a day past its prime. Perhaps she should talk to the owners about doing flowers for them. Her eyes rested on Jack. With a start she realized she might never get tired of looking at him. He had a tiny spatter of white paint on his left earlobe. His sunburnt nose was peeling. She looked at his big hands. His left hand was resting on the tabletop and he was clutching a glass of red wine in his right hand, and she noticed his thumbnail was blackened.

Her day?

"Where do I start? The Colonel continues to hound me about my bad debt and bad business decisions. Also, another contractor showed up at the shop this morning, all set to come in and look around on behalf of Cullen Kane."

"That guy," Jack said.

"And on top of everything else, I fired Bert."

"For real?"

"He left me no choice. He's been coming in late, leaving early, just generally slacking off. I figured he had some new boyfriend, but he kept pushing the limits. And this thing with Lillian Fanning's missing epergne, he kept acting as though I was the one accusing him of stealing it. I never accused him. Whatever else he might be, Bert is no thief. Finally, today, I'd had it. I told him if he left early he could stay gone. So he did."

"Nothing else you could do," Jack said.

"Not long after that the second contractor showed up. He had a key to my place. He let himself in the back gate. That was the final straw. I was so mad, Jack, I couldn't even see straight. Who the hell does this guy think he is?

"I drove over to his shop—I mean, excuse me, Cullen Kane Floral Design Studio. And you'll never guess who was working as Cullen's new receptionist. Bert. My Bert!"

"Kane hired him that quickly?"

"Cullen Kane is Bert's new boyfriend. That's who Bert's been sneaking around with all these weeks now. And that's how Cullen found out my landlady died. Bert 'just happened to mention' to Kane that Bernice Bradley had died, and that Sylvia Bradley was refusing to fix my air-conditioning."

"Bert was spying on you for Cullen Kane? I thought the guy was practically your best friend."

"I thought so too," Cara said sadly. "Bert was probably planning to quit and go to work for Cullen all along. And he didn't even have the decency to feel guilty about betraying me. He just sat at that stupid desk wearing that stupid Cullen Kane T-shirt, smirking at me. He even had the nerve to ask me if I wanted a bottle of Perrier, or some champagne!"

"Did you let him have it?"

"I did. And then I went barreling to the back room to let his boss have it too."

"I'd like to have heard that."

"No you wouldn't have. You would have been ashamed of me. I'm such a spineless jellyfish. I ended up groveling at his feet—begging him to give me a new lease and let me stay in my building."

"I'm guessing you weren't successful?"

Cara nodded. "Big mistake. Kane was actually enjoying himself, telling me all about his big plans to gut the place and put on a new roof and all new systems, and then raise the rent—which he said he knew I could never afford. Finally, I flat-out asked him why he was so determined to destroy me. And he just looked at me—like I was nothing. And he said what every megalomaniac says these days when they do something unconscionable. 'It's nothing personal. It's just business.'"

"Bastard," Jack said. "So, what now?"

It was noisy in the restaurant, the tables were close together, so close she could hear snatches of conversation from all directions. A woman, her voice slow and syrupy: *"I told Mama you have to be firm with these people. Otherwise they walk all over you, but you know Mama."* A man's deep voice: *"You can't get there direct from Savannah. We'll lay over in Atlanta and get into Kansas City after five on Monday."*

Cara heard her own voice, too. It sounded tinny and somehow disembodied. "I've got to leave my building. Two weeks. That's all the time I have before I have to get out. Two weeks. To pack up and find a new shop and a new apartment."

All day long, she'd managed to push *that* reality to the back of her mind. She'd busied herself with the tedium of what had to get done, ordering flowers and answering emails and feeding Poppy, and dozens of other little things. But the enormity of what she was facing was gaining strength and velocity. And as she thought about it now, it felt like a huge boulder, inescapable, careering down a mountain, threatening to crush her under its weight.

She hadn't realized she was crying until she felt the big sloppy tears sliding down her cheek. And then she was full-out sobbing, sitting in the middle of a crowded restaurant, bawling like a baby.

"Oh, God," she said, choking back the tears. The voices around her quieted, and she knew people were staring. She crushed the linen napkin to her face, wishing she could crawl under the table.

"Heeyyyy." Jack scooted his chair beside hers. He put his arm around her shoulder. Her chest heaved, and she couldn't catch her breath. He put a glass of water in her hand. "Drink this."

She managed a sip. "I'm . . . so . . . sorry. . . ." The words were wobbly.

The waiter came with their meals, crispy flounder for him, shrimp bisque for her. He stood—statuelike, unsure of the proper thing to do in such a situation.

"Could you box that up for us?" Jack said quietly. "And bring the check?" Of course Jack Finnerty would know exactly what to do.

Despite Cara's feeble protests, he called a cab, and five minutes later he'd unlocked the door to the shop, and they were upstairs, and he'd sat her down on the sofa. While he went out to the garden to check on Shaz and Poppy, she went into the bathroom to try to pull herself together.

She was a mess. Her face was blotchy, her nose was red and running, and there were mascara trails down both cheeks. She washed her face and combed her hair and put on some lip gloss.

Jack was waiting in the living room with a glass of wine. She took a sip, and then another.

"Better?" he asked.

She nodded, afraid if she tried to speak the tears would start anew. He sat down on the sofa beside her, and gathered her into his arms. She pressed her face into his starched shirtfront, he rested his chin on the top of her hair.

"It's gonna be okay," he said.

The phone in his pocket buzzed. He swore softly and ignored it, but five minutes later, it buzzed again.

Jack shifted onto his left hip, took out the phone, and looked at the text.

"Dammit, Zoey," he muttered.

Cara looked up. He held out the phone so he could read the message.

Battery dead. No way to get to motel. Found unlocked window. Bring me some pizza?

"I never leave windows unlocked over there. I'm sure she broke one so she could get back in the house," Jack said.

"You should go home and check on her," Cara said, hoping he wouldn't.

He was already typing, and held up the phone again, so she could read his response.

Call a cab. Get out of my house and get your own pizza.

"You sure have a way with the ladies," Cara said.

"Zoey ain't no lady."

After a while, Jack heated up their dinners, and was surprised to find she was actually hungry. They drank another glass of wine and rinsed out the dinner dishes.

"Will you stay here tonight?" Cara asked, drying the glasses and putting them back on the shelf where she'd so carefully arranged them on moving day two years ago.

"Do you want me to?"

Cara grasped his shirtfront, pulled him to her, and whispered in his ear. "There's a time and a place for everything, remember?"

"I'll bring in the dogs," Jack said.

"Better text Zoey and tell her not to wait up," Cara teased. She really was feeling a little better.

48

As soon as he pulled up to the house with the peeling pea-green paint on East Forty-Fourth Street Tuesday morning, Jack Finnerty felt the old familiar sensation of dread seep into his pores. He hadn't been to this house in more than twenty-five years, but not much had changed. The grass was still bone-dry, because the old lady was too cheap to turn on a sprinkler. The shrubbery near the house still needed trimming and the concrete sidewalk was still cracked and potholed. The one thing that surprised him was how small it looked now.

But then, the last time he'd been here he'd been what, ten years old? He'd pedal slowly over here every Wednesday after school let out at Charles Ellis School on nearby Washington Avenue, lean the bike against the kickstand, and reluctantly drag himself up this same sidewalk, with the white envelope and the five-dollar bill tucked in his pants pocket.

He rang the doorbell, and felt his stomach muscles suck in, out of some decades-old force of habit. If he'd had a shirttail he would have tucked it in, and removed his ball cap, too.

The heavy front door, still painted that same mud brown, was open, and as he looked through the screen door, he could have sworn he saw that same ghostly-gray moth-eaten Siamese cat of his childhood flit from beneath the marble-top console table in the entry hall.

A moment later, Sylvia Bradley was peering out at him through the screen. She wore a flowered print blouse and baggy blue polyester slacks, and her ever-present old-school Keds. Like the house, she looked smaller now, too. And he was startled to see that she walked with a cane.

"Jack Finnerty?" Her voice was fluty, and overly loud.

"Yes ma'am," he said.

"Well, come on in then," she said, unlatching the hook.

The house was stifling, but in his memory, it had always been stifling. She plied him with a Dixie cup of warm Hawaiian Punch, and he was certain it came from the same can she'd opened twenty-five years ago, and that it had been sitting on her kitchen counter all this time. Sylvia motioned for him to sit down in the parlor, on an excruciatingly stiff tufted red velvet sofa. He pointed at the upright piano on the opposite wall, with its books of sheet music propped above the keyboard, and the metronome sitting on top.

"Do you still give lessons?"

"Unfortunately no." She held up her right hand, its knobby joints red and swollen. "Arthritis."

"That's too bad," Jack said. "You must miss your students."

"Not really," Sylvia Bradley said. "Children today don't want to study piano. They want to play 'keyboard' and be in rock bands."

"I suppose so."

"You don't play piano anymore, do you?"

"Uh, no ma'am."

"Good. You were a terrible student. One of the worst I ever had. I never understood why your poor mother insisted you should try to learn."

Jack laughed. He thought it was probably the only time he had ever laughed in this house. "It was my dad's idea. He thought everybody should learn to appreciate music."

"Appreciate it, yes. Play it, no. What was your little brother's name?"

"Ryan."

She nodded. "That's right. He was a ginger, as I recall. Nice boy. Totally tone deaf, of course. And your baby sister. Maureen?"

"Meghan. I think by the time she came along, Dad gave up on piano. Meghan took ballet, instead." Jack cleared his throat. "I was sorry to hear about your mother."

"Thank you. You know, she was nearly ninety-one, and still cooked for both of us and did all the grocery shopping. I took her car keys away a year ago, but she was still sharp as a tack right up until that last stroke."

Sharp as a tack, Jack thought, and mean as a snake, that would describe Bernice Bradley. And her daughter.

"You said you had a business matter to discuss with me?" Sylvia said, regarding him through glasses with lenses so thick and convex they gave her the look of a giant insect. "What type of business are you in these days, Jack?"

"I'm a contractor. Specializing in historic restoration. Ryan and I are business partners."

She looked at him with distaste. "I have contractors leaving flyers and business cards in my mailbox every week. As though I would hire somebody who has to resort to passing out flyers to get work."

"Um . . . that's not really why I wanted to talk to you. Actually, I came here today to ask you about a piece of property you own downtown."

Suddenly the room got very quiet, and the ticking from the grandfather clock in the corner seemed synchronized with his own pulse-beat.

"Mother and I own quite a few properties downtown. My father worked for the C&S Bank, you know, but he believed in buying real estate, not stocks and bonds."

"Smart man," Jack said. "I'm probably not anywhere near as smart as your father, or as successful, but I believe in buying real estate too. Especially in this last economic downturn, Ryan and I found that we were able to pick up some distressed properties for a pretty modest investment."

"I don't own any distressed properties," the old lady shot back.

"Oh, no, no ma'am. I didn't mean to insinuate that," he said quickly. "Not at all. The thing is, I've always admired that three-story building you own on

West Jones Street. I like the retail mix on the ground floor, with the residential above it. And of course, that's one of the most desirable streets in the historic district."

"How do you happen to know I own that building?" Sylvia asked. "Are you one of those scam artists who hang around the courthouse records room, looking to make a quick killing?"

"Not at all. I only know about it because I got a call from a man named Cullen Kane—a florist here in town. Somebody gave him my name, and he called me up and asked me to take a look at West Jones Street. To give him estimates to do some work on the building. And he mentioned that he was buying it from you."

"That's right," she said cautiously. "We close on the thirtieth. Mother and I always kept our properties up, but, well, tenants these days are so demanding, especially the young woman who's renting the space right now. She's another florist, you know, but every week she had a new complaint. Mr. Kane called me up out of the blue, asked me what I wanted for the building, and I thought, Mother is gone. Why not? I named a price, and he countered, then I countered, and we agreed to it."

"Just like that?" Jack asked.

"He sent me a beautiful orchid plant," Sylvia confided. "And he has lovely manners, for a homosexual, I mean."

Jack almost choked on his Hawaiian Punch. "Miss Sylvia, would it be nosy of me to ask how much he offered you for the building?"

She told him, and he nearly choked again. Sylvia Bradley might be old, but she'd managed to squeeze top dollar out of Cullen Kane.

He put his Dixie cup carefully down on the marble-top coffee table. "I wish I'd known you were going to sell that building, Miss Sylvia. Because I would have been able to offer you more than what Cullen Kane did."

"Is that so?"

"Yes, ma'am," Jack said.

"How much more?"

He did some quick, painful calculations and named his price.

She sighed loudly. "I wish I had known you were interested, Jack. It would have been nice to sell it to one of my former pupils. I think Mother would have liked that. She always used to say she liked those Finnerty boys."

This was news to Jack. As far as he knew, Bernice Bradley hated all little boys, especially if they were named Jack or Ryan Finnerty. He'd once made the mistake of leaving his bicycle lying down in the driveway during a piano lesson, and Bernice had run right over it in her dark blue Pontiac.

"I guess you have a legally binding contract with Kane? No way to get out of it?"

Sylvia pursed her lips. "I could tell him I'd changed my mind and decided not to sell."

"He might make trouble for you," Jack warned. "From what I hear, Cullen Kane is a pretty astute businessman. He usually gets what he sets out to buy."

"Maybe not this time," Sylvia said. "My father taught me more about buying and selling real estate than either of you two will ever know. You leave him to me."

Jack's face lit up. "So we have a deal? For the price I named?"

"All cash?" Sylvia asked. "It will make things simpler."

Now Jack understood that foreboding feeling he'd experienced coming up Sylvia Bradley's front steps. He'd been a lamb led to slaughter.

"All cash," he said. He held out his arm and helped her to her feet, and as she was showing him to the door, she stopped suddenly.

"There is one other thing," she said. "A little leak in the roof over my back mud porch. My laundry room. I'm sure a reputable contractor could take care of that in no time."

Half an hour later, he slid behind the steering wheel of his truck and looked down at the dark dress pants he'd worn especially for this meeting. They were covered with fine gray cat hair. As he pulled away from the curb, he saw Sylvia Bradley, silhouetted in the doorway. Cullen Kane had gotten off easy with a potted orchid. As for Jack, he and a helper would be returning that afternoon to tear down the termite-infested mud porch and rebuild it. Gratis.

Materials alone would probably cost a couple thousand, but all he could think about was the look on Cara's face tomorrow when he would tell her what he'd done.

49

You did what?" Cara had been about to take a bite of her sandwich, but instead she put it down on her paper plate and picked up the sheaf of papers he'd just presented with a flourish.

The look on her face was not anything like what he'd pictured. Her jaw tightened and her eyes narrowed as she skimmed the sales contract for West Jones Street. Her face paled when she got to the page with the sales price.

"Is this some kind of joke?" she demanded. "Because if it is, I don't get the punch line."

"It's no joke. I bought it. Sylvia Bradley was my piano teacher when I was a kid. I went to see her yesterday morning, and I bought this building. For you."

Cara stabbed at the contract with her fingertip. "You paid twice what it's worth! Are you crazy? Where would you get that kind of money?"

Now Jack put down his own sandwich. He was confused. Where was the jumping up and down? Where were the screams of joy and wild kisses of gratitude he'd been anticipating for the past two days?

. . .

Earlier that day, Jack and a helper arrived at Forty-fourth Street at dawn. They carted Sylvia's ancient rusted Kenmore washer and dryer down the crumbling driveway and into the back of Jack's truck for the trip to the dump. It took only a couple hours to tear down Sylvia Bradley's mud porch. He was shocked that it hadn't just fallen off of its own accord.

Even with a cane, the old lady was pretty spry, and she stood in the weedy backyard, in her flower-print blouse and old-school Keds, and supervised as they tossed the rotted timbers into the Dumpster he'd rented.

Late Wednesday morning, after she could see the yellow pine skeleton of her new porch, Sylvia finally called him into the kitchen, offered him a paper cup of warm Hawaiian Punch and the sales contract for West Jones Street.

He reached into the pocket of his cargo shorts and brought out a white envelope with the cashier's check for the earnest money inside, just as he'd offered those five-dollar envelopes from his mother every Wednesday the year he was ten. As he handed this one over to Sylvia Bradley, he halfway expected her to ask him if he'd been practicing his finger exercises.

She ripped open the envelope and studied the check, running a swollen forefinger over the embossed bank logo.

"How did you leave things with Cullen Kane?" he asked, signing the contract with a flourish.

"Never you mind," Sylvia said. She opened a kitchen drawer and rummaged around among the rubber bands, balls of string, and nubs of pencils until she found a set of keys with a white plastic C&S Bank key fob. "Here are the keys. My father bought that building in 1953. He was always partial to West Jones Street."

Jack pocketed the keys. "I'm partial to it too. Thank you, Miss Sylvia."

At lunchtime, Jack picked up sandwiches and chips at a deli on Habersham Street, and he headed over to Bloom to share the good news with Cara, and bask in the warmth of her admiration.

"You must be insane," Cara said, shaking the contract, as though she might shake the numbers right off the paper. "This is a lot of money."

"It is a lot of money, but no, I'm not crazy," Jack said calmly. "The price is a little on the high side, but it's not terribly out of line with comparable prices in the district. I checked the tax records. It's a decent deal, Cara."

And it might have been considered a decent deal, if you didn't factor in the cost of rebuilding Sylva Bradley's mud porch, replacing her washer and dryer, and having his painters sand, prime, and repaint her house. But those were details he didn't feel the need to share with Cara at this time.

"Where did you get the money to buy this building?" Cara asked. "You told me that you and Ryan were struggling to keep your business afloat, just like me."

"That's right. It *was* a struggle. Still is. But my dad helped us out a little. In a business like ours, we're sometimes in the position to pick up a house or a building on the cheap. So that's what we did. We bought crappy houses and crappy buildings for pennies on the dollar, fixed them up, and resold for a good profit. Right now, I'm not doing a lot of flipping, so a property like West Jones, that's one I want to keep. I'm not saying we're rich, but we've done okay."

Cara tossed the papers back in his face. "I didn't ask you to do this. I didn't want you to do this."

He was dumbfounded. "I wanted to do it. For you. You were so upset the other night, about having to move and everything. And I'd been thinking about it, ever since I found out Sylvia Bradley owned your building. So I went to see her yesterday."

"Without even asking me. You just took it upon yourself to go behind my back and buy my building. Just like Cullen Kane did. And you expect me to be happy about that?"

"Hell yeah," he said. "I thought you'd be delirious. Don't you see? Now you don't have to move out. I'll start working on the building right away. Well, right after we finish up the Strayhorns' barn. We'll have to run new electrical first, and then I'll get my HVAC guy over here to see what kind of tonnage he recommends, especially if we open up the third floor."

"*We'll* run the electric. *We'll* open up the third floor? Who is this magical 'we'? You and your brother? When were you going to consult me? Or were you just going to show up here one day and start tearing down the walls?"

"Whoa, whoa, whoa." Jack held his hands up in surrender. "Don't go getting your panties all in a bunch. It's just a figure of speech. Of course I was going to consult you before I started any work. But we talked about this. The day I helped you put in that window unit, we talked about how much work this place needed."

"No. *You* talked about it. And *you* decided what would be best for me. Just like the Colonel. Just like my ex-husband. Poor, helpless Cara is too dumb to figure out life for herself, so we'll just step in and take charge and tell her how to run her life."

"It's not like that!" Jack exclaimed. "You're twisting everything all around. I thought we could fix this place up together."

"With you supplying all the money and most of the labor," Cara said. "Did it occur to you that after you make all these amazing improvements I won't be able to afford the rent here? Or were you planning to go looking for a new tenant and move me to another building in your vast array of real-estate ventures?"

"Cara, for Chrissake—I don't understand why you're getting so worked up about all this. You know I'm not going to raise your rent or kick you out. I care about you, not the money. That's the only reason I got into this."

She felt the rage bubbling up from her gut. "Men always say that, and they always lie. Because it's *always* about the money. Look at my father. He loans me money, and when I run into problems repaying it, he starts with the emotional blackmail. It's not about the money, he says. It's about financial responsibility. What he really means is, it's about control. And as long as I'm in his debt, I'm in his control. We've slept together what, Jack, five times? And you're just going to give me a building that you spent three-quarters of a million dollars to buy? How do you amortize that out? About a hundred and fifty thousand per fuck? I had no idea I was that good."

"Since you seem to be keeping track, we've slept together exactly three times," Jack said quietly. He pushed away from the table and gathered up the lunch wrappers, tossing them into the waste basket. "So it looks like you've undervalued yourself. And underestimated me, and my motives."

"Guess I'm just a typical flighty female. No head for numbers," Cara shot back. She took the sales contract, shoved it into the manila folder he'd brought it in, and held it out.

"Here. You can keep your building," she said. "I can be out of here in by the end of the month. I don't want any more gifts from any more men."

"Fine." He grabbed the envelope and headed for the shop door. "But you owe me six bucks for the lunch."

50

Ginny Best was sitting at the worktable when Cara, still bleary-eyed, got downstairs at eight o'clock. She'd made coffee, rolled the garden cart out to the street, and was already on the computer, scrolling through the day's emails.

The day was already looking up. Cara mentally congratulated herself for having the sense to offer this woman the job immediately after her interview the day before.

"Good morning." Ginny beamed. "I hope it's okay that I came in a little early. I wanted to get a jump on the hospital orders first thing."

Cara yawned. "Early is good. Early is amazing. Just make sure you write down your hours so I remember to pay you for the extra time. I'm glad you're here, because I've got a crazy day today. I'm gonna go look at a couple properties with my real-estate agent, then I've got to meet Harris and Brooke over at Cabin Creek to walk through plans for the reception and after-party. Think you can hold down the fort here by yourself?"

Ginny's serious brown eyes blinked rapidly behind the thick lens of her glasses. "How long will you be gone?"

"Better part of the day," Cara said.

Cara heard scratching coming from the back of the shop. "Back in a sec," she told her new assistant. She hurried down the hallway and opened the back door to let Poppy in from the garden.

"Good girl," Cara said, scratching the puppy's silken curls. "Come on, let's go get you a treat." The dog followed Cara back into the shop, and when she saw the newcomer standing at the flower cooler, barked happily and lunged for her.

"Ack!" Ginny stumbled backward, flailing her arms wildly. "Get off, get off!"

"Poppy, down!" Cara called. But Poppy was intent on greeting the newest member of the Bloom staff. She lunged again, planting her muddy front paws on Ginny's pale pink blouse.

"No! Bad dog, bad dog," Ginny shouted, shoving the dog violently away.

Cara grabbed for Poppy's collar. "Poppy! No." Poppy sank to the floor and looked embarrassed at her outburst.

"I'm so sorry," Cara said, standing up. "She gets excited when somebody new comes in. I know it's terrible manners, and I've got to take her back to obedience school, but really, she wouldn't hurt a fly."

Ginny looked warily at Poppy, who was now crouched under Cara's side of the worktable, gnawing on a chew toy. She glanced down at the front of her blouse, brushing at the mud stains. "I'm not really a dog person," she said, frowning. "She doesn't have to stay here all the time, does she?"

"Actually, she does. Not necessarily in the shop, all day, because I let her out into the garden to play, but yes, since I live here, or wherever we move to next, Poppy does too. Is that going to be a problem?"

Ginny bit her lip. "Don't your clients think it's kind of . . . I don't know, unprofessional—your having a pet in your place of business?"

"I've never had any complaints. In fact, most of my clients love having Poppy around."

"It's just that, when I interviewed, you didn't say anything about a dog." Ginny went to the kitchenette, wet a paper towel, and began dabbing at the front of her blouse.

"I'll be happy to pay to have that cleaned," Cara said.

"No need. It'll probably come out," Ginny said. She looked over at Poppy, who, misinterpreting the moment, lifted her head, tongue lolling, tail thumping enthusiastically. "Down," Ginny said sternly.

Cara tied a pale blue satin ribbon and wrapped it around a potted azalea in a rattan basket. "Okay," she said, standing and reaching for her purse. "I'm off. You can load everything in the van by yourself and make the deliveries, right? There are just six this morning, three for St. Joe's, two for Memorial, and one for the Rose of Sharon apartments."

Ginny nodded vigorously. "Right. That won't be any problem."

"I may be back late," Cara warned, her hand on the front door. "Alice, my real-estate agent, has several properties to show me, and I don't know how long I'll be in South Carolina. If I'm not back by five, just bring the garden cart in, and lock up, like I showed you."

"Wait," Ginny called. "What about the dog? Aren't you going to take her with you?"

"I can't," Cara said patiently. "She gets carsick unless I medicate her. Anyway, it's ninety-two degrees already. I can't leave her in a car while I look at buildings. Poppy's really no trouble, Ginny. She's house-trained, so you don't have to worry about letting her out while you run the deliveries. If you do let her into the garden, please make sure the back gate is closed and locked, and check her water bowl to make sure it's full. I'll see you in the morning."

Alice Murphy pulled her Cadillac alongside a stretch of curb on Waters Avenue. "Okay, Cara," she said, her New England accent making it sound more like "Carer." "This is the last one."

She gestured at the single-story brick building. It was boxy, with a vaguely 1960s reference, but over the years multiple owners had successfully erased any kind of architectural personality it might once have possessed. Now it was painted the color of brown mustard. The tattered remnants of a tan awning stretched over a pair of dusty plate-glass windows, which were still painted with the name of the building's most recently departed tenants—ACEY-DUECY AUTO DETAILING.

Cara eyed the building with disbelief. "Really? You think this is a good option?"

Alice sighed. "Oh, Cara, sweetheart. With your budget and the time frame we're working with, this is the best I can do."

She held up her hand, ticking off the building's many desirable qualities. "One, it's available immediately. You could move in today, if you wanted. Two, it's dirt cheap. The owner's desperate to get somebody in here. Three, it's big. Huge. You can have a big workspace up front, and make a nice-sized apartment in the back. And four, you've got plenty of parking."

"Wait. Back up, Alice. It doesn't already have a living space?"

"Well . . . the owner says the last tenants were sort of illegally squatting. He thinks there were at least three families staying there."

"Great. A combination flophouse and auto-detailing shop. I can't wait to see it."

Alice held out the keys and gave her an approving smile. "That's my gal."

Ten minutes later, the two women burst through the front door, alternately gagging and gasping for air.

"Oh my Lawd," Alice exclaimed, wiping at her watery eyes. "Oh my Lawd."

Cara slumped against the door of the Cadillac. "I wish I could unsee what we just saw."

"I had no idea," Alice said. "I should call that owner. I bet he doesn't know the roof caved in."

"Or that raccoons have taken up residence. Or that the last tenants left a year's worth of rotting garbage in the so-called kitchen," Cara added.

Alice shook her head. "We cross this one off the list. That just leaves us the dry cleaner's shop on Paulsen."

"Which is too small and has no yard for Poppy," Cara said.

"Or the duplex on Hall Street," Alice added. "It had parking, a courtyard garden for Poppy, and a nice apartment upstairs for you."

"And it's twice as much as I can afford, and I'm not crazy about that block. Other than that, it's perfect," Cara said.

Alice unlocked the Caddy, turned the air-conditioning on the polar-ice-cap setting, and rolled the windows down to allow the hot air to escape. "We rode by a dozen properties today, hon. You nixed everything except for Paulsen and Hall. What do you want to do?"

"I want to stay right where I'm at," Cara said stubbornly, dabbing at her damp forehead with a tissue. "But since that's no longer an option, I guess we should call the duplex owner. Do you think you can talk him down any on the rent?"

"I doubt it. She told me she had two other showings this week. If you think it's a possibility, we probably need to jump on it pretty quickly, or we risk losing it."

"I know, Alice. But I'm really scared. I've got a big check coming from my next wedding next week, and with that, I can just barely scrape up enough for first and last month's rent for Hall Street, plus moving expenses. But what if something goes wrong? I'm one wedding away from skid row."

Alice patted her arm sympathetically. "I admire you young single gals so much. Starting and running your own businesses, I never could have done anything like that when I was your age. I got married at nineteen, started having my babies. John was always the boss. Don't get me wrong. He's always been a wonderful provider, but I went from living in my father's house to being somebody's wife and mother. I never would have had the guts or the smarts to do the things you've done, Cara."

Cara smiled ruefully. "I'm not so smart, Alice. I've had a rotten marriage, my business could come crashing down around me at any minute, and in the meantime, I've been so busy trying to save the business, the one promising relationship I've had since my divorce just went up in flames.

"At least you have your kids, and your grandkids, and a solid marriage," Cara went on. "What have I got to show for the last ten years? A crappy van, a website, and a dog who's an obedience-school dropout. I don't even own my own house."

"You will," Alice said. "You're having a run of bad luck right now, but I know things are going to change for you. I'm Irish. We know these things."

"I hope you're right," Cara said. She sank back into the Cadillac's buttery leathery upholstery as Alice turned the car back toward the real-estate office.

"Sure I can't take you out to a late lunch?" Alice asked, as she pulled alongside Cara's own car. "My treat."

"Thanks, but I've got to get over to South Carolina. We're doing a walk-through and site visit with the bride and groom and their parents, and I need everything to be perfect," Cara said, reaching for the passenger-door handle.

"Cara?" Alice put a hand on her arm. "Are you sure you don't want me to call the new owner of your building? See if we can't come to an agreement that would allow you to stay put? It seems a shame to leave a place that's so perfect for your needs, just because of some misunderstanding."

"No misunderstanding at all, Alice," Cara said soberly. "Jack Finnerty deliberately misled me. Jones Street is just a shrewd real-estate investment as far as he's concerned. He's just as bad as Cullen Kane, just as bad as my former assistant. Just as bad as my ex-husband. I wouldn't trust him as far as I could throw him."

"Okay," Alice said slowly. "Shall I call about Hall Street? See if we can get moving on a lease?"

Cara's shoulders slumped. "Yes. Go ahead. But I can't write any checks until next Friday. Make sure they understand that."

51

Her car's air conditioner thrummed ineffectively against the glaring midday heat. Sweat stung her eyes, and her pale blue linen shift, which that morning she'd thought would look so cool and effortless, now stuck to the back of her legs and resembled a limp, slightly used Kleenex.

The Eugene Talmadge Memorial Bridge was a suspension bridge that separated Georgia from South Carolina. Cara glanced down, toward the brownish green water of the Savannah River below, and saw a huge container ship gliding toward the port. Her arms were rigid as she gripped the steering wheel with two damp hands.

Alice had just called with the news that she was drawing up the lease for the duplex on Hall Street. Cara honestly didn't know whether to laugh or cry.

She had ten days to pack up her apartment and shop—her life, in essence—and move out of Jones Street and over to Hall. And she had to do it by herself. This time around there would be no Bert, to make her laugh and help pack and unpack boxes, and moan and bitch about schlepping stuff up and down stairs.

He'd only been gone less than a week, but she missed her former assistant more than she'd ever admit. Ginny seemed pleasant and efficient, but Cara knew that she and Ginny would never sip from the same cup of snark sauce.

And there would be no Jack, either. The angry words they'd hurled at each other the night before had guaranteed that.

So, fine. She was too busy for idle gossip and casual sex anyway. Cara pushed a strand of hair out of her eyes. Time to concentrate on today's meeting.

She and Marie had finally managed to bully Brooke and Harris into agreeing to meet at Cabin Creek to walk through the plans for the reception and after-party. Libba Strayhorn was anxious to show them the progress on the old barn, and if all went well, they'd even be able to finalize placement of all the tables, chairs, and "lounge furniture" Cara had already rented from the tents and events house in Savannah. And, of course, Patricia Trapnell would be there, too.

Cara's stomach was already in knots. She wondered if Patricia was aware of the way her "dear friend" Cullen Kane had managed to so thoroughly torpedo her personal and professional life.

She relaxed her grip on the steering wheel just slightly after her car was finally speeding along the flat, featureless low country on the South Carolina side of the bridge. Glimpses of marsh flashed by, of elderly men with cane poles fishing on muddy creek banks, of elegant white egrets soaring over the green-gold grass, of rusted, aging mobile homes separated from the highway by little more than a weedy patch of dirt.

Thirty minutes later she slowed the car for the turn down the crushed-gravel drive to Cabin Creek. It was five till two, and she felt relief at the sight of Brooke's white Volvo sedan parked behind her mother's sedate gray Mercedes. There was always a fifty-fifty chance their harried bride might not show up.

Libba Strayhorn met her at the back door, dressed in a short, mint green cotton dress, pearls, and low-heeled sandals. Her blond hair curled just below her chin. Cara realized she'd never seen her client's hair, because Libba was never without her baseball cap.

"You're staring," Libba said, as she ushered her inside.

"It's just that I've never seen you so dressed up before," Cara admitted.

"Doesn't happen very often," Libba said cheerfully. "I had an altar guild meeting at church this morning, and I haven't had a minute to change. But I'm going to, right this minute."

She gestured toward the kitchen wing. "Everybody's out in the kitchen getting something cold to drink. Go on in, and I'll be right with you as soon as I get out of this rig and into something comfortable."

As soon as she walked into the kitchen, Cara sensed something was amiss. Marie sat at the kitchen table, her hands folded in her lap, glancing anxiously in the direction of the French doors that led to the patio. Patricia sat at the far end of the table, her head bent, furiously typing something into her Blackberry. But where were the bride and groom?

Ahh. Finally, she saw Brooke and Harris, outside on the patio. They stood close together, talking quietly, but Cara could tell from the angry set of Harris's usually placid face and the animated flashing of Brooke's hands that they were arguing.

Marie winced. "They've been out there for about ten minutes. Brooke is really wound up about something. I've never seen her like this before."

Patricia looked up from her typing. "I heard them when I walked up to the house, they were so involved, they didn't even notice me. It's all over this silly bachelor party tomorrow night. Brooke is being ridiculous."

"Why do you say that?" Marie said, her voice uncharacteristically sharp.

"She's making this big fuss about nothing. It's a bachelor's party, for God's sake. A bunch of guys hooting and hollering at a strip club. So what? It's harmless. A rite of passage. My son's friends all do it before their weddings."

Marie stared down at her iced-tea glass. "Brooke won't see it like that."

"Then she needs to get over herself," Patricia shot back. "Harris is a big boy. He can take care of himself."

Marie's eyes narrowed. But before she could respond, Libba bounced into the room. She wore faded blue jeans, a loose-fitting T-shirt, tennis shoes, and her ever-present Cabin Creek baseball cap again, and her dog was right on her heels.

"Thanks for your patience, ladies," Libba said. "I feel soooo much better. You know, every year I swear I'm not going to dress up for these darned altar-guild meetings, and every year, I bow to peer pressure, and put on the dress and heels and pantyhose. And every year, I want to kill myself. It's torture! And I'll tell you right now, I am *not* wearing hose at this wedding. My mother-of-the groom dress is floor length, so nobody but me and Jesus will be any the wiser."

"Ooh, good idea," Marie chimed in. "Mine is long too. And I despise pantyhose. Let's make a pact. We'll call it a hose-free zone." She looked over at Patricia. "What do you say? Are you in?"

Patricia stopped typing on her Blackberry and slipped it back into her Louis Vuitton tote. "Sorry, girls. My dress is cocktail length. And Gordon thinks sheer black hose are terrifically sexy."

"You're wearing black to the wedding?" Libba blurted. "Isn't that considered bad luck, or taboo or something?"

"Not for stepmothers," Patricia purred.

Two pink spots bloomed high on Marie's cheeks. The awkward silence was broken when the French doors opened and the bride and groom stepped inside.

Brooke's eyes were red-rimmed, and Harris was stony-faced. He looked from his mother to Cara to Marie. "Can we just get through this, please? Brooke says she has a meeting back in town."

"Sure thing," Libba said. "Let's start in the ballroom."

The ballroom had been freshly painted and wallpapered, and Libba Strayhorn was tickled to be showing it off. She linked her arm through Marie's as they walked around the room.

"I don't know why we waited so long to freshen this room up," she said, pointing out the new window treatments, and the polished floors. She looked over her shoulder at Brooke, who hadn't uttered a single word since the tour had started.

"Thank you so much, Brooke, for agreeing to have the wedding over here. Even that old skinflint Mitchell is pleased with how things have turned out."

Brooke forced a smile. "You're welcome, Lib. It looks great."

Cara paced off the room and showed the women the floor plan she'd drawn up for the bandstand, dance floor, ten-top tables and chairs.

"Do we have the fabric samples for the tablecloths yet?" Patricia asked, studying the sketches.

Cara blinked. "I thought you'd seen them, Patricia. I sent them to Brooke two weeks ago. The seamstress called yesterday, she thinks she'll have them done early next week."

Patricia glared at Brooke, who blandly looked away. "Sorry, I guess I forgot. I think I still have the sample in my car, if you really care."

"Not at this late date, I don't."

"Okay, good," Brooke said, smirking.

"I just love paying for something I haven't even seen," Patricia said under her breath.

Marie glanced helplessly from Cara to her daughter to Libba. The tension in the room was nearly as thick and unpleasant as the June humidity.

"Let's go out and see the barn," Libba suggested brightly. "You're simply not going to believe how it looks."

Cara let out an inward sigh of relief when they approached the barn and Jack's pickup wasn't there.

But there were signs everywhere that he and Ryan had worked their magic. A wide new walkway of worn flagstones wound through the newly mown field toward the barn. Nearby, an old farm wagon had been planted with white geraniums, trailing Swedish ivy and swirls of blue plumbago.

"After the guys cleaned the barn they dragged that out, and I told them to just take it to the dump," Libba said. "The next time I walked over here, it looked like that."

"The flagstones were Jack's idea," she said. "He pointed out that walking through the field would ruin everybody's shoes, and particularly Brooke's wedding gown, if they had to trail in the grass. And God forbid there might be rain that night."

"It looks like it's always been here," Marie said approvingly. She glanced at Brooke, who trailed a few yards behind. "Isn't it lovely, Brooke?"

"Nice," Brooke said.

Cara stopped dead in her tracks as they got closer to the barn. It had been a month since she'd last been out to Cabin Creek, and the transformation in that time was dramatic.

The cracked and faded exterior barn boards had been pressure-washed and patched, with the new boards carefully stained to blend with the old. The standing-seam tin roof gleamed brightly in the glaring afternoon sun. Wide new windows had been cut into the walls, but the glass was old and wavy, with true divided lights picked out in a deep gray that contrasted with the original silvery exterior color.

Libba walked up to the newly painted glossy black barn doors. "This is one of my favorite things," she crowed. She touched a black iron latch, and both doors slid open on the wrought-iron sliders.

"Isn't that amazing? Those old doors, I could hardly yank them open anymore. Jack and Ryan found these doors and rigged some system of weights and counterweights, and I can open them with no problem."

Libba spread her arms wide, her face wreathed in smiles as she stepped inside the barn. "Ta-da!"

Brooke stood in the middle of the barn and burst into tears.

"Honey?" Harris gingerly wrapped his arms around his fiancée. "Don't you like it?" He rested his chin on Brooke's shining hair and looked to his mother for help.

Libba shook her head, speechless.

It was Patricia who finally broke the silence. "It's spectacular."

"It's . . . it's just so beautiful," Brooke said, her voice breaking. She turned and hugged Libba. "I can't believe you did all of this just for us."

"Well, to be honest, it was for me too," Libba said, rubbing Brooke's back. "Just call it a labor of love."

Their footsteps echoed in the high-ceilinged room. Cara craned her neck to see the exposed trusses and beams overhead. Sturdy industrial-looking galvanized light fixtures hung from thick ropes, illuminating the space below.

"Should we take off our shoes?" Patricia asked, already slipping out of her own Prada pumps.

"Not at all," Libba said. She leaned down and ran a hand lovingly over the burnished wood floors. "These boards came out of a closed-down textile mill in Spartanburg. They're old-growth pine. If you look carefully, you can see old grease stains and holes where machinery was bolted to the floor, and gouges and dents. I love them just the way they are, and Jack and Ryan agreed. The more beat up they get, the better they'll look."

"If you say so," Patricia said, her tone implying that she thought otherwise.

"It's a barn," Libba said, chuckling. "A really expensive barn, but I didn't want it too tarted up."

"Look up there, Brooke," Harris said, pointing to the gabled east end of the barn. "The old hayloft."

"Harris and his high-school band used to practice up there," Libba said. "Mitchell used to say the racket they made would make the neighbor's cows go dry. Brooke, I bet you didn't know you were marrying a musician."

"I didn't," Brooke said.

"That's because we sucked," Harris said. "Called ourselves the Chiggers. We were trying to be badass, but mostly we were just bad. And asses."

"I'll bet you weren't that awful."

"Actually, they were," Libba volunteered. She drew Marie aside and pointed again at the hayloft. "I had the guys reinforce the floors with steel beams, and that rail is reinforced too. Someday, my grandbabies will play up in that loft, just like Harris and Holly did, and their daddy before them."

For a split second, Cara saw a tiny pucker form on Brooke's smooth brow.

"Jack had a great idea," Harris said. "He said we should put the DJ booth up there for the after-party."

Brooke pointed at the sturdy ladder leading up to the loft. "But how would he get his equipment up that ladder?"

"If you open that door back there behind that partition, you'll see how," Libba said. "The guys put in a nice wide staircase. And underneath it, there's a new bathroom too."

Marie shook her head. "Libba, I'm just stunned at everything you've accomplished in such a short time."

Cara was already pacing off the room, admiring the honest grace and simplicity of the old structure's lines. She reached out and touched a silvery board and felt a deep twinge of regret. Jack Finnerty had rebuilt this barn, poured his sweat and passion into every detail and rediscovered its beauty. She wished she could tell him how moved she was by the artistry of his work.

But that ship had sailed.

Libba was still beaming as she led the group out of the barn. "I asked Jack for a fireplace back in the barn, but he talked me out of it. There just wasn't going to be time to build a suitable rock chimney before the wedding."

She pointed to a cleared area on the south side of the barn. "Instead, he's giving me a fire pit over there. He and Ryan will build some benches from wood left over from the barn."

"I've got an idea," Cara said. "If you don't mind, maybe we could move that old cart over near the fire pit. We can use it to set up the bar and the dessert buffet."

Cara turned to Marie. "Layne is baking homemade chocolate-dipped graham crackers and her own marshmallows for s'mores at midnight. And we're going to do a signature Cabin Creek cocktail. It's basically an old-fashioned, but we'll use this new bourbon from a distillery in Americus. And we'll serve them in pint Mason jars."

"Americus as in Georgia?" Patricia laughed. "No thanks. Give me a dry martini any day."

Cara couldn't resist the challenge. "You might be pleasantly surprised, Patricia. I've had this bourbon, and it's really quite good."

"I think this all sounds great," Marie said. She looked around to seek her daughter's agreement, but Brooke and Harris had drifted away from the others. They were standing under the shade of a pin-oak tree several yards away, deep in discussion, and from the looks of their expressions, things had gotten heated again.

"Brooke, Harris," Marie called, determined to draw them out of their argument. "Did you hear what Cara said about the Cabin Creek cocktail?"

Brooke shook her head, tears spilling down her cheeks, and stomped off.

"That sounds fine, Marie," Harris called. Then he hurried off in his fiancée's wake.

A few minutes later, they heard car doors slamming, then Brooke's Volvo, roaring up the road in a cloud of dust.

"Oh my," Libba said, shading her eyes with her hand as she watched Harris's car follow a moment later.

Marie sighed and shook her head. "I'm sorry, Libba. Brooke's just a bundle of nerves these days. It's this trial she's working on. I'll be so glad when it's over. This is classic Brooke. She's so intense and driven when it comes to her job. She was the same way when she was in school. She'd make herself sick worrying and studying before a big test. She'd convince herself she couldn't possibly pass, and of course, she always did. I don't remember her ever making anything lower than a B-plus."

"Brooke is so unlike Gordon in that way," Patricia piped up. "He's always so calm and confident. I think he actually thrives under pressure."

Marie gazed wordlessly at her ex-husband's new wife. She started to say something, but stopped herself.

"Never mind," Libba said soothingly. "Whatever is going on between the kids, they'll work it out."

"I hope so," Marie said.

52

Cara felt like a wrung-out dishrag by the time she finally parked her car on the street outside Bloom. It was nearly 5:30, but she was surprised to see that the garden cart was still on the sidewalk, and through the window she spotted Ginny Best, still seated at the worktable, poking daisies and zinnias into a round glass bowl.

"Oh hi," Ginny said. She held up the arrangement. "What do you think?"

"Mmm. Needs something else. Maybe some of those little miniature blue irises." Cara looked around the shop. "Where's Poppy?"

"Out back," Ginny said, going to the cooler for more flowers. "Some guy came by to see you earlier. I told him you'd be back late in the day."

"What guy?" Cara asked, grabbing a bottle of cold water from the fridge in the kitchenette. She left the fridge door open, uncapped the bottle, and swigged deeply as the cool air chilled her damp skin. She felt a tiny prickle of hope. Could it have been Jack? Was it possible that he hadn't totally written her of?

"He didn't tell me his name," Ginny said. "He was kind of a hottie, though. Blond hair, Ray-Bans. Your boyfriend?"

Cara choked, spewing water over her chest and chin. She grabbed a paper towel and mopped her face. "Not even," she said.

"Oh." Ginny nodded. "I think I get the picture."

"Thanks, Ginny. You can go on home now. I don't want you working a ten-hour day. I can finish that in the morning," Cara said.

"Okay," Ginny said, hopping down from her stool.

Cara fished a puppy treat from the jar on the counter and unlocked the back door, bracing herself for Poppy's typical rocket launch of unbridled puppy love.

At first glance, she thought the dog was sleeping. Poppy lay motionless on the sun-baked bricks.

"Here girl!" Cara called gaily. "Treat time!"

Poppy raised her muzzle and whined. That's when Cara saw the taut rope leading from the trunk of the crepe myrtle to the dog's neck. That's when she noticed the reddish trickle staining Poppy's platinum curls.

"Oh my God!" Cara cried. She dropped to the ground, her fingers shaking uncontrollably as she worked at the knot attached to her pet's collar. Poppy whined again, but she didn't squirm. All the fight had already gone out of her.

The bricks beneath Cara's knees scorched her skin as she fumbled helplessly with the tangled cord. "Oh my sweet girl. My poor sweet girl," Cara crooned. Finally, after what seemed like an hour, but was probably less than a minute, she tossed the rope aside. Cara unbuckled the dog's collar, flinching at the sight of the bloodstained fur.

She felt Poppy's nose. It was dry. She looked around for her water bowl and saw it, just out of reach, turned on its side.

Cara carefully gathered the forty-five-pound puppy in her arms. She found the hose bib, turned it on, and, placing a finger over the nozzle, gently sprayed the dog's face and the top of her head with it. Poppy's pink tongue worked furiously, lapping at the sun-warmed water. At some point, Cara searched for the thermometer attached to the courtyard wall. Ninety degrees, and it was now nearly six o'clock.

Somehow, she got to her feet, with Poppy still cradled in her arms. She jerked the back door open, sprinted toward the front of the shop.

Ginny Best was standing by the front door, her pocketbook over her shoulder, smiling into her cell phone. "Okay, if you're sure you've done your spelling words, we'll go out for ice cream when we get home." Her eyes widened when she saw her employer.

"I'll see you in a bit," Ginny said hastily, ending the call.

"Did you do this?" Cara demanded. "Did you tie my dog to a tree and leave her out there all day with no shade and no water?"

"She had water," Ginny protested.

"What kind of heartless, stupid bitch are you?" Cara felt her whole body shaking with barely contained fury. "It was nearly a hundred degrees out there today. You tie her up with four feet of rope, so she can't get to shade, can't get to water? And you leave her there? She could have died!"

"She was fine," Ginny said. "You weren't here. You don't know. She kept whining to go out, then whining to come back in, and the phone was ringing, and when I went to load the van, she tried to get out of the gate. She would have run away! So I tied her up. And I gave her water. I did. She had a whole bowl of it. I figured she'd be okay."

"How about this, Ginny? How about I take one of your kids and tie a rope around their neck and leave them out in the sun all day—with no water and no food? And dressed in a fur coat? Would that be okay?"

"She's a dog, for God's sake," Ginny said. "I'm sorry. It won't happen again."

"It certainly won't," Cara said. "You're fired. Now get out of my sight before I do something we'll both regret."

The vet tech at the after-hours animal clinic found Cara in the waiting room, sitting beside an elderly man whose dachshund had eaten a remote control.

"Ms. Kryzik? Poppy's fine. Why don't you come back and see her now?"

Poppy was sprawled out on her side on an examining table, damp towels draped over her head and body, a small fan pointed toward her face. It reminded Cara of a spa treatment she'd once had. When the dog saw Cara, her tail thumped against the vinyl tabletop.

"My girl," Cara whispered, kissing the towel on top of Poppy's head. "My sweet, sweet girl. You had me so worried."

"It's a good thing you found her when you did," the tech said, giving Poppy's rump a fond pat. "Her body temp was right at a hundred and two. She was one degree from stroking out. You did the right thing too, wetting her down like that and getting her over here immediately. You'd be surprised how many people try to put a dog in an ice bath. They mean well, but that's totally the wrong thing to do. It makes the surface blood vessels constrict, and that can kill a dog."

Cara realized she'd been holding her breath. She exhaled slowly now. "I guess I just reacted. I was so scared, and then so furious, I didn't really have time to stop and think."

"We gave her some Pedialyte and her urine checked out okay, and her heart's fine," the tech said. "So you can take her home now. Just try to keep her quiet tonight, and cool, of course. Let her have as much water as she wants, but don't try to force her to drink."

"I will. I mean, I won't. I mean, I'm still pretty freaked out. Can you write all that down for me?" Cara asked.

She dragged Poppy's dog bed downstairs and placed it in the workroom, near the air conditioner, which she turned on high. Screw the electric bill.

Poppy flopped down on her bed, but seemed restless, getting up every few minutes to stand in front of the front door, staring out at the now-dark sidewalk. Cara didn't know if the dog was watching for enemy squirrels, or even worse, Ginny Best.

Cara was restless as well. She opened her laptop and checked her emails. There were at least forty more responses to her Craigslist ad. She read a few, silently, her reaction to the contents ranging from hopeless to hilarious. Finally, Poppy gave up her sentry post and returned to her bed.

"Here's a good one," Cara said, turning toward the drowsy dog and reading aloud.

"'Hello sweet mommy. My name is Khalika and I am living in Gambia. I have read your requirements and am saying I am excellent candidate for professional job you are wanting. Please be immediate wiring two thousand dollars (American) for air travel expenses.' "

Poppy's bright pink tongue lolled from her mouth.

"Wonder if he's single?" Cara mused.

She was still reading when the laptop dinged, signaling the arrival of a new message in her inbox.

"I don't believe it," Cara said, staring at the message.

"Poppy, listen to this. It's an email from that stupid bitch Ginny. The one who tried to kill you earlier today? Here's what she says."

Poppy opened one eye, lifted one ear.

" 'Hi. I'll come by the shop tomorrow to pick up my paycheck for ten hours worked. I'm assuming you won't be taking out taxes or social security? Sincerely, Virginia Best.' "

Cara's fingertips flew over the keyboard.

Hi Ginny. The bill for the emergency after-hours vet clinic for treating Poppy for heat stroke and deyhydration came to four hundred and fifty dollars. How about we call it even and you never come near here again? Otherwise you won't have to worry about a dog attacking you. I'll bite you my ownself. Sincerely, Cara Kryzik.

She read it aloud for Poppy's approval. "What do you think, girl?"

The dog's eyes were half closed. Her tail switched, and emitted a short, noxious blast of gas.

"I'll take that as a yes." Cara hit the Send button.

53

Poppy seemed good as new by Friday morning. Cara took her out for a brief early-morning stroll at 7:30, taking a cautionary interest in her urine output, as the vet tech had suggested. All was well.

Except that she was running a one-woman show again. Reluctantly concluding that there was no way she could do it all, Cara referred phone and email orders to another downtown florist, and even paid the florist to deliver the few arrangements Ginny Best had finished before her Thursday banishment.

Cara was working on placing the Trapnell order with her California shipper when the office phone rang. She grabbed the receiver.

"Bloom. This is Cara."

"Hi Cara, it's Meredith. Have you talked to your bride today?"

"Which bride?"

"Brooke Trapnell. She was supposed to sit for her wedding portrait in my studio today. She's nearly an hour late."

Cara squeezed her eyes shut in frustration. "Have you tried to call her?"

"I don't have her number. I made the arrangements with you, remember?"

"Okay, okay. I'll call and suggest she get her tiny little heinie over there pronto. Sorry for the hassle."

She considered her best strategy for contacting Brooke Trapnell. Emails were a waste of time, and phone calls were iffy at best. A text just might get the girl's attention.

Brooke! Call me ASAP! Very important! Cara

Ten minutes later, when she'd still had no reply, she tried again.

Brooke! Don't make me call Patricia.

Her phone rang almost as soon as the text sent.

"Very funny," Brooke said, chuckling. "What's so important that you had to threaten to bring in the big guns?"

"Do you know what day it is?" Cara asked.

"It's Friday. Lunchtime. I only know that because everybody else in my office is eating lunch, while I'm still sitting at my desk buried in Georgia code."

"You're supposed to be at the photographer's," Cara said pointedly.

"Oh hell! I completely forgot. I had a deposition that ran long this morning, and my whole day has been screwed up."

"You were due there almost an hour ago."

"I can't get away now, that's for sure. Give me her number, and I'll call and rebook."

"Do both of us a favor and see that you do, okay? Otherwise your stepmother is going to hound me into an early grave. She wants that wedding portrait as a belated Father's Day gift for your dad."

"Why? Gordon's not her daddy. He's mine."

"Take it up with her, not me," Cara said. "Um, while I have you on the phone, did you and Harris kiss and make up yesterday? Your mom and Libba were pretty upset when you left the way you did."

"Geez," Brooke said. "I should have known blabbermouth Patricia would tell you we were fighting about the damned bachelor party. My girlfriends keep saying it's no biggie—just a bunch of overaged frat guys getting hammered and cruising strip clubs. And Harris insists it's harmless. They've rented a van and a driver to take them to Atlanta and back. 'Good dirty fun' he calls it."

"But you don't see it that way."

"No. When I was a first-year associate I had a pro-bono client—a girl who'd worked in one of those clubs. She was barely twenty-one and had a five-year-old son and a string of prostitution and solicitation arrests. And a raging meth habit. She told me what it was like working in a strip club. They treat those girls like . . . trash. They post rules telling them they're not allowed to fraternize with the customers, but the only way the girls make tips is by coming on to the guys, offering them, you know, hand jobs or whatever out in the parking lot. My client got busted for meth, and her little boy ended up in foster care. I've never forgotten her."

"Did you tell all that to Harris?"

"I told him I hated the idea, and he said he couldn't cancel, because all the guys would say he was pussy-whipped."

Cara could see both points of view. They were both right, but there would be no winner over an issue like this.

"It's just one night," she pointed out.

"You sound like my mom. I know, I'm a bitch. I'll get over it. I guess I'm just really, really tired. This sounds awful but I wish I didn't have my own bachelorette party tomorrow night."

"Aww, you don't want to miss your bachelorette party," Cara said. "What are you doing?"

"Holly won't tell me. It's supposed to be some big surprise. All I know is, there better not be any male strippers involved."

"I'm sure they'll have something fun planned for you. Look, Brooke. I know you have a lot on your plate right now with the trial and the wedding. And it probably doesn't do much good for people to tell you to relax and stop stressing, but I've done tons and tons of weddings, and I'm telling you, relax. Your wedding is supposed to be fun, you know?"

"Fun," Brooke said dully. "Got it."

"Magical."

"Right."

"Never mind," Cara said, finally. "Please, please, I beg you, call Meredith and get over there and have your wedding portrait taken. And while you're at it, you might practice smiling."

54

Because her real-estate agent knew how to make things happen—or maybe just because her new about-to-be landlord had a certain laissez-faire attitude about legal matters—Cara picked up the key to the Hall Street duplex Saturday afternoon.

Friday night must have been a happening scene on this block. Empty malt-liquor bottles, fast-food wrappers, cigarette butts, and even something she feared might be a condom littered the sidewalk out front of the building. Cara made a mental note to bring a hose, a bottle of Pine-Sol, and a scrub brush on her next trip back.

Poppy sat down on the sidewalk while Cara unlocked the front door. "Come on, girl," Cara said, stepping inside and flipping the light switch. "Let's see our new place."

The dog wouldn't budge. "Let's go," Cara urged, gesturing toward the doorway. "Check it out. I'll bet there's a whole bunch of squirrels out back."

Cara couldn't bear to tug at the dog's neck, with its fresh abrasions from Thursday. In the end, she simply picked Poppy up and plopped her down inside the building.

The inside of the shop wasn't much cheerier than the exterior. Alice Murphy said the last tenant had been a dry cleaner and alterationist. The faded linoleum floor was gritty underfoot; the wide plate-glass window was streaked with dust and what looked like remnants of masking tape.

She forced herself to overlook the negative and focus on the positive. The walls were the original exposed brick, and there was a handsome fireplace with a carved Victorian mantelpiece and stained marble hearth. The walls would be charming once she pressure-washed them, and the fireplace, which was intended to burn coal, could perhaps be fitted with gas logs, which might be nice on what passed for a cold winter day in Savannah. The front room was much wider and deeper than the shop on Jones Street. Eventually, maybe she'd have a large showroom here, with a counter and display shelves, with the workroom separated by a partition or finished wall.

For now, though, with the huge bump in rent, she'd have to leave things as they were.

Before being turned into commercial space, Cara knew this floor of the building, like most of the others on the block, had been residential. There were still a small kitchen and a tiny, squalid bathroom here, and a back door that led out to a large fenced area.

She opened the thick fire door and frowned at the sight that met her eyes. Impossible to find anything to like here. The space couldn't even be called a yard, and it certainly wasn't a garden. It was overgrown with weeds, and a tall, narrow, sickly-looking magnolia tree blocked whatever sunlight might otherwise have shone there. She could see a couple of bashed-up Dumpsters next to the stockade fence, and next to them was an abandoned supermarket shopping cart, probably stolen from the Kroger a few blocks away. Cara shuddered, sure the area was probably teeming with rats, snakes, spiders, and God knew what else. She would have to have the yard cleared out and mowed before she'd dare let Poppy out there.

One more thing to add to her to-do list. She closed the door, locked and bolted it.

"Let's go upstairs," she told Poppy. The dog yawned and dropped to the floor. Only a puppy, and she was already a prima donna.

The staircase was narrow and steep, with worn risers and a handrail and balustrades thick with gummy layers of old paint.

At the top of the stairs she stood and took it all in. Her new home. The wallpaper was a dusty blue pattern of baby ducks and tulips, circa 1982, Cara thought. She knew there were probably wooden floors under the cheap commercial carpet, but she also knew she wouldn't be pulling that carpet up to find out anytime soon.

"It's a nice, big space," Alice Murphy had pointed out. Big, yes; nice, not so much.

Whoever had installed that fugly wallpaper back in the eighties had also seen fit to install a dropped ceiling of stained and yellowed acoustical tile. She was standing in the living room, which had a fireplace that roughly matched the one on the first floor. It was also much bigger than her apartment on Jones Street, but with not a scintilla of appeal. An arched doorway led from the living room to the dining room, which led to the kitchen.

The kitchen was about what you'd expect. Yellow vinyl floor, cheap orangish-stained pine cabinets, laminate countertops littered with cockroach corpses, rusting stove and fridge, no dishwasher, tiny sink. Depressing. A window over the sink overlooked the Dumpster graveyard.

Cara meant to head up to the third floor, where her bedroom would be, but suddenly found she lacked the energy.

Poppy was where she'd left her in the living room. "Come on, girl," she said, opening the door. "Let's go back home. While we still can."

She stripped down to shorts and a tank top in the Jones Street apartment, and halfheartedly began packing boxes of books. After an hour or so, she gave up, and plopped down on the sofa. She'd brought her laptop upstairs, and out of boredom, logged on to Facebook.

Cara had a business page for Bloom, and in the past, she'd made a regular practice of posting pictures of happy brides and beautiful bouquets. It was good marketing, and most of the "likers" on her page were former clients or other vendors in the wedding business.

She was scrolling down the page when a bubble popped up on her screen—a private message from Layne Pelletier.

OMG—have you seen this? There was a link, and Cara clicked it, the link taking her to Harris Strayhorn's Facebook page.

The OMG-inspired item Layne referred to was a timeline photo at the top of Harris's page. It was definitely a cell-phone picture, with bad lighting and fuzzy focus, but there was no mistaking the subject matter: Harris Strayhorn, leaning back in a chair, his eyes heavy-lidded, his mouth slack, with a very naked, voluptuous redhead straddling his lap. And just to make it clear who the subject of the photo was, the caption read HARRIS STRAYHORN TAKES IT LIKE A MAN.

There was a whole album of photos, and each one was worse than the one before—fifteen in all, fifteen photos of a bunch of overaged frat guys in a cheesy strip club, including five or six starring the bridegroom and man of the hour, Harris Strayhorn, receiving lap dances from two different naked women.

Cara felt a little sick. It was nearly four in the afternoon. The photos had been posted hours ago. Why hadn't Harris taken them down? Brooke had to have seen them by now. She glanced at the post again. There were forty-two comments and sixty-eight likes.

She closed the laptop, went to the refrigerator, and got a bottle of cold water. She felt like she also needed a cold shower, to rinse away the ugly images she'd just viewed.

Dinner was a slice of pizza at nine o'clock. She wasn't really hungry, but she needed to get out of the house, so she and Poppy strolled over to Mellow Mushroom on West Liberty Street.

Cara ordered a slice of the Philosopher's Pie and a glass of wine, and sat at a table outside, with Poppy crouched at her feet. This was a college hangout, and SCAD kids swarmed the sidewalk around her, laughing, talking, swearing, smoking. They rolled by on bikes and skateboards, and the atmosphere was noisy and electric. There were old-timers in Savannah who hated SCAD, with its artsy, avant-garde faculty and wacky, and some said entitled, student body, but Cara loved the energy they contributed to her neighborhood.

She took her time finishing her wine, enjoying eavesdropping on the swirl of conversations going on around her. Finally, when she could stand the hot sticky air no longer, she walked home, being vigilant about staying under streetlights and away from dark doorways.

They were only a few steps from her own door at Bloom when a tall, slender figure suddenly emerged from the shadows, stepping directly in front of her. Poppy gave a startled bark, and she had to choke back a half-formed scream.

"Cara? Sorry. I didn't mean to startle you."

It took a moment for her heart to stop racing and to gather her wits.

"Startle me? Jesus, Bert, you scared the living beejesus out of me." She held up the can of Mace she'd been clutching in her right hand. "Another second and you'd have gotten a faceful of this."

He laughed nervously. "Yeah. Rookie move. Can I talk to you for a minute?"

She fetched them both bottles of water, and they sat in her living room, with Poppy's head placed contentedly on Bert's lap.

He was dressed oddly, and acting strange, even for Bert. He wore his usual weekend attire of baggy shorts, flip-flops, and white "wife-beater" undershirt, but tonight, despite the stifling heat, he'd seen fit to throw a calf-length raincoat over the ensemble. His hair was cut shorter than she'd ever seen it, and he was obviously on edge.

Cara had no time for subterfuge. "Why are you here, Bert? Did Cullen send you?"

"Cullen? God, no." He kept running his fingers along Poppy's ears.

She raised one eyebrow, expectantly. "I'm waiting."

"I guess you were right. I guess this is where you get to say 'I told you so.' "

"About?"

"Cullen. Us. Everything. You were right about all of it. He doesn't give a damn about me. He was just using me to get to you. He's evil, Cara. Evil and twisted, and smart as hell. Scary smart."

"How did you figure it out?"

"I started putting things together almost as soon as I left here and went to work for him. I'm such a twit. I actually thought he cared about me. I bought everything he was selling—that he'd make me a designer, and I'd get to do my own events. But you saw where he had me at his studio—answering the phone. I never even touched a flower. My actual job was to pour champagne for clients and tweet photos of Cullen's fabulous creations. And empty his cat's litter box. When I moved in with him? I had to stay out in the carriage house. I was a glorified house boy. With fringe benefits."

Cara knew she should have felt vindicated—everything she'd predicted about Bert's experience with Cullen Kane had come true—but it felt like a hollow victory. He looked so sad and defeated.

"So you broke up with him?"

Bert snorted. "There was nothing to break up. It was like you said. I was just an easy lay for him. He's got half a dozen guys just like me between here and Charleston."

"I'm so sorry, Bert," she said gently. "Truly I am. I feel partly to blame, because he did use you to get to me."

"No." Bert shook his head vehemently. "This was all me, Cara. Me falling into my old bad habits."

"Are you drinking again?" She had to ask it.

"I wanted to," he admitted. "Cullen did everything he could to make it easy for me. But somehow, I didn't. Maybe that's how I had the nerve to walk away. I started going to meetings again Friday. And that helped."

"I'm glad," she said. "At least you've got your sobriety."

"Two years, three months, sixteen days," Bert said. "But that's not the reason I came here tonight."

"Tell me you came to ask for your old job back," Cara said.

His face lit up. "That'd be great, but that's not really it." Then he reached into the raincoat and brought out a medium-sized linen bag that he'd shoved into an inner pocket. "This is the real reason I came."

Cara took the bag and loosened the drawstring opening. An heirloom-quality eighteenth-century sterling-silver epergne slid out onto her lap.

"Lillian's?"

"Uh-huh."

"Where on earth did you find it?"

"In Cullen's gym bag. The bastard has had it all this time."

"But *how* did you find it?"

Bert laughed bitterly. "House boy take Mercedes to get detailed. House boy empty trunk, think maybe he wash boss man's stinky gym clothes, score extra points with boss. Instead, house boy find missing shiny silver doodad."

"Unbelievable," Cara said, holding up the epergne. "I can't even process it."

"I can," Bert said. "Cullen must have swiped it from the van that weekend after Torie's wedding." His face flushed and he looked away, embarrassed. "That's when I first met him. I'd gone to an after-hours club in midtown with a couple friends, and he was there, kinda window-shopping I guess you'd say. He sent a drink over to my table, but I told the waiter to take it back, because you know, I don't drink. A few minutes later, Cullen came over. He said he recognized me from Torie's wedding, talked about what a great job we'd done with all the flowers. He bought cocktails for the whole table, and we sort of hit it off, and after a while . . . I can't believe I'm telling you this shit . . ."

"You went out to the van?"

"Yeah," Bert whispered. "I think he was kinda into that."

"Remind me to have that thing steam-cleaned," Cara said.

"So . . . what now?" Bert asked, after he'd related the whole tawdry Cullen Kane affair.

Cara put the epergne back into the linen bag. "First thing tomorrow, we take this thing back to Lillian Fanning. You know she's been going around town trashing my reputation, right?"

"Cullen was loving that," Bert said. "He's got quite the network of ladies who lunch."

"I can't wait to see her face when she sees the epergne," Cara said.

"What will you tell her?"

"Just that we figured out who took it from the van, and we were able to recover it. Don't worry. I'll leave you out of it."

"And what about that Detective Peebles? Won't she be asking a lot of questions?"

"If she asks, we'll tell her the truth," Cara decided. "Let Cullen Kane deal with it. He's got a lot to answer for as far as I'm concerned."

"And he's still not done," Bert warned. "He's seriously obsessed with grinding his heel in your face. He went all batshit when he figured out that contractor friend of yours managed to buy this building out from under him."

Bert looked around the living room and for the first time noticed the packing boxes. "Hey, what's up with all this? I figured you wouldn't have to move now, since Cullen got outmaneuevered."

Cara shrugged. "Long, sad story. Things didn't work out with the new guy. I'll be out of here by the end of next week."

"Oh." Bert sank lower into the sofa cushions. "Well, shit."

"Yeah." Cara finished off the last of her water, wishing it were wine.

"Bert?"

"Yeah?"

"You didn't give up your apartment when you moved in with Cullen, did you?"

"Yup."

"So . . . you're basically homeless now?"

"Sorta."

She patted the sofa cushion, then stood up. "I'll get you a pillow and a sheet. And PS. You're hired. Again."

55

In the morning, Bert was gone. The sofa bed was folded up, the pillow and sheet neatly stacked on top of one of the boxes of books. The smell of brewing coffee wafted from the direction of the kitchen. Poppy was missing, too.

Cara poured herself a mug of coffee and took it out to the courtyard garden. Out of habit, she deadheaded a spent rose and pulled a weed from the side planting bed. The big bell from St. John the Baptist was booming eight as she sat down under the shade of the café umbrella.

She wondered if she'd be able to hear the church bells over on Hall Street. Geographically, the new place wasn't all that far away. Emotionally? That was a different story. She tried not to think about how much she was going to miss this little garden, miss all the work she'd put into it, and the enjoyment it had brought.

There was a big new yard over at Hall Street. It had seemed so hopeless yesterday, but things had shifted just a little last night. Bert was back. Bert had a strong back and he was a hard worker, when he wasn't whining.

The timing of Bert's return couldn't have been more fortuitous. There was no way she could get through the Trapnell wedding without help.

Thinking of the Trapnell wedding made her remember what had triggered the sense of uneasiness that had propelled her out of the apartment the night before. She went inside and fetched her laptop, clicking onto Facebook and Harris Strayhorn's page.

Thank God! The stripper photos had been deleted. Maybe, through some divine providence, Brooke hadn't seen them after all. Just out of curiosity, she clicked over to Brooke's page.

The bride-to-be wasn't what you'd call a Facebook fanatic. It looked like she posted irregularly, whenever the mood struck. There were photos of Brooke and Harris toasting on the beach at Tybee at sunset, of Brooke in running clothes finishing a marathon, of Brooke and Marie at Mother's Day brunch. The most recent item had been posted yesterday morning at 10 a.m. by Holly Strayhorn.

Bachelorette party tonight for my almost-sister BROOKE TRAPNELL! Woot, woot! #CosmoCraziness #Alertthemedia #Whosgotthebailmoney?

There were six responses to Holly's post, including Brooke's.

Can't wait!

Cara was just about to post something on her own Facebook page about the Trapnell wedding when the kitchen door opened and Poppy came bounding out to the garden, with Bert right behind. He was waving a large white paper sack.

"Guess who went to Back in the Day for bacon cheddar biscones for breakfast?"

She called ahead to make sure the Fannings would be home. Lillian's voice dripped ice. "We've got brunch plans at eleven. What's this about Cara?"

Cara ignored the question. "It won't take long. I can be there in twenty minutes."

It didn't get much better than Isle of Hope on a warm June morning. The live oaks lent cool shade, the sun sparkled off sailboats skittering over the river, and not a single blade of jade-green grass at the Shutters was anything less than perfection. It could have been a cover for *Southern Living* magazine.

Lillian Fanning sat stiffly on a wicker armchair on her porch and looked down at the epergne, which Cara had handed over without a word.

She picked it up, turned it over, and studied the hallmark. She held it up to the light, turning it this way and that, looking for dents or scratches, or any other clue to where the epergne might have been for these past weeks.

"It doesn't look any the worse for wear," Lillian admitted, her lips pursed. "And you won't tell me how you managed to find it?"

Cara had been rehearsing her response all morning. She delivered her lines as practiced.

"Somebody . . . who has a grudge against me took it. Not because it was so valuable or to sell it. To cause trouble for me, and ruin my reputation. A friend found where this person had hidden the epergne, and last night, he brought it back to me. And now, I'm returning it to you."

"I don't know what to say." Lillian's face was flushed. "Torie was right. I should have known better. All these weeks, I've thought, and I've said, really terrible things about you. To that police detective, to my friends." She shook her head. "I am deeply, deeply ashamed of myself right now, Cara. And I'm afraid an apology won't even begin to make things right with you."

"An apology is all that's needed," Cara said. "Thank you, Lillian. I'll let you get to your brunch now."

Lillian reached out and touched Cara's bare arm. Her fingertips were cool.

"You know, Cara, we Southerners pride ourselves on good manners. Torie says I'm a big snob about these kinds of things, and that's something else she's probably right about. You're from up North someplace . . . Michigan?"

"Ohio."

"I knew it was one of those places. Anyway, I just want to tell you that the way you handled this whole episode, with such dignity, and the way you just accepted my totally inadequate apology with such grace, says a lot to me about who you are and how you were raised."

Cara smiled. "My mother would have been happy to hear you say that."

"Where was your mother from?"

"Actually? Kentucky."

Lillian's eyes twinkled. "That explains everything. Seriously though, Cara.

I guess that's a lesson learned for me. You don't have to be Southern to have good manners. And you don't have to be a Yankee to make a total ass of yourself."

That got a laugh from Cara. She was halfway across the lawn when Lillian called out to her. "I'm going to make it up to you, Cara. You wait. Your phone is going to be ringing. There won't be a bride within a hundred miles of this town who won't be calling you."

"Man, I hate it when you have to act all classy and grown-up, instead of going *off* on a bitch," Bert complained, after Cara gave him the blow-by-blow of her encounter with Lillian Fanning.

They were upstairs in the apartment, and he was helping her finish packing books. "Grown-up is definitely not as fun," Cara agreed. "But I'd much rather have Lillian as an ally than an enemy. Now she owes me, or she thinks she does. And that's a good thing, considering the rent on Hall Street is double what I paid here."

Bert gave her a quizzical look. "What happened with Jack Finnerty? I got the impression you two were pretty hot and heavy."

"Where'd you hear that?"

"Cullen has spies everywhere," Bert explained. "After Jack took a pass on doing the work over here, he started asking around. I think Patricia Trapnell probably helped him put it together because of all the work Jack and his brother were doing over at the Strayhorns."

"I can't believe Cullen Kane was that interested in my personal life."

Cara's cell phone was sitting on the coffee table. It buzzed and Bert picked it up and handed it to her. "It's Marie Trapnell. You want to take it, or should I tell her it's your day off?"

"Give."

"Hi, Marie," Cara said cheerfully.

"Cara?" Marie Trapnell's voice crackled with agitation. "Have you heard from Brooke?"

"Nooo, we haven't spoken since Friday. Should I have? Is something wrong?"

"Brooke is gone."

Cara felt a cold whisper at the base of her neck. "When? Where?"

"We don't know how long she's been gone. Holly went to pick her up for the bachelorette party last night at eight, but she wasn't there. She tried calling and texting, but Brooke never answered."

"Has Harris talked to her?" Cara's mind flashed on the pictures from the strip club. "Did they have another fight?"

"No. Not that I know of. I just talked to Harris. He hasn't seen her since she left for work Friday morning. He and his friends went up to Atlanta Friday, and he didn't get back till nearly ten last night. He went straight to bed, and he wasn't really worried about her until just now, when Holly called to ask him why Brooke skipped out on the party."

"Oh no," Cara said.

"I'm trying to stay calm, but I'm afraid I'm not doing a very good job of it," Marie said shakily. "It's just that Brooke is so emotionally fragile right now. The trial and the wedding, it's all just too much for her."

"Have you called her friends? When I talked to her Friday, she mentioned that she was sort of dreading the bachelorette thing. Because she was so tired."

"All of her friends were with Holly last night. Brooke was the only one missing. And none of them talked to her on Friday or Saturday."

Cara's mind was racing with possibilities. "Is her car there?"

"Her car?"

"Brooke's Volvo. Was it at her house last night?"

"I don't know. I didn't even think to ask, when Harris called to see if Brooke was with me."

"You might want to check on that," Cara said gently.

"I will. I'll call Harris right now and ask."

"Marie? You might also ask him if Brooke saw the pictures on his Facebook page."

"What pictures?"

"Just ask Harris. He'll know which ones."

Ten minutes later, Cara's phone rang. This time it was Harris Strayhorn. No surprise there.

"Marie says you asked whether Brooke saw some Facebook pictures? What are you talking about?"

"I saw the pictures from the strip club yesterday, Harris, before you took them down. I saw all of them. And I wasn't the only one."

"Fuuuuck." His voice sounded distant. "I'm gonna kill Mike Bingham. He swiped my phone and posted them on my page. We were all pretty hammered. I didn't even know they were on there, until another buddy texted me to warn me to delete them. Which I did as soon as I saw them."

"Did Brooke see the pictures?"

"Christ, I hope not. Maybe not. She doesn't look at Facebook on a regular basis." He groaned. "But if she did see them . . ."

"Exactly."

"They look awful, I know. But I swear to God, it was just a lap dance. Okay, two. Maybe more. I can't remember. I got so drunk I passed out in the back of the van after the third or fourth club. That's why I didn't come home until last night. I didn't want Brooke to see me until I got sobered up."

"Do you have any idea where she might have gone?"

"I've called everybody we know. Nobody's seen or talked to her. Wherever she went, she took her car. Marie told me you were asking about that."

"Did she pack any bags? Take a lot of clothes?"

"I'm walking in the bedroom now to check." Cara heard footsteps, and the sound of a door opening.

"She's got this duffel bag she takes when we go over to my folks' house for the weekend. It's not in the closet."

"What about clothes?"

She heard the sound of hangers on a wooden rod, of drawers being opened and closed.

"It's hard to tell with her clothes. Wait. Yeah, her favorite jeans are gone. Maybe some shorts. Definitely her running shoes, although she sometimes leaves those in her car if she's working out at lunch."

There was a long silence at the other end of the phone. Had he hung up?

"Harris? Are you still there?"

She could hear him breathing heavily. And then, a sort of muffled sob.

"Harris?"

"I should never have gone. I knew she didn't want me to go. We had a fight about it. And we almost never fight. I never should have gone to those stinking clubs."

"Maybe it wasn't about that," Cara said. "Was there anything else worrying her, something she was upset about?"

"Not that she talked about," Harris said. "Brooke was . . . moody sometimes. She needed her space. I tried to give it to her. I love her, you know?"

"I know," Cara said. "And she loves you. She told me so."

"Then why would she leave? Where would she go?"

"We'll find out," Cara said soothingly. "Brides . . . sometimes it all becomes too much for them. Sometimes they just have these little meltdowns. That's probably all this is. Like you said, Brooke needs her space."

"You really think so?"

"I do," Cara lied.

56

Holy shit," Bert said. "Brooke Trapnell is a runaway bride?"

"Looks like it. Harris hasn't seen her since she left for work Friday morning. They'd had a fight, because she hated the idea of his doing the strip-club stag-night thing with his buddies."

Before Cara could explain any more, Marie Trapnell called back.

"What did Harris tell you?" she asked urgently.

"Her car is gone, and she apparently packed an overnight bag. So we know she went of her own accord. She wasn't abducted or anything."

"Thank God for that," Marie said. "I can't tell you all the things running through my mind right now. This is just such a nightmare. Why would she do something like this? If she needed to get away, why not at least tell me? She knows how I worry."

"I talked to Brooke Friday, to remind her about her portrait sitting, and she did seem stressed." Cara said. "She even admitted she was dreading the bachelorette party, but she never said she was thinking of skipping it. So it looks like she probably left sometime Saturday."

"Why did you want me to ask Harris about his Facebook page?" Marie asked. "He told me he didn't know what you were talking about, but I know he was lying."

Cara hesitated. She hated to rat Harris out, but on the other hand, Marie had a right to know what might have triggered her daughter's flight.

"One of Harris's buddies posted some pretty risqué pictures of him from the bachelor's party on Harris's Facebook page."

"Risqué, how?"

"There were pictures of him getting a lap dance from a stripper."

"That's revolting. It doesn't even sound like Harris."

"He said he was pretty drunk. I saw the pictures, and he looked like he was about to pass out. Which he apparently did later that night."

"And you think maybe Brooke saw those pictures, and that's why she left?"

"That could be part of it. Brooke told me she and Harris had a fight about it, because she didn't want him to go to those strip clubs. But maybe that's just part of it. I don't really know, Marie. I'm not a therapist. I'm only a florist-slash-wedding-planner."

"I'm just trying so hard to understand what was going through Brooke's mind. I don't dare say this to Harris or Gordon, but I'm terrified Brooke will hurt herself."

"Oh, yikes. I hadn't even thought about Gordon. How's he handling this?"

"In typically Gordon style. He's furious at Brooke for quote 'pulling a stunt like this.' It doesn't occur to him that perhaps his daughter is in some kind of emotional distress. All he can think about is how it affects him. How embarrassing it will be if the wedding doesn't come off as planned. He's already talking about hiring a private detective to track her down."

"Would he really do that?"

"Maybe. I don't know. Gordon's not somebody who just sits around waiting for things to happen. He's used to making them happen. Right now. Times like these, I have no idea how we ever ended up marrying or staying together for as long as we did."

"But you did, and the two of you raised an amazing daughter. I'm sure Brooke is okay, and she wouldn't hurt herself, Marie. Like I told Harris, she probably just needs some alone time."

"Have you ever had a bride do anything like this before?"

Cara had to think. "Just disappear? Without saying anything to anybody?"

"Exactly."

"No."

"Oh God." Marie was weeping. "I'm so sorry, Cara. I'm trying not to fall to pieces, but I can't stand not knowing where she is, or what she's going through."

"It's all right, Marie," Cara said. "I don't blame you for being upset. Let me think a moment. Does Brooke have any special 'happy place'—someplace she likes to retreat to? Maybe a friend's mountain cabin, or a beach cottage or something?"

"Gordon and Patricia have a condo down at St. Simon's, but I doubt she'd go there. I don't think she even has a key."

"You might ask Gordon to check on that. Where else?"

"She and Harris have rented cottages in Highlands, North Carolina. They usually go in the fall, with other couples."

"Maybe ask Harris to call the real-estate company they rent from, to see if they've heard from Brooke."

"That's a thought. You're making me feel better already, Cara."

"I'm just taking stabs in the dark here Marie. There's just as good a chance that she found a motel room on the interstate and she's lounging by the pool, drinking a Margarita."

"No. That doesn't sound like Brooke at all."

Cara threw her hands up in exasperation. "I'm sorry. I'm out of ideas."

"I am too," Marie said, her voice nearly a whisper. "But I've got to keep trying."

"If I think of anything, I'll let you know," Cara promised. "Try not to worry too much, Marie. Brooke's a smart, resourceful woman. She can take care of herself."

"I hope so."

Cara hung up the phone and turned to Bert. "I've got a really bad feeling in my gut about this."

Bert's eyes widened. "What? You really think she might be in some kind of physical danger? Like, maybe somebody really did abduct her?"

Cara shook her head. "No. It's not that. Her car's gone, she packed a suitcase. Brooke went of her own free will. And that's what's got me so worried. If she doesn't come back—if that wedding doesn't come off? I'm through. That's a twenty-five-thousand-dollar paycheck that doesn't get written. I absolutely promised the Colonel I'd get him the rest of his money by next week. And I've got all these bills coming due, first and last month's rent on the new place, plus the expenses of getting moved in over there."

She swallowed hard, trying to suppress the tide of fear and panic that had begun bubbling just below the surface as soon as she'd heard the news that Brooke Trapnell was missing.

"Technically? It's not really your problem, Cara. As of yesterday, per your contract, Gordon Trapnell owed you the balance of your fee, whether the wedding happens or not."

Cara sighed. "That's true. But if this wedding doesn't come off, there's no way, short of suing, that Patricia will write that check. Anyway, I really care about Brooke and Harris."

Bert rolled his eyes. "So what are you going to do?"

"I wish I knew. I honestly do think this is just a classic case of pre-wedding jitters. If I could find Brooke, and talk to her, I really believe I could help her see that this is totally normal. I've never done a wedding where the bride didn't freak out, in some way."

Bert nodded agreement. "What was that girl's name—the one who kicked her maid of honor out of the wedding party because she wouldn't grow her hair out long like the rest of the bridesmaids?"

"Cherish Scanlon," Cara said. "And don't forget about Vanessa Pettigrew. She literally plucked out all her eyebrows and eyelashes three days before the wedding."

"Poor girl looked like a Chihuahua," Bert said.

"When I worked for Norma we had a bride who was so nervous during the ceremony she literally passed out cold, right at the altar. When she fell, she somehow bit her own tongue, there was blood everywhere. . . ."

"Maybe Brooke knows something we don't," Bert said gently. "Even in bizarro bride world, running away is pretty radical, don't you think?"

"No. This is just how Brooke Trapnell operates. I've been working with this girl for weeks and weeks now. It's just stress, that's all. If I could just talk to her . . ."

"Give her a call," Bert suggested.

"Everybody has tried calling her. Her mom, Harris. I'm sure Gordon's tried to reach her too. This is typical Brooke behavior. She never returns phone calls. The only success I've ever had reaching her is with a text."

"So text her. What have you got to lose?"

Cara stared at Bert. She grabbed her phone and started typing, her fingers flying so quickly over the keyboard she had to start over three times. Finally, she got it right.

Brooke. Where are you?

She hit send and held her breath. A minute later, Cara's phone dinged.

Promise u won't tell?

Cara looked over at Bert. He nodded.

Promise.

She waited five long minutes before her phone dinged again.

Brooke had typed only one word.

Loblolly.

Bert had been reading over her shoulder. "Huh? Is that a typo? Was she trying to write LOL—you know, laughing out loud?"

"No," Cara said slowly. She smacked her forehead. "I can't believe I didn't think of it. Loblolly is the name of some house that used to belong to Brooke's mother's family. It's on Cumberland Island."

"Why would she go to Cumberland Island of all places?"

Cara thought back to her lunch at Johnny Harris, of the lanky park ranger who'd dropped by their table, and Brooke's confession about their secret romance. What was his name? Pete something?

"I've been to Cumberland Island. There's nothing over there," Bert was saying.

"Wrong," Cara said. "There's a house, someplace that used to be special to Brooke. And a man. He used to be special too. Maybe he still is."

"And how do you happen to know all this?"

"When I had lunch with Brooke at Johnny Harris last week, we ran into this guy—he was kind of geeky-looking, not at all somebody you'd picture Brooke Trapnell with. But she got all flustered after they spoke. It turns out he was this secret college flame she'd had. She actually told me she was sleeping with him the summer before she started law school—even though she was unofficially engaged to Harris."

"Oooh. Quel scandal!"

"Right. Anyway, he came by the table before leaving, and was sort of hinting that he wanted to get together with her. He works as some sort of park ranger or something, and he's temporarily posted on Cumberland Island. Cara told him straight up that she was getting married. She even introduced me as her wedding planner. But she gave him her business card."

"Which you don't do unless you want somebody to call you again," Bert pointed out.

"He asked her if they still went to the family place over there. Loblolly. And Brooke said no, not in years. Listen, where exactly is Cumberland Island? Is it somewhere around Savannah? Or Hilton Head?"

"It's about two hours south of here. Almost to the Florida line. The whole island used to belong to the Carnegie family—the steel magnates? They had a couple big spooky old mansions and a farm and a few other houses for their staff going all the way back to the late 1800s. But a few years ago they deeded or sold almost all of it over to the National Park Service. One of the mansions burned down years ago, you can still see the ruins, and some of the Carnegie heirs run a really expensive inn you can stay at, but other than that, it's all just wilderness.. I remember, we went camping out there when I was a Boy Scout. I was totally traumatized when I figured out there was no outlet for my hair dryer in the outhouse."

"You were a Boy Scout?"

"I liked the uniform," Bert said. "Are you sure this Loblolly place is on Cumberland? I thought the only people who still had houses over there were Carnegies. Is Marie Trapnell a Carnegie?"

"Who knows? It doesn't really matter anyway. What matters is, I need to go down there, and find Brooke Trapnell."

"Is that a good idea?" Bert asked. "Why don't you just leave that to her fiancé, or her parents?"

"Because I promised her I wouldn't tell. Anyway, if Brooke really is on that island, I think there's a chance she's with that old flame, the park ranger. What do you think Harris would do if he figured that out?"

"Call off the wedding, probably."

"Which is why I've got to go myself," Cara said. "I'm going to go down to Cumberland Island, and find Brooke Trapnell, and then I'm going to drag her back to Savannah and put on the most amazing wedding anybody in this town has ever seen."

"High five," Bert said.

57

Cara raced into her bedroom and unearthed her backpack from her closet while Bert sat on her bed and researched Cumberland Island on Google.

"There are only two ferry departures a day from the Park Service dock at St. Marys, at nine and eleven-forty-five a.m.," he reported. "You're supposed to call weekdays before five p.m. to make a reservation."

"What if you decide on Sunday afternoon that you want to go on Monday morning?"

"Mmm, looks like if you don't have a reservation it's first-come, first-serve. You're supposed to be there half an hour before departure time. Only two return trips a day, at ten-fifteen a.m. and four-forty-five p.m."

Cara started folding a T-shirt to put in her bag.

"Bad idea," Bert said. "Long sleeves are the way to go over there. The place is crawling with bugs. Make sure you throw in some insect repellent and some sunscreen too. Can I ask about your plan of attack?"

"You can ask, but I don't really have one. I guess I'll get over to Cumberland, track Brooke down, and then hope and pray she'll listen to good sense."

"About the tracking-down thing. You do realize the island is like twenty miles long, right? And most of it's either woods, swamp, or beaches. And only rangers or residents are allowed to have cars."

Cara threw in a pair of running shorts, a long-sleeved T-shirt, and a pair of blue jeans, then added hiking boots, socks, panties, and a toothbrush to her pack.

She frowned. "Check that website, see if you see a place called Loblolly on it."

Bert skimmed the website, and clicked around until he found a reference.

" 'Loblolly is a circa-1912 hunting lodge built to house overflow guests from Plum Orchard, the Carnegies' opulent hundred-room Georgian Revival mansion. In 1930, Loblolly was deeded to Jasper O. Updegraff, a wealthy friend of George Carnegie, who reportedly won the property in a high-stakes poker game.' "

"Updegraff." Cara turned the name over in her mind. "Vicki Cooper told me that Marie Trapnell came from a family with even more money than Gordon's, but I can't remember if she told me the family name."

"One moment," Bert said, typing in a Google search. "Okay, here it is. Brooke's engagement announcement from the *Savannah Morning News*. Mary Brooke Trapnell, daughter of Gordon Vincent Trapnell of Vernonburg, and Marie Louise Eagleton Trapnell, of Savannah."

"Gotta love the Savannah newspaper for running those engagement announcements so everybody in polite society can keep a scorecard on who's marrying whom," Cara said.

"Cullen reads the engagement announcements in the Savannah and Charleston papers religiously, and if he sees an upper-crust name, he always sends flowers to the bride-to-be," Bert said. "You'd be amazed the amount of business it generates."

"Yes, he's quite the entrepreneur," Cara said. "I wonder if he makes it a habit to steal heirloom silver from any of those brides?"

"Updegraffs," Bert muttered. "Updegraff?"

"Keep looking," Cara said. "If the house belonged to Marie's mother's family, maybe that's the Updegraff connection."

"Okay . . . yeah. Here we go. There's a story about Brooke's debut from a few years ago. Daughter of Gordon and Marie, stepdaughter of Patricia, granddaughter of so and so Von Moneybags the Third, and great-granddaughter of the late Dr. and Mrs. Warner Updegraff of Sea Island, Georgia."

"Bingo." Cara found a bottle of bug spray and threw it into the bag. "So, the question is, how far is Loblolly from the ferry dock, and if there are no cars, how do I get there once I'm on the island?"

"Checking. This says Loblolly is five miles from the dock. That's a pretty good hike in June. But it does say you can rent a bike." Bert looked up at her. "Did I mention there are no motels? Just primitive tent camping. And the Greyfield Inn, where rooms without a private bath start at around five hundred dollars a night."

"I'm not planning to need a room," Cara said. She hoisted the backpack to her shoulder to test its weight. "If I do have to hike, this shouldn't be too heavy."

"Ugh," Bert grimaced. "I wouldn't mind hiking and camping, if it weren't for the fact that you have to do it outside, in nature. They have boo-koodles of nature over on Cumberland. All these bugs buzzing around, and random animals. I mean, in addition to your garden-variety raccoons and possums and deer they have herds of wild horses pooping everywhere, not to mention alligators." He glanced down at the Park Service website. "Just listen to this: 'Venomous snakes present on the island include diamondback rattlesnakes, timber rattlesnakes and cottonmouth moccasins.' "

"I'll be sure to watch where I walk," Cara promised. They went back out to the living room, and Cara gathered up her cell phone and charger.

"What needs doing in the shop while you're gone?" Bert asked. "What do we have coming up?"

"The usual baby shower, retirement, and hospital stuff," Cara said. "Check the inbox on my desk. We've also got the Loudermilk wedding next Saturday, but it's a second marriage for both of them, very small, simple ceremony in the best friend's town house on Charlton Street. The couple are very sweet, very low maintenance. We're doing a bouquet for BeBe, one for Weezie, her maid-of-honor, boutonnieres for Harry and the best man, and a couple of arrangements for the mantel and the buffet table. But that's not until Saturday, and hopefully, I'll be back here tomorrow afternoon."

"Hopefully," Bert said.

"You'll stay here and take care of Poppy?" she asked. Her face darkened at the memory of the last, temporary assistant she'd hired, with such disastrous results. "And walk her and make sure she gets plenty of water?"

"When have I not done those things?" Bert asked. "You know I'll take care of everything around here." He grabbed her hand. "Hey. You trust me, right? I mean, I know I messed up, with Cullen. But that's history. This is the new Bert. Reliable, responsible Bert."

"Okay. Yeah, that's the Bert I need," Cara said. She hugged him tightly. "That's the one I missed. I was really starting to panic about doing these next three weddings without you."

"Three? Who do we have besides the Loudermilk wedding, and then Brooke's?"

"The week before Brooke and Harris we've got the Schroeders."

"Ohh. Wait. Is that the beach wedding?"

"Afraid so."

"Who gets married at the beach on Tybee in late June?"

"Somebody who's never been there in June," Cara said. "She's from out of town. The whole wedding party is from out of town."

Cara was raiding the shop's petty-cash drawer when she heard the sound of a car door slamming on the street outside. She looked up in time to see Jack Finnerty heading toward the shop door. She considered running out the back door to evade yet another confrontation with him, but it was already too late. He'd spotted her, and Poppy had spotted Jack, and she was barking and pawing at the door, eager to see her old friend.

As soon as he stepped in the door, Poppy pounced, slapping her front paws on his chest, and slathering his neck with her big pink tongue.

"Hey, girl!" he said, ruffling the fur on Poppy's neck. "Have you missed me?" He looked up at Cara, and it was obvious he was addressing them both.

Jack had obviously come directly from the job site. His work boots were covered in mud and sawdust, and his T-shirt and jeans were grimy.

Cara felt her heart pounding in her chest. Damn Jack Finnerty. He was the only man she'd ever known who looked as good dirty as he did clean. Come to think of it, she couldn't remember another man who made her palms sweat and her pulse race the way Jack did. Too bad he'd turned out to be such a world-class jerk.

"I've started packing, if you've come to check up on your investment," she said coolly. "I move over to Hall Street next week." She gestured around the small room. "And just in case Sylvia Bradley didn't mention it, all the shelving and fixtures are mine. And I intend to take them with me."

Jack's face flushed under his sunburn. "You know that's not why I came here. Look. Maybe I didn't express myself too well the last time. I was pumped, you know? So let me be clear. I bought this building for you. Not to give to you, or hold over your head so I'd have demonical power over you. It's a great building, and I thought it deserved something better. And you deserve something better, too."

"I see."

"Okay, so yeah, maybe I also bought it because I'm a typical competitive male and I wanted to keep that creep Cullen Kane from getting his hands on it. So yeah, my execution was pretty clumsy. But don't I at least get credit for . . ."

"What? Having a pure heart?"

"Yeah, that," he said belligerently.

She felt her spine weaken a little. Damn, she really was such a jellyfish. But his face was so damn earnest, and yes, deep down inside, she did have a sneaking suspicion that his heart was pure.

"Why didn't you tell me you were thinking of buying the building, instead of all this sneaking around? What is it with you men? Why do you all have to be so . . ."

"Devious?"

"Exactly! I'm just so sick of all the plotting and power plays and the secrets and the subterfuge. Can't you just communicate?"

Jack stood with his hands on his hips. "Fine. This is me communicating. Even if you and I are through, I'd really rather not have to find a new tenant. If you feel so strongly about not taking any favors, we can talk about escalating your rent, eventually. What do you say?"

She had to stick to her guns. This was a matter of principle, not a matter of the heart.

"Thanks. I appreciate the offer, but I've signed a lease for Hall Street. It's a bigger space, and when I get it fixed up, Poppy will have more room. Plus, I've already started packing."

He shook his head, then shrugged. "Have it your own way, then." He was on his way out the door when he noticed her backpack. "What's up? You've taken up hiking?"

She debated whether or not to tell him the truth. But why not?

"I'll tell you where I'm going, but this is strictly on the low-down, okay? Brooke has disappeared."

"That explains a lot. Ryan and I were going to get some stuff done at Cabin Creek today, because we're starting to get down to the wire with the wedding, but Libba just waved us off, which was kind of weird. She's been out there every day we've been working, taking pictures and coming up with things she wants done. So, wow. Brooke—what? Just vanished?"

"She and Harris had a fight Friday, and then sometime Saturday, while he was still in Atlanta for his bachelor's party, she took off. Skipped her own bachelorette party."

He whistled softly. "That sucks for Harris. And Libba too, of course. Does this mean the wedding is off?"

"Not if I can help it," Cara said fiercely.

That took him by surprise. "What? You're going after her? Cara Kryzik, finder of lost brides?"

"As a matter of fact, yes. I'm the only one who knows where she's gone."

"Cool. Tell Harris. Let him deal with it."

"Negative. I promised Brooke I wouldn't tell. Anyway, I don't want to hurt Harris. He's a sweet guy. If he went after Brooke this whole wedding thing could blow up in our faces."

"And why is that?

"I don't think Brooke is by herself. I think maybe she's with another guy."

Jack shook his head. "Oh shit. Another guy. That's a deal-breaker. What do you hope to accomplish by going after her?"

"Brooke is emotionally overwrought right now. Lots of brides get like that. Most of them, in fact, freak out in some form or fashion. I'll explain that to her, calm her down, and bring her home to get married."

"And what about this other guy? The one you said she might be with?"

"He's just somebody from her past, an excuse she's probably clinging to for why she should run away."

Jack's eyes narrowed. "You don't know that. How could you?"

"I met him. By accident. He's totally wrong for Brooke. He's a park ranger. Can you imagine Brooke Trapnell living on some wilderness island somewhere?"

"Why are you so dead-set on meddling in this thing, Cara? Why don't you just let Harris and Brooke sort things out for themselves?"

Instead of answering, Cara picked up her backpack and her car keys. "I don't have time for this, Jack. I've got to go."

He followed her out to her car, and before she could stop him, he'd slid into the front passenger seat. "I get it. If this wedding gets canceled, you're out a crapload of money, right?"

Cara went perfectly still for a moment. If that's what he thought of her, why let him know otherwise?

"Yes!" she cried. "That's right. I finally figured out that the only way to win at this game is to play by the big boy's rules. I'm going to find Brooke Trapnell and bring her home and by God, this wedding is going to come off and I am going to finally be out from under my father's thumb. Okay? Happy now?"

"Yeah," he said, his mouth twisting downward. "I'm just great."

The motel room in St. Marys was tiny, but cheap. And most importantly, it had air-conditioning. Cara took a shower, brushed her teeth, and fell into bed. It was barely 9 p.m., but after the jarring encounter with Jack and the two-hour drive south from Savannah, she was exhausted.

In the morning, she had a convenience-store breakfast of coffee with a stale cheese Danish. As an extra precaution, she bought a bottle of water and two protein bars, which she tucked into her backpack.

By eight o'clock, she was in the ticket line at the ferry dock. A group of giggling Girl Scouts and their mothers were ahead of her in line, as were a pair of solidly built gray-haired ladies who were decked out for a day of bird-watching, with canvas rain hats, hiking boots, and cameras and binoculars strung around their necks.

After she bought her ticket for the early ferry, Cara took a brochure about the island from a display by the ticket window, found a seat in the shade, and watched with interest as cars and vans pulled up, disgorging campers and day-trippers loaded down with coolers, tents, beach chairs, and more.

It was an eclectic group, families with young children, gung ho hikers, and half a dozen college students, who stealthily swigged beer from brown paper sacks.

At 8:45, a voice came over the loudspeaker, and a couple of uniformed deckhands appeared, to direct them in loading onto the *Cumberland Queen* ferry.

With the sun beating down, Cara chose a seat on the lower deck and spent the forty-five-minute ride across the St. John's River watching as seabirds wheeled in the sky above, and dolphins chased along in the boat's wake.

She also studied the map in the Park Service brochure. The island's major sightseeing spots were clearly marked. On the far north end was something called the Settlement. She found Plum Orchard, something called Yankee Paradise, Stafford Beach, Sea Camp, and Dungeness. Nowhere on the map was there a spot marked Loblolly.

But according to the internet, Loblolly had been built as a guest house/hunting lodge—adjacent to Plum Orchard. So. Find Plum Orchard, and Loblolly would be nearby. Wouldn't it?

In her mind, she rehearsed what she would say when she found Brooke Trapnell. Occasionally, doubt crept in. What if she couldn't find the bride-to-be? The brochure she clutched in her sweaty hands described Cumberland as nearly 17 miles long by 3.5 miles wide, with over 36,000 acres of beaches, marsh, mudflats, and wilderness areas.

And poisonous snakes, Cara thought, remembering Bert's description. And alligators. But this wouldn't matter. She wouldn't be hanging around Cumberland long enough to experience any reptile confrontations.

Planning a wedding or any event required organization, clear thinking, and flawless execution. By the time the *Cumberland Queen* was chugging toward the ferry dock on the island, Cara had worked out her game plan. Step 1. Get bike. Step 2. Find Loblolly. Step 3. Grab Brooke. Step 4. Take Brooke home. Step 5. Payday.

Bert had warned her about the primitive facilities on the island, so she hurried toward the ferry's bathroom, and spotting the snack bar, bought another bottle of water.

. . .

The middle-aged woman at the bike-rental concession smiled as Cara stepped up to the counter. "Day rate or overnight?"

"Day," Cara said firmly. She paid for the bike from her petty-cash stash, then held out the now-creased map of the island. "Could you please tell me where I can find Loblolly?"

"Loblolly? You mean, like the pine trees?"

Cara shrugged. "Loblolly, like the house. It's supposed to be near Plum Orchard, I think."

"Sorry, never heard of it. Just be sure you have the bike back here thirty minutes before the four-forty-five ferry this afternoon. Okay?" The woman looked over Cara's shoulder. "Next?"

She'd been relieved to find that her bike was a fat-tired beach cruiser. Cara wheeled it away from the concession area, and looked around. Campers were loading gear into large beach carts and headed down the crushed-shell pathway, bikers were wheeling away, and the hikers were setting off down the road on foot. But which way should she be going?

Spying a young woman in a khaki Park Service uniform addressing the group of Girl Scouts, Cara hurried over to her. She waited while the ranger explained the rules—no touching or approaching the wild horses, stay on the trails, leave no trash anywhere on the island.

When there was a pause in the drill, Cara touched the ranger's arm. "Excuse me, could you help me with some directions?"

"I'll try."

Cara showed her the map. "I'm trying to find a private home called Loblolly. I think it's near Plum Orchard, but I'm not really certain."

The woman shook her head. "This is a national park. There aren't any private homes here anymore."

"Right. Well, I mean, I know it's a park, but I read on the internet that there were still a handful of private homes on the island, right? Aren't there still some Carnegies and Candlers who still own homes here? And also, Loblolly is one of them. Owned by the Updegraffs?"

"Sorry. Yes, there are still a very few private homes whose owners have retained rights, but I don't know about one called Loblolly, and I don't know any Updegraffs. I can tell you that those homeowners are pretty vigilant about their homes being private property. And most of them are reached through privately maintained roads, which are not open to the public."

"Oh." Cara adjusted her backpack straps, which were already cutting into her shoulders. "Well, now I'm more confused than ever. I know this place is called Loblolly, and that my friend is staying there."

"Let me just go check with one of the other rangers," the young woman said. Five minutes later she was back.

"You were right," she said, handing Cara's map back to her. "There actually *was* a house called Loblolly. But it wasn't at Plum Orchard. It was actually on the south end near the Dungeness ruins."

"Was?" Cara felt her stomach lurch.

"Loblolly was torn down last year, because the former owner's life lease expired, and the Park Service didn't consider it historically significant," the ranger said. "That explains why I'd never heard of it. I've only been on Cumberland for about nine months."

Cara felt her jaw drop open. "Torn down?" she said stupidly. "But my friend's family owned it. She told me she was staying there."

"I don't know what to tell you," the ranger said. "Maybe she was mistaken?" She took the map and pointed at a red circle. "This is Dungeness, if you want to take a look at where your friend's house was. And this," she said, stabbing another point just north of Dungeness, "is where you are right now. Sea Camp. Good luck!"

"Good luck," Cara muttered, pedaling south. "Good luck, my ass."

Any other time, Cara would have been entranced by Cumberland's natural beauty. Grand Avenue wound beneath a canopy of live oaks whose heavy, curving limbs reached out from both sides of the hard-packed road. Lush green ferns grew up the trunks of the oaks, and the branches were festooned with thick, silvery Spanish moss. Beyond the oaks, Cara saw stands of pines, magnolias, palmetto, and palm trees whose names she'd not yet learned.

Far ahead of her on the road she could see a few specks of humanity, the

Girl Scouts, on foot, but if she looked behind, all she saw was the road and the trees.

Birds twittered from the treetops, and she saw an occasional winged flash, but the aloneness struck her. Maybe that was what Brooke had come here looking for. Solitude.

There had been a picture in the brochure of Dungeness Castle as it had looked when it was built by the Carnegies, before it had been torched, in the fifties, by a poacher. Now, looking at the brick and tabby remains of the once grand home, Cara could see the outlines of the great house, and the way nature had already begun to encroach and overrun the ruins. Vines crept up walls and chimneys, palm trees sprouted where rooms had been. Cara held her breath when she spotted a group of three horses, two adults, and a colt, grazing on grass just inside the stone entryway, oblivious of her presence.

She circled the outskirts of the mansion, looking for some sign of Loblolly. She found collapsed and charred outbuildings, wound with what looked like decades' worth of honeysuckle and kudzu vines, and even what looked like an old car graveyard, with the rusting hulks of the Carnegies' once-splendid touring cars.

Finally, on the west side of the ruins, on a rise overlooking the river, she spotted what looked like a recently cleared spot of land. Neat piles of old bricks and worn timbers had been stacked to one side, but the outlines of mature boxwood hedges, bushy camellia shrubs, and a pair of twin palms were the only remnants of what must have been the foundation plantings for a fairly large house.

Cara laid the bike on the ground and walked around the property. The Park Service had done an admirable job of dismantling whatever had been here. From the siting of the palm trees, she guessed where the home's porch would have been. She stood there now, wondering what her next move would be, kicking frustratedly at the pale sand with the toe of her sneaker.

"Ow." Her toe hit something solid. She kicked it again, then knelt down to get a better look. She dug at the damp sand, brushing it sideways, until she spied a glimpse of dark gray granite. Her backpack swung awkwardly to one side, so she took it off and resumed digging. Five minutes later, she'd dug away enough sand to reveal a block of tile mosaic lettering. L-O . . . She dug on, until she'd exhumed a three-foot patch of granite threshold with the word Loblolly spelled in tile.

Cara sat back on her heels. So. The ranger had been right. Loblolly was gone. But where was Brooke Trapnell?

She glanced down at her watch. It was nearly noon, and she was hungry and thirsty, and the back of her sweaty T-shirt clung to her skin. She looked around for a shady place to take a lunch break. Just a few yards away was another of Cumberland's enormous live oaks. And this one had a picnic bench beneath it. Perfect!

She sat in the shade, uncapped her water bottle, and devoured one of her protein bars while reading the dozens of names and dates that had been carved into the wooden bench, leaving barely an inch of ungraffitied space. The earliest one she found was from 1972, inside a crude heart with the names "John + Marsha." The most recent entry was from 2013.

Cara leaned back on her elbows and sighed. The first year they'd moved into their house in Savannah, Leo had carved a heart with their initials into the trunk of a tall, spindly pine tree in their front yard. Less than a month later, the tree came crashing to the ground during a violent lightning storm, leaving a huge dent on the hood of Cara's car, and an ugly uneven stump, which, as far as Cara knew, was still there. Had that been an omen of things to come?

She was contemplating omens and their meanings and staring at the Loblolly home site when the sun caught a gleam of metal nearly hidden in the canopy of another live oak close to the house site. She took another swallow of water and walked closer to take another look.

A tree house! It had been built on and around the tree's thick main trunk, and the glint of metal she'd seen was a bit of its tin roof. As a child, Cara had always longed for a tree house, but of course, they'd lived in base housing in those days, and the Air Force didn't consider playhouses for little girls as standard issue.

She was almost directly under the plank floor of the house when she noticed the foot ladder nailed to the oak's trunk. And at the base of the trunk, she spied a pair of expensive-looking Jack Rogers sandals. Cara had seen a pair of sandals like those not so many days ago. She tilted her head as far back as it could go.

"Brooke?"

There followed an almost imperceptible rustling of branches, but the tree's foliage was so dense, she could see little besides brown branches and green leaves. Cara pulled herself onto the first rung of the foot ladder, holding on to the step above it. She climbed another step, and then the next. Finally, when she was nearly six feet off the ground, she saw the hatch that had been cut into the floor. Two more steps and she poked her head through that hatch.

Brooke Trapnell sat in the corner of the wooden house, her legs folded beneath her Indian style.

"Olly-olly-oxen-free," Cara said.

59

Brooke smiled wanly. "I saw you come riding up on your bike. I was hoping you wouldn't see me. What were you digging for over there? Buried treasure?"

Cara hoisted herself up and onto the floor of the tree house. The floor platform was a little larger than a king-size bed. The side walls were actually three foot railings, and the roof was held up by four-by-four posts. This must be what a rich kid's tree house looked like.

"When I was kicking the sand I felt something solid under my shoe. I guess it was the old threshold for your family's house."

That perked her up. "The one that said Loblolly?"

"Yes."

"I can't believe you found that. It must be the one thing the fucking Park Service didn't destroy."

"You didn't know they'd torn the house down?"

"No! I had no idea. When I got down to St. Marys on Saturday, I'd already missed the ferry. I should have just gotten a motel room and come the next morning, but in the frame of mind I was in, all I could think of was getting over here to Loblolly. I went to the marina and took a charter boat to the Sea

Camp dock. By the time I'd hiked down here, it was almost sunset. For a minute there, I thought maybe I'd somehow gotten turned around and gone the wrong way. Which made no sense. I mean, Dungeness is right over there."

Her finger stabbed the still, humid air, in the direction of the brick-and-stucco ruins. "So where was our house? I mean, how could it have just disappeared? Then, I saw the pile of bricks, and of course, you can still sort of see the outline of where the house was. I kind of went a little crazy. Okay, I was already halfway there, but the house being gone, that pushed me over the edge."

"What did you do?" Cara asked.

"You mean after I cried and carried on and stood over there on the bluff and screamed so loud I scared the feral horses and nearly gave a hiker a heart attack because he thought I'd been bit by a rattlesnake?"

"Yes. What did you do after that?"

"I turned around and started to walk back to Sea Camp. But then I realized there wouldn't be a ferry back to the mainland until the next morning. I had my overnight bag, but no tent or sleeping bag—and it was getting dark. I didn't know what else to do, so I called Pete."

"Your ranger friend?"

She nodded. "That day after we ran into him at lunch and I gave him my business card? He texted me after I got back to the office. I texted back, just to say how glad I was to have seen him, and that was it. He asked me to meet him for a drink, even suggested I should bring Harris, but I said no. I never intended to see Pete again."

"Then why come over here to Cumberland?" Cara asked. "You knew he'd be here, right?"

"I knew Loblolly would be here." She laughed ruefully. "Anyway, that's what I told myself. But with Loblolly gone, what else was I going to do? I had Pete's number in my phone, so I called him and told him where I was, and he came and got me, no questions asked."

Cara looked around again at the tree house. "I'm guessing you didn't stay up here."

"God, no. Pete has one of the little ranger cabins, so I stayed with him. The mosquitoes would have carried me away up here. Anyway, I'd forgotten all about the tree house until I came back over here yesterday, to see if there was anything left of the house that I could salvage. You know, a doorknob, anything at all. The Park Service was very efficient about obliterating every trace of Loblolly."

"And you really didn't know the house was going to be torn down? When was the last time you were here?"

"Mmm, maybe my senior year of high school, so that's like, ten years ago."

"Nobody in your family mentioned that the house was gone?"

"No, but that's understandable. My mom was never really crazy about staying at Loblolly. It was too much like camping for her, but I adored being here. We used to come over a couple times a year for a week or two at a time with my uncle Les and his family, but Les has been dealing with his own family stuff for the past couple years. His wife has breast cancer, and my cousin was nearly killed in a car wreck last Christmas and is still in rehab. I don't even know if Mom knows Loblolly has been torn down."

Brooke propped her elbows on her knees and looked out toward the riverbank. Cara took the time to study her. Her short, uncharacteristically messy hair was held back from her face with a rolled-up red bandanna, and she wore a pair of too-big wrinkled khaki shorts and a lime-green tie-dye T-shirt. It looked like she'd gone shopping at the St. Marys Goodwill.

"Did my mom send you to get me?"

"No. I promised not to tell where you'd gone. The only other person who knows where we are is Bert, my assistant. It was his idea for me to text you."

"Then why are you here?"

Cara didn't answer at first.

"Shhh. Look." Cara nodded in the direction of Loblolly. A herd of horses had drifted up and they were nosing about the vegetation around the foundation. There were six of them, four mares and two colts. They were so close, she could hear them whinnying.

"They're so beautiful," Cara whispered. "Where did they come from?"

"Nobody really knows. When we were kids we used to pretend they were pirate horses. Some people think they came over with Spanish explorers in the 1500s, but there would have been horses on the early plantations too, plus the Carnegies had their own stables. The Park Service has tried to figure out ways to manage the size of the herd, because they say the horses eat the sea oats and beach grasses that are needed to control beach erosion, but a lot of people love those horses, so it's just another hot topic on the island."

"Did you ever try to ride one of those horses?" Cara asked.

"You still haven't answered my question."

"I came here to Cumberland to find you and make you understand what a big mistake you're making. Now you. What are you doing here, Brooke?"

Brooke hugged her knees to her chest. "I guess I'm looking for me too."

"Oh God," Cara groaned. "Spare me the existentialism."

"I just wanted things to slow down a little, okay? I've been working all these hours for this trial coming up, and then Friday, my boss came in and said the other side had decided to settle out of court! It was like this huge load had been lifted. But I still had all the wedding stuff to contend with, and my dad and Patricia, and yes, even my mom, although she means well, it was all too, too much."

Brooke studied Cara. "Haven't you ever wanted to run away?"

"Sure," Cara said. "All the time. Everybody wants to run away at some time or another."

"But not everybody does."

"True that." Cara paused, trying to remember the speech she'd rehearsed on the ferryboat. "Harris and your mom are worried sick about you, Brooke. Your mom knows the pressure you've been under, and she told me she's afraid you'll hurt yourself."

"Me?" Brooke looked shocked. "Mom thinks I'm suicidal?"

"She doesn't know what to think. And Harris—he really loves you, Brooke. He broke down in tears when I talked to him. He blames himself for your leaving."

"He did?" Brooke looked away.

"Why didn't you just let them know you were going to take a few days off?" Cara asked. "They would have understood."

Brooke was looking down at something on the floor. She lowered a fingertip to a plank, then lifted it up so Cara could see a tiny ladybug perched there.

"I didn't plan to leave. I'd been dreading the bachelorette party. I've never understood why a girl feels the need to get dressed up in some stupid 'I'm the Bride' tiara and beauty-pageant sash and go riding around town with her girlfriends in a limo, getting shit-faced on candy-colored cocktails."

"Then why have one?"

"Holly—she's my best friend. And Harris's sister. I couldn't hurt her feelings and tell her I didn't feel like going clubbing. It's not normal to not want a bachelorette party. Finally, I made myself put on my game face. I was almost ready when I got a text from a number I didn't recognize. There was no message, just a link."

"To Harris's Facebook page," Cara said. "And the stripper photos."

Brooke's head bent over the ladybug, who was beetling her way up her wrist.

"We had another fight about the bachelor party Friday morning, before I left for work. Harris offered not to go—said he'd stay home if it was going to make me that upset. Which made me even angrier. I knew all the guys would blame *me* if Harris didn't go, and they'd say he was pussy-whipped."

"Damned if you do, damned if you don't," Cara said.

"He sent me a beautiful bouquet of flowers at work Friday, with the sweetest note, apologizing again and telling me how much he loved me." Brooke's face softened.

"He sent you flowers from another florist?" Cara said indignantly.

"He's a guy. I'm sure he got his secretary to send the flowers," Brooke said. "Anyway, so then I was feeling guilty about making him feel guilty, but I was still dreading going out. And then that text came Saturday afternoon. And I saw those pictures of him—with that woman—riding him—with her boobs pushed up in his face. . . ."

"I saw the pictures too, Brooke. He was drunk. So drunk he passed out in the van afterward."

"Harris told you that? Is he the one who told you the pictures were on Facebook?" She buried her head in her arms. "Did everybody in Savannah see them?"

"Layne, your caterer, saw them, and she sent me the link. Harris deleted the pictures as soon as he found out his friend Mike Bingham had posted them. Brooke? Did you ever figure out who texted you with the Facebook link?"

"No." She looked up. "I deleted it afterward. Does it matter? Somebody would have told me sooner or later anyway."

Cara felt herself grinding her back molars. "I have a pretty good idea who wanted to make sure you saw them."

"Who?"

"I can't prove it, but I bet Cullen Kane was behind it."

"The florist? The one Patricia wanted to hire?"

"That's the one. He'll do anything he can to mess with me."

"I don't get it," Brooke said.

"It's a long story. But let's get back to you. That's why you left? Because of the photos?"

"Yes." She held her right hand up to her left and let the ladybug cross over the fingertip bridge. There was a faint band of pale skin where her engagement ring had been. "Honestly? No. That's the lie I told myself the whole drive down here. I thought I wanted to hurt Harris as much as he'd hurt me. I decided I'd come over here, stay a couple nights at Loblolly, and then go back and get married."

"You can still go back and get married. Harris won't care where you've been. He just wants you to come back."

Brooke shook her head. "It's too late for that now. I can't marry Harris. I won't marry him." She looked over at Cara. "And nothing you can say is going to change my mind."

She tilted her right hand slightly, and the ladybug nimbly transitioned into the palm of her hand. Brooke stood up and leaned over the wooden railing. She raised her palm to her lips and blew gently.

60

Brooke sat back down and looked at the thin gold watch on her wrist. "If you leave now, you can still make the afternoon ferry back to St. Marys."

Cara's mind was working frantically. Where was that rational, well-planned speech she'd rehearsed? All she could think of was—why? Why not marry sweet, lovely, loving, wealthy, wonderful Harris Strayhorn? Why not return to her loving family in Savannah? Why not beg forgiveness and get on with a wedding that might mean the difference between financial success or suicide for Cara Mia Kryzik?

Her mind went haywire. So she asked the burning question.

"Are you sleeping with Pete?"

Brooke looked up at her through lowered eyelashes. She had such long, luxurious dark lashes, Cara had major lash envy.

"Who wants to know?"

"I do. It might help me understand what's going through your head right now."

"I wanted to sleep with Pete. That first night in his cabin, I tried to seduce him. Does that shock you?"

"A little," Cara admitted. "What happened?"

"He turned me down. He was the perfect gentleman. Pretty depressing, huh? I mean, you're alone on an island. You're naked. Well, I was naked. He was dressed in some kind of ranger boxers. And then nothing. Zero. He wouldn't even kiss me. Just patted me on the head and suggested I might be more comfortable if he took the sofa."

Cara couldn't help herself. She just blurted it out. "Is he gay?"

"He says not." Brooke giggled. "And, um, from the looks of his boxers that night, I'd say he's not immune to feminine wiles."

"What did he say?"

"Oh, the usual. 'I care too much about you to let you do something you might regret in the morning.' And then there was 'I wouldn't feel right about sleeping with another man's fiancée.' And let's not forget the old 'I don't believe in rebound sex.'"

Brooke sighed dramatically. "What is it with me and nice guys? Harris is nice. Pete is nice. I've never dated a not-nice guy. Just once in my life, I'd really like to go to the dark side. You know, do it with some really smoking hot, gnarly semicriminal bad boy."

"Who *are* you?" Cara gave her a quizzical look. "What happened to the sedate, conservative, dark-suit-wearing debutante lady lawyer from Savannah? Did they give you some kind of mystic Indian Kool-Aid when you got off the ferryboat Saturday? Because this is totally not the Brooke Trapnell I know."

"That's sort of the root of my problem," Brooke said. "You asked me earlier why I left. I'm just beginning to figure that out. I do know it's not because Harris went to some titty show. It's not because I want to punish my dad and Patricia for pushing me into a giant wedding that I didn't really want. And it's not because I'm in love with Pete Haynes. Although yeah, I'll admit I'm attracted to him. Which in itself should be a reason not to get married to Harris, don't you think?"

"Do you love Harris? I mean, really love him?" Cara asked.

"I thought I did," Brooke said softly. "I knew I *should* love him. Harris is perfect for me, right? So why was I having panic attacks in the middle of the night? And throwing up every morning? Why did I deliberately miss those dress fittings and portrait sittings?"

Now, thought Cara. *Now is the time to tell her how normal it is to have doubts and fears and panic attacks. Tell her about the hairless Chihuahua bride, or the girl who lost so much weight her mother ended up force-feeding her Ensure every day for two weeks before the wedding. Tell her this is all perfectly normal, and then drag her butt back to Savannah and collect her daddy's check.*

"The wedding is still two weeks off," Cara pointed out. "Maybe if you come home, let Harris know that you're feeling confused and unsettled, or speak to a therapist, go to couple's counseling or something, you'll realize that this is all just a severe case of pre-wedding jitters."

"Is that what you'd do?" Brooke asked, regarding Cara carefully. "If you were me, knowing what you know about what I'm feeling and what I've done, would you go back to Savannah and go through with the wedding anyway?"

"Dammit, that is not a fair question," Cara said.

"Sure it is. You've been married. And divorced. You've seen what, a couple hundred weddings up close and personal? You're battle-scarred. So tell me, what would you do?"

"I guess . . . I guess maybe I'd try to find a graceful way out of this mess. There's no way to do this without hurting people you care about, but from what you've told me, I don't think you should marry Harris. Not now, anyway."

Brooke nodded and reached over and squeezed Cara's hands. "Thank you for being honest with me. And for not ratting me out to anybody."

"You have to talk to Harris right away," Cara said. "He's in agony. And so is your mom."

"I know. And my dad too." She winced. "What's Dad's reaction to all this drama?"

"He was getting ready to hire a private detective to track you down and bring you home, but your mother managed to talk him out of it," Cara said.

"That sounds like Warden Gordon, all right."

They both laughed, and then Brooke stood up and dusted off the seat of her shorts. She pulled Cara to her feet, too.

"Will you go back with me? And talk to Harris face-to-face?" Cara asked, as Brooke lowered herself onto the top rung of the foot ladder.

Brooke hesitated, then shook her head. "I can't. If I go back, Harris will probably succeed in talking me into going through with the wedding. And I just can't risk that. It's the coward's way out, I know."

Cara dropped her backpack to the ground, and then climbed down after Brooke.

"What will you do?" Cara asked. "Savannah's a pretty small town. It's going to cause quite a stir when word gets out that you jilted Harris."

"Ow," Brooke said. "Jilted. It sounds so cruel."

"I tell it like I see it," Cara replied. "Remember, it's not just Harris who's going to be devastated. You say his sister is your best friend, and his parents adore you . . . I'm not trying to guilt-trip you, Brooke, but you need to be aware of what the consequences will be. For everybody involved."

"I'm fully aware," Brooke said calmly. "I borrowed Pete's computer and emailed my boss this morning and resigned from the law firm. Cell-phone service here most days seems to depend on which way the wind is blowing. I guess maybe I'll catch the ferry back with you this afternoon and try to call Harris tonight, when he gets home from work. I need to get some more clean clothes from my car, anyway. I'll call Mom and Dad too."

"Attagirl," Cara said. "And then what?"

Brooke shrugged. "Who knows? I can't stay with Pete too much longer, that's for sure. Park Service regulations." She made a face. "I do love it down here, though. I'd like to see if I could rent one of the little caretaker's cottages on the north end for two or three months. Just hang out and chill. See if I can make my brain and body slow down long enough to enjoy life. I want to spend fall on the island. It's my favorite time to be on Cumberland. Mom knows people, so maybe she could get me the hookup."

"And after the fall?" Cara asked. They were walking in the direction of Loblolly, where Cara had left her bike. The horses were gone now, and the sky had started to cloud up.

Brooke wasn't listening. She was looking down at the spot Cara had excavated, and in the next moment, she was kneeling on the ground, brushing sand away from the Loblolly threshold. "Hmm?"

Cara walked her bike over. "I said, what will you do after the fall? How will you make a living?"

Brooke looked up. "I'll figure that out, right after I figure out me. Who knows? Maybe I'll hang up a shingle in St. Marys. There must be somebody over there who needs suing, right?"

"Right."

A wide, mischievous grin lit up Brooke's face. "I'll start with the Park Service."

61

Bert was seated on the living-room floor in what looked like the lotus position, his hands palm-up, resting lightly on his knees. He opened his eyes when he heard Cara come clomping up the steps from the shop.

"How did it go?" he asked. "Did you manage to lasso the runaway bride?"

"No." Cara dropped her backpack on the floor and collapsed onto the sofa. Poppy took that as the signal to rest her muzzle in Cara's lap, nudging Cara's hand until she obliged with a head scratch.

"The wedding is off. Brooke called Harris and her parents this afternoon to let them know where she is and to say that she's not coming back."

"Oh, wow. Major bummer."

Cara looked idly around the room. Bert had managed to pack up everything from her bookshelves, and now boxes lined the living-room wall. "What exactly are you doing?" she asked.

"Yoga. My AA sponsor says sober means sober, so no more drugs. He says the yoga will help with keeping me grounded and quitting the weed."

"Sounds good. How long have you been doing yoga?"

"Counting this morning, twice. It's very relaxing. You should try it."

"Maybe later," Cara said.

"Was Brooke shacked up with the geeky ranger like you figured?" he asked.

"She's staying with him, but not sleeping with him. And she swears that calling off the wedding is not about the strip club or the geeky ranger or even about torturing her father and stepmother. I think she basically wants to hit the reset button with her life."

"Hmm." Bert slid forward with his hands under his shoulders, straightening his legs, lowering his head, and pointing his butt toward the sky. He held the pose for only a few seconds before dropping back onto the floor. "Ugh! Now I remember why I hate the Downward Dog pose. It makes all the snot run out my eyeballs."

"Just out of curiosity, how are you learning yoga? Are you going to class?"

"Nah. Classes cost money, and I don't like the idea of being in the same room with a lot of stinky, sweaty women. I just watch YouTube videos."

"Makes sense. By the way, thanks for packing up all the stuff, Bert. I was dreading coming home to face that. But mostly I was dreading coming home without Brooke in tow."

"I really thought you would pull this one off, Cara. I was sure if you found Brooke you'd be able to talk her into going through with things."

"Me too. I even had a brilliant five-point plan worked out."

"What happened?"

"I was outgunned. So that's it. No humongous two-hundred-and-fifty-thousand-dollar wedding means no humongous check. Patricia called me to make that perfectly clear. I called most of our vendors during the drive back from St. Marys. Everybody's disappointed. Nobody more so than me. I'll have to talk to the Colonel in the morning to break the bad news. He's going to pop a vein when I tell him I can't send the rest of his money the way I promised."

"He called today, by the way."

"My dad?"

"Yup." Bert got up and handed her a stack of pink message slips from the console table. "He tried calling your cell phone too, but said the calls wouldn't go through."

"Thank God for crappy reception on that island. I don't think I could have dealt with talking with the Colonel today. Wait a minute. How'd he get my cell number?"

"Not from me," Bert said.

Cara shook her head, then held up the other message slips. "Who are all these people? I don't recognize the names."

"Ahhh. Well, it seems your former nemesis Lillian Fanning has transformed herself into your own personal patron saint. The top three slips are all from brides or mothers of the brides wanting an appointment to talk wedding flowers, and two of them said Lillian referred them. The third girl, Taylor Vickers, and her mom, you're seeing tomorrow at eleven because she just had a tragic breakup with her former florist, and the wedding is only three weeks away."

"What florist did she break up with?" Cara asked.

"Some old mean queen named Cullen Kane."

"What! Bert, I appreciate your trying to make things up to me, but I do not want to be poaching Cullen Kane's clients."

"It's not poaching," he assured her. "I met Taylor while I was um, seeing Cullen. You know he wines and dines all these brides when he's trying to get them to commit, but she just discovered he's doing another big wedding the same date and time as hers, at a church across town, and when you meet Taylor's mama, you'll understand that she is *not* having a florist double-book on her date. I ran into Taylor at Whole Foods this morning, and she remembered me and told me the whole sad story. I might have slipped her one of your business cards. Not an hour later, her mama called here."

"You are shameless," Cara said.

"You say that like it's a bad thing."

"I told the other two brides you'd call them in the morning. This one"—he plucked the top slip and waved it in front of her—"is from the general manager of that new boutique hotel that opens at the end of July in the old Kresge's store downtown on Broughton Street."

"The Ibis? Did he say what he wanted?"

"*She* would like to discuss your developing a signature floral look for the hotel. I told her Wednesday noon would be good for you."

"Here? She can't come here. The shop is going to be all torn up. We've got to be of here by Friday. And we've got to finish up all the stuff for that beach wedding Saturday. . . ."

"Relax," Bert said. "Deep, cleansing breaths. In, out. Release the tension. You're meeting her at their new lobby restaurant. She'd like you to bring along some concepts, which I told her you'd be pleased to do."

"Concepts? I can't just come up with a whole look out of thin air by Wednesday. I don't know anything . . ."

Bert grasped her by the shoulders. "I got this. Okay? I went online and looked at the chain's website. There are seventeen Ibis hotels, all over the country, mostly out West, in California, Oregon, Washington, and Colorado. This is their first property in the South. Each of the hotels has a different name and theme, keyed to the location. I printed out photos I found of their hotels in Portland, San Francisco, and Seattle. I think they go for a pretty eclectic, bohemian look."

"You did all that? Today? On top of packing up my stuff?"

"I also finished off one of the oyster-shell chandeliers for Saturday."

"How many do we have left to do?"

"Two."

Cara groaned. "Then I guess I better go fire up the glue gun, huh?"

Jack found Libba in the barn Wednesday morning. She'd left the big sliding doors open, and she was standing in front of one of the windows, staring out at the pasture, where a mare and her foal drank from a galvanized watering trough.

She turned at the sound of his footsteps. It seemed to him that Libba Strayhorn had aged ten years since he'd seen her last. Her gray-streaked hair was pushed behind her ears, and the sunlight revealed the network of fine lines and creases radiating out from her warm gray eyes and downturned mouth.

"The wedding is off, Jack."

"I heard."

"Already? Yeah, what am I saying? The gossip mill in Savannah must be working overtime."

"Ryan's mother-in-law, Lillian, is friends with Marie Trapnell," he said.

"I should call Marie," Libba murmured. "Let her know I don't blame her."

Libba thrust her hands in the back pocket of her jeans. "Right now, I feel like a big old fool putting all this time and money and work into this place. Libba's Folly, that's what the neighbors around here have been calling it, and they haven't even gotten the word yet that the wedding is off."

Jack set his toolbox down on the floor. "I don't know what to say, Libba. How is Harris dealing with all this?"

"About like you'd expect. He's crushed. Hurt." Her laugh was bitter. "Pissed off. He and Brooke lived together for six years. Six years! That girl was like family to all of us. Nobody understands it."

Jack nodded. "Uh, we don't have to finish the work here if you don't want to. We can leave off tiling the bathroom. The kitchen fixtures have been delivered, but I can probably send them back and just pay a shipping and restocking fee."

"No," Lillian said sharply. "Mitch and I talked about this last night. We want you to go ahead and finish everything, just as planned. Harris is going to get past this. We'll all get past it. He will find somebody who has her head on straight and eventually get married to a girl who can appreciate what she's found in him. Holly has a new boyfriend, and that's gotten pretty serious. They will get married, and eventually we will have a large time right here. And someday, my grandbabies are going to laugh and run and play in this barn."

With that, Libba Strayhorn burst into tears.

Not knowing what else to do, Jack awkwardly patted her back.

Libba took a crumpled tissue from her pocket and blew her nose. "Please forgive a crazy old fool. I know this must be embarrassing for you. Go on and do what you need to do. I'll get out of your way in a few minutes."

"It's okay," Jack said. He hesitated. "I don't know if this is any consolation, but earlier this year, my live-in girlfriend left me, too. It came out of nowhere. She met some other dude and blew town with him. At first, I was destroyed. I mean, what the hell? But then . . . the longer she was gone, the more I saw that things hadn't been going that great between us. We didn't have much in common. Zoey wanted me to be somebody I wasn't. This sounds mean, but when I look back on it now, I realize we were just a habit. She did me a favor by leaving. But it still hurts like hell when the other person does what she did."

"Don't I know it," Libba said, sniffing. "What happened to the girlfriend?"

Jack rolled his eyes. "She's back in town, pestering the hell out of me. I let her stay at my place one night, while I was away, and now she keeps turning up, claiming she's just visiting the dog. I'm gonna have to get the locks changed to keep her out."

"But I gather you were able to move on," Libba prompted.

"A couple months ago, I met somebody new." His face darkened. "Okay, I don't know where I was going with this, because that didn't have such a happy ending either."

"Cara?" Libba asked gently.

"Yeah."

"You two broke up? Already? I'm so sorry. She's a lovely girl. A joy to work with, and so creative."

"She's all of that," Jack admitted.

"Do you mind my asking what happened?"

He made a helpless gesture. "The thing is, I don't know what happened. One minute, things were going great. We had fun together, we like the same things. We even have the same kind of dog. Cara has had some bad luck and tough times, financially, and it seemed like everything was coming down on her at once. I wanted to help out. Her shop is in this cool old building downtown on West Jones Street, and some asshole was gonna buy it and put Cara out on the street, out of professional jealousy. It just happens that I used to take piano lessons from the old lady who owned the place. I went to see her and I guess I sort of sweet-talked her a little because I was able to outbid the other guy."

"That's so thoughtful," Libba said.

"I thought so," Jack said wryly. "But apparently I was mistaken. I kept it a secret because I wanted to surprise Cara. The building hadn't been maintained at all, and it needs a lot of work, but I thought we could work on it together, you know? Really transform the place."

Libba squeezed his arm. "You could make anything awesome. I still can't get over the miracle you worked with this old barn. That's the one good thing that came out of all this. I'm just telling myself I didn't lose a daughter-in-law, I gained a fabulous barn."

"Thanks, but that's not how Cara saw it. She was mad as hell. Furious. Accused me of going behind her back, and making some sinister power play to get control of her and her business. She actually thought I was going to jack up the rent on her after making the improvements, and when I insisted I wasn't, that pissed her off even more, because she said I was insinuating she couldn't pay her own way."

He shook his head again. "I just don't get it. I did this for her. Out of, you know . . ."

"Love?" Libba raised one eyebrow.

"I guess."

"Had you two talked about your feelings, or how serious things had gotten between you?"

"Not really. I didn't think we needed to. I mean, we were together, and it was going good. . . ."

"And then you bought her building, out of love." Libba laughed. "Some guys would have settled for a nice piece of jewelry, Jack."

He looked confused. "Why would Cara want jewelry? She was going to lose her shop, and her apartment. Her father's breathing down her neck to repay him some money she owes him, and this seemed like a good solution."

"I'll tell you a little story, Jack. Back in the early eighties, Mitch and I had been married a couple of years, and we were renting a crummy garage apartment on Washington Avenue, when I got pregnant with Harris. One day, some friend told Mitch about a little fixer-upper in Kensington Park, so he went to see it on his lunch hour, then came home that night and proudly announced he'd bought us a house."

"And you weren't thrilled?"

"I was enraged! I had three years' worth of back issues of *Southern Living*, bookmarked with ideas for our first house. And this place was a dump. Two bedrooms, one tiny little bath that didn't even have a shower. No washer or dryer, and the kitchen was a nightmare. If Mitch had bothered to show me the place, I could have pointed that out. I could have pointed out the fire station across the street, and predicted that every time there was an alarm, those fire trucks would go racing out of there with sirens wailing, waking our sleeping baby. But most of all, I hated that my husband didn't understand me enough to know you don't make that kind of a decision without consulting your partner."

"Point taken," Jack said.

"I tell you, I stewed and fumed over that house every day, until when I got pregnant with Holly, I laid down the law, we sold that house, and we picked out another house together in Ardsley Park."

"And you lived happily ever after."

A smile crept across Libba's round, ruddy face. "We did, didn't we?"

"I don't see that kind of ending for us," he said. "Cara is determined to move into another building, over on East Hall. The guy who owns it is a bottom-feeder, had it on the market forever, and couldn't unload it. I took a look at it, just out of curiosity, and it's a real piece of crap. That block is no place for a florist's shop, and it's no place for her. But I've learned my lesson. I'm staying out of it."

"No chance of a reconciliation?" Libba asked.

Jack shook his head vehemently. "I tried. Now I'm done. A man can only crawl for so long."

63

Cara heard heavy footsteps on the stairs. She stuck her head around the kitchen doorway. "Bert? Is that you?"

A blond head came into view. "It's Leo." He topped the last stair and flashed her his trademark Southeastern Region Salesman of the Quarter smile. "The shop door was open and unlocked, but there was nobody around downstairs, so I thought I should come up here and check things out. You shouldn't leave your door unlocked in this neighborhood, Cara. Anybody could walk right in here, like I just did."

"Thanks for the helpful advice, Leo. What do you want?"

He glanced around the kitchen. "I saw all the boxes downstairs. You're moving?"

"Yes." She slammed the packing-tape dispenser on the top of a cardboard box of dishes and dragged it across the closed flaps, snapping off the tape at the end.

"How come? I thought you liked it here. It looked like a pretty sweet setup."

"The building has been sold." Cara moved over to the next box. Leo leaned over and plucked a mug from a nest of wadded-up newspaper.

"Hey, I remember these. They were a wedding present from my aunt, right?"

"Keep it," Cara said.

"That's okay," Leo said, handing the cup back. "I got plenty myself."

He leaned back against the counter, crossed one foot over the other, oblivious of the fact that he was in her way.

"Where are you moving to? Not out of town, right?"

She put the tape down on the countertop. "Is there a point to this drop-in, Leo? Because if there is, I wish you'd get to it. Bert will be back with the van any minute now, and I want to finish boxing up this kitchen."

He glanced around the kitchen. "What happened to your new boyfriend? How come he's not the one doing all the heavy lifting?"

Cara flushed. "None of your business."

"Sounds like he's out of the picture now. Just as well. The dude was not in your class, at all."

Leo reached in his pocket, brought out a Chap Stick, and ran it across his lips, smacking them noisily, and in the process reminding Cara of how much she'd loathed that particular nervous habit of his.

"Again. Why are you here?"

"Well yeah," Leo said. "The thing is, your dad called and asked me to look in on you."

"Why would the Colonel do that?"

"He's worried about you. He said he'd tried calling you several times, at the shop and on your cell phone. . . ."

"Who gave him my cell-phone number?" Cara demanded. "I didn't."

"Okay, I might have shared that with him. But only because he was really concerned about you. He called me because he said he hadn't heard from you, and he was even thinking of flying down here to see if you were okay."

"I knew I should have changed that number after we split up," Cara said. "He actually asked you to come over here and spy on me?"

"It's not spying. We were married for Pete's sake. I care about you." He ran an index finger down her cheek, and Cara flinched. "You dad cares about you. "

"The Colonel cares about the fact that I still owe him money,," Cara said. "Did he appoint you his new collection agency? Or are you his idea of a leg-breaker?"

"He never said a word to me about money. He said you're having some challenges, that's all. He thought maybe I could help. I would help, if you'd let me."

"'Challenges'?" Cara hooted. "I'm pretty sure my father never used that word in reference to me. He probably told you I'm a screwup and a failure. Did he tell you he wants me to close up the shop and move back home?"

"He mentioned that," Leo said cautiously. "Your mom is gone and you're his only kid. He's lonely. Why is that so hard for you to swallow?"

"Because I know the Colonel. If he's lonely, why has he never, not once, come to Savannah to visit me? And don't give me any bullshit about him hating to travel. He goes to Vegas two or three times a year. If he was so worried about how my business was doing, why didn't he come down here to see for himself? Since I moved here, I'm the one who has to fly or drive up to Ohio, to see him on his own terms."

"I can't answer why your dad does or doesn't come down here," Leo said. "Okay, he's set in his ways. That's the military, right? He's always been like that. The Colonel just wants what's best for you, Cara. I want it too. You say you're moving because this building was sold, maybe that's true. But I think you're moving because business stinks, and you can't make the rent here. It's no big crime to admit it, you know. So what? Walk away. I don't happen to agree with the Colonel about you moving up home again. There's nothing in Ohio for you. On the other hand, I think enough time has passed, we should take another shot at making things work between us."

Cara blinked. "You really think so?"

"Yeah." He nodded thoughtfully. "We've both changed a lot. Matured. Maybe we got married too young to be able to appreciate what we had. But now, I know where I'm going, and what I want." He leaned in so close Cara could smell his cologne. "I want you, Cara. That's all. Just you. What do you say we load all these boxes in my car and take them over to my place?"

She took a step backward, and then another step. She could actually feel the blood rushing to her face, her fingertips tingling—with what? He'd caught her off-guard, that was sure.

"Move in with you again? Is that what you're saying?"

"Yeah. Exactly."

"Close up the shop. But how do I pay off the Colonel?"

"I got money. I'm doing great. They just gave me the two biggest accounts in the territory. I've actually been thinking of selling the condo, buying a house again. Have you seen those houses out at Southridge? Four bedrooms on the golf course, swim and tennis club. You could decorate it like you like. . . ."

"And then what?"

"Whatever you want. I don't know, you could maybe keep doing flowers if you wanted, work for somebody else, not as much pressure. And I was thinking, maybe next year, we could start a family."

"Have a baby?"

He nodded. "Yeah. My mom is crazy to have another grandchild. . . ."

She felt a roaring sensation in her ears. "Are you crazy? I'm not moving in with you, Leo. I'm not closing up my business and moving to some country-club development. I am not taking money from you to pay off my dad, and I am most definitely not having your baby."

"We could wait on the baby like another year or so. . . ."

"Leo!" Cara was shouting. "We are over. We've been over. I don't need your money, or your pity or your advice. Maybe you have matured, but I seriously doubt it if you were able to convince yourself that this fantasy of us remarrying and moving to the suburbs could ever become reality."

"You don't have to shout," he said, putting on that hurt look of his. "I was just trying to help out, okay? You want to talk about fantasy?" He gestured around the kitchen, with its chipped laminate countertops and faded linoleum. "This right here is a fantasy. You can't even afford this place, and you think moving someplace else is going to fix things? Who are you kidding? The Colonel is right—you are a screwup. You're pathetic, Cara. Really. So you just keep on doing what you're doing. Stay right here in your dreamworld. Move on over to the next roach motel. You're all about doing everything for yourself, not accepting help from anybody. Maybe that's why the boyfriend left you.

Great. Keep it up. Be a ballbuster. You're going to end up the crazy dog lady of Savannah, broke and alone."

"Get out," she whispered. "Don't call me again."

"Not a problem," he snapped, heading for the stairs. She stood in the hallway, watching him go. She heard the front door open, and now Bert was heading back to start retrieving the moving boxes. "Some asshole parked a black Lexus in the loading zone out back," he called. "I had to park the van a block over."

Bert stood in the downstairs hallway, glowering when he spotted Cara's ex.

"I'm just leaving," Leo said curtly.

"Shitbird," Bert muttered.

Cara couldn't help it. She had to have the last word. She ran down the stairs after Leo. "Tell the Colonel he'll get his money. Tell him I have three weddings and a big fat contract to do all the flowers for a new hotel in town. Tell him . . ."

It was too late. She heard the back door slam.

64

It was nearly six by the time Jack got back to Savannah from Cabin Creek. He told himself he was only driving past the shop to see if Cara really meant what she said about moving out. He slowed the truck to a roll as he approached the shop, but when he saw the large, hand-lettered MOVED TO NEW LOCATION sign in the window, he pulled up and parked in the loading zone.

BLOOM HAS BEEN TRANSPLANTED TO EAST HALL STREET, the sign said in smaller letters. Trust Cara to make that seem like a good thing.

He fished the set of keys with the C&S Bank key fob out of his pocket and unlocked the front door. The first thing he noticed was that the little tinkling bell that announced visitors was gone.

The second thing he noticed was the smell of antiseptic. True to her word, Cara had stripped the walls of the reclaimed-pine shelves and the chippy wrought-iron trellis, the mirrors and the chandeliers. A slight indentation in the wood floor was the only sign that a flower cooler had once occupied this space. The shop was spotless. And empty.

He walked through to the back of the first floor, glancing into the kitchenette and noticing that this, too, had been cleaned out. The undercounter dorm-size refrigerator was gone, but he noticed that the coffeepot had been left behind.

Jack unlocked the door to the courtyard patio. To his surprise, the space looked the same as it had the last time he and Cara and the dogs had sat out here. He was relocking the door when he spotted a small yellow Post-it that must have fallen to the floor.

J—I won't be needing patio furniture in the new place until I get backyard cleared out. Hope it's ok to leave here for now.—C.

He shrugged. This was her idea of a good-bye note. No "Dear Jack," no "Fondly, Cara."

The second floor had been as thoroughly cleaned out as the first floor. The walls bore the faded outlines of where Cara's pictures had hung, and there were depressions in the carpet left there by the now departed bookshelves.

Curtains still hung at her bedroom window, and when he brushed the thick linen panel aside to look out onto the street below, it released a scent he realized was Cara's. Her box fan was still wedged inside the window casing.

Jack slid down to the floor, his hands on his knees, his back against the wall. He inhaled and the faint floral bouquet of roses and some other flower—maybe honeysuckle—filled his nostrils. He thought about the night they'd danced at Ryan and Torie's wedding, the way she looked in that pink silk dress and how she felt in his arms.

Sweat trickled down his shoulders to the small of his back. It was unbearably hot up here. How had Cara stood it up here for these past few weeks? He stood slowly and started toward the stairs, but then he backtracked to the bedroom, where he unplugged the fan and tucked it under his arm.

As he was passing the kitchen, he spotted a lone coffee cup sitting on the kitchen counter. All the cabinets and shelves had been emptied. He wondered if Cara had meant to leave this one behind. He picked up the cup, and on the rim saw the faint pink remains of her lipstick. He told himself he would return the cup when he returned her fan. That's what he told himself.

. . .

The prospect of returning home alone to the cottage on Macon Street did not appeal. Anyway, there was a good chance he wouldn't really be alone. Zoey's check still hadn't arrived, so despite her sketchy description of a job offer in New Orleans, she was still hanging around, sleeping on the sofa at a friend's house, but "dropping by" Jack's place, ostensibly to be with Shaz.

Tonight he was in no mood for Zoey's laughably obvious attempts to seduce him. What he was in the mood for was a cold beer and some hot wings. He called Ryan.

"Hey bro," Ryan said. "What's shakin'? You finish up over at Cabin Creek? Pick up the rest of the tools and stuff?"

"Change of plans," Jack said. "Libba wants us to go ahead and finish everything. Including the kitchen."

"Even with the wedding off?"

"Yep. She wants it finished. How did you guys do today over at Sylvia Bradley's?"

"You don't want to know," Ryan said. "That old lady is driving me nuts. We put the new roof on that mud porch yesterday, and this morning when I got over there, she'd somehow managed to climb up on the ladder, and she proceeded to bitch me out about how the new shingles were a different color than the ones on the rest of the house!"

"Did you explain that those old shingles probably hadn't been manufactured since the Eisenhower administration?"

"I tried, but you don't explain nothin' to Sylvia Bradley. She wants you to call her. I think she's gonna try and talk you into giving her a new roof for the rest of the house."

"Not happening," Jack said succinctly. "Hey, I'm headed over to the Exchange to grab a bite. You wanna meet me?"

"Awww, man. Wish I could. We've got our first childbirth class at the hospital tonight."

"Okay, no problem. Listen, in the morning, I'm gonna get the HVAC guy to walk through Jones Street with me, to see when we can get started on that."

"Oh. So . . . Cara went ahead and moved out?"

"Yeah. Probably for the best. You know what a pain in the ass it is to rehab a building when somebody's living there. Anyway, good luck tonight. I hope you do better with childbirth class than you did with high-school algebra. Cuz I am *not* helping out with that homework."

"Smart-ass," Ryan growled.

Jack sat in a booth by the window. The tables around him were filled with groups, families with young kids, gray-haired couples there for the early-bird specials, and groups of office workers stopping in for happy hour after work.

He drank a beer and ate half a plate of wings before deciding he was tired of avoiding his own home. Zoey had managed to find his spare key. By God, he would go back to Macon Street right now, and if she was there, he would kick her ass to the street. And then he would go to Home Depot and buy a new lockset and install it himself.

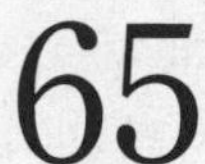

65

I forgot the coffeepot," Cara said.

Bert dumped the last box of dishes on the dining-room table. Which was sitting in the middle of the large open space that would allegedly someday be Cara's living quarters.

"Forget about it," he said, collapsing onto one of the chairs. "We've still got to get your bed set up, and anyway, there's no telling where your dishes or pantry stuff are. I'll go over to Back in the Day in the morning and get us coffee and muffins."

"No more takeout coffee," Cara said stubbornly. "Our overhead here is going to be killer. We've got to start economizing. And that means no more five-dollar lattes. I'll just run over to Jones Street and get the coffeepot. I think the pantry stuff, with the coffee and the sugar, are in that box there." She pointed to a large carton on the floor. "If you'll start unpacking that, I'll take Poppy with me, and we'll bring back pizza for dinner.

"Come on, Poppy," Cara called. "Let's go, girl."

The dog came running and happily allowed herself to be loaded into the front seat of the pink Bloom van for the short ride back to their old home.

. . .

Cara let herself in the front door and felt the gloom descend on her, like a heavy wool blanket. She wouldn't allow herself to look at the barren walls, at the swept-clean floor. Get the coffeepot and get out, she told herself.

Poppy raced down the hall. She stopped in front of the back door, glancing back expectantly at Cara, and pawed at the door.

"Okay," Cara said with a sigh. "One more try. Maybe that squirrel will get careless, and you'll get lucky." She opened the door and Poppy was out like a shot.

She went back to the kitchenette and unplugged the coffeemaker.

"Hey!" a woman's voice called from the front of the shop. She banged on the glass window. "Hey, are you in there?"

Cara poked her head out of the kitchen nook. A willowy blonde stood on the sidewalk, peering in through the window.

She opened the door. "Can I help you?" Over the woman's shoulder she spied a yellow VW bug parked in the loading zone. A familiar fluffy white dog's head hung out the open passenger window.

"Rowlf!" Shaz barked a greeting.

Zoey was a stunner, even with her long blond hair pinned carelessly atop her head. She wore a tight-fitting turquoise tank top that showed off impressive cleavage and a span of flat, tanned abdomen above low-slung white denim shorts. She had dancer's legs, long and toned, if just the slightest bit bowlegged, and she stood at least four inches taller than Cara, making her feel like a dwarf. A dowdy, depressed dwarf.

Zoey was studying Cara, too, and not bothering to pretend otherwise. "So you're the new girlfriend," she said, her lips flickering amusement. "Sorry for the intrusion, but I just had to check you out for myself before I leave."

Cara was looking at the VW. The backseat was loaded with boxes, and there was a bike on a rack strapped to the rear bumper.

"You're leaving town?" she asked. Stupid question.

"Sure am. My severance check from the cruise line finally came today, so I am out—like the fat kid in dodgeball." Zoey laughed at her own little joke.

Shaz had managed to wriggle her whole upper body out of the toylike VW window.

"Does Jack know you're leaving?" Cara asked.

"He'll figure it out when he gets home and sees that Shaz is gone."

"Where are you moving?" In her mind's eye, Cara could picture Jack arriving back at Macon Street, opening the door, and waiting for the dog to nearly knock him down with her bad-mannered adoration.

"New Orleans," Zoey said brightly. "I'm going to teach at a new studio that just opened in the French Quarter. It's called Sweatbox. Cool, huh? And I've rented the cutest little furnished efficiency you've ever seen, on the third floor above it."

Cara frowned, thinking of Shaz cooped up in a third-floor studio all day. Jack's cottage might be small, but it had its own fenced backyard, and these days, she knew, more often than not, Jack took Shaz with him to his job sites.

She turned her attention back to Zoey. "Why are you telling me all this?"

Zoey's laugh was deep and throaty. She could have had a great career doing phone sex. "That's a very good question. First off, before I leave town, yeah, I wanted to check you out, see what the hot attraction was between you two. Honestly? I don't get it. But you know what? I have no regrets. You want Jack Finnerty? Honey, you can have him. Yeah, he's cute, and he's great in bed. But you already know that, right?"

Cara stared up at the blonde, wondering where this was going, and whether she should admit that she and Jack were no longer an item.

"But here's something you might not have realized yet. He might have a hot body, but deep down, Jack is cold. He's cold and he's emotionally unavailable. He walls himself off from you, and there's no breaking that down. And did I mention he's a tightwad? We lived together for over a year, and he never bought me the first piece of jewelry."

And yet, Cara thought. She and Jack had slept together exactly three times by his accounting, and then he'd gone out and bought her a building. A three-story $750,000 building. And to thank him, she'd thrown it right back in his face. Figuratively speaking.

Shaz barked, and Zoey looked over her shoulder and frowned. "Quiet, baby, we're leaving in just a minute."

Cara's mind was working. She kept picturing Jack, walking into that cottage and realizing just how empty it really was.

"It's a long ride to New Orleans," she said, trying to sound casual. "And it's so hot. You don't want her to get dehydrated. Why don't you let me take Shaz out back to my courtyard, where my dog is? I'll give her some water and she can have one more potty stop before you hit the road."

"Okay, yeah, whatever," Zoey said carelessly. She opened the VW's door and Shaz bounced out, like an overinflated helium balloon. Zoey pulled a cell phone from the pocket of her shorts and leaned back against the car. "I'll just wait here for her."

Cara opened the door to the courtyard, and on spotting Poppy, Shaz barked a happy greeting. Poppy dropped the headless rubber doll she'd been chewing on, and came over to sniff Shaz's muffle, and then her butt. A moment later, Shaz grabbed the toy Poppy had dropped, and lay down on the bricks to give it a chew.

"Come here, Poppy," Cara called softly, looking back over her shoulder to make sure she was unobserved. For once, the dog obeyed. Cara wrapped her arms around the dog's shoulders, inhaling the smell of her freshly shampooed fur. Poppy licked Cara's neck and chin, while, with trembling fingers, Cara unbuckled her pink plaid collar and slipped it from her neck.

"I'm so sorry to do this to you," she whispered in the dog's silky ear. "But you're just going to have to trust me. Okay? Do you trust me?"

Poppy's tail beat a happy tattoo on the bricks.

"Okay," Cara said, leading the dog out to the VW. "She's all set to go."

Zoey put her phone away, opened the car door and gestured. "Come on, Shaz. Let's go! Let's go for a nice ride."

The dog planted its butt on the curb and looked from Zoey to Cara.

"Damn it, Shaz," Zoey cried. She grabbed the dog's neon-green collar and tugged. "Come on!" The dog resisted, even backing away from the VW.

Cara held her breath. "Let's go, Shaz," she said cheerily, giving the dog's butt a gentle push. Finally, between the two of them, they managed to wedge her back into the VW's passenger seat.

"Jack spoiled her rotten while I was gone," Zoey griped, crossing around to the driver's side. "Which is hysterical, since he claimed he never wanted a puppy in the first place. Now, he treats her way better than he ever treated me." She gave Cara an appraising look. "You watch, he'll do the same with your dog, now that Shaz is gone."

"Maybe so," Cara said. She stood back from the curb, and when the VW lurched away, she gave a sad little wave as it drove off, with the dog's big fluffy head hanging out the window, looking backward.

Cara raced inside the shop and picked up her cell phone. She touched the icon with Jack's number, praying he would pick up.

Fifteen minutes later, he pulled the truck around to the lane in back of the shop. He used his key to unlock the courtyard door.

Cara sat at the table under the umbrella, clutching her phone in her hand, her face etched with worry.

"Are you nuts?" he exploded. Shaz jumped up and planted her paws on his chest. "Down!" he said sternly, but she was not to be deterred. Finally, he scratched her head and her ears. She dropped to the ground, rolled over, and allowed him to scratch her belly.

"What if this doesn't work?" he asked, glaring at Cara. "You don't know Zoey. She's a total flake. There's no telling what she'll do. She could drive straight through to New Orleans, and you'll never see Poppy again. And then what? You'll blame me, even though if you'd run this harebrained idea past me, I would have told you how crazy it was."

"Five more minutes," Cara said, glancing down at her watch. She reached her hand out for Jack's phone. "Let me see Zoey's number, so I can type it into my phone."

"She might not answer," Jack warned. "She won't know who's calling. Or maybe she won't even hear it. She plays the radio in that car at full volume."

"Just give me the phone, please," Cara said.

He handed it over and she tapped in the number.

"Why did Zoey even come over here?" he asked.

Cara was still staring down at her phone, but she looked up now. "She wanted to check out what she thought was the competition. And she clearly didn't see what you could have seen in me."

"That's textbook Zoey. She's about as deep as an Arizona mud puddle."

"She had a lot to say about you, Jack. And none of it was very flattering. She says you're cold and emotionally distant."

"Sounds about right."

"And cheap. She says you never gave her a single piece of jewelry."

His answering smile was grim. "Seems like I'll be buying her some now, whether I like it or not. I'd just walked in the door five minutes earlier when you called. She wasn't content to just take Shaz. She also cleaned out my sock drawer."

"Zoey stole your socks?"

"She left the socks, but she took my stash. Sometimes my subs want to be paid in cash. I figure she got about two thousand dollars."

Cara held up her phone so Jack could see it. "Okay, keep your fingers crossed. It's been thirty minutes. It usually only takes about twenty minutes for Poppy."

She tapped the Dial button on her phone. Zoey's phone rang once, twice, three times, before the voicemail recording came on.

"Hi, this is Zoey," the sultry recorded voice said. "You know what to do."

Cara shook her head and disconnected.

"See? I knew this would happen. She probably thinks you're a bill collector or something."

"Or maybe she's got her hands full right at the moment," Cara said, swallowing her fear.

She dialed again, and this time Zoey picked up. Cara could hear the rush of traffic in the background.

"Oh, Zoey," Cara cried with absolutely authentic relief. "Something awful has happened."

"You're telling me," Zoey said.

"I must have gotten the dogs mixed up. Poppy and Shaz were both running around in the backyard, and they look identical, and somehow, I must have given you my dog, Poppy, instead of Shaz."

"Thanks a lot," Zoey said. "This damn dog has been barfing for ten minutes. She barfed all over the car, herself, me, it's everywhere. It's disgusting."

"I am so, so sorry," Cara said. "I just realized my mistake."

"Yeah, ten minutes too late," Zoey said. "Okay, I'm turning around right now. I can't take much more of this."

Cara hung up and turned to Jack with a triumphant smile. "She's coming back."

"Thank God," he breathed. "But Zoey's not going to give up this easily. Once she hands over Poppy, she's gonna insist on taking Shaz with her, if only because she wants her revenge against me."

"I've got another idea," Cara said. "Do you trust me?"

Jack looked down at Shaz, who was curled up at his feet. Despite all the excitement, she was asleep, softly snoring. "Do I have a choice?"

Exactly twenty-seven minutes later, the VW zoomed up to the curb in front of Bloom. The motor was still running as Zoey jumped out, ran around, and opened the passenger door. "Out!" she screamed. Poppy's head hung limply over the edge of the seat. "Get out, dammit!" Zoey repeated.

Cara stepped up and gathered the reeking puppy into her arms. "Poor baby," she crooned. "My poor baby."

"*Your* poor baby," Zoey exploded. "Look at me! Look at my car! I can't go anywhere like this. I've gotta get out of these clothes, shower, get my car cleaned up. I was gagging the whole way back here. I mean, what the fuck?"

"I'm sorry," Cara said, setting Poppy carefully down on the sidewalk. "But

I'm surprised you haven't encountered this with Shaz when you go on car trips. The vet says it's something to do with the breed."

"I've never taken Shaz on a car trip before," Zoey replied. "What are you talking about?"

"Carsickness," Cara said. "The vet says it's hereditary with goldendoodles."

"The breeder never mentioned it to me," Zoey said. "And come to think of it, when I brought Shaz back from Atlanta, that was a four-hour car ride, and she was fine. She slept the whole way home."

"Exactly," Cara said. "My vet says it's something the breeders downplay. Like hip dysplasia in Great Danes. When they're really young, it doesn't affect them so much. But once they're seven or eight months old . . . bleaaahhhh." Cara pantomimed an Oscar-worthy rendition of canine carsickness. "Poppy's fine for a short ride, like to the vet or the grocery store, but if she's in the car for more than fifteen minutes . . . bleaahhh."

Zoey shuddered, then tapped her foot impatiently. "Jack never said anything about Shaz getting carsick."

"Like you said, he's totally selfish," Cara pointed out. "He was probably hoping you'd take Shaz with you so he doesn't have to deal with her himself." She gestured toward the shop door. "If you want to come inside and get cleaned up, I'll take Poppy out to the garden and hose her off, and then you can get Shaz. I've probably got some old towels you can take with you for the rest of the trip. Just in case, you know . . . bleahhh."

Zoey crossed and uncrossed her arms. It took less than thirty seconds to make up her mind.

"Yeah. Thanks but no thanks. I think I'm just gonna let Shaz be Jack's problem from now on."

"You sure?" Cara asked helpfully. "I've got plenty of towels."

"Positive," Zoey said. "I gotta get to a car wash before this mess soaks into my upholstery." She looked over at Poppy, and then at Cara. "Gross."

Cara stood perfectly still while Zoey slammed the VW into first gear and pulled away from the curb.

She held up her right hand and gave a soft finger wave. "Buh-byeeee."

66

The bells at St. John's were just tolling six. Cara led Poppy through the lane and into the courtyard garden. She fetched the galvanized tub and the bottle of dog shampoo from the toolshed, and filled it with water from the hose. Then she held a dog treat beneath Poppy's nose, and gently coaxed the puppy into the tub. Cara squeezed shampoo into her hand and worked it into the dog's fur, training the nozzle over Poppy's fur.

"Zoey's gone," she told Jack, who still held a tight hand on the pink collar around Shaz's neck. "And the coast is clear."

"I was inside, crouched down, watching through the front window," Jack said. "I figured, if Zoey tried to argue with you, I'd come out and try to buy her off. What did you say to get her to leave Shaz behind?"

Hearing her name mentioned, Shaz stood, her ears pricked up. Jack released his hold on her collar and she edged over to watch the proceedings.

"Does she like a bath as much as Poppy does?" Cara asked, looking over at Jack.

He looked chagrined. "Uh, I guess. I mean, when I take her to the groomers, she's okay with it."

Cara gave him a look of reproof. "She's half golden retriever. Most retrievers love the water.

"Come here, you," Cara said, and Shaz propped her front paws on the edge of the washtub. She looked over at Jack. "Put out your hand."

He did as he was told, and she squeezed a dollop of shampoo into his open palm. He gave a disdainful sniff. "Smells like flowers."

"Deal with it," Cara said. She trained the hose on Shaz's head and then body, deliberately splashing Jack's legs.

"Come on," he said, choosing to ignore the water. "What did you tell Zoey?"

Cara scrubbed at Poppy's coat with both hands, working up a thick lather of suds. "I told her my vet says all goldendoodles are subject to carsickness. Because it's hereditary."

"That's bullshit. Shaz has never gotten carsick. I've taken her over to South Carolina, to Cabin Creek, plenty of times. It's a forty-five-minute drive, one way. She loves riding in the truck."

"Mmm-hmm," Cara said. "I totally made it up. Luckily, Zoey was happy to buy my lies."

"Luckily," Jack said.

"In the end, she basically told me I was welcome to the guy, and the dog. I guess she decided you were both more trouble than you were worth."

He got up from the chair and gazed down at Cara, still bent over the tub, washing her dog. He'd never noticed the fine sprinkling of freckles across her shoulders and the back of her neck. Then he stood up, grabbed the hose, and trained it on her exposed neck and back.

She gave a yelp of surprise. He grabbed her hands and pulled her to her feet. "I don't know about the dog, but I do know that I'm definitely more trouble than I'm worth. I still can't believe what you just did for me out there. Thank you. Thank you so much, Cara. You let Zoey take Poppy, not really knowing if she'd bring her back, if your crazy scheme would work. You risked everything for me."

Cara sighed. "Sometimes, you just have to trust your gut."

He took her hands and placed them on his own hips, then wrapped his arms loosely around her shoulders and tilted his forehead until it was resting on hers.

"Sometimes you have to trust your heart, too. You give what you think the other person needs, and hope they know that you're doing it out of love."

Cara raised her chin and smiled. "It took me a while, I'll admit. I wasn't very gracious about accepting your gift. But I think maybe I'm ready now, for whatever you have to offer."

His lips found hers. He pulled her tighter, then whispered in her ear. "All of it. Everything. Darlin', everything I have is yours."

She felt her knees buckle, which forced her to clasp herself tighter against his chest. "I love it when you call me darlin'."

There was a chattering just then, from the top of the crape myrtle. Poppy scrambled out of the washtub, and dashed after the squirrel in mad pursuit, with Shaz hot on her heels. The two wet, soapy dogs crouched at the foot of the tree, snouts pointed upward, barking in perfect unison.

"We are not taking those dogs on our honeymoon," he muttered.

"Honeymoon?"

"Will you marry me, darlin'?" Jack asked.

She fluttered her eyelashes like a true Southern belle. "Since you put it like that, of course I will."

Epilogue

Afterward, Ellie Lewis, the wedding coordinator, would swear that this was the sweetest, most romantic wedding she'd ever witnessed. But in the middle of the melee, she merely swore.

When she arrived at Cabin Creek shortly after five that sunny day in early October, all was chaos. She found the bride in the barn, dressed in blue jeans and a faded T-shirt, putting the finishing touches on the tables for the reception, and the groom, also clad in jeans and a T-shirt, standing at the top of a ladder, fastening the last of the vintage-wagon-wheel chandeliers he'd made under Cara's tutelage.

A pair of nearly identical fluffy white dogs lounged in the vicinity of the kitchen, staring with hopeful black button eyes at the crew of caterers who were starting to chop the pork butts that had been on the smokers all afternoon.

Each of the fifteen handmade tables was draped in an artfully paint-spattered canvas dropcloth, and Cara was buzzing from table to table, fluffing the centerpieces of local wildflowers mixed with sunflowers, pink and coral dahlias, and lime-green bells of Ireland arranged in a variety of mismatched antique white ironstone vases, pitchers, and jugs.

"Cara!" Ellie was out of breath by the time she caught up with the bride. "What are you doing? Your guests start arriving in an hour. You've got to get dressed, get your hair and makeup done. . . ."

"Almost done here," Cara assured her, pinching a less-than-perfect petal from a stem of blue salvia. Cara stood back, hands on hips, and nodded in approval. "Okay, that's it. Now I can get dressed."

"And you!" Ellie stood at the bottom of the ladder, staring up at the groom. "Jack, you were supposed to finish those chandeliers last night. You promised, after the rehearsal dinner . . ."

"They're done now," Jack said, climbing down. "Anyway, it's Cara's fault. She decided at midnight last night that we had to wire vines and flowers and moss around those old wagon wheels. And by we, she meant me."

"Scoot!" Ellie made shooing motions toward the open barn doors. "And what about your brother? And your sister and Harris? And Torie? Are you telling me that not a single member of my wedding party is here yet?"

Jack grinned. "Torie's up at the house nursing baby Betsy." He glanced at his watch. "Ryan ought to be back any minute. He just made an emergency bourbon run. Meghan and Harris? Hell, I don't know." He jerked his chin skyward. "Check up there in the hayloft. Everytime I look for those two I seem to find them in some kind of compromising position."

His voice echoed in the high-ceilinged barn. Sure enough, a moment later, Harris Strayhorn poked his head over the loft railing, frantically buttoning his shirt. "Hey, I heard that! We were just, uh, checking the acoustics up here. For the bluegrass band."

"Since when does a sound check require the removal of clothing?" Jack demanded. "You better not be dishonoring my baby sister up there."

Meghan Finnerty peeked over Harris's shoulder. "Mind your own business, Jack Finnerty!" She deftly plucked a stalk of hay from Harris's hair. "And don't you say a *word* to Mama or Miss Libba, or I'll tell both of 'em what I caught you and Cara up to in that hay wagon after the rehearsal last night."

"I don't care what any of y'all have been up to," Ellie screeched. "I need everybody who is going to be in this wedding to get up to the house right this minute and get themselves cleaned up and dressed for this wedding."

Harris scrambled down from the loft, with Meghan following a moment later. He turned, caught her by the waist, and swung her to the ground, his hand lingering at her waist just a second longer than was absolutely necessary.

"Tell 'em, baby," he urged.

"Tell us what?" Jack asked.

Meghan gave a quick shake of her head. "Nothing." She grabbed Harris's hand. "Come on. Ellie's right. My mom will have a fit if I'm not dressed and ready for the photographer in fifteen minutes."

"Wait." Jack grabbed Meghan's left hand and held it up. A large diamond solitaire twinkled in the late afternoon sunlight. "What's this?"

Meghan gave Harris an exasperated look. "It was supposed to be a secret. Until after the wedding. I don't want anybody to think we're trying to upstage you and Cara. . . ."

Jack pounded Harris on the back. "You son of a bitch! Congratulations! That's great." He gathered his sister into a hug. "Do Dad and Frannie know?"

"I managed to get your dad alone to ask his permission after the dinner last night," Harris said.

"Daddy burst out crying!" Meghan said. "And when Mama walked over and saw Daddy crying, she started in. . . ."

Harris rolled his eyes. "Which will be nothing compared to the way my parents are gonna react when we tell them. . . ."

"You can tell everybody later," Ellie said. "After the wedding. Which starts in forty-five minutes." She fumbled in the pocket of her all-purpose light blue wedding-reception dress and pulled out a small bottle of pills. "I swear, I am never doing another wedding professional's wedding. Ever again." She popped a pill, swallowed, and mopped her face with a crumpled lace hankie.

Torie Fanning Finnerty tucked her slumbering infant into the bassinette, kissed her fingertip, and touched it to her daughter's velvety cheek. She turned and gave the bride an appraising look followed by a smiling thumbs-up.

"You are absolutely the only girl I know who can get away with wearing an antique pink wedding gown and still manage to look fabulous," she said.

"Thanks." Cara turned with her back to her almost sister-in-law. "Can you zip me up? My hands are sweating, I'm so nervous."

Torie grasped the metal zipper and slid it upward. "How old is this thing, do you think?"

Cara turned around and tugged at the dress's heavy satin bodice, revealing an additional inch of her cleavage. "Hmm. Well, portrait necklines and cap sleeves like these were all the rage in the fifties. And the full ballet-length skirt with the tulle petticoats were in back then too. So it's at least sixty years old."

"Do you think somebody dyed this wedding gown this shade of pink?" Torie asked.

"Oh no. This is the original color. And it was a cocktail dress," Cara said. "I bought it years ago, when I worked at a vintage-clothing shop in Columbus. It's a knockoff of a Pierre Balmain, who was a famous couturier back in the day."

She fluffed her skirts and stepped into her pink satin pumps. "And I'll tell you something I haven't shared with anybody else. I bought this dress thinking I would wear it to my first wedding. But Leo—and my dad, and Leo's mom—were *appalled* that I'd even consider not wearing white . . . or a brand-new bought special wedding gown."

Cara shrugged. "So I did what I always did back then. I gave in and bought this big, stupid expensive virginal white dress that made me look like an over-decorated lampshade."

Cara twirled in front of the three-paneled mirror in Libba Strayhorn's guest bedroom, and smiled when she caught her own reflection in the mirror.

"When Leo and I moved down to Savannah, I couldn't wait to donate my wedding dress to Goodwill. But I kept this one." She smoothed her hands over her hips. "It's been tucked away in pink tissue paper all these years. Just waiting for the right moment."

"And the right guy," Torie said. "And here you are." She reached for the velvet-lined box on the dressing table and carefully lifted a single strand of pearls from the satin lining and fastened it around Cara's throat. "Here's your something new. Jack's dad gave me a set of pearls just like this the day I married Ryan."

The bathroom door opened, and Meghan hurried into the room, dressed in bra and panties. "I'm late, I'm late, I'm late," she singsonged, grabbing her deep coral dress from a hanger and slipping it over her head. She turned her back to Torie. "Zip me?"

Torie picked a piece of hay from her sister-in-law's hair and held it up for Cara to see. "Can you guess where baby sister's been and what made her late?"

"I don't judge," Cara said, laughing. She gave Meghan a wink. "What goes on in the barn, stays in the barn, right?"

"Mmm-hmm." Meghan leaned into the mirror, a mascara wand poised in her right hand.

"Hey!" Cara said, grabbing Meghan's left hand. She held it up to Torie.

"Whaatttt?"

"You're engaged?" Cara asked. "Since when? I can't believe it!"

Meghan smiled and flashed a set of dimples. "Harris asked Daddy's permission last night, at the rehearsal dinner. But he didn't bother to ask *me*, until just now, in the, er, barn."

Torie held Meghan's hand and studied the ring with an experienced eye. She held her own left hand up to Meghan's. "Baby girl, that is a serious ring. Bigger than my diamond, for sure."

Cara held her left hand on top of the others. Her engagement ring was made up of a circlet of smaller stones, with a single raised one-carat cushion-cut diamond in a platinum band. "Mine too," she said carelessly.

"Way bigger than the ring Harris gave Brooke," Torie pointed out. "By at least a carat."

Meghan frowned for only a moment. "This was Harris's grandmother's engagement ring. She left it to him in her will, but he bought a new ring for Brooke, because he thought that's what she'd prefer."

Torie gave Meghan an apprehensive glance. "Has anybody heard anything from, uh, her?"

Meghan laughed. "It's okay. You can say Brooke's name in front of me."

Cara said, "We text. That's the only way you can communicate with Brooke. She's still down on Cumberland Island. I think the thing with Pete, the park ranger, is heating up, but she says she has no plans to marry anytime soon. She's working for the Georgia Conservancy, and is still feuding with the Park Service over any issue she can think of. I think Brooke is finally in a good place."

"I'm glad," Meghan said earnestly. "Because of her, Harris and I found each other. And that's the best place of all, for me."

"This ring is beautiful, Meghan, and it's totally you," Cara said. She hugged Jack's little sister. "I'm so happy for you. Have you set the date yet?"

"Nope," Meghan said. "And I made Harris promise that he will not go around talking about it today at your wedding. Although I can't promise he won't, because he is so excited."

"He should be excited," Torie drawled. "After everything he's been though these past few months. Have you told Libba and Mitch yet?"

"Libba caught me coming into the house from the barn just now. She admitted she knew something was up when Harris 'casually' asked her where his grandmother's ring was last week."

"I'll bet she's over the moon," Cara said. "And Mitch too."

"She was very, very happy," Meghan admitted. "She wants us to have the wedding here, too, of course, and I promised her we would. Oooh. I almost forgot."

She disappeared into the bathroom and came out with a small creamy satin drawstring bag, which she handed Cara. "Libba thought you might want to borrow these." Cara untied the string, and a pair of diamond-and-pearl earrings dropped into the palm of her hand.

"Gorgeous," Torie said, picking up one of the earrings. "And real, too."

"I don't know," Cara said. "I've got my little fake pearls I was going to wear. . . ."

"No way," Torie said, pushing her gently down onto the dressing stool. She handed the earrings back to Cara. "It's just a loaner. I'll be in charge of getting them back to Libba after the wedding."

The bedroom door opened, and Frannie Finnerty stepped inside. She was dressed in a short sage-green velvet cocktail dress that accentuated her hazel eyes.

"My girls!" she exclaimed, beaming. "My three, beautiful, amazing girls!"

Baby Betsy stirred in her bassinette, and Meghan scooped her up and handed her to her grandmother. "Four."

"That's right," Frannie murmured.

The door opened again and Ellie Lewis poked her head around the doorway. "Everybody dressed and ready? The photographer wants you all out in the foyer for a few pictures before the guests start stampeding."

Cara took a deep breath. "All ready."

"Oh, just one more thing," Frannie said. She picked her gold pocketbook off the bed, opened it, and handed Cara a frilly, beribboned garter. "Here's your something blue. It's probably not really your style, but my sister Betty made it especially for you. . . ."

"I love it," Cara assured her. She hiked up her dress and slid the garter above her knee.

"Good. Now, can we please get moving?" Ellie said, dabbing at her damp face with her hankie. The other women filed out of the bedroom, with Cara bringing up the rear.

"Wait," Ellie said. "Where's your bouquet? We can't take your picture without your bouquet."

"Bert was bringing it," Cara said. "He insisted on making it himself, as a surprise for me. Isn't he here yet? I swear, if he's late today, I'll . . ."

"You'll what?"

Bert stood in the hallway at the end of the guest wing. He wore a pair of dark green linen pleat-front trousers with dark red suspenders, a billowy cream-colored dress shirt, a vintage brown tweed three-button vest, and a brown felt fedora.

"You'll fire me? You can't fire me, now, I'm your business partner, remember?"

"Oh, never mind," Cara said, remembering her vow to stay calm. "Did you bring my flowers?"

Bert had been standing with one hand hidden behind his back.

"Ta-da!" he said, bowing deeply.

Cara had been holding her breath. But she exhaled slowly now, holding the bouquet in both hands, turning it slowly to take it all in.

"Oh, Bert," she breathed. "It's exquisite."

"Better than Martha Stewart March 2009?"

"Better than anything, ever," Cara said.

And this was no exaggeration. The bouquet was an explosion of creamy coral roses, light and deep pink dahlias, and hypericum berries. Tiny sprigs of white feverfew and celosia plumes were interspersed with the larger flowers. The flower stems were tightly wrapped with coral pink satin ribbon and fastened with a sparkly pink vintage starburst rhinestone brooch.

Cara inhaled sharply. "My mother's pin! This is just like her favorite pin. How did you . . ."

"You didn't think I'd skip our trademark Bloom touch now, did you?"

"But . . . where did it come from? My mother used to wear this when my parents had a fancy-dress party to go to. I used to call it her fairy-princess pin. I haven't seen it in years. . . ."

Cara hadn't seen any of her mother's belongings since before her funeral. She'd come home from college the day before to find that all her mother's possessions, her clothes, books, paintings, everything, had been removed from the house, overnight.

Valerie, her mother's best friend, confided in Cara that she'd done the packing at the Colonel's request. "It's too painful for him," Valerie said. "Seeing her clothes in the closet, her hairbrush on the dressing table, it was just too much. He thought it would be easier for you this way too."

"Easier," Cara had mumbled, her mind numb with the pain and confusion of her mother's sudden death. "Yeah, probably so."

But in the months and years that followed Barbara Kryzik's funeral, Cara would silently pine for anything that would be a tangible reminder of her mother.

"The pin was Jack's idea," Bert admitted. "He thought you might like to have something of your mom's. You know, for something old."

"I still don't understand how he found it," Cara continued, shaking her head.

"He called me and asked me if I'd mind bringing it down here."

Cara's head jerked up. The Colonel stood in the doorway to the hallway.

"You came," Cara breathed. "You're really here."

Bert took her by the elbow and steered her toward her father. He gave her a quick peck on the cheek and whispered in her ear before handing her off to her father. "He's nervous as hell. So go easy on the old guy, okay?"

Cara nodded, and then Bert was gone, and she and the Colonel were alone, in a small alcove just a few feet away from the entry hall.

With a start, she realized she hadn't seen her father in over two years. Since before her split with Leo. Was that possible? He'd let his military-issue brush cut grow out a centimeter, and now his once-dark hair was more salt than pepper. He stood erect in a proper charcoal suit with a burgundy tie, but Cara noticed that the collar of his starched white dress shirt gaped a bit. In her memory, the Colonel had always towered over her, but now they were almost at eye level.

"You're so beautiful," the Colonel said, his voice shaky. He took her bouquet and placed it on the gilded settee, then took both her hands in his. And true to Bert's warning, the Colonel's hands were shaking. As were Cara's.

He touched a lock of her caramel-colored hair, which she wore down, with a single coral rose pinned behind her right ear. "Your hair is longer," he said. "I like it that way."

"Yours too," Cara pointed out, and they both laughed awkwardly.

"When did you get in?" Cara asked. "I had no idea you were coming. You said you weren't sure. . . ."

"I got in just now. Jack's brother Ryan picked me up at the airport in Savannah and brought me straight here."

"They told me Ryan was making a bourbon run," Cara said.

"Oh, we stopped for the bourbon, all right," the Colonel said ruefully. "I was pretty nervous about seeing you again . . . after everything."

"I'm so glad you came," Cara said, her eyes misting up. "I've missed you, Dad."

"I've missed you too, Cara Mia," he said, squeezing her hands tightly.

"Ahem."

Ellie Lewis was beckoning them. "I'm sorry, Cara, but if we are going to start this wedding on time, you have to come have these photos taken with the wedding party right now! Jack and Ryan and Harris have already gone over. The barn is filling up, and we only have ten minutes till go time."

The Colonel shook his head. "Late again. Some things never change."

"We're coming," Cara said, tucking her hand through her father's elbow.

Cara peeked around the barn doors. She could see Jack and Ryan standing in front of the makeshift altar he'd built just for the occasion, from barn boards and leftover roofing tin. A violinist was playing softly up in the hayloft.

"Go!" Ellie Lewis said, sending Torie and Meghan on their slow march up the carpet runner Jack had tacked down earlier in the morning.

Cara twirled her bouquet in her hands again. "Dad?" she whispered. "Mom's pin. Where did you find it?"

"Right where it's been since she died," the Colonel said. "Valerie put together a box of her things for you. Some of her jewelry, her favorite blue sweater, her watch, that painting of pink flowers that she liked. It's been at the house, on the top closet shelf."

Cara raised an eyebrow. "All this time? I thought you got rid of everything."

"Not everything," the Colonel said. His piercing blue eyes met hers. "I have so many regrets. About her, about us. You. I thought if I wiped the slate clean, it would all go away. All the hurt. And the guilt. I wasn't there for her, or for you. And I regret that more than I can ever say."

"Doesn't matter anymore," Cara said, smiling. "You're here for me now, today."

"Thanks to this young man of yours," the Colonel said. "He called me, multiple times. I wasn't going to come down here, but he doesn't give up easily, does he?"

"No, thank God," Cara said fervently. "He wouldn't give up on me, either."

"I like him," her father said. "He suits you." He took a deep breath and took a step forward, then a quick step back. "Who are all those people in there?"

Cara looked again. Heads were turned in their direction. With a start she realized the barn was full. Full of familiar faces. Vicki Cooper sat on the end of one of the plank benches with her husband, and her son and her daughter-in-law Kristin, Cara's first bride. Other brides and their families were scattered around. Jack's extended family took up row after row, aunts, uncles, cousins, and second cousins. As an only child of only children, she continued to be amazed at how close and intertwined her new family was.

She felt a warm surge of happiness, at the surprising recognition that these were her people, and that finally, she belonged.

"I know Ryan tried to explain this, but tell me again how you're connected to the people who own this plantation?" the Colonel asked.

"Mitch and Libba Strayhorn are friends," Cara said, liking the way the word sounded. "And clients. Jack and Ryan totally rebuilt this barn," she added proudly. "And pretty soon, they'll be family. Their son Harris just got engaged to Jack's little sister Meghan. You'll meet everybody at the reception."

From inside the barn, they heard a piano softly playing, accompanying the violin. And the first strains of Mendelssohn's wedding march.

"Okay. Now!" Ellie whispered. The Colonel stiffened and froze.

"Now!" Ellie repeated, waving her hankie like a starter flag. "Go. Go. Go."

"Dad?" Cara squeezed the Colonel's arm. "Just this once, maybe I could be on time?"

Every head in the room was turned in their direction. Somebody, probably Ellie, had remembered to turn off the overhead lights and switch on the dozens of strings of café lights that crisscrossed from the barn beams. Their guests' faces were a blur of golden light.

She floated up the aisle on her father's arm, hurrying a little to match the Colonel's measured march steps. At one point, it occurred to her that she hadn't actually hired a piano player for the wedding. When she glanced toward the altar, she was shocked to see an elderly woman with a shock of white hair pounding the keys of an upright piano she'd never seen before.

Sylvia Bradley? Only Jack Finnerty could have managed such a feat.

Finally, they were at the altar. Jack and Ryan stood at ease, dressed in dark gray dress pants, open-collared white shirts, and mismatched vintage tweed vests. Cara had made their boutonnieres herself, from flowers she'd planted in the courtyard garden at Jones Street, sprigs of dusty miller, lavender, tiny white asters, and blue salvia wrapped with raffia, backed with a single quail feather.

The minister, one of Jack's high-school classmates, wore a dark suit, and a jaunty straw boater with a sprig of lavender tucked in the hatband.

The Colonel reached out and shook Ryan's hand vigorously, then shook Jack's, and after another moment, gave the bridegroom a hug.

He turned, kissed Cara on both cheeks, and stepped quickly away to a spot on the front bench next to Jack's mother and father and Bert.

Cara was dimly aware of all the faces watching theirs. She heard the minister's words, heard Jack's deep voice, firmly pledge to love, honor, and cherish her. She heard herself breathlessly promise to do the same.

"I now pronounce y'all husband and wife," the minister said. He grinned at Jack. "She's all yours, buddy." He nodded at Cara. "And he's yours."

Jack Finnerty swept Cara into his arms. She felt her legs buckle, gasped as he dipped her backward, low to the floor, felt his warm lips on hers. When he finally released her, she stood unsteadily.

"Okay?" he asked, his hazel eyes crinkling at the corners.

"Okay," she assured him, breaking into a smile that lit up the room.

Ellie Lewis, standing to one side of the altar, exhaled for the first time that day.

The Colonel stood and shook hands with Bert again, as the guests stood and began to make their way to the bar at the back of the room. "Nice wedding," the Colonel said, doing his version of polite conversation. "I think Cara finally got it right this time, don't you?"

"Absolutely," Bert said. "I'm kind of an expert on these things. They both got it one hundred percent right."

Bill Miles

Mary Kay Andrews is the *New York Times* bestselling author of *Sunset Beach, The High Tide Club, The Beach House Cookbook, The Weekenders, Beach Town, Save the Date, Christmas Bliss, Ladies' Night, Spring Fever, Summer Rental, The Fixer Upper, Deep Dish, Savannah Breeze, Blue Christmas, Hissy Fit, Little Bitty Lies,* and *Savannah Blues.* A former journalist for *The Atlanta Journal-Constitution,* she lives in Atlanta, Georgia.